TERRESTRIALS

THE COMPLETE DUOLOGY

GRETCHEN POWELL FOX

AUTHOR'S NOTE

I first published *Terra* in December 2012, back when self-publishing was still the new kid on the block, before BookTok and Bookstagram existed, and long before a myriad of life's curveballs had me putting my writing dreams on pause.

It took me more than a decade to finally bring its sequel, *Underground*, into the world—a fact that could easily paralyze me with shame over how long I let those dreams simmer on the backburner. Instead, I choose to take pride in the fact that, though I may have been waylaid for a time, I still did the damn thing. I finished that story.

And now, with a new chapter in my author career unfolding—thanks to the incredible readership I've found with *Smoke and Scar*—I wanted to return to this story and ensure I do it justice.

So, I've polished and repackaged *Terra* and *Underground* in this single-volume omnibus edition, complete with a beautiful new cover by the amazing Kim at Spirit of Ebullience.

For those of you who have read the earlier versions, I hope you find new joy in revisiting this world with Terra, Adam, and Mica. For those of you reading for the first time: Enjoy the fall.

Love,
Gretchen

CONTENT WARNINGS

This is an upper YA dystopian sci-fi romance duology that contains themes that may not be appropriate for readers below the age of 12.

Content warnings include strong language, violence, psychological torture, parental death, depictions of grief, and closed-door romance (sometimes referred to as "fade to black").

Our greatest strength lies not in never having fallen,
but in rising every time we fall.

Unknown

BOOK 1: TERRA

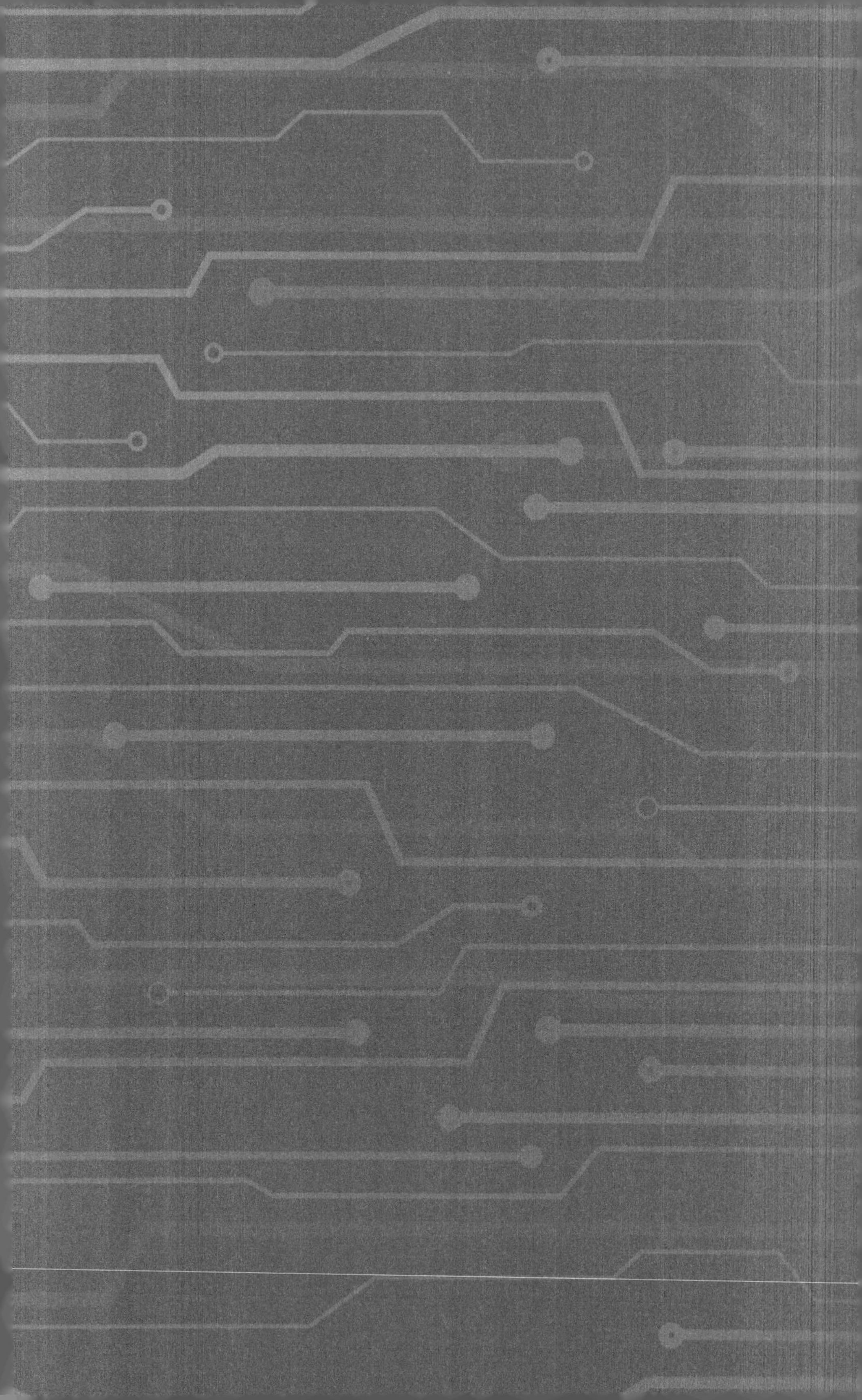

ONE

"TERRA?" Mica's voice, heavy with sleep, seeps from his half-open door. "Where are you going?"

Damn, I think. *I was trying to be quiet.*

I pause in his doorway, resting my shoulder against the frame. "Don't worry about it," I say softly. "It's still early. Go back to sleep."

His ancient computer blinks softly on his desk. With silent steps, I walk over and shut off the monitor, then peer up through the grime-streaked window above my brother's head. The soft gray light of early morning is beginning to peek through. I need to get moving.

"No argument here," Mica mumbles as he buries his face in his pillow.

I hover over him for a few moments, waiting for his breathing to slow before quietly drawing his door back to its half-open position. I'm careful not to close it all the way. Even now, after all this time, he still won't sleep with the door shut.

I retreat to the main room. Our apartment's layout is based on Floor Plan #4, which means our bedrooms empty out into one large, square room that serves as living area, dining room, and foyer in one. In one deft movement, I grab my bag from a hook near the front door and I am off.

Thankfully, at this hour, it's still cool out. The sun has barely crested over the horizon. I sling the strap of my blue scavenging bag over my shoulder and zip my black jacket up halfway.

The air is thick, as it always is. I know that the sun will be blazing by the time I get back, but I take it as a good sign that there's even the slightest of breezes this morning. It's two miles to settlement limits, and I'm headed a good deal farther than that; the longer I can go without breaking into my water canteen, the better.

The streets are empty. The few people who are up at this time of day will all be out by the docks, getting ready for the bustle of morning business. Nonetheless, I choose my route to the southern wall carefully, skimming along the outskirts of town, darting down side roads and occasionally throwing a glance behind me to make sure I'm not being tracked.

It might be a little paranoid of me, but you really can't be too careful around here. Last month, a boy from the East Quadrant was nearly beaten to death by a group of men who swore they saw him sneaking extra food pills into his pack after the Rationing. When they ripped the bag off his back, there was nothing inside but his scavenging spoils from the day before. The mob fought over the bits of copper wire and scrap metal anyway.

Once I clear the limits of the South Quadrant, I start to breathe a little easier. Slowing my pace, I root around in my bag for breakfast, pulling out a white pill bottle. I twist off the cap and shake a large brown pill into my palm, the bottle rattling noisily. There are only a couple of pills left inside, I realize with a grimace.

Mmm, delicious, I think sarcastically as I read the bottle's label. B-E665. I unhook my water canteen from the side of my bag and pop the pill in my mouth, trying not to shudder as I wash it down. Bitter as the "meal" tastes, however, I feel energized immediately and pick up my pace as I head toward the edge of town.

Reaching the boundary wall, I toss a wary eye behind me before I begin to climb. I'm alone for now, but others will be venturing into the plains soon enough, competing with me in scouring the fields for whatever useful bits and pieces might have dropped from the trash barges that pass overhead. I want to ensure there's plenty of distance behind me when they do.

Gran told Mica and me once that, long ago, before even her father's father was born, the walls surrounding Genesis X-16 stood fifty feet high, and the black dystridium brick was smooth as glass. Still feeling the scars of the Skyfall—the catastrophe that brought civilization to a grinding halt centuries ago—the founders of Sixteen built a protective dome that enshrouded our entire settlement. The giant ceiling acted as a UV filter that kept out both the acid rain and the harsh sun, akin to the ones that still encapsulate the skycities floating above us.

A single gate was built into the northernmost wall as the sole way in and out of the settlement. Of course, after the UV filter inevitably broke down and broke apart from lack of maintenance, it didn't take long for scavs to find more convenient routes to the outside.

Since the gate is located in the North Quadrant, most scavs don't bother going that way to get to the plains. It's not just that it's out of the way; most of us don't like dealing with the hoity-toities who live in that part of Sixteen. I've only used the main gate a handful of times myself, on the few occasions when I've brought Mica out with me.

It's not like what we're doing is illegal—scavenging is a regular part of life down here. But scavs don't exactly like to have guardsmen breathing down our necks, so we prefer to climb over the western or southern walls instead.

As it stands now, the south wall is no more than fifteen feet at its highest point, so I have little trouble climbing up. As always, I'm careful to avoid the remnants of jagged bricks and broken glass that still decorate certain sections. Soon, I'm jumping down on the other side, kicking up a cloud of dry earth behind me when I land.

The sun has settled in a spot halfway up the cloudless sky; in this light, the dusty brown landscape seems to stretch on forever. Patches of dead weeds line the sides of my path, the light breeze my boots make as I sweep past causing them to crumble.

The glint of something buried halfway in the dirt catches my eye. I stoop down and see a pair of small metal plates, maybe three or four inches across, slightly bent in the middle and with holes in the corner where screws would normally go.

Meh, I think, shrugging as I stand. They're not a bad find as far as generics go, but I decide to leave them for the other poor schleps to fight over. It is Collection Day, after all. The scavs will be out in full force. The more stuff that's available just outside the settlement, the less likely others will venture further out. I kick some dust over my boot prints and set off again with light steps.

No trails, I remind myself. I don't want some curious latecomer following me and cashing in on the poor-man's-treasure trove I've managed to keep to myself all these months. As I trudge on, the ground begins to slope and before long I see the tips of barren trees in the distance.

Another half-mile covered and I've reached the Dead Woods. I make my way south through the empty forest; the farther I walk, the less space there is between the trees. Scavengers rarely bother coming this far out from town. The woods are the only physical barrier between Sixteen and the District—the sprawling landscape of crumbling buildings that used to be one of the groundworld's greatest cities. A quarantine line wraps around the ruined city to warn us away too, but a few beams of red light don't provide quite the same sense of security as a petrified forest. Plus, the spoils are hardly ever worth the journey out to the woods for most, given the risk of your findings being stolen by raiders on the way back.

For those of us who know where to look, however, the odds of finding something worth collecting are much higher out here. Metal generics drop all over the place, but plastic is where the real money is. Something to do with dried-up fuel sources or something along those lines—I admit I never cared for the specifics. They don't really matter anyway. All that does matter is that plastic is worth a pretty penny to the folks at the recycling center, and the placement of the petrified trees out here makes it far less likely for the acid rain that regularly pours down to dissolve it before someone can scoop up a rare scrap of the stuff.

As for the raiders . . . thankfully, I know these woods like the back of my hand. I make an X over my heart and throw a prayer of thanks toward the sky that they've never had the chance to get close to me. Though I wish I could say the same for everyone else.

I weave my way through the thick trunks, the path I forge growing narrower as the roots that have broken through the ground begin to overlap, overtaking the forest floor. I'm less than a quarter-mile in when I start to see the first recyclables, discarded by skyworld citizens without a second thought.

One man's trash, I think, a bitter taste on my tongue.

I doubt the skyfolk even realize how quickly they would run out of their luxuries if we weren't down here, working in their recycling plants and scavenging for their leftovers. It's not like these resources just grow in the ground, after all.

Not anymore.

My eyes fixed on the dirt, I am methodical about how I walk between the withered trees—back and forth, then over two paces and back again. I stop occasionally to pick up lengths of wire and screws that sparsely pepper the ground and add them to my bag. They jangle as they mix into the pile I gathered earlier this week.

The work is consuming, and at one point I have to force myself to choke down my last few food pills.

The sun has long since peaked in the sky, beating down through the leafless branches. Sweat slicks my neck and arms. I roll the sleeves of my jacket up and wish I could just shuck the whole thing off, but the thin brown tank I'm wearing underneath provides little protection against the burning rays. My shoulders are freckled with more than my share of sunspots as it is.

Time for a break, I think, having just snatched up a cracked square of plastic. I grin as I calculate how much steel it will net me; it's got to be at least fifty credits' worth. My trek out to the woods has been worthwhile.

I straddle the trunk of a large fallen tree lying a few feet away and take a few grateful sips from my water canteen. I pull off the stretched-out elastic band that is knotted around my wrist and tie my sweat-dampened hair into a bun on the back of my head, grimacing as I twist it a little too tightly. When I pull my hand away, several dark strands come with it.

I groan as I swing my head from side to side, my neck stiff from hours of staring at the ground. I cock my head to the left in an attempt to work out the kinks and hear a dull series of pops as my vertebrae resettle. I then hang my head to the right for a few moments, stretching my neck muscles, and from this new sideways perspective, something catches my eye.

Sunlight glints off of something small and silver, and I see the vague outline of whatever it is tucked under a raised root about a yard over.

I crawl over and gently dig around the object. After some maneuvering, I pull out a small machine, consisting of dozens of little interlocking tubes and shafts. The device is slightly larger than the palm of my hand and surprisingly heavy. Underneath the caked-on dirt, it looks shiny—brand new, in fact. It's missing that matte sheen, a telltale sign of having been processed through the recycling center. Some small pieces might be missing—a few loose wires hang out, a lonely peg sticks out from the side —but, for the most part, it seems intact.

"Jackpot." This thing has got to be worth at least a hundred credits, easily. Enough to cover an entire month of Rations. I can't help but smile. Between this little machine, the plastic, and the myriad of generics already lining my bag, this is going to be a stellar Collection Day.

I carefully tuck the piece of machinery into the inner pocket of my bag and survey the spoils inside. Toting around a week's worth of generics is bothersome, but I'd rather deal with the annoyance than with the line that will form outside the recycling plant in the time it takes me to collect my spoils from home. Sweat drips down the crook of my arm and I decide that this should be more than enough to carry us through until the next biweekly Collection.

Not bad. I swing the strap of my bag over my shoulder and start back toward Sixteen. The bag bounces softly against my side with each step, and I can hear its contents jingling as the generics roll against each other —a soft symphony commending me on my success.

I steadily work my way back, still on the verge of overheating but in good spirits. As the trees begin to thin, I vaguely make out the silhouettes of other scavs scouring the fields. I peel off my jacket and shove it down into my bag to mute the sound of metal on metal before striding into the field.

"Ahoy, Terra!" Mal is the first to see me, and I wince slightly as he shouts his friendly greeting in my direction. He and I have always been on good terms, but he's one of very few to regard me with such enthusiasm.

Several men in the surrounding area sneer as I pace toward them. I've been a scav for over three years and they still can't stand that, at just eighteen, I pull bigger payouts most weeks than they do. I guess the fact that I'm a girl doesn't do much to draw their favor either.

"And just where are you coming from? You look kinda . . ." Mal trails off as I come close, dusting off his brown pants as he stands. I can tell by his expression that I'm not exactly at my most gorgeous. He runs his hand through his salt-and-pepper hair, leaving a streak of dirt on his temple.

"What? I can pull off the dirty, sweat-soaked look just as well as you can, old man," I respond with a grin, though my words sound stiff and formal compared to Mal's easygoing South Quadrant drawl.

Mal grins. "So ya can. Good haul?"

"I've just been cruising the Southern Plains for a while. Picked up a few more generics, nothing too exciting," I lie smoothly, shrugging my shoulders. A rugged-looking guy who's been surreptitiously observing me returns his gaze to the ground.

"Same here. Just some screws mostly, but I did find half a spool of copper wire right outside the wall." He shoots his eyes in the direction of our eavesdropper before adding in a hushed voice, "Chrys scored the real jackpot though. Found two metal plates just south of the wall, with a battery core underneath 'em. That's, what, a hundred and fifty credits for the core alone? At least? Lucky bastard was hardly out here twenty minutes. Turned tail and headed straight back to turn 'em in."

Damn it, I think, kicking myself for dismissing the plates earlier.

"Wow, good for him," I say, failing to keep the bitterness out of my voice. Jealousy is a normal reaction to that kind of find though, so Mal doesn't seem to think anything of it. "Lucky is right."

"Yeah, well, at least he only got those twenty minutes in 'cause of it. Means there's more left for us, right?"

"Right," I respond, smiling at him. "Well, I should get back."

"Heading in already? If you didn't find that much . . ." he says with a concerned look, and I know he's thinking of Mica. I feel a twinge of guilt for lying to him but remind myself that he wasn't the only one who was listening.

"Nah, it's okay, really. We still have credits left over from the last Collection. I just have to get back. I don't like to leave the little bro alone for too long, you know how it is. He's . . ."

"Mica," we say at the same time.

We both laugh. I wave goodbye to Mal and start back toward the wall, pinning my bag to my side with all the nonchalance I can manage as I pass through the other scavs' lines of sight.

TWO

THE LINE outside the recycling center is blissfully short. The rain kept us trapped inside for two days this week, so I'm not surprised that most scavs are still out searching, putting in last-minute efforts to boost their credit totals as high as they can.

I get in line behind a tall, lanky boy with reddish-brown hair that sticks up in the back. He looks a few years older than I am, but I know I recognize him from somewhere.

E-something, I think. His name definitely starts with an E.

A tired-looking woman with dirty blond hair loosely braided down her back approaches the drop-off station, which is set up right outside the recycling center doors. She empties her bag on the table, though since I'm stuck behind Something That Begins With E, I can't quite see its contents.

I can, however, hear the pathetic clink of each item hitting the metal tabletop.

The Collection Agent purses her lips as she pokes the items with her white-gloved hands, then holds her computer tablet over the collection to scan them. She prods at the screen for a minute before looking up.

"Total: thirty-seven credits," she announces curtly, sweeping the items into a bin that hangs off the edge of the desk.

A pang of sympathy hits me behind my ribs. That's barely enough to get by between Collections. The blond woman doesn't move. She mumbles something feebly to the attendant.

The agent stares vacantly, her right eyebrow raised, while the woman speaks. After a moment, she gives a small but distinct shake of her head. I don't know what the question was, but the answer is very clear. The woman bows her head low as she's ushered off by a guardsman.

"Next." The agent motions for the next person to step forward, flicking a speck of dirt off her crisp uniform. A bearded man limps up to the table.

"What was that about?" My tendency to think out loud rears its ugly head. E-something turns and gives me a quizzical look.

"That was Hess Underwood," he says quietly, in a way that makes it clear I should already know this.

I furrow my brow in response.

"Loran Underwood's wife."

"Oh," I say. It's all I can muster as a response as I recall what happened to the well-established scav. How he was making his rounds a few days ago when raiders jumped him.

In most instances, raiders might rob a scav of whatever spoils he's carrying and give him a light beating—the severity of the latter directly corresponding with resistance to the former. If it's a woman, though . . . Well, there's a reason there aren't too many female scavs.

It's pretty much an unwritten rule that if you get caught, you just give up your stash and the raiders won't bother with the more violent part. Loran would have known this better than anyone with as many past run-ins as he'd had with them. And it'd been months since a scav had been seriously injured, even longer since one's been killed.

Not since Lee, I think, something constricting in my chest.

So, it was a bit of a mystery when the guardsmen were seen dragging Loran back to his home that night, on the verge of death. He was unconscious for over a day, and when he finally woke up, he had a shattered kneecap and head injuries bad enough that he couldn't remember a lick of what happened.

It appears Hess has had to take over his scav duties while he's recovering, which is a slow process down here even under the best of circumstances.

"Total: eighty-nine credits," I hear the agent say. "Next!"

"I thought they had a son," I whisper to E-something, the edge of accusation in my voice. "A year or two above Mica. Trip Underwood, right?" I remember seeing him out scavenging alongside his father on occasion.

E-something doesn't reply.

"So, why is his mother the one out scavenging?" I continue.

He stares at me for a long moment before slowly exhaling, an act that sounds suspiciously like a sigh.

"Traders." He says the word matter-of-factly, before turning to the front again.

"Oh," I say again, unable to come up with a better response.

I don't know if he means that Trip has been recruited into the ranks of the infamous band of thugs and lawbreakers, or if the Black Traders have done something else with him. Either way, it explains why poor Hess has been stuck with scavenging as a means of providing for her injured husband. The couple will be lucky if they get to see their son again.

"Next!" It's E-something's turn. He steps up to the metal table and gives a wary glance in the direction of the guardsman to his right.

"Name?" the agent asks as she takes his palm and scans it with her tablet.

"Garren, Emery," he replies.

A small grin plays at the corner of my lips. *At least I was right about the E.*

Still, not being able to remember where I know him from nags at me. I can't place him in my memories from school but, then again, it's been years since I've set foot in the place.

Gran's passing had sealed the deal for me: Higher learning was never going to be my bag. Mica's smart enough for the both of us and after what I put him through after she passed . . . Well, stepping up and starting to provide for the two of us was the very least I could do. I never even bothered to find out if I passed my secondary examinations.

A vague memory begins to stir as I watch Emery stand in front of the Collection Agent. There's something about the set of Emery's shoulders that sends me back to my classroom days. Before I can fully recall the memory, however, I'm snapped back to the present by the agent's shrill voice.

"Total: Two hundred and eighteen credits," she says through pursed lips.

Wow. Go Emery, I think.

I've never broken the two hundred mark at a single Collection before, though I'm hopeful that my little machine will help me do so today. Our electric bill's a day overdue, Mica needs new school supplies, and the next Rationing is less than a week away, which means most of this payout is already allocated. I need to bag at least one hundred and fifty credits if we're going to make it without dipping into our paltry savings.

Plus, I think, scraping the worn-down heel of my right shoe in the dirt, *I was really hoping to get a new pair of boots this month.*

There are a few impressed murmurs from the people in line behind me, still appreciating Emery's haul. I turn around briefly and take in the length of the queue. Good thing I came back when I did.

Emery turns away from the drop-off station with a poorly suppressed smile on his face. I give him a subtle thumbs-up as he passes but he simply stares at me in response, his expression impassive.

Well, fine then.

"Next!"

I step up to the table and automatically stick out my hand.

"Name?" the agent says, placing my palm on the tablet.

"Rhodon, Terra."

"Let's see what you've got," she says, her eyes still plastered to her handheld computer's screen.

I lift the flap of my bag and remove my jacket, setting it on the table in front of me.

"I think I'm going to need a container," I say quietly.

The agent peers up at me quizzically with large hazel eyes.

"There are a lot of little pieces," I explain.

She nods curtly to a guardsman, who places a shallow metal tray on the table.

I slowly tip my bag over it; the piece of plastic is the first to fall out, quickly followed by dozens of screws, wires, and other scraps. They ring loudly as they pour onto the tray, and I can hear speculative murmurs coming from the line behind me.

With pursed lips, the agent immediately holds her computer out and scans the contents of the tray before I have a chance to interject.

"One hundred and seventy-five credits," she says briskly.

An appreciative whistle rings out from behind me. I glance back to the crowded line and see several beaming faces beaming among the standard, pissed off ones. At least some of them, Mal included, seem pleased that I've gotten a good haul. They're happy for me. Well, happy for Mica.

The agent looks at me with an impatient cock of her eyebrow. "Your credits have been transferred to your account, Ms. Rhodon. You may go."

"Sorry," I say quickly, "I wasn't done."

She stares at me apathetically.

"You scanned before I had a chance to . . ." I trail off as I reach into the pocket of my bag. Wrapping my fingers around the machine, I pull it out and place it gingerly on the table, keeping my eyes down.

Annoyed, the agent taps around on her computer screen for a few moments, then holds it over the machine. After a minute, I look up. The scan is taking much longer than usual.

Suddenly, I hear a sharp intake of breath. The agent's eyes dart from the screen to my little machine and back again. She looks up at me with wide eyes and it seems to take a second to find her words.

"C-correction," she stutters. "Make that . . . six thousand, two hundred and fifteen credits."

A collective gasp rings out from the queue, and I hear the number repeated over and over again as it moves through the crowd. After a moment, the onlookers' hushed voices fall into total silence. My heart hammers in my ears as I process the number.

"W-what?" My voice barely registers above a whisper. "Are . . . are you sure?"

The agent simply nods. There has never, in all my recollection, been a credit payout this large before. Ever. The crowd's silence breaks with my whisper, and their murmurs begin to take on a considerably different tone.

I risk a furtive glance behind me to find that the smiling faces have changed. Some look confused, some outraged. Several people in the back of the crowd have begun to argue. I force my eyes back to the agent, who is staring at me with her mouth agape.

Taking a deep breath, I gently place two fingers on my little machine, still shining on the metal tabletop. It already looks different to me; the tubes wrap around each other, interlocking in a way that seems more intricate in light of its hidden value.

"What is it? What did I find?" I blurt out.

The agent gives me a puzzled look and closes her mouth as if she's debating how to respond. Ultimately, she says nothing, and her mask of composure quickly returns.

"That information is classified," she says brusquely. She surveys the crowd that has edged up behind me, all semblance of a line forgotten, then summons a stony-faced, brown-haired guardsman forward. "Guardsman Brant will escort you home, Ms. Rhodon. You may go."

The guardsman's green eyes are wide as he approaches, flashing with something that almost looks like recognition as he searches my face, but I don't think I've seen him before. He says nothing. He simply grips my arm and pulls me away from the crowd of onlookers, many of whom are still sending angry glares in my direction.

Just before we turn out of the square, I look back to see the agent pick up the machine and walk directly inside the recycling center, shutting the doors behind her.

It appears Collection Day is over.

THREE

I BARELY REGISTER the feel of Guardsman Brant's hand around my upper arm until we're two blocks from the square. Then it hits me.

Six. Thousand. Credits.

I swallow noisily and try to compose myself, but my heart is racing. It's insane. It's unheard of. It's . . . troubling, to say the least.

In an attempt to hide my shock, I force Brant to take a quick detour to the Marketplace. Actually, I try to convince him to let me go by myself, but he insists he is to accompany me all the way home.

Despite his protests, I'm dead set on picking up the few items that I had already intended to purchase after what I thought would be a fairly ordinary payout. My hand shakes as I offer it to Mr. Copper, my favorite stallkeeper, to scan.

"What'd you do this time?" he asks jokingly, glancing pointedly at Brant.

"You know me, Copp," I say, trying to keep my voice light. "Natural-born troublemaker. Brant here's keeping me on the straight and narrow."

Copp chuckles as he runs the credit scanner over my palm. My breath hitches when my credit balance flashes over the register, and his eyebrows shoot straight up his forehead.

"Time to go, Miss Rhodon," Brant says brusquely, shepherding me out of the stall before another word is exchanged.

I leave the Marketplace with Mica's school supplies, half a dozen freshly purified water canteens, and my much-needed boots, feeling the burn of a dozen pairs of eyes on my back.

The walk home has never felt so long. I pepper Brant with questions once the shock wears off a little—why did they close the recycling center early? Had he ever seen anything like my machine—but I receive nothing in response.

"It's just a few blocks down," I say to Brant as we finally near my apartment complex, "I got it from here."

His silence, though typical for a guardsman, has left me tense and anxious. If he won't answer any of my questions, the least he can do is leave me alone with my thoughts.

"My instructions are to escort you home, Miss Rhodon," he replies, polite but perfunctory.

"I know, but we're basically there already," I persist. "Really, it's fine if you go. I'm a big girl."

Brant raises an eyebrow and gently places his hand on my shoulder as if to prevent me from running away. My cheeks burn; I'm being led like a child.

He walks me inside my apartment building, only releasing me once we reach my doorstep. As I fumble to find my keys, he suddenly reaches out and grabs my wrist. I look up at him, indignant, only to find him darting his head from side to side like he's ensuring we are alone.

"You have to be careful," he whispers, his eyes full of urgency. "Don't ask questions. Keep your head down."

Before I can ask him to explain, he's already walking away, his face stoic once again. I'm not sure if he meant them as a warning or a threat, but either way, his words leave me with my breath caught in my chest.

When Mica returns from school, I'm bursting at the seams to talk about it, but somehow I manage to refrain from telling him about my discovery and the resulting payout. The last thing I want is to get his hopes up—this could very well be some kind of error, a glitch in the system. I need to learn more, to be sure.

Brant's warning echoes in my head, but I need answers. Is this legitimate? Why did they insist upon escorting me home—am I in danger? Far more importantly, is Mica? And, in the back of my mind, less urgent but still there: What was it that I found?

FIRST THING THE NEXT MORNING, I find myself heading back to the reopened recycling center. Unfortunately, my initial efforts to find answers are decidedly unsuccessful.

"If you do not have goods to drop off, you have no business here," the guardsman tells me for the second time, his face vacant.

I let out a huff, my patience already thin after waiting an hour just to talk to this new guard. He wasn't there yesterday, but it feels clear from just how dismissive he's being that he knows why I'm here.

"Just let me talk to someone, anyone. The Collection Agent, another one of the guardsmen . . ." I refrain from mentioning Brant by name, just in case. "I just have a few questions, it won't take long."

"Do you have goods to drop off?"

"Well, no, but—"

"Then *you* have no business here," he repeats, his emphasis on the word "you" giving me pause.

"*I'm* not leaving until *I* get some answers," I say, crossing my arms stubbornly.

I hear a sigh and look over to see today's Collection Agent, a young man with wavy, chin-length brown hair and a crystal stud in his ear, seated at the drop-off station, watching me. He squints, studying my face. After a moment, he holds a finger up to the scav he's been speaking with as if instructing him to wait, then beckons me over. The scav scowls at me as I approach.

"What exactly is the problem here?" the Agent asks.

"I was here yesterday," I say. "I had the . . . I'm the one who . . ." I can't quite bring myself to say it, like speaking it aloud will either wake me from this dream or cement it into reality. I'm not sure which one I'd prefer.

Comprehension dawns on the agent's face, before quickly being replaced with the same indifference as before. "And . . . ?"

"And I have some questions. I need to talk to someone about it."

"You have questions. You need to talk to someone," he repeats slowly, pursing his lips at the end as if the words themselves taste bad.

I feel incredibly small.

"I'm afraid I can't help you," he says. "If we stopped to flag down an agent every time someone in this settlement wanted to 'talk to someone' about their Collection, we'd never get anything done at all. So, if that's all . . . "

He moves to dismiss me with a wave of his hand and I bite the inside of my lip, weighing my options.

"Brant," I say after a moment. *Sorry, Brant.* "Let me speak with Guardsman Brant."

The agent raises his eyebrows and surveys me with a look of what feels like amusement. It's unnerving.

"Jarvis!" he calls, summoning the guardsman I'd been arguing with. "Call up the main office. Get Brant out here."

Without as much as a glance, Jarvis walks into the recycling center with his hand at his ear.

"Wait until he arrives, ask your *questions*," the Agent sneers, "then leave. You are being very disruptive."

With a nod, I walk around to the side of the building, away from the glares and murmurs coming from the people standing in line. Eventually, a black transport vehicle rolls up in front of me. Brant steps out of the vehicle, a weary expression already on his face.

"Miss Rhodon," he says guardedly as he approaches.

"Brant," I respond.

A tense moment of silence passes between us.

"Well?" he says finally. "I assume there is a reason you summoned me? What is it?"

"What do you mean, 'What?' You know what," I say, trying to keep my voice low. "I have about a thousand questions about what happened yesterday—actually, make that *six thousand* questions."

"I have no answers to give, Miss Rhodon," he says, the words sharp, his tone clipped. "You delivered your findings on Collection Day, you were compensated accordingly."

I stare at him.

"You should leave it alone," he adds quietly.

With the smallest possible head movement, he checks the peripheral area for onlookers. I look around too. We're out of sight from the scavs now lining up for Collection Day 2.0, but there are still a few people milling about.

"Maybe there's somewhere more private we could speak?" I suggest.

He shakes his head, though it seems more like an indication of his exasperation than an actual response.

"Look, I'm sorry I called you back out here. I'm just . . . I'm nervous," I say softly. "All that steel, it's not normal. I have no idea if this whole thing is legitimate, I have no idea what it even is that I found. And after what you said yesterday, I just thought—"

"You have been compensated for your discovery," he repeats, a hard edge to his voice.

Frustration burns through me. "That's all I get? You're not even going to explain why you were suddenly assigned as my protection detail? Or what the hell your little warning meant? Is it because of the Black Traders? I deserve to know if I'm at risk or if there's some other reas—"

"We're done here." He cuts me off and turns back to the idling transport. Without so much as another glance, he gets into the vehicle and takes off. My eyes follow the path of the transport in disappointment as I return to the front of the building.

"Back for seconds, Rhodon?" an unfortunately familiar harpy-like voice rings in my ears.

I search the line until I see Yttria Coal standing next to her father, her jet-black hair tied in a tight knot on top of her head. Our eyes meet and she starts toward me, her open jacket flapping in the wind, revealing a stomach-baring cropped top underneath. Arc Coal clucks disapprovingly but makes no motion to stop his daughter.

"Take the hint," she says as she gets close to me, breathing so hard that I can see her stomach muscles flexing beneath her caramel skin. "Why don't you and that precious little brother of yours take your undeserved payout and use it to get out of our lives, *Terror*?"

"Mind your own damn business, Yttria," I say quietly, rolling my eyes at the nickname she still thinks she's clever for coming up with when we were ten. There are far too many ears listening for me to say what I really want to. Maybe that's a good thing, though. Holding my tongue is still something I'm working on. After all, had I been smart enough to do so when I caught my father sneaking around with Yttria's mother, maybe she wouldn't hate me so much.

"Oh, I will, when you finally keep your cheating scav paws out of *our* business so the rest of us can make a living too." She storms back to her father.

I shake my head and turn to leave, but not before I see Arc place a reassuring arm around his daughter's shoulders as she sidles up to him. He plants a fatherly kiss against her forehead and the inner corners of my eyes prickle for a reason I don't quite understand.

<hr>

NOT EVERYONE EYES me with hostility as I head home. I've barely made it back across the road when I am greeted by an old acquaintance of Gran's, an elderly woman I have seen maybe twice before in my life.

"Terra, my dear!" she cries, a wide, toothy grin decorating her wrinkled face. "You look wonderful, darling. Simply wonderful! You certainly have grown up well. A little skinny, perhaps, but what a beauty you are turning out to be!"

She is hunched over slightly as she hobbles in step alongside me. I slow my stride so she can keep up. Her white hair is tied back in a wispy bun, and she has a purple scarf draped over her clean blue dress. Around her neck hangs a fine silver necklace that is suspiciously lacking in tarnish.

"Thank you, Mrs . . ." I trail off, having vaguely recognized her but fully blanking on her name.

"Why, it's Gem Kuipers, child! Surely you haven't forgotten me? I was the very closest of friends with your old Gran." She flashes another smile. "I remember when you were just a tiny little thing."

"Of course, Mrs. Kuipers," I reply politely. "How are you?"

"Oh, my sweet girl," she says, her face falling into a dramatic frown. "You're so kind to ask, but I'm afraid I'm not very well at all. My Frankie —well, you remember my son Frank, of course—he's laid up at home with a twisted ankle. He can't make it twenty feet outside the wall these days, and with my stall not doing very well these past months . . ." She continues for another few minutes as I sympathetically nod along. I use the time to prepare myself for the question I know she—and everybody else—will be asking.

"So, you see," she says finally, "all we need is a bit of steel to tide us over until he's all healed up and the spring sales have begun. And when I heard that you had the good fortune to come into a little extra . . . I just knew that you would be more than happy to help out your Gran's dear old friend."

"Ah, Mrs. Kuipers . . ." I begin awkwardly.

"Please, dear, call me Gem."

I respond with a hard smile. "Mrs. K—Gem. I am genuinely sorry to hear about your troubles."

She stares at me eagerly.

"It's just that I think there's been a little confusion with my credit balance, so I'm afraid I'm not really in a position to help at this precise moment."

Guilt seeps into every cell of my body as I brace myself for the incoming backlash, but there really is so much I still don't know, don't understand about this payout. I can't just go giving it away. Anybody in my shoes would feel the same.

Her filmy eyes narrow and I grimace at the look that flashes across her face. It only lasts a moment, though, and before I know it, her kindly mask is back.

"Well, of course, my dear," she says, her voice alarmingly chipper. "I completely understand. I'm sure that Frankie and I will survive somehow, don't you fret about us one bit. It was lovely to see you." She touches her fingers absentmindedly to her necklace, turning to leave. "Do give my love to darling Miko."

"It's Mica," I call after her, but she is already gone, weaving through the crowd with strong steps and a straight back.

BEFORE I'M EVEN HALFWAY home, three more of our "friends" have stopped me. Just to say hello, of course.

At least I don't have any real friends to refuse, I think grudgingly as I finally reach the sanctuary of the apartment. I busy myself by cleaning the entire apartment, glad for the distraction while I wait for Mica to return from school. I need to tell him everything. The news of our payout is traveling fast, and I'd rather Mica hear it from me than from a nosy neighbor. As soon as he bursts through the door, however, it's clear that I'm too late.

"Terraaaaaa," Mica calls in a sing-songy voice as he pulls his backpack off, dropping it carelessly in the middle of the room. "Anything you feel like telling me?" His eyes are bright, his smile beaming.

"Whatever do you mean?" I say with an innocent shrug, though I'm unable to refrain from returning his radiant smile. I can't even remember the last time I saw him so full of light, full of life.

"Alright, let's try another one. Guess who I sat with at lunch today?"

"Prime Whitlock?" I ask, retrieving his bag and tossing it at him.

"Juniper Coal," he says, ignoring my sarcastic reply and catching his backpack before plopping onto the couch. "And Lark, and Brim, and Cyrx. Wild, right?"

Aside from Yttria's sister, I've never heard of these kids before, but Mica's enthusiasm makes it clear enough that they must be a big deal around the schoolhouse.

"Juniper Coal," he says again, sighing her name. "Or, Junie, I guess. She told me to call her that." He wiggles his eyebrows and I stifle a laugh. "They were practically fighting over me."

"Well, you must feel like royalty now," I say, bending at the waist in a mocking bow.

"Don't take it out on me just because you were never this popular."

If that isn't the truth.

I furrow my brow and try to choose my words carefully. My little brother, who has always been just a bit too smart to really fit in, even without our family's reputation dragging him down, is suddenly a star. Mica, who usually stalks through the door at the end of the day, sullen and despondent, is finally feeling the glow of popularity.

It breaks my heart a little to know why.

"Sorry, Mic," I say, sitting down next to him. "Something did happen yesterday."

"Duh," he says with a roll of his eyes. "Honestly, it just would've been nice if you had, you know, told me we're rich and famous now." His face lights up, as if he's been struck with a sudden idea. He springs up from the couch and walks quickly to the kitchen, where he starts to pull cans of Rations from the cabinets.

"We're not rich and famous. I still don't know if this is all some kind of mix-up," I say. I understand his excitement. But I don't want to encourage it. We're sitting on more steel than either of us have ever seen. More than Gran left when she passed. Far more than we got when our father left us in her care.

Granted, that isn't saying much.

I just can't help feeling like I'm still waiting for the other shoe to drop.

Mica ignores me and continues rooting through the cabinets.

"Chill out, would you?" I call from the couch. "I'll make dinner soon."

"We can afford food that tastes like actual food now. I'm throwing this garbage out."

"What? Stop!" I say, my tone more forceful than I intended. I stalk into the kitchen and snatch a can out of his hand, then proceed to reshelve the rest of the Rations he's pulled out. "We're not spending a single credit until I figure out exactly what is going on."

Mica glares at me, staring down his nose in a way that somehow makes me feel like I'm not the big sister anymore.

"Why do you have to question everything?" he says. "Why can't you just be happy that something good has finally happened to us?"

I slam the cabinet door closed. "Too bad it's not your decision, kid."

With a huff, Mica stomps out of the kitchen and into his bedroom. He doesn't come out for the rest of the night.

THE RAIN STARTS the next morning, and for the first time, I'm happy to hear the warning alarm. People are far less likely to come begging for handouts when they risk death or disfigurement by going outside.

For once, being stuck inside this apartment's acid-proof walls is a blessing, even if it means being confined with Mica's temper tantrum.

As if life with a thirteen-year-old isn't hard enough.

He's still mad, and I can't really blame him. His inclination to want to jump up and down, shout from the rooftops, marvel at this change of fortune . . . it's not like I don't get it.

This life hasn't been fair to him. It hasn't been fair to a lot of people, granted, but especially my brave, brilliant brother. Sure, we may have lived through the same circumstances, experienced the same losses. We were abandoned by the same father. Lost the same mother, even if Mica might not ever have gotten the chance to know her. Grieved the same Gran.

And through it all, he was still able to be, well, Mica.

I've always envied his ability to see through the gloom, the jeers and snide remarks, the hunger, to the light on the other side. To keep reaching for that light, however faint it might be. To never let the spark inside him go out, however dim it might get.

To hope.

Even when the last person he had to rely on, the only person he had left, shut down and shut him out. When my inability to see past my own pain left me frozen and my little brother, still just a kid, had to figure out how to make it one day to the next all alone.

If I could rewind time, there are so many things I would do differently. There's so much I can't take back.

So, yes. He probably wouldn't believe me if I said it aloud, but I get it. I really do.

When you've been living at the bottom of a hole for so long, a rope descending from above is a lifeline. Your first instinct is to grab for it, hold fast, and use it to crawl back up.

You don't stop to think who might be holding the other end.

FOUR

"SERIOUSLY?"

It's three days into the storm. Mica looks down at the dinner plate I've placed on the table in front of him, his sand-colored hair falling into his face.

"Six thousand credits in the bank and we still gotta eat slop?" He prods the glutinous brown lump in the middle of his dish, causing it to jiggle.

I groan, massaging my temples with two fingers on either side of my head. "I'm so done arguing about this. We still have three days' worth of food left over from the last Rationing, so we will be eating Rations for the next three days. We can talk about what to do next after that."

He rolls his eyes at me and I grin at him, trying to alleviate the tension.

"Suck it up, bro," I say. "It was between slop and glug, so honestly you should be thanking me."

I eye the cans of D-T04U peeking out of the pantry and shudder. If I'd gotten to last month's Rationing on time, I could've stocked up on some better stuff. Unfortunately, I had spent most of my morning retrieving a bent steel pole that was caught in the branches of a tree out in the Dead Woods, and it was slim pickings by the time I arrived. D-B334, D-T04U, and food pills were all that was left.

As it is, the slop vibrating on our plates is by far the lesser of two evils.

Mica stares at me, his gold-kissed brown eyes squinting in scrutiny. My eyes, peering back at me from his face.

People constantly tell us that we wouldn't even look related if it weren't for our perfectly matching eyes. Where his shaggy hair is a light, sandy color, mine is a sheet of brown so dark it's almost black. Though my skin is tan and freckled from the years of scavenging, he remains pale. And where Mica inherited our mother's flat Exodusian nose, I received our father's: thin with a high bridge and rounded tip.

But our eyes.

Color-wise, everyone in Sixteen ends up with pretty much the same muddy brown eyes. Even those that aren't born brown-eyed end up that way as their bodies acclimate to the atmosphere down here. Just another of the many reasons skydwellers despise being assigned to jobs on the groundworld. If they spend enough time in the settlements, their precious baby blues might be affected; that easy indicator of status and superiority, tainted.

But even though all terrestrials share a similar color, people still point out that there's just something different about Mica's and my eyes. Almond-shaped, long-lashed, with the subtlest flecks of gold echoing out from the middle.

Like the sun itself is trying to burst through, Gran used to say. So that's what she called me: Her little sunburst.

I smile at the memory and take a moment to listen to the rain hiss as it hits the solar panels on the roof, still audible over the low murmurs of the television in the main room. A new special is airing tonight, something about some skycity technology that the Tribunal is eager to unveil. I think Prime Morrigan Whitlock is making the announcement herself. I couldn't care less about what goes on up there—it never affects us in any significant way—but Mica always insists on watching.

"I know you're annoyed," I say, snapping my attention back to my brother.

Mica huffs in confirmation.

"You have to see it from my side here. I'm just not convinced that this is legit. Maybe that dinky little computer messed up, and our account will be back to empty again before we know it. What would be the point in getting a taste of nice things if it all gets repo'd in a week?"

Mica pierces a slice of slop with his fork and quickly shovels it into his mouth before it can slide off.

"If it was just some computer error they would have told us by now," he says, his words garbled in his full mouth. He swallows before continuing, "I mean, wouldn't they want to keep that kind of steel for themselves if they could?"

I ignore the little voice in the back of my mind that wants to point out that though it might be a fortune to us, six thousand credits is likely nothing to the skydwellers.

"Oh, just shut up and eat," I say.

A few moments of tense silence pass.

"It's not like we don't have enough to spare now. You're being so selfish." Mica's eyes are dark as he glares across the table.

"*I'm* being selfish? How is it selfish to want to be smart about this? We are not spending unnecessary steel just so you have something to brag about at school. I'm still in charge here."

"But you're not being smart. You're not *doing* anything! God, you do this every time, Terra. Every time something big happens. Something has to change. You can't just freeze up on me anymore."

I flinch at his words and want to respond, but the memories of the dark time that followed Gran's death are already rushing back to me.

Overwhelmed with the burden of responsibility and the ache of Gran being gone, I had just . . . stopped. Did nothing beyond the basic, perfunctory motions required to stay alive. And every time Mica, not even ten years old yet, tried to shake me out of it, every time he cried, I would shut him out. Literally. The pain would crest and I would fall into it, locking myself in my bedroom while he howled and pounded at the door, the days ticking on without me.

We ran out of money first. Then, food.

It wasn't until the guardsmen delivered my starving baby brother after he collapsed at school that I finally woke up. Seeing his body, limp and ashen against their stark uniforms, was an ice-cold shock that yanked me back to reality. The way his wrist dangled lifelessly over the edge of that guard's arm . . . I swore then and there that I would never fail him like that again.

The guilt alone would kill me.

I went scavenging for the first time that very day. Too young and inexperienced to get a job doing anything else, it was the fastest way I could think of to get credits. And as luck would have it, I turned out to have a knack for it.

By the following Collection Day there was steel in the bank and food in our bellies once again, but the scars of my failure are still there.

To this day, Mica won't sleep with his door closed.

With a glance toward his always partially open bedroom door, I snap back to the present.

"That was different," I say. "When Gran died, I was—"

"You know I don't just mean her. I'm talking about—"

"Don't." I cut Mica off, clenching my jaw and staring him down. His eyes widen in response. He knows he's toeing the line, if not stepping over it.

It's been over a year since Lee died, the last tragic victim of raider violence taken too far. Well, the last one that was publicized, at any rate.

The funny thing is, I was never really all that sad about it. Angry, yes, but not sad. It kind of felt inevitable. After all, raider attacks had been on the rise. Scavs were getting torn up left and right. It was only a matter of time before something happened to someone I knew.

Besides, Lee and I hadn't even been together that long. We weren't in love. I didn't fall asleep thinking of the way his hair stuck up in the back, like he had perpetually just rolled out of bed. I didn't dream of how he kissed me—softly, like he was always just a little shy.

Of course, after he died, I couldn't stop thinking about those things.

I had no idea if he was The One. In all probability, he wouldn't have been. But it's the not-knowing that kills me. The regret that fills all of the space he'll never occupy again.

Lee was one more person snatched from my life before we even got our chance. Where Gran's death had paralyzed me with fear and sadness, with Lee's it was all anger. Enough rage to keep me holed up in my room for a solid week.

At least Mica was better prepared that time.

My nostrils flare as I inhale slowly, attempting to calm myself down. Mica is trying to distract me from the matter at hand, and I can't let him.

"Don't you think your future is *slightly* more important than getting darling Junie to let you stare at her adoringly while she eats lunch?" If I were a better person, my voice would be soft with sympathy, my words comforting. But I'm not. I can't quite keep the jibe from slipping out.

"You don't even know her. She's not like that."

"Please," I scoff. "I know her sister. Siblings are never really that different from each other."

"Well let's hope for my sake that's not true," he says, venom on his tongue. "This town doesn't need another pariah to shun."

Ouch. I know he doesn't really mean it; he's a pissed-off teenager and I'm insulting the girl he likes. But it still stings. I do my best to shrug off his insult and return my attention to my plate.

"Ugh." Mica shudders, shoveling the last forkful into his mouth and pushing his plate away. It may taste like dirt, but it's not disgusting enough for a boy in the middle of a growth spurt to pass up. He's barely started growing and he's already almost eclipsed all five-foot-eight of me.

"Put your dishes in the sink, please," I remind him gently.

With a derisive look, Mica picks up his plate and cup, walks over to the sink, and places them squarely on the counter *next* to it before storming off to the living room.

I sigh. He just doesn't understand. If moochers were all we had to deal with, that would be one thing. Unfortunately, there are far more dangerous threats out there. For one, there's no way the Traders aren't also aware of our recent stroke of literal good fortune.

It's been a few months since the last credit theft, which makes it feel like it's only a matter of time until the next one. There are only two ways to obtain someone else's steel: it is either gifted or it is taken, and the only way to *take* someone's credits around here is to . . .

The thought makes me run cold. It feels like targets have been painted on our backs now that we've become the richest orphans to grace the West Quadrant. If Mica didn't have school, I doubt I'd want either of us to leave the apartment again.

I laugh humorlessly under my breath, contemplating how this time, it feels like I'm shutting us both in rather than shutting him out.

Some improvement, I think to myself as the wind whistles outside.

40

FIVE

I WAKE in the middle of the night to the sound of nothing. The rain, after three days of unceasing pounding, has finally stopped. A couple more hours and the ground will be dry enough to walk on without eating through the soles of my shoes.

The silence is disconcerting, though, and I know I won't be able to fall back asleep. As I wipe the sleep from my eyes and roll over onto my back, my mind starts racing with the same unanswered questions.

What did I find? Why won't any officials speak to me? And what the hell do I do with all this steel now that we have it?

In my solitude, I am forced to acknowledge the idea that maybe I have been using Mica, mooching neighbors, and fear of the Black Traders as excuses not to take action.

What is wrong with me? I squeeze my eyes shut for several heartbeats before reopening them. Here I am, again. Avoiding instead of confronting, again. Ignoring instead of planning. Again.

But receiving a large sum of money, no matter how suspicious, is nothing like inheriting the sudden responsibility of caring for your kid brother on your own, right? So what am I afraid of? Aren't I supposed to be both older *and* wiser than I was at fifteen?

Mica is right. There's no use sitting on this fortune. I need to start considering how we're going to spend it. And I need to be smart about it too.

Mica will have all the supplies he'll ever need for school. We can even start shopping in the North Quadrant instead of bargaining over every pair of socks purchased from the Marketplace. Maybe we can even afford a transport of some kind. Four-wheelers are still too expensive, of course, but maybe a scooter or a refurbished minicycle . . .

I force myself to take a breath. Food, supplies, new clothes, and a transport vehicle? I'm already getting ahead of myself. Six thousand credits may seem like an insane amount now but spread between Mica and me? It won't last forever. Steel only lasts as long as you can go without spending it. What happens when we start to run out? And am I supposed to just sit around and do nothing until then?

My relationship with the other scavs has always been tenuous at best. I can only imagine the endless stream of remarks I'll have to endure if I try to return to the fields:

"Spent your fortune already, have you?"

"What, you need more steel to spruce up your wardrobe?"

"Here she is, fellas, ready to show us up again."

"You just can't leave any for the rest of us, can you?"

No, the other scavs definitely won't tolerate me edging in on their own future payouts after this, and I don't blame them. If I was on the other side of this kind of thing . . . I get it.

Unfortunately, a job in town is pretty much out of the question for me too; I have neither the skill set nor the desire to work down at the docks or in the recycling center. And somehow I suspect that my sunny disposition is not quite what they're looking for in a shopkeeper.

I flip my pillow to the cool side and press my face into it, counting my shallow breaths. Had you asked me a week ago, I would have told you that something like this would be a blessing. I never considered how complicated it could be.

I start to recall how normal the events of That Day felt, scavenging out in the Dead Woods, my friendly conversation with Mal. I am recounting my terse chat with Emery when, suddenly, I remember why I recognized the set of his shoulders, the shade of his hair. It's from watching him walk in and out of my classroom, back when he came to speak at school about his scholarship. Emery Garren: the first person in fifty years from Genesis X-16 who would be attending school in the sky.

Technically, the universities up top are open to anyone, citizens of the groundworld and skycities alike. At least that's what the commercials say. Of course, the kids up there don't have acid rain that prevents regular school attendance, and their teachers actually like being assigned to teach them.

Here in Sixteen, kids with test scores high enough and wallets deep enough to qualify for entrance are pretty much nonexistent. We don't have access to the technology or the resources that the skydwellers have, so achieving those scores takes a particular kind of brilliance. And even when kids do make the grade, the cost is what really keeps us out.

Emery was a special case because he managed to land himself one of the exclusive Skyline Scholarships reserved for terrestrials who score highly on their tertiary examinations. Most years, nobody from Sixteen even bothers applying. Our chances are already low and the disappointment just isn't worth the effort. Most years, no scholarships are awarded at all.

So, why is Emery back here doing scavenging work? I think briefly, though my curiosity is soon eclipsed by one glowing thought: Mica. He's already passed his secondary examinations, an achievement most kids don't hit until they're much older. Under the right circumstances, and with the right resources, my brilliant little brother might actually have the smarts to make it up top.

Our circumstances have never been right, though. Not until now.

I can see it.

I can see Mica shutting the apartment door behind him, bags slung over his shoulders, the two of us beginning the long trek toward the Skyline Transfer together. I see him, sitting at a tiny table in a tiny room with real, sky-grown food on his plate—the kind of stuff we've only ever seen on TV: colorful fruits and vegetables that have actual names instead of coded numbers stamped onto their labels.

It would be the chance for a real life for Mica. A life in which his potential wouldn't be wasted as a scav or recycling plant laborer down here. One where he'd have the education to become more than some self-important skydweller's personal servant once he got up top.

He's smart enough, no question, but more importantly, he deserves that chance. He deserves all of it. And with the right education, the ability to meet the right people, the right opportunities . . . He might even be able to become someone who matters. Someone who could *change* things.

My heart swells but I can only let my imagination run away for so long before I shake myself back to reality. How much steel am I honestly talking about here? Skyline Transfer tickets must cost hundreds and hundreds of credits, and who knows how much he would need once he got up there.

I suddenly realize I might have already figured out why Emery is back.

Even if Mica were able to obtain a scholarship, logic tells me that what it takes to live up there is a hell of a lot more than what it takes to survive down here. The voice in the back of my mind returns, alerting me to the idea that even if my payout was indeed some sort of computer-generated glitch, they might not care enough to fix it. The thought that this much steel really might be mere chump change to the Tribunal puts a sour taste in my mouth.

No, if I want even a chance of making this happen for Mica, I know I'll need more. We need more.

I glance at the window, imagining I can see the Dead Woods through the foggy panes. What if there's more out there? I'm not foolish enough to hope that I'd find the exact same thing, another machine, another six thousand credits. But I was so excited about my find that I didn't even bother digging around the spot where I found it. What if that little machine wasn't the only valuable thing there? What if—

I push back against that little voice in my mind, but I can't help the additional thought from slipping through: What if finding whatever else is out there means I could go with him?

I bolt upright. The other scavs will be riotous if they find out that I've broken the unwritten rule and tried to collect less than a week after a huge payout. It's as bad as stealing in these parts. But to be honest, I think they'll riot if they see me scav ever again after a payout this large anyway. If I sneak out and get back without anyone seeing me, I can sit on my findings until the next Collection Day rolls around, cash in, and we can get out.

I contemplate waiting a while to give the hysteria time to die down a bit. Hardly anyone ever scavenges in the Dead Woods, so there's a fair chance that anything that's still out there will stay undiscovered, untouched. But I can't count on that.

Has Mal already pieced together that I had not, in fact, come from the Southern Plains that day, as I said? What about one of our eavesdroppers? No—if there's anything else out there like my machine, I need to go now, before anyone else goes looking.

I whip myself out of bed. Tying my hair back in a tight ponytail, I shimmy into an old pair of dark cargos and zip my jacket over a thread-bare t-shirt. It's a risk to venture out so soon after the rain, so I want to make sure my skin is well covered. I pull a pair of gloves out of a drawer and shove them into my pocket.

I tiptoe out of my bedroom and dart over to the kitchen table with my boots gripped tightly in one hand. A glance in the direction of Mica's room reveals his door still ajar in its standard position. The thought that he still won't close it, as mad as he is at me, simultaneously warms and wrenches my heart.

I reach over to unhook my bag from its usual resting place but pause before removing it. The electric blue sack, while great for avoiding being run over in the dark, is definitely unfit for secret excursions. I look around for an alternative and, through his half-open door, I notice Mica's worn black backpack hanging from the back of his desk chair.

I creep in, tossing a furtive glance at his snoring form: hair sticking up on one side, a growing drool spot on his pillow. I quietly pull out the contents of his bag: two textbooks, a notebook, some pens, and a handful of comic books. I smile as I peek at the cover of one of the comics—a giant, floating alien waving its tentacles as it descends on a green planet—before stalking back out of the room.

As I leave, I toss a look at his closet, where his old silver backpack still hangs from a hook on the wall. Being able to replace that dingy thing was a proud moment for me, the happy result of the last time I found plastic during a scav run and ended up with a larger-than-expected credit haul. Mica was so palpably delighted to receive the new bag, it was almost painful.

I chew my lip, feeling the tiniest tinge of guilt for borrowing it, but shake off the thought. He can manage for one day. And if I'm quick, I'll be back before Mica wakes up and notices anyway.

I take a canteen of water out of the fridge and toss it into the bag, along with a small flashlight. With one strap slung over my shoulder and my boots still in my hand, I steal out the front door and close it behind me as gently as possible.

I quietly tiptoe down the stairs. The air outside is brisk and still. There is no movement on the street. I quickly bend over to put on my shoes, sheltered under the apartment building's awning, and inspect the area around me. Most of the ground seems dry enough to walk on, though I can still see a few steaming puddles that have collected where the gravel is uneven. Easy enough to avoid. I take a deep breath and silently hopscotch across the road in the moonlight.

The route to the southern wall takes three times longer than usual. In addition to having to navigate around the small lingering pools of acid rain, I find myself looking behind me with every other step. All it would take is one nosy insomniac to spot me and figure out what it is I'm trying to do.

Thankfully, by the time I finally reach the wall, I'm confident I haven't been followed. I pull the gloves out of my pocket and put them on to protect myself against any residual water that might have pooled in the wall's cracks, then begin to climb. As I scramble up, the moonlight casts an eerie glow on the black brick, making me feel uncomfortably visible.

My anxiety is high as I reach the top, and I climb down the other side without checking the ground below. My boot lands in a shallow puddle of rainwater, splashing up a cascade of droplets that land on the arms of my jacket with a sizzle.

I bite the inside of my lip to keep from crying out. Mentally cursing myself for not looking at where I was landing, I leap out of the puddle and instinctively wipe down my arms with my gloved hands. Drawing a deep breath, I survey the damage. Fortunately, the thick soles of my new boots seem virtually unscathed, and there are only a few light scorch marks on the sleeves of my jacket. My gloves, on the other hand, are completely shredded.

"Well, those were a good investment," I mutter under my breath, peeling off what remains of the gloves and inspecting the pink skin on my palms. My hands feel a little raw, but they don't actively hurt. It appears the still-smoking material of the gloves absorbed most of the damage from climbing.

Throwing a silent prayer up to whatever Powers That Be that the rain will have fully evaporated by the time I return, I toss the gloves into the puddle. I offer up a sarcastic salute as they disintegrate, leaving nothing but decorative metal studs floating on the surface.

BY THE TIME I reach the Dead Woods, the ground is almost entirely dry. I pick up my pace, jogging through the brush until I'm back at the fallen trunk next to where I found my little machine. I take a long swig of water and survey the area. It's been less than a week since I was here, but it feels like eons have passed.

I pull the flashlight out of the backpack and, with my eyes on the ground, feverishly begin my search. First, I check the exact spot where I made my discovery, digging down, pushing back into the roots I found it under. When it's clear there's nothing more there, I widen my search and start to trace a path that spiders out through the tightly knit trees. I head in one direction, then, after a few dozen feet, retrace my steps and start over at a different angle. It isn't long before the tedium gets to me, though, and soon I give up on sticking to the pattern and start forging forward in a single direction.

Sweat gathers on the back of my neck as I check underneath tree roots and paw at the dirt with the tip of my boot, finding nothing but newly fallen bits of scrap metal. Every now and then I stop to snatch up an errant bolt or length of wire, unable to ignore the practiced scavenger in me.

I am so caught up in searching that I don't notice the sky's transition from black to increasingly light gray. With its slow brightening, I start to see beyond the immediate circumference of my flashlight's beam and it invigorates my search. After a while, thirst convinces me to look up. The trees have begun to thin out, and I can just make out the hazy outline of the District ruins in the distance. I've ventured so deep into the woods that I'm almost out the other side. This is unfamiliar territory.

I mentally calculate how far I must have come and, consequently, how long it will take me to get back. The answer makes me stop short and, as I do, my boot catches on the edge of a large rock and I start to fall. I reach out to catch myself and skid forward on my hands, my already raw palms burning as they run over the rough ground.

Hissing through clenched teeth, I roll onto my back, crushing Mica's backpack underneath me before I sit up. I slip it off and scoot so I can lean against the trunk of a nearby tree. Wincing slightly, I hold my hands out in front of me and flex them a few times. I haven't broken through the skin, but between this and their earlier exposure to the puddled rain, they definitely sting.

I tilt my head back against the tree trunk and stare up at the sky. What had I honestly expected to find? It's almost daylight, I'm miles from town, and all I have to show for my efforts are skinned hands and a few measly generics. Mica's sure to wake soon, and there will be no avoiding the morning scavs by the time I get back, which means I'm in for some serious verbal thrashing at best. I don't want to think of what "at worst" might be.

Tap, tap, tap. I gently knock the back of my head against the hard trunk and sigh. I know I need to go back, but I can't bring myself to get up just yet. I pull out the canteen again and gulp down half my remaining water as my unfocused gaze drifts across the landscape.

Beyond the last few trees, the hazy fog is evaporating/ Gray-tinged morning light illuminates the ruined metropolis that lies beyond the woods. I stare at the deteriorated silhouette of the District—just one of thousands of once-great cities that have been turned into decaying shrines, or tombs, forever reminding us of the Skyfall.

NOBODY KNOWS why the city of Intheria, that bastion of scientific research and medical knowledge, fell from the sky centuries ago. Only that when it did, the hundred thousand souls who worked and ate and slept and *lived* there weren't the only ones lost that day.

Something else was unleashed when the great city fell.

Nobody knows exactly how the plague came to be either, only that it did. Some say that those Intherian scientists grew it in a lab. To this day, the religious folk insist it was sent down from God. Punishment for the sins of humanity and all.

The plague had spread like wildfire. The major cities were the first to go, but it wasn't long before the disease made its way across even the smallest towns. They tried to isolate the contamination to the ground-world, but eventually it hit the skycities too. Millions succumbed. Those who might have been able to help had perished when Intheria fell, and historians conjecture that any hope of an antidote or cure was lost with them.

Within the year, Earth's population was decimated. Our great global civilization, reduced to ashes.

No survivor's story was exactly the same. Some had fled far and fast enough to outrun it, some were too secluded to have ever been at risk, and some, miraculously, were simply unaffected. The religious folk really go nuts over that last one.

Eventually, those who survived began to rebuild. With the government of old collapsed, the Tribunal took control and declared themselves our leaders; their progeny still lead us today. The skycities were temporarily evacuated so they could be cleansed, with skydwellers begrudgingly moving into ground settlements they would later abandon. Meanwhile, the infected areas on the ground were simply cordoned off and quarantined.

Urban survivors became refugees, forced to leave everything behind. Homes and belongings were automatically condemned as contaminated and, thus, quarantined as well. Occasionally, someone would cross the quarantine line in an attempt to recover their belongings, landing them in observation for weeks to ensure they showed no signs of infection.

Isolation, observation, decontamination. That was the drill. That is, assuming they didn't end up dead first.

Survivors who still had money or connections ultimately returned to the sky while the rest banded together down here. The Tribunal restored what technology they could, and gave us terrestrials our role to play, sustaining what few resources we had left.

And here we still are today: salvaging, scavenging, recycling.

Surviving.

IT'S BEEN centuries since the Skyfall, but the Tribunal still keeps an active quarantine on all the old major city sites. They say the plague is still a threat—dormant but looming. I'm not sure how much of that I believe, since, as time has gone on, the enforcement of the quarantine has certainly loosened.

The occasional crossing does happen, and it never seems like a big deal. The Tribunal videos we were shown in school said that the disease was spread through contact, so as long as we don't touch anything inside the quarantine line, we're fine. But we never forget what happened. We never forget the risk.

I tear my eyes from the city's silhouette. *Guess all that schooling wasn't completely lost on me.*

I take a deep breath and exhale slowly, willing myself to get up. Bracing myself against the tree, I attempt to stand without the aid of my hands. Stumbling upward, the toe of my boot catches beneath me and I begin to tilt to the right. I grit my teeth and grasp the rough bark behind me with my left palm, a low curse tearing from my lips.

"Now, now, little girl." A deep voice emerges from the shadows behind me. "Hasn't anyone ever told you to watch your language?"

SIX

I FREEZE.

The crunch of multiple footsteps sounds in my ears, and I know the unseen speaker is not alone. With achingly slow speed, I bend my knees to pick up Mica's bag and pivot in the direction of the voice.

Three huge men stand about a yard in front of me, lined up in a row. All three of them sport shaved heads, making them almost indistinguishable from one another, save for their differing skin tones. Their long brown coats hang open, revealing bare chests covered with tattoos that creep from below their waistlines up to their chins.

Raiders.

The man in the middle has a chain of thick golden links hanging around his throat. As I watch it bounce against his dark chest, I realize I've never actually seen raiders this close before. All that time spent thinking about Lee's final moments, what his murderers had looked like. Turns out I had it pictured all wrong.

My heart pounds behind my ribs and my breathing quickens. I tighten my grip around the backpack, my pulse radiating through my still-raw palm. Not to protect anything of real value inside, but to stop my hand from shaking.

The man in the middle appraises me with dark eyes. Smirking, he draws one hand up to his face and rests his thumb and fingers on either side of his chin. The back of his hand is branded with a word, one letter inked on each knuckle, but I can't make it out.

"Well, girlie? Didn't your mother teach you any manners? Ladies don't swear," he says darkly.

"You'd be hard-pressed to find anyone who considers me a lady," I spit before I can stop myself. "Not that you'd be able to tell, I'm sure. Run across many classy gals in your line of work, do you?"

The lackeys that flank his side exchange a wary look, but their leader simply shakes his head and laughs.

"Looks like we got ourselves a live one, boys. A real firecracker." His eyes narrow on my face. "Tell me, what's a pretty thing like you doing way out here?"

"Can't a *lady*," I stress the word, "go out for a nice post-rain stroll in peace?"

"No." His gaze darkens.

"Sorry to disappoint. All that rain gave me cabin fever. I needed some fresh air. Didn't even realize how far I had wandered until now." I try my best to look sheepish.

He laughs again. "Why don't I believe you?" he says, taking a step toward me.

"Trust issues?" I shrug, mirroring his movement to maintain the distance between us.

The humor drains from his face. "You're a long way from home, little girl. Lady or not, you should know better than to push your luck with us."

He runs his gaze up and down my body and I force myself not to squirm. After a moment, he gestures for me to hand over the backpack.

"I'd be the one worried about luck if I were you." I toss the pack in front of his feet. "I don't think you have much of it going for you today. There's nothing worthwhile in there."

"Locke, check it out." Without breaking his gaze, he motions to the man on his right, who picks up the bag and hastily unzips it.

"Couple pieces of scrap, canteen, flashlight . . ." Locke's accent is stilted as he paws through the pockets. "Like she said." He darts his eyes to me, his expression unreadable. "It's not much, boss."

"Like I told you. Nothing to brag about. Sorry you've wasted your time," I say.

The boss strokes his chin slowly before answering. "I wouldn't say we've wasted anything yet. Am I right, boys?"

"Always are, Ryk," the other lackey says with a guffaw.

My heartbeat picks up, and the warning bells that have been pealing in my head start to clang.

"I'll just be going then," I say, taking another step back. "Feel free to keep the bag. You know, gesture of goodwill and all."

"I don't think so, firecracker." Ryk bridges the space between us with one giant step, wrapping his fingers firmly around both my upper arms. He pulls me into him, smashing my face against his sweaty chest. "You smell nice," he growls into my hair and moves one of his meaty hands to grip the back of my neck.

Bile rises in my throat. Over Ryk's shoulder, I toss a panicked glance at his companions. One is openly grinning; Locke, still holding my backpack, tries not to meet my gaze but fails. His lips are in a tight line as I silently plead with him, my eyes wide with fear, and to my utter shock, he opens his mouth.

"Don't . . ." Locke says weakly.

I'm not sure if he simply can't stand to see my silent begging, or if he's actually trying to get his boss to stop. Either way, it's enough to make my captor turn toward him.

"The hell did you say?" Ryk snarls.

The single second of distraction is all I need. With as much strength as I can muster, I bring my knee up swiftly and ram it into Ryk's groin as hard as I can. A strangled, animalistic moan falls from his lips as he collapses, and the grinning lackey lets out a single, booming laugh before smacking his hand to his mouth in horror.

I turn on the spot, wrenching myself out of Ryk's grasp. Digging my heels into the ground, I sprint in the opposite direction. His whimpers fade as I run, but I'm not fast enough to avoid hearing the crunch of fists on bone as both lackeys receive their respective punishments. I can't help but wonder who committed the worse offense—the one who might've pitied me, or the one who laughed at the boss's expense.

I race on, not daring to slow down or look behind me. For a single minute, I think they might actually have let me go, but my hopes are dashed as my ears pick up the patter of heavy boots behind me.

There's no way I'll be able to circle around them to get home. My only option is to outrun them until one of us can't run anymore.

I bolt out of the forest and aim for the closest structure within sight. About half a mile ahead, down a slight slope, sits an old outpost station. Squat and square, the battered building wears decades of graffiti, and the early morning sun casts low shadows on the outpost, making it appear larger than it is. The blinking red lights that mark the quarantine line lay behind the building, three beams spaced six inches apart and suspended in midair, separating the outpost from the city ruins that begin just a few hundred feet beyond.

Grateful that the past three years of hiking, climbing, digging, and outrunning other scavs has bolstered my speed and stamina, I run toward the front of the outpost as fast as I can. I crash into the front door, violently jiggling the handle.

Locked.

I curse aloud and run the perimeter to check the windows. Though the majority of them are broken, they're too high up for me to climb through. I peek back around the front, only to see the raiders' dark outlines closing the distance between us, one trailing behind the other two.

I slip around to the rear of the building and flatten my back against it, hiding in the long shadows. My lungs scream for air and I hastily comply, gulping it down as adrenaline and fear pin me to the wall. The blinking boundary between the plague-infested District ruins and my post against the station wall stands about ten feet ahead. My chest heaving, I stare at the quarantine line. If I cross it, I risk contaminating myself with whatever strains of disease might still linger in the ruins. But if the raiders get a hold of me . . .

"Jax, get the door!"

One of them tries to turn the locked handle, rattling it with increasing annoyance.

"She's locked herself in, boss."

They think I'm inside.

Ryk lets loose a string of expletives, and the pain checkering his voice is almost enough to make me smirk. Almost.

"I'm gonna break her in half," he says soullessly, and I swallow hard.

I hear a couple of clicks and buzzes, like the sound of an intercom, followed by some low muttering. I can't make out what's being said, but the situation becomes clear enough when I feel the wood shiver and hear a crash as one of them kicks in the door.

"Th-there's no one in here, Ryk." The choked voice filters through the window directly above my head. I tense as their heavy footsteps stomp overhead, and a few moments of silent shuffling pass before a booming voice swears loudly and jolts my body into movement.

They've seen me.

I launch myself forward just as a hand reaches through the window above me. I feel a sharp jab of pain as the raider grabs at my ponytail, but he's half a second too slow.

In five steps, I've crossed the quarantine line. I imagine that somewhere in the sky an alarm must be sounding, but I don't care. Right now, taking my chances with the plague seems far preferable to whatever Ryk and his boys have planned for me.

There is unintelligible yelling at my back as I run toward the ruins, the dusty dirt of the valley floor giving way to crumbling pavement. The District is no longer simply a silhouette, a distant backdrop to life in Sixteen, the setting for stories of lives long since lost. In an instant, it has become real. I race past decaying brick houses—skinny but tall, and falling apart from the top down—that seem to beg, "*Imagine what we used to be.*"

The houses give way to tall, gray buildings that loom over me, forming the outline of the ruined city that I know. After about a hundred feet, I realize the raiders haven't pursued me. I risk a glance back in their direction and slow to a stop.

The trio hovers just behind the quarantine line, the red lights illuminating their forms. Ryk is hunched over, fury etched on his dark face. Jax is distracted, his fingers trying to stifle the outpouring of blood from a clearly broken nose. Locke simply stands there, clutching his side. The look of pain on his face, however, tells me that his wounds may not be so easily remedied.

Suddenly, all three of them turn their heads to the right. I follow their gaze just in time to see a huge black transport truck barreling toward the outpost, four other raiders perched in its long, rectangular wagon. I can just barely hear the truck's engine humming as the vehicle screeches to a stop and one of the riders tosses something out to each of my pursuers, but I don't stick around long enough to see what it is.

Wind whipping past my ears, I race down the cracked city street, failing to blot out the truck's crescendoing engine as it gains on me. I run past the brick houses and charge into the shadows of the skyscrapers, turning blindly down a narrow alleyway. I leap over fallen rubble and piles of scrap metal, emerging on a parallel street where ancient-looking transport vehicles have been abandoned on the road like rusted monuments. Their round tops have been crushed by falling debris, the dyminium glass in their windows shattered. A few paces ahead, a tall black gate with a thick chain wrapped around it bars the entrance to a set of stairs that appear to go underground.

Behind me, the truck speeds past the alley entrance in search of a clear path. Turning toward the sound, I see Ryk, Jax, and Locke have joined the other raiders in the transport's cab. They have all donned gas masks, adding weight to my growing worries about contamination.

I tell myself that as long as I don't touch anything, I will be fine. "No contact, no contamination," I remember. I pull the sleeves of my jacket over my hands just in case.

One life-threatening issue at a time, I remind myself.

Between the obstacles that block their transport's path and the cover of the surrounding buildings, it's now much easier to put distance between the raiders and me. The transport fades into silence and a hopeful thought emerges. This city is huge and their mobility is limited. If I can just get back to the Dead Woods while they think they're still tracking me in here, I could make it home.

I double back, my body aching. I can't remember the last time I've run this far, let alone this fast. The heat is stifling, and sweat has already bled through my shirt to my jacket. I round a corner and find myself back on the street with the gated stairwell.

I've almost reached the alley when I stop short.

"There you are, firecracker," Ryk says, stepping out of the shadows. His voice is garbled through his mask, but the malice in it still rings clear. Without giving him time for another word, I turn and take off in the opposite direction, only to be forced to a stop by two new raiders as they step into the road.

Trapped.

The alley is out of reach behind Ryk, thirty feet away, and the next cross street lies just behind the newcomers. The long buildings on either side of me leave no gaps, other than the black gate to the right.

"City people are so predictable," says one of the raiders, balancing a long metal staff on his shoulders. "The first sign of freedom and they head for home."

"What was that you were saying about luck, again?" Ryk says arrogantly. I throw a sneer at him and he snarls.

The third man's shoulders shake with silent laughter. "This one's going to be a lot of fun, I can tell."

I pivot, my back toward the black gate and Ryk and the two raiders now on either side of me. They watch me predatorily as I step back. Then, simultaneously, they move.

My head whips from left to right as the threats on either side of me close in. All three men move slowly, leisurely. Like they want to build up my panic, like they're savoring my fear. I take one final step backward and feel cool metal bars of the gate through the material of my jacket. The padlock hooked into the chain digs into my hip.

This is it. I close my eyes for half of a second and take a deep breath. *Contact.*

Gripping the sleeves of my jacket over my fists, I spin around and stick my boots through the bars of the gate, hoisting myself up. I hear the raiders' pace quicken as they realize what I'm doing, but I have the advantage of the past three years spent climbing over walls. Holding my breath, I quickly scale up and over the top of the gate.

I drop down on the other side, unable to suppress the victorious smile that breaks out on my face. It is short-lived, however, as I'm suddenly yanked backward. I hit the gate, hard, the back of my head slamming into the metal bars.

"Enough." I hear Ryk's growl over the ringing in my ears. His hand tightens around the fistful of my jacket he's grabbed hold of and thrusts his other arm through the bars, pinning me across my neck. "I have you now, little girl. Fun's over."

He is so strong. I struggle against his crushing hold, barely able to unzip my jacket with what little arm movement I have. My movements cause the sleeve of his coat to ride up, and a gap of skin appears at his wrist.

"You're right," I gasp. "It is." I turn my head and bite down on his wrist as hard as I can, tasting blood on my tongue as Ryk hollers. He momentarily loosens his hold around my neck, giving me just enough room to wiggle out of my jacket which is still gripped tightly in his other hand, my arms stinging painfully as I wrench myself free.

I flee in the only direction I can—down.

I bound down the stairs two at a time, holding my arms to my chest as I descend into darkness. The loss of my jacket has me feeling vulnerable, but it's still the least of my concerns. Is it one less layer of protection? Yes. And if I become contaminated, there is a chance I could die.

If Ryk catches me at this point, though, I'm pretty sure I will be begging for death.

I hear the protest of metal wrenching against metal as the raiders break through the gate behind me. I hit the bottom of the stairwell with a thud, and the sudden lack of a next stair throws me off balance. I am a long way down. I reach out instinctively and blindly grab hold of a railing, steadying myself before following it forward in the pitch black.

So much for not touching anything.

Faint beams of light come from behind me as the raiders' flashlights search ahead of them. By the sound of it, they aren't running, but they're still gaining on me. I try to speed up, using the dim light to avoid the debris on the ground, but my legs feel weak. My adrenaline is evaporating and I don't know how much further I'll be able to go.

The railing runs out abruptly and I catch myself to avoid plunging headfirst into a pit that has appeared in front of me. The wavering light from the flashlights is too dim to see how wide it is or how deep it goes, but I've run out of pavement.

Sucking in a nervous breath, I sit on the edge of the platform and dangle my legs over the edge. I flip around and slowly lower myself down, breathing through my teeth as my still-raw palms press against the rough floor, prepared to hang off the side until I find the bottom. My careful descent turns out to be unnecessary though, as my feet hit something firm before the platform has even passed my chest.

Releasing myself, I let my eyes adjust to survey the area. The pit is narrow but long, a tunnel within the tunnel I'm already in. It stretches out seemingly infinitely on either side.

I quickly recollect a history lesson we were given on the Skyline Transfer. Our teacher told us that the technology was loosely based on an underground train system that used to run below all the major cities, a maze of connecting tunnels and shafts. When solar power became the name of the energy game and cities took to the skies, however, the underground system was shut down. The tracks were pulled up to be recycled and the entrances were sealed off. Thus, the Skyline Transfer was born and the rest fell into the history books.

As if on cue, the flashlight beams suddenly brighten. Across the pit, I can see the entrance to another passage on the opposite platform and I can only pray there's a stairway that leads back to the surface at the end of it.

The surface. I never thought I'd want to feel the blistering sun so badly.

I stumble forward across the pit until I hit the platform on the other side, but my arms give out when I try to hoist myself up, my head slamming against the edge of the platform when my hand slips out from under me.

I squeeze my eyes tightly shut to halt the tears that immediately spring up in response to the pain, and when I reopen them, my vision is slashed with streaks of white. Desperately, I try to lift myself onto the platform again, to no avail. I can't get up. With my head pulsing and the raiders closing in, I blindly choose a direction within the pit and set off.

I see the tunnel suddenly illuminate around me before I hear the raider's yell.

"We got her!" The sound is victorious and terrifying, and with my path lit from behind, I immediately understand why. An enormous wall made up of huge metal panels stands twenty feet in front of me, blocking off the path from top to bottom.

A small cry escapes my lips. Barricaded in front, raiders at my back. Nowhere left to run. I dart toward the wall and pound on it hopelessly, my fists echoing against the steel as I sink to my knees. The adrenaline that has been propelling me drains from my body as my impending defeat washes over me.

A muffled ringing fills my ears, pressing against my brain, and I feel an icy chill in my cheeks, even though I know they should still be hot from the chase. The throbbing rhythm in my head calls forth a cool darkness that begins to seep into the edges of my consciousness, but I keep pounding on the wall, oblivious to the minutes or hours or seconds that must be passing as I wait for the raiders to descend upon me.

I know they've finally gotten to me as an abrupt surge of light blinds me. Strong arms wrap around my torso, wrenching me from the wall. The arms are bare; the skin smooth against my own. I wonder with detached interest why the raiders would take off their jackets after going through the trouble of using masks and gloves up top.

My instincts tell me to struggle but my body feels so weak, my head full of swirls, my vision full of stars. It all just seems so futile. So, I simply let my captor pull me back, and through the fog of the spreading blackness, I hear screams of outrage.

Why are they mad? They've caught me.

My captor shoves me from behind and I burst through a door into impossible sunlight. I blink rapidly, my eyes burning in response to the sudden brightness. I reach up to rub them and find them wet. The light must be making them water. Yes, that must be it.

A heavy hammering echoes from behind, fists banging against metal, but the darkness and pain in my head are finally consuming me, and I spin just in time to see bare arms reaching for me as I crumple to the ground.

SEVEN

MY HEAD THROBS, a relentless, pounding ache—the kind that starts in one spot but slowly spreads with each pulse. A twinge in my throat tells me that I'm thirsty too. Really thirsty. How long have I been out?

I am lying down, I know that much. It feels like I'm level with the ground, but something softer than dirt cushions the length of my body. The backs of my eyelids are a bright, fiery red; apparently, I didn't hallucinate the brightness that encompassed me before I passed out. I grasp at the memories of those last moments in the underground tunnel, but everything is still fuzzy.

Green. I remember seeing the color green before I blacked out. There was green and there was sunlight and there was . . . someone.

My eyes fly open. The eruption of light forces me to immediately shut them again, but the cursory glimpse, along with my instincts, tells me that I am alone. I could have sworn someone caught me before I fell, though. A raider? Couldn't be. Aside from the hammering in my head, my parched throat, the soreness I feel in my muscles, and the stings running down both arms, I am relatively unharmed. I highly doubt that, after the chase I gave them, the raiders would do me the courtesy of letting me die by way of a headache.

I slowly open my eyes again, squinting against the brightness. I don't understand how I'm back outside. The last thing I remember is desperately pounding against a metal wall in an underground tunnel, raiders closing in. I recall the despair that washed over me with the realization I had nowhere else to run. I felt it in my bones like a death sentence.

Yet, somehow, I made it back to the surface? And not just back to the ruined city from where I descended either. My hasty preview of the area overhead was decidedly lacking in tall, dilapidated buildings, so somehow I'm back outside the District?

I shake my head, trying to make sense of my fuzzy thoughts, and immediately regret it.

Ow.

In addition to the relentless pounding radiating through my head, a sharper sting pulls at me from one side, making me wince. I gently prod the painful region on top of my head with my fingers, grimacing when I draw them back and see they are covered in still-drying blood.

With the smallest movement I can manage, I lift my head and start to soak in my surroundings, quickly realizing why the color green sticks out so vividly in my memory: it is everywhere.

My senses are on overload. Green blankets the ground, dangling above me, surrounding my body on all sides. It lines the edges of a small, clear, freestanding pool of water that sits a few yards away. It bursts from the tips of trees overhead.

I've never seen so much green. I never realized so much green even existed.

In addition to the news, reality shows, and occasional special events that air on TV, the Tribunal often features educational programming. The topics range from the history of the Skyfall to the water purification and food manufacturing processes. Once, during a show that focused on the latter, I saw shots of an agricultural plant in the skycity, Daedryl. Up there, above the cloud layer, under the protection of a UV filter, where the rain can't burn through them, things grow.

It's the only time I remember seeing what food looks like in its natural state, before it's processed into the nutrient-rich but thoroughly disgusting stuff we terrestrials subsist on. Given the unceasing dusty brownness of the groundworld, it's no wonder my favorite part was getting to see the rainbow of produce they have up there: vibrant reds, oranges, and greens.

That was nothing compared to what I'm seeing now.

I prop myself up on my elbow a little too quickly, and the change in elevation causes pain to immediately rush to my temple. Waiting for the ache to subside, I flex my hand against the green ground and feel soft, springy blades poke up in the spaces between my fingers. I grasp one and try to pull it up, but it tears halfway, leaving behind a tiny jagged base that I quickly lose sight of as the rest of the blades sway in the breeze and swallow it up.

Grass. Not the fake plastic turf that decorates skycity residences. Real grass.

I sit up, watching in wonder as the breeze slowly sweeps across the ground, skimming the surface of the pool and causing delicate ripples to spread through the water. The air is so clear and weightless, I hadn't even noticed it until now. I suck in a deep breath, amazed at the temperature. It's cool and dry, so unlike the thick, stifling air I'm used to. It might even feel cold if the sun wasn't pleasantly warming my skin.

Ha, I scoff mentally. *Never thought there'd be a day I'd consider the sun pleasant.*

I turn my eyes skyward, only to realize that, while I can see the effects of its illumination and can feel its rays beaming on my shoulders, there's no actual sun in sight. The sky is vividly blue but entirely empty.

I stand up, slowly. The pain in my head has subsided to a soft thud, but the thirst burning in my throat is more acute now. I look longingly at the clear water in the pond, almost within reach, and desperately wish it was safe to drink.

I force myself to look away and that's when I see it—the metal barricade behind me, an exact copy of the one that had barred my way in the underground tunnel. It suddenly occurs to me that maybe I'm not back on the surface after all.

The wall stretches twenty feet straight up, made of dark matte metal panels bolted to one another with shiny silver rivets, and the top, incredibly, seems to meld right into the calm blue sky. Lush landscape stretches on all sides of it, as if the plates just happened to fall into place in that spot—an expanse of exposed metal, unattached to anything. I'm not sure how it's even staying upright.

I walk over to the wall and touch a single finger to its surface. Tracing a line along the cool metal until I reach the edge, I attempt to curl the rest of my fingers around the side, but I hit firm resistance in what should be thin air. I push against the spot with both hands. Beneath my palms, I feel the same smooth metal, even though my brain tells me that I should be falling forward into the open space.

I step back and blink, slowly and purposefully. Maybe I hit my head harder than I realized.

I run my eyes up the wall in disbelief. Though my eyes tell me that the landscape continues far beyond where I'm standing, it actually ends right in front of me. It's so subtle, I probably would never have noticed if I weren't right next to it. I can just barely make out where the cloudless sky ends—right where it meets the panels at the top of the wall.

I knock on the fake landscape lightly. A moment passes. Then something on the other side thumps back at me, hard.

"What in the name of . . ." I back away from the boundary, eyes fixed on the wall of sky at my front until my feet stutter as I collide with something behind me.

"Pretty neat, isn't it?"

The voice, soft and calm in my ear, immediately sets me back on red alert. I have backed up not into some*thing*, but some*one*.

Instinct takes over, and before my brain has even digested what's happening, I swing my fist up behind my head. It connects with something soft but firm, and I hear a stunned yelp as I pull away.

I whirl, both of my hands curled into fists and raised comically in front of me like I'm preparing for a boxing match.

He is bent over, his hands at his face. "You're stronger than you look," he mumbles into his palms.

The stranger in front of me is pale. That's the first thing I notice. The light skin covering his arms is smooth and spotless, starkly lacking the freckles and sunspots that pepper my own golden skin.

"Who are you?" I shout.

He ignores the question as he straightens, one hand grazing against his ribs, like he's checking for something, the other still prodding gently at his mouth.

I note with satisfaction that his lower lip is bleeding.

He runs his other hand over his head, brushing his fingers through cropped blond hair, still mumbling. The words "grateful" and "know better" jump out at me.

The stranger looks to be about my age, maybe a little older. He's nearly a full head taller than me. His blue eyes, squinting in pain, are framed with thick, dark blond lashes. Eyes that simultaneously alarm and fascinate me.

The fact that they're blue makes it clear he's a skydweller. But his eyes are not the icy, fragile blue that peers out from the faces of elite skydwellers like the Primes of the Tribunal or the Elders—those who have never even set foot here on the ground. It's a bold, iridescent hue I have never seen before—swirls of cobalt and indigo, sapphire and cerulean.

It is the most beautiful color I've ever seen.

He releases his face to hold up his arms, palms out in surrender. Through the fabric of his shirt—a thin, metallic weave I'm not familiar with—I can see the outline of the muscles in his forearms, flexed in response to my attack. His nostrils flare with each sharp intake of breath, and his expression seems to fall somewhere between fear and curiosity.

I decide that he doesn't seem particularly inclined to attack. He certainly doesn't look like a raider, at any rate. I drop my arms but keep them loose and ready.

"Who are you?" I ask again, each word sharp.

He doesn't respond.

"What is this place? Where am I?"

After what feels like an unnecessarily long pause, he draws a slow breath. "Earth?" he says, his voice smooth and rich even as it's flattened with apprehension.

I groan and lift a hand to my face, pinching the bridge of my nose. "Fantastic," I grumble. "I'm having some sort of dehydration-induced hallucination, but at least it's got a sense of humor."

His mouth curves up on one side, as though he's fighting a grin. "Who are you?" he asks.

"I asked you first."

He looks at me with amusement and we stand for another few moments in a silent stalemate. "My name is Adam," he finally says.

"Wow." I fail to stifle a giggle. It burns my dry throat as it leaves my lips.

He frowns. "What's so funny?"

"It's just that I don't think I've heard that name in . . . Maybe my Gran's gran might've had a friend named that?" I say, the words slurring together slightly. "Guess your parents must have a serious soft spot for old-fashioned stuff, huh?"

"Must be," he says.

"So. Adam." I can't help chuckling when I say his name. "What exactly are you doing here?"

He says nothing and my frustration returns.

"At the very least, can you tell me what the hell that is?" I jab a finger in the direction of the wall, still looming ominously over us.

"It's a wall," he says slowly.

I stare at him. "I know it's a wall. You said something about it back before I . . ." I glance guiltily at the fresh split in his bottom lip and trail off. "What did you mean?"

"You already figured it out, didn't you? I saw you pushing on the camouflage. You know we're not actually outside, right?"

Even though I had already considered the possibility, it is still jarring to hear my theory confirmed. "So, right now, we're still underground?"

"Of course," he replies, as if this is a perfectly natural thing. "This is a really well-made encapsulation dome," he continues as he looks around speculatively. "I've never seen one quite this . . . beautiful before. Usually it's more obvious where the boundary is, but this is pretty finessed. I mean, obviously, these panels right here are broken," he walks over and runs his hand down the front of the metal plates, "but it does make it easier to find the door."

"Door?" I rush over to him and run my fingers over the seam between panels. "Where? How do I get out?"

"It's just a normal exterior exit," he says matter-of-factly. He presses in on a camouflaged spot just to the left of the metal wall. Looking closely, I can see that it's a slightly different color than the rest of the "air" around it. Three of the plates shift to reveal a shallow doorway and my jaw goes slack. I've never seen anything like this.

"It's tiresome to search for the exit panels normally, but since these camo panels are malfunctioning, it's kind of like a landmark. You're not going to want to go out that way though," he adds.

"Why not?"

Adam shifts on his feet, an uncomfortable expression on his face.

"Okay, look, I don't have time for this. I need to—" I attempt to stride past him, but my still weak legs have a different idea. My right knee quivers as I step forward and I collapse into Adam instead.

"Whoa." He catches me with one arm, propping me up like a rag doll.

"I'm fine," I say sharply, pushing myself off of him.

"You're not, clearly."

"I'll *be* fine." I stumble forward a few steps, but the dehydration and probable concussion make it hard to walk straight. I nearly bite it when my foot catches on something soft, but before I have time to fall, Adam has caught me again.

"Stop helping me," I hiss. I look down to see what I tripped over and have to stop my mouth from falling open entirely. Mica's backpack: dirty but completely intact. I pick it up with hasty hands before swiveling around.

"Where did you get this?" I blurt.

"One of those guys was carrying it," Adam replies with an infuriating air of nonchalance.

"Yes," I sigh. "I know. But how did *you* get it?"

He shrugs.

"Those raiders, they took it from me. How did you get it from them?"

He fidgets with the hem of his shirt. "Look, I really didn't mean to make them any angrier than you already had. It's just that when I grabbed you and saw that he—the, uh, big one—wasn't about to let you go . . . I had to subdue them. But as I think you can tell, they're awake now, and I think I may have just pissed them off even more. They've set up a guard right outside. You heard them pound on the wall a minute ago."

I gape at him.

"Don't worry," he adds, "this exterior wall is over two feet thick, and I've locked the outside controls. There's no way they're getting in."

I ignore, for the moment, the fact that most of what he just said makes no sense to me. "So, right through that doorway is the underground tunnel?"

"Yep."

"And you pulled me out. You brought me in here."

"Yeah."

"You saved me."

"Yes." His eyes blaze with a sudden seriousness that makes me want to ask why.

I don't.

"Well, thank you," I say, as a surge of humbled gratitude flares in my cheeks. "Wait, what do you mean when you say you 'subdued' them?" I ask skeptically, eyeing his frame. Adam looks like he's in pretty good shape from what I can tell, but the thought of him up against Ryk's massive form is still ludicrous.

He shrugs again. I attempt to repeat my question, but my throat catches, starting an uncontrollable coughing fit. All this talking has leached the remaining moisture from my mouth. My free hand rushes to my throat, and my tongue sticks to the roof of my mouth as I attempt to swallow.

With elation, I remember the canteen in my backpack. I tear open the zipper and pull it out, only to find it completely empty. A strangled sob rips through my throat and I sink to my knees.

"What's wrong?" Adam says, crouching down with me.

"I'm just really thirsty." I try to say the words casually, but they emerge on a whimper, making me sound as pathetic as I feel.

"Hang on." He snatches the bottle from my hands and returns less than a minute later. "Here," he says, handing the canteen back to me. I hear the water sloshing inside and grab it without hesitation, drinking feverishly. I feel the cool liquid slide slowly down my throat and hit my stomach.

A moan escapes my lips as I exhale, sitting back on my heels once I've drained the entire canteen. "I think you just saved my life. Again. So . . . thanks. Again."

He smiles, a lopsided grin. "Want more?"

"I don't want to deplete your supply," I say, trying to mimic his consideration despite how thirsty I still am.

He laughs. "I hardly think you have to worry about that." He points to the pond.

The pond of unfiltered water.

District water. Contaminated water.

And the realization of what I've just poured into my body hits me like a Skyline train.

EIGHT

"WHAT HAVE YOU DONE?" My eyes are wide as I wrap both hands around my throat, grasping wildly as if I might be able to pull the poisonous water out.

"What are you talking about?" Adam looks at me in bewilderment.

"That water isn't purified," I gasp. "Why did I even bother running? I really am going to die out here . . . Mica doesn't even know where I am . . ." My thoughts are frantic as I speak them aloud.

"Are you always this dramatic?"

I peer up through my lashes to see Adam staring at me like I am deranged.

He looks at me pointedly. "You think I'd just give you water from an open source? Of course it's been filtered, look." He points to the canteen in my hands, and I notice an unfamiliar metal ring wrapped around the neck. "I've been drinking the same water, using the same portable filter, and I'm still standing," he finishes.

I lower my hand from my neck and assess myself. "How is that possible?" I think aloud, staring at the pool. The purification process for drinkable water takes days. There's no way the toxins could have been filtered out so quickly. My system should already be shutting down.

Granted, it doesn't *feel* like I'm dying.

"Surely you can understand why I was alarmed," I say, my cheeks flushing with sudden embarrassment.

"Sure," he says, though I feel like he's just placating me.

"So, this . . . thing," I say, rapping my fingernails against the metal ring, "is some kind of water filter?"

He nods.

"And you just . . . fill it up. And it purifies the water. Instantly?"

"Nothing gets past you, does it?"

I disregard his barb as my eyes dart back and forth from the bottle in my hands to the pool, my disbelief leaving a long, awkward silence between Adam and me.

"So, who's Mica?" he says offhandedly, finally breaking the silence.

I scowl, part of me annoyed by his casual attempts to breeze past something that feels so momentous. The fact that he has a water filter like this, that something this small can be this effective, this instantaneous, is blowing my mind.

"My younger brother," I finally say, standing. I'm pleased to find I'm feeling stronger already. I throw the backpack over my shoulder and walk over to the pool, then squat down, rip a few green blades of grass from the ground, and toss them into the water. They fall gently to the surface, and the absence of hissing and steam confirms that the water's not acidic.

Tentatively, I dip the canteen into the pool and fill it halfway. I shoot Adam a guarded look and, after he nods, I take a small swig. There's no burning, not even that metallic aftertaste I've become so accustomed to from Marketplace canteens.

The bottle is empty again before I know it. I dip it into the cool water a final time, filling it to the top before I screw the cap on and put it back in Mica's bag.

"Well, thanks." I blow out an awkward breath. "Again."

Adam nods and I take off in the opposite direction of the wall, toward the tree line. I am moderately irritated, though thoroughly unsurprised, when I hear him start to follow me.

"So, now that we've established that you'll live to see another day, how about your name?" he calls to my back.

I ignore him. Now that I'm conscious and rehydrated, I have to get home. How long have I been down here? How long was I passed out? Mica must be losing it.

All I need to do is reach the other side of this encapsulation dome, or whatever Adam called it. If it is a dome, I'll have to hit another wall eventually. As soon as I find it, I can look for another door panel and hopefully get back to the surface far away from wherever the raiders have set up camp.

"If I save your life a third time, will you tell me?"

I frown. I can't deny the fact that he's already helped me more than any stranger should. And how have I shown my gratitude? By giving him a bloody lip and ridiculing his name.

Gran would be so proud.

I slow my stride to let him catch up and he falls into step beside me. My gaze drifts down to his mouth, searching for the place where my fist connected with his lip. It takes a second for me to locate it, my eyebrows lifting in surprise as I see the cut has already sealed over.

Adam clears his throat gently and heat blooms in my cheeks as I realize I've been staring at his mouth.

"My name is Terra," I say, darting my eyes back to the forest ahead of us.

"Terra?" he says, forcing a raucous laugh. "What kind of outlandish name is that?" I whip my head back toward him, affronted and ready to dole out a few choice words, but he's grinning. He's mocking me. "You know, because I'm so old-fashioned, remember?" he adds.

"In my defense," I say, "I was delirious from dehydration when I said that. I can't really be held responsible for my words." My eyes flit back to his lower lip. "Or actions."

"Does that mean I can hold you responsible for both from now on then?"

"Not that anyone would blame me for my initial reaction, but I do apologize for sucker-punching you. And I am grateful for your assistance."

"Can't say you bursting onto the scene hasn't made things more interesting, at least," he says.

"I really am fine now, though. I don't need an escort."

"Precedence begs to differ."

I scowl but don't say anything else as we fall into a quiet rhythm, trekking side-by-side through the greenery.

FALLEN leaves and twigs crunch beneath our feet as we work our way further into the woods. There are no clear paths marked, so I occasionally have to force my way through thick bushes and groups of branches in order to continue forward.

I can't keep my eyes from wandering as we trudge along. This forest is so vastly different from the Dead Woods. The trees here are not nearly as tall, nor as thick, but they still take up more room, due to the foliage bursting from their branches.

The entire scene is so peaceful. The only sounds other than our footsteps come in the form of the wind rustling through the leaves and the distant babble of running water. Sunlight filters in through the canopy above us, making delightful shadowy patterns on my skin. I'm so captivated that I almost walk right into a low-hanging branch.

I look over to find Adam watching me, his eyes crinkled in a smile. With a huff, I return my gaze to the front.

"So, where exactly are we going?" he says.

"*We* aren't going anywhere. *I'm* going to find another one of those door panels so *I* can go home." I push a particularly swishy branch out of my way and it snaps back at me, leaving a harsh red welt on my upper arm.

"Wouldn't it be easier just to ask someone for help? Maybe someone who already knows of another way out? Someone who—oh, I don't know —has been living down here for over a week and actually knows where he's going?" he says, graciously ignoring the tears stinging my eyes.

I am so shocked by his words, I barely notice. "You know where to go? You've been living down here? Why? How did you get here? Why haven't you left?" The questions spill off of my tongue in a flurry.

"I've got questions too, you know. You're the first person I've had contact with since coming down here. And other than the whole being-cornered-by-a-pack-of-large-men thing, I don't know anything about you either. So forgive me if I don't feel like spilling my guts," he says calmly, one eyebrow raised. "I've already answered more of your questions than you have of mine."

I purse my lips. "Will you at least tell me if I'm going in the right direction?"

"Yes," he says.

"Yes, you'll tell me? Or yes, I am?"

"Yes," he repeats, smirking.

"Fine." I roll my eyes. "How about this: a question for a question. You give me an answer, and I give you one. Fair?"

"I won't say it's fair, precisely, but sure. Go ahead."

My head is swirling with questions, so I decide to start at the beginning. "How long was I unconscious?"

"A little while," he says vaguely. "How did you get here?"

I raise an eyebrow. *That's hardly an answer,* I think, but I figure the best way to get him to talk is to humor him. "I was just really in the mood to take a leisurely stroll through the contaminated ruins," I answer. "What do you think? I was running from those raiders. How did *you* get here?"

"Same way you did," he says with a shrug. "Minus the chase. I just kind of stumbled into it. What did those guys want with you?"

"Same thing they want with any girl, most likely. Something tells me they're not used to running into female scavs."

Adam's eyebrows knit together as he absorbs my words, but doesn't ask me to clarify.

"Who are you?" I ask.

"I'm Adam. I thought we'd met."

"I'm being serious."

"So am I."

I sigh, loudly.

"My turn again," he says. "I probably should've opened with this, but are you alright?"

My forehead creases as I contemplate the sincerity of his concern. "Sure," I say after a moment. "I mean, I will be. I do feel much better already." My headache has faded, and though the wound on my head still stings when I touch the hair surrounding it, the pain has subsided substantially.

I duck below an overhanging branch. "Thanks," I add as an afterthought.

"You're welcome," he replies earnestly.

"So, what are you doing down here?" I ask, unsure of whether I mean here, in this underground paradise, or here, on the groundworld in general.

He contemplates for a minute. "I got lost," he says.

I can tell he's trying to keep his tone light, but something else lurks behind it. Another vague non-answer.

"Are all raiders like that?" Adam asks before I can insist he elaborate. "What did you do to make those guys so mad?"

I pause for a second. "I may or may not have kneed the big guy—their leader—in the balls."

"Yeah, that'd do it," he replies with a laugh.

"What were you doing in the ruins in the first place?" I ask, though my hope that he might finally provide a real response to any of my questions is rapidly waning.

"Exploring." He plucks a large leaf from above his head. He holds it by the stem and twirls it between his fingers. "I'm on assignment for . . . my job. I'm trying to get more familiar with things down here." He lets the leaf fall from his fingers; it floats gently as it joins the rest of the foliage decorating the forest floor. "How old are you? Your brother? Your parents?"

I scrutinize his face. That's really what he wants to know? How random. "I don't know how it works for you all up *there*, but people down *here* are usually just about the age they look. I'm eighteen. Mica is thirteen, which, as you probably remember, is just a really lovely time in male adolescence."

Adam laughs.

"Why? How old are you?" I ask back, eyeing him shrewdly.

"Just turned twenty," he says with a smile. "But you didn't finish answering. What about the rest of your family?"

"What family?" I let out a bitter laugh. "Doesn't really matter. They're gone."

Adam slows to a stop. I look back at him over my shoulder, then pause my steps as well. His smile fades, an unfamiliar expression settling on his face before he moves to catch up to me.

"Can I ask what happened?" he asks, tone tentative.

I shrug. "It's not like it's a secret. Our mom died shortly after Mica was born and our *father*," I can't quite contain my bitterness as I spit the word out, "took off some years later. Chances are he's dead now too. Our grandmother was taking care of Mica and me until . . . Well, now she's gone too." I try to keep my voice indifferent, but it hitches over the last few words. "I don't like talking about it."

Whatever emotion had sparked behind Adam's former expression has melted into compassion. It makes me instantly uncomfortable.

I clear my throat and start to walk more quickly again. Adam matches my pace. "Right. My turn again," I say. "If you know how to get out of here, why haven't you left?"

"Don't have anywhere else to be," he says lightly, though a frown plays at the corner of his lips. His face perks up again after a moment. "I've done some exploring in the city up top, but don't have any idea where to go from there. Where are you from?"

"Sixteen."

"I thought you said you were eighteen." Adam looks at me blankly, and I stifle a laugh. No surprise that a skydweller wouldn't be familiar with groundworld settlements—how they're referred to or what they're even named.

"No, not my age. Sixteen is what we call my settlement. Genesis X-16."

"Genesis X-16," Adam repeats quietly, as if he's testing the words out. "That's a mouthful."

"The sixteenth settlement on the eastern seaboard of the Genesis continent. It figures they don't even bother teaching you guys the basics about the groundworld up there. "

Adam scrunches his face, like he's trying to remember something, but it relaxes after a moment. "So, where is Sixteen exactly? How big is it? How many people live there? How did you get here from there?"

"Tsk, that's more than one question, and it's not even your turn," I chastise affably.

Adam just shrugs and grins expectantly again.

"Let's see, how did I get here? Do you mean physically or metaphorically?" I say with a smirk, ignoring his first few rapid-fire questions. "It's kind of a long story. Scavenging and raiders and running . . . God, so much running. I normally never venture out this far. Let's just say it was never my plan to cross the quarantine line into this city, but desperate times and all." I eye him up and down. "I suppose I don't need to bother asking where you're from."

"Oh?" he says.

"Who can even tell one skycity from the next? Bright lights, big city here. Slightly brighter lights, slightly bigger city there. Rich snobs here, richer snobs there."

Adam looks like he wants to interject, but I continue. "Yeah, yeah, I get it. Each skycity is *special*, each has its *thing*. Korbyllis is the capital, Lexicon's a dream for entertainment junkies, and most modern tech is manufactured on Altara. Blah, blah, blah. They're all the same when you're stuck down here."

I cut myself off, literally biting my tongue to keep the rest of my contemptuous speech at bay. This is my first real interaction with a skydweller who's even close to my age, and so far, hard as it is to admit, Adam seems all right. A little cocky, maybe, but he's not completely terrible.

He did save me, after all.

"It's obvious enough you're a skydweller, what does it matter which city you've deigned to descend upon us from?" I finish, even though I know I'm still not being fair. I hate it when folks from above generalize about us terrestrials, looping us all together as if we're just one huge group of uncouth, uncivilized plebeians. I shouldn't sink to their level.

"It's obvious, huh?" Adam says, amusement edging his tone.

"Need me to list it out for you?"

"Please do."

I roll my eyes and start to tick the reasons off one by one on my fingers. "One, you've never heard of Sixteen, even though we're one of the largest settlements left on Genesis. Two, somehow you know a ton about the technology in this place, whereas I've never even heard of, let alone seen, anything like this. They must teach you all a little something extra up there." I keep myself from adding commentary about the implicit unfairness in that.

"Three, it's blindingly clear you've hardly spent any time in the sun without a UV filter over your head," I say, gesturing toward his body. "And lastly, even if all of those other factors weren't present, your eyes would still give you away."

Adam cocks his head to the side.

"I've never even seen eyes that blue down here. You should probably get back up top soon if you want to keep them like that, by the way," I tease. "Sure, right now it's early days. But you stay down here too long and you'll end up with a set of greeners. Or maybe a light hazel. And if you're truly unlucky, you'll end up with these muddy things for the rest of your life." I widen my eyes and blink purposefully into his face, affecting an angelic expression.

"Noted," he says with a laugh, though his expression turns surprisingly intense as he looks at me, like he's taking note of the golden flecks decorating my irises.

I cough. "Whose question is it now?"

"I'm not sure," he says.

"Me either." I'm not quite sure why I'm smiling as I say it.

"Pretty useless to strike a deal if you're not keeping track."

I stick my tongue out at him and he laughs. "Okay, fine. I have one more," I say after a beat. I take a slow breath and notice him looking at me with renewed curiosity.

"Why did you save me?" My voice comes out quieter than I intended. "There could have been a dozen raiders closing in on me. You could have gotten hurt."

My mind flashes with the image of Adam prostrate on the tunnel floor, heavy boots kicking at his side, and I feel a surprising pang in my chest. I shake my head slightly, like doing so will purge the vision from my mind.

We slow to a stop again, and Adam looks down at me for a moment before replying. "How could I not?"

His cerulean eyes meet mine with such fierceness that I have to look away. This time, the heat that burns in my cheeks is not from embarrassment. I force my feet forward and continue plodding along through the forest, Adam a step behind, our mutual inquisition over.

IT TAKES me a rather embarrassing amount of time to realize that Adam has subtly taken the lead. We've been traipsing along for what feels like hours, and I've been following him for a while now without even noticing.

I scowl at myself for falling into such complacency, as I scamper past him. "I thought I told you, I don't need your help. I can find my own way out of here." I pivot slightly to diverge from whatever path Adam had set us on, turning back into the forest just to prove a point.

"Uh huh, sure," he says. "I'd love to see just how far you think you're going to get."

I glance back and see the ghost of a smile on his mouth. My eyes narrow at the challenge in his voice, and I speed up.

"Wait up." I hear his footsteps quicken behind me.

I do no such thing, breaking into a jog as I toss a grin back in Adam's direction. But whatever humor might have been there moments before is gone. There's no smile on his face.

"Stop."

The air becomes suddenly serious. Threatening. My stomach flips as I glance behind Adam and see the outline of a pair of squat gray buildings behind the tree line. Where has he been leading me?

Pulse thundering in my ears, my jog turns into an all-out run.

"Terra, stop!" he yells.

I cringe at the power in his voice; I don't think I have another chase in me today.

"Watch out!" His shout comes after I've already heard the snap. I throw my gaze skyward and see an enormous branch plummeting toward me.

I fling myself to the ground with my arms wrapped protectively around my head, whimpering as my hand grazes my wound.

A heartbeat passes. Then another. But there's no impact. No crash sounds.

Banking on the hope that the branch got caught somewhere above me, I open my eyes and stifle a gasp.

The thick tree limb hovers three inches from my face, suspended in midair. It's even bigger than I thought, easily ninety pounds of solid wood. I hear a grunt and turn my head just in time to see Adam, ten feet away, waving his outstretched arm. The branch drifts to the side before dropping to the ground next to me with a thud.

I lie still, my arms peeling away from my head but otherwise paralyzed by what I've just seen. What *have* I just seen?

Adam has one arm over his ribs, bearing a pained expression. One second he's standing there, his chest heaving from obvious exertion, the next he's at my side, concern etched into every angle of his face as he offers me his hand.

I take it cautiously and he pulls me upright.

"Are you okay?" he asks.

"Well, I have another question." I pull my shaking hand from his grasp and dust myself off. "What the hell was that?"

NINE

"WHAT WAS THAT?" I say again, the accusation in my voice stronger, sharper this time. "What did you just do?"

"Are you okay?" Adam repeats, ignoring my question. "You're so lucky, if you'd been just a few inches over, that branch would've nailed you."

My eyes narrow into a glare. "Don't you dare do that."

"Do what?"

"Play dumb with me. I know what I saw. You . . . you moved the branch. You stopped it from hitting me. From killing me."

"How might I have accomplished that?" he asks blankly. "I was back there when it fell."

"I don't know!" I yell, throwing my hands up in frustration. "I don't know how you stopped that branch in midair. I don't know how you got over to me so fast. But I know you did *something*."

"You're injured, you were scared. It's perfectly understandable that you might have gotten confused," Adam says placatingly. "But what you're saying is impossible." His demeanor is calm and comforting, but I glimpse a flash of unease in his eyes.

"I'm not an idiot. I know what I saw. What I don't know is how, and the only thing I'm confused about is you."

Adam opens his mouth, then closes it again.

"I don't know anything about you. You won't tell me anything real. I can barely get a straight answer out of you."

"You're not exactly an open book yourself."

"I'm not the one who can move things without touching them!" I sway on my feet. The renewed spark of adrenaline that surged through my veins as the branch came crashing down is leaving my system, taking with it what little strength I've regained. I'm suddenly very aware of just how hard I've pushed myself today.

Adam draws a deep breath and lightly touches his middle finger to his almost-healed lip. "Okay," he says solemnly. "Fine. I'll explain, just come with me."

"Where?" I eye the gray buildings, still visible in the background despite my panic-driven detour. "You said you knew a raider-free way out of here, so where is it already?"

"It really is all questions, all the time with you, isn't it?" he says with a shaky laugh.

"Trust's a two-way street, my guy."

He searches my face, but I lock it into a scowl. "You look like you're about to keel over," he says. "When's the last time you ate something?"

"Don't change the subject," I say, but he has already turned away and started walking toward the buildings.

I balk as my stomach growls loudly, right on cue. My dinner with Mica last night feels like an entire lifetime ago. I briefly try to calculate how much time has passed since I left on my clandestine scavenging run, all too aware of the faux-sunlight streaming from above, how it's gotten heavier and warmer as we've walked. Like the sun is setting.

I'd only intended to be gone a few hours at most, and all I can do now is hope that Mica isn't full-on panicking. He's used to waking up to an empty apartment, me having already left on a scav run, but he's also used to me being back by the time he returns from school. With the attitude he's been serving me lately, though, maybe he won't mind the extra alone time.

My stomach growls again, and I return my gaze to Adam, his back still to me as he continues walking toward the buildings.

I feel safe in the assumption that if he wanted to hurt me, he would have by now. So, despite my pride telling me I should probably do otherwise, I move to follow after him.

"All right," I call out. Adam is already a good distance ahead. "Hold up."

I fall into step behind him and we approach the twin buildings in silence. As we get closer, I see that they're not separate buildings, but two towers that share a base. A continuous row of windows wraps around the first floor, broken only by a set of double doors.

"What is this place?"

He rolls his eyes at me, a perfect imitation of the looks I've been shooting at him all afternoon.

"Patience isn't one of your virtues, I'm noticing."

He leads me around the side of the building, where one of the floor-to-ceiling windows has been smashed in. I raise my eyebrows and he chuckles.

"It was like this when I found it," he says with a twinkle in his iridescent eyes.

"Have something against doors?"

"They're all on lockdown. I've tried overriding the system to open them, but I think they're synced to a biometric lock. It was enough of an effort getting the ancient system to power on in the first place."

He hops through the makeshift doorway, giving a wide berth to the broken glass still clinging to the edge of the window frame, then turns back and offers me his hand. I reluctantly take it, and with one easy pull, I'm inside; I barely even felt myself move. I yank my hand back as soon as I've cleared the glass.

We are inside a small, empty, white room. Adam opens the door on the far side and ushers me into a dark, windowless hallway. The light from the room illuminates the hall just enough for me to see where I'm walking.

I follow Adam down the corridor until we reach a set of swinging doors that he pushes open to reveal a cavernous room filled with workspaces. Rows of shiny metal desks cross the room lengthwise, all facing a heavily windowed wall that looks out onto the forest. Light streams in through the windows, and at the end I see the double doors that indicate we're just on the other side of the main entrance.

Adam immediately heads for the back of the room while I take in the setup. Chairs with wheels attached to their legs are intermingled with the tables, some upright, some tipped over. Computer monitors sit on each desk, their casings cracked open, wires and components spilling out. I walk up the row in front of me and can confirm that Adam was right—these machines are ancient. They look far older than Mica's secondhand PC, the one luxury our father left to us after pawning the rest of our belongings on his way out of dodge.

The back row of desks stands out from the wreckage, and I make my way over to inspect it more closely. A computer on the end boasts a small green light, blinking wildly. Unlike the others, this unit has power.

An array of silver instruments is laid out next to it, arranged by size. Beside them is a tablet computer that resembles the ones Collection Agents use, as well as a lockbox, an innocuous-looking metal cylinder about the length of my hand, and several thick metal rings like the one currently attached to my canteen.

I take off Mica's backpack and lay it on a nearby desk, then pull out my canteen to confirm the rings are the same. A portable filter, Adam called it.

A flare of rage suddenly bubbles up inside me. With these little things, skydwellers have access to instantaneous clean, drinkable water whenever they want. Meanwhile, we're stuck with the choice of purchasing canteen refills every week from the Marketplace or risk getting sick—or worse—by drinking from the tap.

I glance back at Adam, primed and ready to fill his ears with complaints about the disparity between our two worlds again. I locate him crouching in the corner of the room near a small pile of blankets and pillows—a crude bed.

My anger dissolves into surprise as he lifts his shirt and pulls it off, revealing an enormous yellowing bruise along his right side. A swirled mass of green, yellow, and gray stretches from the dip of his waist to his shoulder.

My first thought is that the raiders must have gotten a few good hits in while Adam was coming to my rescue, and guilt washes over me. But, jarring and grotesque as the bruise looks, I quickly realize it's already been healing for a while.

Adam discards his silvery shirt—it shimmers slightly as he drops it to the floor—and pulls a clean white undershirt from a short stack of clothing at the foot of the makeshift bed. He crouches down to root around in the blankets before tossing a small rectangular packet in my direction, then puts on the clean shirt.

I reach to catch the packet but get distracted by the brief flash of pain crossing Adam's face as he pulls his shirt on, and I miss. The packet lands on the desk next to me, displacing the metal tools with a jingle.

Adam laughs as I eye the blue and gold packaging with suspicion.

"Food," he encourages, just a hint of exasperation lacing his voice.

My stomach rumbles as I snatch up the packet and rip it open. Inside is a bar of tiny round grains, pressed together. I take a tentative bite. It's chewy and sweet.

"Thank you," I say, my voice garbled as I cram another bite into my mouth. The bar may be small, but I'm surprised and pleased at how rapidly my hunger is disappearing. "Am I allowed to ask questions again now?"

"I suppose," Adam says with a sigh. He sits down in a nearby chair and rolls over to me.

"How did you stop that branch?"

Adam avoids my eyes, his lips set in a line. He's guarding himself.

"You promised me answers," I remind him.

"Technically, I never *promised* anything," he says. An indignant look crosses my face, but before I can say anything, he continues. "It's just not that simple to explain."

"It can't be that hard. Just say it."

"So you're allowed to have things you don't want to talk about, but I'm not? How about I make you talk about your parents some more before you get all the nitty-gritty details of my life?"

His defensiveness catches me off guard. "Okay," I say after a moment of stunned silence, "I'll start with something easier then. Where are we?" I pick up one of the filter rings and thread my finger through it.

"We're in the research complex for this biodome," he says, visibly relaxing.

"Oh, right. Of course. How silly of me. The research complex. The *biodome*," I say, rolling my eyes.

He shrugs.

"We are underground, in the ruins. Supposedly, nobody's been here for centuries, and yet somehow you just happen to find this whole world down here. With green trees and sunlight and wind and fake walls that look like the sky." I start to pace, the volume of my voice rising. "How do trees grow underground, Adam?"

"It's all self-contained. There's an irrigation system that runs underneath the dome, cycling the water through a series of reservoirs and filters. It can't physically rain down here, so that's how the grass and trees get their water."

I fidget with the filter, spinning it around my finger with the pad of my thumb, but don't interrupt.

"The sunlight isn't really coming from the sun, either," he continues. "There are UV lights built into the ceiling panels. This entire biodome was created to simulate the outside atmosphere. I suspect that this complex was built to monitor and observe it, hence all the windows."

"And you know all this, how?" I ask skeptically.

He makes a flippant gesture toward the computer sitting idly on the table. "It's amazing what a little research will get you."

My mouth hangs open as the weight of where we are settles in, wonder and horror warring inside me. My understanding of the technology that powers the skycities is limited, as is my knowledge of what life in Sixteen was like when the settlements were first formed, but I know enough to connect the dots.

"This is the precursor to the skycities," I say.

Bitterness creeps up my spine as generations of "what ifs" flood my mind. What if Sixteen's UV filter had never faltered? What if it had been repaired before it shattered completely? What if Sixteen was still a place like this—self-contained, self-sustaining? A place where things grow and bloom and thrive unaffected by the environment outside.

"This is how the groundworld settlements used to be."

"Possibly," Adam says.

I narrow my eyes.

"Probably," he concedes.

"What are you doing here, really?" I ask.

"I already told you, I've been exploring. Let's call it a fact-finding mission. I came down here to collect data on this city, and just happened to find this place. You can't blame me for wanting to set up camp here rather than roughing it topside."

"So, what, you're a scientist? You work for the Tribunal?"

"Something like that." His eyes dart away, suddenly fixating on a spot just behind my head. I turn to see what he's looking at, but there's nothing there but the blank wall.

I walk over to an overturned chair and pull it upright, my gaze fixed on Adam's face, trying to figure out what he isn't telling me. As I bend to sit down, the backs of my knees hit the seat and it rolls out from under me. I yelp as my backside connects with the hard floor.

"Graceful," he says with a laugh.

"Shut up." I pull myself into the chair, my cheeks blazing. "What are you looking for? With your research, I mean. It must be pretty valuable intel for you to be willing to live down here for it."

Adam swivels nervously in his chair. "I wasn't originally meant to stay. And it wasn't supposed to just be me. There were four of us on the . . . my research team. We all came down together but I got separated from them. And I'm not able to reach them." I can tell he's trying to make the explanation sound casual, but there is emotion behind his words.

"You got lost," I say, repeating his words from earlier.

Adam nods.

"Won't they be looking for you?"

"They have work to do too. It's a long-term mission. Job's not done."

"They just left you here?" I say, unable to keep the disapproval out of my voice. Now that sounds like the skydwellers I know—the ones who are always first to pick up and leave when things get rough.

"It's more complicated than that."

I'm sure it is, I think. Every answer he gives just brings more questions with it. Why would the Tribunal send a research team down to the ruins now? If there was some kind of valuable technology or data to be gleaned here, surely they would have retrieved it long ago.

"Try me," I say. "Whatever it is, I can handle it."

Adam considers me for a moment, like he's weighing his options. His broad chest rises as he takes a deep breath and slowly lifts his arm and extends it toward me, then flicks his wrist back toward his face. I feel the soles of my shoes scrape against the floor as my chair glides toward him through no effort on my part.

I let out a surprised shout and leap from my seat, kicking the chair away from me. It hits one of the desks with a clang, leaving the table askew. "Okay, that!" I yell. "What *is* that?"

"It's just something I can do," Adam says calmly. He holds his hands up in front of him, palms out, the way he did when we first met. Admittedly, I'm having trouble forcing myself to remember that was only hours ago.

"I knew it. I knew that you did something to the branch."

His shoulders bounce in another infuriating shrug.

"Right. Telekinesis. No big deal," I say, swallowing a nervous laugh.

Tense silence fills the space between us.

"Can everyone do that? Is this some kind of secret ability everyone has up there?"

Is this just another thing you get that we don't?

"Up there . . ." he repeats softly. "No, not exactly. Not everyone. And it's not exactly an ability." He looks me up and down as he considers his words. "It's more like . . . an advancement."

My face contorts in confusion as I contemplate what he means by that.

"Still feel like you can handle it?" His words are as smug as I'd expect, but there's something sad in his voice behind them.

I hop up onto the table behind me and cross my arms defiantly, my legs dangling off the side. I force a nonchalant expression onto my face, arching a brow. *Bring it on.*

He smiles, and with another flick of his wrist, the chair I had kicked aside comes rolling back, slowing to a stop right in front of me. I prop my feet up on the seat of the chair, rest my hands on my knees, and give Adam an expectant look.

"I'm listening."

TEN

FX. That's what Adam says his ability, his "advancement," is called.

I've seen enough superhero movies and read enough of Mica's comics to be familiar with the concept of telekinesis. Adam can interact with things without touching them. Move and maneuver objects, other people —even himself.

That pretty much sums up the extent of what I understand.

To his credit, Adam is finally giving me some answers. It's not his fault I can barely comprehend an iota of what he's actually telling me. He throws around words like *bioengineering* and *nanotechnology*, terms like *attraction fields* and *microgravity manipulation* like they're confetti. Mica would pass out from excitement if he were here right now, but it takes everything I have in me to even keep up with what Adam is saying.

He answers my clarifying questions patiently, confirming not only that his FX is how he stopped the branch, but also how he's able to move so fast. How he was able to incapacitate Ryk and the raiders all on his own. How he got to the wall so quickly in the first place, after hearing my desperate pounding from the other side.

He insists that telekinesis is not the right term for it, but I think he's just harping on semantics. Maybe he doesn't like the way it sounds, how it makes it seem even more fantastical and inconceivable, when in fact it's very, very real. If I couldn't have attested to that before, I certainly can now.

As he speaks, Adam flicks his hands and gesticulates with his fingers, punctuating his words while simultaneously utilizing his FX. He flips on a light switch. He straightens the instruments on the desk. He slides my backpack closer to me.

I can tell that it's not a case of him trying to show off. He uses his ability casually, like it's an extension of his body. His gestures are loose, his shoulders visibly relaxed, like telling me about his ability has unwound any lingering pretense he had been maintaining, and he can finally just . . . be. The thought sends a warm trickle down my spine.

"You're taking this a lot better than I thought you would," he says.

I look at him pointedly. "The initial shock wore off a while ago. Does it still seem kinda crazy? Of course. Is it incredibly unfair that you and who knows how many other skydwellers basically have superpowers? Sure."

Adam clucks his tongue at my choice of words.

"But welcome to the life of a terrestrial," I continue. "We're used to getting the short end of the stick. So, somehow, I guess even this really isn't all that surprising."

Adam's face starts to morph into something that looks a little too much like pity so I quickly change the subject. "You still haven't explained what it is that your team was sent down here to research. What exactly is it that you're looking for?"

Adam gets out of his chair and picks up the tablet computer. I can't see the screen from my perch, but after a few moments of tapping, he turns it toward me. Words and numbers scroll across the screen, too quickly for me to read.

"Data," he says matter-of-factly. "Anything and everything. Evidence of what life was—is—like down here."

He reaches into his pocket and pulls out a small metal square that he plugs directly into the side of the tablet. "Thanks to you, I was actually able to net a lot of useful information from those raiders."

"You're so welcome," I reply, voice dripping with sarcasm.

Adam taps the device and my stomach lurches as Ryk's face pops up. I scoot a couple of inches back in surprise.

"Don't worry, he's not going to break out of the screen and get you," Adam says with a half-tilted smirk, earning a new glower from me.

"It's just data I collected after . . . after you were safe," he continues, putting the tablet down on the table next to me so I can view it more clearly. Upon closer inspection of the image, I see that Ryk's eyes are closed, his head hanging to the side.

"So, this is what a 'subdued' raider looks like, huh?" I glance at Adam, who has leaned in unsettlingly close to swipe to the next image on the tablet. I swallow nervously. "What did you do to them?"

"Gave them all a bad headache to wake up to, that's all. Then I scanned their images, jotted down some notes, and took a couple of samples."

"Samples?" I say skeptically.

Adam reaches back into his pocket and pulls out a silver cylinder, identical to the one already on the table. He flicks open the top, revealing a stack of glass slides inside.

"Anyway, it's just like I told you. Me." He points to himself. "Research assignment." He gestures to the room around us. "Fact-finding." He looks pointedly at the tablet and grins. "I'm finding facts. That includes ones about the people living down here."

"Are you going to take samples from me too?" I look him squarely in his cerulean eyes as if daring him to try.

"Only if you want to give them to me," he says, voice softer than I expected.

"You didn't ask the raiders for their permission."

"They didn't really give me a chance to ask nicely, did they?" Adam picks the tablet up and unplugs the drive. "I *could* use a picture, if you're willing."

A flash emanates from the little square in his hand before I have a chance to object, and when my eyes refocus, Adam has a wide smile plastered on his face.

"Nuh-uh. No way. Delete that."

"Okay, okay, sorry." He plugs the drive back into the tablet, and my own startled expression is staring back at me a second later. I grimace at my appearance—face caked in dirt, wild hair barely contained in my ponytail, dried blood creeping out from my hairline. Even if I were inclined to allow him to take my picture, this is not exactly how I would want to be committed to memory.

Adam runs his fingers over the screen and my image disappears. "There. Gone forever. Happy?"

I roll my eyes at the notion that I could possibly be happy about any of this. From the minute I woke up and allowed myself to get carried away with this harebrained plan for Mica's future, not a single damn thing has gone the way I wanted. Hell, from the minute I spotted that infernal machine in the Dead Woods five days ago, nothing's turned out the way I'd hoped.

Things keep happening, to me, around me, and every reaction I have, every action I take turns out to be wrong. Even the one small thing I thought I could do, securing Mica's future by doing what I do every damn day . . .

Scavenging is supposed to be the one thing I'm good at, and I barely survived it today.

Happy? I hardly know what the word means anymore.

I open my mouth to say as much to Adam, but his attention is back on his tablet, swiping and tapping through whatever data he's collected. He bites his bottom lip in concentration and a bloom of heat rises from my chest as I watch him, before I shove it back down with a grit of my teeth.

What's the matter with me? I shush the voice in the back of my head before it tells me something I don't want to hear.

I'm just checking on the status of the split lip I gave him, I tell myself. It's perfectly natural to be concerned. Perfectly understandable that I can't keep my eyes from lingering on his mouth.

Perfectly understandable.

Perfect.

How *is* his mouth so perfect, I wonder. Is it natural how quickly his injury has healed? I can't even see a mark anymore, and with the way he's chewing on his lip, it doesn't seem like it still hurts at all. Did he use some kind of healing balm when I wasn't looking? Or is this his FX at work?

Resentment floods through my veins like ice as the inequality between skydwellers and terrestrials is pushed to the forefront of my mind once again. They have medicine and technology and goddamn FX at their literal fingertips, while folks down here starve and scrape by and just try to survive one day at a time. While we laugh away our dreams of a better life because even imagining it is a foolish waste.

The very place I'm standing is proof that it didn't have to be this way. That it wasn't always this way. The skydwellers allowed the settlements to erode into their current desolate, destitute state because they couldn't —or wouldn't—help us beyond the absolute bare minimum we need to stay alive, stay functioning. Wouldn't even give us the resources to repair our shattered filters. All of which is a hard enough pill to swallow, but at least it's in the past.

But this, this is now. This place is still here, in the present, mere miles from Sixteen, and we never knew. How different would our lives be if just one person had known this was here? If we'd been able to bring this technology back to the settlement somehow, reverse engineer it, reclaim it, repurpose it? If we could have used this space to grow and build and live?

It dawns on me with bitter clarity that the rules and regulations about not crossing into the District, the fear and anxiety about contamination and the plague resurfacing, have likely all been a means of protecting this secret. Deterring us common folk from finding out about this.

The dreamy gaze that had adorned my face just moments ago morphs into a dagger-like glare. Adam doesn't notice, though, too engrossed in his work, the tablet full of observations about antiquated terrestrial life on the wild and primitive groundworld.

The purpose of his questions during our mutual interrogation suddenly clicks into place. Asking about my age, my family situation, Sixteen . . . He really was just mining for data. The realization makes me angry, though more at myself than at him. Sure, I'm not exactly eager to get my personal info in the hands of the Tribunal, but it's not as if anything I told him is top-secret.

It's the way his questioning made me feel, the realization that I truly am just another datapoint to him that makes mortification settle like a rock in the pit of my stomach. It's not his fault. I can't blame him for any of it. But did I honestly think he was interested in getting to know me?

Silly, stupid girl.

"I think it's time for me to go," I say abruptly, standing.

Adam immediately looks up from his tablet and blinks at me. "I don't think that's a great idea, Terra," he says after a beat.

Despite myself, hearing my name on his tongue melts the ice in my veins by a degree. I shake my head, masking my wince as the motion makes pain shoot from the wound there. "I don't think it's up to you," I snap.

A perplexed expression crosses his face. "Look at yourself. You're exhausted. It's late. You're in no shape to go anywhere right this second."

My gaze drifts to the windows, where, sure enough, the fake sky has darkened to a dusky color. I curse myself mentally for not paying attention to how long we've been here.

"Mica has to be absolutely beside himself. I can't—"

"I understand how anxious that must make you," Adam interrupts. "Truly, I do. But you won't be doing him any favors by taking off now and getting lost or hurt even worse. Rest here overnight and I promise, you'll be on your way first thing in the morning. I'll get you out of here."

I sway slightly on my feet as I contemplate his suggestion, and the fact that I am considering it at all goes to show just how silly and stupid I really must be. Because even though it would mean putting myself in a vulnerable position, the idea of sleeping here doesn't spark fear in my chest like I know it should.

Exhausted doesn't even begin to describe how I feel right now. The mere thought of sleep has my eyelids feeling heavy, and I know if I were to lay my body down and close them, I would be out in seconds. And despite a lifetime of telling me I should feel otherwise, I know in my bones that I am safe here. With him.

But still, Mica . . .

Adam seems to guess at the debate raging silently between myself and my better judgment. "At least let me take another look at that wound on your head before you decide anything," he says.

"Another?"

"I tried to treat it as best I could when I first pulled you through from the tunnel, but you got yourself a pretty nasty gash there. I just want to see how it's healing."

I purse my lips but offer a frail nod, prompting him to step closer. He gestures for me to take a seat, then proceeds to tenderly move his fingers through my hair, parting it so he can get a better look at my injury. There's no masking my wince this time as a segment of my hair, matted together with blood, tugs on the edge of my wound.

"Sorry," he murmurs. "Your wound is healing well, though I can't do much about the lovely bruise you'll have underneath. If you can bring yourself to rest here tonight, I guarantee you'll feel whole again in the morning."

With the flick of his wrist, he summons a small tin from over near his makeshift bed. It flies into his hand and his gaze drifts to my face as he untwists the lid.

"If you'll allow me, this should help speed the process along."

I nod again. He dips a long finger into the tin and gently applies the balm to my wound. I brace myself for another wave of stinging pain, but a slow warmth spreading across the crown of my head is all I feel.

"There," he says, pulling away. "Should be all closed up by the time you wake up." His cerulean eyes meet mine and my breath catches.

"Quite remarkable," he murmurs.

"What is?"

"The little bits of gold in your eyes. Almost as if there's a star behind your irises, ready to burst right on through."

"That's what my Gran used to say," I admit in a quiet voice. "She called me her little sunburst."

Adam just looks at me, a soft smile on those perfect lips.

"Is there a facility here?" I say suddenly, breaking the charged silence. "I have to . . . you know . . ."

"Hmm? Oh. *Oh.* Yes, of course. Back through those doors, to the left. Sign with a bald person in a dress on the door, you can't miss it."

"Thanks." My cheeks blaze as I charge out of the room.

The bathroom is long and narrow with several walled-off stalls on one side of the room, and a row of sinks on the other. I note the half-sized window at head height on the far end before hopping into one of the stalls.

When I emerge, I brace my hands on either side of one of the sinks, staring in astonishment at my reflection in the cracked mirror hanging above it.

The pink blush in my cheeks is just barely visible through the dirt streaked across the right side of my face, as well as down my neck. There is a rip in the fabric of my t-shirt near my collarbone. Ugly red scratches run down both of my arms. I run the tap and gently wash my hands—they still feel a little raw—making sure to scrape out the dirt from beneath my fingernails.

I splash some cool water on my face, careful to avoid my mouth and eyes. I wouldn't be surprised if this water is already semi-filtered, like the tap water at home—not quite clean enough to drink, but good enough to wash in. Still, better safe than sorry.

My hands washed, I gently prod around the injury on the side of my head, and though I can feel a lump and the scabbed over edges of the gash, there's barely any pain. When I pull the rest of my wild hair from its ponytail, my dark brown strands stay flattened in that spot.

I lean over the sink, pool some water in my hands, and gingerly attempt to wash the blood out of my hair as best I can without getting too close to the cut. The water runs pink as it swirls down the drain.

I wring the water from my locks and attempt to draw my hair back into a bun, but I guess even Adam's magical pain-relieving balm has its limits, because pulling at the hair near my wound stretches my skin in a way that has me hissing aloud. Somewhat begrudgingly, I settle for leaving it down in its wild state: wet and flat on one side, tangled and erratic on the other, with a large crimp from my hair elastic running through the middle.

"You've never looked better," I tell my reflection before striding back out into the hall.

***

ADAM'S lopsided smile greets me when I walk back into the main room. "You're looking slightly less worse for the wear," he says.

I huff in affirmation, then look down at his feet where he's broken down his makeshift bed into two separate ones, spaced a few feet apart.

"This okay?" he asks.

A cursory glance shows me the difference in how each bed has been set up. His original bed is basically just a single blanket on the hard floor now. "You gave me all the pillows," I mutter.

"Between the two of us, I think you've had the harder day," he says lightly. "I don't mind."

I recall the giant, grotesque bruise stretching across a third of his body and attempt a half-hearted protestation, but he dismisses me with a wave of his hand.

Groaning, I settle onto the pile, gratitude sweeping through my sore bones. I close my eyes immediately and savor the impending relief that only the beckoning blackness of sleep can provide, casting out a silent prayer that Mica is doing okay, that he knows I'll be back to him soon.

I hear shuffling beside me as Adam lays down, and I let my head fall to the side and crack my eyes open one last time to see him observing me with keen interest.

"That's creepy," I say, sleep slurring my words.

"What?"

"You, staring at me."

"Who's staring?" He makes a show of looking everywhere except at me.

I snort. "You absolutely were staring."

"Just making sure you're comfortable, Sunburst," he says, and hearing the nickname causes my heart to ache. If I weren't nearly asleep, I might've objected. Or at least been able to think of something clever to say back.

"Focus on yourself, superhero," I whisper, and the sound of Adam's soft chortle brushes my ears as I finally fall into sleep's embrace.

ELEVEN

"HOW'D YOU SLEEP?"

My eyes have barely cracked open before Adam's voice pipes into my ears. He's perched at a desk nearby, working on his tablet.

"Like the dead." I sit up in my makeshift bed and stretch my arms above my head, noting with incredulity how painless the movement is. The gray light of morning is just barely starting to peek through from the windows outside.

"I don't think the dead snore quite that loudly," Adam says without looking up from his screen.

With a flick of his wrist, he deftly deflects the pillow I've thrown at his head and boomerangs it back to me. I can't help but marvel as I catch it, both at the instant reminder of his FX and at the state of my body after just a single night's rest. The pain and soreness in my muscles have dissipated almost entirely, and the scratches that were still raw just yesterday evening have been reduced to faint pink lines.

I touch a tentative hand to the side of my head, still somewhat tender to the touch, but have to bite back a gasp as my fingers dance over the small raised scar there, now the only remnant of the open gash that had my hair matted with blood yesterday.

"H-how . . . ?" I stutter, and Adam finally breaks his gaze away from the tablet.

"Didn't I tell you," he says, "a good night's rest and you'd be feeling whole again?" His words tumble out with an easy grace, but there's an edge of uncertainty in his voice.

My eyes narrow as I contemplate levying back a petulant reply, as it's beyond clear to me that something more is going on. Even the world's deepest, most restorative sleep couldn't possibly heal injuries this quickly, and my suspicion is that this is far more than what a healing balm—no matter how advanced—could do. But what does it really matter? I've vastly improved thanks to his ministrations one way or the other, and something in his tone makes me feel like he won't appreciate being grilled about the specifics.

I survey the various tools still laid out on one of the tables around me as I stand. "You sure have a lot of stuff for someone who was stranded down here without the rest of your team," I say, offering the change in subject like a peace offering.

Adam loosens a breath as he follows my gaze. "Not particularly. This is really just the basics. Scanning equipment, water filters, nutrition bars, and a sustenance generator. Odds and ends."

"Sustenance generator?" My curiosity piques.

"In the pack by the bed," he says, turning his eyes back to the screen in his hands. "Along with a few other things. Feel free to check them out if you're so fascinated."

"I think I should probably get a move on," I say, surprising myself with the flash of disappointment I feel as the words leave my mouth. "You're still going to make good on your promise to give me directions out of here, right?"

"Just give me five minutes," he says without looking up. "Feel free to find yourself something to eat for breakfast."

I trot over to his bed and grab another nutrition bar from a box on the floor. I rip it open—the striped packaging red and orange this time—and take a few hurried bites as I survey the rest of Adam's impossible wares. There's the pile of undershirts I noticed yesterday, but aside from the box of bars and various empty wrappers dotting the floor, there isn't much else to observe. I can't help but wonder where the shirts—not to mention the blankets and pillows I slept on—came from.

I run my hand lightly over the blanket on the floor, and the pristine fabric is silky and cool to the touch. It feels the same as the one I slept upon last night too. All the pillows, blankets, and—I can now see—Adam's shirts seem to be made from this same material, all of them too new, too unmarred by time to have come from somewhere here in the research facility. But they're definitely too big and bulky to possibly fit in the silver pack sitting near the foot of his improvised bed.

Frankly, I'm not sure I can even call it a pack. Rectangular and thin, the two straps on one side are the only things that make it seem remotely bag-like. In fact, with the stiff set of its open flaps, it looks more like a large book. If it weren't for the strange-looking box laying half-inside the pack's open mouth, I wouldn't have believed it could hold anything at all.

"What's this?" I ask, picking up the small metal box and showing it to Adam. It's just slightly larger than the palm of my hand, with a wide slot in the middle surrounded by metal teeth.

He looks up for a split-second before returning his gaze to the screen. "That's the sustenance generator. Put any organic matter in there and it'll churn out the nutrients in edible form. I haven't had to use it yet, but I'll be glad I have it when I run out of bars."

"Huh," I murmur, intrigued. "*Any* matter?"

"Yep, although plant-based tends to be preferred."

"You skyfolk have it even better than I thought. I guess a sustenance generator might not do us much good anyway, though. You may not have noticed, but it's not *quite* as lush on the surface as it is down here."

"You never know. Tree bark, rocks . . . you'd be surprised what that thing can shake out. And worst comes to worst, there's always hair. Tastes legitimately awful, but you'd also be surprised what you're willing to stomach in a pinch. Just don't put your finger in there," he cautions. "I know more than one person who's made that mistake."

My face screws up in disgust and Adam laughs. "I kid, I kid. Lighten up."

Annoyed, I kneel to replace the generator in Adam's pack and almost choke on the final bite of the nutrition bar I've just popped in my mouth. The pack seemingly sucks the machine inside itself as soon as I drop it in.

Cautiously, I peer inside but see only blackness that stretches on far past where I'd expect the bottom of the pack to be. Testing a theory, I take one of Adam's shirts, accidentally knocking the pile over, and drop it into the pack as well. Just as before, the pack sucks it inside, and there's no further sign of it. Suddenly, I understand how he's been able to travel with all this stuff.

Shuddering slightly at the technology required to create a *bottomless bag*, I'm standing back up when a glint of shiny metal catches my eye, just to the side, half buried underneath the remaining undershirts that have flopped onto the floor.

My eyes widen.

It's a bit bigger than I remember, but there's no mistaking it.

Rows of interlocking tubes and shafts. A shiny silver casing. It's missing the stray, disconnected wires that were sticking out from the first one, but other than that, it's basically identical to the one I found in the Dead Woods.

Another little machine. The one that began all of this.

I reach out and pick it up, testing its familiar weight in my palm.

"And this?" I call to Adam, trying to maintain an air of indifference. "What's this?"

He looks up and his eyes meet mine for a split second. I quickly look away.

"Oh, that's nothing really," he says, returning his gaze to the screen in his hands without missing a beat. "Just part of an old biostatic conversion unit. It's basically useless now, I should probably just trash it."

"Ah," I say as if I have any idea what that means, turning my back to him, afraid that uttering another syllable will betray my wondrous disbelief. There's another six *thousand* credits attached to this. That would be enough for Mica, for me, for us—it'd have to be.

It's trash anyway, Adam said so himself . . .

I know it's wrong to take it, but explaining my interest in a piece of broken skyworld technology might elicit too many additional questions from Adam, and it feels like I've already given him more than enough information about myself. My mind runs through a list of justifications as I slip the slight machine into my pocket, causing the fabric to bulge out so noticeably that I might as well have a sign attached to my leg.

I quickly stand and head to grab Mica's backpack, hoping to toss the machine inside, but the movement draws Adam's attention and I can't make the switch. Instead, I hold the bag in front of my leg in an attempt to conceal my swollen pocket.

"Look," I say as his gaze meets mine once more. "I really need to get going. All of this has been fascinating, but I think I'm about maxed out on crazy underground technology and lost skyboys for now. I've been gone for way too long, and given that I don't even know exactly how far I am from home . . . My brother—"

"Of course," Adam says. He pushes a button on the side of the tablet and the screen goes blank. "Just give me two more minutes to pack up and we'll go. I have to admit, I'm pretty intrigued to see what Sixteen is like. If all of your fellow residents are as charming as yourself," he says with a lopsided grin.

"Pack up? What? No," I protest. "You're not coming with me."

"Why not? You need me to show you how to get out of the dome, don't you?"

"I assumed you were just going to give me directions."

"Why tell when you can show?"

I look around the room before settling my eyes back on his face. "Why would you even want to go to Sixteen?"

"Shocking though it may be, I don't intend on living down here for the rest of my life by myself," he says, his voice hitching on the final two words. "I need to continue my research and now that I have someone who might actually know where to go once we're up top . . ."

He looks at me as if he's trying to decide if that's truly the case and I have to work very hard to keep myself from saying something particularly rude in response.

"It's win-win, Terra. I get you out of here, you get me to Sixteen. Show me around a bit. What better way to conduct my research than with a local guide?"

"I can't just bring you home with me. How would that look? I don't need to give people any additional reasons to keep an eye on me."

"What do you mean?" Adam says, his expression suddenly curious.

I mentally curse myself. The last thing I want to tell Adam about is my recent fortune. Questions about the payout might lead to questions about what I was paid out for. And that will lead right to the machine I'm currently trying to smuggle in my pocket. "You would just stand out too much, a skydweller like you, slumming with us. How am I supposed to explain how we even met?"

"I think the truth makes for a pretty good story," Adam says with a smirk.

"Ha. Right. Whilst scavenging in the middle of the night, I was chased by raiders over the quarantine line. Then, when trying to escape, I found a friendly telekinetic skyworld scientist in a magical underground forest. Yeah, I'm sure that'll go over real well with the guardsmen."

"I think, technically, I'm the one who found you."

"Whatever. While you probably have some kind of Tribunal-signed permission slip to be here, if they find out that I've been in the ruins this long, it'll be isolation, observation, and decontamination for me. Who knows when—or if—I'll come back from that." I think about the conclusion I drew yesterday, how outlandish the idea of contamination feels in light of everything I've learned being here. "I mean, I guess there is a *chance* I could be infected but I certainly don't feel plague-ish. How about you?"

"Fit as a fiddle," Adam says, patting himself down.

I arch a brow at the outdated expression. "Anyway, you see my point, right? It will be a lot less suspicious if I go back on my own."

"I disagree."

"As you're fully entitled to. Regardless, I need to go." I shift my weight as I move to leave, trying not to draw attention to the awkward way I'm still holding the backpack against my leg.

"What if I gave you something? In exchange for taking me back with you," Adam says suddenly.

"Like what?" I'm already heading toward the door.

"I don't know. A water filter, maybe."

I turn back to face him. "You already gave me one of those, remember?"

His forehead creases, his mouth tipping to one side. "I didn't realize that was a gift."

I feel heat in my cheeks. Of course he would want it back. And I've already taken something that isn't mine. I squirm a little, unsure of how to respond, but the smirk on Adam's face has already been replaced by a kind smile.

"Take it easy. You can keep that one too. I could give you another one though. It's not just you, right? You take care of your younger brother. It'd be much easier if you each had your own filter. Or you could leave one at home—they attach to faucets too—and keep the other one portable. Or if there's anything else here that strikes your fancy, it's yours, with a few exceptions."

I purse my lips. He's right, of course. These water filters would make a world of difference for Mica and me. I can only imagine how much steel we'll save if we can cross canteens off our weekly purchase list. The voice in my head reminds me I've already got another thing that was definitely *not* a gift in my pocket.

Still, I'm not sure I want to bring Adam to Sixteen. His willingness to part with his belongings in order to get me to agree feels suspect. His eagerness makes me uneasy. Why would his "research" necessitate a visit there, when he didn't even appear to know what or where it was until I told him?

"So, what do you say?" Adam asks.

I feel the pressure building as he waits for my response, guilt and gratitude warring inside me. I go back and forth—yes or no, risk or reward—before I get an idea. The plan is already half-formed when I finally open my mouth.

"How far are we from the dome exit?" I ask.

"Not far at all," he says. "Just a little ways east of here."

"All right, fine. You can come. We'll figure out a story on the way. But I want the water filter first."

Adam grins. "You got it." He picks up a filter ring from the top of the table and tosses it at me. I reach out to grab it with my free hand but it zooms over my head, ringing as it bounces on the floor behind me.

"Nice catch," he teases.

"Nice throw," I retort.

Adam scoops up the rest of his tools from the desk and retreats to the back of the room to pack. I snatch up the filter from the floor and open the backpack, keeping an eye on Adam while I pull the machine out of my pocket, dump both items in the bag, and zip it back up before he has time to turn around.

"Right, I need to hit the"—I nod my chin in the direction of the bathroom—"again." Adam waves his hand in acknowledgment and I slip out of the room.

East, Adam had said. The exit is to the east, and it's close. I might be able to get all the way to the wall before he notices I'm gone. I hoist Mica's irrationally heavy backpack high on my shoulders as I hurry into the hall, and can't help but feel like my guilt is what's weighing it down.

Back in the bathroom, I stride straight over to the window at the far end. Not the easiest escape route, but it'll do. Hinged at the top and shut with a simple latch at the bottom, the window is about two feet wide and a foot and a half tall, just big enough for me to shimmy through. I twist the lock and it pops open at an angle.

I unzip my backpack to take a quick inventory. Though the raiders left me the empty canteen, they appear to have taken everything else, including my flashlight. I instinctively groan as I think about how much it will be to replace, before remembering that cost isn't really a concern anymore.

I secure the machine by tucking it into an interior pocket, then zip the bag closed. I shove it through the open window first, then hike my foot up onto the sink nearest to me and hoist myself up. Not without difficulty, I squirm through the opening and drop down onto the grass outside. I search around my feet for the backpack, but it's nowhere to be found.

"Looking for this?"

I spin around to see Adam leaning against the side of the building, one leg propped up behind him. His voice is filled with amusement as he holds the bag out in front of him, dangling it from two of his fingers like bait.

"How did you—"

"I wasn't born yesterday, Sunburst. Let's go." He tosses the bag to me and I cringe as I catch it. Did he look inside? I doubt he had time to, but the thought still makes me nervous.

"Sorry," I say sheepishly, though I'm not sure if I'm apologizing for trying to leave him behind, or for taking the machine in the first place.

"Don't worry about it."

"You're not angry?"

He shrugs. "I wouldn't be too inclined to trust me either."

"Where's your stuff?" I say after a beat, desperate to change the subject.

Adam turns around to show me the thin pack slung across his back.

"All of it fit in there?" I ask, feigning incredulity even though I already know the answer.

"It's bigger than it looks," he says simply as he peels himself off of the building and strides toward the trees.

Reluctantly, I follow.

I PLUCK a leaf off of a low-hanging branch, twirling it between my fingers the same way Adam did yesterday. "I'm still trying to wrap my head around the fact that all of this is fake."

"Well, it's not really," he says. "This is real grass, these are real trees, you drank real water. It just all happens to be down here. The sunlight is the only thing that's fake."

"That feels real too, though."

"Yeah, it really is something, isn't it? The panels mimic the normal cycle of day and night. It's not a perfect match, but the sunsets in particular are quite accurate. And beautiful. I'm sorry you missed it yesterday." He looks sideways at me for a moment.

I avoid meeting his gaze. "Sunsets aren't really my thing," I say, stalking ahead of him.

Adam suddenly grabs my arm.

"Hey!" I object.

"I'm sorry, did you want to walk into the wall?"

I reach out into the air in front of me. Less than a foot from my face, I feel the cool resistance of metal beneath my fingers. "Oh."

Adam pushes on an invisible plate and, just like before, the scene before me shifts. A shallow doorway appears and I realize he was right; there's absolutely no way I would have been able to find this on my own, even if I had walked straight into the wall. "After you," he says, sliding open the door inside.

I tilt my head to peer through it and am met with the familiar blackness of the underground tunnels. "You wouldn't happen to have a flashlight, would you?" I ask.

Adam grins and pulls a tiny tube, no bigger than his index finger, out of his pocket and hands it to me.

"Er, thanks," I say as he offers the laughably small light to me. "I guess this is better than nothing."

"I imagine it will be," Adam says knowingly. "Twist the top to turn it on."

I venture forward into the darkness, twisting a ridge at the top of the tube as instructed. Light flares, so bright that I yelp in surprise. The entire tunnel is illuminated. From behind me, I hear poorly muffled laughter.

"Think it'll do?" Adam says innocently, and it's all I can do to stop myself from smacking his arm.

The tunnels on this side of the dome are less cluttered with debris than the ones I'd entered from, so we move through them quickly. Adam guides me with gentle direction, and before long, we're standing at the bottom of another stairwell.

"You're sure this goes back up to the surface?" I ask for the third time.

He sighs.

"Okay, okay," I say, beginning my ascent. The steps feel much steeper going up than they did running down, and I find myself struggling for breath. My injuries may be healed, but two nutrition bars and one night's rest is not enough to undo the strain of yesterday's events. Mercifully, Adam keeps any comments about my lack of stamina at bay.

After climbing for a while, the stairwell becomes noticeably brighter. I twist the flashlight off and hand it back to Adam as we emerge into sunlight in front of another locked black gate, the padlock facing us this time.

Ugh, more climbing.

I take quick breaths through my nose to mask my labored breathing, shoving my foot between the bars and prepare to climb, but Adam places a gentle hand on my shoulder to stop me.

"Let me try something," he says. He walks over and plants himself squarely in front of the padlock. His shoulders tense and the muscles flex in his back. A second later, I hear the grating sound of chains uncoiling.

"Carry a lockpick in your pocket, do you?" I say.

Adam looks at me warily before responding. "Not exactly." He holds up his hand and wiggles his fingers.

"Ah." *Of course. He can pick locks with his mind.* "No need to be all secretive about it on my account. Feel free to utilize your talents as you see fit."

"I didn't want to freak you out again," he replies.

"Why don't we just assume from now on that I'm just generally freaked out at all times?"

Adam chuckles quietly as he pushes the gate open and scans the street. "No raiders," he confirms, stepping onto the pavement.

Sucking a deep, slow breath into my lungs, I walk out beside him.

TWELVE

"DO you have any idea where we are?" I ask.

"You're the local," Adam says with a shrug.

"This hardly qualifies as my neighborhood." I scan the area. Buildings box us in on three sides, a block out in each direction, but the area where we have emerged is flat and empty. The ground, cracked and dry, slopes in front of us to form a dusty brown hill where the bottom half of a gargantuan stone obelisk is planted ceremonially in the middle. The top portion has broken off and lays in two pieces on the ground.

"I already miss it down there," I say with a sigh. Wherever we are, the landscape of the District here differs drastically from the cityscape I ran through yesterday. The area surrounding us is barren and still; I doubt there's another underground entrance nearby.

"Tell me about it," Adam says. "We covered at least two miles in the tunnel. I haven't had a chance to collect data around here yet."

I scan the horizon. The artificial sun in the biodome had felt real enough, but the unforgiving way the actual sun beats down, even at this early hour, is a stark reminder of reality. I squint into the distance, then glance back at Adam. His pale skin practically glows in the morning light.

"Let me ask you something," I say.

His brow creases. "All right . . ."

"You've been on the ground for over a week, and you yourself said that it's not like you've been down in the biodome the entire time, right? You've been out here, in the ruins, collecting data and whatnot?" I'm talking as if it's a question, but it's not really.

"Yes."

"So, why hasn't your skin started to darken? I didn't see a giant tube of sunscreen amongst your belongings." Though I suppose he could be hiding any manner of things in that black hole he's got strapped to his back.

"I . . . don't need sunscreen," he says after a beat, the words spoken cautiously, like he's bracing for their impact.

"What?" I don't bother hiding my shock. "So, in addition to portable water filters, you have some kind of, what, wearable UV filter too?"

"Not exactly. It's more like another advancement. A . . . procedure." He purses his lips. "My skin doesn't absorb the sun the same way yours does."

"Oh, of course. Heaven forbid anything sully your perfect paleness," I say bitterly. Apparently, slathering on tube after tube of expensive sunscreen lotion isn't enough anymore. Skydwellers have become so vain that they're actively getting procedures done to preserve their vanity. Or, maybe they're just getting lazier. Probably both.

Adam becomes quiet, sensing my sudden upsurge of anger at the continued revelations of imbalance between our worlds. After a minute, he clears his throat. "Do you recognize anything?"

I blink a few times, refocusing on the task at hand. "That building kind of looks familiar." I point to a tall structure in the distance that has exposed girders where the roof should be. "But I'd need to see further out to tell where to go." As much as I hate the idea of heading back toward where the raiders might still be patrolling, it's our best bet for getting out of the ruins.

"Let's get you a better vantage point then," Adam says.

The barren ground shifts back into crumbling city streets as we make our way to the familiar building. We stop at the bare brass frame of what was once a double-door entrance, shards of glass dusting the ground.

"You sure about this?" I ask.

"Not especially," he answers. He steps through the doorway and offers his hand to pull me through.

I shove past him without taking it, but don't miss the way his eyes roll up toward the sky, as if he's praying for patience.

The room we enter is dark, the late-afternoon light that streams in from the doorway behind us only reaching so far. Adam pulls his flashlight back out of his pocket and places it in my free hand, twisting the top for me as I hold the base. Light flares out and I see we are standing in an ornate lobby. It reminds me of the casino in the skycity, Lexicon—or of the photos I've seen, at least.

The lobby's walls are made of smooth, polished marble— grandiose and elegant, even if they are webbed with cracks. The ceiling seems miles above us, and threadbare sofas that have been leached of their color are set in fours across from each other. The sofas form square booths that sparsely dot the room, their legs sunken into fissures in the patterned tile as if the floor is trying to swallow them. An elaborate chandelier lies in pieces in the middle of the room, delicate crystals and heavy golden candelabras strewn unceremoniously across the floor, twinkling under the flashlight's beam as it passes over them.

I step forward into the room, awed by its grandeur even in its decayed state. As I walk, a thick cloud of dust rises around my ankles. I point the flashlight at the floor, and swirls of dust dance along the shattered tile beneath my feet, the motes twirling around each other in the shadows.

"This is wild," I say, running the flashlight back and forth across the giant room.

"What is?" Adam asks.

"Being here. Seeing this. We might be the first people to set foot in here in hundreds of years. It's a little . . ." I search for the right word in the stillness, while the dust cloud settles at my feet.

"Creepy," I say finally.

"Sad," Adam says at the same time.

A beat of silence passes.

"Looks like we can get up this way," he says, pushing my hand so that the flashlight shines on a doorway off to the side where I find myself staring up at a rickety, winding stairway. The stairs are too steep to see how far up they go.

"More stairs?" I grumble.

"You can handle it."

"I'm starting to rethink the merits of this idea. What if the floor collapses?"

"I've caught you every other time, haven't I?" Adam places his palm against the small of my back and ushers me forward. My body instinctively wants to lean back into his touch, but his fingers brush against the bottom of the backpack, my contraband still inside, and I speed up so he's forced to pull his hand back.

We climb.

My thighs burn as I lose count of the number of small landings we pass, each one indicating a new level, another floor. The stairs become increasingly unstable as we ascend and, eventually, debris blocks our path to the point that we can't go any further. We return to the previous landing and exit the stairwell into a long hallway lined with doors on either side.

"Pick a side," Adam suggests.

I walk up to the first door on the left. The handle turns, but the door doesn't open. I pivot back to Adam, who winces as I accidentally flash the light into his eyes.

"It's locked."

"Honestly," he says with another roll of those cerulean eyes. He steps back and lunges at the door shoulder-first. It gives immediately, the latch falling to the floor as the door flies open.

"Why didn't you use your . . ." I flick my wrist in a poor imitation of the motion I now associate with Adam's FX.

A wrinkle appears in his forehead. "It's not good for me to use it all the time," he says after a moment. "Little stuff is simple, but . . ."

But even superheroes have their limitations, I think. My mind flicks back to how he looked after he'd prevented the branch from hitting me—his chest heaving, his hands at his ribs. I find myself even more curious as to how exactly he got the giant bruise that mars his abdomen.

Adam clears his throat, and I turn my attention to the now-open room. Inside, there are two neatly made beds, a chair, and several pieces of dark wooden furniture. Lengths of threadbare fabric hang above the open windows. It's all barely worth noting, however, compared to the gaping hole in the middle of the floor. It's mirrored by a similar opening in the ceiling that looks into the room above, as if some huge object crashed into the building from above and tore straight through each level.

"Yep, creepy," I confirm.

Adam saunters over to the window, giving a wide berth to the hole in the floor, and looks down at the street below. "You go ahead and get your bearings. There's something I want to look into." He sounds excited as he heads back to the open doorway.

"Where are you going? We only have one flashlight," I say. "Just wait a sec, I won't be long. You won't be able to feel your way back down in the dark."

"I'll manage. Meet you out front." Adam looks at the opening in the floor before adding, "And please, *please* try not to fall."

"What are you—" I start, but he's out of sight before I can finish my sentence. "Okay, bye then."

I walk over to the edge of the room, treading lightly over the unsound floor, and peer out the window. I'm just above the skyline, and over the surrounding buildings I can see the Dead Woods in the distance. From up here, it doesn't look that far, but I know better. Leaning out the window to get a better look, a gust of wind blows what remains of the curtains into my face. I wobble, grabbing the windowsill to steady myself.

Glad that Adam wasn't there to witness that, I quickly scan the sky and reel myself back into the room. The cool light of early morning is already changing as the sun has risen in the cloudless sky, and my anxiety spikes as I think about just how long Mica has been alone now, though I couldn't say the exact number of hours.

If I make it to next Collection Day with this second machine, I think as I head back down the stairs, *I am definitely buying a watch.* My legs ache as I reach the bottom of the stairwell and make my way through the lobby, but when I step back out onto the street, Adam is nowhere to be found.

"Adam?" I call out. A minute passes. Then another. I pull my hair over one shoulder and twist it nervously around my finger.

I call Adam's name again, louder this time, moving away from the building and toward the nearest cross-street.

Did he ditch me? My eyes flit nervously down the expanse of road. I suppose it might be for the best if he did, but then why would he have been so insistent about coming with me?

"Terra." Adam's voice echoes over to me, faint at first but growing louder as the seconds tick by, accompanied by a mechanical rumbling that drowns out his words. Beyond my name, I can't make out most of what he's saying, and I don't understand where the sputtering sound is coming from until Adam finally turns a corner and barrels into my line of sight.

He sits astride a motorized bike-style transport vehicle, with one wheel in front and two in the back. How the hell he got its centuries-old motor to run is beyond me. What remains of the paint tells me that the bike was originally black, though the shell that would customarily cover the engine is missing. At least that explains why it's so loud. Adam's yells are frantic over the buzz of the bike, but I still can't tell what he's trying to tell me.

He races toward me with no signs of slowing down and I finally hear a frenzied "Move!" just in time to lunge out of the way as he rushes past.

My shoulder hits the side of an abandoned vehicle that's been pushed up onto the sidewalk, and I scrape my elbow as I career onto the broken pavement. Outraged, I wrap my fingers around a large chunk of rubble that has landed next to my arm, seconds from hurling it in Adam's direction when I hear the second transport round the corner.

Before I can react, the transport slows down, only yards away from me. The truck's wagon is empty but I spy two raiders sitting inside the cab. A small, curious part of me wonders if they're part of Ryk's gang, or some other, fresh threat.

Convinced that they've spotted me, I crawl around the vehicle I fell against, my heart pounding even while dejection spreads across my insides. I don't think I have it in me to go through another chase. A few moments pass though, and the truck is still moving. I risk a glance back through the vehicle's broken windows and realize I'm not the reason the raiders have slowed down.

At the end of the street, trapped between the raiders' truck and a barricade of abandoned vehicles, is Adam. He faces away from his pursuers, who angle their truck to block the street. Only a sliver of sidewalk remains open, and I doubt it's wide enough for the motorbike to fit through.

I inhale sharply. Why isn't he turning around? Does he not realize how close they are? With his back to them, he's a sitting duck.

I curse under my breath, turning my head toward the open road behind me. It would be so easy to run. The raiders haven't seen me, and they're obviously preoccupied. I have the machine. Now that I know which way to go, I could outrun them.

I could go home.

I hear the raiders' boots crunch on the gravelly road as they exit their truck and step onto the street. They're maybe thirty feet from Adam, and they're laughing. I can't help wondering if the raiders who killed Lee laughed beforehand too.

"Damn it," I say quietly. Crouching low, I creep down the sidewalk toward the still-running truck. The raiders have left the doors open and the engine churns noisily. My palm begins to pulse around the heavy chunk of rubble still clutched in my hand.

"Tsk, tsk, pretty boy," one of the raiders taunts. "You didn't really think you were gonna get away on that thing?"

Adam continues to face the blockade of broken-down vehicles, his head cocked to the side, like he's pondering how to get past them. The raiders grow visibly irritated by his lack of reaction and start rushing at him just as I reach the driver's side door. I peer in cautiously, taking a split second to assess the interior of the truck. In the foot bed sits a pair of matching pedals, just inches beneath the sloped underside of the dashboard that houses the steering wheel.

I bite my lip as I try to remember which pedal is the accelerator, and which is the brake. I only have one shot.

I take a deep breath and jam the chunk of rubble onto the pedal on the right, wedging it between the pedal and the dashboard's undercarriage. I yank my arm back as the truck jolts forward, hitting the side of the door with my hand as I withdraw it, but the pain barely registers as the raiders' black truck careens into the side of a building. Both the raiders and Adam turn just in time to see the transport smash into the wall with an ear split-ting crash.

I casually dust my pants off as I stand. "Sorry, did you need that?"

Adam gapes at me. One of the raiders growls and immediately breaks into a sprint. I pivot on the spot and take off running, confident that if I can just get back there fast enough, I can lose him amongst the maze of rooms in the grand building I just left.

But the raider is much faster than I anticipated. He closes the gap between us before I have a chance to get away. As quickly as I feel his hands grab hold of my upper arms, though, I am released. I whip around to see the raider flying backward. Half a second later, he slams into the side of the truck and slinks to the ground. Adam stands on the other side of the vehicle, arm outstretched, panting, the other raider collapsed at his feet.

"What were you thinking?" Adam roars, stomping over to me.

"You're welcome?"

"I told you to run."

"Is that what you were saying? I had a little bit of trouble hearing you as you were trying to flatten me."

"This isn't a joke, Terra." Adam places his hand over his forehead, his middle finger on one temple and his thumb on the other, shielding his eyes.

"I was helping," I insist.

"Well, you shouldn't have. You'd think after all the trouble I've gone through saving your life, you'd maybe want to stop risking it so often."

"I—you—I—As if you weren't risking your own life? You could've been hurt too," I seethe.

"I had everything well under control."

"It sure as hell didn't look like it from where I was."

"That was the point. You think I couldn't take them out?" He gestures to the unconscious raiders. "I was keeping them distracted so you had time to get away."

I open and close my mouth, searching for another retort. Despite my best efforts, I'm still the one who needed saving.

I stare at the ground. "I couldn't just leave you," I finally say, my face flushing.

Something in my voice seems to soften Adam's ire. Still breathing heavily, he retrieves the motorbike. "Need a ride?" He beeps a comical-sounding horn as he mounts the vehicle. "We probably don't want to stick around here too much longer. I doubt their comrades are far."

I eye the bike and have half a mind to ask how he found a working transport in this dead city, but humiliation stays my tongue.

"Hop on." He scoots forward and pats the bench behind him with his palm.

I throw one leg over the bike and before I've even fully settled into the seat, Adam floors it. The sudden burst of speed blasts me backward, and I immediately wrap my arms around his waist. He winces and, remembering his bruise, I move my hands to rest somewhat awkwardly on his shoulders instead.

It is not a smooth ride. The ancient transport, paired with the destroyed city streets, makes for wild dips and bumps that have my stomach rising into my throat. My hair flies up around my head in all directions, whipping around me, and I press my cheek into the slim pack on Adam's back to shield my face.

I clench my thighs tightly around the seat as Adam weaves in and out of alleys, using my arms to direct him toward the Dead Woods. Unlike the raiders' truck, which had been forced to go around the more crowded streets, Adam maneuvers the bike nimbly between obstacles and we clear the District in no time.

The bike deals with the unpaved stretches outside the ruins surprisingly well. With fewer bumps comes a much smoother ride, so I unhook one of my arms from Adam's shoulder and use it to hold my hair to one side.

"Go left," I yell into Adam's ear as we near the woods. Despite its dexterous steering, there is no way the transport will fit through the trees. He yells something back, but the wind eats his words.

I guide us on a broad arc around the Dead Woods and am surprised when I see the glint of black dystridium in the distance. Having never actually driven a transport, and not having ridden in one since I was a child, I never had a chance to appreciate how fast they are. We've made it back to Sixteen in a fraction of the time it would normally take me.

I can't help the smile that flits across my wind-whipped face as we approach the settlement. I know I'll have some serious explaining to do, but, for now, I'm just relieved to be so close to home. Already exhausted again, but so, so relieved.

As we approach the southern wall, I realize that Adam isn't slowing down. "Stop just up ahead," I shout. He shakes his head. I'm not sure if he is disagreeing with me or if he simply can't hear me. He follows the curve of the wall around the settlement, circling it fully before we finally come to a stop less than a foot from where I'd originally indicated.

"Sorry," he says, cutting the engine, "I just wanted to get a full view. Why are we stopping here? There's a gate on the other side."

"It'll be hard enough to come up with an explanation that accounts for you, let alone this thing," I say, gesturing to the bike. "We can climb over here."

"You worry too much, Sunburst," Adam responds. He flicks his hand and the bike pops back to life.

"What are you doing?" I scramble to get off, but I'm not fast enough, and the bike lurches forward while I'm still half-seated. I grab at Adam for balance, wrapping my arms tightly around his torso. His back tenses, adjusting to the pressure on his bruise, but I don't move my hands this time. *Serves him right.*

We zoom back around to the North Gate, slowing as we enter. I try my best not to meet the curious gazes of the guardsmen stationed there. As we ride through town, I notice more than a few disapproving looks from North Quadrant residents on the street, though I suspect it has more to do with the noise of the bike than anything else. Up in this part of town, owning transports isn't so rare. I think of Councilman Loxley's matching roadsters—one red, one black. Even as dinged up as they are, the lower quadrants couldn't stop talking about them for weeks.

I pat Adam's shoulder twice, urging him to speed up. After a few minutes of me directing him through the settlement, we putter to a stop outside my apartment complex.

I groan, rubbing the inside of my thighs lightly as I stand. I guess I was holding on tighter than I thought.

Adam parks the bike at the side of the building. "So, this is home?"

"The one and only," I say. "The good thing about having all the adults in your life either die or abandon you is that everyone feels too bad to kick you out of your apartment." I run my fingers through my hair, and they get caught in its tangles immediately. As I work on retrieving my digits from my hair, my gaze shifts and a movement catches my eyes. I turn my head and see the unmistakable glint of a transport window being rolled up. The sight of the black vehicle on our street fills me with unease.

"Come on skyboy, let's go inside," I say, doing my best to keep my voice level, even as I rush the words. I'm eager to get off the street. "I'll draw you a map or something so you don't get lost again. And maybe you can distract Mica from wanting to kill me the second I step inside."

I open the door to the apartment building, and with slow steps, Adam and I climb the three sets of stairs to my floor, my thigh muscles pulsing painfully with each step. When we finally reach my front door, I take a long, steadying breath before turning the doorknob.

"Mica?" I say tentatively, swinging the door open.

I duck as a couch cushion comes flying toward me, moving out of the way just in time for it to hit Adam squarely in the chest.

I stand back up and find myself eye-to-eye with Mica, his arms crossed over his chest. His mouth is set in a hard line but his eyes are wide and alert.

"Where the *hell* have you been?"

THIRTEEN

"WHAT WAS THAT FOR?" I ask Mica as Adam shuts the door behind him.

"Where have you been?" Mica repeats, his voice cracking. "I've been looking for you everywhere! No idea where you were, no idea if you were okay, no—"

"I'm so sorry, Mic. I'm fine, really. I just . . ." I bite the inside of my lip, uncertainty making my stomach feel queasy. "I got caught up in something," I finish lamely.

"Caught up in something?" Mica scoffs. "You disappeared for more than a day! You didn't even tell me you were going scavenging. And when the guardsmen showed up—"

"Guardsmen came to talk to you? What did they say?" I flick my eyes toward Adam as he steps forward to stand beside me, his proximity dulling the blade of the panic rising in my chest.

Mica follows my gaze and shoots a curious look at him before returning his attention to me. "They came yesterday evening, asking about you. Where you were, when the last time I saw you was, stuff like that. I told them I didn't know, that I hadn't seen you all day and had looked for you, but you were probably out scavenging. I asked them why they were asking, and they said they just wanted to check up on the two of us, to make sure we were doing all right."

"How courteous of them," I say wryly.

"But after they left, I kind of freaked. I thought you might've been nabbed by raiders, or gotten hurt, or the Black Traders got a hold of you, and I . . ." His eyes glisten as he trails off, and I feel a pang in my chest.

"Oh." The sound exits my mouth more like a breath than a word. "God, I'm so sorry you were worried, Mic."

"I can't—You can't do that, Terra," he says.

"I know."

"I didn't know—I thought . . ."

"I know. I'll explain everything, I—"

"And you stole my backpack!" His voice jumps an octave on the last word and I have to swallow a laugh because of course that's the biggest offense.

"Another thing that I promise I'll—"

"*And* you were *this close* to missing the assembly."

I pause. "What assembly?"

"You didn't hear? I figured that's why you're finally back. It's a Full Council," Mica says.

I gawk at him. Sixteen has its fair share of periodic meetings. There are monthly public forums and quarterly status addresses that deal with citizen-specific and settlement-wide issues respectively. Then, there's the Full Council Assembly. It occurs once a year and is the only one that's mandatory, since the Tribunal sends down a high-ranking official to run it. We're not due one for another six months, though.

"Is there a problem?" Adam asks.

"Who's he?" Mica says, finally acknowledging Adam's presence.

"There's no problem, not exactly," I say, my mind whirring with new anxieties as I rush through introductions. "Mica, Adam. Adam, Mica." Suddenly, explaining the telekinetic skydweller who saved my life to my brother is not my top concern.

Mica cocks his head at me but doesn't say anything.

"When does the meeting start?" I ask him.

"Noon. We've got a little less than an hour so we should get ready to leave soon."

"We can go in a minute, I just need to . . ." I gesture to my general state and Mica nods a little too enthusiastically.

"Yeah, you do. You certainly look like you've been dragged through the muck, Terra. Are you going to tell me what happened?"

"Yes, absolutely," I say, already halfway to my bedroom. "It's just that it's kind of a long story." I strip off Mica's backpack and kick it under the bed—I'll deal with the machine later—before casting a longing look at my pillow. I snatch a set of clean clothes from my dresser, not even bothering to see what they are.

I turn to Adam as I cross over to the bathroom. "They check all the residences during Full Counsels to ensure compliance, and if you're caught skipping we could be fined, or worse. You'll have to come with us. Just try not to catch anyone's eye, okay? The fewer questions we get right now, the better." My eyes drift from his messy blonde hair to the silken white undershirt he's wearing, then back up to his cerulean eyes. "Mic, can you help him? Just find him, you know, something to cover all the . . ."

"Sky-ness?" Mica offers, and I bark a laugh of confirmation before shutting the door.

I hear my brother say something to Adam but the door muffles his words. Judging from his tone, though, he's not pleased.

One thing at a time, I tell myself.

I peel off my clothes and thrust a washcloth under the running tap to wipe myself down. After washing just one of my forearms though, the sink is already brown with dirt.

"To hell with it," I mutter. I close off the tap and jump into the shower instead, squealing as the cold water hits my skin—I don't allow it time to warm. I quickly set about rinsing off the grit, grime, and gunk—literal and metaphorical—of the past thirty-something hours. As my body adjusts to the temperature, I feel my muscles start to relax under the pressure of the stream, even as the goosebumps on my skin keep me tense and alert.

I grab the thin sliver that remains of the soap bar and lather the suds into my hair, the slick foam helping me unsnarl my tangled locks. I grimace as I pull through the knots surrounding the scar on my head, not because it hurts, but because of everything that little raised line represents. My utter failures yesterday and the fact that I likely wouldn't be alive—let alone have made it back home—were it not for Adam. I shiver and it's not entirely from the temperature of the water.

As soon as the water runs clear in the bottom of the tub, I shut off the valve. I reach around the shower curtain for a towel, only to find nothing there.

"Mica," I call out, annoyed. "What did you do with the towels?" I wring my hair out as I wait for a response. Several seconds later, there's a knock on the door.

"Come in," I say, pulling the shower curtain around me. A moment passes. "Come in," I repeat, louder. The door clicks open and a sliver of Adam's face appears as he peeks through the crack.

"Mica is changing but there's a pile of towels out here so . . ."

I mutter my brother's name under my breath like it's a curse. "Bring me a towel then."

"Are you . . . You're sure?" Adam asks.

I sigh. "Just hurry up already."

Adam slowly swings the rest of the door open to reveal his shirtless chest, a threadbare towel folded in his arms. I rip my eyes from his torso and meet his eyes—just for a second—before we both look away.

"Here you go," he says, holding it at arm's length with his eyes fixed on the ceiling.

Heat rises in my cheeks as I tighten the shower curtain around me, then yank the towel from his hand. Several beats pass.

"You can go now," I say.

"Right—Sorry. Right." He rushes out of the bathroom, but not before he clips his shin on the edge of the toilet.

Good, I think as he inhales sharply before closing the door. The half-naked guy standing in my bathroom is the absolute last thing I need to deal with, I remind myself. Attraction, relationships—they're just distractions, more ties that will eventually be severed.

Lee certainly proved that.

I've been more than fine on my own. I've got the guys—Mal, Chrys, and the few other scavs that still like me—when I need a little male camaraderie from someone other than Mica. We all hang around after the occasional scav meeting. They tell their crude jokes and I laugh, or I smack them, depending on exactly how offensive they are.

It works for me. It's been working for me.

I've kept the idea of wanting anything more buried in the back of my mind for over a year, and I don't plan on unearthing it anytime soon.

I rub my face with the towel like I'm trying to rub away the thoughts trying to claw their way back to the surface. Even if I did want to go down that road, it definitely wouldn't be with Adam. At least Lee was like me. Scav. Sixteener. Terrestrial. Adam being a skydweller makes this a whole different matter.

It's not as if relationships between us and *them* never happen. Mica and I are proof of that. It's just that I'm of the firm belief that, well, they shouldn't. Even if a couple were able to get past the judgment and disapproving looks from others, the canyon of difference in backgrounds, the logistical nightmare that is a cross-world relationship, romance is rarely destined to succeed.

Just look at how well things turned out for Dad. There he was, the skyboy who'd sacrificed everything for the terrestrial he loved, only to have her die on him. How ungrateful.

I suppose that, to some, abandoning your kids is a perfectly understandable reaction, given the circumstances.

I grimace, quickly finish toweling off, and slip on my bra and underwear. I gingerly comb through my hair and twist it back in a low bun before donning the rest of my outfit: a long blue tunic that ties at the waist and a pair of dark leggings. It's a little fancier than I would have picked had I been paying attention, but I guess it doesn't hurt to dress up a bit. Full Council Assembly and all.

When I emerge from the bathroom, Adam is respectably clothed, waiting at the kitchen table. He stands as I approach, looking at me with a mix of appreciation and awkwardness. He wears a pair of slim-cut black pants, and a long-sleeved white button-down on top—nice and innocuous. The clothes fit him surprisingly well, especially considering Mica is a good six inches shorter than he is.

"Where did you find those clothes?" I ask Mica, who walks out of his own bedroom wearing a green collared t-shirt and a pair of khaki pants, holding a faded blue cap in his hands.

He shrugs, averting his gaze as he tosses the cap to Adam.

"Ah." I didn't realize he had kept any of Dad's things. Adam smoothes his blonde hair back as he dons the cap and pulls it low over his brow. My eyes linger on a missing button at the collar of his shirt and I shake my head, freeing my mind of whatever memories are trying to creep back in. "All right. Let's go."

THE ASSEMBLY STARTS the way they always do. An enormous white screen descends from the ceiling just as Mica, Adam, and I enter the auditorium, ready to broadcast the opening video transmission from the Tribunal.

The Assembly Hall is one of the only buildings in Sixteen used for official Tribunal business, so it is also one of the nicest. Rows of seats on three separate levels face a broad stage, though the screen currently blocks it from view. The Town Council will be seated behind the screen, along with whatever Tribunal patsy has been sent to address us. After the transmission is over, the screen will recede and the representative—almost always the same old man with thinning hair and a wavering voice who Mica refers to as "Wompy"—will begin his speech.

The lower levels of the hall are already filled, so the three of us climb up to the balcony and make our way to the back. As we pass, I recognize Emery sitting squarely in the front row. A little further back, a pretty, petite girl with wavy black hair waves to Mica. Juniper Coal. A redheaded girl I don't recognize sits on Juniper's left, and Juniper's sister, Yttria, is on the other side with a sneer already fixed on her face.

Yttria's eyes widen briefly as she catches sight of us.

Mica shoots me an unapologetic look before hurrying over to Juniper, who shoos her friend over to free a seat for him. I think briefly about snatching him back, but I have enough to deal with right now as it is, and really don't want to add the Coals to that list today. I settle for making sure Mica hears my irritated sigh as he scurries away.

I pull Adam over to a pair of empty seats at the end of the second-to-last row just as the lights begin to flash, signaling the start of the assembly.

On screen, the three Tribunal Primes form a triangle behind a podium. Prime Whitlock takes front stage. Her auburn hair is styled in a sharp chin-length bob, and she wears a tailored, ice-blue pantsuit, the color reflecting her ghostly white skin. Her pale blue eyes pop from behind sleek, rimless spectacles. Behind her stands Prime Donovan, his greasy black hair slicked straight back, and Prime Laraby, complete with checkered bowtie, slightly askew. They both look bored.

"Good evening," Whitlock begins. "I am sure you are all wondering why you have been called here so unexpectedly. It has recently come to our attention that an unprecedented number of quarantine violations have occurred in the vicinity of Genesis X-16."

A low murmur echoes over the Assembly Hall and my cheeks flare with color. There's no way they would have called a Full Council Assembly because of me, is there?

No, no, I reassure myself. We might not have learned about the meeting until the last minute, but this kind of thing takes more than a single day to organize. It couldn't be just about me.

Prime Whitlock continues speaking, her voice somehow simultaneously ice-cold and utterly saccharine. "The Tribunal understands that there is a degree of curiosity surrounding quarantined areas. As Genesis X-16 is located in closer proximity to a quarantine site than other settlements, however, we cannot stress enough the importance of upholding and respecting the quarantine line. These boundaries exist for your protection, and to ensure the safety of not only you, but of the entire human race. Contamination is still a very real, though thankfully scarce, threat. Lest we forget the Skyfall."

Prime Whitlock removes her glasses and folds them neatly before tucking them into her breast pocket, allowing a moment of threatened silence to settle over the audience. Several people make a gesture of prayer.

"We also recognize that, in most instances, quarantine line violations are relatively harmless. Perhaps whilst scavenging, one saw something valuable just across the border. The Tribunal understands this temptation. However, the number of recent violations has caused much concern, and we have determined an official inquiry is to commence. In order to limit further violations that might impede the sanctity of our investigation, scavenging restrictions are to be imposed on the areas surrounding Genesis X-16."

There is a shout from the bottom level, and a chorus of grumbling grows from it.

"This is a temporary measure, we assure you. However, attempting to violate these restrictions would be most unwise. As a proceeding of the investigation, those who have recently been in violation of the quarantine, regardless of their intentions while doing so, should report themselves to the guardsmen immediately. This is for the safety of Genesis X-16, as well as your own personal health, of course, and will not reflect on you negatively in any way. We also ask that if you witness someone exhibiting strange behavior, or if you know anyone whose whereabouts cannot be accounted for, please notify an official without delay. I reiterate, these are temporary measures that serve to aid our investigation in its initial stages."

I've been gripping the armrest between Adam and me so hard that my knuckles are white when Prime Whitlock ends her speech. An investigation? Folks may not be gallivanting around the District or camping in underground biodomes on the regular, but plenty of people have crossed just over the quarantine line in the past. Kids daring each other, scavs venturing just a foot or two beyond the line to snag a find . . . Violations have never elicited a response like this before.

"Representative Tallis will now explain the restriction guidelines," Prime Whitlock announces. "You may direct any questions to him. Thank you." She signs the Tribunal's trademark symbol to sign off, waving three fingers from left-to-right, then up and down in a T shape.

The screen goes black and withdraws into the ceiling as a dark-suited Tribunal official takes the stage in front of us. I can't see him too clearly from this far up, but it is immediately evident that this is no Wompy. Broad-shouldered and imposing, Tallis dwarfs the small metal podium in front of him.

"Questions will be held until the end," he says in a low voice that booms with authority. The few people who were already making their way to the front of the auditorium to ask their questions, as is customary, retreat.

"First, I will review the new rules that pertain to the quarantine line . . ."

Adam's hand brushes against mine, like he's checking to make sure I'm still there, and I can feel the tension roiling off him. My eyes point forward, watching Tallis intently, but his words rush through my ears unheard.

Out of the corner of my eye, I see Mica, ten rows in front of me and to the right. With the slightest turn of his head, he meets my gaze. His eyes are wide with worry. He already told the guardsmen that he didn't know where I was, and now we all know why they were asking. I offer him what I hope is a reassuring smile.

I think back through all the people I've come into contact with today who might know I crossed the quarantine line. The raiders, of course, but they're not exactly in a position to go tattling on me. The guardsmen at the North Gate perhaps—why did Adam insist on going through the gate? I should have stopped him. I should have insisted. We could've ditched the transport outside the wall, and then all those people we passed when we drove through town on that stupid thing wouldn't be an issue either. Even if they suspect something, though, they can't prove it. The only person here who really knows what happened with me is Adam, and he seems just as tense about this investigation as I do.

Did his research really necessitate him entering the ruins, or was it just a mistake he doesn't want to own up to? With his interest in the raiders, my family, and Sixteen, his research seems like it's more about the people down here than anything else. Is it possible he didn't even realize he'd crossed into a quarantined area when he got lost? I can't imagine most skydwellers know what the line looks like, or what it's for. Why should they? The plague isn't a real threat to them, and they've worked hard to keep it that way. If they even suspected one of their own of being contaminated . . .

Whatever the consequences may be down here, I can only imagine what "decontamination" entails up top. Like it or not, we're in similar situations.

Without thinking, I grab hold of Adam's hand and clutch it tightly. He squeezes it reassuringly, but I can feel his unease. I can't be sure, but I imagine we're thinking the same thing: *What the hell have we gotten into?*

FOURTEEN

HOURS LATER, we are finally released from the Assembly Hall, the seemingly endless onslaught of questions from the citizens of Sixteen finally exhausted. Representative Tallis had answered each inquiry with the same infuriatingly cool, detached tone, even as questions—especially from my fellow scavs—became increasingly indignant. Folks are understandingly concerned with the minutiae of what these new restrictions could mean for our livelihoods.

A surge of guilt washes over me anew as I wonder again if this is all my fault, and doesn't ebb when I realize that even if it isn't, Mica and I won't really be impacted. I don't plan on scavenging here again for a long, long time—possibly ever, once I secure the credits from the second machine.

The walk home is tense and silent. Mica doesn't dare ask in front of Adam what I know he's dying to ask, and I don't want to talk to Adam about anything while Mica's around. But at least the walk itself is easy, the sun dipping low and painting the sky in the swirling colors of sunset.

My stomach rumbles and I speed up as our apartment building comes into view, intending to head straight to the kitchen as soon as we get home. As we near the building, however, a white uniform and familiar face is already there to greet us.

Guardsman Brant waits on the steps of the complex, the shadows growing long on his face under the rapidly setting sun.

"Evening, sir," Mica calls out politely as we approach.

"Good evening. I have a few questions for you."

"I already answered all the questions the other guards had yesterday. I'm not sure what else I can tell you," Mica says earnestly.

"Not you," Brant turns to me. "You."

Mica glances at me nervously.

"Sure thing," I say lightly. "Mica, why don't you and your friend head inside? I'll be there in a minute." I make my voice as natural as I can. Adam keeps his head down, cap on his head pulled low, as he follows Mica into the building.

"Hello, Guardsman Brant." I offer a tentative smile. "How's it going?"

"Terra Rhodon, I have been instructed to determine your whereabouts between the hours of 04:00 yesterday and 10:30 today." He pulls out a rectangular device from his pocket, no bigger than the palm of his hand. A red light blinks evenly in the corner and I am suddenly very aware of the fact that this isn't a private conversation.

"You are unaccounted for during that time frame," Brant continues, "and were last seen leaving your apartment building early yesterday morning. Can you explain this?"

"Seen by whom?"

"That's not relevant."

"Of course it isn't." I chuckle nervously under my breath.

"I assure you, Miss Rhodon, this is no laughing matter." He lowers his voice. "The Tribunal is taking the quarantine violations very seriously. I need to record your official report."

He deliberately looks down at the device in his hand, then back at me. "I'm going to ask you some questions, and you will answer them as best you can." It's not a request, but he says it gently.

"All right," I say, bracing myself because I'm just not sure what he is— or, rather, they are—looking to hear.

"Have you been outside settlement limits in the past day?"

"Yes."

"Why?"

"I . . . needed some fresh air. Cabin fever. From the rain and all." It feels strange to parrot back the same weak excuse I gave Ryk yesterday, but it's the one that makes the most sense. "I wanted to clear my head. My brother and I have been having some disagreements lately and I needed some time alone to think."

There. That's kind of the truth.

"Explain your need to go outside the settlement limits."

I shrug. "I just kind of started walking, and before I knew it I was at the wall. So I just kept going. It's not like that's unusual for me."

Brant nods and looks down at his device for a moment, like he's reading from it. When he looks at me again, his eyes are wide and his lips are set in a stern line.

"Did you, purposely or accidentally, cross the quarantine line at any point?"

I shake my head.

"I require a verbal response, Miss Rhodon."

"Right. Sorry." I take a breath. "No, I did not cross the quarantine line." My resolve hardens as the lie comes out. Time to go big or go home. Or rather, go big or go to a Tribunal holding cell for further interrogation —though that doesn't have quite the same ring.

"I wasn't even gone that long. I just took a walk around the outside of the city. I don't even think Mica was awake when I got back. It was early, so I went back to bed. When I got up again, he had left. Whoever you had keeping tabs on me must have stopped paying attention," I say accusingly.

Brant's eyebrows fly up as I speak. "Your own brother claimed not to know where you were all day and reported as much to the guardsmen he spoke with."

I shrug. "Mica's always at school, so I don't usually see him until later in the day anyway. And I guess I was out again when he got home."

"We have no record of that."

"You've already asked every single citizen of Sixteen if they've seen me today? Give me a break."

"Why did you leave for a second time?"

"I got a lead on someone looking to unload their old transport," I say, jutting my chin at the bike leaning against the side of the building. "Wanted to get to it before anyone else did and also . . . Well, I'm sure I don't need to remind you of our current circumstances, but I haven't exactly been clamoring to engage with other people since Collection Day. Can you blame me for trying to be a little discreet?"

My mind races as I realize it would only take a few minutes to check my credit balance and see I haven't made a single deduction since that first day. "I also didn't realize it was a crime to leave my own house," I say, forcing harshness into my voice. At this point, anybody would be starting to get riled up, even if they weren't blatantly lying, so I'm hoping my visible irritation is helping to sell it.

"Is there anyone else who can attest to your whereabouts?"

"Considering how people have been treating me lately, I've been trying to keep my head down," I say with a shrug. "Whether or not someone noticed me is not my problem."

"According to your brother, he looked for you fervently, without success. Can you explain why you were essentially unreachable?"

"Right. Because a thirteen-year-old boy is really going to spend his extracurricular hours searching high and low for his big sister. I can assure you he was not that worried about me."

"Then why would he have said that?"

"Because teenagers are *never* melodramatic, right? They *never* stretch the truth, or try to get a rise out of someone. I told you we've been fighting. He was probably just trying to get me into trouble. Mission accomplished, apparently."

"And will he be able to corroborate this?"

"I'm sure he won't be thrilled to admit it. But yes, he will." I regret the words as soon as they leave my lips. There is no guarantee that Mica will play along. It's too late now, though. All I can do is trust the voice in the back of my mind, the infinitesimal part of me that thinks Brant might be on my side.

The device in the guardsman's hand beeps twice, and he reads the screen quickly. "All right, Miss Rhodon. There may be some follow-up, but that's all for now. Thank you for your cooperation."

He taps a button on the top edge of the device and slips it back into his pocket. With it powered off, I look up at Brant expectantly, hoping he'll offer another warning, some advice, anything. But he simply nods his head in silence, his eyes soft, and strides off in the opposite direction.

"WHAT WAS THAT ABOUT?" Mica asks as soon as I step through the apartment door.

I stroll past him and try to make my way to the kitchen, but he blocks me. I wearily shove past him and flop down into a chair at the kitchen table. The sun has barely set but the siren call of my pillow rings loudly in my ears, beckoning me to put this day behind me.

"Is everything all right?" Adam asks guardedly as he peers around the corner.

"No. Maybe. Yes. For now, at any rate," I say.

"What did that guardsman want?" Mica persists.

"What do you think? Apparently the Tribunal is getting a head start on their quarantine investigation." I look at my brother with a sheepish expression. "And I'm actually going to need you to do me a favor."

"What kind of favor?" Mica eyes me skeptically.

"If they come by to ask you any more questions . . . I'm going to need you to tell them that you made up all that stuff about looking for me."

"But I did look for you."

"I know."

"Then why—"

"Because I told Guardsman Brant you only said that because you were trying to get me into trouble."

"And I would do that because . . . ?"

"Because you're pissed at me."

"What?" Mica is incensed. "You think I'd be so petty—"

"Oh, calm down. Of course not. I just needed to tell him something to make him back off. So that my story would be a little more plausible."

"Why does your story need to be more plausible? What the hell were you really doing yesterday? You haven't even told me where you fucking slept last night!"

"Mica! Language," I scold.

Adam walks over and stands behind me, placing his hands on the back of the chair. His knuckles press gently into my shoulder as I lean back, steadying me—physically and otherwise.

"Let me get this straight," Mica says, inhaling deeply. "You lied to that guardsman, and now you want me to lie too. That about cover it?"

"I mean, if you insist on making it black and white . . ."

Mica stares at me.

"Fine. Yes. I lied. I am a terrible role model. Go ahead, call Brant back and have me arrested." I put my wrists together in a mock show of being handcuffed, then turn to Adam. "Aren't you glad you're getting such a classy introduction to life in Sixteen? I'm sure the rest of your research team will just love hearing about this."

Adam's expression shifts from vague concern to amusement.

"Look, Mic," I say. "Who knows if they're actually going to bother coming back to ask you more questions. I'm clearly the one on their watchlist. I'm just asking for your help in case they do."

"Fine," Mica says.

I raise an eyebrow. "Fine?"

"Yeah, fine, okay. I'll play along. But only if you tell me what you really have been doing."

"I . . ." I trail off, unsure of how to respond. I don't want to burden Mica with everything that's happened.

"Come on, Terra. You know you're going to tell me eventually. You're just not that great at keeping secrets."

"Maybe that's just what I want you to think. Maybe I'm actually so good at keeping them that I led you to believe I wasn't."

Mica looks at me expectantly. I shoot Adam a questioning look and he nods. "All right," I say, stifling a yawn. "But we'll talk about it in the morning, okay?"

"No way," Mica says. He swings his leg around and falls into a chair on the opposite side of the table, interlacing his fingers on the tabletop. "Spill."

ADAM and I spend the next hour detailing the events of yesterday and this morning to Mica while we scarf down some Rations. I'm so ravenous that I don't even care that all we have left are a couple cans of glug. I shovel spoonful after spoonful of beige curdles into my mouth, only pausing between bites long enough to chuckle at the look of revulsion on Adam's face.

"What did you say this was again?" Adam says, swirling his spoon in the mess on his plate.

I swallow another bite before responding, barely shuddering as it slides down my throat. "D-T04U, but everyone just calls it 'glug.' "

"I can see why." He uses the back of his spoon to push the glug into three piles, then sweeps the spoon across the bottom half of his plate in a crescent-motion. I rise out of my seat slightly to see what he's doing, and almost spit when I see the frowning face he's drawn in his food.

"What are you, five?" I say, choking down a laugh. "Just eat. If Mica can stomach the stuff, surely you can suck it up too."

Adam glances at Mica, who looks back at him with an expression that I imagine says something like, *I feel your pain.*

Adam begins recounting our journey back to Sixteen as I scrape my plate clean, my eyes darting to the kitchen cabinets. My ravenous hunger, as well as the addition of Adam, has caused us to work through the last of our Rations faster than I had initially planned. With the next Rationing still a few days away, I'll need to pick up some food from the shops to tide us over. At least Mica will be elated about that.

My brother takes in the story with surprising acceptance, though I suspect that's at least partly because Adam glosses over some of the more outrageous parts. In particular, he leaves out the whole thing where he can move things with his mind, which makes me frown. I don't want Mica to be blindsided the way I was, but don't have the opportunity to interject with the waterfall of questions overflowing from his mouth.

"You have to take me there," Mica says after asking his tenth question about the workings of the biodome. "I've got to see it."

"No way," I say immediately. "We literally *just* sat through a Full Council Assembly explaining why that's a terrible idea. Guardsmen will be crawling all over the place. Sorry, bud. Not worth the decontamination time."

Mica pouts, but doesn't press the issue. I'm a little surprised he gives up so easily; he must realize how serious the Tribunal is about the quarantine violations.

"I'll be right back," Adam says, excusing himself to use the restroom.

As soon as the bathroom door is shut, I grab Mica's wrist across the table. "Mica," I whisper, "there's something else you need to know about Adam."

"Man, he is the coolest. I've never met someone from up top who was so, I don't know, normal. And he's so smart. I can't believe you almost didn't bring him back with you," Mica gushes.

"Yeah, yeah, he's awesome, I get it. Still, you need to be careful, Mic. We barely know anything about him."

"What are you talking about? And why are you whispering?"

"I'm just saying, don't get too attached. There's still a lot he's hiding from us."

"You're just being paranoid," he says.

"Shut up and listen to me, okay? Adam has . . . abilities."

"Huh?"

"I know it sounds crazy, but he can move things. With his mind. Without touching them."

"What, like telekinesis?" He scoffs loudly.

"Shh!"

"You cannot possibly be serious. You really must have a concussion, sis."

"Something that might be easily remedied if you would just let me get some rest," I grumble. "But I'm telling the truth."

"She's not lying." Adam's voice makes me jump.

"I'm sorry," I say immediately, feeling the burn in my cheeks as Adam returns to his seat. "I just wanted to—"

"It's fine. If he's even half as much of a danger magnet as you, I'd have ended up using it in front of him eventually." My face scrunches into a scowl. "I would appreciate it if neither of you spread this around while I'm in town though," he continues.

"Can we backtrack for a second?" Mica says. "You're seriously trying to tell me you're telekinetic?"

"Afraid so," replies Adam. "Except we call it 'FX.' "

"Prove it."

I spin around in my chair to face Adam. "You don't have to do that."

He seems to deliberate for a second, then cracks his lopsided grin.

Without warning, a pillow from the couch zooms into the back of Mica's head.

"Hey!"

I burst out laughing. "You get what you asked for, brother."

Mica eyes Adam cautiously. "Do that again," he says.

With a flick of his wrist, Adam sends another pillow careening toward my brother, who catches it deftly this time.

"Amazing." Mica whoops with elation as Adam begins spinning his dinner plate. It rings softly as it twirls on the kitchen table. He jerks his wrist in rhythm with the spinning dishware and, as the plate pirouettes, bits of stuck-on glug fly off; a fleck lands on my cheek.

"Whoops," Adam says, breaking his focus. The plate clatters to a stop.

"Thanks for that," I say, flicking the speck off my face. "Are we done now?" I'm somewhat bemused by the fact that the casual exhibition of Adam's FX already seems so normal to me.

"How does it work?" says Mica. "It's got to be some kind of, what? Magnetics? Nanorobotics? And why haven't we heard about it?"

"Well, not everybody can—"

"You really think that people up there would want us knowing about something like this?" I interrupt before Adam has a chance to finish explaining.

"I guess not," Mica says, his brow furrowed. "And you did say that not everybody is able to—but then why would you need this kind of ability as a researcher? If you were military or something then sure, maybe . . ." He trails off as he dives deeper into thought.

Under normal circumstances, I might wonder the same things. But I've long since accepted that nothing about the past day and a half has been normal, and all I can do is yawn.

"I think we should probably call it a night. Your sister's been through a lot today," Adam says.

I pump my fist in victory and they both laugh.

"Okay, okay," Mica says as he walks toward his bedroom. "Your secret's safe with me, man."

Adam nods appreciatively at my little brother, and then we are alone.

A moment of awkward silence passes.

"So, I guess you'll want to get going," I finally say. "There's a place at the edge of the East Q you can stay. I'll give you directions."

"That'd be great," he says, and I'm not quite sure what to make of the contrast between his eager tone and the resigned way he picks up his pack and throws it over his shoulder. "Hey . . . Do you know if there have been any other people who have passed through town recently? People like me?"

"I don't think there are many people like you." I rise from my seat, slightly surprised at the boldness of my words. "But the only new skydwellers we ever see around here are part of the guardsmen rotation."

"Oh, okay," Adam says with forced casualness.

"Are you . . . are you thinking about the rest of your research team?"

He shrugs and moves toward the front door. "I was just wondering if they might've passed through here at some point. Not a big deal. Now how about those directions?"

As I reach for the doorknob, Mica wanders back out of his bedroom with a pillow and a pile of blankets stacked in his arms. "Where are you going?" he barks.

"Adam's going to go check into the hostel," I explain.

"What? No way," Mica protests, dropping the pile of bedding on the couch. "Why wouldn't he just stay here?"

I cross the room to stand next to my brother. "That's not a good idea." I say, voice low.

"Why not?" Mica says defiantly.

"We've already got too many eyes on us," I say. "We don't need to provide any more reasons for someone to sniff around our business, and that most definitely includes harboring an errant skydweller."

"Don't you think that kicking him to the curb, knowing you're being watched, would be more suspicious than letting him stay? Plus, skydwellers don't exactly flood the hostel on a regular basis."

I glance guiltily at Adam, who is shifting his weight from leg to leg and fidgeting with the straps on his pack. "Don't worry about me," he says to Mica. "I really should head out. I don't want to impose any further."

"You're not imposing." Mica turns to me with pleading eyes. "Come on, Terra."

"Mica, I—"

"He saved your life." Mica puts the final, guilt-tripping flourish on his plea, and I'm too exhausted to argue further. My brother's hero worship aside, I guess there are worse things than Adam staying here. At least I'll be able to keep an eye on him.

"Fine," I say to Adam. "You can sleep on the couch." A brief flash of disappointment crosses Adam's face as he glances subtly from the couch to the door. But when he looks back at Mica, the hesitation has shifted into a lopsided grin.

"Will do, boss," Adam says, lowering his pack.

I'm too tired to coherently bid either of them good night. I simply wobble into my bedroom and close the door behind me as I kick off my shoes and pull my hair out of its bun, still wet where I coiled it in the middle after my shower. Without another thought, I flick off the lights and collapse into bed, fully clothed.

Not twenty seconds after my head hits my pillow, there is a gentle knock on my door. With a groan, I prop myself up on one elbow just as Adam pokes his head into the room.

"Just wanted to say goodnight, Terra."

"Oh. Sure," I say, flopping back down. "G'night."

"And thanks," he adds softly.

"For what?" I murmur, already half asleep.

If he says something else, I don't hear it. All I hear is the soft click of the door closing behind him before I drift off.

FIFTEEN

CLANG.

I wake with a jolt. It's too warm; my sheets are damp with sweat, and the clothing I fell asleep in but apparently stripped off at some point during the night sits in a discarded heap on my floor. Bright light streams in through my window, a far cry from the gray morning light I'm accustomed to waking to. I don't think I've slept this late, well, ever.

I sit up and stretch my arms over my head, savoring the pops of my vertebrae as they settle. I smack my tongue a few times in my dry mouth, thirst burning my throat.

Swinging my stiff legs over the side of my mattress, I bend down, feeling blindly under the bed for Mica's backpack. I yank it up and pull out my water canteen, greedily draining it before unscrewing the filter ring from around its mouth. I pull the other filter from the backpack and slip both rings onto the middle finger of my left hand. Mica will want to see these.

My thirst temporarily sated, I pull out the machine, anxious to inspect it more closely. But before I can begin my examination, something interrupts me.

Clang.

The familiar sound rings from outside my bedroom door.

Clang. Clang. Clang.

I jump out of bed—the muscles in my legs aching with every step—and shove the machine haphazardly into one of my dresser drawers, grabbing some clothing that I hope is clean.

I limp out into the main room, pulling my arms through the sleeve holes of a black tank top, just as a metal bowl rolls out of the kitchen and clatters to a stop at my feet. Mica, his shirt untucked lazily, chases after it with outstretched arms.

"Morning," he says brightly, grabbing the bowl and quickly straightening.

I scowl. "What's with the noise?"

"Sorry, sorry," Adam calls as he appears from the kitchen. Another one of my father's shirts hangs open, revealing his chest. "That was my fault."

"What was your fault?" I turn back to Mica. "And why aren't you at school?"

"It's my off day, Terra." He rolls his eyes and takes the bowl back into the kitchen.

"Oh. Right." Suddenly I am very tired again. "What time is it?"

Adam shrugs. "Almost noon, maybe."

My mouth pops open in shock. I slept *that* long?

"Did you get enough rest?" Adam says.

I can't tell if he's mocking me, so I ignore his question and follow Mica into the kitchen. The contents of our pantry are strewn about the kitchen, pots and pans littering the floor. Mica is on his hands and knees, pulling pieces of flatware from underneath the refrigerator.

"What exactly have you two been doing in here?"

"Nothing?" Mica says innocently as he pulls himself upright.

I arch a brow at him.

"I was just trying to find some breakfast. Or, I guess it's more like lunch now. The kitchen just got . . . kind of messy in the process," he confesses. I open my mouth to protest his blatant understatement, but Mica continues, "Turns out we did finish off the last of our Rations last night." He doesn't bother keeping the glee from his voice.

"If you already realized that, why did you have to tear the kitchen apart?"

"I don't know, I thought maybe you had some extra cans hidden away, a secret hoarder stash or something. Seems like the kind of thing you would do."

I glare at him.

"Adam wouldn't let me wake you up to ask, so I was just double-checking we were out."

"Uh-huh." I look at Adam. He shrugs. "I meant to get up earlier and pick up more food," I say.

"No worries," Mica says lightly. "Adam gave me one of his bar things this morning, so I've been good until now." He returns to the mess at hand, humming a little as he puts our kitchen wares back in the entirely wrong spots.

I can't remember the last time he seemed in such high spirits. I surreptitiously pinch the underside of my forearm, just to make sure I'm not still sleeping.

"Mica got a little overzealous with the search, I think," Adam says with that lopsided grin on his face. "Sorry we woke you."

"No, it's fine," I say. "I should've been up a long while ago. I never sleep this late."

"You never snore that loud either," Mica chimes in.

Adam barks a laugh and I scowl.

"What does it matter anyway?" Mica says as he pops out from the cabinet he's been restocking. "It's not like you have anywhere to be. You sure aren't going scavenging right now."

I widen my eyes warningly at Mica. I've made it this far without mentioning our credit balance to Adam, and I don't want him asking questions that might lead him to the machine sitting in my dresser drawer. I wish I'd taken the time to conceal it a little better. "That's enough, Mic," I warn.

"What?" Mica pipes up. "Adam's on my side about the payout. *He* thinks we should be buying things."

My heart sinks into my stomach. "Ah, so you two have already been chatting away," I say, trying to mask my nervousness. I shouldn't be surprised; did I think they'd just be sitting in silence as I slept half the day away?

"I just think you can afford a weekend off." Adam's blue eyes scrutinize my expression. If he knows exactly what it is that got us that payout, he doesn't show it.

"It'll be a lot longer than that. The other scavs around here don't exactly like being shown up, especially by me," I explain. "It is going to be easier if I lay low for a while. Considering everything that's happened, we should *all* probably follow that rule for the time being. No need to draw more attention to our . . . situation."

"Lame," says Mica.

"Totally," says Adam. They both grin widely at me.

"Great. The two of you are in cahoots now? This bodes well for me," I mutter.

"Don't forget, we do still need something to eat," Mica says.

"I tried to get him to test out the sustenance generator," Adam says, "but I don't think he was convinced."

Mica laughs. "Extremely, extremely cool in concept. Less so in execution."

I wrinkle my nose as I remember Adam's description of what the generator produces, and can't say I disagree. "I'll pick up a few things to tide us over until the Rationing next week."

"We're still going to participate in the Rationing?" Mica's gold-flecked eyes stare at me with incredulity. "No way."

"Yes way. We've been over this. Just because we *have* the steel doesn't mean we have to *spend* it." I don't want to sour Mica's good mood with this argument again, but I'm not ready to tell him my plan for our fortune. Not yet.

Even though that's what got me into this mess, I think.

"I hate to break it to you, my oh-so-frugal sister, but if you think we're going to be allowed to participate, you're nuts."

"Why's that? What's the Rationing?" asks Adam.

"Oh, to live a skydweller's life," I say with a sigh.

Mica shoots a silencing look at me. "The Rationing happens after the monthly delivery of foodstuffs from up top comes," he patiently explains. "After all the good stuff goes to the shopkeepers, we get to fight between the leftovers. I mean, we still have to pay but it's like—what's the word for it—"

"Wholesale," I finish for him.

"Right. Wholesale. Most people in the North and East Quadrants don't even bother with the Rationing, it's such a madhouse. They have enough credits to buy their food directly from the shops."

"I see," says Adam. "So, the other people from around here, knowing about your payout..."

"Yeah. They're not going to be okay with us trying to get in on the Rationing," I say. "Mica's right."

"As usual," he mutters.

"All right, little bro, you win. Here, Adam," I pull the filter rings off my finger and toss them to him, "you said these things work on sinks, right? Mind popping one on the kitchen faucet? Mica, tuck in your shirt. Looks like the two of us are going grocery shopping."

"He should come too." Mica hastily shoves the tails of his shirt into his waistband as Adam fiddles with the filter at the sink.

"We just went over this," I say as I stalk over to the bathroom. "Why is the concept of laying low so difficult for you to understand?" I close the door before giving him a chance to respond. After some much-needed bodily relief, I splash some water on my face and run a brush through my hair, grimacing as the bristles skim over the bruise on my head.

Mica is waiting for me the second I step back into the main room. "When was the last time you went grocery shopping for real, Terra? How are you even going to know what's what? I bet Adam does it all the time, he could help us."

Adam chuckles. "I've been on research assignments so long, I barely remember the taste of anything that doesn't come in bar form."

"I think I can handle it, Mic," I say, rolling my eyes as I quickly retrieve my boots from my bedroom. "You're just afraid I won't let you get anything good unless he's there so you can gang up on me."

"I mean, I'm not going to say you're wrong," he says with a grin. "But you can't just expect him to sit here and wait patiently. Brant said there could be follow-ups to your questioning yesterday. Won't it be way more suspicious if the guards come back here only to find this guy hanging out, without reason or explanation?"

My head fills with an image of Adam pulling open my dresser drawer and finding the machine. He doesn't necessarily seem like the snooping type, but who knows what kind of samples he intends to collect while he's here.

"I should try to go out and collect some data," Adam interjects, as if on cue. "Yesterday caused a bit of a setback." He smirks at me.

Mica makes a disappointed noise and I sigh a little too loudly.

"Please just try to lay low?" I beg Adam. "I don't know how easy it'll be to convince people you're our long-lost cousin, twice removed or whatever. Come on, Mica. Let's go."

MICA'S WHINING ASIDE, the walk to the North Quadrant shops is surprisingly pleasant. I'm not confronted by a single heckler or moocher, and once we cross out of the West Quadrant, the dirty looks I've come to expect are replaced with ones of total indifference. Either they don't know about our recent fortune up in this part of town, or they simply don't care.

We're more careful with our steps once we're in the North Q, quick to avoid the occasional transport that rumbles down the road. It occurs to me that I haven't even shown Mica the motorbike yet. That should win me a few sibling points.

We spend a little time window-shopping once we reach the shopping district, Mica planting himself at the front display of the comic store while I walk a few storefronts further down until I'm at the window of a local jewelry purveyor. I can't keep myself from ogling the watches neatly lined up on display. For refurbished skycity hand-me-downs, they look pretty damn good.

My eyes linger on a delicate-looking piece with a round face, the engraved band of silver links reminding me instantly of the watch our mother used to wear. Memories flash through my mind, unbidden. Her gentle smile at my father as he fastens her watch around her wrist. The silver links gleaming brightly against her tawny skin as she braids my hair. The warm lilt in her voice as she teaches me how to tell time, and her whispered promises cascading across my cheek when she thought I was already asleep.

I don't realize how hard I'm pressing my palms against the store window until I hear the shopkeeper clear her throat loudly from next to me. Offering her a conciliatory grimace, I peel myself away from the display, and the mess of red curls atop her head bounce as she returns inside.

I cast another longing look through the window. I know it's not *actually* my mother's watch, it can't be. But it's close—so close—to what I see in my memory, and I want to retrieve Mica so I can show him the resemblance. He was too young to remember our mother, let alone her favorite piece of jewelry, but I think he'd still appreciate the sentiment.

I walk back toward the comic shop, only to see he's wandered to the far side of the road, deep in conversation with a pair of people. One of them I recognize as Hess Underwood, but the other has their back to me.

I sigh and go to retrieve my brother, approaching the conversing trio in a huff, but my footsteps falter on the gravelly road as I get a clearer view of the set of the third person's shoulders, the blond hair peeking out from beneath a brimmed cap.

"It was very nice to meet you, Adam," Hess says fondly, her words becoming audible as I approach.

"And you," he replies. "Thank you for your help. I know I had a lot of questions."

"No, thank you for taking the time to listen," she says. "Do feel free to stop by while you're still in town. Loran's not in much shape to move around, but his memories have been getting clearer every day. I'm sure soon he'll be able to tell you much more about his accident, and I know we'd both welcome the company." She smiles warmly at Mica, nods in my direction, and then leaves.

"Look who I found," Mica says happily.

"Hi there," Adam says.

"What do you think you're doing?" I whisper harshly, all the lingering warmth from my trip down memory lane gone.

"I'm laying low—look, I wore the hat." He flicks the brim with his fingers.

"Pardon me, what was I thinking? Of course, *you wore the hat*. Now you fit right in."

"Calm down, Terra," Mica says. "It's not a big deal."

"How did you even get here so fast?" I say bitterly. "Or know where to go? Did you follow us? And what were you talking to Hess Underwood about?"

"All questions, all the time," Adam says with a soft chuckle, shaking his head.

I scowl.

"Well, he's here now," Mica says. "Can we get some food already? I'm starving."

"You two carry on with your shopping trip, I'm fine on my own," Adam says.

I glance around—several people passing by are already stopping to gawk at our unusual trio. "If *someone* hadn't felt the need to come running over as soon as he saw you," I say, glaring at Mica, "then I'd be inclined to agree. But given that we're already causing a bit of a spectacle out here, you'd better just come with us."

"But—" Adam starts to protest, just as Mica blurts, "Yes, come with us, please!"

I feel a prickle in the back of my throat at the sheer elation in my little brother's voice, how he's so damn happy to be reunited with this skydweller he just met.

Adam furrows his brow for a split second, then his face relaxes into an easy smile. "All right, lead the way, kid."

"Let's just get this over with." I march over to a red-doored storefront with a sign above the door that says "Grocer" in large, welcoming letters. Adam and Mica follow me robotically as I push open the door and enter the shop.

A pretty young woman, maybe in her early twenties, looks up in surprise from the counter at the back of the store. She stares at us for a few moments of awkward silence. I instinctively look down at my shirt, wondering if there's something wrong with the dark pants and black tank I threw on. Mica is in gray shorts and a polo shirt, and I smile inwardly knowing that the outfit was probably just his way of showing off for Adam this morning, but I'm glad for it nonetheless. If we're going to be in the North Q, it's a bonus for us to look presentable, especially since my recent adventures haven't exactly left me in the best-looking shape.

I catch a glimpse of myself in the wall of mirrors behind the shopkeeper and self-consciously flatten my hair. The bruise on the side of my head has crept down past my hairline, lining the side of my face with a ring of deep purple. It only takes another second for me to realize, however, that the attendant isn't looking at me at all. I suddenly feel like it wouldn't matter if I was standing here buck-naked; the only person she seems to see is Adam.

"Hello," I venture. "We're here to purchase some groceries?"

"What?" the shopkeeper says lazily, darting her eyes over to me. "Oh. Of course. Feel free to take a look around." She returns her gaze to Adam. "And *please don't hesitate* to let me know if there's anything I can help you with."

"Will do." Adam winks at her and my eyes nearly roll out the back of my head.

"Don't go too crazy," I tell Mica. I grab a basket from a stack near the door and hand one to him. He takes it without looking at me, his gaze already fixed greedily on the aisles of goods in front of us.

"Yeah, yeah," he says, his eyes gleaming as he takes off down an aisle. I'm going to need to double-check his choices before we leave.

"Shall we?" Adam says. He bends his arm at the elbow and offers it to me, a ridiculously formal gesture. The attendant scowls noticeably.

"Thanks." I loop my wrist through his arm and pull him quickly over to the shelves. So much for not drawing attention. I suppose expecting a preening skyboy to turn down female attention is simply asking too much.

I drop his arm as we enter an aisle marked "Consumables." I scan the shelves for familiar-looking cans, but I don't recognize any of them. There are quite a few rows of canned goods, but nothing so methodically labeled as the D-B334 I'm used to seeing. Instead, the cans are color-coordinated and boast labels like "Beef" and "Chicken"—complete with quotation marks.

I'm quickly reminded that real meat isn't available to the public down here, even in the North Q; it's much more practical and cost-effective for the Tribunal to ship down their synthetic versions than to worry about raising enough of their genetically perfected livestock for us primitive terrestrials.

Even the pets that skydwellers dote upon are genetically engineered. I've never seen one in person, of course, but every year they show a

"Best Pet" competition on TV. I hate to admit it's one program I kind of enjoy.

Further down the aisle, we pass boxes of crackers, packages of noodles, and shiny, foil-wrapped candy bars—things I haven't seen since I was a little kid. I pick up a fancy-looking box and check the price tag on the bottom.

"Ten credits for *crackers*?" I blurt out. That'd buy more than a dozen cans at the Rationing. "What a joke."

"Hmm?" Adam says, examining a jar of dark blue jelly.

"It's just . . . all of this. People who can afford to live like this every day. It's crazy." I don't care if my statement offends him; I'm sure he's used to all this and more where he's from. "Being here, just being able to do this . . . it feels like I'll never be able to go back to how things were." The pragmatic part of me understands that isn't a bad thing. But as for how I *feel* . . .

"Mica told me what it's like for you, being a scav," Adam says gently. "Out there, every day, for hours on end, basically picking up trash. Why would you ever want to go back to that? It sounds like you've been dealt a much better hand than you had before. Seems to me like you've earned a break."

I bite my lip. The thing is, I don't feel like I've earned anything. Finding the machine, the payout, Adam saving me . . . it's all just been dumb luck. And I can't let my luck run out before Mica gets to benefit from it.

"Stop trying to convince yourself that you don't deserve better, Terra." Adam squeezes my shoulder in a way I'm sure he thinks is comforting, letting his fingers brush down my bare arm, and my breath hitches. For a second I think he's going to say something else, but he seems to think better of it and quickly retracts his hand, moving further down the aisle.

"I guess," I say noncommittally, letting the box of crackers fall into my basket and surveying the rest of the shelves. "Don't tell him I said this, but Mica was right. I don't know what I'm supposed to be getting here. A little help? I might even let you eat some of it if you give me a hand."

Adam glances around the aisle. "Uh, sure," he says, somewhat hesitantly. His expression brightens a second later. "I never pass up an offer for a free meal."

I follow him down aisle after aisle, trying to pay attention to the items he tosses into my waiting basket, but I can't get his words out of my head. *Stop trying to convince yourself that you don't deserve better.*

But do I?

"That should do it," Adam says, and I blink, looking down to see the basket in my hands is full. I'm not even sure what Adam pulled from the shelves.

We meet back up with Mica in an aisle marked "Libations."

"Nice try, buddy," I say as I walk up behind him and pluck the huge bottle of crystal-clear alcohol out of his hands. I check the tag: Forty-three credits.

"I was just looking," he says as I place it back on the shelf. I glance into his basket—only a dozen small items are inside. His practiced restraint warms my heart.

"Maybe when you're older," I joke, tossing my arm around Mica's shoulders. As we approach the still-gawking attendant at the register, Adam chivalrously takes both baskets from Mica and me.

"Did you find everything okay?" she purrs.

"Ab-so-lutely," Adam says, flirtatiously drawing out each syllable. An involuntary snort escapes me and the attendant sucks in a breath as she starts to scan our items.

"Ninety credits even," she says, her bottom lip jutting out in a pout as she bags the last item. I suppress a mirthless laugh as I hold out my palm so she can scan it for payment. We're leaving with barely a week's worth of food and it cost more than a month of Rations.

Mica immediately digs through a bag and pulls out a candy bar. He rips open the packaging and races out the door after Adam, who's carrying the rest of the groceries. Looping the remaining bag over my arm, I follow them out of the store.

SIXTEEN

"WHAT! ARE YOU KIDDING?"

Mica grins like he's just been told he gets a second birthday, his gleeful gaze following the line of my pointer finger to the motorbike parked against the side of the building.

"Kinda neat, huh?" I say, unable to suppress a smile of my own.

"*Kinda*? Understatement of the century. This is *awesome*."

I glance at Adam, whose shoulders shake with silent laughter when Mica sprints over to get a closer look at the bike. Add this to the list of things I owe him for.

"I'll put this stuff inside," Adam says, taking the bag I've been carrying and adding it to his load.

"Hang on a sec. I'll come with you." I appreciate his willingness to help, but any time spent alone in the apartment is time he could end up finding the machine.

"You should be here to enjoy this." He nods his chin at Mica, who is already straddling the bike and fiddling with something on the dashboard. Mica turns a knob and I hear a series of empty clicks.

"More like I should be here to bear witness in the inevitable case something goes wrong."

Adam chuckles as I hesitantly hand him the apartment key, then disappears inside.

"So, how does this work?" Mica asks.

"You got me." I shrug. "Adam's the one who . . . you know, come to think of it, I don't even know what he did."

"What's the deal with you two anyway?"

"What do you mean?" I try to keep my voice level but that traitorous blush is already blooming in my cheeks.

Mica looks at me pointedly. "Come on, Terra."

"*You* come on. I've known him for, like, a day."

"Two days," Mica corrects. "And so?"

"So, nothing. He helped me out, now we're helping him out. Giving him opportunities to conduct his research or whatever, and that's all."

"I'm just saying, I think I know my sister well enough to be able to tell—"

"Tell what?" I snap.

"That there's something going on here other than *research*." He draws out the word suggestively and suddenly it's taking considerable effort to stop myself from smacking my brother upside the head.

"It's not—We're—He's not—I'm—"

Mica grins.

"He's a skydweller," I say with finality. "There's nothing to talk about."

"Whatever you say." Mica shrugs innocently and turns his focus back to the motorbike as I lean against the side of the building. I contemplate sitting down, but my thighs scream in protest as soon as I begin to squat.

Damn stairs.

"Man, this thing is, like, prehistoric. Except for this." Mica points to a shiny lever poking out from just below the ignition. "What is it?"

"How should I know?" I say. "It's probably whatever miraculous skytech Adam used to get the transport to run."

Mica flicks the lever up and twists one of the handles at the same time. The bike roars to life.

How does he do that? My brother's knack for technology has always been a bit astounding. It's so intuitive for him. And then there's me, who took almost an entire day just to figure out how to login and check his grades on our computer.

Mica looks at me with wide, pleading eyes, and I know what he's asking. I bury a smile as I nod permission cooly, and he takes off with a jolt . . . only to stall out just as quickly.

"That doesn't count," he says hastily. He restarts the engine and takes off again, accelerating and braking with alarming frequency as he weaves back and forth.

"Be careful," I shout.

He lifts one hand to wave in acknowledgement . . . and stalls out again. I swallow a laugh, and after a few minutes, he starts to get the hang of it.

"Not too long," I call, waving to him before turning to go back inside.

Adam is exiting the kitchen as I enter.

"I wasn't sure where everything went," he says. "I can move things around if it's wrong."

"You already put everything up?"

Adam shrugs, and I'm momentarily taken aback by how familiar the gesture feels already.

"Well, uh, thanks." I breeze into the kitchen and open up a cabinet to inspect the goods. He's thrown them haphazardly onto the shelves, and I have to smother the look of disbelief I'm tempted to give him.

He was trying to be helpful, I remind myself, darting my eyes to where Adam now leans against the kitchen entryway, his hands in his pockets. His cheeks are a little pink, like he's embarrassed, and damn it all if it isn't cute as hell.

I swallow, trying to bury whatever the hell this feeling is. "Mica is having the time of his life on that thing," I say casually, straightening a tall green box that has tipped on its side. "Pretty sure you've made his entire year."

"It's fun for me too," Adam says, coming up beside me. His voice is low when he adds "Sorry if my organization skills aren't the best." He reaches into the cabinet to straighten a different fallen box, his hand brushing against mine as he sets it upright.

"Did you see what you needed today? Get all your notes down?" The words fly out in a jumble as I yank my hand back.

"Huh?"

"I figured you'd be scribbling on that tablet of yours. For your research?"

"Oh, right. I'll get to it." He rotates a jar in the cabinet so that its label faces forward—*jellied blueberry concentrate*, it says.

"You might as well take your chance now, while Mica's preoccupied. I'm sure he'll have about a million more questions for you once he gets back up here."

"I don't mind," Adam says. "Honestly, it's kind of nice. I have a brother too."

"Oh?"

"Yeah. Older though. And he doesn't have much of an interest in me." He clears his throat, like the words burn a little as he says them.

"Careful what you wish for." I run my finger over the embossed lettering on the blueberry jar. "Or you'll end up with mine attached to your hip."

"Could be worse. At least Mica had the courtesy not to punch me in the face when he met me," Adam says with a laugh.

I turn to make a face at him, but the small space between us feels suddenly charged. I tuck a lock of hair behind my ear self-consciously and we both pull away from the cabinet.

"He shouldn't get so attached," I say suddenly. "He's had enough people duck out on him."

Adam shuts the cabinet door. "Mica has, huh?" He takes a step toward me.

"Yes." It comes out like a whisper.

There is a sudden and noticeable silence, followed by a burst of thundering footsteps, and I barely have time to step back from Adam before Mica crashes through the front door.

"Holy crap," Mica says, his face flushed with excitement. "That was awesome."

"Before or after you stalled out?" I tease.

"As if you could do any better."

"Now, now, children," Adam teases.

I can't stop the smile that breaks out across my face. "So, who wants to see how good a ten-credit cracker tastes?"

AS SOON AS we've finished eating, Adam busies himself with his computer tablet. Hours pass with him perched on the couch, poking around on the screen, Mica glued to his side as the TV blares in the background. I'm just grateful he's too consumed in his work to bother going back out again, and before I know it, the sun is sinking.

When Mica gets hungry again, we repeat our lunchtime production, opting to fill up on samples of our grocery store haul instead of making a real dinner. Every package I open is as delicious as the last, and Adam has to forcibly wrench a sleeve of tiny yellow cookies out of my hands.

"Okay, okay," I say, throwing my hands up in surrender, "I'm done." Adam eyes me skeptically. "No, really, I'm good."

"I'm not going to lie, I could get used to living like the other half," Mica says, patting his stomach. "Well, the other half of *our* half. I'm sure this is still 'roughing it' by skycity standards." He pokes Adam in the shoulder and laughs.

"If this is roughing it, what does that say about the D-T-whatever you fed me last night?" Adam says.

"I'm pretty sure it says, 'shut up.' " I'm smiling as I close up the rest of the open packages and return them to the cabinet. "Anyway, if you thought this was good, just wait until tomorrow morning. I picked up a carton of synthetic eggs. Mic, remember eggs?"

"Not even a little," he says, "but I'm excited regardless."

"All right, I'm going to go for a walk," I announce, eager to have some time alone with my thoughts. It feels like I've barely had a free moment to think in the past few days. Free from . . . certain distractions, that is. "Hopefully work off some of this sucrose buzz."

"Oh, great idea. I'll join you," says Adam.

I shift on my feet. "That's okay, you don't have to."

"Remember our deal? I show you out of the biodome, you show me around Sixteen."

I sigh. "Mic, you want to come too?" I ask hopefully.

"Pass," he says. "Homework." I don't miss the way his lips quirk up at the edges.

"Shall we?" Adam says, already waiting at the front door.

The sun is just beginning to set as we step outside, tingeing the sky with soft swirls of pink and orange.

"What do you want to see first?" I ask.

Adam shrugs. "How about we start with you showing me around this —what did you call it—quadrant?"

"Yeah, the West Quadrant," I say as I start walking. "That's where we are now. Two-point-two square miles of dust and gravel. Welcome."

"So, the North Quadrant has the shopping district and the main gate," Adam says, falling into step with me. "What does this one have?"

"A little of everything and nothing," I say. "Half the Marketplace is in this quadrant, we share it with the East Q. Other than that, it's mostly housing developments. There's Mica's school, and I guess we have the West Square, which is the closest thing Sixteen will ever have to a park."

"Sounds resplendent."

"Nobody says you have to stay," I snap. West Q might not be much, but the only people who are allowed to talk shit about it are the ones who call it home.

Something that looks a little like regret flashes over Adam's face, and he is quiet for a moment. "What's that?" he asks, pointing to a squat, square building with black-tinted windows. An obvious attempt to change the subject.

"It's our mini library."

"Mini library? As opposed to . . . giant library?" He smirks at his bad joke.

"As opposed to the main library server housed over in town hall," I explain flatly. I refuse to muster the chipper demeanor necessary to be an enthusiastic tour guide for Adam, especially considering he's ruined my first chance to clear my head. "The mini branches allow us access to information without having to make the trek all the way over there. There's one in each quadrant, and they have a bunch of computer stations set up inside. They're kind of like little study halls. This way every school-aged kid doesn't flood town hall every time a paper is due. We're lucky, we have a computer at home. Not everyone does."

I glance at Adam, who is observing the building with a speculative expression, ever the researcher. Eventually, he tears his eyes away and we forge onward, but he takes in our surroundings in silence. There are only a few other people out on the streets as we walk across the quadrant, and the quiet that settles over us starts to make me uneasy.

"So, what kind of data are you hoping to ascertain here in Sixteen anyway? Is there something in particular I should be trying to show you?" *What can I do to make it go faster?*

He takes a moment to answer. "It's mostly observational. You know, seeing how things run down here, how you operate."

"I didn't think the Tribunal cared so much," I say.

"You might not believe me, but it's not exactly my first-choice assignment either. All this waiting around, watching, data collecting, note-taking . . . it's all more my brother's area."

"He's a researcher too?"

"Sort of," he says after a moment. "But I don't just mean it as a job thing."

"How do you mean it?"

Adam looks sideways at me. "He's always been the patient one, the one who plans things out. Since we were kids, he was always on my case about needing to be more careful, more thoughtful. Less reckless. What I wouldn't have given for him to just let me live a little." He tenses and I suddenly regret venturing down this line of conversation.

"I didn't realize how late it had gotten," I say, glancing toward the sinking sun and feeling pressure to change the subject. "My schedule is thoroughly messed up."

"I'd say that's more than understandable, considering all you've been through recently," he says, relaxing his shoulders.

"I guess. Still, I can't help but feel like we've wasted this whole day."

"That's a pessimistic way to look at it. At least there was shopping, right? I thought girls were supposed to like shopping," he teases.

It is very, very hard not to roll my eyes. "That's not exactly a progressive thing to say, my friend." I bite my lip, then add, "Maybe normal girls do."

"Which makes you, what, abnormal?" he says, that lopsided grin of his making another appearance.

"There are numerous people who would attest to that."

"I'm sure they don't know what they're talking about," he says softly.

Heat creeps up my neck. "Well, thank you. But considering the fact that we've known each other for roughly two days, I'd say your expertise is questionable."

Adam laughs. "Come now. It's been *at least* two and a half."

I crack a smile. "Oh, well, of course, then. You obviously know me better than I know myself."

"Scoff all you like, but I think I do know you better than you'd like to admit."

"Is that so?" I raise my eyebrows as defensiveness instinctively stirs in my chest.

He slows to a stop, looking at me with that speculating gaze again, his head cocked to one side. "You're not that hard for me to read. For other people, you probably are. I think they have a hard time seeing through you."

I frown. "Is this some kind of FX thing? I'm transparent to you?"

"It doesn't take FX to see you're a smart girl, Terra. You know how you're supposed to act. You pretend like you want to be normal, like being ostracized is something that saddens you, because you think that's how you're supposed to feel."

"That *is* how I feel."

"It is? I think you like the solitude. That's why you like being a scav. You like that there's nobody out there depending on you, except Mica, and we both know that if push came to shove he could take care of himself. You want to prove to yourself that you don't need anybody."

"I *don't* need anybody." My neck is hot, my cheeks are flushed, and every word from Adam's mouth has my emotions churning. I am not some research specimen for him to analyze, some case study for him to deduce.

Even if he might be right.

"Because if you don't need anybody, it won't hurt as much when they leave you, right?"

His words are like a blow to the gut and my mouth falls open.

Adam's eyes soften. "That's how you feel, isn't it? You were forced to grow up fast, in the wake of so much loss. It's natural you'd want to protect yourself from experiencing more of it. It makes sense that you'd become so overly cautious."

I suck in a deep breath. "So, in addition to being a transparent loner," I say, anger punctuating every syllable, "I'm overprotective *and* overly cautious now too?" My fists clench at my sides. "You don't know anything about me. You think that dropping into my life makes you some kind of expert? Who are you to judge me?"

I start walking again, faster now, eager to distance myself from him.

"That's not what I said," he calls after me.

I don't slow down, not even as I realize we've made it as far as the West Square. I'm almost to the Intheria Memorial statue in the center when I hear Adam running up from behind me.

"Hey, I'm sorry," he says, a gentle grasp on my arm pulling me to a stop as he catches up. "I didn't mean to upset you. Sometimes my mouth works faster than my brain and things come out wrong. The last thing I want is to offend you."

I spin to face him, throwing off his grip. "You don't know me!" I yell, alarmed at the tightness I feel in the back of my throat, a precursor to tears that I refuse to let him see. "You don't *get* to know me. And you certainly don't get to judge me."

"I wasn't." He calmly takes a step toward me. "Honest. It's not my place to judge, and even if it were, I would never judge you for being independent. I admire your ability to take care of yourself."

"You *admire* me?" I say skeptically. I want to step away from him, but the Intheria statue's large stone base blocks my path.

"I think you are strong." He reaches his hand to my face and, with surprising tenderness, brushes a lock of hair behind my ear. His fingers linger as they reveal the bruise underneath my hairline. "And I'm sorry this happened to you."

I don't know if he's talking about my physical injury or something much deeper than that. I swallow the lump in my throat, my mind teetering on the edge of something. The heel of my boot presses against the statue's base and, before my mind can tell it not to, my body propels itself forward and folds into Adam's arms.

He doesn't hesitate, leaning into me even as he releases a breath of surprise, his strong arms wrapping around me. I stand there, my cheek pressing against his chest, the steady rhythm of his heart pulsing in my ear.

"Looks like sunsets are growing on you," he says with a soft laugh.

I don't look up at him, or the setting sun. I don't even move.

"Well, what do you know? Look who it is!" Yttria Coal's voice echoes out over the square. I push Adam back, embarrassment and anger replacing the real reason for the color in my cheeks. I'm angry at myself for callously letting my guard down; I'm embarrassed for getting caught.

"Good evening, Terra," she says as she approaches, Juniper at her heels. I can't even remember the last time she addressed me by my actual name. "You look . . . well."

"Uh, thanks?" I say awkwardly, sidestepping away from Adam.

Yttria's smile is uncharacteristically sweet as she toys with the ends of her black locks. They flow over her bare shoulders, emphasizing the cut of her sleeveless top. "We were just on our way to your place. Junie wanted to stop by and see Mica."

Juniper squirms as she plays with the yellow ribbon belted around her hips, the color spotlighting a sliver of honey-brown skin that shows between her shirt and pants.

"I guess we can all head back that way then." I deliberately avoid Adam's gaze as I start walking, not completely sure if the emotions I'm feeling after Yttria's timely intrusion are ones of relief or resentment.

"I'm Yttria," I hear her coo. "And this is my sister, Juniper. We saw you at the Assembly yesterday."

"It's nice to meet you," Adam replies.

I quicken my pace. *Resentment. Definitely resentment.*

Adam waits outside with Yttria and Juniper once we reach the apartment building.

"Mica," I shout the second I get inside the apartment, my legs burning from racing up the stairs. "Micaaaaa!"

"What?" he says. He's still buttoning his pants as he emerges from the bathroom. "Yeesh, what is it?"

"You have a visitor. Juniper's outside . . . with her sister," I say. As if on cue, Yttria lets out an over-the-top laugh so loud I can hear it from here.

"Seriously?" Mica flies out the door without another word. I follow him out just in time to see him wipe the stupid grin off his face.

"Hey," he says coolly to Juniper.

"Hi," she says back, a sweet smile on her face.

I press my lips together to keep my amusement bay as they stand there, looking at each other expectantly.

"Want to see something cool?" Mica finally says.

Juniper nods and my brother disappears around the side of the building, returning a minute later with the transport in tow.

"Whoa," Juniper says in a low voice. "Is this yours?"

"Yep." His chest swells with pride as he swings a leg over and climbs on the bike.

Oh, is it? I want to say as Juniper steps closer and Mica makes quick work of showing her the controls, but I hold my tongue. I'm not trying to ruin my little brother's moment but we'll be discussing that line of thinking later, given that the bike actually belongs to . . . I dare a glance at Adam for the first time since we left the Square and find him looking at me with an expression that, if I didn't know better, almost looks like—

"Want to go for a ride?" Mica asks Juniper, interrupting my thoughts.

"Yes!" Juniper replies immediately.

"Mica," I caution. "I don't know if that's such a good idea. It's getting dark."

"You can't be serious," he says.

"It's not safe."

"Terra," he says pleadingly.

"I say go for it," Adam interjects.

Mica looks at Adam with optimistic excitement and my eyes narrow into a glare. "Fortunately, your opinion doesn't really carry a lot of weight in this situation," I tell Adam.

"Come on, Sunburst, let the kid live a little," he says.

"Yeah, don't be such a downer," Yttria chimes in. "They'll be fine. Let them have some fun."

Mica looks from Adam to me with wide, hopeful eyes. "Fine," I say irritably, and Juniper immediately hops on behind Mica. "But just a quick spin."

Juniper squeals as the bike comes to life. She wraps her arms around Mica's waist and they speed to the end of the street, and I don't hold in my laugh when he stalls out this time. It only takes a second for him to kick the bike back to life, though, and they disappear around a corner. When I turn back to Yttria, she's batting her eyelashes at Adam.

"Looks like they're off," I say quickly. "Thanks for bringing Junie by, Mica will make sure she gets home. You'd better head back before it gets too dark."

Yttria's eyes narrow slightly as I dismiss her. "All right." Her words come out sluggishly like she's trying to come up with a reason to stay. "I guess I'll . . . see you later. It was *wonderful* to meet you, Adam," she says, extending her arm.

"Likewise," he says pleasantly as he shakes her hand.

Yttria's fingers linger on his palm as she pulls it back, and Adam flexes his hand as they break contact. Then, with one final, smug look thrown my way, she's gone.

***

"WHAT DO you think you're doing?" We've barely crossed the threshold back into the apartment before I'm whirling with a finger pointed purposefully in Adam's face.

"What?" One eyebrow quirks up, puzzled.

"You just undermined me in front of my brother."

He sighs. "I wasn't trying to *undermine* anyone. I was trying to help you out. I mean, you didn't want Mica to take that girl for a ride because it's getting too dark? He's thirteen, not three. And I know it's a sensitive subject for you but given that we were *just* talking about someone's overprotective tendencies . . ." He's grinning but his words cut deep.

"This is not your family," I say coldly. "I think I know what's best for *my* brother."

"Look, I told you how my brother was with me growing up," he says, his voice gentler. "Babying Mica is only going to strain things between you two, especially if you do it in front of a girl. One he clearly *likes*."

"Of course he likes Juniper," I say shrilly. "But if you think that any of the Coals would ever actively encourage her to reciprocate . . ." I release a hollow laugh, flopping down on the couch. "I just don't want him to get hurt. The Coals aren't exactly our biggest fans."

"How come?"

"It's complicated," I say dismissively. I certainly do not feel like airing out our family's dirty laundry in front of him. "Whether it was your intention or not, you did show me up with Mica out there. And that's bad enough on its own, but did you have to do it in front of *her?"*

"Who, Yttria? She seemed nice enough."

"She was falling all over you, of course you'd think she's nice. She only came by in the first place because she wanted to meet you. Juniper was just the excuse."

"So," Adam says as he sits beside me, "I'm a commodity, huh?"

"Don't go getting a big head," I say, and I'm irritated with myself at the way my annoyance with him is already softening.

Adam grins but says nothing else. With no distraction, awkwardness quickly settles in and I switch on the TV to fill the silence. Adam pulls out his tablet and starts poking around on the screen. He sits lazily beside me on the sofa as he concentrates on his work, and though I try to engross myself in the moving figures on the screen, my posture is unusually straight and the sofa feels very small.

Mica returns an hour later, goofy and elated.

"What's up?" he calls from the kitchen. I hear him open a cabinet and rustle through the packages of food again.

I don't answer. I can't even recall the name of the show I've been staring at in his absence. While the TV droned on, I'd replayed my argument with Adam in my head, over and over, trying to make sense of my emotional whiplash.

Hot and cold, up and down, back and forth . . . How can anybody feel so many conflicting things in such a short time? At the *same* time? How can I be wildly pissed off one minute, laughing and at ease the next, then ready to completely break down by the third?

One second, he's looking at me with the detached interest of a researcher observing a mildly entertaining subject, and the next he's just . . . looking at me. Looking *into* me. Like he really does see everything about me, down to my very core.

Why am I letting this guy get under my skin? Why does his opinion of my makeshift parenting skills even matter?

It doesn't, I tell myself.

So, why do I care? Why does *he* even care enough to offer his opinion in the first place? And why, the entire time Mica was gone, couldn't I concentrate on anything else?

My mind was held hostage by Adam's proximity to me as we sat side-by-side on the couch. How he was so close I could feel the heat radiating from him, my skin prickling at the memory of how his arms felt when they were wrapped around me in the West Square.

And how I don't think I've ever wanted anything as badly as I wanted him to move just two inches closer.

SEVENTEEN

ADAM DOESN'T BRING up what happened in the square the next morning. Doesn't bring up our argument. So, I follow suit. And since our tour of the West Q was cut short and I'm not particularly eager to talk about why, I don't object when he insists on tagging along to school with Mica. He spends two hours conversing with Principal Conifer about lesson plans, teacher assignments, and test scores, while I try my best not to look bored—failing miserably—and create a mental countdown until the next Collection.

Five days.

I have five days to guide him through whatever research points he has to hit here in Sixteen. Five days, and he'll be on his way without ever finding out about the second machine. I don't know why the thought makes me a little sad.

After departing from the school, we make our way to the town center, where Adam wants to sit in on a public forum. We hide in the back, where no one can notice me sulking while Adam scribbles down more notes. I quickly decide there has to be some kind of gene that allows you to become a Tribunal researcher because there is no way that a normal person could find such mundane things so unremittingly fascinating.

The following day, we spend the afternoon walking the docks in the

East Quadrant. Adam spends an inordinate amount of time inspecting the structure of each building, questioning the who and where and what and why of the workers going about their day. His notetaking is relentless.

Blatantly disregarding my request to lay low, he converses with almost every person we come across. At first, I think the constant conversations are his attempt to quell the stares we receive. I'm never sure whether those looks are because of me or because of Adam, though. It's probably both.

Regardless of the reason, Adam introduces himself to anyone who even glances in our direction from the side of their eye. The conversations are all over the place, though more often than not they end up somewhere decidedly boring. Sometimes he barely has to say five words and he'll get someone's entire life story in response. The most interesting thing Adam asks about is Loran Underwood's raider accident, though even that gets old quickly, because he asks about it *a lot*. I guess running into Hess in the North Q must have piqued his curiosity.

I try chiming in on the conversation when we run across a cheery Mrs. Kuipers, but as soon as I open my mouth she shoots me a look so devastatingly cold that I immediately shut back up.

If only I were so charming, I think, as the old woman returns her gaze to Adam with a sweet smile plastered back on her face.

"I THOUGHT you might want to finally check out the Marketplace today," I say to Adam.

Collection Day is tomorrow, and my anxiety has risen exponentially with each passing day. Adam has made no indications of getting ready to move on from observing Sixteen.

It's partially my own fault. I don't want to have to wait another fortnight before securing the credits from the second machine, but Mica's attachment to the skydweller has made me hesitant to actively kick him out.

My brother has bloomed in the past week. He's more animated when he talks—sharing more about his friends and how school went. He's even started to *look* different. More confident, more grown up. Like simply being around Adam has brought out a whole new side of him.

Or maybe it's because cans of slop and glug aren't the only things he has to subsist on anymore. Could also be the permanent smile he has on his face lately, thanks to Juniper Coal.

My feelings about all of it have been confusing, to say the least.

On the one hand, I'm elated my that little brother is coming into his own. How could I not be? He holds his head high when he bursts through the door after school. He has color in his cheeks and a spring in his step that almost makes me forget there ever was a time when he nearly wasted away—*almost*.

But a sad, small, selfish part of me resents these changes for what they might mean. The unspoken truth underneath. Because it feels all too clear to me that he's only like this now because . . .

Because just having me here wasn't enough.

Once I woke the hell up, sure, I took care of him. Well enough to survive, at least. But not enough for him to *thrive*.

I don't want to think about what might happen between Mica and me when Adam does leave. Because he will. Whether it's tomorrow or another week from now, he's going to move onto another area for observation, or he'll return home and be reunited with the rest of his team . . . and we'll still be here.

Until we're not.

Until we have what we need to get out of here too.

I've been racking my brain all through breakfast, trying to figure out what's left in Sixteen for Adam to see, to try and urgent him along. The Marketplace is pretty much the last place left of interest that we haven't covered. Hopefully, it'll be packed with people he can prod for data, and he'll have finally gathered enough research to move on.

But even though it's my idea, even though I know it needs to happen, the thought has me frowning. It's true that I don't want Adam to find out that not only was our recent payout due to his technology but that, broken or not, I've been hoarding another one of his machines without telling him. I should be elated to be so close to getting rid of him, shouldn't I?

It's just because of Mica, I tell myself. I feel guilty because of my brother's attachment to the skydweller. That's all it is.

All it can be.

I glance over at Adam, seated at the kitchen table, and shake my head. "The forecast calls for rain later, so we can't stay out too long," I say, peeking up at the sky through the living room window. "But we should still have enough time to hit up the Market. Doesn't sound like it'll be a big storm, anyway." I can barely contain the glee in my voice. Rain forecasts usually mean being stuck inside for twenty-four hours or longer. Predictions for short showers are few and far between.

"Oh," he says. "I was kind of hoping to go see the Underwoods."

I arch a brow. "Why are you so interested in Loran's accident?" I ask. It's the one thing he's brought up with almost every person he's come across while out on our tours. I suppose that after running into Hess, it was only a matter of time before he'd want to go straight to the source, but I still don't know why. "It was a raider attack. They happen. You practically saw one firsthand with me, remember? I hear he's healing up just fine. Slow, but fine."

Adam shrugs. "You go ahead to the Market then," he says, avoiding my question, "and I'll meet up with you later." His evasiveness does nothing to quell my curiosity.

"It's fine. There should be time for both." I lace up my boots, still not understanding his obsession with the incident. If it's about learning more about raiders, Adam already collected samples from Ryk and his cronies back in the ruins, and I don't know what else Loran can tell him that I haven't.

Admittedly, now that pretty much everyone in town knows Adam has been staying with us, I can't say I'm crazy about him chatting with other scavs on his own. Something's bound to come up about my payout and the quarantine restrictions, and I'd prefer to be there to squash the rumors when it does. "Besides, you don't even know where they live."

Frustration flashes across Adam's face. "I've gotten a pretty good idea of where things are by now," he says. "I don't need a chaperone every time I leave the house."

I raise an eyebrow at the defensiveness coloring his tone. If I wasn't already determined to figure out the reason for his interest in Loran Underwood, I certainly am now.

"You're not the only one with business at the Underwoods," I say, thinking up an excuse on the spot. "Hess has been having some difficulties since she's taken over Loran's scav duties. I feel bad that I haven't had a chance to visit since his accident. This is a good chance for me to offer to help. In any way I can."

Adam sighs. "All right," he says resignedly. "Who am I to get in the way of such humanitarian kindness? Let's get going, Sunburst."

WE HOP on the motorbike and I direct Adam south to the Underwoods' apartment complex. They live at the edge of the West Quadrant, right on the border of the South Q. People on the street stare longingly at our transport as Adam parks it around the back of the building.

"Look, it's really important that I speak with Loran today," Adam says as we enter the building, "so can your *business* with Hess wait until I'm done?" His tone makes it clear he doesn't really buy my do-gooder act for a second.

Cheeks burning, I rap my knuckles on the Underwoods' first-floor apartment door. "Yeah, yeah, sure," I say. "I hope your obsession with him helps you nab that Most Spirited Researcher trophy you're gunning for, or something else that makes all of this worth it."

Footsteps shuffle from inside the apartment. Adam says something under his breath. It sounds sort of like, "Me too."

Hess Underwood opens the door wearing slippers. A raggedy bathrobe hangs open over threadbare pajamas and she looks at me with curiosity. "Yes?"

"Hi, Mrs. Underwood. I'm Terra Rhodon and—"

"I know who you are. Can I help you?"

"Hello again, Hess," Adam says before I have a chance to respond. Her eyes dart to Adam and she beams.

"Oh, Adam! I didn't realize it was you. Please, come in."

I have to work very hard to keep from rolling my eyes as we're ushered inside. I recognize the apartment as Floor Plan #7, with all the rooms connecting via a long hallway that runs through the center of the home. I shuffle awkward into the small entryway and take up a spot along the wall.

"Thank you," Adam says. "I thought I might take you up on your offer to speak to Loran about his accident?"

"Of course, of course," she says eagerly. "I'll go wake him, he's just been resting."

"That would be great," Adam says.

"We don't want to disturb him," I say, glancing from Tess's open robe to Adam and back again. "We can always come back at a more convenient time."

Adam's expression darkens as I speak, and a chill runs through the room.

"Nonsense," Hess says brightly. "I'm sure he'll be thrilled to have a visitor. The house is rather quiet these days." I remember what Emery told me about her son, Trip, and the Black Traders, and I feel a pang of sympathy in my chest. Regardless of whether Trip joined the Traders or was taken by them, it can't be easy for Hess to have both her husband injured and her son gone.

"Thanks very much, in that case," I say. "I just wanted to make sure we weren't interrupting anything."

I mistakenly glance at Hess's pajamas again and she follows my gaze. Her cheeks suddenly flare pink. "Please, have a seat, make yourselves at home. I'll be right back." She turns on the spot and flies down the hall.

"What was that?" Adam whispers roughly once Hess is out of earshot.

"What was what?"

" 'We don't want to disturb him?' I just told you that I needed to talk to him. Why would you say that?"

"It's called being polite," I hiss, trying to keep my voice down. "You should try it sometime."

I walk out of the entryway and into what I assume is the living room, taking a seat in a cushioned recliner against the back wall. Adam follows me into the room and sits on a small sofa set diagonally across from me. The fabric of the sofa perfectly matches the chair I'm occupying, painting the room a comforting shade of plaid.

"What's your problem?" I mutter, picking at a loose thread on the armrest as Adam scowls at me. "You didn't want me to come with you in the first place. You got mad when I suggested we come back later. You've been asking about Loran's accident all week. What kind of *data* can you possibly get talking to some random raider victim that you can't get from me?" The words come out sounding far more petulant than I intended.

"Look, I'm sorry if I was short with you," Adam says, his voice heavy. He drums his fingers on the armrest of the sofa. "I just . . ."

When he doesn't continue, I look up to find his face drained of emotion, his expression difficult to read. "What is it?"

"I just have some questions for him, that's all," he says. "Important ones."

"About what?" I press, though before the words have fully left my mouth, the realization hits me like a crack to the head. Adam was in the biodome for a week before I found him. Loran's accident happened several days before I found the first machine. The timing is too close to be a coincidence.

I lean forward, touching the back of his hand—his fingers still-drumming an anxious pattern on the armrest. "Did you . . . did you see what happened to him? Do you think he might know something about the rest of your team?"

Adam's jaw clenches, and he draws his hand into his lap before dipping his chin in a single curt nod. My mouth drops open, but before I have a chance to ask anything further, I hear slow-shuffling footsteps making their way down the hall.

"Here they are," Hess exclaims, turning into the living room with her husband's arm over her shoulders. She has changed into a cheery pink dress and brushed her hair back into a neat braid. Loran Underwood wears a baggy sweater and long pants, but under his right knee, I can see the bulge of a large bandage. Yellow bruises pepper his arms, just short of being fully healed, and I grimace at the thought of just how deep his injuries must have been if they're still visible now.

Adam hops up and helps Loran limp to the couch. He settles into the middle of the sofa with Hess on one side and Adam on the other.

"Thank you, m'boy," Loran says, already out of breath from his short journey down the hall. "Terra Rhodon?" he says, suddenly noticing me in the corner.

"Hi, Loran. I mean, Mr. Underwood," I say, offering a timid smile.

Loran laughs, a booming guffaw. "*Mr. Underwood,* eh? You never called me that out in the fields, no need to start now. How's that little brother of yours? And how's the scav business treatin' ya?"

Hess clucks her tongue softly and Loran turns to her, confused. A second later, comprehension dawns on his face and he looks suddenly embarrassed. "Oh, I meant . . . that is to say . . . of course, it's been going real well, eh?"

"No complaints here," I say lightly, trying to skate through the sudden awkwardness. "And Mica's doing fine, thank you for asking."

Loran nods, then turns his head to the side. "So, you're Adam then?"

"Yes, sir," Adam responds.

"Well, you certainly made an impression on my Hessie," he says. "We don't meet many skydwellers like you. She's been hoping you'd stop by all week."

"Oh, hush, you," Hess says, slapping her husband lightly on the shoulder. I can't help but chuckle.

"So, what can I do for you?" Loran asks.

An air of seriousness falls over the room as Adam glances at me.

I hold his stare. *I'm not going anywhere.*

Adam's mouth presses into a hard line, as though he can hear the challenge in my thoughts. The corners quiver, though, like he's holding in one of those lopsided grins. "I hope you don't feel this is too intrusive," he says, turning back to Loran, "but I was hoping you might be willing to talk to me about your accident."

"Are you part of the investigation team? 'Cause some other skydwelling folk already came and asked me about everything when it happened."

"No, I'm . . . on a different assignment. I apologize if you'll be repeating information."

"It's all right," Loran says slowly. "Things are a little clearer these days than they were then anyway. Though, I'm sure I still sound just as crazy."

"What do you mean?" Adam asks.

Loran takes a deep breath and looks at his wife. Hess nods. "I was out in the fields, like normal," he says. "It was pretty late in the day—I think I was probably the only scav still out there. But I'd been following a trail of broken tech down through the Southern Plains and I wanted to make sure I'd gotten 'em all. I must've been down past the Dead Woods by the time I decided to pack it in." He glances at me and I nod knowingly.

"Suddenly, I'm swept off my feet, out of nowhere. Something just blew me straight back, like—like I got hit with . . . a cannonball made of air or something. I go flying and hit the ground—hard. Next thing I know, I'm back home with a screwed-up knee and a head that's fuzzier than usual to boot."

"So, it wasn't raiders?" The question flies out of my mouth before I can stop it.

"Raiders? Ha! Almost wish it had been," Loran says, a tinge of sadness to his voice. "The other investigators told me that's what must've happened, that a raider must've hit me from behind or something but . . . I might be gettin' on in years, but I ain't that old. I would've known if somebody hit me." He slumps back into the couch, like he wishes he could sink into it. "All I know is what I said. I didn't feel anything but the air. If it had been a raider, I would've seen him—or at least felt him—touch me, right?"

Alarm has me whipping my head to look at Adam, whose face is contorted, his brow deeply furrowed. Loran catches sight of my expression and starts to laugh.

"Believe me, I know how it sounds," he continues, and my eyes track the way Hess pats his hand—a gentle comfort. "Everyone says the accident messed up my memory. And maybe they're right. All that matters now is that I'm home, and I'm healing. Even if I might be a little crazy, at least there's that." He places a hand over his wife's, stilling it, then gives her a slow smile.

"Nobody here thinks you're crazy," I say, still looking at Adam. My comment seems to bring him back to the present, and he shoots me a wary glance.

"I know it's a lot, asking you to relive it like this," Adam says to Loran, "but is there anything else—anything at all—that you remember? Sounds, smells, something in your peripheral vision? Even the smallest detail could help."

"Well, there is one thing, but if you didn't already think I was nuts . . ." Loran trails off, chuckling nervously.

"I promise you, we won't," Adam says, looking at him hopefully.

"It happened so fast, of course, so I can't be sure. But when . . . when I was knocked into the air, when I was sent flying? I could've sworn I saw something overhead."

"Like what?" I ask. "A trash barge? A Skyline shuttle?"

"Maybe," Loran says. "Maybe there was a shuttle of some kind up there. But if I'm being honest . . . It looked more like a person. Arms splayed out, spinning in the sky, it almost looked like . . ."

"Like what?"

"Like someone was flying."

Adam's face falls in unmistakable disappointment, and silence takes over the room once more. After a few beats, Loran and Hess exchange a wary look, and I poke Adam with my foot, prompting him to rearrange his expression.

He clears his throat. "Terra, didn't you have something to talk to Hess about?"

"Huh?" I say. Adam raises both his eyebrows at me. "Oh, right. Of course."

"What is it?" Hess asks quietly.

"I just . . . I wanted to see if you needed anything. Any help." My words come out in a nervous jumble, as my mind continues processing the details of Loran's accident. It was a flimsy excuse when I came up with it at the apartment, and it feels even flimsier now. "I know things have been a bit rough since the accident. And, you know, with the situation with Trip."

Hess blinks. "The situation with Trip?"

"Y-yeah," I stammer, "I know your son isn't—I mean, it can't be easy with the Traders and—"

I know I've crossed a line the instant Hess's eyes widen and hear her sharp inhale. If I didn't know better, I'd swear the temperature in here drops a few degrees from her icy expression alone.

"I'm sorry," I say, attempting a preemptive apology.

"We're doing all right," Loran says quickly, rubbing Hess's back in slow circles. Something clenches around my heart at the way she leans into her husband's touch, her expression softening, even there still seem to be daggers in her eyes when she returns her gaze to me. "But we appreciate the offer."

"I guess we should get going," Adam says. "Thank you again."

I get to my feed, nodding hurriedly. "Well, if you ever need anything, the offer stands."

Loran's answering smile is warm and reassuring as we walk away, and it eases a touch of the anxiousness I'm feeling over having overstepped.

I whirl on Adam as soon as we've shut the front door behind us. "Do I get an explanation of what that was all about now?"

"There's nothing to explain," he says with a dismissive wave of his hand before climbing onto the motorbike. "I thought there was a chance that he saw something—something that could help me. But you heard him. There was nothing to tell."

"Nothing to tell?" I say. "The man said he felt like someone knocked him off his feet without touching him, Adam. That sure sounds like something to me."

"But it's nothing that helps me now, Terra!" My eyes widen at the sharp rise in Adam's tone. "It's a dead end. Nothing he said tells me where my team is, or if they even came through here. Nothing. I thought —I hoped—" He sighs. "Look, can we just drop it?"

He looks so crestfallen, so disappointed, all I can do is nod and take my place on the bike behind him.

"Still up for the Market?" I ask quietly.

He doesn't respond. He simply brings the bike to life and takes off toward the Marketplace.

EIGHTEEN

THE MARKETPLACE IS A LONG, rectangular building with wide doors on both ends and individual stalls built into the sides. Mica likes to show off his nerdy side by reminding me frequently that buildings like this were originally meant to keep livestock—back when there was livestock to be kept down here. Now, merchants of all specialties sell their wares for more reasonable prices than you'll find in the North Q. That said, you can't always be sure what you'll get.

Adam weaves quickly through the people crammed into various stalls while I avoid the stares of surrounding shoppers. They're understandably wary; much of Marketplace culture is based on haggling, and someone with the kind of steel I have now could easily skew the dynamic.

Mr. Copper's stall is at the very end, near the back of the building. His long, gray hair spills familiarly from his bowler hat.

Copp, in addition to being my favorite stallkeeper, is an old friend of our family. As kids, he would often regale Mica and me with stories of my mother. I haven't been brave enough to come back to the Marketplace since That Day, when I found the machine and Copp got his first glimpse of my new credit total. I'm not sure how welcome I'll be now, even here.

"Hello, Terra," Copp says stiffly as we approach.

"Heya, Copp."

An awkward silence fills the space between us.

"Been a while," he says after a minute. "Wasn't sure we'd be seein' ya here again."

"Guess old habits are hard to break." I offer him a timid smile.

"Ha!" he booms. "Shoulda known all that steel wouldn't change ya."

I let out a sigh of relief. "This is Adam," I say, pulling him forward by his forearm.

"Hello," Adam says, smiling. Back in public, all traces of his disappointment from our conversation with Loran have disappeared.

Copp stares at Adam just a little too long. I clear my throat several times.

"Ah . . . well, welcome!" Copp says after he's composed himself. "Any friend of Terra's and all that. If ya got questions, just let 'em rip."

Adam nods and starts to inspect Copp's wares. He holds up a lightweight windbreaker, gray instead of black, but otherwise similar to the jacket I lost in the District, and dives into a conversation with Copp about it. My eyes immediately glaze over.

Here we go again. How interesting can a jacket be?

I entertain myself by perusing Copp's collection of tarnished silver pendants until three sharp blasts ring out from unseen speakers.

Rain.

I step outside Copp's stall, where the doors at the end of the building are open to the outside. The clouds are already rolling in: massive and threatening swirls of dark purples and blackish blues. We've got maybe twenty minutes before the downpour begins.

"C'mon," I tell Adam. "We've gotta go."

"Why?" he asks, his eyes now glued to another jacket—navy blue this time—pinned to the wall behind Copp's head.

"Rain, dummy." I roll my eyes and tug on his arm. "We'll pick up Mica on the way. They should be releasing him from school now."

"Right, of course. The rain." Adam looks wistfully at the jacket.

"Oh, for the love of—" I say, my exasperation making the words blend together. "Copp, we'll take this."

"No, you don't have to—"

I silence Adam with a look, then turn back to Copp. "Throw in that blue one too," I say, pointing to the navy jacket. "Buying double means a discount, right?"

"Ya *definitely* haven't changed," Copp says with a laugh.

Adam holds up a hand in protest. "Terra, I can't just let you—"

"I need a new one too. You can pay me back later." I ignore my credit balance when it comes up on the register.

"Thank you," Adam says, his gaze just a little too intense.

I shrug. "It's just a jacket."

Adam says a brief goodbye to Copp, who tips his hat at the skydweller—something I've never seen him do. Adam really brings out the most unusual reactions in people. Copp stuffs the jackets in a bag, then hands it to Adam, who steps outside.

"Always a pleasure," Copp says to me as I turn to leave. "And I gotta say, it's kinda nice."

"What is?"

"Seeing ya with someone."

"No, we're not—"

"Never figured ya for a skychaser," he continues with a wink, "but this one seems all right."

Before I can clarify the situation, Copp's already turned to help the next customer in line, eager to finish her shopping before the rain starts.

I join Adam outside, avoiding his eyes as I take the bag with the jackets from him and climb onto the bike. "Okay, let's go."

"Mica?" he asks.

"Mica," I say, and we rumble off toward the school.

***

"WHAT DO you mean he's not here?" Annoyance has my nostrils flaring as the redheaded girl I saw with Juniper at the assembly stands in front of me outside the school. Her name, I learn, is Brim Lyle.

"Don't know what to tell you, Miss Terra," Brim says coyly, twisting a lock of hair around her finger. "He's not."

"Do you know where he went?"

"Yep."

I sigh. "And . . . ? Feel like telling me where?"

"I saw him take off with Junie. He's walked her home every day this week. Guess he wanted to make sure she got home nice and dry." Brim bursts into a fit of giggles as her mother arrives to collect her.

"Great." I pinch the bridge of my nose and turn back to Adam. "What a time for him to become a gentleman. I blame you for this, you know."

"Should we go get him?" Adam asks.

I bite my lip and glance up at the sky. The clouds are almost directly overhead. They're moving much faster than they normally do.

"I don't think there's time," I say finally. "Let's just go home. Maybe he's already back. And if not . . ." I let the rest of the sentence fall away. I know Mica will be fine, that's hardly the issue. I just hope that the Coals tolerate his company much better than they do mine.

Our detour at the school took longer than I thought it would, and we're still speeding through the deserted streets of the West Q when the first drops start to fall.

The rain starts slowly, as it always does; beads of water descend sporadically, as if patches of the cloud layer have sprung very mild leaks. They're spaced out far enough for us to avoid, and we still have a few minutes before it evolves into a full-blown downpour.

I sigh with relief as we turn the corner and my apartment building comes into view, then gasp as a fat droplet grazes my shoulder. I feel Adam tense—he must have gotten hit too. He drives straight under the awning that hangs above the building's front doors, and we dash inside.

"Are you all right?" I ask once we're safely inside, checking my shoulder for damage. There's a small pink dash on my skin, but I've definitely had worse.

Adam breathes through his teeth as he inspects his arm. It only takes me a moment to see exactly where he got hit, and then another to realize that he got it much worse than I did. A circle on top of his forearm—an inch from his elbow—has risen into a grotesque bubble. After a second, it settles back down into a raw, red welt. Adam grips his arm from underneath, still breathing harshly, and marches upstairs without saying a word.

"How do you live like this?" he says once we've reached the top of the stairs.

"What?" I say, distracted as I wrestle with the lock on the front door. "You mean the rain?"

"Yes. It's just so . . ."

"Inconvenient?" I offer.

"I think it goes a little beyond that," he says darkly, following me inside.

"I don't know. I mean, it's a pain, sure. But this is life. The UV filter that used to encase the entire settlement broke down ages ago. We never had the resources to maintain it, let alone build a new one." I hold in the part about how the primary reason for that is because the Tribunal—the skycities—refused to help. "But forecasts are down almost to the minute at this point, plus there are the warning horns. Nobody's gotten seriously hurt in ages."

He holds out his arm. "I find that hard to believe."

"There's usually more time," I say, guilt gnawing at my insides. "If I'd known the rain was going to start so soon after the horns, I wouldn't have said we should go by the school."

Adam frowns. "Timing would be the least of my concerns if I had to deal with this on a regular basis."

I give a noncommittal shrug, fighting the resentment rising in my chest. It's not that I've forgotten Adam is a skydweller—the proof literally stares me in the face every time I look him in the eye. But I've gotten so used to his presence that it's no longer the first thing I think about, so whenever he comments on the hardships of groundworld life, it's extra jarring.

"How unfortunate it is that we can't all be born into a life of skyborn luxury," I say bitterly. I toss the bag with the jackets onto the kitchen table with too much force, and it slides right over the opposite edge and lands on the floor.

"I didn't mean it like that." He walks around the table to retrieve the bag, placing it squarely in the center, like it's some sort of decoration.

I suck in a deep breath. "Sorry, old habit."

"I understand," he says, and the look on his face makes me think he actually might.

I walk into the bathroom and pull a box of bandages and a tube of antiseptic from a cabinet. "Here, let me see your arm." We pull chairs from the kitchen table and face each other so I can clean his wound. "You have to understand that I'm still getting used to all of this," I say, trying to be gentle as I wrap his forearm with a bandage.

"All of what?"

"You. You're . . . you're this total anomaly. The officials, the guardsmen, even our own teachers . . . People from up top barely associate with us. They're paying their dues, serving their time down here in the hopes of netting something better for themselves when they get back—a promotion, a raise, whatever."

I secure the bandage with a knot, my fingers lingering on the frayed edges of the fabric. "You could treat us like the rest of them do—like we're nothing more than your innkeepers, people who provide a place for you to bunk," I continue. "But you, I don't know, actually seem to like spending time with the people here. You're interesting. And you're interest*ed*. In Sixteen. In us. You don't immediately try to sanitize your palms after shaking someone's hand down here."

I look at Adam earnestly for a moment, his blue eyes warm and inviting, a smile lurking behind the serious set of his lips.

"Don't get me wrong, it's nice," I add. "It's also strange. There's a reason why we don't spend time with you all, why we don't get to know you. My father is a perfect example. He was from up top, born and raised in Korbyllis. Did you know that? And as he loved to remind me, he threw it all away—his life *up there*—to be with my mother. Then she died, and he hated it down here so much that he left. Didn't even have the decency to say goodbye to his own kids.

"I get that you're down here because of work, but there's no benefit for you getting to know us at all. No reason you should *want* to be here." My lips close clumsily over the last words, and I'm struck with the urge to crawl to my room and smother my embarrassment under my pillow.

I stand and start to walk away, but Adam catches my wrist, pulling me back toward him as he rises from his chair. In an instant, we are face-to-face. "You feel like you're not allowed to think the things you think," he says, a sudden intensity in his voice. "Or feel the things you feel."

"Welcome to the human condition," I say wryly.

He releases my wrist and brushes aside a few dark strands of hair that have fallen into my eyes. His hand lingers on my cheek and I can't stop myself from leaning into it.

"Don't," I say faintly.

"Why not?"

I don't have an answer at first. "Look, it's been a long day, and you're upset, and we're . . . we're not the same." The moment the words fall from my lips, I regret them.

He laughs, a breathy sound. "So what? What's so great about being the same? The same is boring. And you, Sunburst, are most decidedly not."

He leans forward and brushes his lips against mine, his kiss soft and appraising. He pulls away and evaluates me tentatively, his eyebrows raised in question, as if to ask me if this is all right.

I don't know if it is right. But it certainly doesn't feel wrong.

So, before I can second-guess myself, I press my lips back to his, and we ignite.

Adam's hand glides from my cheek to the back of my neck, pulling me into him, and I wrap one arm around his shoulders, meeting his urgency with my own.

His fingers brush through my hair, tangling in my locks, and he tugs gently, pulling my head back. He trails his lips down my chin, feathering kisses down my neck, making me shiver. I draw Adam's face back to mine, his skin soft and warm beneath my fingertips as our lips meet again.

My emotions pulse and mingle and flare—desire and longing and gratitude all mixed in one. The voice in the back of my mind is at war with my more logical self.

This is wrong. *Is it?* This should feel wrong. *Should it?*

It doesn't. Somehow, it feels like this is what was meant to happen all along.

Two people, from two opposite worlds, lost and left behind in our own ways, finding each other.

His hand presses into the small of my back, brushing the gap of skin between my shirt and pants and tugging me closer. My breath becomes ragged as his fingers edge up beneath the hem of my shirt, my skin hot under his electric touch. He moves his other hand to cradle my cheek, his lips fluttering over mine until he catches my bottom lip between his and grazes it with his teeth. It kindles something primal in my core and I push my entire body into his—one hand on his chest, the other still wrapped around his shoulders—feeling his muscles roll under my grip.

Our bodies aligned, we move backward until we hit the back of the couch, and a laugh escapes me as we tumble right over it. Our limbs tangle as we right ourselves on the sofa before Adam leans back and pulls me onto his lap, my legs dropping to either side of him. I run my hands up the back of his neck, one stopping where the buzzed bristles fade into the silky crop on his crown, the other trailing a path north until my fingers catch in his golden tresses. A groan escapes his lips as I part my own, inviting him in as a week's worth—or has it been a lifetime?—of want consumes us both.

———

ADAM IS the first to break away.

"Listen," he says, gesturing toward the window.

I peel myself off his lap to go see what he's pointing at, immediately missing the warmth of his skin, the pressure of his touch. Thankfully, it doesn't last long, as he joins me by the window, spinning me deftly around so my back is to him and wrapping his arms around my middle, rooting me to the spot.

Save for the breath I'm still rapidly trying to catch in my lungs, the air around us is silent.

"Rain's stopped," I say. "Guess that really was a short shower." I don't add that it's the first time I've ever wished it rained longer.

"How long until you think Mica will be home?" he asks, resting his chin on my hair. His breath is a flame on my skin as the words vibrate into me and he brushes the hair off my shoulder to plant soft kisses along my neck.

I shiver. "I don't know. Not much longer, probably."

"Well then," he says, and I can feel him grinning. "I guess we should take advantage of whatever time we do have." He turns me back around and starts to lean back into me, but I put my hand on his chest to stop him, his reminder of Mica flooding me with sudden clarity.

What am I doing?

Whatever spell I was under breaks.

"What's wrong, Sunburst?" he asks, stepping back and dropping his hands from my waist.

"I can't."

He laughs softly. "I thought we went over this already."

"I'm serious, Adam. This was a mistake."

It wasn't really though, was it? says the voice in the back of my mind, louder than usual.

I shake my head as if that'll shut it up. "It's wrong."

Adam's face falls, his lips forming a line, and a chill sweeps over me that has nothing to do with the temperature as he takes another step back. "Why do you keep saying that? What is so damn *wrong* about this?"

I swallow. "I—it just is. I've already told you, you and me, them and us, we don't work. Sooner or later, you're going to take off, and I don't want to be the trampy terrestrial you end up telling all your skybuddies about once you're gone, okay?"

A muscle tightens along his jaw. "Nice to know you have such a high opinion of me."

"It's just better for everyone if we don't go there."

"Not sure if you've noticed, Terra, but we're already there."

I stare at him in silence, afraid that my willpower will dissipate if I utter another word. Even as I try to strengthen my resolve, that little voice inside just gets louder, screaming at me to stop being so stubborn, so stupid. To take it back, to fall into his embrace again, to pick up right where we left off.

"All right, if that's how you want it," he finally says, and my heartbeat stutters. He trudges over to the front door and yanks it open.

"You can't go outside yet," I say. "The ground is still too wet, it's not safe."

"I'll take my chances." He slams the door behind him as he storms out, leaving me in thunderous silence.

NINETEEN

"I KNOW, I KNOW," Mica says, a sheepish expression on his young face when he walks through the door.

I finish putting the final clean dish away—my last in the series of mindless housekeeping tasks I've been tackling in an attempt to keep myself out of my head.

"How much trouble am I in?" Mica asks, rounding the corner and peering at me from the edge of the kitchen alcove.

"What? None," I say quickly, flattening the back of my hair nervously. Even though I've already brushed it twice, I can't help feeling like evidence of my incident with Adam—*oh, is that what we're calling it?*—is still visible in its tangles. "You're not in trouble. I'm just glad you got back all right. How was school?"

I nearly cringe at my own words. They sound too formal, too forced.

Mica eyes me curiously. "Okay . . . I was just with Juniper, hunkered down at her folks' place."

"I know," I say. "We stopped by the school and your friend Brim told me. But maybe next time leave a message with a teacher or something." I pause. "Were the Coals okay with you being there?"

"I guess. I mean, her sister wasn't half as nice to me as when she was here the other day, but it's not like she threw me out."

"That's good."

"Are *you* okay with me being there?"

I shrug. "You turn fourteen in a couple of days, Mic. I assume by now you're perfectly capable of keeping yourself thoroughly un-disintegrated during a rainfall."

"That's not what I meant."

"It's fine," I say, but the look on my brother's face is wholly unconvinced, so I add, "Really. I mean, I'm not a fan of the Coals, generally speaking, but it's whatever. Juniper seems nice and I'm . . . happy for you."

"So, where's Adam?" Mica asks, and I silently thank the Powers that Be that he's already turning to sit down at the table before he can see my grimace.

I blink, not knowing how to respond. It's been over an hour since he left, and I have no idea when—or if—he's coming back. "He's, uh—"

Right on cue, I hear a knock at the front door. Mica slides his chair back and lumbers over to open it. The wave of ice I feel immediately taking over the apartment confirms that Adam has returned. Face burning, I flatten myself against the back kitchen wall to keep myself out of his line of sight, though I can't help continuing to peek at their interaction.

"Perfect timing," Mica says with a grin before noticing the bandage on Adam's forearm. "Ouch, guess the rain got you?"

"Yep, it nailed me pretty good."

"Sucks." Mica lets out a low whistle. "So, where've you been?"

I hold my breath.

"I finally made it to the Marketplace today." Adam's voice is bright, and I exhale, thankful that whatever front he puts on for the public also apparently applies to little brothers.

Or maybe he really is already over it—whatever "it" was.

"Fascinating stuff," he continues. "Haggling, bartering . . . it's all unheard of where I'm from. Makes for a completely different kind of shopping experience."

Mica walks into the kitchen and notices me cowering against the wall. I pretend to straighten a picture hanging beside me, but I know it's not fooling him. He eyes me with an arched brow as he sits down at the table.

A few seconds later, Adam enters and takes a seat as well. I shoot a nervous glance at him, but his face is impassive. He is still angry with me but is reining it in for Mica's benefit. I flash what I hope looks like a grateful, close-lipped smile, which he dutifully ignores.

"What'd you get?" Mica asks, reaching into the bag on the table and pulling out the two jackets. He lays them out side-by-side before donning an impish grin. "Matching outerwear? How adorable."

"Quiet, you," I say, finally lugging myself off the wall.

"You get these from Copp?" Mica asks. "How was he? Were things . . . different?"

"At first," I say, grabbing the navy jacket off the table. "But you know Copp. It didn't take long for him to get back to normal. Can't say the same for just about anyone else there, though. I must've gotten twenty death stares."

"Yeah, guess that figures. They'll get over it." Mica shrugs, then turns to Adam. "You've pretty much covered the whole town now, huh? Will you be leaving soon?"

Mica's question sparks a wave of self-righteousness in my mind. I was right to have stopped us. Adam's going to leave—and soon. I've been counting on it. Hoping for it.

But I still can't stop my stomach from clenching as the reality sinks in that once he's gone, he'll be . . . gone.

I know it's nothing like when Gran died, or when Dad left, or when Lee was killed, but the end result is still the same. I'll probably never see Adam again.

"Why, getting sick of me already?" Adam jokes.

"Of course not, man. Having you around is great." Mica sinks his voice to a faux-whisper. "Makes dealing with her much more tolerable."

I ball up the jacket and throw it at Mica's head. He catches it with a taunting laugh.

"No, but seriously," he continues, tossing the jacket back at me. It misses me by a long shot and drifts lamely to the floor. He shrugs unapologetically as I recover it. "Isn't there someone up there wondering where you are?"

Adam glances at me. "I'm sure they've been surviving without me. But you're right, it's probably time for me to move on. I'll leave tomorrow."

Mica's mouth shifts into a frown, but he nods slowly, signaling his acceptance.

"I'll be right back." I walk to my bedroom and close the door behind me. Leaning against the back of my door with the jacket clutched to my chest, I suck in one deep breath, then another. Despite all my efforts spent trying to resist my attraction to Adam, despite what I told him barely an hour ago—what I told *myself* twenty seconds ago—the thought of him leaving hurts more than I want to admit.

I pull my dresser drawer open to put the jacket away and a glint of metal catches my eye. I push aside a sweater to reveal the broken machine. It feels like ages since I unceremoniously shoved it into the drawer. I can't believe I almost allowed myself to forget about it.

I eagerly pull the machine out to take a good look. What had Adam called it? A bio-something converter? Whatever the hell that means.

I bounce it in my hand, familiarizing myself with its weight—and worth—again. Despite letting my plans momentarily slip to the back of my mind, I'm still on schedule. Collection Day is tomorrow. I put the machine back in the drawer and lay my new jacket on top of it.

Just one more day of secrets.

As I close the drawer, my heart starts to race with my reinvigorated plan. I've been so distracted by Adam and accompanying him on his exploits across Sixteen that I'd almost forgotten the reason this all happened in the first place.

Not anymore, I think, steeling myself against the wave of emotions roiling inside me. *Time to get back on track.*

TWENTY

I WAKE EARLY the next day. Collection Day.

Tomorrow is Mica's birthday and I want to wait until then to surprise him with my plan for his schooling. I form a loose script: I'll say I need his help running a few errands. He'll be annoyed, which will only make the revelation sweeter when I bring him to the Skyline ticket office by the Assembly Hall, where an undated shuttle pass with his name on it will be waiting.

I sit up in bed and smile as I imagine Mica's face shifting from confusion to comprehension, from irritation to excitement.

God, I hope he's excited, I think. I could use the boost to my mood. Even with my renewed determination to make this happen, I'm finding thoughts of Adam difficult to shake.

It doesn't matter anyway, I suppose. Adam's leaving today, he said so himself. There's no better time to make sure that the second machine will get us the additional steel we need to make it up top. I can't risk making a promise to Mica that I won't be able to keep.

And if I get to the recycling center early enough, at least I won't have to deal with the dirty looks. People will still hear about it, of course. They always do. But hopefully, I'll be back, safe and sound, before I have to deal with them, and once the steel is safely in my account, there's nothing anyone will be able to do about it . . . provided I stay out of the Black Traders' line of sight.

I get ready slowly, taking the time to brush back my hair and fasten it in a secure bun. I slip on a pair of slim-cut pants that end at my ankles, and throw my new jacket on over a white tank top, rolling the sleeves up to my elbows and leaving the front unzipped.

I slip the machine into my jacket pocket, pleasantly surprised to find how deep the pockets are. The machine's weight pulls one side of the jacket down, but it's not in any danger of slipping out. The bulge isn't even that noticeable.

I creep out of my bedroom and glance at Adam splayed out on the couch. The back of the sofa blocks most of him from view, but his feet dangle clear off the end, hanging over his pack, which is propped up on the side. I tiptoe to the door, hopeful I'll be able to slip out unseen, then silently curse when I realize my boots are sitting at the foot of the couch.

I creep over as quietly as possible, trying not to wake him, but my plans are immediately foiled as I peer around the corner of the couch and find myself staring directly into his wide-open cerulean eyes.

"Morning," he whispers.

"Damn, you're a light sleeper."

"Where are you off to?"

"I have to run a quick errand." I keep my voice low so as not to wake Mica.

"Want company?" Adam says, sitting up.

"I thought you were mad at me."

"I was." He shrugs. "Maybe I still am. But I think it'd be a good chance for us to talk."

The machine suddenly feels very heavy in my pocket. "I thought you were taking off this morning." I'm careful to keep the emotion out of my voice. "You've been all over Sixteen and back now. There's nowhere left to see." I motion toward his new jacket, bundled up in a ball next to his pack. "You even got yourself a souvenir."

"Doesn't mean my business here is done."

"We can talk when I get back." I let the words fall out casually, hoping it'll mask my uneasiness. "I won't be gone long and Mica will be getting up soon anyway. Maybe you can make breakfast for once, huh?"

I quickly turn away to hide my reddening face. I'd counted on avoiding him today so as not to bring attention to my plans for the second machine. Then again, why should I care if he finds out now? Maybe the revelation will be just the push he needs to leave us behind for good.

"Just wait a second," he says, gently grabbing my hand and breaking through my thoughts. I reflexively pull it back and I swear, something akin to pain flashes across his features.

Maybe I just imagined it.

"I have something for you." He throws his blanket off, revealing he slept in nothing but his boxers. I avert my gaze as he reaches into his pack and pulls out a small, rectangular box.

My eyes widen in surprise and I cock my head to the side in curiosity as he holds it out to me. "What's this?"

"There's an easy way to find out," he says, and the humor in his voice makes me want to melt. "Open it."

I lift the lid to reveal a shiny glint of silver. A band of engraved links that lead up to a smooth bezel. Three elegant hands that sprout from its center.

The watch from the jewelry store window.

"How did you . . . ?" I breathe.

"Observing is kind of my thing." He lifts the watch out of the box.

"Adam, this is—"

"This isn't anything," he says, his voice even. "We don't need to make it a bigger deal than it is. I'm just returning it to you, that's all."

"Returning it?"

He flips it over and hands it to me. On the back of the watch face is a scuffed inscription. I tilt the watch until the light hits the metal at the right angle for me to read the words.

To my wife, my love, my life. Yours always, Auron.

"How did you know?" My words catch in the back of my throat as I turn the watch back over, tracking the seconds hand as it ticks around the perimeter.

"His name is stitched onto the labels of some of his clothes." Adam takes the watch from me and hooked it delicately around my wrist. "I couldn't be positive it was your father, but I figured it was worth taking the chance."

I take in the shape of my mother's watch as it sits on my wrist, the silver gleaming against my skin. "I don't know how to thank you." My eyes glisten as I look up at Adam. I think if I were to move a single muscle, my body would fold itself right back into his arms.

Like he's reading my mind, he takes a step closer, then seems to think better of it. "No thanks necessary. I was just getting it back to you, like I said."

I give him a pointed look, weighing his words against the obvious significance of his actions. The machine feels like lead in my jacket pocket, and remorse bubbles up from the pit of my stomach.

"Is the time on this correct?" I ask, finally acknowledging the practical purpose of the timepiece.

"Should be."

"I really need to go. But . . . I agree, we should talk." About Mica and us and stolen machines and best-laid plans for the future. About everything. "I'll be back soon."

He flashes that lopsided grin at me. "Well, now you can time yourself."

THE WALK to the recycling center is quiet, giving me no choice but to work through the thoughts noisily buzzing in my head.

This was a mistake, I told him yesterday. *It wasn't really though, was it?* said the voice in my head that I refused to listen to, the small part of myself that knew the truth.

Maybe the mistake was how quickly I tried to dismiss whatever this is between us. The pull that called me to the Dead Woods that day, that chased me underground, that led me to him.

Or maybe the mistake is what I'm doing right now. Operating in secrecy to secure another payload for my little brother's future. Keeping every plan close to my chest because trusting another person—even if it's him—is the most terrifying thing I could do. Hell, I'd go another round with Ryk and his boys over this any day.

I'll tell him everything once I get back, I decide as I toy with the clasp on my watch. *The whole sordid tale.* No more half-truths and no more secrets

—from either of us. And from there, who knows? If Mica and I are bound for a skyworld life, isn't there a possibility that Adam could still be part of it?

EVEN AT THIS EARLY HOUR, it's surprising how little movement there is on the streets. When I reach the center itself, the roads are completely dead. There isn't another scav in sight.

A twang of guilt runs through me as I think about Mal and the other guys—going on about their lives under the Tribunal's new restrictions, while I eat boxes of ten-credit crackers with a skyboy.

A solitary Collection Agent sits at the drop-off station, flanked by the standard guardsmen on either side. I don't recognize any of them, and I have to stifle a giggle as I approach. The contrast between the guardsmen is ludicrous. The one on the left is tall but incredibly thin, his chin-length hair black as night, framing a pointy jaw. He looks so gangly, that it's hard to imagine how he was accepted to the Academy at all; I've heard the physical requirements are pretty demanding.

The second guardsman, on the other hand, must be three times the width of his partner. The muscles in his arms bulge under the sleeves of his uniform, and his shaved head is almost perfectly square. Neither of them pays me any notice as I walk up to the station.

"Hey there," I say amiably.

The agent, a young-ish man with spiky hair that's so blond it's almost white, looks at me resignedly with turquoise eyes. I suppose spending time with Adam has made me much more comfortable around skyd-wellers; I'm sure the agent is rarely addressed so genially.

"I have a drop-off contribution." I stick out my hand as the agent robotically picks up his tablet.

"Name?" he asks as he runs my palm over the screen.

"Rhodon, Terra."

A beat passes as he reads the information on the tablet, his jaw set stiffly as he looks back up to me.

"And what is it that you are dropping off?" His eyes are wider, but his voice remains steady.

I glance around again. Not a soul in sight. The guilt bubble in my stomach returns as I pull the machine out of my jacket pocket and lay it on the table.

The agent presses his lips into a hard line as he scans his computer over the machine. I stare at him expectantly, bracing for a repeat of what happened last time: shock when he sees the machine's value followed by the hushed announcement of my payout. Instead, the tablet starts to beep.

I freeze, dumbfounded, but if the agent is surprised, he doesn't show it.

"There seems to be an issue with this device. Please wait here for a moment." He stands abruptly, leaving the machine on the table, and half-walks, half-runs into the recycling center.

Time ticks by in hypnotizing spirals as I stare at my mother's watch. Five minutes pass. Then ten.

There continues to be a distinct lack of other scavs lining up for the Collection, which is disconcerting. By now, there should be at least a few early risers coming to stake their spot in line. My anxiety spikes with each tick of the seconds hand.

The mismatched guardsmen watch me with tempered expressions. Their white uniforms remind me of Brant and his warning, which suddenly feels like it's clanging in my brain. Just as I am considering leaving, however, the Collection Agent returns. In one hand, he carries a square container with a clear lid. The tablet is hooked under his other arm, still beeping relentlessly. He carefully picks up the machine, places it inside the container, and locks the lid in place.

"What's going—"

The agent cuts me off with a flourish of his white-gloved hand. A signal. Before I can react, the lanky guardsman has swooped in on me, pinning my arms behind my back.

"What the hell?" I protest, struggling against his grip. "Get off me!"

"Terra Rhodon," the agent says, his voice underpinned with a declarative authority that wasn't there before. "You are under arrest."

TWENTY-ONE

"YOU ARE under arrest for quarantine boundary violation, as well as for being in possession of illegal technology," the Collection Agent reads from his still-beeping tablet.

"What?" My mouth goes dry and I stop my futile struggle against the guardsman's hold. This can't be happening—illegal technology? I can't be understanding this correctly.

"You have withheld information from the Tribunal, obstructed an official investigation, and have attempted to leverage this knowledge for personal profit. You will be immediately extradited to Korbyllis to await further judgment."

"Korbyllis?" I repeat in a strangled voice. Even if I understood the charges the agent is levying against me, judgments and punishments are always handled directly by the Council here in Sixteen. It's rare that a lawbreaker would commit a crime that warrants being sent to the capital —even the worst of the Black Traders aren't sent up top.

The agent flourishes his hand again, and this time it's the gargantuan guardsman who sweeps me out of his partner's grasp and crams me into the back of a waiting transport vehicle that seems to have appeared out of nowhere.

"You can't do this," I yell. "You're making a huge mistake. Let me go!"

The guard doesn't say a word as he slams the transport's door in my face.

I jiggle the handle. Locked.

I scoot to the opposite side of the transport to try the other door, but it's bolted shut as well.

I pound on the window with my fists, then lie back on the seat and slam my feet into the door, hard. It doesn't budge.

My eyes well up with angry tears as I watch the agent issue instructions to the two guardsmen. The thin one runs off with alarming speed, and a new kind of panic settles in my gut as I realize the direction he's headed in. Before my fears have fully formed, however, the brutish one is wedging himself into the driver's seat.

I catch a glimpse of his badge as he settles in: Titan. How appropriate.

I begin hurling as many obscenities as I can muster through the gated partition between the front and back of the vehicle. Steadfastly ignoring me, Titan turns on the transport and we take off.

"Help!" I cry, pounding again on the window as we drive through the shopping district, where there are finally people out on the street. Whether it's because the passers-by can't hear me, can't see me, or are simply choosing to ignore me, I don't know. But not a single person even bothers to look my way as we pass.

After a few minutes, the transport slows down, and for a moment I think we're going to turn into the parking lot at the Town Hall—where the local guardsmen's office is—but Titan drives right past it. Instead, he heads straight toward the North Gate.

"Wait," I say, lowering my voice in the desperate hope that he might respond if I'm calmer, "where are you taking me?"

"As Agent Pyke said, you are being transported to Korbyllis." His voice is low and rough, like chunks of gravel are rolling around in the back of his throat.

"Now? Right now?" I ask frantically. "No, you can't. You can't just send me up there. I haven't done anything! What about being processed? Isn't there some kind of protocol?"

Titan says nothing else, and the tears that have been threatening to spill over finally do. They fall in heavy drops, warm against my skin as they cascade down my cheeks in waves. I feel helpless. Will they even bother telling Mica what has happened? Is that why the other agent was heading for the West Q? Or will I just be . . . gone?

How did they know about the quarantine violation? I think, recalling Agent Pyke's words. And what does *illegal technology* even mean? All I did was turn in the same kind of machine I had turned in before. The one they already paid me for once. Adam's machine.

Adam.

My chest heaves violently and a sob escapes my lips. What will he think has happened? Will they tell him the truth? Will he think I . . . ran away from him? From Mica?

Will he be able to help?

"Please . . ." I say, catching Titan's eye in the transport's rearview mirror, one last desperate plea for mercy as we speed away from the settlement. For a heartbeat, it feels like I'm back in the Dead Woods, pleading with the raider, Locke. Feels like maybe there is still hope.

Where Locke's pity was my saving grace, however, all I get from Titan is a solitary glance, his eyes cold and unyielding.

I turn around to face out the back window, clutching my jacket tightly around me, my tears still falling as the black walls of Genesis X-16 fade into the distance.

"WE'RE HERE." Titan's rough voice wakes me from an uneasy sleep. My eyes meet a darkening sky as I look out the window, and a quick glimpse at my watch confirms that it's almost evening. We've been driving all day.

"Move it," he says, yanking the transport door open. I catch a glimpse of a sign behind him as he pulls me roughly from the vehicle, indicating we are at the Skyline Transport station. More specifically, we are in a parking area at the back of the complex, which I guess is where they take the people they don't want the paying passengers to see.

This is really happening.

Titan shoves me forward, forcing me to walk ahead of him as we approach a large set of metal doors. He knocks twice, pauses, then knocks twice more. A slot in one of the doors slides open, revealing a set of green eyes that look oddly familiar. The rest of the door opens a second later.

"Brant!" I cry, relief flooding through me. "Brant, please. There's been a huge misunderstanding. You have to help me."

Brant turns to Titan, ignoring me. "Transfer authorization?" he asks, holding out a tablet, and the single spark of hope that had just flared inside me is snuffed out.

Titan places his palm on the screen and holds it there until it beeps. "Transfer complete," he says brusquely. Without so much as another glance in my direction, he leaves.

Brant ushers me inside. Several other guardsmen are lined up in a windowless hallway, the fluorescent lights overhead casting harsh shadows on their faces. Aside from the color—a light, cloudy gray—their uniforms are identical to those worn in Sixteen. I realize that Brant's is gray as well.

"When did you get promoted here?" I ask quietly.

His arm is on my shoulder, holding me in place the same way he did that fateful day when he escorted me home. He tightens his grip for a moment but stays silent.

Maybe it wasn't a promotion.

We weave through a maze of hallways, all lined with guardsmen who appear to be waiting for something. It's not until we pass through a set of swinging doors and into an empty hall that Brant finally opens his mouth.

"What did you do?" he asks, his voice quiet but distressed. He yanks me by the arm into a tiny room off the main hallway—a closet, perhaps— and shuts the door behind us. "How did this happen?"

"I'm not even sure *what* happened. One minute it's Collection Day and I'm turning in another one of those machines, and the next thing I know I'm being arrested for violating quarantine and '*possession of illegal technology*' and being dragged out here," I hiss, making quotation marks in the air with my fingers. "Care to enlighten me?"

"What do you mean, another machine?"

"Like the one I turned in before. I found another," I say, leaving out Adam's involvement.

Brant's chin drops sadly. "Why would you do that? Did you really not realize you were already on their radar?"

"On *whose* radar?" My voice rises hysterically.

Brant shushes me. "Shh, you have to calm down. If they catch me . . ." He sneaks a furtive glance toward the door. "Look, the Tribunal has been interested in you since you turned in that machine. It's technology that should never have been found by anyone, let alone a scav. That initial payout? It was supposed to be more like a pay*off*, except it quickly became clear to them that you weren't interested in dropping the subject. And when you disappeared that day . . ." He trails off, no doubt remembering his terse interrogation during our last encounter.

"We've been issued instructions to expedite your transfer," he continues, "and send you up to Korbyllis on the next shuttle, which happens to be a luxury liner. Try to lay low. Once you're up there . . ." Brant takes a deep breath. "Terra, listen to me. They are going to want *answers*. I don't know what happened that day and I don't want to know. But stick to your story, okay? The one you told me. You never even set foot across the quarantine line. Got it?"

"I don't think I—" I start, but Brant cuts me off.

"I don't know how you're going to explain this second machine, but you have to try. Come up with something."

"I just don't understand why this is happening to me."

"This isn't just about you, Terra. This is something much bigger than you. It's not about the machine. It's about what they think you *know*."

"But I don't know anything," I protest.

Brant pauses. "I believe you," he says after a moment. "But they won't." He checks the black watch on his wrist. "We have to go."

"I'm not ready," I say weakly.

Brant puts both hands on my shoulders and squeezes them. "You're strong," he says, and I have to bite my lip to keep it from quivering as the deja vu from hearing those exact same words tumble from Adam's mouth hits me. If I let myself think about him again right now, I really am going to lose it.

"They just want their answers," Brant continues. "Prove that there's no reason for them to keep you, and they'll have to let you go."

Brant ushers me back into the hallway and toward a heavy sliding door with a sign nailed to it that reads "Loading Dock."

"It's just through here. Another guard will accompany you on the shuttle. I don't have the clearance." With a grunt, he slides the metal door open and, without walking through it, beckons me to move forward. It opens up into a tunnel with clear walls; outside, the silhouette of mountains frames the brown and barren landscape.

A gleaming white shuttle with polished wings waits at the end of the tunnel. The ship's oval body is dotted with double-decker windows, coming to a point at the hull, and wings balloon out at the back end, giving it the appearance of a giant spade.

I step through the doorway but turn back to Brant just as he begins to pull the door shut.

"Why are you helping me?" I ask through the remaining sliver of open doorway.

Brant looks at me, his green eyes burning. "Stay strong." His voice is shaking. "Your father would want you to be."

The door slides shut and locks into place with a finite click. I stare at the closed wall of matte metal in front of me, my jaw agape. I want to shout through the door at Brant, to force him back here and make him explain. Just as I ready my fist to start pounding away, my outraged thoughts are interrupted by the hollow sound of boots stomping toward me.

"Terra Rhodon?" says the guard, a stocky woman with tightly braided blond hair and a heavy brow. Her high, sparkly voice is a total disconnect from her appearance. "Come with me."

TWENTY-TWO

WHEN BRANT SAID this was a luxury shuttle, he wasn't kidding. The ship is possibly the most lavish thing I have ever seen.

Upon embarking, I am immediately led into a small elevator with shiny gold doors. We ride up a single level, then exit into the main cabin, where the velvet-lined walls are a deep shade of pink, the lower half stamped with a golden leaf pattern. Ten neatly coiffed female attendants stand against the walls, ready and waiting. Wearing starched yellow blouses with pink crossover ties neatly folded under the collar, they look as much a part of the ship's decoration as the sparkling crystal chandeliers that hang overhead.

The upper level of the shuttle is sectioned off into individual seating compartments, separated by embossed half-walls that come up to my stomach as I walk past them. While folks walking past can easily see into the stalls on either side, one could just as easily ignore whoever might be sitting inside. Either way, they're empty for now.

The guard leads me straight through the main area to a small, plain booth tucked far into the back of the cabin, situated between the restrooms and the galley. Its purpose becomes clear when I see a pair of attendants enter a similar one on the other end of the cabin. A staff compartment.

While the other compartments boast plush, cream-colored benches, this one sports a pair of metal chairs bolted to the wall, with seats that fold up when they're not in use. My escort gestures to the chair next to the window, buckling me into my seat before plopping down in the one next to me. The half-walls of our booth are slightly taller than those surrounding the regular compartments, but if I sit up straight and tilt my chin, I can still observe the rest of the cabin as passengers begin to board.

I expect there to be some sort of forward motion or pressure as we lift off, but all I perceive is a slight jingling from the chandeliers. I lean as far away from the window as possible, not eager for the visual reminder that everything I've ever known is hundreds of feet below me, getting farther away every second.

My escort's name, as she happily informs me, is Akryn.

"They don't even showcase the inside of this class of shuttles on TV." Her hazel eyes are bright as she flicks a piece of fuzz off of her uniform. "You are very lucky to experience it for yourself."

"Sure. Lucky," I reply.

"To be honest, I was surprised to learn you were to be taken up today," she says. "I know another shuttle wasn't scheduled to arrive until the day after tomorrow, but still. Shuttles like this are generally reserved for the most elite skydwellers. You know, coming down to go on guided tours of the settlements, see the monuments and landmarks of the old world, that sort of thing."

"Of course," I mutter. "Who wouldn't want a tour of our beautifully barren wasteland?"

Akryn continues without missing a beat. "I bet you're the first lawbreaker in a hundred years to get this kind of treatment. You might as well make the most of it."

I'm not exactly sure what treatment she is referring to. The brown-eyed staff has been steadfastly ignoring us since we boarded. They must already be aware of my status as a detainee. I watch them as they bustle about, serving the other passengers with broad smiles on their faces that disappear whenever they glance in my direction.

One of the attendants, a petite brunette woman with a frilly apron wrapped around her waist, pours out a glass of champagne and hands it to a man in a pinstriped suit seated in the compartment in front of ours.

He accepts the drink but waves her away rudely, like he's aggravated by her proximity. She smiles acquiescently as she steps back, but I don't miss the momentary flash of irritation on her face.

I can't help but wonder what it takes for someone from Sixteen to get a job like hers. Catering to upper-class skyworld snobs seems a small price to be surrounded by luxury like this. To get to see so much more of the world than the settlement we are born in. This is probably the closest thing to skyborn life most of us could hope for.

An older woman in the compartment next to the pinstriped man has a catlike creature sitting in her lap. I try not to stare too overtly, but it's hard to look away; this is the first pet I've ever seen in real life.

The woman strokes the animal's fluffy white fur between its floppy ears, then adjusts the yellow ribbon tied around its neck. It chirps happily in response—a pleasant, uplifting tune that could only have been engineered in a lab.

The attendant with the champagne retreats to the back of the cabin. Passing our booth, she glances at me with a creased brow before heading into the galley behind us, then returns with a small cart in tow and a bright smile plastered on her face. As she pushes the cart past us, she pauses and looks at me more decidedly, her smile plummeting into a conflicted frown. She quickly pulls a small covered tray from the cart and offers it to Akryn, who declines with a shake of her head.

I watch the attendant deliver the tray to the woman with the pet instead. She lifts the cover, revealing half a dozen miniature cakes, each roughly the size of her palm, lining a shining silver platter. A pang of annoyance—or is that a pang of hunger—ripples through me as the woman bites into a flower-shaped cake with overlapping peaks of purple frosting before offering a morsel to the creature in her lap.

I chew on the inside of my cheek, knowing full well I shouldn't want the cakes anyway, even if Akryn had accepted them.

I am a prisoner, not a passenger.

Averting my eyes, I pin my gaze to the floor, folding my hands in my lap and running my thumb along the links of the watch band around my wrist.

I don't want to see any more.

IT ONLY TAKES a few hours to reach Korbyllis—I spent more time in the transport vehicle with Titan than onboard the shuttle—though the thoughts running through my mind the entire time make the trip feel much longer. When I'm not consumed with what might be happening on the ground—is Mica safe? Is Adam with him?—I'm desperately trying to figure out what the hell I'm going to say when I'm processed.

I'm still formulating the details of my story when the shuttle begins to slow. I lean closer to the window, peering outside just in time to watch us dip below the sprawling metropolis, then jut straight up into the Skyline Transfer terminal from underneath.

After the other passengers have disembarked, Akryn ushers me out of the shuttle and into a spacious hangar. It is completely bare, aside from a scattering of workers in neon green shirts running to and from the shuttle's docking bay. A second docking bay sits empty on the opposite end of the hangar.

We exit into a bustling terminal with a vaulted glass ceiling. When I look up, I can see the stars.

"Last call for Skyline train passengers traveling to Daedryl," blares a robotic voice that comes from the speakers dotting the smooth white walls.

The main terminal is long and wide, with doors that mark individual hangars spaced along both sides. Akryn and I step onto a moving sidewalk and I read the names of the hangars as we glide past.

Altara, Daedryl, Echor, Lexicon . . . They're listed in alphabetical order and look identical, save for one. Intheria's hangar has been closed off, its entrance converted into a memorial for the Skyfall. A few travelers stand beneath the golden plaque bearing the city's name, their heads bowed in reverence.

Unsurprisingly, inter-skyworld travel seems much more popular than trips to and from the ground. Though our shuttle housed only a handful of passengers, plenty of skydwellers roam the terminal. They shoot wary looks in my direction as Akryn and I make our way to the exit.

It's dark outside, but the air is crisp and clean. I close my eyes and inhale deeply in an attempt to steel myself against what's to come. When I blink them open again my jaw drops.

The stars.

From beneath the terminal's glass ceiling, they didn't look too special, but out here . . . I stare in rapt wonder at the stars glittering outside the crystal clear UV filter that domes the city, cosmic confetti sprinkled across the night sky.

The terminal sits on a hill overlooking most of the colossal city, and Korbyllis blazes beneath us with so many lights that it looks like it's on fire.

"Impressive, isn't it?" Akryn says, chuckling at my expression. "There's nothing else quite like it." She allows me another moment of enthrallment before hurrying me into the back of a vehicle that's been waiting at the curb.

The transport's windows are tinted black from the outside, and a dark screen separates us from where I assume the driver sits. The vehicle takes off with a jolt, and we zoom through the lively streets of Korbyllis. Unlike in Sixteen, where hardly anyone stays out after dark, people are all over the place here.

We pause at a stoplight and I see women giggling in gaggles of three or four as they wait in line outside a thumping nightclub. Elegant couples exit a restaurant with a sign written in fancy script. Men wearing suits gather together at the base of a skyscraper, waving their cigars around animatedly as they chat.

It truly is a different world up here. On the face of every beautifully made-up woman and cleanly shaven man is a look of pure, unencumbered delight. A look that makes it very obvious they have never known the hardship of the groundworld. And they never will.

Not while we are there to endure it for them.

HALF AN HOUR LATER, we finally come to a stop. We pull up to an intimidating gate with spikes decorating the tips of its tall black bars, beyond which sits a palatial building at the end of a long, winding driveway. The mansion's polished walls are so white that they glow under the light from the streetlamps.

"The Capitol Building," Akryn informs me as the gate opens and the transport delivers us to the front. The building's columned façade makes it seem both historic and intimidating at the same time; I'm not sure whether to be impressed or scared, which, I suppose, is the point.

I step out of the transport and turn to Akryn. "So, what happens now?"

She purses her lips and looks me over. "You will be processed."

I get the distinct feeling that lawbreaker processing up here is not *quite* the same as it is in Sixteen.

Akryn bypasses the set of golden doors at the building's front, leading me instead to a small entrance to the side. "After you," she says, pulling a black card from the inside of her jacket and swiping it in a slot next to the handle.

We walk through brightly lit halls for several minutes in silence before finally stopping in front of an innocuous white door with a frosted window cut into the top. A plate on the wall says "Processing Room A," and through the opaque glass I can see someone standing on the other side.

"This is where I leave you," Akryn says, rapping on the door three times. In a low voice she adds, "I'm sorry."

Before I have a chance to ask her what she means, the door flies open, revealing a black-suited guardsman with beady blue eyes. He looks me up and down with an eager grin that immediately has me ill at ease. I turn back to Akryn only to find she's already gone.

"Welcome, little bird," the new guardsman says, his voice hoarse. He places an arm, gloved in black leather, around my shoulders and shepherds me into a windowless room with musty gray walls. Two stiff, uncushioned chairs face each other in the center of the room, a small, rectangular metal table sitting between them.

The guardsman takes a seat and gestures to the chair across from him. "Please, sit."

I hesitate, eyeing the chair dubiously.

"Sit," he repeats. It is not a request.

I unobtrusively scoot the chair back a few inches as I take my seat.

The guardsman extends an arm. "Allow me to take your jacket."

I unzip my jacket with trembling fingers, goosebumps promptly pebbling my skin. As he moves to take it, he grabs my hand.

"This is very pretty," he says, tracing a gloved finger along the band of my watch.

I recoil, yanking my arm back and instinctively wrapping my other hand around my wrist.

He smirks. "Here." He pulls a shallow box out from under the table, methodically folding my jacket into a tight square and placing it inside. "We wouldn't want to ruin it."

He flicks his eyes from my wrist to the box and back again—a silent command. I reluctantly remove the watch and lay it atop my jacket. I start to draw my hand back, but he snatches it again and I yelp in surprise as he clamps a ring of metal around my wrist. He attaches the other end to my chair, cuffing me to my seat just as a knock sounds at the door.

"Enter," the guardsman says.

A thin, balding man in a white lab coat enters the room, a silver tray in his hands. He places it on the table and I cringe at the scraping sound of metal against metal before he makes a wordless exit.

My nostrils flare as I take in the contents on the tray. There is a cup filled with what looks like water next to a clear plastic bottle filled with tiny round orange pills and a syringe boasting a murky blue liquid.

I look up at the guardsman in alarm.

"All right, now that we're all set up, I think some introductions are in order." The placid expression on his face is the epitome of unsettling. "My name is Wolfe. I am your Inquisitor. Welcome to your processing, little bird."

"Why do you keep calling me that?" I say, finally breaking the silence I've maintained since stepping inside the building.

A smile plays at Wolfe's mouth as he glances from me to the tray and back again. He pulls a small black device—identical to the one Brant used to question me after the Assembly—out of his pocket and sets it on the table.

"Because, little bird," he says, picking up the pill bottle, "I am going to make you sing."

TWENTY-THREE

"STOP. . ." I whimper as Wolfe forces another orange pill between my lips. "Please . . . stop."

The first pill thrust me into the worst day of my life. It felt so real, as if I was reliving every aspect of my mother's final moments, as if it was happening all over again. An infant Mica crying in the background. My mother's limp wrist dangling off the side of her bed. My father, stone-faced and silent, kneeling beside her.

The second pill jerked me back to the day my father left. I walked through the front door into the same empty apartment. I took in the expression on Gran's face when she returned home with the same confusion. I watched the curve of her mouth as she announced his abandonment with the same outrage.

On and on it goes. I don't know how long I am buried in the memories, but when I return to the present, the collar of my shirt is wet with tears I don't remember crying. And every time I snap back to reality, ravaged by sadness and rage and fear, Wolfe continues his line of questioning.

"Where did you find the illegal tech?" His voice is as calm and detached as it was when we first started.

"The Dead Woods," I say, my voice weak. My throat burns from screaming my cries, yelling my rage. "I've already told you that."

"I'm referring to the *second* machine."

I grit my teeth. "So am I. I found them both at the same time, I just didn't turn them both in on that first Collection Day." Somehow, in my haze, I'm still able to remember the story I rehearsed during the shuttle ride.

"And do you know what they are? What they do?"

"No," I answer honestly.

"Why would you have held onto the second one if you found them together?"

I suck in a deep breath. "I—I didn't know it would be *that* valuable, but I knew it had to be worth a lot. The other scavs, they get so upset when anybody gets a big payout, so I only turned one in at first. And then when it all turned out the way that it did, and everyone was making such a big deal about it, I got scared. I couldn't let them know I had another. It wasn't just the other scavs, either. The Black Traders . . ." I trail off.

"So, what changed? Why bother turning in the second machine at all if that was your concern?"

"I got . . . selfish." *At least that much is true*, I think.

"See, that I believe. What I *don't* believe is that you were restrained enough to hold back on a sure bet," Wolfe says condescendingly. "If I were a groundling," he doesn't bother hiding his sneer as he says the word, "and was sitting on that much steel, do you think I would be able to resist locking it safely away in my account? Away from the Traders?"

I bite the inside of my cheek.

"No, I wouldn't," he continues. "I've read your report. You lied to us about not crossing the quarantine line, and you're lying to us now."

"I told you, I found them together," I repeat. "I was just scared. Please, there's no need to—"

I jump in my chair as Wolfe bangs his fist on the table, causing the bottle of pills to tip over. They clink as they spill onto the metal tabletop, some of them rolling over the edge, decorating the floor with tiny orange polka dots.

"You're trying my patience, little bird," he says, pinching a pill between his thumb and pointer finger. "Let's try again."

I shake my head.

"I can continue to force you if that's really what you'd prefer."

My free hand instinctively flies to my face. I rub the still-sore spot on my jaw where Wolfe gripped it after each of my former refusals. Where he squeezed until my lips were forced to part, shoved a pill inside, and then clamped my mouth shut until it dissolved on my tongue.

My hand quakes as I reach for the pill. Within seconds, another hallucination starts. This time, instead of a memory, it's a nightmare. Mica, being sworn in as a Black Trader, his smile curving maliciously as he grips the handle of the still-steaming brand he's just used to mark his forearm with their trademark black T. His voice is familiar but harder, colder, as he laughs at me. "What did you expect, sis? *A fairy tale ending in the sky?*"

Wolfe bangs on the table again, and I gasp back to the present. Over and over, the cycle repeats. The lines of my memories and the nightmares start to blur until I'm no longer sure what's real and what's imaginary.

Gran's death.

Our home burning to the ground.

Ryk and the raiders, only they've caught me this time.

Adam, shot before my eyes, his cerulean eyes unseeing.

I know it's not real. I know that. But it *feels* so . . .

"Please," I beg again. "I've already told you everything I know. Please, let me go."

Hours pass. Or it could be minutes. It feels like days, years, decades. We stop only twice. Once, when there's another knock on the door and a meal is brought in. Wolfe consumes it greedily in front of me, watching me with a narrowed glare as I fruitlessly attempt to stifle the sound of my rumbling stomach.

The other interruption comes when I vomit and I am given the briefest of reprieves to clean myself up.

"When did you find the crash site?" Wolfe says, ripping me back to the present. My whole body is shaking; the image of Mica, broken and bleeding, is branded on the inside of my eyelids. I clutch my unshackled arm around myself tightly, trying to control my trembling. "How long have you been helping them?"

For the fifteenth—or maybe the fiftieth—time, I scream back, "I don't know what you're talking about!"

Wolfe sighs. "And I don't know why you won't cooperate with me."

I whimper. Every question he asks makes less sense than the last. He asks me about things that I honestly don't know the answer to—people I've never heard of, places I've never been—and I stop needing to lie.

Another eternity passes before he walks around the table and crouches next to me.

"Who are you protecting?" he asks, his voice dropping to a near whisper. "And why? I think you need to ask yourself, little bird, if it's worth it."

He reaches out to push aside the hair sticking to my sweaty forehead. I hold in another whimper, my lip quivering with the effort.

"It's time to come clean. Help us, and we'll help you," he continues, molding his features into an expression of what he must think benevolence looks like.

It doesn't look like that.

Whatever it is they think I know, one thing feels clear: Brant was wrong. The Tribunal is not going to let me go.

I muster the infinitesimal amount of defiance I have left in me and spit it directly into Wolfe's face.

He sighs as he wipes my saliva from his cheekbone. Slowly, he pulls the black gloves off his hands, finger by finger, and lays them carefully on the table.

"Fine," he says. "If that's how you want it, that's how we'll play it. Just remember, I tried to go easy on you."

I gasp as his fingers curl into a fist and his eyes narrow. He rears his arm back, and I grip the underside of my chair with white knuckles, bracing for the bone-crushing impact.

But I don't look away.

Wolfe slams his fist into the left side of my face with such force that it momentarily blinds me. When my vision returns half a second later, it is dotted with white spots. Tears pool in my eyes. I feel them run down my free hand as I cradle my cheek, praying the tears are all that's making my face wet.

Nearby, a beeping noise sounds and the table vibrates.

I blink slowly and see Wolfe shaking out his hand as he walks around the table to retrieve the beeping device. He reads something on the screen and curses under his breath.

"Looks like you're off the hook, little bird. Your processing is over." He gives me an appraising once-over before adding, "You must really be something special."

I want to ask him what he means, to demand an explanation, to curse him and his whole family and the day he was born. I want to say anything at all. But I know if I open my mouth, all that will come out are the sobs I am struggling to contain.

Wolfe slips the device into his pocket and grabs the syringe. I should be terrified of the blue liquid, but something is broken inside me and the fear doesn't come. Instead, I just feel . . . relieved.

At least this part is over.

Wolfe rubs a piece of wet cloth on the side of my neck. I don't remember seeing the cloth on the tray, but it has the burning odor of alcohol and makes my skin tingle as it dries.

"This might hurt a little," he says, and the irony of that statement coming from the man who just punched me in the face is not lost on me. I release a small gasp as he pushes the needle into my skin, but within moments, the throbbing in my cheek begins to fade. My eyelids droop, and the last thing I see before they close completely is Inquisitor Wolfe, reaching for me.

THE ROOM IS TOO BRIGHT.

I squint against the harsh light, sucking in a few slow breaths as I attempt to discern where I am. Gone is the room with the tiny metal table and the tray of orange pills. Blessedly, also gone is Wolfe.

Like with apparently everything in this godforsaken building, the room is stark white and almost entirely empty. Two black-suited guardsmen stand near a door on the opposite wall, and a row of tall cabinets—also white, go figure—line the other side of the room. A table piled high with electronics is off to one side.

I inspect the guardsmen quickly, tensing when I notice the silver handguns strapped into holsters on their hips. I don't remember those being part of the standard uniform.

I wish I could see more, but as I awaken further, as my sensibilities return to me, I realize I am restrained. I am standing, but not of my own volition. I couldn't sit or lie down even if I tried. Cuffs are clamped around my wrists and ankles, a large plate pinning my chest to the wall, holding me upright. The only thing I can move is my head, though the painful pulse over my left cheek doesn't make that particularly easy either.

As my eyes fully adjust to the room's brightness, my ears begin to prickle with the sound of labored breathing next to me. With not a small amount of effort, I manage to wiggle my head to the left to determine the source.

"No." The word escapes my lips unbidden, a reflex.

My eyes are frantic as they roam over a mess of blonde hair, a familiar-looking gray jacket.

Because next to me, passed out and chained up in exactly the same way, is Adam.

TWENTY-FOUR

"ADAM? ADAM!" A smarter woman might have tried to keep her voice low, but there's no hiding my hysteria.

Adam's eyes flutter weakly as he turns his head in my direction and I exhale in relief. He's conscious. He's alive.

"Hey, Sunburst," he says feebly, attempting his lopsided grin. His lower lip is puffy and there's a shadow over his right eye, like he's been in a fight. I grimace as I realize that after my session with Wolfe, I probably look much worse.

"Are you okay?" I ask, although I'm not sure why. As though the answer isn't blatantly obvious.

"Oh, sure. You know me. I'm a trooper," he says, but as he turns his head to face forward again, he visibly winces.

"How—why—what—" My words come out in a jumble. A small part of me is relieved to see him, but that fear that went missing before I was knocked out? Well, a much larger part of me just found it. Terror ricochets through my veins, bringing with it a thousand questions. Why is he here? *How* is he here? Is this part of their tactic to get me to talk? And if they took Adam to get to me, then . . .

"Where's Mica?" I say suddenly. "Is he—"

"It's okay," Adam says, cutting me off. "Mica was gone

when . . . when they came for me. He's just a kid, they aren't interested in him."

My eyes burn, more of that relief and fear warring in my chest. "Oh, God, I'm sorry, Adam. I'm so, so sorry. This is all my fault."

He turns to look at me again, his brow creased. "What are you talking about?"

"It's me. I . . . I took that broken machine that you had, back in the . . ." I trail off before I let the word "biodome" slip out. I want to explain everything to Adam, but considering what I went through to keep Wolfe from confirming my jaunt into the ruins, there's no way in hell I'm risking one of the guardsmen hearing me.

I lower my voice to a whisper. "The converter. It looked exactly like this other machine I found before we met, and they'd paid out so much for that one so when I saw another, I just couldn't help myself. I'm sorry. They flagged me the second I turned it in. And when I couldn't answer their questions, they—" I swallow. "It's my fault you got dragged into this."

I suck in a deep breath and wait for Adam's reaction, preparing for the worst. To my complete and utter shock, the emotion that pours from his brilliant blue eyes is not anger. It's something that looks a lot like pity.

"Sunburst, this is not your fault," he says, and my own brow furrows. "Should you have let me know about the conversion unit? Maybe." He barks out a fractured laugh. "But this? This isn't about you."

"What is it about then?"

Adam doesn't answer.

"My interrogator said something," I press. "Something about a crash and . . ." The details of my processing are hazy. I try to regroup my thoughts. "Was the converter—conversion unit, whatever . . . Was it stolen or something? Is that why we're here? When I was being ques-ques-tioned"—I stutter over the word—"they said I was in possession of illegal technology."

"What does that mean, when you were being *questioned*?" His eyes finally seem to focus on my face, lingering on the space under my left eye before he meets my gaze. "What did they do to you?" he demands.

"Nothing that can't be undone," I say unconvincingly. "Eventually." I can't maintain his stare; the drug-induced visions are too fresh. Of course,

I don't know what I'm expecting to hide from him. It's likely he is a victim of a similar interrogation.

"Terra . . ." His voice is soft, but the knowing way he says my name wrenches something in my chest. His sympathy—his *pity*—hits me like a physical blow, and something inside me snaps. "What have we done?" I yell at the guardsmen. "Let us go!"

"Try to stay calm," Adam says. The guardsmen glance over with impassive expressions before turning their backs to us.

I drop my voice again. "Can you . . . can you do your thing?" I ask Adam. "FX your way out of these?" I wiggle my fingers as much as the cuffs will let me.

He looks at me warningly. "Shh," he says, throwing his eyes toward the guards. His forehead creases in concentration, but after a few moments he shakes his head. "Can't focus it like this. I need my hands." His voice is barely louder than a breath.

"Why is this happening?" I whisper. I'm desperate for his assurance that everything is going to be okay, that this is all just some kind of misunderstanding.

Instead, he simply faces forward once more. "You'll find out soon enough," he says, setting his mouth in a hard line.

I hear a door slide open and the clack of high heels on the floor. A woman wearing a mint green blazer crosses the room to stand directly in front of us, her auburn hair slicked back into a tight bun.

She pulls her spectacles from the breast pocket of her blazer and frames them over icy blue eyes.

Prime Morrigan Whitlock.

"Excellent, you're both awake," she says cheerfully. She turns to me. "Hello, Terra."

I stare at her, words refusing to form on my tongue. What is one of the most important people in Korbyllis—the world, even—doing here?

Delusion settles in my chest as I summon the idea that she's somehow connected with Adam, that she's been called here—by his team, his research department, somebody—and is here to help. But as soon as I note the way her gaze narrows on the two of us, my theory is snuffed out, along with that singular spark of hope.

She sighs, crossing her arms across her chest. "Let's try that again. I am Morrigan Whitlock, Prime of the Tribunal. Hello."

"I know who you are," I muster.

"Of course you do," she says. "This is your first visit to the skyworld, I understand. Tell me, Terra, what do you think of it?"

I huff a breath. "It's not quite what I expected."

Prime Whitlock laughs—a cold, high-pitched squeal. "Understandable. It is unfortunate that your first taste of Korbyllis had to be under these circumstances. I heard your processing with Inquisitor Wolfe did not go well."

"That's one way to put it."

"He's one of our most talented Inquisitors, you know. Most people crack within minutes. But not you. Which is why we had to put our secondary plan in motion." She gives a casual wave of her hand in Adam's direction. "We initially went looking for your brother, of course. A bargaining chip, if you will."

"What?" My voice jumps an entire octave before I turn to face Adam again. "You said they didn't want him."

He refuses to meet my gaze. "I didn't want you to worry."

"You young people are so dramatic. Fear not, Terra. Your *man* was there to save the day." Prime Whitlock purses her lips and focuses her attention on Adam, looking him up and down. "The arresting guardsman said you offered yourself up in her brother's stead immediately. Very noble. Especially in light of what I'm sure you knew would happen."

My mouth falls open. Adam grits his teeth.

"Of course, it was you we were looking for all along, wasn't it?" She pauses for a moment, turning her gaze back on me and peering through her spectacles with feigned sympathy. "Which, sadly, makes everything this poor girl has gone through pretty much moot. Pity."

My thoughts are like mud, a sticky mess swirling together in my mind. "What is she talking about?" I ask.

"Yes, why don't you explain things to her?" says Prime Whitlock, her mouth curving into a smirk. "Though I have to say, with all your gallivanting across her settlement, all that time spent *bonding*, I'm a little surprised you haven't taken the time to tell her already."

Adam glares at Whitlock, his expression so dark, he's almost unrecognizable. "Why don't you take those pseudo-intellectual glasses and go find yourself a different toy, you skydwelling witch?"

In an instant, her smooth smile is gone. "Right, I think that's enough from you." With a snap of her fingers, one of the guardsmen swoops down to wrap a black cloth around Adam's mouth.

"Don't—" I start to object, but there's no point. Before I can finish my thought, the gag is in place. Adam grunts against it for a moment, biting down on the thick fabric, but quickly falls silent.

"We've been watching you quite closely since that day at the Collection, Terra. We wanted to give you the benefit of the doubt, of course. Even rewarded you handsomely for your trouble. But you couldn't let it be, could you?"

My heartbeat pounds in my ears. "I didn't know what it was. I was just curious."

"Imagine my surprise when, a few days later, you simply . . . disappeared. Gone—all day, all night. Nobody knew where, and nobody seemed to know when you'd be coming back. And when you did finally return, you had this one in tow." She jerks her head toward Adam.

"We weren't completely sure who he was at first, of course, so we had to keep our distance. Lucky for us, his sense of self-preservation seemed to be overtaken by his desire to find the rest of his team. The more he pranced about throughout your sad little settlement, the surer we became of his identity. Then, it was just a matter of getting a hold of him. Which is, of course, where you came in."

Muffled shouts pour from Adam's mouth.

Prime Whitlock only raises her voice. "Really, we should be thanking you, Terra. We knew he'd be much too slippery to nab right off the bat, so we had to think of another way to reel him in. You and your brother were the obvious choices, given how much time you all were spending together, but finding a legitimate reason to get to you proved a bit problematic. You saved us a lot of trouble by being so delightfully predictable." She glances over at the guardsmen and releases a wistful sort of sigh. "Terrestrials, am I right?"

One of the guards chuckles in response, and my anger feels like fire burning a hole right through my chest.

Prime Whitlock clucks her tongue. "When you turned in the second machine, you gave us just the excuse we needed to scoop you up for questioning. I suppose I can't even blame you. Were I in your shoes, and suddenly had access to all that technology—"

"I. Don't. Know. What. You're. Talking. About!" I scream, confusion, concern, and contempt clashing inside me. "I don't know what *technology* you're talking about. I just found the machines. Two machines, that's all."

She peers at me overtop her glasses. "I'm sure."

"Just tell us what you want," I plead. "If this is about the quarantine violation, I swear, there's nothing wrong with us. We didn't contract anything or—"

Prime Whitlock's eyebrows shoot up her forehead, her gaze darting from Adam to me. "My, my," she says. "You really don't know."

"Know what?" I half scream, half sigh.

"Even after Wolfe couldn't get you to talk, we still assumed you had to know *something*," she says, and it suddenly seems like she's only speaking herself. "The proximity of the landing site to the ruins . . . the conversion unit . . . the quarantine breaches . . ."

"Know *what*?" I repeat, clenching my jaw.

Adam jerks against his restraints.

"Didn't you ever wonder, Terra?" Her icy eyes are piercing as she paces in front of me. *Clack, clack, clack.* "How he knew so much, but still had so many questions? Why he was so interested in Genesis X-16? In *you*?"

"I got over it," I spit.

"Once again, I guess I can't blame you," she continues, ignoring my remark. "If you had bothered to finish your schooling, you might have picked up on it sooner."

The insult is more cutting than it should be. "You don't know anything about me."

"Oh, please. We know *everything* about you." She reaches down to unhook a small computer tablet clipped to her belt, and begins reading aloud. "Terra Eryth Rhodon. Eighteen years old. Two living blood relatives. A resident of the Western Quadrant of Genesis X-16. Ceased schooling at the age of fifteen. To take up scavenging, of all things," she adds.

Disdain drips from her voice as she continues to pace. Clack, clack.

"Legal guardian of one younger brother, Auron Mica Rhodon, age thirteen. Oh, would you look at that? Age fourteen, as of today. How sweet." Her smile is full of falsities as she looks at me, and my heart sinks.

Happy birthday, Mic. I'm sorry.

"You aren't exactly a superior example of the groundworld education system, are you?" she continues. "Not that education down there amounts to much in general, but still. Your knowledge of Earth's history is almost as antiquated as his."

Adam's restraints rattle as she jerks her head in his direction again.

"Plus or minus a few centuries, I suppose." She laughs appreciatively, as though she's just told the most hilarious joke. Abruptly, she stops pacing, hooks her tablet back onto her belt, and plants herself directly in front of Adam.

She reaches out with long, manicured fingers and grabs his chin, forcibly turning his head from side to side. He stifles a groan as her fingers press into his bruised jawline.

"Get your hands off him," I snarl, straining futilely against my bonds.

"Ooh, touchy." She smirks, but releases him. "All right, fine. If you haven't figured it out by now, allow me to be the bearer of bad news."

Adam's eyes widen with something that looks like a plea.

"Your boyfriend is not like you," she says, each word spoken slowly, like she's talking to a child.

"I know that," I reply, rolling my eyes. "He's one of you. Any idiot can tell that."

Prime Whitlock laughs again, her screech ringing in my ears, a sound I'll never be able to forget. "What an apt choice of words. But no, my dear. What I meant to say is, he is not from *here*."

I blink at her.

"Not from Earth," she clarifies.

I snort. "Please don't tell me our government is being led by some space nut conspiracy theorist. You're trying to tell me he's, what, an alien?" The word sounds so ludicrous slipping off my tongue that I can't help but laugh.

"You're smart to be skeptical. Surprisingly so. But it's true. He and his crew crashed their—for lack of a better term—*spaceship* near the ruins of the District. I'm still not sure how we missed him during the extraction.

We didn't even know he existed until he came back with you. The others were all quite tight-lipped on the subject."

"Others?"

"While the two of you have been playing house, we've been putting the rest of them to good use."

Adam attempts to lunge forward against his chest plate, screaming in his throat.

"It's clear that whatever resources they used to learn about our culture are rather outdated. Aside from that, however, their technology is quite astounding. We decoded his companions' datapads, not without difficulty. Their plan was quite clever, really. They look just like us, after all. Barely even extraterrestrial. So, they come down here armed with a basic understanding of human history and, hey, what do you knw? They almost blend right in."

My jaw is slack, though it tenses when she reaches a hand toward Adam's face again. She stops just before touching him this time, like she's thought better of it.

"Almost," she adds, turning back to me. "You understand now, don't you, Terra? Whatever he's been telling you, whatever he's been having you do for him, he's just been using you for information. Settlement locations, population numbers, military tactics . . . and before you know it"— she bangs her fist on the wall between our heads—"invasion."

"This is ridiculous," I say, shaking my head. "I don't believe you."

"No? What, he's never displayed knowledge or produced technology beyond what you know to exist? He's never done anything suspicious, anything you can't quite explain? Given the time you've spent together, *that's* what I find hard to believe."

I stare at her, keeping my eyes narrowed to mask the thoughts running amuck in my mind. Something *does* feel out of place—maybe it always has. The miraculous portable water filters, his anxiety at the Assembly, his lack of groundworld knowledge, his FX, what happened to Loran Underwood . . .

Even when I had suspicions, I easily wrote them off as symptoms of his skyworld background. But a researcher working for the Tribunal should have been prepared for a quarantine investigation. And just a few minutes ago, he didn't want the guards to know about his abilities.

"Still not convinced?" Prime Whitlock says. "Fine, ask him yourself." With a brutal pull, she rips the gag from Adam's mouth and tosses it to the ground. He coughs violently.

"Adam?" I say softly, turning my head back toward him. I search his face, looking for some sign that Prime Whitlock is lying, that she's just trying to drive a wedge between us. Instead, his blazing blue eyes meet mine with fear and uncertainty.

"I—I . . ." he stutters, but he looks away before any actual words come out, like he can't bear to meet my gaze.

A rock the size of my fist sinks into my stomach. I taste bile in my throat, feel the blood drain from my face.

"Terra, no, it's not like that. She's twisting it, we just—" Adam starts, but the tablet at Prime Whitlock's waist starts to beep, interrupting him.

"Well, as much as I enjoy watching dashed hopes flit across this pretty young thing's face," she says loudly, talking over Adam as she pulls out the tablet again and reads a message on its screen. "I've got places to go, *people* to see." She stresses the word, staring right into Adam's dejected face.

Prime Whitlock tucks her glasses back into her blazer pocket and turns to me. "I'll allow you five minutes to . . . say your goodbyes. When you're done, you will be escorted home. It's clear enough to me that you have not been aiding and abetting him, so we have no reason to detain you further." Her icy gaze flits between Adam and me before she adds, "The guardsmen will be waiting for you outside if you decide you don't require all five minutes."

She chuckles to herself as she unlatches my wrist and ankle cuffs, then pulls a key from a chain around her neck to unlock the plate on my chest. I fall to the floor and catch myself with my hands, wobbling unsteadily.

Prime Whitlock hovers over me for a moment. "I do apologize for how you've been treated, Terra," she says with thinly veiled insincerity. "We had to assume the worst, you understand. Better safe than sorry, and all that. Speaking of which, we'll be leaving him locked up. Safety first!"

With that, she tucks the key back into her shirt and leaves, the guardsmen following her out, and it isn't until the door shuts behind them that the clacking finally fades.

TWENTY-FIVE

"SO, YOU LIED TO ME."

"Only a little?" Adam says, and though his tone is light, his eyes are glued to my face, tracking every shift in my reaction.

"This is not a joke." I try to look at him with new eyes, but all I see is the same Adam. Despite what Prime Whitlock said, I can't just leave him tied up and helpless. I loosen the bindings on his wrists, but I don't have a way to unlock his chest plate. I imagine that once his hands are free, his FX can take care of the rest.

"Technically, I never lied to you. You made assumptions based on the information you were given, and I simply failed to correct you." The side of his mouth starts to edge upward, forming that lopsided half-smile of his. It looks foreign now.

No, not foreign. *Alien.*

"You think you're going to get off on a technicality? Don't you think the whole 'I'm from outer space' thing should have come up at least once?" My voice rises and I take a deep breath to steady myself. I can't get carried away; who knows how alone we truly are.

"It's not that simple, Terra. I didn't want to scare you. I didn't want you to react like—well, like this."

"How am I supposed to react, Adam? Or, I'm sorry, is that even your real name? Or is it Zorqblatt, or something with a lot of Xs and Qs that our primitive human tongues can't pronounce?"

He rolls his cerulean eyes. "This isn't some sci-fi movie. It's not like Mica's comics."

"What is it, then?"

"It's complicated."

I snort. "So complicated you couldn't—wouldn't—even *try* to explain? Not once? Not when we were marveling at your ridiculously expansive knowledge, or the technology at your disposal, or your *fucking* telekinesis?

"You couldn't have pulled me aside and said, 'Oh hey, Terra, by the way, it's not a big deal or anything, but I just wanted to let you know that I'm not actually a skydweller. In fact, I'm not even from this planet. Okay, carry on.' " I throw my hands in the air and start pacing around the room. "God, I feel so stupid. I *am* stupid. I should have trusted my gut. I should have known something was wrong with you."

Adam flinches at my words, and for a second I regret them. Before I can even contemplate taking them back, however, he's already speaking.

"I was just trying to protect you," he says. "That's all I have done, all I've wanted to do, since the moment I first saw you."

"No. Don't give me that. You were lonely down there, you said so yourself. You were separated from your team, you felt abandoned, and I was the first living, breathing thing you came across." My hands ball into fists at my sides, and the sharp pressure of my nails digging into my palms is grounding. "All you've done is string me along with your charm and your wit and your goddamn grin, and the whole time you knew. You *knew*."

Adam's face falls.

The inner corners of my eyes prickle. "You knew that every minute you spent with us put Mica and me in danger."

"Please, just listen to—"

"And the worst part is that I believed you! Research? Sure! You came down here to explore? Came here to learn? Of course! Never mind *where* you came from in the first place. Never mind the fact that it was preparation for, what, some kind of invasion? Never mind the fact that you're not even *human*." My voice cracks on the word. "That's how you're so good, I see it now. You answered just enough of my questions, I never even thought to ask the one that really mattered."

"But it *doesn't* matter, Terra," he says, and his gaze is so piercing, his voice so earnest, I can feel my will already threatening to falter.

I refuse to let it.

"There is a reason that all of this has happened," he continues. "Our ship was malfunctioning. We were going to crash. My team told me not to, but I went out to fix an external part, and when I did . . . I was thrown. I fell. I shouldn't even have survived, but I did. Though by the sound of it, it was partly at Loran Underwood's expense, and believe me, I feel awful about that.

"By the time I woke up, I was alone. I thought my team might've stopped to look for me, but there was no sign of them. Not even landing marks. I figured they thought I was dead and had moved on. They had good reason to. I had no way to communicate and no idea where I was or where to go. The only city within sight was the District, completely devoid of life, but I couldn't stray too far. What if they came back? Came looking for me? If I left, it'd be just another thing to blame on my reckless impatience. For days, I was completely alone. I was so close to losing hope."

I exhale sharply through my nose. "You're just proving my point. I was your first living contact, that's it. It had nothing to do with me."

"It had everything to do with you! I could have landed anywhere, but I landed near Sixteen. Anyone could have found the conversion unit, but it was you who did. You could have run in any direction when the raiders were after you, but you ended up running into me. And finding you . . ." He swallows, and his voice is thick when he says, "Don't you see? We were *meant* to save each other."

My fists shake as I dig my nails in deeper. I don't want to hear this. I don't want any of it.

"So, I'm supposed to believe that this is all part of some greater plan? That it was, what, fate? I was meant to save you, huh? Why? So you could reunite with your extraterrestrial comrades and then what? Invade, enslave us, destroy us?"

"No, that's not even—" Adam tries to protest, but there's no stopping the inferno of words tumbling from me now.

"How long were you going to wait until you told me the truth? Until you could lock me up yourself? Until the rest of your *people* got here to back you up? I can't believe I thought—You made me think—You made me want—" My words catch in my throat. I glare at him, chest heaving, tears stinging threateningly behind my eyes.

No. He does not get this too.

I need to get away. I stumble toward the door as quickly as I can, despite the sudden blurring of my vision.

"Terra, don't," Adam says. "They aren't just going to let you go. Please tell me you see that. She's only doing this to mess with us. Don't give her what she wants."

I'm ten steps from the door.

"We can talk about this. I can help you understand. It's not what you think. It's not like she said!"

Five steps.

"Please," he begs. "I . . . I would never hurt you. I care about you. I—"

I reach the door just as the first tear spills down my cheek.

"Go to hell, Adam," I say, my hands curling into fists as I shove the door open. "Or, at the very least, go back to wherever the hell it is you came from."

TWENTY-SIX

"I'D LIKE to go home now," I say to the guardsmen standing sentry outside the holding room. I don't stop myself from crying; I don't think I could even if I tried.

The tears roll down my face as one guard catches his compatriot's eye, and they both nod in sync. They pincer me in as we walk down the hall: one leading in front, one at my back. We stop in front of an elevator and one of the guards hits the "Up" button.

"Where are we going now?" I ask, wiping my cheek with the back of my hand.

"There is some final paperwork you need to complete before you can be discharged," one of them says, his tone clipped, formal. "Your outprocessing."

"Oh." *Fine. Paperwork, I can handle.* "And my personal effects?"

"Those too."

I consider whether I'll be able to stomach wearing my mother's watch again. I can't bear to leave it behind, but I know that all it will do is serve as a reminder of this insanity. Of *him*.

The elevator dings, the doors open, and I am steered inside. I try not to, but I can't help wondering if Adam has freed himself from his restraints yet. Will he be able to get out? Where will he go when he does?

It doesn't matter, I tell myself. *He's not my problem anymore.*

The elevator dings again as we arrive on the fifth floor. A cursory look at the elevator's button panel indicates that this is the top floor of the building. Based on the number of sublevel buttons there are, however, it goes down much further than it goes up.

The guardsmen lead me down a hallway. Halfway down, there is a row of chairs lining the right side, facing wide windows that look out the front of the building.

"Wait here." One of the guardsmen guides me into a chair, while the other continues to the end of the hall and disappears inside a door. My body feels so heavy, I wish I could melt right into my seat.

I can still see through the windows from where I sit, and try to steady my breathing as I take in the scene outside. The sun casts a soft glow on the city, and everything looks completely different in the light of day; the glitz and glamour of Korbyllis nightlife have been replaced with polish and elegance. Potted plants frame the front doors of residences and small trees decorate the sidewalks every few yards and I'm instantly reminded of the biodome. I pinch the underside of my arm to stop that train of thought in its tracks.

Well-dressed citizens meander slowly through the streets below, engaging each other with pleasant expressions. It infuriates me to see how normal things are on the outside when, here, inside this building, my entire world has been forever altered.

I watch a sandy-haired boy cross the street, guided by a woman I assume is his mother, and I feel a pang in my chest.

Today is Mica's birthday. My baby brother's fourteenth birthday, and I'm not there. I don't even know if he's all right. The best I can hope for is that he's been left alone.

How ironic to be here in the very place I had wanted to send him. I'd been so consumed with how the skyworld could change his life for the better, but here I am, irreparably distorted by it instead.

I wait for a long time, gazing out the window and watching the sun glide slowly across the sky. The light grows warm and soft, and I watch it for so long that I nearly doze off in my seat—or maybe I did fall asleep and didn't realize it. I finally look up when the guard clears his throat, signaling the other guardsman's return.

"How much longer will this take?" I ask, standing on still somewhat shaky legs.

The guard ignores me as we rejoin his partner. We reach the door at the end of the hall and enter a laboratory. The room itself looks almost identical to the one I was held in with Adam—white walls, bright lights, and lots of open space. Along the walls, the restraints that bound us have been replaced by metal worktables, and instead of guards, a dozen white-coated workers bustle about. The back of the room is lined with a row of cots that have metal bars around them.

"What are we doing here?" I stop mid-stride. Something feels wrong.

"Outprocessing," one of the guardsmen says gruffly.

"I just want to go home."

"And you will." The guardsmen grip my shoulders firmly and tug me forward, toward the cots in the back. "After you are outprocessed."

"Stop," I say, struggling against their hold. A few of the lab workers look up at me. As we near the beds, I see a small silver tray with a syringe of blue liquid resting on top. A shiver runs through my entire body as my mind flashes back to my inquisition with Wolfe. "No!"

I'm not strong enough to force my way out of the guardsmen's grasp, so I let my legs fall limp and the dead weight of my body suddenly lurches toward the ground. It surprises the guards just enough that I'm able to wrench myself free. I turn on the spot and race back across the room, the surrounding lab technicians fading into a white blur as I pass.

Before I can reach the door, another guardsman enters through it. He sees me running toward him and draws his gun.

"Stop her!" yells one of the guards behind me.

The new guardsman pulls the trigger and I collapse, shuddering uncontrollably as an electric pulse races through my body.

The guard who stunned me loops his arms under my shoulders and starts to drag my convulsing, immobile body across the floor.

"Adam . . ." I mutter feebly, the words slipping off my tongue uninten-tionally. My brain feels like it's vibrating against my skull. "Adam, help . . ."

I can barely keep my eyes open. My brain and body, ravaged by the stun gun, are in total disarray. All I feel is the hard floor beneath my legs as I'm hauled backward, until I'm suddenly dropped and my head smacks against the tile.

A crash sounds.

Somebody curses.

The smell of burning.

A chorus of shouting.

I try to focus my eyes but the room is a watery blur. Fuzzy shapes race back and forth in front of me.

A siren goes off and suddenly there is a shadow crouching over me.

"Hey!" the shadow says harshly, barely audible over the commotion. "What did you just say?"

I stare blankly at the ceiling with unfocused eyes before a sharp sting echoes across my face as the shadow slaps my cheek. The pain pulses into the spot where Wolfe had punched me, making me slightly more aware. Just slightly.

"Ow," I say.

"What did you say before?" The shadow has a woman's voice. She wears a white coat. "Why did you say 'Adam'?"

"Because Adam's going to save me," I slur. "We were meant to save each other."

"Is he here? Is Adam here?"

"Of course he is," I say, my words garbled. My tongue feels like it weighs twenty pounds. "Where else would he be?"

"Get up," she says.

I try to sit up. I don't. My head flops to the side, my body refusing to listen to me.

"Oh, for crying out loud."

There is an explosion, then more shouting.

With half-open eyes, I see the desks around me start to move. No, wait. They're not moving. I am. My vision slowly starts to clear as my body slides across the floor, the rest of the room consumed in chaos.

"Luke! Come on, we've got to go!"

I am weightless. I float through the air as the shadow and I head for the door where we are joined by another white coat. This time, it's attached to a man with dark hair.

They move stealthily through the halls and into a stairwell. I glide along behind them as they descend, as if toted by an invisible rope.

"What are we doing, Charlie?" the man asks.

"You heard her. She said his name. She said he's here." Charlie pulls at the bun on the back of her head and a cascade of burgundy hair falls down her back.

"Impossible. We don't even know who she is." He scoffs. "She's been tazed—she's talking nonsense. Or worse, this could be a trap."

"I know what I heard, Luke. And you saw what happened in there. They wouldn't have been prepping her for outprocessing if she didn't know something. What other reason would there be to make her forget?"

"Well, she's not exactly in a state to tell us anything right now, is she?"

"Sorry, but it's not like we can go back," she says, not sounding sorry at all.

"And whose fault is that?"

We stop moving. Charlie opens a door and we enter what looks like a storage room. The mysterious force keeping me afloat breaks its hold on me, and my ass hits the floor beside a pile of crates. With the modicum of bodily control I've regained, I hoist myself into a seated position, leaning back against the boxes.

When I finally look up, Luke is barricading the door with a large crate. A few floors above us, the alarm is still going off.

"We should be okay for now," he says. "That was . . . chaotic. I don't think anyone noticed us because of the fire. But it's only a matter of time before they come looking. We need to get Tom and get out."

"Not before we hear what she has to say."

I blink. My vision restored, I am finally able to get a good look at my rescuers. Or are they my new captors? Luke towers over me, concern pouring from turquoise eyes that are framed by thick, dark eyebrows. Streaks of gray run from his temples back through his dark hair, though he doesn't otherwise look much older than Adam.

Charlie assesses me with an entirely different expression. Her violet eyes are narrowed and her jaw is stiff as she sheds her lab coat, revealing a form-fitting metallic jumpsuit. Svelte and leggy, her deep red hair looks a little listless and there are dark circles under her eyes, but she is otherwise stunning.

"Come on, out with it. What was that about back there?" she says abruptly. When I don't respond, she kicks the side of my foot with her shoe. "Hello, we don't have all day."

I stare at her in disbelief.

"Take it easy," says Luke. "She's clearly been through a lot."

Charlie crosses her arms but steps back to allow Luke to approach me.

"What's your name?" he asks kindly.

I bite my lip. "Terra."

"Oh, now she can talk," Charlie says.

"I . . . I . . ." I stammer, still regaining control of my verbal faculties, though there's *a lot* I'd like to say to her.

Charlie looses a melodramatic sigh, and my tongue finally unlocks.

"Just give me a minute," I say sharply.

"We don't *have* a minute," she spits back, but a scalding look from Luke has her backing off, her palms raised in supplication.

I suck in a deep breath, inhaling and exhaling three times before I'm ready to speak. "I don't know if you noticed, but I wasn't exactly in any shape to chat back there."

"And I don't know if you noticed, but we saved your scrawny ass back there."

"What is your deal?" I grit out.

"My deal? What's yours? How the hell do you know Adam?"

"Charlie," Luke cautions.

Realization slams into me. "It's you. You're the rest of his team. How you got me out back there, transported me here—that was FX."

I don't say it like a question, but Luke nods in affirmation anyway.

"How do you know about that?" Charlie asks angrily.

Luke ignores her. "Yes, we're his team. Most of it, anyway. I'm Luke. This ball of sunshine is Charlie. You obviously already know Adam. And there's a fourth, Thomas."

Charlie slaps him on the shoulder. "Stop talking. She's not the one who needs answers."

Luke rolls his eyes but takes a resigned step back.

"How do you know about us?" she repeats.

"He told me."

Charlie's nostrils flare. "Look, either you start giving us some real answers or—"

"Or what?" I challenge, getting to my feet and hoping my legs don't collapse beneath me. The fact that this woman thinks she can bully me into compliance after what I've been through has rage churning in my gut.

"Or—"

"Shh!" Luke holds his hand up, immediately silencing her. I listen intently for whatever sound is causing him alarm but hear nothing.

"I don't hear anything," I whisper.

Charlie shoots me a death glare.

Seconds later, a shadow passes over a crack of light at the bottom of the door, still visible despite the barricade. Charlie raises her hands defensively while Luke quietly pulls a small box from beneath a pile of linens on one of the storage shelves. My eyes widen when he lifts the lid and pulls out a gun.

I hold my breath.

The crate barring the door scrapes on the floor as the intruder pushes against it. Charlie's brow creases, beads of sweat gathering along her hairline. I can tell she's using her FX to try and keep the door shut, but whoever is trying to get in from the other side is just barely stronger than she is. The door creaks open an inch at a time.

Luke raises his gun and gestures for me to get behind him. With no small effort, I will my shaky legs to comply.

Charlie lets out the tiniest groan as her focus falters.

The door swings open.

Charlie sucks in a deep breath.

The gun falls to Luke's side.

"Well, this looks like quite the party." Adam's voice, warm and familiar, sounds from the doorway. "Mind if I crash it?"

TWENTY-SEVEN

DEAD SILENCE FALLS over the small storage room. The grin on Adam's face falters as Charlie, Luke, and I stare at him in bewilderment. Finally, Luke clears his throat, and the impasse breaks. My emotions churn up inside of me like a geyser, propelling my feet into motion before I can stop myself.

I don't think. I don't care. I just stumble straight into Adam's arms.

"It's okay," he says gently, stroking my back. "You're okay."

I lift my head from his chest and am unsurprised to see wet marks on his shirt. "You were right," I say bitterly. "They weren't just going to let me go."

Adam's embrace tightens. "What did they do to you?"

"Nothing. They didn't get a chance to, thanks to them." I look over at Luke, who is watching us in awe, and Charlie, who merely looks irritated. "I'm sorry I didn't listen."

"You have nothing to be sorry for. I, on the other hand . . ." He rakes a hand through his hair. "You must know I never meant to hurt you. And you know Whitlock was lying, right?" He glances at his teammates. "We don't intend to hurt anyone at all."

"I know," I say, and it's the truth.

"As adorable as this little reunion is, don't you think there's a slightly more pressing matter at hand here?" Charlie rolls her eyes as she repositions the barricade in front of the door.

"Nice to see you too, Chuck," Adam says with a grin as he guides me over to a box of supplies and helps me sit down. "You're sure you're okay?" he asks. I nod and he spins to face Luke.

There's a moment of hesitation as if neither of them knows what to say. Another second passes, awkwardness settling into the space between them. And they're laughing, having exploded into a clash of grins and back slaps and hugs.

"We thought you were dead," Luke says, his hands clamped on Adam's shoulders.

"I should be." The words come out on a laugh, but there's something broken about the sound. "I fell a long fucking way."

"How did you survive?" Charlie asks, and I'm surprised to see the raw emotion glistening in her violet eyes.

"My FX might not be quite at Charlie-like levels, but I guess it's a bit stronger than I thought."

She gives him a playful slap on the back, but says nothing, her lips pressed into a line like she's trying to keep herself from smiling.

"I managed to slow down just enough to save myself from shattering every bone in my body," Adam continues. "Still hurt like a mother though. Cracked a couple of ribs, I think." He looks guiltily in my direction. "And someone else got hurt because of it."

A few silent seconds pass before Luke speaks again. "Where have you been this whole time?"

Adam is still looking at me.

Luke follows his gaze. "Ah."

"I swear, I had no idea what was happening to you all. The fall knocked me out pretty good, and by the time I came to, there was no sign of you guys. No landing marks, nothing. My datapad was damaged when I hit the ground—I kind of got it to work? But the communicator function is all jammed up. I figured you thought I died and had moved on."

Charlie scoffs. "Give us a little credit. As if we would've left you behind."

"Maybe *you* wouldn't have."

"C'mon, man. You know better than to think that." Luke gives a sad shake of his head. "Tom's the one who insisted we land and look for you. We just never really got around to the second part."

"The Tribunal."

"Yep. With the ship malfunctioning, it was a rough landing. but we made it. Unfortunately, that ice queen Whitlock nabbed us before we even had a chance of finding you. Took us by complete surprise—I don't even know how they got there so fast. They grabbed us, the ship, everything. Then got rid of the evidence. Aside from you, I guess."

"How are you here? How did you find us?" Charlie asks.

"The abridged version? I got picked up from the groundworld and was shipped up here." Adam shrugs. "The next thing I know, I'm waking up in a holding room with Terra chained up next to me and I'm finding out you guys have been captive this whole time." He looks from Charlie to Luke and back again, his expression pained. "I am so, so sorry."

"You didn't know." Charlie's tone is softer now.

"A little while after they released Terra, a couple of guards came in to get me. I gave them the slip and went looking for you. Eventually, I overheard a few people talking about some commotion in the lab, and figured that'd be a good place to start. I caught sight of you all just as you were sneaking out and followed you down."

"And to think, all those hours you spent whining about how you can't track worth a damn," Charlie says with a grin.

For a few heartbeats, the three of them simply look at each other, the relief that's spun out of their reunion tangible. It's touching, and I hate to ruin the moment, but it feels like there's a clock ticking over our heads.

"Look, I don't want to offend anyone or anything," I say, voice breaking the silence, "but I'm having a hard time understanding why you guys are still, uh, here. If it's really like Prime Whitlock said, and the Tribunal fears some kind of alien invasion, why wouldn't they just kill you? And me, for that matter?"

"I don't really have an answer with regard to you," Luke replies. "Maybe it would raise too many questions, be too difficult to cover up. Or, I don't know, maybe the Tribunal actually does have some kind of conscience."

Charlie snorts.

"At least when it comes to the potential murder of an innocent civilian," he caveats. "But as for us? They need us."

Adam's brow furrows. "What do you mean?"

Luke scratches at his chin. "When we're not under lock and key, they have us working around the clock. They have Charlie updating the schematics of their oxygen generator; Tom's been practically living in the engine room. They monitor our conversations pretty closely, but from what we've been able to glean from each other we think they're—"

"Shh!" Charlie interjects, gesturing at me.

"She's fine," Adam says, taking my hand. "She's with me." I feel that familiar bloom of warmth under my skin.

Charlie rolls her eyes. "Figures you'd end up picking up a pet."

"Shut up, Charlotte."

"Don't call me that," Charlie replies, stiffening.

Adam rolls his eyes at her before turning back to Luke. "You think they're what?"

Luke hesitates. "We think they're trying to convert the city."

"Convert it into what?" I ask. They ignore me.

"But that would mean—" Adam starts.

"Exactly," Charlie says.

"And their plan is to launch?"

"Yes. I've seen the specs. They've got a ways to go, but still."

"Do they know . . . ?"

"Not that we can tell."

"Would full conversion be possible?"

"It's clear they've been working on it for a long time. Our being here has just . . . expedited things," she says bitterly.

"And the people below?"

"We have our theories," Luke says, "but they all end in pretty much the same outcome."

There is panic in Adam's cerulean eyes when he meets my questioning gaze.

I squeeze his hand. "What is it? What are you talking about? What conversion? What theories?"

Charlie lets out a frustrated sound—somewhere between a grunt and groan. "We don't have time to dumb it down for her. We need to get out of here. Now." She charges over to the entrance with her arm outstretched, moving the barricade aside with her FX like it's nothing and cracking open the door to peek outside.

I'm not sure when the alarm upstairs stopped sounding, but I am suddenly very aware of how quiet it is.

"We're clear," she says.

"The ship's on the main level," Luke says. "It's in some kind of shuttle bay out back. I imagine they've been messing with it, so we won't know if it'll still fly until we get to it."

"What about Tom?" Adam asks.

"He's down in the engine room, like always. Sublevel five."

"Okay, okay." Adam drops my hand to pace in a small circle, like it might help him formulate a plan. "We head to the ship together. Once we clear the guards, it'll only take one of us to make sure it'll fly. The other two go get Tom, and we'll all reconvene here. If the shuttle's operational, great. If not . . . we'll just have to figure something else out."

Charlie and Luke nod.

"So, who's getting us airborne? Chuck?"

"Hell no," she says. "You're not leaving me on mechanic duty while you two get to play hero. Make Luke do it."

Adam rolls his shoulders, like his irritation is physically weighing on him. "Fine. Luke?"

Luke nods. "Sure."

Adam nods right back, his brow furrowed in thought. Luke and Charlie look at him expectantly, like they're waiting for instructions. The instant deference they show him is honestly a little shocking.

"We've been stockpiling supplies as we've been able to get our hands on them, sneaking them onto the ship, hoping we'd get the chance to do this," Luke offers after a moment. "There should be more than enough to get us back."

"What about her?" Charlie gestures to me with her thumb.

"Terra will stay here with the supplies." He turns to me. "Don't worry, I'll be back for you."

"No way. I'm coming with you." I try to stand taller, to put on a brave face, but my legs still feel weak, and I have to keep one hand on the boxes behind me for support.

Adam shakes his head. "It's too dangerous."

"Besides, look at you. You can barely stand," adds Charlie. "You'll only slow us down."

I ignore her and steady myself enough to move next to Adam. "What do I have to worry about?" I say to him, forcing a note of dismissiveness into my voice. "You always save me anyway."

The breath he exhales sounds a little bit like a laugh as he laces his fingers through mine, and it makes me smile.

"Well, that was cheesy," Charlie says, and Adam's hand locked on mine is the only thing keeping me from returning the slap she gave me earlier.

"I'm not staying here," I tell her. "What if they find me? Then all your collective rescue attempts would have been in vain. Nobody wants that, right?" I crack a grin.

Charlie rolls her eyes. "You'd better keep up."

"You can stay with me while they pick up Tom. Here, take this." Luke hands me the gun. "Keep it on stun mode. It's better than nothing."

I wince as I take the weapon, remembering the immediate incapacitation my own run-in with a stunner caused. "To say the least."

Luke grins and I decide right then and there that I like him.

"All right. Let's move out," Adam says.

With a movement so smooth it seems choreographed, the three of them head toward the exit. I sidestep them, blocking the door just as Adam reaches for the handle.

"Wait," I say quickly. "Just wait. Somebody needs to explain to me exactly what is going on."

"Terra." Adam's eyes blaze. "There's no time."

"In the past day, I have been arrested, drugged, psychologically tortured, punched in the face, knocked out, tied up, stun gunned, and dumped with the equivalent of a Skyline train's worth of emotional cargo. I am still coming to grips with the fact that you all even exist in the first place. And, all things considered, I think I've been pretty damn understanding."

"Just make it snappy," Charlie says with a melodramatic sigh.

"Fine, look. It sounds like the Tribunal is trying to use our technology to convert this skycity," Adam speaks quickly, pulling me in close.

"I heard. What does that mean?"

"The skycities are in stasis, right? They stay in the same location."

"Of course," I reply. "Otherwise, how would anybody know where to find them?"

"Exactly. But conversion means the city would become mobile. It would have all of the capabilities of an aircraft—able to go pretty much anywhere."

I try to imagine an engine capable of moving an entire city. The thought is daunting, but I don't see why it's so horrifying to them.

"It's not just that though." Adam hesitates. "You know how because of the UV filter technology already in place, the environment inside each city is self-contained?"

"Sure?" I say, though it's obvious I'm anything but.

"This far above the cloud layer, the temperature and oxygen levels have to be regulated," Luke explains, "which is why the cities are fully encapsulated."

"Right, right." A vague recollection of various school lessons start to surface in my mind. "Which is why shuttles enter and exit from underneath."

Adam squeezes my hand. "So, it wouldn't take much for a city like this to be able to sustain itself without any oxygen on the outside at all."

I look at him blankly. "But when would that ever happen? Under what circumstances would that possibly be necessary?"

Adam looks at Luke and Charlie uneasily. Pity and regret flash between the three of them, and the answer comes to me.

Space.

There's no oxygen in space.

"The Tribunal wants to convert Korbyllis into a spaceship," I say, my voice hollow.

"I know how it sounds," Luke says quickly. "But this technology has been in development for a long time. Since before the skycities were even launched."

I want to ask him how he knows that. More than that, I want them to tell me that I'm wrong, that I've jumped to an utterly insane conclusion. But the sudden image of green grass swaying in a manufactured breeze takes over my mind, and I frown.

The biodome.

I can still feel the stems of the leaves I rolled between my fingers. The environment down there, almost entirely self-sustaining, has been able to thrive for hundreds of years. A precursor to the skycities.

"Skyfall," I say abruptly.

"What?" Adam, Luke, and Charlie say simultaneously.

"The Skyfall," I repeat. "The city of Intheria. Nobody knew what could have caused an entire skycity to fall, to simply plummet to the ground without warning. What if . . . what if it's because they tried to convert it? What if it's because something went wrong? I mean, Intheria was supposedly the stronghold for all scientific research back then. I suppose it makes a kind of sense that they would be testing conversion technology there."

"And not only did the conversion fail," Adam suggests, "but suddenly there was the plague to contend with too. Which explains why it took the Tribunal centuries to recreate the technology and get back on track."

"And why they want our help, our knowledge, so badly," Luke adds.

"Exactly," I say. "This planet is dying. The Tribunal instills that concept in our minds before we're even old enough to walk. They're always stressing how few resources there are left, how important it is for us to scav, to recycle, to maintain. If we had the ability to leave, to start over . . ."

"You can't possibly think it's a good thing that we've been kept here, forced to work on this," Charlie says, crossing her arms angrily.

"Don't be absurd, Chuck. She wasn't saying that." Adam squeezes my hand.

"I'm horrified the Tribunal has acted this way. I've gotten a crash course in what they're capable of." I point to my bruised cheek. "But you have to admit, the idea itself is kind of remarkable."

Charlie purses her lips.

"Why all the secrecy though?" I continue. "If the plan is to leave Earth for literally greener pastures, wouldn't it be more efficient to have all of us—skydweller, terrestrial, whoever—working toward the same goal? Helping with the conversion? Why the stealth, the secrets, the hush money?"

I see the sadness in Adam's eyes as he watches me work through this new information, and the answer clicks into place.

Oh.

"The plan isn't actually for all of us, is it? They're going to leave us here." My eyes widen in horror as I consider how long we would be able to survive without the skycities. They provide everything. We'd be goners within months.

A laugh bubbles up in my chest—a completely inappropriate response to the crushing realization that I'm unable to contain. By the time it reaches my mouth, however, it comes out as a sob. "We're dead."

Adam pulls me into him. "It's not going to happen," he says. "We won't let it."

"We've stalled their progress the best we can, provided them with fake algorithms, false information," Luke says. "They won't be able to finish the conversion without us."

I nod mechanically against Adam's chest.

Charlie clears her throat. "I know this must be difficult for you to process," she says to me, her tone surprisingly gentle. "But we really have to go."

"Ready?" Adam asks, and I nod again, though I don't think there's any possible way I could ever have been ready for this.

So, with the stunner gripped tightly in one hand and crushing Adam's fingers in my other, I follow them out.

TWENTY-EIGHT

WE CREEP INTO THE HALLWAY—CHARLIE in front, Adam at my side, Luke bringing up the rear. I keep the stunner at chest level as we move through the halls, my finger next to the trigger. We're almost to the stairwell when Charlie suddenly curses.

"Get back," she whispers.

We duck into a nearby restroom just as two guardsmen pass by. I listen at the door until their footsteps fade.

"Just a patrol," Luke says, cracking the door open before slinking back into the hall.

We dash out of the bathroom and into an empty stairwell. Muting our footsteps as much as we can, we descend to the main floor.

"There." Charlie points to the frosted panel inlaid in the stairwell exit door. A dark silhouette moves behind the glass; a guardsman is standing on the other side.

With a wave of his arm, Adam uses his FX to knock the guard's head back against the wall. He slumps to the floor, and Luke opens the door to drag him into the stairwell.

"Done this before, have you?" I say quietly to Adam.

Grinning, he tucks the guard's gun into his waistband, and we exit onto the main floor.

Despite its spacious, open layout, we fail to encounter any other guards or workers as we work our way toward the back of the building. The lack of activity unnerves me. The Tribunal has to know something is amiss. Even if they hadn't picked up on Charlie and Luke's absence, the trail of incapacitated guardsmen that Adam left in the wake of his escape must have raised some alarms. So, where's the siren? The mayhem? The search party?

"This is too easy," I whisper as we rush across yet another empty room.

"Maybe luck's finally on our side," Luke says. "This door should take us outside."

"All right, remember the plan," Adam says, halting our steps. "We need to be faster than fast. We subdue the guards, get Luke and Terra a clear path to the ship, then make a break for Tom. Chuck, you know where he'll be?"

Charlie nods. "I can get us there."

"Then we're gone."

I don't ask where it is we'll be going. I don't think I want to know.

We exit into a deserted courtyard at the side of the building. The dusky light hitting the Capitol Building casts long shadows over us, concealing our movement.

"That's the shuttle bay there," says Luke, pointing to the back of what looks like a massive metal box missing its lid. "Entrance is on the other side. They keep two guards on duty at all times, so be ready."

"We'll take them from both sides," Adam directs. "Luke, Charlie, head up from the left. We'll go right." He turns to me. "Stay behind me."

Adam and I sneak up one side of the building, our backs flat against the wall. He looks at me and lifts his eyebrows. I nod.

Quick as lightning, he darts around the corner. I take a deep breath before following him, only to crash straight into his back.

"What are you—" I start to whisper, cutting myself off as soon as I look up. Ten guardsmen stand in front of us, guns at the ready, Luke and Charlie already lined up before them.

They were waiting for us.

With a jerk of his gun, one of the guards summons us forward. I catch a flash of silver behind their heads, and clock the very alien-looking ship docked at the back of the shuttle bay.

I stay tucked halfway behind Adam, holding my gun against my chest as if I might bully my heartbeat into slowing down.

"So, in retrospect," Luke says quietly as he and Charlie line up beside us, "I take back what I said about luck."

"We were wondering when you'd get here," I hear from the throng of guardsmen.

The voice makes my heart jump into my throat. The guardsmen part as Inquisitor Wolfe walks out of the bay entrance. "What an unexpected treat," he says coolly, his eyes piercing right through me. "Hello again, little bird."

My entire body seizes and I grab Adam's arm with my free hand. He tenses and lets out a snarl, but it takes me a second to realize it's not on my account.

Two paces in front of Wolfe is a blond man with a slim build. He stares at the ground, but I don't need to see his face to know who he is.

"Tom!" cries Charlie.

Her outburst causes an immediate reaction from the guards. All ten guns turn toward her. She and Luke simultaneously pull hidden guns from their waistbands and point them back at the firing squad. I follow suit, raising my weapon with shaking hands, while Adam raises a gun of his own and points it directly at Wolfe.

Tom looks up and his eyes meet mine.

Cobalt. Indigo. Sapphire. Cerulean.

That bluest blue—Adam's blue—staring right at me.

"Oh, good," Tom says tiredly as his eyes lock onto Adam. "You're alive."

"Hey, Tommy," Adam says. "Good to see you too, brother."

Wolf clucks his tongue. "I'd drop those weapons if I were you."

"And I'd let him go if I valued staying alive," Adam says darkly.

"Tsk, so hostile. What happened to all that 'We come in peace' stuff?"

Adam clicks the safety on the side of his gun off.

"I wouldn't be so hasty if I were you." Wolfe turns to the side to give us a clear view of the gun pressed between Tom's shoulder blades.

Tom looks apologetic as I sense every muscle in Adam's body coiling with tension.

"Now, here's how this is going to work," Wolfe says. "You're all going to come with us quietly, and we're not going to kill any of you."

Charlie lets out a single laugh.

"It's a good deal. I suggest you take it."

"You won't kill us," she says. "You need us."

"It's true, Prime Whitlock did make it clear that we were not to use any fatal means of detaining you. Of course, the Prime isn't here, is she? And she certainly wouldn't be able to blame me if one of you was, say, putting the lives of these good men at risk."

"You're bluffing," she replies steadily.

Wolfe laughs. "Maybe I am, maybe I'm not. I guess you'll have to ask yourself if that's a risk you're willing to take." Tom inhales sharply as Wolfe presses the barrel deeper into his back.

An eternity passes. Nobody moves. The silence is deafening. I feel each rapid beat of my heart, hear each pulse in my ears. Sixteen people with fifteen guns, poised and ready. Deadlocked. One stray twitch of a trigger finger and we all go down.

"All right, fine. Since we seem to be at a bit of an impasse, allow me to further emphasize my point. I am going to disable this gun's stunner safety. If you do not immediately drop your weapons, I will kill him. Simple as that."

Wolfe clicks his gun into kill mode.

Not even half a second later, Adam reluctantly drops his.

"Good boy. Now, the rest of you."

Luke and Charlie lower their weapons to the ground, where they are quickly retrieved by nearby guardsmen.

"You too, little bird."

I glower at Wolfe as I crouch down and place my gun on the grass. When I stand back up, Adam, Luke, Charlie, and Tom all have their hands raised—palms up—in surrender.

"You win," Adam says. "We'll come with you. Just don't hurt him."

Wolfe smiles—a wicked, toothy grin. "Now those are words I like to hear." He pulls his gun off of Tom's back and shoves him forward.

In the split-second Wolfe breaks eye contact to holster his weapon, eight arms simultaneously fling downward. All fifteen guns career out of their owners' hands and fly into the open shuttle bay at the behest of the team's FX.

"No!" Wolfe shrieks.

"Now!" Adam yells.

Luke turns on the spot and sprints into the bay, making a beeline for the sleek silver ship.

With a grunt and a wave of her arm, Charlie sends six of the approaching guardsmen off their feet. Adam clotheslines one of the guards, knocking him to the ground, then body slams another. Tom throws an elbow backward and connects with Wolfe's nose before launching himself into the melee.

They move like a dance: graceful, lithe, powerful. The now-unarmed guards never stood a chance.

A lone guardsman hurtles toward me and instinct kicks in. I drop to the ground just as he's reaching to grab me, jutting my leg out and causing him to trip. He hits the ground face-first. I roll him over, my fingers curled into fists, but he's already unconscious.

Luke's victorious cry suddenly rings out from the shuttle bay, followed by the unmistakable roar of an engine. Charlie, Adam, and Tom all immediately turn and run toward the sound.

"Terra, come on!" Adam shouts as he races past me.

I pick myself up off the ground and am just about to charge after them when I see it.

Wolfe, with one hand still blocking the blood pouring from his nose, reaches into his boot and draws a small gun. It is no stunner special. It's old. The kind that I've only ever seen in movies. The kind that is actively outlawed due to the shatter risk it poses to the UV filter.

With a bloody grin, Wolfe raises the pistol and aims it directly at Tom's back.

"No!" I cry, leaping forward. I don't have a goal. I know I won't be able to reach him, won't be able to push him out of the way. I just know that I have to do something.

The pistol goes off with a deafening bang.

I fall to the ground.

Adam curses and rushes back to crouch next to me as I clutch at my right leg, a strangled cry held hostage in the back of my throat. Blood seeps from the bullet hole in my thigh, painting my hands red as I try to stem its flow.

Wolfe raises his gun again; with a flick of his wrist, Adam knocks the weapon out of Wolfe's hands before slamming him backward into the ground.

The pain is like nothing I've felt before. The bullet hit me high on the outside of my leg, almost at my hip. It feels like my thigh is both on fire and being doused in ice. In one moment it's burning, and the next it's as if the same spot is being stabbed over and over.

Adam pulls off his shirt and wraps it around the wound, tying it as tightly as he can—a makeshift tourniquet. The fabric is soaked with crimson in seconds.

"Adam! Let's go!" Charlie calls. She and Tom are already at the shuttle.

"Can you stand?" Adam's voice is strained, desperate.

The mere act of lifting my leg is unbearable. I choke on air as I try to breathe through the pain, but it's too much.

"I can't," I sob.

He says nothing, gives me a single, solemn nod before throwing my arm over his shoulder, his other hand stretched out as he uses his FX to telekinetically bear some of my weight.

We've barely gotten upright when I hear the shouting. I look back to see a sea of black uniforms barreling toward us.

Reinforcements have arrived.

The wave of guardsmen begins preemptively firing off stun shots. One clips Adam in the arm and we both collapse.

I scream in pain. Adam jumps up, hooks his good arm around me, drags me inside the shuttle bay, and tucks me into a corner where the oncoming guards don't have a clear shot.

I gag my cries with my fist, biting down to muffle my wails. Falling has more than renewed the pain; it's sharper, more piercing now. Adam looks at me, his face filled with terror as the pings of missed stun shots reverberate off the bay walls. They're getting closer.

"Shit," he says, his voice constricted, panicked. "What do I do? What can I do?"

I bite my cheek to distract myself from the pain enough to speak. "Go. You need to get out of here."

"No."

"If you don't go now, you'll never get out."

"I'm not leaving you."

"You have to. I'm not the only one who needs you. Please, Adam, you have to run."

"Adam! What the hell are you doing?" Tom's voice is barely audible between the sound of the ship's engine and the oncoming horde.

Adam stands. He hesitates.

"Go!" I scream.

"I *will* come back for you." Time stands still as he crushes his lips to mine before dashing to the back of the shuttle bay, his speed boosted by his FX. He hurtles himself at the ship just as it lifts off, latching his good arm onto the rungs of a short ladder on the side.

The engine's thunderous roar vibrates in my bones as I turn my gaze back to the cavalry that has almost reached me. I put my hands flat on the ground to help me rotate into a better vantage point when I feel something hard beneath my palm.

My fingers curl around Wolfe's pistol just as the first guardsmen arrive. They don't even notice me. The ship rising overhead throws them into a frenzy—they begin firing directly at the hull. Their shots deflect uselessly and I almost laugh, though whether it's in response to their failure or because of the blood loss, I can't say.

My delirium is quickly replaced with panic as the ship spins. I watch in horror as Adam, still hanging from its side, is fully exposed to the guards.

No.

My arm acts of its own accord, raising the pistol and aiming it at the nearest guardsman, his gun pointed clearly at Adam. I close my eyes.

Bang.

There's a yelp and the sound of rushing footsteps. I open my eyes to see one of the other guards fire off three stun shots in my direction. One grazes my outstretched hand and sends it into spasm, forcing me to drop the pistol.

The rest of the guardsmen rush toward me and I know it's over. My leg throbs in rhythm with my heart, and the adrenaline drains from my veins. I am simultaneously sweltering and freezing. My body is shutting down.

Two guardsmen drag me out of the shuttle bay by my wrists, and there is a dull pop as one of my shoulders is wrenched from its socket, though it's nothing compared to the still-searing pain in my leg.

My vision starts to blur. I watch the ship glide away, and try to focus on what little I can see of Adam's form, still hanging onto the side. Someone thrusts an arm down to pull him up—Tom, maybe—but blackness overtakes me and I don't get to see what happens next.

TWENTY-NINE

I WAKE IN A DAZE. The room is, once again, too bright, and my eyes are bleary. I try to lift a hand, to wipe at the wetness gathered along my lashline, but I can't.

I can't move at all.

Something pins me to whatever I'm laying on, but when I look, nothing appears to be holding me down. A clear tube runs out from the inner crook of my elbow, but I can't see what it connects to.

Two blurry figures loom over me, speaking in hushed tones. Panic swells in my chest and I try again to sit up, to roll over—to do *anything*—but I'm frozen in place. All I manage to do is send a jolt of throbbing pain through my shoulder, and a stab of sharp pain to my thigh.

"She's waking up," someone says. A man, I think.

"Do it quickly then, before she's fully lucid," responds a second voice, feminine yet coarse.

Firm hands grip both sides of my shoulder. There's pressure, then a pinch, then an ear-splitting wail; it takes a full second before I realize I'm the one making the sound. The agony of my shoulder being popped back into place momentarily eclipses the searing pain in my leg, but not for long.

Every sense is heightened, worsened by my inability to move, trapping me in torment. Tears stream down my temples and mix with my hair, which is pooled loosely around my head.

"Seems we didn't administer enough," the man says.

Through my panic, the pain sharpens my senses, allowing me to absorb my surroundings. I'm back in the laboratory, lying on one of the cots lined up along the rear wall. My attendants wear white masks and caps, their blue eyes exposed as they stare down at me.

"Just sedate her again," instructs the woman with a wave of dismissal. "Enough to knock her out until tomorrow. The morning shift can deal with her."

Light purple liquid runs down the tube into my arm. Warmth spreads up my body and the pain starts to dissipate as darkness edges my consciousness again.

"Wait . . ." I say feebly.

My attendants suddenly straighten up and turn to face the same direction; someone is speaking, someone new. I can't make out what they're saying, but as I slip back under, I could swear I hear something that sounds a lot like *clacking*.

I AM SITTING UPRIGHT when I awaken again. The cot has been adjusted so that the top half is raised, giving me something to prop up against. A wire is pinned to my chest just below my clavicle, connecting me to a monitor that beeps idly.

I'm draped in an oversized hospital gown. A wave of relief washes over me as I realize I can move my limbs again, and I grab a fistful of the gown's scratchy white material, rolling it between my fingers. My leg is tightly bound with a hefty bandage covering the entire upper section, and my shoulder pulses with a muted ache. I'm still hooked up to the IV, but whatever chemical had rendered me immobile appears to have worn off.

"Finally," says a bored voice. "Took you long enough."

Prime Morrigan Whitlock sits in a comfortable-looking chair next to my bed, observing me over the top of her glasses.

"Leave us." She dismisses two guardsmen I hadn't noticed.

"What happened?" I say groggily.

"What do you remember happening?" she asks.

I squeeze my eyes shut as I try to recall those last moments in the shuttle bay. "There was shooting . . . Shooting and chaos and—" My eyelids snap open as the image of Adam dangling from the side of the airborne ship flashes through my mind. "They were going to kill him. They were trying to shoot him down."

"Mmm, yes, I can see how that would be a very alarming scene to witness. Which is why, I assume, you felt the need to interfere?"

"Oh, God," I say, remembering the way Wolfe's pistol had shuddered as I pulled the trigger. The beeping on the monitor accelerates. "Did I . . . did I . . . ?"

"Did you what? Oh, you're talking about Guardsman Yao. That was *days* ago."

A gasp slips from between my lips.

"Don't worry, you're not a murderer," she adds, giving a condescending pat to the back of my hand.

She thinks I'm reacting to what I might've done, but it's the sound of devastation, not fear. I've lost so much time. Again. How long has Mica been alone? Does he know what happened? Is he okay?

"You barely even grazed him," Whitlock finishes.

I let out a long, slow breath, and it's as I draw in another that who I'm speaking with actually hits me. "Prime Whitlock, why are you here?"

"I came to make sure you're all right," she says.

"Right," I say, drawing out the vowel. "Because my wellbeing is of the utmost importance to you."

"It is, Terra." She blinks at me as though honestly affronted by the suggestion that it's anything but. "Your alien bodyguards may have escaped and we may have lost track of them for now, but I have full confidence that they'll be back for you." She stands and paces around the end of my bed, her heels clacking.

I say nothing.

"I will admit, their telekinetic abilities took us by *complete* surprise. I'm impressed they managed to hide them from us for so long. Admittedly, we should have been more prepared." She purses her lips. "Though, really, how can you prepare for something like that? Ah, well. When they return, we will be ready."

I dismiss the glimmer of hope that springs up at her words, shoving down the memory of Adam's lips brutally crushing mine for what might very well have been the last time.

I will come back for you, he said. Half of me is praying he does; the other half hopes he's already long gone.

"They barely broke a sweat taking out Wolfe's team," I say. "You're kidding yourself if you think you'll be able to recapture them. And even if you did, you can't seriously believe they'd ever help you again. They know what you were using them for."

"Oh? And what might that be?" A malicious grin plays at her lips, making my stomach churns. Have I said too much?

Prime Whitlock surveys me with raised eyebrows. "You know about the conversion project."

I loosen my clenched jaw but manage to keep my mouth closed, my eyes narrowing in defiance.

"Oh, come on, out with it," she says. "You must have something to say. Or am I giving you too much credit here? I mean, how much could *you* possibly know?"

She's goading me on purpose. Unfortunately, it works.

"I know you're trying to leave this planet in the dust," I spit. "Simultaneously leaving us to rot."

Something that almost looks like pride flickers across her face. She doesn't even bother trying to deny it.

"You're talking about *genocide*." My voice cracks with my barely-contained fury. "If you abandon the groundworld, the Tribunal would be single-handedly responsible for the death of every terrestrial—well over half the human race. How can you live with yourself?"

She sighs. "Progress requires sacrifice, Terra. You think we're these great villains, hellbent on destroying your peace and happiness. But we are only trying to protect the longevity of our species. You talk about the human race? We are here to ensure it continues. Sadly, we can't do that on a dying planet. So, yes, we want to leave. And, no, there isn't enough room for everyone. But we are not the bad guys."

There's no stopping the derisive laugh that bursts from my mouth.

"Please. Covering all of this up, misleading your citizens, deceiving the very people who trust you, who work tirelessly for you? Kidnapping people, holding them against their will, exploiting their knowledge, and forcing their labor? You can't be serious. Not the bad guys?" My derisive huff cuts through the air. "You are tyrants, taking advantage of our trust and harnessing our labor to fuel your own selfish plans."

Whitlock rolls her eyes. "Take advantage of you? We gave you *purpose*. Where would you terrestrials be without us? Before the Tribunal stepped in, your precious groundworld was a cesspool. Crime? Endless. Violence? Unceasing. At least with our guidance, we've crafted you into something useful."

"That's all we've ever been to you, isn't it? Pawns in your game, a means to an end." There's a bitter taste on my tongue as I think about Sixteen, the days when Mica and I had to stretch a single can of glug just to survive until the next Rationing. I recall Hess Underwood's crestfallen face at the Collection. I think about Lee.

How dare she act like the Tribunal has done us some kind of favor.

"We would've been infinitely better off without your 'guidance.' We didn't need you before, and the only reason we need you now is because you made it that way."

"You honestly think life would've been better if the government of old had pieced itself back together after the Skyfall?" She barks one of her high-pitched, ear-grating laughs. "I would think a government that purposefully manufactured a means to wipe out an entire group of people would be far worse to contend with. You want to talk about genocide? Let's talk about *that*."

Whatever words I might've had ready on the tip of my tongue evaporate into smoke. I just look at Prime Whitlock, and the confusion I'm feeling must be evident on my face because there's a renewed glint of victory in her icy eyes.

"What, you don't know about that part? Didn't catch the part where our forerunners set the entire plan for conversion in motion long before we even came into the picture? At least we have the decency to let you live out the rest of your lives. Their original design, on the other hand? Included a means of separating the wheat from the chaff."

I blink rapidly, my eyes widening as I try to make sense of her words. "What are you talking about?"

Whitlock draws a hand to her clavicle in mock surprise. "Surely someone as smart as you would have figured it out by now."

I fix her with a hard look.

"*The plague*, Terra. Where do you think a disease that devastating comes from? It doesn't just spring up out of thin air. It is born, cultivated, developed. In a lab. Under the direct orders of our oh-so-benevolent predecessors. For the very explicit purpose of weeding out the weak."

"You're trying to tell me the plague was engineered to wipe out all terrestrials?" The words drag heavily off my tongue.

She nods. "Precisely. Of course, their timing was absolutely atrocious. Too eager to put their plans into motion. Took too many shortcuts. They didn't foresee the havoc Intheria's botched conversion would wreak. The plague erupted when Intheria fell and, before they knew it: contagion.

"The disease hadn't been perfected yet. It was still a prototype, really. So, it ended up ravaging those above as much as it did it below." She removes her glasses and polishes them against her blouse. "Such a pity. Well, live and learn, I suppose."

Something inside me snaps. "These are human lives you're talking about. Millions—billions dead! And here you are, ready to sentence the rest of us to join them. Fuck you."

Whitlock cocks her head to the side with an amused expression. "Have you finally reached your tipping point for life-altering revelations?" she says. "It's about time."

"Fuck you," I say again, and she *smiles*. I violently shake my head, as if doing so might dispel the words now echoing in my ears. "I don't want to hear any more of this."

She clucks her tongue. "So melodramatic."

"Why are you even telling me this?"

"Why not? It's not like you'll be telling anyone."

And there it is.

My breath hitches. "Are you going to kill me?"

Whitlock seems genuinely taken aback. "Kill you? Of course not. How rude to even suggest such a thing."

I snort. "So, genocide is fine, but the thought of murdering me is where you draw the line?"

Her eyes are piercing as she looks down her nose at me. "We are not murderers. We are survivors."

"Keep telling yourself that," I retort. "What's the plan then? Keep me locked away here forever? Seems like a waste of resources."

Whitlock sighs. "It'll be useful to keep you around, for now. Assuming they actually are planning on returning for you . . ." She arches a brow, but I don't react to the implied insult. "Once they are back in our possession," she continues, as if Adam and his team are items to be repo'd instead of living, breathing people—or whatever it is they are, "we'll proceed with your outprocessing. You'll be released and sent home."

"So I've been told," I say, already tired again. "You'll forgive me if I don't quite believe you. And if by 'outprocessing' you just mean 'more torture,' I feel I should remind you that it didn't work so well on me the first time."

"Torture?" She laughs. "Please. We have no reason to torture you, Terra. Memory removal is a standard part of the outprocessing procedure. Oh, don't fret," she adds as she takes in the sudden flare of my nostrils, my sharp inhale, "we won't take *everything*. Just the recent things. The bits having to do with your extraterrestrial friends."

My memories, gone? Adam . . . *gone*?

"Then you can live in blissful ignorance once again," she finishes. "Everybody wins."

"I don't believe you," I say bitterly.

"Believe what you want," she says dismissively. "But it was always our intention to return you home."

"If you all take off and leave the groundworld to fend for ourselves, you're killing me anyway. Why even go to the trouble?"

She rolls her ice-blue eyes. "Oh, come now. We aren't monsters. If we killed you, who would take care of that brother of yours?"

"Leave him out of this," I say, rage simmering in my chest. "Mica doesn't know anything."

"Oh, we are aware. We've already sent someone to attend to him."

I desperately want to keep a neutral expression on my face, though I can't stop another breath from escaping at the thought of Mica being questioned. Worse, *inquisitioned.*

"We already confirmed he's clean. A good thing too. We wouldn't want to risk jeopardizing that brain of his. His intellect really is quite astounding for his age. It's funny, really; if it weren't for you, we never would have seen his potential. I think he could end up being quite useful."

Prime Whitlock smiles cruelly, but before I can ponder what she means, the tablet on her waistband begins to beep. She pulls it out, her brow furrowing as she reads the message on the screen.

"Well, that's unfortunate," she says with a scowl.

"What is?"

"Your friends have left the party."

I lean back with a sigh, pinching the bridge of my nose. "Do you get some kind of special kick out of being cryptic? Is it really that difficult to just speak normally?"

Prime Whitlocks huffs like she's actually affronted. I roll my eyes, then close them entirely. I've had enough of this.

"Our scanners are reporting that their ship has left Earth's atmosphere," she says. "They've gone . . . *home.*"

My eyes fly open.

I will come back for you.

My teeth come down on my bottom lip so hard, I taste blood.

He wouldn't leave me here.

"Well, I don't know what to tell you," she barks, making me realize I said that second thought out loud. "I'm not exactly thrilled about it either, but our scanners don't lie. They're gone." She places the tablet back in its holster and begins to rub at her temples in frustrated circles.

I suck in a deep, slow breath as my heart sinks into the bottom of my stomach. Her outrage feels real. I think she's telling the truth.

I will come back for you.

He probably meant it when he said it.

I will come back for you.

He still could mean it, I suppose. He still could be planning on coming back to help me, to help all of us. Maybe they just need supplies, maybe they're getting reinforcements . . .

The thoughts dissipate almost as quickly as they form inside my mind, the reality of my situation suddenly all too clear. I am just one girl on this godforsaken planet. They have a wealth of superior alien knowledge and technology that the Tribunal desperately wants. They're not going to risk letting it fall back into their hands.

Not for me.

I will come back for you.

Maybe he might have. But this isn't just about him.

And I am not worth coming back for.

Something cracks in my chest.

I want to pull my knees up, to physically brace myself against the waves of disappointment I feel crashing over me, but the pain in my hip reminds me that I can't. I wrap my arms around my torso instead, as if it might do anything to keep the cracked thing inside from falling apart completely.

Gone.

Whitlock snaps her fingers in front of my face, yanking me back to the unfortunate present. "Don't look so tragic. It's pathetic. You're better off this way. Your relationship with that boy was based on a lie. And not some insignificant little white lie. One big, colossal disaster of one. One that put you and your brother in danger." She looks deliberately at my bandaged leg. "But I know I don't need to tell you this. Surely, *smart* as you are, you see that."

Every part of me feels heavy and useless and fragile all at once, as if the smallest movement could shatter my very bones. Prime Whitlock's final insult echoes hollowly through my head, and I'm too drained to even be offended.

We lapse into silence.

"So, now what?" I ask vacantly after a minute. "Time to launch the Tribunal's secret space robots in pursuit of them?"

"If only." Whitlock exhales slowly, coming back around to the side of my bed. "We've barely regained the technology necessary to launch satellites, let alone compete with a ship like theirs. Alas, it looks like we're on our own for the conversion. Which, hey, is good news for you." I wince as she claps me on my still-healing shoulder. "You'll get to live out the rest of your menial little life before we can even dream of matching the progress they might've made for us."

I should be relieved. We have more time. Distantly, I wonder if it might even be time enough to stop them. But even if I weren't still absorbing the news of Adam's departure, caring feels pointless. By the time I'm outprocessed, I won't remember there's anything that needs to be stopped.

"And as for me?"

"Unlike your former beloved, nothing I've told you has been a lie. You'll be outprocessed as we discussed, after which you will be returned home."

I don't have the energy to muster anything other than a slow nod of acknowledgment.

"I'm really doing you a favor here, Terra. Now you won't have to live with the knowledge that you've been abandoned by the very person you risked everything to protect."

Whitlock walks to the door and pokes her head out to address someone in the hall. A few minutes later, the medical attendants return. I shudder as they approach.

"No hard feelings, yes?" Whitlock stands, folds her glasses into her blazer pocket, and offers me her hand.

I instinctively recoil, as if her touch is poisonous.

"Have it your way." She withdraws her hand with a shrug. "Make sure you give her the full workup. I don't care how long it takes," she says to the attendants on her way out, her high heels clacking as she leaves.

If being outprocessed means never having to hear that sound again, maybe it'll be worth it.

The two attendants flock around my cot, checking monitors and adjusting my IV. The female attendant reclines the top half of the bed until I'm lying down again.

"Try to relax," she instructs.

There's no point in fighting anymore. Nobody's coming to save me. I stare up at the ceiling as one of the attendants hangs a bag of viridescent solution and connects it to my IV. Within seconds, my eyes are too heavy to keep open.

I hold on to consciousness, trying to conjure one final image in my mind before I succumb, but I can't get it to fully form. All I see is two pools of deep water, multifaceted swirls of cobalt and indigo, sapphire and cerulean that hold the gentle whisper of a better future.

Goodbye, I tell them.

And I let go.

I expect to see that familiar blackness behind my eyelids, to feel the cool, beckoning serenity of sleep. Instead, there is a flash of white—brighter than anything I've ever experienced—and then overwhelming silence.

THIRTY

I AM in the Western Plains. At least, I think that's where I am. For some reason, my perspective seems a little skewed. I turn in a complete circle, trying to get my bearings, before finally catching sight of Sixteen's black walls in the distance.

Sun poisoning, I think, smacking my sandpapery tongue against the roof of my mouth. *Time to call it a day.*

I glance at the sky in disappointment. The sun is still high, and I hate to be giving up so early. I roll up my jacket sleeves and head back toward the settlement, my bag jingling with generics as I walk. At least I'm not going back completely empty-handed.

Even though I've done it a thousand times, climbing back over the western wall is more difficult than usual. My right leg feels stiff as I hoist myself up the black brick, twinging at all the wrong times. I almost slip more than once.

I hop down on the other side and massage my thigh for a few moments. I decide it might be good for me to try and loosen my legs a little, to walk it off. A quick stop at the Marketplace might be just the ticket before heading home. I should still be back long before Mica gets out of school.

The market is crowded. Busy shoppers all seem to give me the same looks of displeasure as I weave in and out of the mob. Some even actively call me names I can't quite make out under their breath. I can guess their meaning easily enough though. I know I've never been the most popular person in town, but this all seems a bit unnecessary.

"Heya, Copp," I say as I amble up to his stall. "How's it hanging?"

He stares at me, his lips parted in shock. "Terra?"

I raise a brow. "Who else would it be?"

"The hell are ya doing here?" His expression instantaneously shifts. If I didn't know better, I'd think he was angry.

"What do you mean?" I look around, searching the bustling Marketplace as if the reason for his reaction will reveal itself. A few nearby shoppers stare at me with disgust. I covertly sniff myself to see if I'm giving off some specific reason for offense.

"Guess your jaunt into the high life didn't last too long, did it?" Copp says sharply. "I didn't expect you'd show your face here again. Ever."

"Excuse me?" The way he addresses me makes me feel like I should be apologizing, though I have no idea why. I stare at him for a few seconds, unsure of how to proceed.

He gives me a cold stare. "Was there something ya needed, or what?"

"Well, I *was* planning on doing some shopping," I say defensively. Everyone's entitled to have a bad day once in a while, but whatever the cause of his fury is, there's no reason to take it out on me.

"If you're not buyin' then you'd best be on yer way." The muscles in his jaw flex as he clenches his teeth.

"No, wait," I say slowly. I'm irritated, but still eager to smooth things over. "I'll take this." I pick up the first thing I see and hand it over. Copp takes the small box out of my hands without looking at it.

"Twelve credits," he says gruffly.

"Twelve?" I say, incredulous. What the hell did I grab that cost that much? "I'll give you ten."

"I don't think ya wanna be hagglin' with me."

I squirm under his glare. I've never seen him like this.

"Fine," I say, anxious to get out of here. I stick out my palm for him to scan and my balance flashes up on the register. I smile inwardly. Even with this unplanned splurge, our savings are still holding strong at around two hundred credits.

Copp crams the box into a bag and hands it back to me with a grunt. I reach for the bag and meet his eye for the briefest of moments. Suddenly, I'm hit with a mental picture of him, tipping his bowler hat. The image feels like a dream, since I can't for the life of me remember ever seeing Copp practice such a formal gesture.

The real Copp, still in front of me with his hat squarely centered atop his head, glares at me. A woman standing behind me clears her throat. I blink twice before collecting the bag and stepping aside. Whatever's crawled up his ass, I'll just have to sort it out with him later.

I quickly dip out of the Marketplace, glares boring into my back as I exit. It feels like they follow me all the way home.

Once I've crossed through the center of town, I slow down. I reach inside the shopping bag to finally take a look at my twelve-credit purchase. I pop open the box and I'm immediately assaulted with a bouquet of sweet aromas. Three bars of colored soap are lined up in a row. I pull out the middle one—a soft, pretty purple—and read the tiny label wrapped around it.

"Lavender, huh?" I say aloud. I glance at the other two: sandalwood and jasmine. Having never smelled the actual things they're named for, the labels mean little to me, but the soaps smell good. Maybe not *twelve credits* good, but at least it'll be a bit of a change.

I toss the box of soaps back in the bag and turn onto my street. A rusty motorbike is parked in front of my building.

Wonder which of the neighbors lucked into that beast, I think with not a small amount of jealousy as I pass it. I walk into the building, rubbing my thigh distractedly as I climb the stairs. I could've used a transport today.

I open the door to the apartment to find Mica staring up at me from the kitchen table.

"Terra!" He leaps up and rushes over, nearly tackling me to the ground as he wraps his arms around me.

"Hi to you too," I say, giving him an awkward pat on the head.

"Are you all right?" he asks with uncharacteristic intensity. His voice is strained, his face flustered.

"Sure, why wouldn't I be?" I plop my scav bag on the table next to a pile of papers and straddle the seat backward, resting my chin on the back. For some reason, he's pulled his computer out of his room and set it up out here. "Yeesh, Mic. This place is a tornado zone."

He pulls his chair up and sits directly in front of me, searching my face. "Where have you been?"

"What are you talking about, weirdo? I was just on a scav run."

He gapes at me, confusion etched into the creases in his forehead. I look at my brother carefully, trying to pinpoint what it is that seems so different about him.

Huh, I think idly. *I hadn't noticed he'd started spending so much time outside.* It's the only explanation for the smattering of freckles that now run across his nose and cheeks. His skin is darker and his sandy brown hair has gotten long—shaggy around the edges, skimming over his neck.

"What are you doing home?" I ask suddenly. "Shouldn't you be at school?"

"It's a holiday," he replies, a little too quickly.

"Right. What holiday would that be? National Talk Out of Your Ass Day?"

"A mental health day?"

I roll my eyes. "Whatever. I guess one skipped day won't kill you. But please tell me you aren't making a habit of this, Mic. You're too smart for that."

He nods solemnly, looking genuinely guilty. I soften my tone.

"I stopped at Copp's on the way back. Picked up a new set of bath bars for us. I call the lavender. You can have your pick of the other two." I pull the small box out of my bag and toss it at him. Mica catches it with one hand and stares at it for a long time. When he finally looks back at me, he is frowning.

"Stay right there," he says, putting the soaps on the table.

I shoot him a quizzical look. "Okay . . ."

He walks over to his bedroom door but pauses before entering. As if he's giving it some serious thought, he eventually walks over to turn on the television before retreating into his room.

"It was bizarre, actually," I call to him over the noise of the TV. "Copp was in a real mood, acting kind of strange."

"Stranger than usual, you mean?" Mica's voice is muffled through the door. "Why, what did he say?"

I debate repeating Copp's less-than-hospitable words but decide it's not worth burdening Mica just because I got my feelings hurt. "It's not important. He just seemed like he was worked up about something. Wouldn't haggle with me at all."

Mica doesn't respond, though I can just barely hear him mumbling inside his room. There's a dull thump, followed by what sounds suspiciously like swearing.

"What are you doing in there?" I walk over to his door, but Mica pulls it open just as I'm reaching for the knob.

"Nothing, nothing," Mica says. He puts his finger in his ear and wiggles it absentmindedly. Standing face-to-face with him, I realize he's grown a solid two inches. He's officially taller than I am now.

When did that happen?

"So, is there a special coming on or something?" I ask.

"What?" he says distractedly.

I gesture toward the TV. "You turned it on?"

His almond eyes refocus on my face. "Oh. Right. Yes." With stilted steps, he goes and sits down on the couch.

"Everyone's being so weird today," I say, ruffling Mica's hair as I join him. "What's on? Anything I'm going to like?"

Mica mutters something under his breath as he sinks back into the cushions. It sounds a lot like, "Not like you'd know if you did."

THIRTY-ONE

THE ATMOSPHERE in the apartment is still peculiarly tense when breakfast rolls around the next morning. Mica and I have been tiptoeing around each other since yesterday afternoon, barely speaking, though I've caught him gawking at me more than once. I chucked a pillow at his head to snap him out of it once, and got hit with the strangest sense of déjà vu.

I've just cracked open a can of B-C4R7 when a light knock sounds at the door.

In an instant, Mica jumps up from the kitchen table and dashes over to the window. He peers out at the street below, then sprints into his room and slams the door behind him.

"Okay, fine, I guess I'll get it," I mutter, rolling my eyes in annoyance. A woman with graying hair and light eyes is waiting patiently when I open the front door, a small cloth briefcase dangling from one of her hands. Beside her stands a lanky guardsman with chin-length black hair. I don't think I've ever seen him before, so there's no reason for it, but I get the strange sense he's deliberately avoiding my eye.

"Hello," I say guardedly. "Can I help you?"

"Terra Rhodon?" the woman says pleasantly.

"Yes?"

"I am Registrar Kilburn. This is Guardsman Clay. The Tribunal is conducting a census of registered scavengers. May I ask you a few questions?"

"Sure." Is this the reason why Copp and the folks at the Marketplace were so on edge yesterday? I don't remember a census being conducted before, at least not since I've been old enough to participate.

I step aside to allow Kilburn and Clay inside, the former taking a seat next to me in the kitchen while the latter stands stiffly by the door. Kilburn clears a spot for her briefcase on the table between Mica's computer and a stack of comics, and a flicker of irritation runs through me. I start to apologize for the mess. She offers me a commiserative smile as she fishes a tablet out of the briefcase, which chimes as it comes to life.

"Please state your name, age, and occupation for the record?"

"Terra Eryth Rhodon. Eighteen. Scav. I mean, scavenger."

"And you live with one sibling, correct? Auron Rhodon?"

Even though I know we're not talking about him, hearing my father's name still makes me blanch. "Mica," I say. "My brother goes by his middle name."

Kilburn taps her fingers across the tablet screen, typing out a note. "Is he here?"

"He's . . ." I want to make a joke about how he's locked himself mid-tantrum in his room, but I'm not so dense that I don't understand why he ran in there. He doesn't want to deal with this—barely seems to want to deal with *me*—and I can't say I blame him. "No, he's not home."

Another few taps on the screen. Another note. "Do you recall the amount of your most recent Collection payout, Miss Rhodon?"

"Don't you guys have that kind of stuff on record?" I ask.

She smiles. "Yes, we do. We would like to get an idea of what kind of records you keep as well, so we can learn how best to support scavenging efforts here in Sixteen, limit redundancies, *etcetera*."

"Oh." I bite the inside of my cheek as I try to think back to the last Collection Day. "I'm not sure. I don't really keep good records of that stuff," I admit, staring at the tabletop sheepishly.

"That's all right," she says kindly.

"I mean, I know how much steel we have right now," I say. "That's all that matters around here, you know?"

"I understand." She scrolls her finger down the computer's screen. An image flashes across my mind: words and numbers scrolling across a flat screen. But once again, it's gone before I can make sense of it.

"Miss Rhodon?" Kilburn asks, looking at me with concern. I didn't even realize she'd been talking. "Are you all right?"

I clear my throat. "I'm sorry, can you repeat your question?"

"I asked how many times you go scavenging on a monthly basis," she says.

"Oh, I usually go out every day. Unless it's raining, of course."

"I see. And how many times would you say you have gone scavenging since the last Collection?"

I purse my lips. "I'm not sure. Remind me how many days it's been since then?"

"Seven."

"Then I guess I went out seven times," I say with a shrug. I can't remember if it's rained recently or not, but I'm sure she can figure out the actual number.

She makes another note.

"Did you go scavenging yesterday?"

"Yes."

"What kinds of materials did you collect?"

"I, um . . ." My jaw tightens as I strain to remember. I know I went on a run yesterday morning. I know I was in the fields, I know I climbed the wall. I just . . . I don't know if I remember actually picking anything up. Which feels as ridiculous as it sounds.

"If you give me just a second, I could tell you." I reach for my bag to show proof of my spoils, and she peers inside before making another note.

"Thank you," she says, "Is there anything of consequence that you remember finding during this last period?"

"I . . ." My mind goes blank as I try to recall my recent trips. I can't even picture myself in the fields recently, other than today, to be honest. There's something there, though, at the edge of what I can remember. It feels far away, like I can't quite grasp it. I interlock my fingers and squeeze my hands together to keep myself from fidgeting. "Can you clarify the question?"

"Have you picked up anything noteworthy on your scavenging runs since the last Collection? Plastics, batteries, anything beyond your typical generics?"

I stare at the table, my eyes wide. "I'm not sure," I admit. "I don't think so."

"Do you recall finding any items of particular note on past scavenging runs? Anytime in the past, oh, let's say, six months?"

I shrug. "Nothing that seems to have made a big enough impression that I could tell you now. And anything I would've found, you would know about. I turn in my findings clean at every Collection."

Kilburn's tablet beeps again. "All right, thank you very much, Miss Rhodon. There are no further questions."

"That's it?"

She nods as she tucks the tablet back into her briefcase and turns toward the door, Guardsman Clay's hand already on the handle.

"But I couldn't really answer any of your questions."

"We have all the information we need. These censuses are not as complicated as you might think," she says with a conspiratorial wink. "Thank you for your time."

"Right. Bye then," I call as they whisk themselves out the door, leaving me slightly baffled.

The floor creaks as Mica returns from his room.

"Welcome back," I say. "So glad you could join us."

"Sorry." His gaze is falling anywhere and everywhere but on me. "Didn't feel like wading through all that."

"It was just some survey thing. It didn't even concern you, you didn't have to run and hide."

He chews on his lip for a second. "Well, thanks for covering for me anyway. You didn't have to do that."

"Heard that, did you?" I shrug. "You'd have done the same for me."

"Yes," he says, his gold-burst eyes finally meeting my own. "I would."

"MAN, I don't know what's wrong with me," I say as I plop down on the couch. "My mind is a mess. I think I must have gotten some legitimate sunstroke yesterday. Or maybe I'm just going insane." I laugh and brush my fingers through my hair, as if the act might also brush away my increasingly real fear that the latter might actually be true.

Mica looks up from his computer and shoots me a look that feels a little too close to pity for my comfort. I switch the television on as a distraction, letting out a celebratory whoop as I see the Best Pet showcase is on.

I smile as a pet owner is pulling on a leash connected to a curly-haired pink poodle as she tries to convince it to cross the arena floor. The owner is visibly frustrated—her cheeks are red, the sheen of sweat glistens on her forehead—as the pup plants its rear on the ground in defiance, chirping angrily at its owner. The sound is strangely familiar.

I cock my head to the side, trying to place the animal's cry; I've never seen a pet in real life before, but there's something tangible about the sound, like I can hear it echoing in my ears. I'm still trying to figure out why when Mica snatches the remote out of my hand and switches the television off.

"Hey, what gives?" I swallow any additional words of annoyance I might've gone on to say as he sits down on the couch next to me and grabs my face with both hands, turning my head so we're looking directly at each other.

"Uhhh, what're you—"

With one hand on either side of my face, Mica stares unblinkingly into my eyes, his forehead inches away from my own.

"What are you doing?"

He just keeps staring.

"Okay, that's enough," I say, my initial flash of confused amusement giving way to something much closer to annoyance. Why is he being so *weird?* I break Mica's hold and throw his hands back at him, watching him with a wary eye.

Maybe *I'm* not the one losing my mind here.

"Sorry," Mica says, slumping back onto the sofa. "I was just checking for something."

"Use your words next time, weirdo. Was there something on my face? Something in my eye?"

"No," he says sadly, flipping the TV on again and dropping the remote back into my lap. "There's nothing there."

THIRTY-TWO

"WAKE UP, sis. There's something I want to show you."

Mica stands at the base of my bed, kicking my mattress with his foot. A quick glance toward the window tells me it's a time of day that just barely qualifies as morning.

I groan and pull the covers over my head. I've been working myself into the ground this week, spending every day in the field in advance of yesterday's Collection. And when I haven't been scavenging, Mica's insisted on taking me all over Sixteen for the most random reasons—window shopping in the North Q, walking the docks in the East, going with him to meet Juniper Coal, of all people, in the West Square.

As if that weren't enough to deal with, Copp's sour mood seems to have spread through the rest of the settlement, and people have been even nastier to me than usual. I know I've never been a contender for Sixteen's most beloved citizen, but even happy-go-lucky Mal has been curt with me lately.

Channeling my frustration into scavenging has helped keep me distracted, but it's been absolutely exhausting. I was looking forward to sleeping in for once.

"Go away, Mic, it's too early," I moan.

Mica kicks the bed harder, actively jostling me out of place.

"For crying out loud." I flip the blanket off myself, simultaneously flipping my little brother off, then hurl my pillow at his grinning face. "This seriously can't wait a couple of hours?"

"Nope," he says, and damn it all if one look at his beaming face doesn't have me wanting to smile right alongside him. I fight the encroaching grin, though. I don't want him to get the impression that shaking me awake before the sun has fully risen is acceptable behavior, after all.

"Get dressed quick, okay? We gotta go." He shuts the door and I hear him rustling about in the main room. I think I hear him talking to himself, but when I listen harder there's nothing.

First the weird memory problems, and now I'm hearing voices. Great.

The strange mental images that pop in and out of my head unbidden haven't stopped, either. I feel like I'm in a constant state of having forgotten something important—with no way to remember what it is I forgot. It's like there's a static charge in the air, always just a breath away from igniting . . . and I'm not sure if I want it to dissipate or if I want to light a match.

If I haven't already gone insane, I'm certainly getting there.

I rise from my bed and immediately stub my toe on the dresser. I swear under my breath as I pull out the first clean pieces of clothing I can find, and I can't help feeling like this is some sort of twisted revenge for all the times I forced Mica to wake up early.

"Happy?" I mutter, joining him in the main room.

"Is that what you're wearing?"

I look down at my worn teal t-shirt—one of my most comfortable—and navy pants.

"What's wrong with what I'm wearing?" They're not the most flattering pieces, but it's not like there's anyone I'm trying to impress. "You're not exactly Mr. Fancy Pants over here yourself." I give a pointed once-over to the dark hoodie and black pants he's donned.

"At least my socks match," he says with a smirk.

I look down to see two starkly different shades of blue staring up at me from each foot. "So? It's the asscrack of dawn, Mic. Fashion is not my first priority."

"Fine, fine. Forget it."

"This had better be worth it," I say petulantly.

"I hope so too," he replies, and the sudden solemnity in his tone makes me uneasy.

I lace up my boots and we amble out the front door. When we get outside, Mica immediately walks over to the motorbike still parked in front of the building. It hasn't budged in the past week, and I'd started to think someone had abandoned it here. Wouldn't be the first time.

"What are you doing? Don't mess with that," I warn.

He throws a leg over and straddles the bench in the middle.

"Mica!"

"Chill out. It's mine."

My mouth drops open as he turns the bike on. "Hop on," he says.

I simply stare at him.

"Come on, Terra."

I don't move, my eyes glistening with disbelief as they roam over the transport. It's absolutely ancient, with two wheels in the back, one in the front, and seems like it's being held together with rust and chipped paint and sheer force of will.

Mica gives me a few moments before he revs the engine loudly, stirring me from my stupor.

"I'm going with or without you, so you might as well come along. I know you can't resist an opportunity to lecture me on my driving skills," he goads.

The bike's electric engine hums loudly, triggering another bout of that strange familiarity in my mind. Inexplicably, I suddenly *want* to go for a ride.

Hesitantly, I clamber behind Mica, and as soon as my butt hits the seat, we take off.

"Want to try explaining this?" I yell over the wind.

"It was a gift," he yells back.

I want to ask him exactly what he means by that, but it's too hard to keep up conversation on the moving bike. I've just resigned myself to waiting until we reach whatever surprise destination he's hauling me off to, when he starts to slow down. We putter to a stop in front of the North Gate.

"One more time," I say, as we wait for the guards to approach. "You want to explain this monstrosity?"

"There's nothing to explain. It's ours. It was a present."

"I think I'd remember being gifted a damn transport."

"Yeah, you'd think so, wouldn't you?" he mutters.

"And just who was this alleged benefactor, may I ask?"

The guardsman at the gate interrupts us before Mica can answer. "What is your purpose for leaving the settlement?" he asks sternly.

"Time for me to learn the family business," Mica says casually. "My sister is taking me out scavenging."

I'm half a second from denying his claim on the basis of my outrage alone, but Mica digs his fingernails into my arm and I close my mouth as quickly as I'd opened it.

The guardsman gives us a thorough once-over before opening the gate. As soon as we've cleared the settlement, Mica turns the bike south. He drives straight through the Southern Plains, barreling toward the Dead Woods.

"Where are we going?" I shout. He holds his hand up to his ear and points, an indication he's not able to—or maybe refuses to—hear me. We ride for a few minutes in silence before we reach the edge of the Dead Woods and Mica slows to a stop. He parks the motorbike against a large, misshapen tree.

"Okay, this is getting ridiculous, Mic. What are we doing out here?"

"I told you, there's something you need to see." He reaches under the seat of the transport and tucks something into the waist of his pants, but pulls the back of his sweatshirt down before I can see what it is. Without another word, he sets off into the woods.

"Enough is enough, Mica," I theatrically stamp my foot on the ground. "You need to tell me where we are going right now."

"God, he was right, your constant questioning really is annoying," Mica says, stepping over a large tree root poking out of the ground.

I huff in frustration as I realize that not only is he not telling me anything, but he's not waiting around for me. "Who was right?" I ask as I catch up to him.

Mica shoots me an exasperated look. "That's not how you're going to get answers."

I press my lips together into a line, trying to determine where my sweet and mild little brother has gone, and where this newfound insolence has come from.

Puberty sucks.

We walk through the forest in silence. I peer at Mica curiously from time to time, impressed and flabbergasted that he seems so sure of where he's going. I've only brought him out here with me once before.

My breathing becomes labored and my leg twinges as we climb over thick roots and fallen trunks. Eventually, the broad trunks begin to space out again, and I can see a small clearing in the distance. Mica seems to be heading straight for it.

As we get closer, I see the silhouettes of three men sitting in an uneven triangle. It sounds like they're laughing. That static energy lingering around me feels particularly charged as I race through the possible explanations for what's going on here. I wonder if there's a scav meeting happening that I didn't know about. But even if that was the case, why would we have come all the way out here?

I lag a few yards behind Mica, squinting to see if I recognize Mal's salt-and-pepper hair or Chrys's signature locs amongst the three figures, but there's nothing familiar about any of the men.

It's not until we've almost reached the clearing that I can finally see their shaved heads and long, tattered coats that make them look nearly indistinguishable from each other.

I feel the blood drain from my face and a rock forms in my gut as I realize exactly who and what they are.

Raiders. And Mica's headed straight for them.

THIRTY-THREE

"WHAT THE HELL ARE YOU DOING?" I call out in a whisper, reaching for Mica. He's just a step too far ahead of me though, and he's speeding up.

I lunge for him. The raiders haven't seen us yet. If I can just get Mica to turn around, we could still run. We'd have enough of a lead on them to get back to the bike, even if they decide to pursue us. But Mica doesn't break his stride. He sidesteps by grasp and walks confidently into the clearing, wholly unaffected by my panic.

All three raiders look up at the same time. They straighten defensively as Mica walks right up to them. Cursing under my breath, I ignore my instinct to run back into the cover of the trees, and I follow my brother into the clearing.

"Morning, gentlemen," Mica says brightly.

The big one in the middle cracks his knuckles threateningly. "Whatcha want, little man?"

"C'mon, Ryk, I thought you were expecting me."

My mouth falls open in shock. Mica, on a first-name basis with raiders? Mica, talking to the biggest, baddest-looking one like he's not a hundred pounds lighter and six inches shorter than him? Like he's the one in charge?

I pinch the inside of my wrist to check if I'm dreaming and am decidedly disappointed to find that I'm not.

The one Mica called Ryk grits his teeth but nods, releasing his fingers from the fists they've formed. "Right," he grunts. "Didn't think he'd be sending someone like you. So, what's the deal, why are we here?"

"I brought you something," Mica says invitingly. He turns toward me and jerks his head, summoning me forward.

My body seizes entirely, rooting me to the spot. Mica sighs and walks over to me. I stare at him, eyes widened in alarm. Whatever game he thinks he's playing, it's a dangerous one. These raiders could crush both of us into pieces. I search my brother's face, looking for a hint, a sign, anything that might explain his apparent madness.

Mica just winks at me, then grabs me by the wrist and drags me forward.

Ryk's lips curl into a wicked smile as I approach. My body tenses, my fight-or-flight response already starting to kick in. One of his lackeys starts to laugh, a dumbfounded sound, like he can't believe what he's seeing. The other stares at me with wide, unblinking eyes.

"Well, hey there, firecracker. Didn't think I'd get to see your pretty face again." Ryk runs his tongue slowly over his upper lip in a repulsing display.

"Do I know you?" I say coldly, hoping that the disgust in my voice is helping to mask my confusion.

"I'm hurt. No love for an old pal?"

"I've never seen you before in my life," I say, though as the words leave my lips, I wonder if they're true. There's something familiar about the way the heavy golden chain around his neck bounces against his bare chest. Like something out of a dream—the kind that's gone within moments of waking.

He lumbers toward me. "I know you remember me."

Regardless of whether we've met before, it's clear this is a guy I do not *want* to know. "Nope, sorry." I take a step back and collide with Mica, who's standing right behind me.

Ryk grabs me by my shoulders and I brace to defend myself. Before I have a chance to, though, Mica knocks Ryk's hands off of me and steps between us.

"What gives?" Ryk says angrily.

That's exactly what I'd like to know, I think, but I don't take my panicked eyes off of Mica.

"Don't touch her," he says sternly. The juxtaposition between the two of them is ludicrous. Ryk dwarfs Mica physically and despite his newfound attitude that would suggest otherwise, my brother looks like even more of a child than he is.

"You don't make the rules, kid," Ryk growls. "And me and her? We got unfinished business."

"You agreed to this experiment," Mica says coolly. "We're not here for you to regain your pride after getting your ass kicked by a girl."

Ryk's eyes darken.

Mica turns around to face me. "Anything?" he asks, something akin to hope shining in his eyes.

"I feel like I'm missing something kind of crucial," I say through clenched teeth, "because I don't have any idea what the hell we're doing here."

Mica's face crumples into a frown.

Ryk snarls and his lackeys edge in closer to their boss. "I don't have time for this. Move aside, little man, or I'll just have to go through you."

I gasp as Ryk rears back, aiming his meaty fist at the back of Mica's head. I try to shove my brother out of the way, ready to take the blow myself, but Mica just sighs resignedly. He stays anchored where he stands, barely moving against the force of my desperate push, and a detached part of my mind notices how strong he is—much stronger than I'd realized or even given him credit for.

With a movement so quick it shocks me, he whips around and pulls a stun gun from his waistband. He fires off three successive shots before Ryk has time to land the blow.

The three raiders fall to the ground, convulsing.

"Well, this was a huge waste of time," Mica says unhappily.

"Give me that," I shout, yanking the stun gun out of his hands. "Where the hell did you get this?"

Mica just looks at me, anticipation shining in his gaze as he scrutinizes my features. A moment later, he looks away, his expression deflated.

Infuriated, I turn back toward the woods, stepping cleanly over Ryk's still-shuddering body as I stomp away. I don't speak again until we've arrived back home.

"WHAT THE FUCK is your problem, Mica?" I bellow, barely having stepped foot inside the apartment.

"Language," he scolds.

I ignore him. "What was that? Is this some new thing you kids are playing at school? Seeing who's brave enough to cross the quarantine line got old, so now you've all moved on to antagonizing raiders? You could've gotten us killed."

Mica watches me with the edges of his mouth turned down. "I just don't get it. I thought for sure that would trigger something."

"What are you talking about?" I scream. I'm so frustrated I could pull my hair out. I settle for twisting it into a too-tight bun, relishing the muted bite of pain radiating from my crown as I wrap a hair tie around the tightly coiled strands.

"Things didn't go quite as planned, huh?" A voice echoes out from behind me.

Terror grips me as I spin around to find a stranger seated at our kitchen table. Even sitting, I can tell he's tall. Wisps of blond hair peek out from beneath a blue cap, the brim low, so I can only make out the bottom half of his face. A strong jaw, unexpectedly full lips, a straight nose. His gray windbreaker is zipped up to his neck, the sleeves rolled partway up each forearm.

I push Mica behind me and raise the stun gun, pointing it directly at the intruder. "Who are you?" I demand. He raises his hands, palms out, as if in surrender.

"Terra, it's okay." Mica peeks out from around my back looking mildly amused. "He's a friend." He tugs the gun from my grip and lays it on the table.

"How did he—" I start to say, but Mica interrupts me before I can finish my thought.

"Could you just give us a second?" he says to me.

Instantaneous indignation flares in my gut. "*You're* asking *me* to give *you* a second with *him*?"

Mica shrugs. The stranger grins.

I storm into the bathroom and slam the door. I wait a few moments, making a show of washing my face, my hands, and letting the tap run for a few extra seconds before shutting it off. I press my ear to the door, and if I don't breathe too loudly, I can just make out some of what they're saying.

"What are you doing here?" Mica says.

"Did you expect me to stay away forever?" the stranger replies.

"This is suicide. If they find you here, we're all—"

"They won't. The tail followed you both the second you left the building. I watched them go."

"That doesn't mean nobody saw you."

"If they thought for a second that I was here, we both know they'd already be breaking down the door."

Mica falls silent for a few seconds.

"Besides," the stranger continues, "I'm not the one we should be worried about here. You risked both of your lives today and it sounds like it didn't even work. Not to mention the suspicion it could have raised with the guardsmen."

"Yeah, well, let's not forget whose idea this was in the first place."

"You just have to be careful, Mic. We have to keep up appearances. They can't ever know that you know."

"Believe me, I . . . I know," Mica stutters, and my heart clenches because he suddenly sounds so young again.

"I guess we're just lucky you're a much better actor than your sister." They laugh, but quickly seem to realize how much their voices have risen and quiet back down. I can almost feel the exact moment their gaze falls on the bathroom door.

I rip open the bathroom cabinet, then slam it closed. Hopefully, it's loud enough for them to think I haven't been eavesdropping. By the time I return my ear to the door, their conversation is dying down.

"Fine. Have it your way. It's your funeral," Mica says haughtily, and I have to swallow a gasp. I've never heard Mica speak so cavalierly to anyone—well, anyone other than me.

I flush the toilet for good measure and they instantly shut up. A moment later, I saunter back out into the living room, where they stand next to each other by the couch.

"So, Mic, who's your friend?" I ask guardedly.

The stranger removes his cap, and this time I can't keep the gasp in as bright blue eyes gaze back at me. His clothes look the same as any groundling's, and he's missing the usual aura of superiority, but there's no denying it: he must be a skydweller.

"Hello, Sunburst," he says, his voice like velvet now that it's no longer muffled by the bathroom door.

My mouth dries up as I hear my grandmother's loving nickname for me fall from his lips. "Um, hi," I say, and I know it sounds as lame as it feels.

My eyes dart to Mica, then back to the stranger, all signs of their argument gone from their faces as they watch me intently.

"Do I know you?" I ask. They're the same words I said to the raider Ryk less than an hour ago, but the meaning behind them feels completely different. Somehow, impossibly, it feels like I do. Or at least, it feels like I *should* know him.

I'm just not sure how. He looks a little too young to be a Collection Agent, and he certainly lacks the bored authority of a guardsman.

So where have I seen him before?

"Do I know you?" I repeat, my voice soft.

The skydweller smiles, but it doesn't meet his eyes. There's so much sadness there, traces of grief concealed behind his stare, and I feel a prickle in the back of my throat. "I'm afraid not," he says.

"Oh." I hesitate. His conversation with Mica was bizarre, but I don't feel any animosity coming from him. And at least it sounds like he knows what that whole raider thing was about. If Mica won't tell me, maybe this stranger will. "Well, any friend of Mica's and all that."

"Thank you. But, if you don't mind, I came here to speak with you."

"With me?" I say, my confusion palpable.

His chin bows, a tight nod.

"All right," I say after a moment. I walk over slowly and take a seat at the kitchen table. The skydweller follows me and occupies the same chair he had been waiting in when we arrived, shifting it so he faces me head-on.

I expect him to start speaking, to ask whatever he means to ask, or say whatever he came here to say, but he just looks at me.

"So . . ." I say, finally breaking the awkward silence, "what can I do for you?" The words feel silly tumbling out of my mouth.

He smiles, a sort of lopsided grin, where one side of his mouth is higher than the other. It's surprisingly endearing. "I have something to show you," he says.

I shoot a quick, piercing glance at Mica as if to say, *Where have I heard that before?*

The skydweller doesn't seem to notice. He reaches into his pocket and pulls out a small, delicate silver bracelet. No, not a bracelet. A watch. He holds it up for me to see.

"That's very beautiful," I say, wondering what his endgame is.

He places the watch in the center of my palm, face up. I pause for a moment, tilting my head as a memory fights its way to the front of my mind.

"What?" Mica says eagerly. "What is it? What are you thinking?"

"It's just . . . it's funny, this looks almost exactly like one our mother used to wear." I run the pad of my pointer finger in a circle around the edge of the watch face, and something is trying to edge its way into my memory.

"Oh." Mica exchanges a look with the stranger.

The skydweller smiles. "It's yours then," he says. He gently plucks the watch out of my palm and begins to wrap the delicate silver links around my wrist.

"Oh, no, please. I couldn't possibly accept this."

"I insist."

Tick, tick, tick. The needle-thin seconds hand makes a complete circle as I stare at the watch face.

I look up into the stranger's blue eyes.

No, not just blue.

It's almost like the colors are shifting right in front of me—different hues compete, shades of cobalt, indigo, sapphire, and cerulean mixing, mingling, overtaking one another, over and over again.

Somewhere outside of my reverie, Mica coughs quietly, then claps a hand over his mouth as if he can't believe he's made a sound. I notice it happening, but I don't bother wondering what it means. I'm too consumed by what's happening inside my head.

I can feel my mind grasping at the fog, blindly trying to force through the recesses of my memory.

The skydweller leans forward and touches his forehead to mine, a gesture far too intimate for strangers. I should be alarmed. I should recoil. I should be upset, repelled, or, at the very least, embarrassed.

But I'm not.

I simply stare at the watch and let him take my other hand in his.

Tick, tick, tick.

"Terra," he breathes.

Something clicks in my brain. A crack in my chest that I didn't even realize was there seals shut, just as my heart plummets to the bottom of my stomach. I feel my face start to flush with new color.

I pull my head back and look up to meet his unparalleled eyes, twin mirrors that reflect the depth of endless horizons, the promise of sunsets and shivers, warmth, home, and a thousand untold stories.

"Adam."

THIRTY-FOUR

ADAM'S TELLTALE lopsided grin takes over his face as I fall forward off my chair and crash into his arms, already sobbing. I don't even know why I'm crying; I can't identify one singular emotion. I feel everything—happiness and desolation and relief and confusion and . . .

I remember.

"I knew you wouldn't leave me," I cry softly into his chest.

"Never," he says.

I look over at Mica, who is grinning like a lunatic. I force myself to break from Adam's embrace, standing up so I can hug my little brother. Then I slap him on the chest, hard.

"Ryk?" I say hysterically. "Really?"

Mica bursts out laughing. "Don't look at me. It was your boyfriend's idea."

"I apologize for nothing," Adam says. He stands from his chair to wrap his arms back around me. I lean back into the warmth of his chest, and he nestles his chin in the dip between my neck and shoulder. "Nothing else seemed to be working. We were getting desperate."

"Leave it to my sister for a dude to affect her more than near-death raider-related trauma," says Mica.

I try to laugh but I'm still crying, so it comes out as a kind of halfgargled moan. I pull myself together, wiping the tears from my cheeks as I try to make sense of everything that's happened—just now, as well as before.

I run my fingers over my thigh and press gingerly on the spot where the bullet entered. I remember the pain as if I had been shot just yesterday, but I feel nothing now.

I whirl around and Adam's embrace loosens, but he keeps his arms clasped comfortingly around my waist. "How long was I gone?" I demand.

Adam and Mica exchange shamefaced looks.

"How long?" I repeat.

Adam inhales slowly, like he's bracing for my reaction.

"It's been three months since my birthday," Mica says quietly.

My breath hitches. Three months. A quarter of a year. So much lost time.

I take a shocked step forward, breaking out of Adam's arms, and stumble into my chair. "How did I not realize . . .?" I say quietly as I sit. "How could I not notice that my life simply jumped from one date to another?"

"Do you remember anything that happened during your outprocessing?" Adam asks. He takes my palm in his and runs his thumb in soothing circles across the back of my hand.

I think back, trying to conjure the last memory I have of being in Korbyllis. Besides the lingering impression of Whitlock's general malevolence though, the only thing I come up with is a white flash.

I shake my head.

"We don't know how they did it," Adam continues, "but if the Tribunal has the ability to wipe memories, they must have a way to control reintegration too. Maybe nothing so powerful as to implant new memories, but enough to alleviate suspicion. It'd be too conspicuous otherwise."

"What about everyone else? Didn't anybody notice? Didn't anyone care that I just—poof!—vanished?" I say.

"Oh, the Tribunal thought of that," Mica says icily. "You'd been gone less than a day when a couple of guardsmen goons showed up and fed me a story about how you had taken off to Lexicon with all our steel."

I bark a laugh. "Me, gone off to gamble away our fortune in a casino? Yeah, that sounds right up my alley. You didn't believe them, did you?"

"Of course not," he says quickly, though he is suddenly unable to tear his eyes from the floor.

"Oh." My face falls and I feel Adam's grip tighten reassuringly on my hand.

"I didn't believe it at first. Honest." He shoves his hands in his pockets. "I knew something had to have gone down, and I tried finding out what happened. I asked everyone. But you gotta see it from my side, Terra. Both of you were just gone. And the longer time went on, the longer you *stayed* gone . . . it started to make more sense. Then, this guardsman came by to drop off your stuff—the watch, your jacket—and a message from you." He furrows his brow in contemplation. "At least, I thought it was from you. It sounded like you."

A vague memory prickles somewhere in my mind, but it's hazy. Reading lines from a screen, the pinch of something sharp in the crook of my arm . . . My body tenses and I gnash my teeth together as it hits me that there's a lot the Tribunal could have done—and probably did—to me while they held me. Adam places a hand on my lower back, moving his palm in soothing circular motions.

"What did the message say?" I ask through clenched teeth.

"It really did seem like you'd just taken off," Mica continues, and I don't miss the way he sidesteps my question. "I checked our credit account too, and sure enough, it was drained. Well, drained back to normal, I guess. They left me enough to get by. But the pieces fit, you know?"

The anger that sparked at my realization fades into a deep sadness, settling into my bones. Mica thought I had abandoned him. Again.

"Maybe I was just looking for excuses to stay mad. I mean, you did miss my birthday." He grins, but I can see real emotion behind his attempt to relieve the tension.

I look at him sadly. His grin falters, remorse swimming in his gold-specked eyes. Our eyes.

"I'm sorry," he says.

I smile and shake my head. "There's nothing for you to apologize for,

Mic. Really. I'm the one who should be saying sorry. I left you here, alone."

"It's not as if you had a choice. And anyway, it wasn't so bad. A little boring, maybe, but everyone has been really supportive."

"I guess that explains all the extra vitriol coming my way from Copp . . . and our neighbors . . . and pretty much everyone."

"Word spread fast, like it always does. The story's a little different depending on who you ask—some people remember seeing Adam and thought you guys ran away together, some think you went to another settlement instead of the skyworld—but the gist is always the same. People weren't exactly thrilled with the idea that you'd left me here. They . . ."

"They what?"

He fidgets with the string on his hoodie. "They said it was just like you . . . to follow in *his* footsteps."

My free hand curls into a fist at my side. The thought of being compared in any way with our father, let alone like this . . .

"How did I not hear about this?" I say. "My return must have been the talk of Sixteen. People are obviously still angry, but nobody's said anything to me directly, nobody's run up and thrown paint on me or cursed the day I was born."

"You know how it is, sis. People love to talk, but actual confrontation? Forget it. They all know you'd kick their asses." Mica grins widely at me and I can't help but return his smile. "Anyway, we should all be relieved nobody said anything to you. You probably would have thought you were going nuts."

"I was starting to think it anyway . . ." I mutter, then add, "I'm still sorry you thought I left you."

Mica waves his hand in the air like he's batting away my apology. "Adam came back after a while. Pretty much jumped me in an alley on my way home from school and told me everything. I almost didn't believe his story at first but, well, there are a lot of things about Adam that seem unbelievable." Mica punches Adam on the shoulder affection-ately. "That's when we started planning how to get you back."

"How did you even know I was still alive?"

"We figured they wouldn't have concocted this big backstory if they were only going to do you in. I mean, they could have said you had an accident or something, you know? Could have just told me that you died."

We fall silent.

"I can't believe I've been gone so long," I say after a few moments, looking at Mica sadly. The physical changes he's gone through are more evident now. It's not just the additional height, the new muscles he seems to be carrying, or the length of his hair. *He* is different. Like he's grown up twice as fast while I was gone.

"We were shocked they kept you so long too," Adam says. "My guess is it had something to do with your injuries. They would've wanted to make sure you were completely healed, so as not to trigger your memories or make you start asking questions about how you got hurt."

I scoff, tracing a circle around the phantom bullet hole in my thigh. "I guess they're not as good as they think they are."

"We wanted to get you back, sis. More than anything," Mica says. "It's just that planning for that became much more difficult than we thought it would be."

"What do you mean?"

"They've been watching him," Adam says. "It didn't take long for Mica to figure out he was being tailed, but it was always unpredictable. One guard, two guards, people pretending not to be guards, different times, different places . . . We couldn't figure out a pattern, a workaround. I guess that was probably the point."

"They know just how smart you are, Mic. Whitlock told me so herself," I say, my pulse accelerating as I recall her threats. "The Tribunal probably assumed—correctly—that you'd figure out any kind of regular schedule."

A flash of self-satisfaction flits across Mica's face, just for a second. "Whatever the reason for my extra special security detail, my hands were pretty much tied," he says, with something that looks suspiciously like pride lingering in his eyes. "And with Adam not exactly being able to walk into the Skyline ticket office and hop on the next shuttle to Korbyllis, planning your rescue was a little challenging."

"If they've been keeping tabs on you," I say, "how have the two of you been communicating?"

Mica scoffs. "Oh, please. We've got alien tech on our side, Terra." He pulls a tiny, flesh-colored earpiece out from inside his ear. "Kind of puts skydweller communication implants to shame, doesn't it? All of the convenience, none of the Tribunal getting to listen in."

"So, what do we do now?" I ask.

"I don't know," Adam says, and for the first time since meeting him, I really don't think he does. "We've been so focused on getting you back, it hasn't left much time for follow-up."

"Well, obviously we have to do something. The Tribunal is planning on taking off to space without half the Earth's population," Mica says angrily.

My stomach drops as I remember.

"Even if it takes another hundred years before they can do it," Mica continues, "that's a hundred more years of babies, and their babies' babies. A hundred years' worth of more people to condemn."

Adam nods gravely. "Yet they feel they're the saviors of mankind."

I bite the inside of my cheek. I feel like there's something more to it, something else Whitlock told me. But my mind is still clearing through the fog. "I think we already know what the next step needs to be," I say.

"Yeah," Mica says. "Making sure the Tribunal never, ever finds out you remember. If they ever realize either of us knows what we know—"

"No, Mic, we have to make sure we're *not* the only ones who know."

"What are you saying?"

"We have to tell the Council, to tell everybody. We need to spread the word to the other settlements. If all of us knew the truth, we might have a fighting chance of stopping them." I stand up and start to pace, too worked up to sit, before remembering the clacking sound of Whitlock's high heels. I force myself to stand still, though I can't keep from bouncing a little.

"*Fighting* is right," Mica says. "Think about what you're saying. You're talking about revolution. Anarchy."

"So? Maybe we need a revolution. Our government has been plotting to *literally* leave us for dead. We can't stay silent."

"So, what, a girl who everyone thinks just came back from a gambling spree, her kid brother, and an alien insurgent are going to save the world?" Mica says. "This isn't something we can just scream from the rooftops. Even if we didn't get swept up by the Tribunal the second they realized what we were doing, why would anyone even believe us?"

"But—"

"We aren't revolutionaries, sis."

"You'd rather have us, what? Sit back and watch TV? Go back to school, to scaving, and just hope that somebody else eventually figures it out?"

Mica exhales with an annoyed huff and throws his hands into the air. "Well, if there was any doubt as to whether she really is back . . ."

I stick my tongue out at him.

"I gotta take a break," Mica says. "You have fun with that, Adam."

"We do have to be smart about this though," I continue, ignoring my brother as he skulks into his room and shuts the door halfway. "Mica's right about one thing: If the Tribunal finds out you're still here—I still can't believe the risk you took—or if they find out that I remember, we're just going to find ourselves in the same position as before. Actually, *a lot* worse than before."

"Terra." Adam takes my hand.

"I don't even know where we would start."

"Slow down for a second, Sunburst." He pulls me over to the couch and directs me to sit down next to him.

"What?" I don't bother masking my annoyance but thread my fingers through his nonetheless. "We have to figure out what to do. We have to make a plan, start to prepare ourselves."

"Yeah, well, there's something else we're going to need to prepare for first," he says, lowering his eyes.

The sudden seriousness in his tone makes my body still, and I lift our joined hands to my cheek. "What's wrong?"

"It's the others. Charlie, Luke." A muscle feathers in his jaw. "Tom."

My mind floods with images: dark eyebrows framing kind eyes. Being handed a silver gun. Red hair, cascading down a woman's back, paired with a distinct feeling of distaste. And blue eyes—Adam's blue—peering at me from someone else's face.

"Luke, Charlie, your brother . . ." I say as the memories churn. "Where are they? Have you all been staying together? Where? And what have you been doing this whole time?"

New images take over my mind, but they're not memories this time. I picture the four of them, holed up in some underground hideout. Sneaking supplies, planning an insurrection . . . whatever it is that rebels do. A bloom of something akin to pride stirs in my chest.

The stern set of Adam's mouth softens and I see the lopsided edge of a grin playing on his lips. "Always with the questions."

"They're all right, aren't they?" I ask.

"Oh, they're just fine," he says bitterly.

My brow furrows.

"They're not here," he says, his eyes darkening. "They left."

"They're not here? They left?" I repeat inanely.

Adam jerks his jaw downward in a single nod. His eyes—darker than usual—are fixed on my face, carefully judging my reactions.

"I don't understand," I say.

"It didn't even take them a full day to decide you weren't worth saving," he spits.

"Oh. They're *gone*-gone. Like Whitlock said."

"Took the ship and turned tail." The muscles in his throat flex.

"I'm sorry," I say, linking my fingers behind his neck and pulling him close. I don't need to imagine the depth of the betrayal he feels. Or the shame. I felt it too, when I thought I was the one who had been left behind. "You stayed for me, this is my fault."

Adam shakes his head, unlocks my grasp, and leans back. "No," he says solemnly, still holding onto one of my hands. He inhales slowly, his nostrils flaring, then blows the air out through his lips. I watch him as he breathes deeply, in and out.

"Adam?" I say tentatively, not knowing if I'm supposed to break his meditation. "What is it?"

"There's more. Something I didn't know until just a few days ago."

I brace myself. "What is it?"

"I got confirmation that they made it back. Made it . . . home. And they told the President everything, including how I elected to stay behind. I doubt folks are too thrilled about that, but that's not the issue."

"Then, what is?"

"I wasn't lying when I told you our original mission was to fact-find and observe," Adam says. "It was. And it wasn't for invasion or destruction or any of the ridiculous things Whitlock said either. But I never explained why we were sent here in the first place."

My fingers feel cold; blood drains from my extremities, pumping through my rapidly beating heart and booming in my ears. I almost don't want to ask, but I know I have to. "What was the reason?"

"They needed to know it was safe. Safe to return."

I stare at Adam in confusion, his blue eyes blazing.

"My people," he says. "They're coming back."

BOOK 2: UNDERGROUND

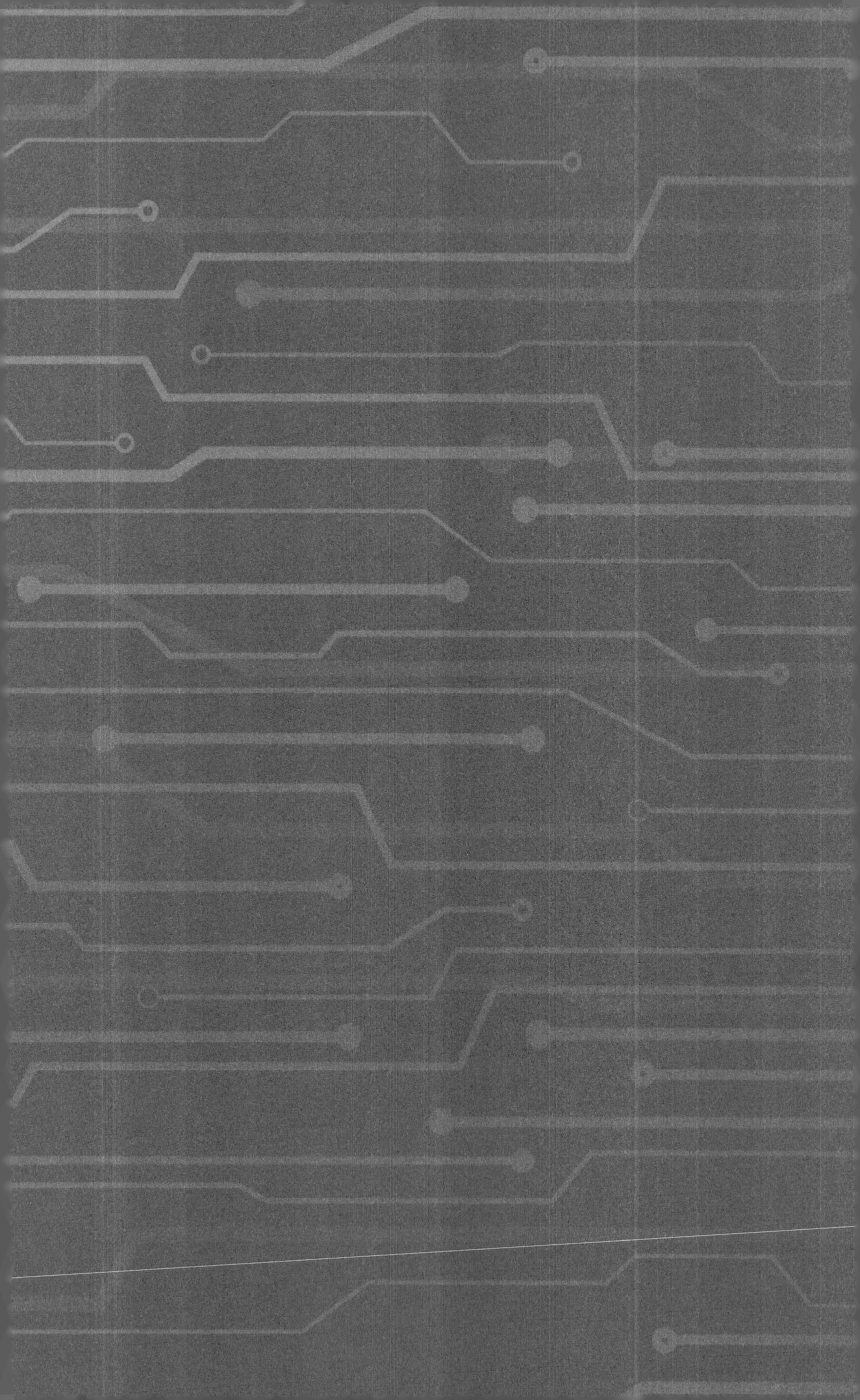

PROLOGUE

ADAM

"HOW MUCH LONGER 'TIL WE LAND?" I unhook the safety tethers from my jumpseat, refastening them to my uniform as I clamber toward the cockpit. My gaze locks onto the back of Tom's buzzed blond head in the captain's chair as I approach.

A long-suffering sigh echoes from the copilot's seat at his right.

"What's your issue, Chuck?" I say with a grin.

Charlie shoots me a pointed look. "Only that the answer hasn't changed since the last time you asked, Adam," she says.

I shrug. "Can't blame me for being antsy. We've been stuck inside this tin can for five days. I'm eager to get down there—see what this planet's all about."

"We're *all* antsy," Luke calls from the back of the ship. "But somehow the rest of us manage to be far less annoying about it."

I chuckle and clap a hand on my brother's shoulder. "So, what's the update, Tommy?"

"As she said, *Ensign* Killian," Tom replies, stressing my rank, "there is no update. We'll be out of the capital's vicinity shortly, and at the Intheria crash site in a few hours. From there, we disembark, set up camp, and begin recon. Now sit back and shut up until we get closer."

"Yes, *Captain*." I give my brother a stiff salute that probably looks respectful to someone who doesn't know better.

We all know better.

With a smirk, I make my way back to my jumpseat. I'm halfway there when several things happen at once.

A piercing boom shudders through the ship.

Metal scrapes against metal. The vessel shakes violently, and I'm thrown from my feet.

An alarm blares. The cockpit dashboard lights up.

And the yelling begins.

"Shit!" Tom shouts.

I scramble to stand, only to lose my footing again as the ship tips to one side.

"We need to level out!" yells Charlie.

"You think?" I brace against the wall and attempt to pull myself upright again. The act is more laborious than it should be. My breathing is strained. "What's happening?"

"The biostatic converter on the right wing has been compromised. The conversion unit was knocked off," Tom hollers over his shoulder. He grips the steering controls with one white-knuckled hand, pressing button after button with the other. "We're losing cabin pressure."

"Knocked off by what?" I bellow over the cacophony of alarms and warnings. No one replies.

Luke unhooks himself from his jumpseat and dashes to the monitors mounted on the wall between Charlie and me. He curses, then presses his nose against the viewport, trying to view the damage. "I can't get a visual," he says, panic in his voice. "Camera on the wing is out. FX is useless if I can't see what I need to *fix*."

I make a split-second decision. With a nod at Luke, I grab my mission pack, slinging it over my shoulder as I head toward the ladder that leads to the overhead hatch.

"What are you doing?" Charlie yells, silencing the alarm with the flick of a lever. Yellow and red lights continue flashing through the cabin.

"What does it look like?" I hook my foot on the first rung of the ladder. Luke hands me a spare conversion unit and I throw it into my pack. "I'll climb up, get eyes on the wing, and replace the unit. Just keep it as steady as you can."

"No." Tom's command is forceful, though his labored breathing belies how the atmosphere inside the ship is rapidly destabilizing without the conversion unit in place.

I climb a few more rungs without replying.

"Stop!" Tom yells. "We'll make an emergency landing." The ship tilts; he has already begun to descend.

"You can't," I snap. "We're still within range of the capital. Get any lower and they'll pick us up on their scanners. We can't risk it."

"What's the more immediate risk, Adam? I can barely keep this thing level." Tom's muscles are taut, his veins popping as he struggles with the controls. "This is no time for one of your reckless stunts. You are not going out there. That is an order, *Ensign*."

"Too goddamn bad, *Captain*," I say, wrenching open the hatch door and launching myself onto the ship's exterior. The collective curses of my teammates echo below as warm, sticky air rushes past me. Wedging my feet between the top rungs of the ladder, I clip a safety tether from my waist to an anchor point on the hull. I pivot my body until the right wing comes into view—along with the small hole and mess of torn, still-sparking wires where the conversion unit used to be.

I glance back down the hatch. Luke stares up, wide-eyed, and gives me a curt nod. A second later, the ship evens out as Tom halts our descent. I'm glad he realized this is a battle of wills he is not going to win.

I inhale deeply, feeling the hum of energy inside me as I muster my FX to the surface. I can *fix* it—slot the spare unit into place from here. Cybernetic enhancements are not without their controversy, but even I'll admit telekinesis has its benefits.

As I move to retrieve the part from my pack, another jolt rocks the ship. My legs fly out from under me and I slam into the open hatch door. Pain shoots through my chest as I slide down the ship's exterior until my safety tether jerks me to a stop down by the left wing. Cursing, I scramble for purchase, grabbing hold of the tether and planting my feet before starting the slow climb across the hull. This time, I bypass the hatch and head straight toward the right wing.

"Forget it, Adam!" Luke's voice whistles through the roar of the wind as he appears at the hatch. "We have to land—the ship's gonna break apart. Get back in here!"

The air goes still. The ship shudders and violently jolts again—just as I've begun rappelling down to the wing—before dipping sharply.

My tether snaps.

Time slows.

I lock eyes with Luke, his turquoise irises pinned open in horror.

And I fall.

I AM WEIGHTLESS.

The air feels thick as it rushes past me, my eyes locked on the ship as it grows smaller, smaller, smaller.

Survive, I think, sending the desperate command back to my team in my mind. This might be the end for me, but it isn't for them. Not for my brother, for our people, for the very future we came here to salvage.

Survive.

I twist my body so I can face the inevitability of my fate head on as I hurtle toward the cracked earth. In the periphery of my bleary vision, I glimpse a crumbling city, a forest of leafless trees, a dirt road, a walled-off town. The ground rushes toward me—closer, closer. I shut my eyes.

Survive.

The hum of my unspent FX swells in my ears. Like a reflex, I throw out my arms as if this is something that can be *fixed,* as if it'll do anything to shield me from the impending bone crush. As if every part of me won't shatter the instant I collide with the earth. Power blasts from my hands, unbidden, and for a second, my fall slows. Unexpected sounds cut through the wind—a yelp of surprise, a panicked scream, a grunt of pain.

My eyes snap open right before I hit the ground.

Survive.

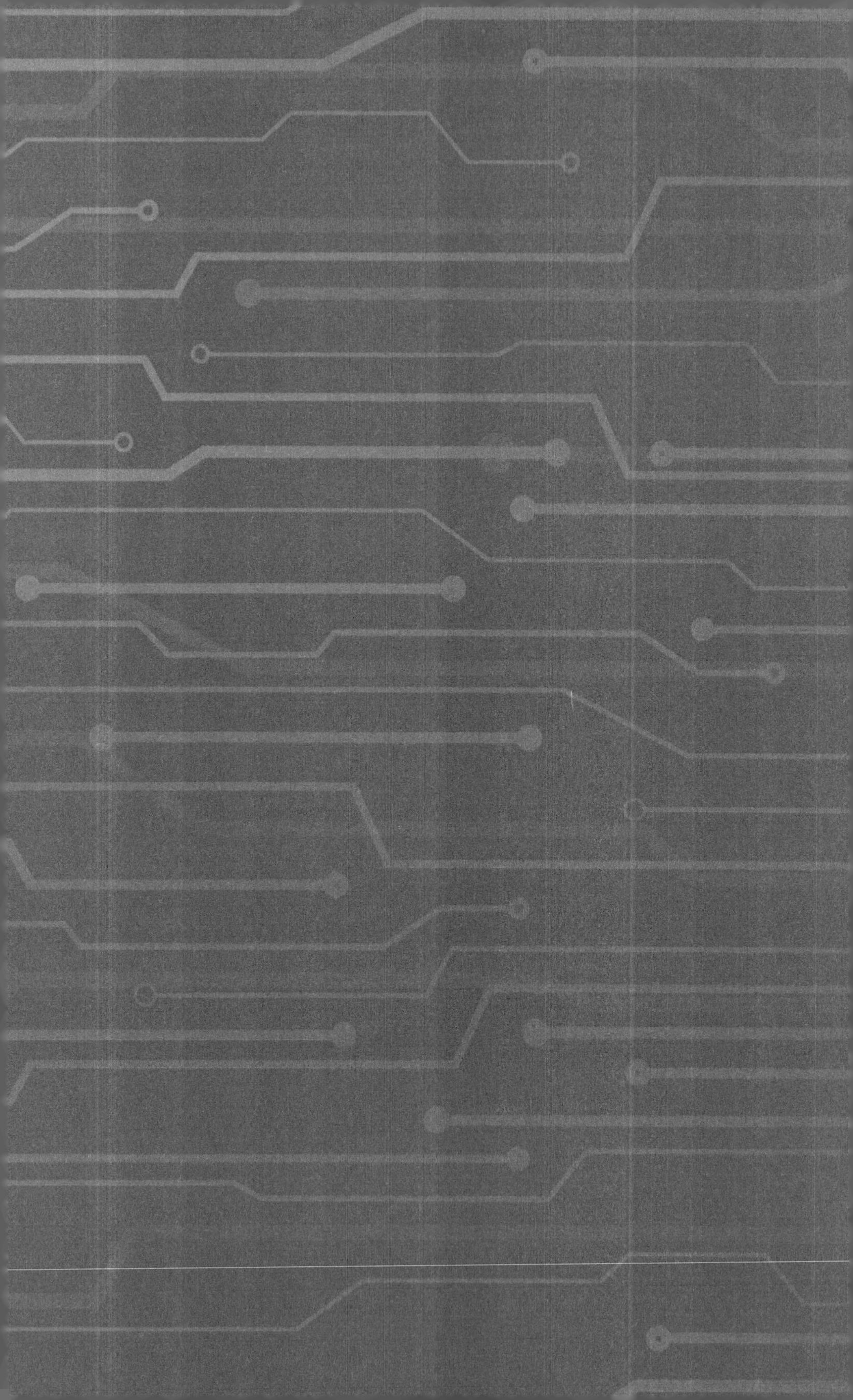

ONE

TERRA

"AGAIN," Mica says, his eyes narrowing.

"Let me catch my breath," I pant.

"No chance." Mica hurtles his fist at my face, and I duck out of the way in time to narrowly avoid the swing, losing my balance in the process. I stumble backward, twisting around and planting both my palms on the wall to steady myself.

"Cool it, Mic," I wheeze as I straighten, "I told you I wasn't ready."

"You dodged this time. That's progress."

I glare at him, my chest heaving. "It's not my fault you got a three-month head start on combat training. I'm still new at this. Cut me some slack."

"Sounds like a personal problem to me, sis," he says with a grin before coming at me with another swing that I miraculously manage to avoid. "Good. You're definitely improving. And after only a few weeks." He leans back, shifting his weight to his back leg, then lunges forward with a low kick.

I lift my own leg in reaction and block his blow with my shin. Well, block it as much as I can. The impact still hurts, and I find myself staggering to the side. In the time it takes me to regain my footing, Mica is already swinging his hand up, his thumb and pointer finger shaped into an imaginary gun.

"*Bang*. You're dead," he says, a little too cheerily.

"Mica," I chastise.

"Fine, not dead. Stunned. And being dragged off to some Tribunal holding cell to be interrogated. Better?"

"I told you—"

"Yeah, yeah, you weren't ready. Fine, we'll take a beat. But just remember, if the Tribunal finds out you got your memory back, the guardsmen sure as shit won't be giving you time to catch your breath."

"Language," I scold.

Mica ignores me, waltzing into the kitchen with an air of superiority. "Inquisitor Wolfe and all those guardsmen, including that poor guy that you gunned down in Korbyllis, didn't wait for you to be ready," he shouts over the running faucet.

"I didn't 'gun anyone down,' Mica," I call to him, my breath ragged from sparring. "It was self-defense." I plop down on the couch, which is pushed up against the back wall with the rest of the furniture. The main room of our apartment resembles a boxing ring more than an actual home now, leaving more than enough space for Mica to run circles around me during these training sessions.

Mica walks back into the room, a glass of water in one hand, a couple of mud-brown food pills in the other. He tosses the pills into his mouth and washes them down with a swig of water before arching his eyebrow at me.

"Fine." My voice is heavy with exasperation. "Proactive self-defense."

"Same difference."

"You sound more and more like Adam every day," I mutter.

Mica's face screws up with disgust. "I don't want to hear that," he says. "Comparing your brother to your boyfriend is gross."

"Don't be a brat." I grab a couch pillow from next to me and fling it at his head. He dodges with ease.

"You're going to make me spill," he taunts, raising the glass of water above his head.

"Shouldn't you be getting ready for school?"

He takes a long sip. "Do I have to?"

And just like that, all traces of the overconfidence that had colored his tone while we were sparring are gone. I look at him pointedly, my response written on my face.

"I hate wasting time there," he whines.

Perhaps I should be concerned that the mere mention of school is enough to sour my brother's mood these days. I find myself fighting a smile instead. Whining is something I wish I heard more often. Since returning from my three-month-long detention in Korbyllis, it's like our roles have been reversed. He's become this entirely new, grown-up person. So, strange as it seems, I kind of love the glimpses I get of him as the fourteen-year-old he actually is. The times I get to step back into my role as his older sister, *his* protector—as it should be.

"How many times have we had this discussion, Mic? Yes, you have to. You can't stop going to school. You barely missed a single day back before I—" I stop short, clearing my throat. "You know . . . *before*. And you've already skipped too many times since I've been back. Honestly, I'm surprised Principal Conifer hasn't already come banging down our door to see what's happened to his star pupil."

"I'm fifteen next summer, Terra. You were barely older than I am now when you dropped out. Nobody would notice if I did the same. They'd think I was prepping to start scavenging—picking up the family business or whatever."

I shake my head. "People *would* notice, Mica. Nobody is going to think that, because if it were true, you would have 'picked up the family business' last year when you passed your secondary examinations. Everyone would know that you're only dropping out now because of me."

Because, according to the Tribunal, I didn't spend three months *up there*, held against my will. I didn't spend three months having my memories tampered with—erased and replaced. No, according to them, I spent three months on some skycity bender, gambling our savings away in Lexicon's casinos and leaving my little brother to fend for himself.

"So?" Mica says with a shrug. "Who cares what everyone else thinks? You never did before."

A derisive laugh escapes my lips. "Everyone in Sixteen will think you're only dropping out because I can't support us anymore. And like it or not, baby brother, you've long been the West Q's golden child. Folks aren't going to look past it if they think I'm failing you."

Failing you again, *that is.*

Mica looks like he wants to interject, but I hold up my finger. "Being ostracized because they think I'm a bitch is one thing. I don't need people to like me. But this is just . . . It's different, okay? We don't want to give anyone a reason to keep an even closer eye on us. And I don't need to add your entire future to the list of things everyone thinks I've thrown away."

Sometimes I wonder if the story that the Tribunal concocted to cover my long absence was less about covering their asses and keeping their secrets, and more about punishing me for learning their secrets in the first place. Designed to crush me under a shadow of shame and disgrace to keep me from looking too closely.

They needed me to forget their treachery. But they *wanted* to make it hurt.

And the worst part? The part that I've barely been able to admit to myself, let alone tell Mica and Adam? It's the doubt. Not being able to trust my own mind.

Because I can't always tell if the things I remember are real.

Which of my memories actually happened? Which are ones they put there? Most days, I think I know. But then, there are moments . . .

Mica coughs, pulling me back to the present. His face is solemn when I look at him. "I'm sorry. I know it's worse for you. Pretending like you don't know anything—the Tribunal's plans, how they used you to get to Adam, even who—what Adam is . . ." His voice is a whisper, trailing off into silence.

"To be fair, I'm still not sure if I wouldn't be better off forgetting the part where I picked up a telekinetic alien in a secret underground biodome." I toss a grin at Mica and he reciprocates my attempt at levity with a half-hearted smile.

"It's just hard. Sitting there, nice and quiet and well-behaved, having to swallow what they are teaching us when *I know*. I know what the Tribunal really thinks of us down here, what they've tried to do to the groundworld in the past. What they still want to do."

"I know, Mic. God, do I know. The Tribunal wants to leave us to rot on this dead planet while they convert their own skycities into spacecraft"—I can't contain my scoff—"and take off for greener pastures. And we can't do anything about it. We have no proof. And without proof . . . I mean, just hearing myself say it out loud, it all sounds absolutely batshit crazy."

"Language," Mica chides with a sniff.

I huff out a laugh. "Who's going to believe us? Not to mention, once word gets out that we're spouting conspiracy theories about the Tribunal, it'd take all of three seconds for Prime Whitlock to send her goons to snatch me back up. And somehow, I don't think she'd be inclined to let me go this time."

Mica shakes his head sadly.

"I know it's rough, but hey, at least we're in it together? You, pretending like you don't know the things you know. Me, pretending I know even less than that. All while everyone in Sixteen hates my guts more than ever. But we do it because we have to."

"I know," Mica says with resignation. "At least until we can get out of here."

"Exactly. We stick to the plan—keep up appearances and stay off their radar. Which, for you, means continuing school until you pass your tertiary examinations and become a proper graduate. The way you were always supposed to."

He nods thoughtfully, and I wonder if he's thinking about the future day when he can take his final exams. The day we'll have the excuse we need to move on from Genesis X-16 without arousing suspicion. I find I've been thinking about it more and more lately, myself.

Tertiaries are the last step in most folks' schooling down here—for the ones who care about completing their education, that is. It's not unheard of for new grads to travel or even move away after they pass their exams —provided they have the means to do so. And given the extra contempt that all of Sixteen seems to bear me lately, I'd say our departure will be a welcome relief for many.

"Once we put this place and all this bad blood behind us," I say, "we might be able to do something about the Tribunal and those plans we aren't supposed to know anything about."

"Adam's specialty," Mica says with a grin, "collecting data. Intel. Proof. Whatever."

"That's the hope. You two geniuses work your technological hocus pocus and hack us a way to freedom."

"Hocus pocus?"

"Shut up. You know what I mean. You two are the tech nerds, not me. And when we get to that point, we'll see what we've got. Hopefully, it'll be enough to get people to listen. Maybe some of them will even believe us." I take a deep breath. "So, long story short, yes, you still have to go to school. It can't be all bad. You've got your friends, you've got Juniper. They must make being at school at least somewhat bearable."

"Yeah, you're right," Mica says, but I don't miss the resignation in his voice. Things must be bad if he no longer finds solace in spending time with Juniper Coal.

"So, until we're able to do more, we just need to concentrate on the not-so-bad stuff. We keep on keeping on. Okay?"

Mica looks at me thoughtfully, his bottom lip sucked beneath his top front teeth, before his mouth curves into a smirk. "We keep on keeping on . . . for now."

I narrow my eyes. "Wait, what does that mean?"

"Well, the next tertiary examination date is only a couple of weeks away."

"Right. For the seventh-year students who are ready to take them—"

"And anybody else who wants to attempt them," Mica finishes.

My mouth pops open. "You're only fourteen. You can't take your tertiaries."

Mica shakes his head dismissively. "You're acting like age is the determining factor in these things. You haven't been out of the system *that* long, you know we are eligible to take our exams as soon as we satisfy the base coursework prerequisites. And I completed those last year."

"Sure, you're *allowed* to take them, but as for whether you're *ready* to . . ."

"I passed my secondaries when I was twelve. You were, what, fifteen? It's not my fault that—" He cuts himself off like he's literally biting his tongue to keep himself from finishing that thought.

"That, what? That you're so much smarter than me? That I'm just an uneducated scav?" Neither statement is a lie. He *is* smarter than me. And, okay, maybe I'm not *un*educated, but I am *under*educated—that's kind of the definition of being a dropout. Though the thought that Mica thinks of me that way stings a little more than I anticipated.

"No," Mica says emphatically. "I never said you weren't smart, Terra. Nobody who knows you would ever think that. You're astute as shit and you know it. I'm just, I dunno. More . . ."

"Cerebral?" I offer.

"More motivated, I guess," he says. "I'm sorry." The guilt that sparks across his face immediately douses my indignation.

"It's fine, Mic. It's not like anybody would argue against the claim that you're the brilliant one in the family."

"Does that mean we're agreed then?" he asks hopefully. "When I pass my tertiaries, I'll be done with school, legitimately. People won't be able to be *suspicious* of anything. It's the same plan, we're still 'keeping up appearances.' I'm just moving the timeline up a bit."

"A bit?" I scoff, then sigh. "*If* you pass, we can talk about it. But you're still young and if you think—"

"Koi Lodgestone passed her tertiary examinations when she was thirteen and a half," Mica interrupts.

"First of all, that happened before you were even born. I think we've hit the statute of limitations on relevancy. And secondly, Koi Lodgestone is a legend. She was a prodigy," I retort. "Are you a prodigy?"

"Hey, you said it, not me," he says with a grin. I give him a playful push, causing the water from the glass that's still in his hand to slosh out, dripping down his wrist and puddling on the floor.

"School." I shove my silver wristwatch—our mother's watch—in his face to prove my point. "Finish getting ready. And clean that up, will you?"

"Fine." Mica deposits his now mostly empty glass on the table that's set up outside the kitchen alcove, then charges into the bathroom. "But let's be real. You just want me out of here so I can lead off whoever the Tribunal has slated to tail us today. So you can go see *him*."

I dash back to the couch and try to chuck another pillow at him, but he closes the bathroom door just in time. With a pathetic *thump*, the pillow ricochets off the door, landing directly in the puddle of spilled water Mica definitely did not clean up.

Perfect, I think. I pick up the now-sopping pillow, as well as the one I had flung at Mica after our sparring session, and dump them back on the couch with a sigh.

As always, Mica's a bit too perceptive for his own good. Of course, I want to see Adam. I've barely been able to spend any time with my personal fugitive. We've only managed to see each other a handful of times since the day he risked everything to come help Mica trigger my memories.

The day he brought me back to myself.

And even those all-too-short times were such a risk. It's dicey for me to be gone for long stretches of time. I fear that with too much time unaccounted for, the guardsmen will come looking, will come to check up on me. That they'll *know*. And if I was only endangering myself, that'd be one thing. But it puts Mica at risk too.

And Adam . . . Should the Tribunal discover that Adam's still down here, that he didn't go with the rest of his team when they fled our pathetic planet . . . Well, I feel confident that the horrors they put me through are nothing compared to what they'll do to Adam if they get their hands on him again.

Not when he and his people—their technology and knowledge—are the key to the Tribunal's despicable conversion project.

"You know full well that I have an *actual* reason to go see him today," I holler at Mica through the closed bathroom door on my way to my room. "I found more of that bipolar wire on my scav run yesterday."

The door jerks open, revealing a suddenly mirthful Mica. "The word you're looking for is 'polarized,' not 'bipolar.' The wire doesn't have a personality disorder." He surveys me with amusement.

I stick my tongue out at him. "Whatever. The point is, that's the last thing on that list you gave me. The list of stuff Adam needs. I was able to find the rest of it at the Marketplace."

"That's great! With his datapad on the fritz, it's been impossible to get the software we need to hack into the network and dig into the Tribunal's records. Not to mention I'm pretty sure it's been driving him a little"—Mica points a finger at his temple and winds it in the air—

"cuckoo. He hasn't been in contact with his team since right before we got you back. But now he should have everything he needs to repair it, and—hmm, but if he—no, no. Once it's synced and we connect it to . . ."

He's talking to himself now, and I know any further contributions I might've made to the conversation have been rendered irrelevant. He's gone full Mica—all technological terminology and muttered observations.

My brother's voice fades as I shut myself in my bedroom. I peel off my sweaty tank top and discard it onto the floor before pulling out a clean set of clothes and quickly redressing. A quick peek in the mirror above my dresser allows me to assess myself—my cheeks are still flushed from sparring with Mica, and the red shirt I selected only magnifies the color. I quickly pull it off and replace it with a soft teal tank.

Better, I think as I pull my dark brown hair out of its unkempt pony-tail. I brush it through twice before putting it back up into the same spot —tightly centered halfway up the back of my head—and coiling the length into a twisted bun. I know it's silly, that there's no need to bother putting any effort into my appearance. That it will likely be ruined in a few minutes by the heat and humidity once I head outside. But it's been long enough since I've seen Adam face-to-face that, though I cringe at myself a little for it, I still want to look nice.

I roll my eyes at myself in the mirror. The gold flecks in the center of my chestnut brown irises shimmer tauntingly in my reflection as I stare. A memory surfaces from the back of my mind: rain beating down outside as Adam pulls me close. Hands roaming, lips crushing, and all the while, losing myself in his iridescent blue eyes.

That memory's real, I tell myself. *That one is mine.*

A dull thump from the main room pulls me back to reality. I point a finger at the mirror as if to scold my reflection for letting my mind wander, then walk out of my bedroom.

"All right, you ready?" I ask Mica. I scan the room for my boots, finding one of them on its side by the front door and eventually rooting the other one out from behind the couch. "Did you let Adam know that I'm coming?"

Mica glances up from his task of stuffing a textbook into his backpack to give me an exasperated look. "As fun as it is playing messenger for the two of you, I have it on good authority that he would *much* rather hear from you directly."

I make a face at him as I lace up my boots, then grab my navy jacket from the back of a chair. Rolling the sleeves up past my elbows, I shrug. "It's quicker for you to do it."

"Wuss. You're just scared to try the earpiece again," Mica says.

I mask my wince with another shrug, remembering with painful clarity what happened the first time I tried to use Adam's communicator earpiece. I was thrilled when I first learned about it—couldn't wait to try it out. Adam had gotten it to Mica while I was still in Tribunal holding. This one tiny piece of alien tech allowed them to talk with each other in secret, across the miles that separated them. And the idea of being able to talk to Adam whenever I wanted, without the Tribunal intercepting, eavesdropping, or even being aware of the communication, had seemed too good to be true.

It was.

I'd barely had the thing in my ear five seconds when the static started, so loud that I swear I felt my brain actually rattle inside my skull. It took days for the ringing to stop.

"You would be too," I say, "if you'd experienced what I did. A twenty-six hour-long headache is not something I'm anxious to relive."

"That only happened because you didn't follow my instructions."

"Did you ever stop to think that maybe your instructions were the problem?"

Mica seems to consider my question. "Nope," he says after a moment. "It's like I told you, all you have to do is—"

"Twenty. Six. Hours."

"Fine, fine." Mica waves his arm dismissively before lifting a hand to his right ear. "I'll tell him, but if his receiver isn't turned on, he won't get the message 'til later anyway."

I nod, and Mica pushes on a spot behind his ear. "Adam, Terra's coming out your way, package in tow. We're leaving now. Ready the waypoint." Mica's blank expression shifts into one of engaged concentration, and I know his warning about Adam not getting the message right away was unwarranted; he is responding right now.

"Yep, exactly. I'll keep my ear to the ground. See ya," Mica finishes, poking behind his ear again to cut off the transmission.

"*Ready the waypoint?*" I mock, unable to stifle a laugh.

"Shut up," Mica says, though he's grinning. "I'm cool and you know it. And as I've said before, this would *all* be much cooler if you two leaned into it. We're basically secret spies now. Think about how rad code names would be."

I roll my eyes. I guess there's still plenty of the old Mica left. "You work on that." I grab my blue scavenging bag from a hook near the front door. "For now, let's get going."

TWO

MICA and I casually walk out the swinging double doors of our apartment building into the clear morning air. Well, "clear" may be a bit of a stretch. Between the constant stink of pollution and the heat that will only intensify as the sun rises, this is about as good as it gets around here.

Mica hooks his backpack over one shoulder and waves me off. His heels kick up little clouds of dust as he ambles down the dirt road. A woman with neatly braided hair and suspiciously clean clothing exits a neighboring apartment complex, walking in a way I'm sure she thinks is nonchalant as she follows Mica.

Tail on the move. I smirk as I consider that Mica might be right—leaning into the espionage angle does make it a little more fun. And goodness knows I'll take any amusement we can get these days. Maybe I'll help him brainstorm code names when he gets back.

I fuss with my bag for a moment, waiting to see if any other oh-so-inconspicuous strangers pop out of the woodwork, then slip into the narrow alleyway behind our building. Our motorbike transport leans against the wall on one side of the alley. I wheel it forward, revealing a discreet manhole cover underneath. With a grunt of effort, I carefully lift the heavy plate, shifting it over far enough to lower myself into the darkness below.

I didn't know what to think when Mica told me about how Adam found him after he escaped from Korbyllis. *Pretty much jumped me in an alley on my way home from school,* he'd said. Turns out, he wasn't being hyperbolic.

"Adam was in a bit of a bind," Mica said. "The new scavenging restrictions and boundary markers made it impossible for him to get back into the District, but he couldn't stay here. It didn't exactly seem like a good idea for him to be seen in Sixteen at all." Adam split the difference by camping out in the old outpost building just outside the District limits. It was several days before he thought about the network of underground tunnels that run beneath the District—the ones that led to the biodome. The ones where I found myself being saved from raiders by a telekinetic spaceboy with the most beautiful eyes on this side of the galaxy.

I'm still not exactly sure how, but Adam was able to procure blueprints for the District's tunnel layout in its entirety, as well as a map of smaller maintenance passageways that run throughout Sixteen. And in what was possibly the only streak of luck any of us have experienced since this all began, he realized that not only does one of the tunnels run directly underneath the outpost, but that a maintenance passage connects there as well.

So, Adam started digging.

Cool air whispers past me as I slide the cover back into place above me. I fish a small flashlight out of my bag and click it on, holding it between my teeth as I climb down into the passageway. I walk quickly, my footsteps echoing softly against the cracked stone walls. The guardsmen don't seem to know these tunnels are here, but every few minutes, I stop and listen anyway to ensure no one is following me.

I noticed the surveillance cameras the first time I ventured down here. It had my pulse racing until I saw their crumbling cases, the grime and cobwebs covering their lenses. Still, I stay vigilant. If there's anything I've learned over the past four months, it's not to take anything for granted. Thankfully, the only sounds I hear are occasional snippets from the soundtrack of the world above—stamping feet, muted shouts, laughing kids.

I think about the people up there, my fellow terrestrials, going about their lives in Sixteen—blissfully ignorant of all the ways the Tribunal has failed them . . . and all the horrible plans still to come. I think about the way their loathing increased exponentially after I returned from Korbyllis. I suppose if I were in their shoes, I'd probably hate me too. They don't know any better. They don't know everything they think they know about me is fiction—a line fed straight from Prime Whitlock's mouth to their ears.

But the fact that I *know* I shouldn't resent them doesn't quite help how I *feel*—which is, indeed, complete and total resentment. Because they believe the lie. Because they're playing right into the Tribunal's hands without realizing it. And the incessant public shunning on every scav run, every time I go to the Marketplace . . .

It's not fun for me.

It helps to remind myself that most of these people weren't exactly my biggest fans before all this happened. Before I found that strange little machine out in the Dead Woods, the one that changed my life forever just because it happened to fall off Adam's *spaceship*.

I laugh, the tunnel walls swallowing the sound. I still can't even think the word "spaceship" with a straight face. Government conspiracies, extraterrestrials, outer space . . . I cannot believe that these are terms I use regularly now. When did this become my life?

The tunnel forks ahead, and I take the right-hand path—toward the old outpost. This section of the tunnel is narrower, the walls lined with rusting pipes and cables. I keep moving, my flashlight dancing over the rough stone as I walk.

After about twenty more minutes, I reach a heavy metal door that looks like it's been carved into the very stone of the wall. Pulling my scav bag around to my front, I take a small circular device from an interior pocket. I run my thumb across the large metal button in the center, affixed with a label that boasts a single word: "Red." I grin as I recall Adam's answer when I asked why he labeled the device—the key—that way.

"Because everything's more fun with a big red button to press," he'd said.

He and Mica are terrible influences on each other, I think with a snort.

Balancing the flashlight between my teeth again, I pull back the sleeve of my jacket to reveal my mother's silver wristwatch—the one Adam had found for me, had gotten back to me. The one that helped me connect the dots back to him after the Tribunal tried to scramble every memory I had of him. I'm right on time.

I hold the key against the door and press the "red" button with my thumb. The door unlocks with a series of clicks, and I slide through before quietly closing it behind me.

Unlike the dark tunnel, the hallway I emerge into is dimly illuminated. Light seeps in from the top of a set of stairs at the far end. My breath is shaky as I make my way up the stairs into the abandoned maintenance outpost. My purpose for coming here is different now, but I still can't quite shake the lingering feelings—the panic, the anticipation, the terror—from the first time I was here.

I glance toward the broken window on one side, right above where I'd hid in the shadows at the back of the building while the raiders who had been chasing me stormed through the outpost. They'd thought I'd gone inside and were none too pleased when they realized I'd been skulking along the periphery instead. One of the raiders had put his hand right through the glass in an attempt to snatch me. Almost got me too.

I pace around the dust-ridden outpost—two lonely rooms, a loft overhead, and the stairwell back down to the passageway. A table with three mismatched chairs sits in the corner. I resist the urge to sit down in a chair with long, spindly legs and a patchwork seat. It's better if it looks as if nobody's been here.

I wait for a few minutes, my ears straining, until I pick up a faint shuffling from beneath the floorboards. I tense. There's a grunt, the sound of something heavy being moved, and finally, soft footsteps in the next room.

A smile breaks out on my face as Adam—all height and muscle and blond hair that's gotten downright shaggy—appears in front of me. There's a smudge of dirt on the edge of his chin. He's slightly out of breath.

We stare at each other for a heartbeat or a minute or a lifetime. My eyes roam over the sharp angles of his face, the way the shades of blue in his eyes seem to eddy and swirl, an ocean in each iris. I reach up to brush a lock of golden hair back from his forehead, my heart stuttering when his breath hitches at my touch.

Adam sweeps me up against him, wrapping his long arms around me.

One hand cradles my head to his chest, and I can feel the gentle thump of his heartbeat through his soft white shirt. He nestles his chin against my hair and I allow myself the moment of respite to soak in his warmth, his scent—sunlight and fresh grass, salt and something so ineffably *him*. I imagine it's the scent of stardust.

He lifts his head and I mimic the movement, pulling back just far enough for his cerulean eyes to lock on my velvet brown ones. I briefly wonder if the flecks of gold in my eyes shine brighter when he's around. It seems like they should. *I* feel brighter when he's here. I don't get a chance to ask him though, because before I can utter a word, his lips are on mine.

The breath rushes from my lungs as I coil both my arms around Adam's torso, leaning into the welcome pressure of his kiss—soft at first, almost hesitant. A reacquaintance. It quickly deepens, firm but gentle, and a small sigh escapes from me as he slides a hand around my waist. He settles it on the small of my back and holds me against him.

For a moment, it's as if it hasn't been weeks since we've seen each other, and he's not what he is, and I'm not who I am, and there isn't a universe of unanswered questions between us.

But too soon, the moment passes, and I remember that I came here for other reasons than this—other than *us*. I brace my palm on his chest and pull myself out of Adam's embrace, meeting his gaze once again.

"Hey there, spaceboy," I say, breathless. "It's nice to see you too."

THREE

ADAM GRINS my favorite lopsided grin—his mouth curving up higher on one side than the other. "Hey yourself, Sunburst."

I smile at the nickname—the same one my Gran used with me as a child. A nod to the streaks of golden color spearing out from the center of my eyes—a burst of sunlight in my otherwise dull brown irises. "I missed you."

Adam brings his mouth back down to mine with exquisite softness. "You have no idea how much I missed you."

"I think maybe I have some idea," I murmur, heat rising in my cheeks as I realize what's pressing against me as he holds me tightly to himself.

He coughs and loosens his grasp, just a smidge. "Any issues getting here?"

I shake my head. "I took the tunnels. No one saw me."

"Good. Ready?"

I nod. He takes my hand and leads me back to where he came in from. Several floorboards in this room have been dislodged and moved aside, leaving a wide, dark hole in the corner.

"After you," Adam says, releasing my hand.

I dangle my legs over the side of the hole and peer down, angling my flashlight's beam into the blackness. It's so dark that even if the bottom was only a few feet below us, I wouldn't be able to see it. Of course, I know from experience that it's actually much, much farther. It's not a comforting thought.

"I don't like this part," I admit, not hiding the tremble in my voice.

"I've got you."

I take a deep breath and slide into the abyss. A tingle runs through my veins as the initial seconds of free fall make my adrenaline spike, but just when I think I'm about to meet my end, my body slows. A few moments later, my feet touch solid ground. It's a gentle landing, but the surprise still has me dropping my flashlight. It winks out as it hits the ground.

Of course. I bend down and grope blindly as I search for the light. I don't find it, but I do soon find myself touching the cool stone of a nearby wall. With a sigh, I lean against it until I finally hear Adam touch down.

"Sorry for the wait," he says, his voice strained and breath labored. I frown in the darkness; I forget how much his telekinesis—his FX—takes out of him.

"I was having some trouble placing the floorboards back correctly," he continues. "You might have to redo it when you go back." Light suddenly flares as Adam pans his own flashlight—brighter and more effective than my own—up and down, revealing the smooth gray walls of the tunnel we've descended into. It stretches off in both directions further than the beam can reach.

"Lead the way," I say, finding my voice. Something glints on the tunnel floor, and I snatch up my runaway flashlight as Adam takes my hand and starts walking. I ignore the quickening of my pulse as I follow, navigating around neat piles of rubble that decorate the tunnel floor—leftovers from Adam's careful demolition into the outpost above.

"You holding up okay back there?" Adam's voice echoes off the tunnel walls. "It's going to be a long haul if I have to end up carrying you."

With a snort, I speed up in an attempt to shove past him, but the tip of my boot snares in a divot on the ground, and I trip.

Adam catches me with one arm. "This again? I thought we were done with the whole 'you fall, I catch you' thing."

"A fluke," I say dismissively as I straighten, and I'm grateful he can't see the heat flaring up my neck. "Don't get used to it."

I swear I can *hear* his answering grin in the darkness.

We fall in line beside each other, our fingers linked, hands dangling between us. We travel through the labyrinth of tunnels in comfortable silence, save for Adam's quiet directions as to where and when to turn. Finally, Adam ushers me around one last corner, and we're there.

The flashlight bounces over a wall of matte metal panels that stretch from floor to ceiling, completely blocking it off. Behind the wall lies the biodome—the underground oasis where I had first awoken after Adam saved me from the raiders.

Fragmented images break through from somewhere in my mind: A desperate woman banging, banging, banging on a metal wall just like this one. A burst of bright white light. The feel of soft grass cushioning my body. Green, everywhere green.

I think it's real. It must be real. But it's like there's a veil over the images. Like I'm not completely sure if the woman in the memory is me.

Adam walks over to the wall and presses in on a spot with his knee. Several panels slide open to reveal a doorway and an embedded keypad. He prods at it for a moment, and there is the distinct sound of something unlocking. Adam pushes open the door and I recoil from the instant brightness, lifting my arm to shield my eyes.

We walk through the doorway into glorious sunlight. It's artificial, I know, but nonetheless welcome after the bleak, unending dark of the tunnels.

"Welcome back," Adam says breezily. He turns around to seal off the entrance, and as the panels slide shut, the doorway disappears before my eyes. The flawlessness of the dome's camouflage panels, there to maintain the illusion of an endless landscape, never ceases to amaze me.

"How much further from here?" I ask, smiling as a warm breeze rustles the flaps of my jacket.

"Not far at all. This is the same entrance we used the last time you came. See?" Adam points to a pair of identical buildings poking up behind a line of lush forest: the research center. I beam as I take in my surroundings: the tall grass swaying in a weightless breeze, the quietest hint of running water babbling somewhere nearby. Every time I leave this place, I think I must be subconsciously forcing myself to forget how beautiful it is. That, or my messed up mind is doing it for me.

Maybe it's a self-preservation thing. An attempt to keep my bitterness at bay, given the fact that everywhere else on this planet is just as dead and barren as the land surrounding Sixteen. All I know is that each time I come back here to the biodome, I'm just as awestruck as I was the first time.

Adam and I hike through the forest, arriving at the double doors that mark the entrance to the research complex. Unlike the previous times I've been here, however, the doors are wide open.

"You finally got them open!" I exclaim. "I thought you said the doors were on some kind of biometric lockdown."

"They were. But I got it eventually, it just took some time." Adam's voice darkens. "And it's not like I don't have plenty of that."

"Beats climbing through windows," I say, trying not to read into his tone as we walk into the observation room. "Done some redecorating, have you?" His makeshift bed is still tucked away in the same spot along the back wall, but that's the only thing that hasn't been rearranged since I was here last.

The desks that used to cross the entire room from wall to wall have been merged into one huge rectangular mass in the room's center. A few archaic computers are set up on one side. Haphazard piles of food and clothing are stacked on the other. Adam's set of strange silver instruments are neatly laid out in the middle, and I recognize his pack lying on the floor nearby. The technology it uses to be able to fit and contain any number and size of items never ceases to astonish me.

Adam shrugs before making a beeline for the computer station. He takes a seat in a rolling chair and picks up a slim black computer tablet— his datapad.

"What did you—" I step behind Adam to get a closer look at the techno-logical carnage in his hands. His datapad has been hacked apart. The back cover is missing. Wires criss-cross one another amidst the mess of chips and circuits. A small metal box—a quantum storage cube, or qube, Adam told me it's called—is attached to the bottom. "What happened to it?"

"Don't worry, it still works just fine." A flash of light emanates from the datapad, and when he flips it around, my own face looks back at me from the screen—my eyes frozen mid-blink, my mouth screwed up like I'm about to speak.

Attractive. "That's a keeper," I snort. "What?" I add, a bit wary of the surprised look on Adam's face.

His mouth quirks up into that lopsided grin. "Nothing, nothing. I just have a rather distinct memory of being in this very lab room and you nearly biting my head off for snapping a picture of you."

"Back then I didn't know if you were a creep who had nefarious plans for me. Now, I'm fully aware of it—and I've accepted that you are." A telekinetic finger pokes my rib and I grin. "Plus, I'm pretty sure my face was, like, sixty percent dirt and blood at that point. Hardly worth capturing in a photo."

"Not true," he says. I blush. With a kick, Adam rolls his chair around until he's behind me. I yelp as he bumps into my legs, sending me down into his lap. "Not true then, and not true now. But it would be nice to get one where you're smiling at the camera for once," he says, kissing my cheek. I roll my eyes, but a grin plays at the corner of my mouth as the datapad emits another flash of light.

"Okay, okay, enough of that." I jump to my feet, the flush in my cheeks deepening. Eager for a distraction from the flustered ripple in my chest, I motion to the ravaged backside of the datapad. "Just seems like a shame to have torn this thing to shreds."

"I know it may be hard to believe," Adam says, "but I don't exactly have all the luxuries of a Dissidian techlab down here."

Dissidian. My brow furrows at the unfamiliar term.

Adam unplugs the qube and uses an instrument with a jagged head to roughly pry off its casing. "I had to improvise to give us even a fool's hope of getting this thing working again. Alas, maintaining aesthetics is not exactly high on my priority list," he finishes, his tone noticeably cooler.

"I didn't mean anything by it."

Adam glances at me, contrition brimming in his eyes. I know he didn't mean to get defensive. I can feel the apology lingering behind the tense set of his mouth, but honestly, there's nothing to apologize for. Being down here alone for weeks would leave my social skills a little on the rusty side too.

"Don't worry about it," I blurt out before he has a chance to speak.

Adam's shoulders sag a bit as he releases a breath. "Mica said you have something for me?" he asks.

"Oh, right." I place my scav bag on the tabletop next to him, displacing the careful order of his instruments—one rolls off the table and bounces on the floor with a soft clang. Adam sighs as he flicks his fingers upward, sending the tool soaring back into his hand with his FX, but the twinkle is back in his eyes.

I lift the flap of my bag and fish out a small fabric-wrapped bundle, neatly tied with a length of black ribbon.

"Speaking of aesthetics," Adam says, the corners of his mouth twitching, "this is so nicely wrapped. Feels like I'm opening a present."

My cheeks heat. "Mica said they were important—I didn't want to lose or damage anything."

Adam wears an amused expression. "Mm-hmm. Sure."

"Fine," I say. "Consider it an early birthday present, then. Or is it belated?"

Adam arches a brow as he opens the bundle, revealing a length of wire, flat batteries of various sizes, and a small box containing the tiniest screws I've ever seen. Those were the hardest for me to procure.

He places the items gingerly on the table and the humor on his face vanishes. "Thank you for finding these," he says, looking at me with an intensity that heightens the burning in my cheeks. "It's exactly what we needed."

I clear my throat. "So, when is it, anyway?"

"When is what?"

"Your birthday."

He pauses. "I don't know."

Now it's my brow's turn to shoot up. "What do you mean?"

"That's not really a thing for us," he says with a shrug.

I gape at him. "But you know what birthdays are."

Adam nods as he begins to coil the wire in a series of small loops.

"And you have, uh, an age. You told me you were twenty."

"I am. It may look a little different than how you do it down here, but we still mark the passage of time. How long we've, er, existed. It just doesn't have anything to do with the day we were . . . born." Maybe I imagine it, but I could swear his voice hitches over that last word.

"I'm confused," I say.

Adam chuckles. "The first day of our annual calendar is called the Turning. My people all turn a year—well, we don't call it a year—older on that day. I suppose it's like . . ." He contemplates for a moment. "It's like if you had the same birthday as every other person on Earth. Only it's not a celebration or cause for exchanging gifts." His eyes dart to the long black ribbon he placed to the side after unwrapping the bundle of datapad parts. "It just *is*. I've had twenty turnings."

"How old is twenty turnings in regular old Earth-years?"

"Why? Worried that you're robbing the cradle here?" he jokes.

I scowl at him. "Given the way you talk, it seems more likely I'm robbing the grave."

Adam laughs as he gently lays the coil of wire on the desk. He takes my hand in his and squeezes it. "Fear not, Sunburst. For all intents and purposes, turnings and regular old Earth-years are the same."

I survey Adam carefully. This is the first time he's offered up any information about his background—where he's from, what it's like—since the day I got my memories back.

"So, before," I start, trying to choose my words with care, "you said a word. 'Dissidian.' What does it mean?"

Adam's grip immediately loosens, and my hand drops listlessly back to my side. "Is that so? Hmm, I guess I did," he says to himself. "Good to know that word's not off-limits."

"Off-limits?"

He sucks in a breath. "You know there's a lot that I can't . . . that I haven't been able to—"

"Yes, I know," I say, more sharply than I intended. "So, it means . . . what exactly? You said something about a Dissidian lab. Is it your word for, like, a technician or something?"

Adam looks at me, his brow deeply furrowed. He takes a long time to reply. When he does, he speaks slowly, as if he's testing his words before he actually says them. "No . . . it's more like . . . the word for . . . what I am. Where I'm from."

My mouth pops open in shock. He's never once said the name of where he's actually from, or what his people are called. The tenuous control I had over my words snaps, questions spewing from my lips in a fury. "What you are? Your people, you call yourselves 'Dissidian' then? Which would make where you're from, what, 'Dissidia?' How far is it from here? How long will it take for your people to reach us? When are they coming? *Why* are they coming? What do they want with us?"

Adam's eyes are wide when my inquisitorial onslaught stops. He considers me for a moment, perhaps surprised at how quickly and frenetically my words spilled out. I eagerly watch his face as he starts to speak, thrilled to finally be getting some of the answers I've been so desperate for. But a few moments pass and his look of surprise is replaced with that same pained expression.

"Yes," he says, slowly. "I am . . . from Dissidia."

I wait for him to continue. He doesn't.

"That's it?" I say, not caring if I sound like a brat. "That's all I get?"

"That's all I can say." He sweeps his eyes over my face, emotion roiling behind his perfect cerulean eyes. Perhaps it's the same abject misery currently sweeping through my gut.

"That's all you *will* say, you mean," I correct him angrily. "Why did I get my hopes up that you might actually *tell me* something? Why did I think this would be any different than last time? Or the time before that?" I sweep my arm out in an explosive gesticulation that knocks my scav bag off the desk. It takes a stack of neatly folded clothing with it; I recognize a few of my father's old shirts, ones that Mica had given to Adam.

"I *did* tell you something," Adam says, finding the capacity to form sentences at a regular pace again. "I didn't think I'd be able to mention Dissidia to you at all, but I could. That's something, right?"

"What are you talking about? You didn't think you'd *be able* to tell me? Who the hell's gonna find out what you say? You think I'm going to report whatever you tell me to the Tribunal? You think I'm planning on selling your secrets?"

Adam shakes his head wearily. "No, of course not."

"Then *why*?" I soften my voice. "If this has something to do with the rest of your team, if it's out of some kind of loyalty to Luke and Charlie and . . ." I trail off without mentioning his brother. "You don't owe them anything. You know that, right? They left you here, Adam."

"I am aware," he says through gritted teeth.

"Then why are you still so loyal to them? You're keeping secrets that could mean the difference between life and death for us when your people arrive."

"And I've told you, *multiple times now,* that it's much more complicated than that. I've told you everything I *can.* Yes, my people—the *Dissidians,*" he all but snarls the word, "are coming here and I can't—not won't, *can't*—tell you exactly why. It's not going to come down to life and death, though, I can say that much."

He reaches for my hand again. I step back, my heart twisting, until I'm just out of reach.

A flash of hurt crosses his face. "I wish I could tell you more," he says. "God, you have no idea. I wish I could tell you *everything*—but I can't. You need to accept that, Terra."

I fold my arms over my chest. "I don't need to accept anything. I need to start lowering my expectations," I spit.

Adam sighs and turns his focus back to the devices on the table, picking the coil of polarized wire back up and resuming his work. With a snort, I turn on my heels and march back through the still-open research center doors.

FOUR

I STORM TOWARD THE TREES. Something settles in my chest as I hide my body beneath the leafy boughs of one particularly large one, and I run my hands over its rough bark.

I suppose, if nothing else, at least seeing these trees again has made this trip worth it, I think. I know I'm being petulant. I know that Adam must have good reasons for not telling me everything—or at least, that he truly believes he does. Logically, I *know* this. But my brain doesn't seem to be operating on the same wavelength as the rest of my body. And I can't shake the unease snaking over me at the thought of what he might still be hiding.

After all, his secrets made me like this. If it weren't for him—finding his technology, getting unknowingly swept up in his mission—I never would have been on the Tribunal's radar. They would never have known about me, or Mica, or our pathetic little life in Genesis X-16.

If I'd never met him, I wouldn't wake screaming in the middle of the night, not knowing if the scenes in my head—Mica's broken and bleeding body, a drop of blood gathered at the tip of a knife held to Adam's throat, the pain of a bullet lancing through my thigh—are nightmares or memories.

But . . . if I'd never met him, I would probably be dead—or worse—at the hands of Ryk and the raiders who almost spelled my doom that fateful day in the District.

If I'd never met him, I wouldn't know the truth about the Tribunal or the Skyfall. I wouldn't know any of it.

And if I'd never met him . . .

I bring my hands to either side of my head and tap on my temples with two fingers, as if it might clear the chaos from my mind. Everything's overlapping—my memories, the confusion, the frustration. Gratitude, attraction, desire. And something . . . deeper. But how can I have feelings for someone who is still keeping so much from me? Is that—that *deeper something*—possible without trust?

But, then again, how can I deny it—any of it? Like the way my stomach flips when I think of him. The way it feels to be in his arms. The way he calms me, even when he's making fun of me. Especially when he's making fun of me. The anguish that floods my every atom whenever we have to say goodbye.

In those moments, it feels like I *can* trust him. Because he's Adam.

He saved me.

He chose me.

He stayed.

But then I think about all the secrets and everything I still don't know, don't understand . . . and everything turns upside down all over again.

The fingers in my right hand start to curl and, before I'm fully aware of what I'm doing, I'm hurtling my fist—once, twice, three times—into the tree trunk. It hurts. It feels good.

I shake out my hand and glance down to appraise the damage. The trunk is, of course, completely unharmed. I, however, have torn through the skin on my first two knuckles.

The wounds aren't deep, barely bleeding, but the pain is clarifying. For the first time, I realize why Mica probably puts so much time and effort into his combat training. It's better than stewing in a labyrinth of unanswered questions and things I can't change.

Yep. Brain. Heart. Not in sync. Get it together, you guys.

I hold my injured hand with the other, gently prodding at the welts— red, raw, and ugly. Something prickles at the back of my mind and I flash back to the moment all my questions started stacking up.

"I WASN'T LYING *when I told you our original mission was to fact-find and observe,*" Adam said. "*It was. And it wasn't for invasion or destruction or any of the ridiculous things Whitlock said either. But I never explained why we were sent here in the first place.*"

"*Then what was the reason?*"

"*They needed to know it was safe. Safe to return.*"

I stared at Adam in confusion, his blue eyes blazing.

"*My people,*" *he said.* "*They're coming back.*"

I felt my breath catch in my chest. A small noise slipped from my throat. "*What—what does that mean? They're coming back to get you?*"

A deep crease appeared between his brows. "*It's . . .That's not . . . I . . .*" *He seemed at a loss for words.*

"What does that mean?" *I repeated, panic lacing my words.*

"*I've told you all that I can.*"

And just like that, I found my breath again. "Are you kidding me?" *I jumped out of my seat.* "You can't tell me? What am I supposed to do with that?"

"*I can't explain it, Terra. There are some things I can't tell you, and I can't explain* why *I can't, either. But you have to believe me when I say I wish I could.*" *There was so much emotion behind his words, I had almost believed him. Almost.*

"*You say you want to tell me, so just tell me!*" *I shouted, my cheeks burning with frustration.*

"*I can't. What I can say is that you don't need to worry about them coming. The Tribunal is a far more dire threat to you than my people.*"

"*Okay, but can you maybe see how I might have a* little *trouble taking you at your word there? I need more than that—I have so many questions.*"

"*Shocking,*" *he muttered.*

I ignored that. "*I see absolutely no reason whatsoever that is preventing you from giving me more details. Other than the kicks you clearly get out of keeping me in the dark. But I can't handle any more secrets, any more surprises. Not after everything.*"

"*You think I'm getting a kick out of this? That I'm doing this for fun?*" *He scoffed, a vein in his throat pulsing.* "*If you honestly think that, then you really don't know anything.*"

"So help me understand. Because you're right, I don't know anything. I especially don't know how you could think that keeping things from me, after everything I went through for you, is the right choice."

He winced at that. Maybe it was cruel of me to say. What happened wasn't his fault. But I needed answers. I deserved them.

Adam was silent as he slowly lowered his head into his hands.

"Just tell me something, Adam, please." I knelt on the ground next to him. "Why are your people coming here? How many are coming? What are they coming for? To take over, to start a war? To come get you? To seek revenge on the Tribunal for how they treated your team? Is it Tom and Luke and Charlie—are they the ones coming? Is that what you meant by 'they're coming back?' "

"Questions, questions . . ." Adam lifted his head and smiled at me. He ran his thumb softly along my jawline, and I found myself leaning into him for just a second, before coming to my senses. I threw his hand back into his lap as I stood.

"Nice try, spaceboy. I won't be distracted that easily."

"I know," he said with a sigh, "but it was worth a shot." He pursed his lips. "My people . . . they are coming back, but it's not . . ." He trailed off. "They aren't coming to . . . They won't want . . . to hurt anyone."

"Okay," I said. A modicum of relief flickered through me. "That's good to hear. But what about—"

"And that is the most I can say," he said, a pained expression marring his beautiful face.

I released a frustrated sigh. "Even if you say they're not coming to straight up annihilate us, I'm supposed to accept the fact that aliens are en route to us, right now? Aliens. With spaceships and lasers and insane tech and freaking telekinetic powers—"

Adam snorted.

"It's not funny."

"It's a little funny."

"Adam, I—"

"Please, stop, Terra. I don't know how many different ways I can say it. I. Can't. Tell. You."

"You are the most stubborn, frustrating, self-righteous piece of—"

Without warning, his lips were suddenly on mine, the kiss swallowing up the rest of my indignation. Against my better judgment, my initial groan of annoy-

ance quickly turned into a wholly different kind of groan. I'd missed him. An hour ago, I didn't remember I'd had anything to miss.

It wasn't until he finally pulled away, just far enough for me to see the self-satisfied expression on his gorgeous face, that I came to my senses. The bastard was proud—his distraction attempt had worked this time.

So, I reared back and punched him.

GRANTED, striking the tree just now was a *bit* more painful than punching Adam's chest had been. But that seems fitting, given how my frustration has only compounded since that day. Hearing about Dissidia had gotten my hopes entirely too high. And being denied answers this time . . . it feels somehow more insulting.

Like I'm the one who can't be trusted, instead of the other way around.

FIVE

FOOTSTEPS SOUND in the grass behind me. Adam has come to find me. I take a deep breath as I turn to face him. He has a cautious expression on his face, like he's halfway braced for an attack.

"Hey." He raises his hands in front of him, palms up, mimicking the way he approached me when we first met—open, cautious, wary. I can't help the way my lips curve as I recall how I'd punched him then too.

There's probably something there that warrants unpacking. I can't help but make the comparison in his expressions—back then, he had looked amused, intrigued, and maybe a little lost.

Now, he just looks tired.

I am too. Tired of secrets, tired of pretending, tired of knowing too much and not being able to do anything about it.

"Hi," I reply.

A beat passes.

Adam drops his hands to his sides. "I've finished with the datapad. Got the qube working. Thanks to you."

We both know I had little to do with it; he's being magnanimous. Not quite sure why.

"Mica knows what to do," he continues. His tone is clinical, his voice carefully void of emotion. "The software on the qube will enable us to hack into Sixteen's directory—and the Tribunal's network."

"That's . . . impressive. Mica mentioned a firewall he needs to get through? He didn't seem too confident he'll be able to though. The Tribunal keeps personal computers pretty locked down in their online capacities. They're mainly meant for correspondence, schoolwork, and basic data entry—bill management, that kind of stuff." I bite the inside of my cheek to stop my babbling.

"I have every faith in that little genius."

My mouth quirks into a small smile.

"But if he can't, he'll need to connect the qube to a computer that's directly wired into the network. One in the West Quadrant mini library should suffice. Ideally, it'd be the main library server, but—"

"But that's in town hall," I finish for him. "And doing so would be a *touch* harder under the scrutiny of all the guardsmen constantly milling about."

"Exactly."

I nod. A charged silence follows.

"So . . . I guess I'll take the qube back to Mica, then?"

"Right."

"You left it inside?"

"Yes."

I stand there for a second, wondering if—hoping?—Adam will say anything else. When he doesn't, I brush past him and walk back into the research center. He follows. My bag is still on the floor, so I pick it up and place it back on the table.

I'm reaching for the qube when Adam grabs my wrist.

"What happened?" His eyes are fixed on my raw knuckles.

"I punched a tree." My words are casual, but inwardly I'm cringing, embarrassed by my outburst.

Adam raises one eyebrow. "Why exactly did you do that?"

"It got fresh with me," I joke.

Adam doesn't look amused.

I shrug. "Seemed like a good idea at the time."

"Here, let me take a look." He gingerly releases my wrist and flattens my palm in his hand.

I yank my hand back. "It's fine. Don't worry about it."

A millisecond of chagrin flashes over his face, before it's replaced with a stern expression. "Give me your damn hand, Terra."

I offer my hand back to him with a sigh.

Adam inspects my wound. "Sit," he commands.

I hop up onto a clear space on the closest desk and pull my legs up so that I'm sitting cross-legged on the table. Adam walks over to his bed and picks something up from a pile on the floor. A pillowcase, or a shirt, maybe. I can't quite tell because by the time he returns, he has already started to shred it. Something in my core tenses as I note the ease with which he tears the fabric apart, ripping it into long strips with his bare hands. All of the sudden my skin feels too hot.

Adam pulls a familiar-looking tin out of his pocket and my stomach does a traitorous flip as his fingers brush over my skin. He applies the healing balm to my knuckles with heart-wrenching gentleness. I keep my eyes pinned to the floor as he takes a long strip of ripped fabric and wraps it around my hand, wincing when he accidentally skims my middle knuckle as he's tying the bandage into a knot. The low apology that he murmurs nearly unravels me.

"Okay, you should be all set," he says when he's finished. "Sorry I don't have a more glamorous solution, but this should at least keep it from getting worse."

"I recall that same stuff mending a gushing head wound overnight," I say, gesturing to the tin of balm. "I imagine I will live, doctor."

"It wasn't *gushing*. But point taken." Adam smiles thinly. It doesn't reach his eyes.

"Well, th—thanks," I stutter. I flex my hand as I hop off the table. "I guess I'll get going then."

"Wait," Adam says abruptly. "Take these with you." He pulls a jingling box out from under the desk and hands it to me. I lift the lid and peek inside to see dozens upon dozens of bent screws, busted pieces of metal, and tangled wires inside. Generics. The kinds of scavenged items I'm used to scrounging for on a daily basis.

"You . . . scavved these?" I ask.

"Yeah," he says, raising a hand to scratch the back of his head. "Last time, you mentioned how slim pickings usually were by the time you made it out to the fields. How the scav restrictions were making it harder and harder to pull a haul worth anything."

"I was just making conversation. It's not so bad." I pause. "I mean, it could be worse. Still, you didn't have to do this."

"It's not a big deal," he says, shrugging his shoulders.

I frown as I look back into the box—it's more than halfway full. It must have taken him a long time to collect this much. "It's not *not* a big deal. In fact, you might have even overdone it," I say with a smirk. "There's more here than I've ever collected in a single run."

"Maybe you're not as good at your job as you think you are," he teases, that twinkle back in his eye. "Consider it an early birthday present."

My shoulders sag in relief at the dispelled tension, the return to normalcy. "I don't really do birthdays either—not my own, at least."

"Why not?"

I grimace. That's a whole other issue I'm not ready to dive into yet. "You know what's not fair?" I say after a moment.

"What?" The word is guarded.

I bite the inside of my cheek. "It's related to the I-can't-tell-you stuff."

"Terra, I swear, I don't know if I can keep having this same—"

"That's not where I'm going with this."

Adam exhales. "Sorry. What is it, then?"

"I was just thinking about how you know so *much* about me and how little I know about you. I don't know your last name, for example. Or if you guys even use last names, actually. Or basically anything at all, except that down here you go by Adam, you have superpowers, and you're an outrageously good kisser."

A blush creeps into his handsome face that's so endearing, I'm tempted to throw my arms around him and let him remind me how good he really is. "And I know there's stuff you won't say"—his eyes narrow—"can't say, whatever. It still doesn't quite seem fair."

Adam considers this, and as his brow furrows in thought I worry I've triggered the slow-talking, cryptic Adam again. The wrinkles in his forehead disappear after a moment, however. "We do have last names," he says. "Mine's Killian. Adam Killian. Nice to meet you." He extends his hand.

"Enchanted, Mr. Killian." I flash a demure smile as I grab his hand and shake it with unnecessary fervor.

Adam laughs. "It's actually *Ensign* Killian if you want to get technical."

"How was your experience as a scav anyway?" I ask. "Did you enjoy—how did you phrase it that one time—picking up trash?"

"Consider me as having fully eaten my words. I have an entirely new level of respect for you now. My back was killing me after the first twenty minutes."

I smirk as I dump half of the generics from the box into my scav bag, then hand the rest back to Adam.

"No, they're for you," he says, confused.

"I told you, this is way more than one person could collect in a single run—maybe in a whole Collection period. You hang onto the rest. For next time."

"So, there will be a next time?"

My heart squeezes at the uncertainty in his voice. I loop my arms over his shoulders, linking my hands behind his neck, and brush my lips against his cheek. "Of course, dummy."

Adam places a hand on my waist and pulls me into him. I savor the warmth of his body as I rest my head on his chest. With a tenderness that makes my throat burn, he tucks a stray piece of hair behind my ear, then trails his hand down my back. "I'm sorry," he murmurs.

I pull my head back to peer into those ocean-deep eyes, so many unspoken words behind them. I'm not sure what he's apologizing for. Our argument? My situation? His? All the things he won't—can't—tell me?

I'm not sure, so I just say, "I'm sorry too."

"I wish we had more time."

I clear my throat, eyes burning, and dislodge myself from his hold. I sweep my arm wide, gesturing toward the rearranged room around us. "Me too. I think it's pretty clear that you are going to go certifiably insane if you're left to your own devices for too long."

Adam chuckles. "True enough. But it's temporary." He picks up the ribbon I'd used to tie the bundle of parts, delicately weaving it in a neat bow around the wrist of my uninjured hand. "And even if it wasn't, if all we ever got are these short visits . . . it'd still be worth it."

I swallow hard, tucking the qube into my scav bag and nestling it amongst the generics Adam gathered for me. I sling the bag over my shoulder. "Ready to head back then, tour guide?"

The right side of Adam's mouth curves up. "Ready and begrudgingly willing," he says, and leads me back outside.

SIX

THE REST of the week is uneventful. Mica makes a few attempts to connect the qube to Sixteen's network from our home computer, but unfortunately, his concerns about the firewall prove true. We'll have to try a networked computer after all, and in order to do that, we need to bide our time until examinations are over. These days, even our dinky West Q mini library is crowded at all hours.

Mica seems okay with the delay, considering his own need to study feverishly for his tertiaries. Every time he brings them up, the conflicting thoughts inside me begin warring anew. I can't lie; staying here is miserable. Our life here has become barely more than a loose set of lies, strung together by sheer force of will. So much pretending. So little Adam.

But I also fear what this is doing to Mica. He shouldn't have this kind of weight on his shoulders. I don't know how to convince him that it's okay—I'm okay. That I can handle staying if he needs more time. That he doesn't need to push himself this hard. He's just a kid.

It feels like I'm losing either way.

THE MORNING of Mica's tertiary examinations, I wake early to find him already wearing circles into the apartment floor. He paces between his bedroom and the front door, concentration and elation warring in his face, as if he keeps figuring out the answer to questions he is asking himself. His anxiety pulses in the air between us.

"Did you get any sleep at all?" I ask him as I cross to the kitchen, the ends of my orange pajama pants dragging under my heels.

Mica shrugs, not breaking stride.

I yawn. "You need to breathe, Mic. You're stressing *me* out." I fish a can of B-6R1T out of the pantry. I pop the tab on the lid, pull two clean bowls out of a cabinet, and evenly distribute the creamy grits between them. I'm actually quite proud of myself for snagging a few cans of this stuff—it's way better than the typical grub I'm able to get from the Rationing, especially lately. I can't prove it, but I swear it's like they hold back all the good stuff on purpose when I'm there, no matter how early I arrive.

I pop the bowls into the confectioner, then set two cups of water and a couple of spoons out on the table. The confectioner buzzes and I take the now-warm bowls out to the table as well. "Breakfast," I tell Mica as he paces by the opening to the kitchen for the fourth time.

"Not hungry."

"You have to eat." I sit down in my usual chair. "Your chances of passing won't be any greater on an empty stomach."

Mica plops down at the table with a groan, but mere seconds pass before he's shoveling giant spoonfuls into his mouth.

"And I don't think choking on your breakfast is going to do much to help your chances either," I add.

He makes a face at me, but he slows his pace. After a minute, he sets his spoon down. "W-what if I don't pass?" he asks. There's the barest tremble in his voice and my chest tightens. He sounds so . . . young.

"Then you don't pass," I respond with a shrug. "Who cares? You take 'em again next cycle. You can use the extra time in school to brush up on the stuff you didn't know. No big deal."

Mica goes quiet again, finishing the last few bites of his breakfast and depositing his bowl in the kitchen sink without further incident. "Guess it's time then," he says, plucking his backpack off the couch.

"Good luck," I tell him. "Remember, no pressure, okay? Just do the best you can."

He nods and moves toward the front door, absentmindedly scratching behind his ear as he does, an action that reminds me of something.

"Hold on a sec," I say, walking over to him. "Hand over your earpiece."

"Huh?" Mica looks surprised.

"The earpiece," I repeat, holding out my palm.

"Why?"

"So that you can't somehow con any answers out of Adam, obviously."

"You honestly think I would cheat?" Mica asks, offended.

I sigh. "I think I know how much you want to get out of here. How much *both* of you do."

Mica rolls his eyes as he pulls the tiny, flesh-colored earpiece out, breezes straight past me and my still-open palm, and sets it down on the kitchen table. "Happy?"

"Ecstatic."

"You should try using it again anyway," he says as he goes to open the front door. "I bet Adam would flip if you finally figured it out. He misses you. It's gross."

I make a face at my little brother. "I don't—"

"It's easy," Mica says. "One long pulse on the little knobby thing behind your ear to turn on the receiver, two quick pulses to open the channel and communicate out. Another long pulse shuts it back down. If Adam's communicator is on and active at the same time, it becomes an open channel. If it's not, you can still send him a message. He'll hear it whenever he does turn his on."

"But, I—"

"Just do it, Terra." Mica wrenches the front door open. "You never know if or when you might need to use the damn thing, so get over your shit and figure it out." And before I can scold him for his language, he's gone.

I eye the earpiece on the table dubiously. I'm not eager to relive the feedback experience but, as usual, Mica's right. I need to start pulling my weight around here on the technology front. I mean, it's pretty pathetic to

have to rely on my little brother to act as my personal messenger. And . . .
I miss Adam too.

Ugh, speaking of pathetic.

I walk into the kitchen and take a thin, worn hand towel from a
drawer, wet it with water from the sink, and then wring it so it's damp
but not dripping. Sitting back down at the table, I wipe the earpiece off
with the towel, poking the fabric into the miniscule dips and bumps to
clean it as best as I can before popping the device into my left ear.

With my pinky finger, I wiggle the earpiece into place. I swallow, then
position my pointer finger over the smooth dip behind my ear where it
connects with my head. I go over Mica's instructions one more time: One
long pulse to turn it on, two quick ones to open the communication
channel and send messages.

I press behind my ear, count to three, then release my finger. Nothing.
I try pushing down quickly twice but again, there's no change. I
remember Mica telling me I should hear some kind of indication that the
earpiece is on—a faint static, or a light beeping if there's a message
waiting to be heard—so I know it's not working.

Irritated, I try again, pressing down in a quick staccato.

Tap, tap, tap.

Silence.

Thinking I must've misremembered the spot I'm supposed to push on,
I start impatiently moving my finger in a path away from my head and
up the back of my ear. For a second, I think I've gotten it. I'm almost positive I hear a beep. Before I can be sure, however, a much worse sound
takes its place.

My eardrum nearly shatters when the deafening screech of feedback
static pierces through my brain.

"Damn it!" I scream, yanking the earpiece out and throwing it onto the
floor. It takes all my bodily willpower not to bring my foot down on top
of it, to smash the device into smithereens.

Mentally cursing Mica, Adam, and the entire goddamn universe while
I'm at it, I stagger into the bathroom and pull a small red bottle out from
the cabinet. I'd haggled with Copp for almost an hour to get my hands on
these precious—and very expensive—painkillers after Mica twisted his

ankle last year. The way the bottle rattles in my hand reminds me of how few are left, but the memory of that twenty-six-hour headache convinces me to grant myself this small luxury.

I pop a bright yellow pill into my mouth and swallow it dry. Staggering over to the couch, I lie on my stomach and press a pillow over my ear—as if that will somehow mute the ringing in my skull. Thankfully, these particular pills do their painkilling by knocking you out. Before I know it, the ache in my head slips away, and sleep takes me.

THE SOUND of a door slamming jolts me awake. I attempt to sit up, but while I was sleeping, I apparently rolled into a rather precarious position at the edge of the couch. I topple off the sofa as Mica angrily stomps past me and into his bedroom, shutting his door with a bang. I rub my sandy eyes and peek at my watch; I've slept the day away.

The events prior to my drug-induced nap take a few moments to come back to me, but once they do, I launch myself onto all fours, searching for the discarded earpiece.

Oh God, please don't have stepped on it, please don't have stepped on it. I scramble across the floor until I locate the tiny device, and slip it into the pocket of the pajama pants I'm still wearing before sighing with relief.

I breathe deeply and look toward Mica's closed bedroom door with a frown. That he's upset is obvious, though it feels like I'm only now realizing how often he's been shutting his door on me lately. A teenage boy slamming the door on his overbearing older sister? Not a particularly noteworthy occurrence . . . if he wasn't Mica. But thanks to my history of locking him out—physically and emotionally—when at my lowest point, he spent years refusing to close his door more than three-quarters of the way. This feels . . . significant. I'm just not sure if it's in a good way or a bad one.

"Mica?" I tap on his door. "Everything okay?"

A thump sounds from inside his bedroom.

"Mica?" I repeat, a little louder.

"I'm fine. Leave me alone."

"As if that's gonna happen," I mutter. I open his bedroom door to reveal my brother standing next to his desk, textbooks and loose papers strewn across the floor around him. He holds a notebook in one hand and a fistful of pages he's just ripped out in the other. He drops the book on his desk, then proceeds to tear the paper into smaller pieces. I stare at my brother as he releases the scraps into the air; they flutter to the ground—a sad, monochrome confetti.

"What the hell are you doing?"

Mica's hand freezes in mid-air, poised to tear out another few pages.

"Stop." I cross to him and wrestle the notebook from his hands. I rest my hand on his shoulder and he tenses up like a coiled spring. His eyes—perfectly matching the shape and color of my own—bore into me, full of fury, and for a quarter of a second, I wonder if he's going to hit me. Instead, he dramatically flings himself onto his bed, facedown.

I sigh and sit down on the edge of his mattress, listening to his stifled breathing slow as he tries to calm himself down.

"So," I say after a minute, "exam didn't go so well, huh?"

"Mmph," Mica garbles into his pillow.

"We don't have to talk about it if you don't want to."

Mica lifts his head. "Sure we do," he says bitterly. "You're gonna want to hear it all, so you can rub in how right you were."

"You know that's not true."

"Why not? You *were* right. I choked. I *choked*," he says, his voice breaking. "I didn't know the answers to, like, half the equations. I completely ran out of time on the essay portion. I ended up leaving the entire last page blank. So, you get your wish. I certainly won't be leaving school anytime soon." He buries his face back in his pillow. "You must be thrilled."

"Yes, because the entire time you were taking your exam, I was actually performing a ritual to ensure your imminent failure."

Mica sits back up and glares at me.

I sigh. "You're being ridiculous, Mic. You don't *know* that you didn't pass. Maybe you just think you performed worse than you did. And secondly, if you did fail, what does it matter? You'll take the exams again next cycle." I gesture to the notebook pages and mistreated textbooks littering the ground. "You might consider keeping some of your notes in preparation for that."

"The next cycle isn't for another four months, Terra," he says, raising his voice.

"And?" My growing irritation has my own voice matching the decibel of Mica's. "So you stay in school and study up for the next four months. I'd be willing to bet that Principal Conifer would be willing to give you an independent study plan or something. And then maybe you'll pass next time."

Mica tries to interject, but I continue, "And if not, you try again, and pass the time after that. Even if it takes you another six tries, you'll still be ahead of your classmates. What is the big deal?"

He presses his lips together.

"I'm serious." I soften my voice. "What difference does it make if it's now or then? Why in God's name are you so eager to be done?"

Mica meets my eyes and I'm startled to see wetness on his lash line. "Because I don't want to be left behind again!" he yells, falling back into his pillow to muffle a sob.

Something splinters in my chest.

Mica had insisted that the time he spent alone was no big deal—fending for himself while I was trapped in Korbyllis. He continually assured me that he was okay, that he knew it wasn't my fault, that he was just fine taking care of himself, and that after a while he was in contact with Adam anyway.

I never pushed the issue. Maybe I wanted it all to be true too badly. Maybe I didn't think I could handle the guilt on top of everything else. Ignorance is bliss, after all.

But now that the truth has slipped out . . . Guilt doesn't begin to cover it.

Of course he wasn't okay.

Because Mica was so young at the time of our mother's death, I'd convinced myself that he wasn't as affected by it. That he wasn't as hurt by our father leaving, either. That his youth and naivete protected him somehow.

But of course he was affected. Of course he was hurt.

I try to imagine if our roles were reversed, how I would have coped if Mica—the one constant thing in my life—was suddenly taken from me. If he'd been the one to disappear. The thought alone is enough to make me want to throw up. If how Mica feels now is even a fraction of that . . .

With sudden clarity, I understand. His newfound growth, his dedication to combat training, throwing himself into our pseudo-revolutionary plans—it's been a bandaid over the bullet hole caused by my leaving. His attempts to cover up and move on from how he's felt all this time.

Abandoned.

Cognitively, I know that he knows it wasn't my choice. He knows I was taken. But semantics don't mean much when it comes to feelings, and for him, I'm sure it still felt like I left him.

I look down at my little brother—his face still buried in his pillow, body gently heaving with sobs I know he is desperately trying to conceal —and my heart breaks.

"Hey," I say, my voice barely louder than a whisper. "You can't possibly think that I would ever, *ever* go anywhere without you." I place a tentative palm on his back. When he doesn't bat it away, I start to move my hand in slow, soothing circles. "What happened, you know if I'd had any choice . . ." I trail off. Mica's logical side already knows this. But this isn't about logic.

"What can I do to reassure you, Mica?" I ask, keeping my tone soft. "What can I do to help you realize I would never—I *will* never—leave you again?"

He lifts his head, leaving two wet spots on his pillow. "That's just it," he says, his voice hoarse. "I do realize that. I know you wouldn't go anywhere without me." He sniffles. "Don't you get it? That's the whole point. It's so dangerous for you here. Every minute you stay, you risk the Tribunal finding out your memory returned, or them figuring out that Adam's still here. And if—*when*—that happens, they'll take you again. They won't hesitate. It isn't safe for you to stay. For *either of you* to stay. But you do anyway . . . because of me. Because you have this notion that the things that used to matter—school, this apartment, this entire stupid town—still do."

My hand stills on his back.

"But they don't matter anymore, Terra. I'm sorry, but everything is different now. You say it's important to keep up appearances, but I know you only want me to finish school because you think it's somehow best for me. Because you always want what's best for me, even when it's not good for you."

I blink slowly.

"You've already been through so much," he continues, "I didn't want you to feel bad. I thought if I could finish up school early, pass my tertiaries, finish this for you . . ." He trails off as he rises into a sitting position, his legs crossed on his bed.

"I—" My words don't come.

"I'm sorry," Mica says, his voice quiet.

"Don't apologize."

"But I really am sor—"

"I'm serious, Mica. If you say 'I'm sorry' one more time, I am going to break in half."

He bites his bottom lip and waits for me to continue. It's another few moments before I do.

"Okay then," I say, sucking in a deep breath. "Screw school."

Mica's eyes widen. "Are you . . . are you serious?"

"Yes. One hundred percent. You're right. I don't know why I've been clinging to . . ." I gesture around us broadly, my words falling away. I don't know what to say. Why have I been so narrowly focused on maintaining some illusion of normalcy? So insistent on keeping up appearances?

I'd like to think it's as Mica said, that I've had his best interests in mind. And I do care about that—his education, his future, his happiness. Of course I do. But if I'm being completely honest with myself, I'm not sure I'm actually that noble.

My priorities have been out of order since waking up in that Western field four months ago. My memories came back, but it's like I'm fighting some kind of programming to try and get back to how things were *before* by any means necessary.

I shake my head. "Who says we can't start a revolution just as easily in Genesis X-8, or T-3, or B-4? There's no reason to stay here. We have everything we need."

Mica chews on his lip. "Well, *almost* everything. We're probably going to want to stock up on a few things if you're serious."

"Sounds like I'll be hitting up the Marketplace soon, then," I reply. "We should prepare to leave after the next Collection. Five days."

"Give me the earpiece," Mica says excitedly. "I'll tell Adam."

I pull the device out of my pocket and toss it to Mica. "Better start packing."

SEVEN

BY THE FOLLOWING COLLECTION DAY, Mica and I have packed our backpacks with as much clothing as we can reasonably fit. The trick, I learn, is to roll our clothes rather than fold them.

Adam, Mica, and I have decided to head for Genesis G-4, located within the skycity Lexicon's territory. It's far enough from Korbyllis that we hope it'll be that much harder to track us down should the Tribunal decide to come checking. Getting there means trekking nearly the entire width of Genesis though, so the trip requires some careful planning.

I've spread out the gathering of supplies somewhat so as not to raise red flags. I still don't think the Tribunal suspects I remember anything, but I also think it won't do us any favors if they learn we're planning on skipping town. Foodwise, we already had a bit stored, and with my surreptitious finagling, we should have enough food pills to last a few weeks. But even with Adam's sustenance generator, a beefed up food supply is definitely necessary. Best to be prepared for the worst.

The last thing on my to-do list is to pick up an acid-resistant tent. We'll need some means of avoiding being melted into oblivion by acid rain should we find ourselves caught in a storm while traveling. Which is why, of course, I needed to wait for one last Collection—camping supplies are neither in high-demand nor plentiful in these parts, which makes them very, very expensive.

"You have everything?" I ask Mica as I peek around the doorframe into his room.

He stands over his overflowing backpack, a comic book dangling from each hand.

"Mica?"

He looks up at me, dilemma etched into every facet of his face.

"What's wrong?" I ask. Has he changed his mind? Is he second-guessing our decision to leave?

"I can't decide which one to bring," he says.

I sigh in exasperation and relief. "So bring both."

"I can't. I only have room for one more."

"They're like, a quarter-inch thick, Mic. I'm sure you can fit them." I walk over and look down at his overflowing backpack. "Or not. Yeesh, what do you have in here? You have this packed all wrong." I begin pulling items out of the bag with the intention of repacking it for him.

"Quit it!" Mica protests, trying to snatch a bundled up sweater from my hands.

"I don't even recognize some of this stuff," I say, holding the sweater out in front of me. It's a chunky knit with a pattern of pink and green berries stitched onto the front. "Wait, is this—"

"It's mine," Mica says, his voice pitching up an octave as he snatches the sweater from me. "Juniper gave it to me. To remember her."

"You didn't tell her what we were doing, did you? That we are leaving?"

"No," Mica says, a little too fast. "I mean, not exactly."

"Mica!" I chastise. "We can't let people know we're leaving, because we can't let *them* know we're leaving. And we especially don't want them knowing where we're planning to go."

"I didn't tell her anything. Even though she asked a million times why I was breaking up with her."

"Oh." With all my stressing over the move, I didn't stop to consider the fact that, despite it being his idea to go, he'd still be leaving at least one thing behind. "Sorry, Mic."

"It's okay. It's not like I'm never going to see her ever again." He peers up at me, hope and a question glistening in his gold-speckled eyes.

"Right," I say without hesitating. Even if we both know it's probably not true. "Here, I've still got a little bit of room. Why don't you let me pack these?" I pull the comic books out of his hands and layer them on top of one another.

"I'm heading to the North Q in a few minutes to grab the tent," I say as I head out of Mica's room and into my own. "So, fill up the water canteens while I'm gone and don't forget to unscrew the filter from the tap. We'll need it." I unzip my own backpack and pull out a few shirts, shoving Mica's comics inside before replacing my clothes on top.

"Will do," Mica replies.

———

THE DRIVE to the North Q shopping district is quiet. Most scavs are out in the fields, trying for a last-minute find, hoping for that jackpot. Normally, I'd be out there with them. Of course, there's nothing normal about my life anymore.

I park my motorbike to the side of Sundry's Supply Shop and dart inside. I'm only four steps in when I'm greeted by the familiar sight of white hair poking out from beneath a bowler hat. Copp's here, looking at a shelf full of tinker tools. The wide-aisled store suddenly feels claustrophobic as Copp catches sight of me. It's just the two of us—Mr. Sundry must be in the back.

I swallow as I pass by, preparing myself for yet another uncomfortable encounter with the man I used to regard as an uncle. But ever since my alleged return from gambling away Mica's financial security, he's barely been able to look at me.

"Terra?" Copp says, surprise coating his voice. "Whatcha doing here so early?"

I look around me, wondering if there's someone else named Terra standing nearby. Copp hasn't spoken so cordially to me in months. "Um . . ." I clear my throat. "Just picking something up from old man Sundry," I say.

Copp nods, looking thoughtful. "How's Mica?" he asks after a moment.

"He's fine."

"Took his exams last week, didn't he?"

"Yeah."

"Always was a smart kid."

"Yeah." My clipped answers feel rude, but I don't want to risk saying anything that might reignite Copp's antipathy for me.

"You mus' be real proud," Copp says, though there's a sad quality to his voice that makes me feel like pride is the last thing I should be feeling.

I nod. A few awkward moments of silence pass.

"So, is Mr. Sundry in the back?" I ask.

"Oh, oh right. Yeah, he is. I'll, uh, go get him fer ya." Copp disappears behind a door, shutting it behind him. After a few minutes, he returns.

"Kilroy's tied up with somethin' right now," he says, avoiding my eye. "He told me to go ahead and ring ya up." He pops behind the counter and starts searching the shelves behind the register. "He said yer item should . . . be . . . right . . . here!" He releases a triumphant sound as he pulls out a flat, plastic package. Vacuum-sealed and airtight, if you didn't already know there was a tent in there, you probably wouldn't be able to guess. Copp doesn't need to guess, however.

"Whatcha need one of these for, anyway?" he asks. "Never figured you for much of an outdoors type."

I'm still a little thrown by how conversational he's being, so it takes me a second to come up with something. "I've been cutting it a little too close with the rain on my scav runs lately," I say. "I figured this would be a good thing to keep on hand out there, maybe give me a bit of an edge on grabbing plastics before they melt off."

Copp wrinkles his forehead. "Pretty pricey edge."

I shrug. A door opens and shuts somewhere in the back of the shop, and a crop of reddish-brown hair pops up along the top of one of the aisles to my right. Emery Garren, a fellow scav, shoots Copp a jovial wave as he heads to the shop's entrance. Then his eyes lock on me and the look that overtakes his face is one of such fierce, unyielding disdain, I'm sure his sneer could cut straight through stone.

What the hell's his problem? I'm used to dealing with scowls and stares, but this is extreme even by my standards. I can still feel the ice from Emery's withering look after the door slams shut behind him.

The register beeps as Copp scans the tag on the tent, and the nauseated feeling caused by Emery's death-glare is replaced with one of equal revulsion—for an entirely different reason. The tent costs two hundred and eighteen credits. More than an entire Collection's worth.

I swallow hard before holding my palm up for him to scan for payment. My credit balance flashes up quickly—three hundred and six credits—before updating to its new total.

"Hope it's worth it," Copp says.

You have no idea.

"Well, thanks," I say awkwardly, "it was, uh, good to see you." I slip the tent package into my scav bag.

He hesitates. "You too, Terra. You'll say h'lo to your brother for me, won't you?"

"Sure will, Copp."

"HOW'D IT GO?" Mica asks eagerly as I walk through the front door.

"Got the tent," I tell him. "And nobody even booed me publicly today."

"Sounds like a stellar morning for you, then," Mica says with a smirk. "Any problems?"

"Not a one. Copp says hi."

"Copp? I thought you said there were no tents at the Marketplace."

"There weren't. Copp was at Sundry's this morning when I went. He was actually kind of nice to me. It was . . . unexpected."

"You don't think he knows?" Mica asks sharply.

"How would he? And does it matter? We're leaving tonight, what's he gonna do about it?"

Mica bites the corner of his bottom lip. "Something feels weird. Maybe we shouldn't wait. Go now."

"You're being paranoid. We talked this through. It has to be at night. We still have to hack into the network at the mini-library before we can leave this place in the dust for good. And for that, *and* to have a chance of leaving without being followed, we need the cover of darkness."

"We should have tried to access the system sooner," he mutters.

"Maybe, but at least now we won't be risking discovery after the fact." We'd spent long hours planning our escape—with the motorbike only being able to seat two, we'll need to swap it for a larger transport once we rendezvous with Adam. Fortunately, there's a whole dead city full of abandoned vehicles right overtop where our resident alien has been hiding out. Adam says he's already found one that's in good enough shape for our needs, and that it'll take no time to hotwire it the same way he did the motorbike.

Mica takes a deep breath. "It just makes me nervous. I mean, we've been cautious, but there are no guarantees. And the longer we wait, the more time that gives someone to figure out that we're—"

"Keep it together, Mic. We're fine. We've been careful. We waited until today to pick up the tent. We haven't told anyone that we're leaving . . ." My mind lingers on Mica's unexplained reasoning for his breakup with Juniper, but I decide not to mention it. "And once we have access to the Tribunal's network, you and Adam will be able to hack new identities— new accounts, records, palm scans, everything—for us. Take a breath. We're almost there."

"Yeah, okay, you're right, I'm probably—" Mica stops mid-sentence, his eyes frozen on something behind me. I turn to follow his gaze, searching for whatever has abruptly commanded his attention, but the room is empty. I glance back at Mica, ready to ask him why he stopped speaking, when three quick raps sound on the front door. I rise from the couch to answer it.

"Genesis X-16 Guardsmen Corps," a low, alto female voice commands from behind the door before I'm halfway there. "Open up."

I glance over at Mica, whose eyes are darting from me to the front door in alarm. He rushes over to the window and peeks onto the street, then turns back to me mouthing the word, *Guardsmen*.

I half-roll my eyes at him. *Obviously* it's guardsmen.

Three more sharp knocks sound out.

"I'm coming!" I call out as I slowly walk over, in less of a hurry to answer now, given their impatience. My fingers hesitate as I reach for the handle.

They knock *again.* "Be aware, if you do not allow us in, we will enter by force."

What the hell? Indignation rises up in me and I yank the door open. Two guardsmen—one female, one male—stand imposingly in front of me. The woman is tall—at least six feet and barely a hairsbreadth shorter than the gangly male standing next to her, though she is at least twice his girth. Her mousy brown hair is plaited on both sides over her ears into elaborate buns that are completely incongruous with the rest of her appearance. The badge affixed to the front of her left breast pocket informs me her last name is Trimble.

"Step aside," Trimble says, barely giving me enough time to jump out before she tramples me. The man follows her, looking down at me disdainfully. A touch of deja vu stirs in the back of my mind as I meet his gaze, but I don't quite understand why.

"You can't just barge in here," I protest as the two guardsmen survey the room. There's a shift in the air as their eyes lock on Mica, still standing by the window. "You have no right."

The man shoves a large flat envelope in my face as if it is proof that, yes, they can. I catch a glimpse of his badge—his name is Clay—and recognition washes over me. He's the guardsman that accompanied the Registrar who came to "survey" me after I returned from Korbyllis, there to ensure my memory was truly gone. And he was also there when I was arrested in the first place.

I swallow hard, a sneaking feeling poking me in the back of my mind like there's something I'm missing, and open the envelope. I pull out a single page of paper, covered top to bottom in neat printed text.

My eyes skim over the letter, not fully comprehending what they're seeing. Words jump off the page at me, one by one, clashing nonsensically and out of order in my mind.

Words like *top-of-class* and *scholarship.* Like *mandatory* and *duty.*

My eyes finally drift back up to the top of the page, and I force them to focus on the words I had skipped right over. Words that—before I even realized what this was about—I knew instinctively that I didn't want to read.

To the Guardian of Auron Mica Rhodon,

On behalf of the Altaraan Academy of Military Refinement and Education, we would like to offer our congratulations to Auron on his top-of-class tertiary examination scores.

In recognition of Auron's remarkable academic achievements and unparalleled examination performance, we are honored to award him with AAMRE's prestigious groundworld scholarship. All tuition fees, room, and board will be covered so he is able to focus entirely on our rigorous training and studies without financial burden.

Attendance at AAMRE is not merely an opportunity; it is a solemn duty. This is a responsibility that must be embraced with dedication and commitment. As a future leader, Auron's presence and enthusiastic participation are mandatory. Please report to Town Hall at 0800 tomorrow for transportation to Altara for enrollment.

Cephalus T. Ilken

Commandant Cephalus T. Ilken
Superintendent, AAMRE

A SHORT BULLETED LIST FOLLOWS—ITEMS Mica will require upon his arrival. There's a code for him to use to access his class schedule and room assignment information once he is logged into the Academy's network.

Detailed instructions on where and when he is to report to town hall are printed last.

And finally, scrawled at the bottom, with a slant to the words that makes it look like they were scribbled in haste, is a handwritten postscript:

I look forward to meeting the cadet I have long heard so much about. I have no doubt your presence at the Academy will be of great consequence.

MY TONGUE STICKS to the roof of my mouth as I stand there, frozen. My forehead is so deeply furrowed that my eyebrows are almost touching as I scan the letter, over and over—as if I can will the words to change.

Once, this might have been a good thing. A great thing, even. For Mica to get out of Sixteen, to enroll at a skycity university, to have a chance of real success in this life. It's the very thing I was working toward, before . . . *Before.* But even at the height of those delusional daydreams, the Altaraan Academy never once crossed my mind as an option.

Not with what it might've meant to our father.

Whether he would ever find out—whether he's even still alive—who knows. I still never relished the idea of Mica attending that particular institution. Not if it means following in his footsteps. If it meant contributing to his . . . legacy.

Stringently militaristic, overtly rigorous, mercilessly strict, the Altaraan Academy is essentially one large pipeline for the guardsmen force. You can usually tell a "Career" guard—someone who gained entry into the force via a low-level position and worked their way up—from an "Academy" guard. I glance back over at Guardsman Clay, who is staring at me with an intensity that has sweat immediately gathering at the back of my neck.

Academy, without a doubt.

Just like Dad.

The real Auron Rhodon.

I glare at his name, peppered all over Mica's summons as if he has anything to do with this—with either of us. As if he's contributed anything to Mica other than his name, anything to me beyond his nose and emotional unavailability.

As if he didn't hightail it back up to the skycities at the first chance after Mom died.

My fist closes around the letter, the paper crumpling in my hand.

And then I laugh.

Trimble and Clay exchange a wary look as laughter spills from my lips —big, heaving guffaws that have me throwing my head back, clutching at my chest. Until a strangled noise bubbles up from inside me, cleaving the hysterical stream of sound. My body shakes as I desperately try to stifle the sobs that want to escape.

This isn't a scholarship.

This is a conscription.

And the signature on the letter might be the Commandant's, but it may as well have been signed by Prime Morrigan Whitlock herself.

She knows. They know.

They have to know.

Or at the very least, they must suspect. Whether it's that I recovered my memories or that I've been otherwise conspiring, that we were planning to leave, they know *something*. I was so naive to think that getting out from under them would be simple—that it would be possible.

I thought we'd been careful. I thought that those months of quiet—of being tailed but nothing coming of it, of getting away with sneaking out to see Adam—meant we had been covering our tracks.

But they were just waiting. Waiting to see if I'd make a move. If I'd slip up. Waiting to pounce.

Because as brilliant as I know my brother is, there's no way that Mica actually passed his tertiaries—let alone with top marks. He said he didn't *finish* the exam, for pity's sake. This is simply the excuse they needed. A reason to sweep in with a calculated reminder of how things work around here, of who's in charge. The one thing they could do to ensure my eternal compliance.

The irony lances straight through me, hitting me like a shard of ice that embeds itself in my bones. My hopes for Mica's future set me on this path. They brought me to Adam. They're what put all of us on the Tribunal's radar.

And now those same hopes are being twisted into the leash that will tie me to them forever.

Screw that, I think. They want Mica to report to them in the morning? Good luck finding us. We'll be long gone by then.

A gentle hand grips my shoulder and the crushed letter is pried from my grip as Mica steps beside me. I stiffen and suck in a deep breath, then another. I will the prickling in my eyes to subside and push down my panic—at least for now.

We don't have time for me to fall apart.

Trimble darts her gaze down to the computer tablet I didn't notice her holding and angles it toward Clay, letting him see whatever is on the screen. He nods before locking that stony stare on my little brother.

Mica's face betrays nothing as he smooths the crinkled letter over his leg and starts reading. "Wow," he says evenly to the guards once he's finished. "Thank you for delivering this missive."

I blink, bewildered by the maturity in his voice, the calm set of his features.

"I understand my orders," he finishes.

"One of us will return in the morning to escort you to town hall," Trimble replies.

"That won't be necessary," I blurt.

She shoots me a cutting glance before dismissing me entirely. "Should you require assistance procuring anything from your necessities list, do not hesitate to let us know." She turns and passes back through our front doorway. The whole exchange has taken fewer than five minutes—we never even closed the door.

"Congratulations, by the way," Guardsman Clay remarks as he follows his colleague out. I have to keep from shuddering as his oily voice slithers into my ears. "Youngest cadet in thirty years." He sounds almost wistful.

He's halfway through the doorway when he turns back to us, his dark eyes falling back to me. "You should be very proud."

I'm rooted to the spot, my features a frozen tangle of bewilderment and rage. Mica's grip on my shoulder tightens, his fingers digging in almost to the point of pain. Guardsman Clay eyes me expectantly—I hadn't realized he was waiting for a response. I force my chin down in a terse nod. "I am."

Clay's gaze doesn't leave my face as he wraps his hand around the door handle, one long, slender finger at a time. "See you soon," he says, and he pulls the door shut.

EIGHT

FOR A FEW MOMENTS, Mica and I stare at each other. The letter hangs limply from his hand, slipping from between his fingers as he drops his arm to his side. Our eyes follow the paper as it drifts through the air, painstakingly slowly despite its many creases—as if buoyed by the tension stretching through the apartment. Finally, it lands on the floor.

The stupor breaks.

We simultaneously erupt in a flurry of silent movement. Mica dashes to the door and presses his ear against it, listening intently until he is satisfied that the guardsmen have retreated. He flips the lock in a deft movement before scooping up the letter from where it landed and pocketing it.

I run to the window and peer down at the street, watching as Guardsman Trimble exits our building and gets into a waiting transport vehicle—sleek, black, and utterly out of place on our West Quadrant street. She rolls down her window and says something to someone standing outside my line of sight before the transport peels off.

Mica is a blur, darting between the kitchen and bathroom before eventually retreating to his room. I follow and take up a familiar stance in his open doorway, leaning my shoulder against the frame. A wave of emotion crests over me as I realize that this is the last time I'll be doing so, triggering a montage of memories. Mornings spent leaning here, an impatient sigh readying in my chest as I waited for him to finish getting ready for school. Nights heavy with guilt and melancholy as I watched the shallow rise and fall of his chest as he slept.

Mica takes a seat on his bed, his backpack still halfway unpacked after our earlier exchange. He pulls the letter out of his pocket and unfolds it, frowning as he scans its contents.

"Okay, yes, good," I say, breaking the silence. "You finish packing. I just need to throw the tent and our remaining Rations into a bag and we can go. Now."

Mica stills. "We can't go now."

I freeze mid-step. "Of course we can. We can't wait until tonight anymore. We need to put as much distance as possible between us and Sixteen by tomorrow."

"Terra."

"You can update Adam on the way. Let him know there's been a change of plans and we're coming."

"*Terra.*"

I blink at my brother, taking in the serious set of his mouth, the tension flaring in his jaw. "No. Just—no."

"We can't leave now."

"We *have* to. There is no other choice."

"There is, and you know it," he says, his voice sedate.

"I won't let them take you," I hiss.

"Be smart, Terra. We can't go. We missed our chance."

"We just—"

"Take another look outside," he says, his voice quiet but stern. I glare at him before storming over to the grime-streaked window over his bed. My pulse thuds in my ears as I take in the scene outside our apartment building —the white-uniformed, stiff-backed guards stationed at each corner. I press my face against the window for a closer view and see none other than Guardsman Clay perched right in front of the building's entrance.

Something cold and viscous slithers through my core. My heartbeat pounds so loudly it sounds like a death knell. "No," I say again, my voice barely more than a whisper.

"It's going to be okay, Terra. *I'm* going to be okay." He bites his lip. "Maybe . . . Maybe this could be a good thing."

My head snaps toward him. "In what world—in what *universe*—would this *ever* be considered a *good thing*? They are only taking you to get to me." Whether they suspect my memories have actually returned or they're putting an insurance policy in place just in case, it's beyond clear that their motivations go far beyond what's written on his acceptance letter.

"I'll be . . ." He struggles to find the words. "I'll be *up there*. On the ground—well, not literally, but you know what I mean. Behind enemy lines, so to speak." He offers a melancholic smile; it slices right through my heart. "I'll be able to help—it should be easier to access their records from there. I might meet people who know things. I could get the proof we need."

I stand there, shaking my head.

He chews on his lip. "And . . . I think it's likely that if they have me, surveillance will lighten up here. You'll be f-free"—he stumbles over the word—"to leave this place behind, like we planned."

I snort. "And what exactly do you think is going to happen to you once I'm gone? When the Tribunal realizes they no longer have me under their thumb? They'd figure out that the only reason I would leave is because I must know something is up. And the only possible way I'd know something was up is if I'd gotten my memories back. Prime Whitlock will—"

"Ugh," Mica interrupts. "Whitlock. More like Prime *Shit*lock."

I try to muster a laugh, a smile, an acknowledgment of Mica's attempt at levity, but I come up short. There's just a kind of hollowness settling into my center.

"It's because of her you have to go along with this," Mica continues, undeterred by my lack of response. "If you fight this, she will figure out that your memories are back anyway."

He's right. Damn it all, but he's right. To anyone else, this would be a good thing. An amazing opportunity. I'd already admitted as much to myself. I curse myself inwardly as I recall the wary look Trimble and Clay exchanged as they took in my initial reaction—that manic laughter, the crazed look in my eyes. They *might* be able to write it off as being due to the shock and surprise of it all. I have to hope that's the case.

Mica takes a slow, deliberate step toward me, resignation weighing down his movement. His face is shadowed with an exhaustion that stretches beyond his youth. "It's not as if I'll never see you again," he says.

And the shackles of my self-control shatter.

I crumple to the ground. Mica is next to me in an instant, his arms around my shoulders, and I hate it. I hate that *he* is the one comforting *me*. I hate that he's right. I hate that six weeks of planning and sacrifice have been for absolutely nothing. I hate that they've *won*.

The sobs I've been struggling to contain since the second I read the letter erupt. Keening wails pour from me. Mica holds me through them all. And when I finally turn my head to look at my brother, his own tears have left track marks down his cheeks.

THE DAY PASSES, somehow.

I help Mica pack according to the list provided in the letter.

We argue over bringing the earpiece with him—he doesn't want to risk it being confiscated. I'm not willing to risk cutting off our only means of communication. I win.

Mica writes letters—to his friends, his teachers, Juniper. He wants to keep up the pretense, let everyone know how excited he is for this *incredible opportunity*. He wants to thank them for everything. He wants to say goodbye.

"It's not, 'Goodbye.' It's, 'See you later,' " he assures me.

We go over a few combat moves, a few defensive stances—ones I've been having particular trouble with. It feels good to lunge, to dodge, to hit.

I scrounge together the nicest meal I can from the Rations we have left. Every bite I take is an effort—it tastes like ash on my tongue.

We clean the apartment to keep ourselves occupied.

And for the first time in many, many years, I tuck my little brother into bed at day's end. Perched in a chair next to his bed, I hold his hand as he falls asleep.

Despite my best efforts to stay awake—partially for fear of what might haunt me in my dreams, and partly because I don't want to waste a single second I have left with him—I finally succumb to sleep in the wee hours of the morning, my hand still clenched around his.

When I jerk awake hours later, Mica is gone.

And someone else is holding my hand.

NINE

ADAM WATCHES ME CAUTIOUSLY, his expression solemn, the eddies of his ocean eyes still.

I look down at our linked fingers, my mind muddled with the fog of sleep. His thumb traces idle circles on the back of my hand as I stare, trying to make sense of what's happening—what's happened. It takes a second. And then it hits me.

The guardsmen must have returned for Mica while I was still asleep. He didn't wake me.

He is gone.

I lift my gaze to meet Adam's, and I can tell from his expression that my anguish must be written all over me. The sympathy in his eyes makes me want to claw my face off.

"I'm so sorry," he says.

"Why? Why did they do this?" My voice is hoarse, my words sluggish. My body is still waking up—my joints aching after hours spent draped uncomfortably across Mica's bed as I slept. I twist my neck from side to side in an attempt to alleviate some of the soreness.

Adam tightens his grip on my hand. "I don't know. They're scared. Maybe they suspect you remember, or that Mica knew more than he let

"

on. Maybe they want to keep you separated to ensure he doesn't trigger your memory."

I nod mutely. I'd already come to similar conclusions. Something pricks at the back of my throat, in the corners of my eyes.

"Or maybe Whitlock is a sadistic bitch who is still pissed about us escaping and is taking it out on you because she can."

My brows quirk upward. I rarely hear him speak so severely. It grounds me a little. "How are you here? The guards—"

"Went to escort Mica. I snuck in as soon as I saw them leave."

"Ah." There's nothing else to say.

"I tried to get here sooner, I really did. Before he . . ." He trails off.

My body feels heavy. The prickle in my eyes has turned into a burning sensation, but the tears refuse to fall. Maybe I cried them all out yesterday. "This is all my fault."

"No, it's not." His voice is unswerving. With one last squeeze, he drops my hand from his grasp, and I hear the words he leaves unsaid: *It's mine.*

I say nothing.

"He'll be alright. He'll be safe. They wouldn't go through all this trouble if they were planning to hurt him."

"No, they just want to hurt me," I say bitterly. "And you and I both know there are any number of things they could still do to him." Images flash through my mind: bottles of little orange pills, syringes filled with milky blue liquid. Reliving the worst moments of my life. Mixing them with nightmarish scenarios I didn't even know were possible.

Nausea swirls in my stomach.

Adam presses his lips into a hard line, his eyes downcast. "We'll get him back."

The resolve in his voice sparks a kernel of hope in my chest before my better sensibilities can douse it. "Can you . . . can you contact him?" I ask. "He still has the earpiece."

Adam shakes his head. "It's not turned on. Or he doesn't have it in. I left him some messages after . . . after he told me what was happening."

My face falls.

"It's smart. We don't know what kind of processing he'll go through.

The communicator should be shielded from any scanning equipment but on the off-chance somebody were to see—"

A faint beeping sound cuts through his words. Surprise lights his features as Adam reaches down and retrieves his datapad from the pack laying next to him. "I—Holy shit." He swipes at the screen. "He did it."

"Did what?"

"Mica got us in. Into the network."

My jaw slackens. "What? That's not possible. Even if they left immediately, there's no way they'd have already reached Altara." I glance at my watch—Mica's barely been gone five hours.

"Maybe he did it before they left?" Adam offers.

"How could he—" I stop myself short, the pieces clicking into place. "They took him to town hall. To rendezvous before departing."

"Clever kid." Adam's tone is utterly reverent. "He must have slipped off. Got away long enough to connect the qube to a networked computer." His fingers flit across the screen—tapping, swiping, typing. "We have access. A backdoor into the Tribunal's system."

Something akin to pride swells in my chest. It's quickly snuffed out by a burst of terror. What if he'd gotten caught? "*Stupid* kid is more like it," I spit. "There were *how* many guardsmen escorting him? What was he thinking? He should never have risked himself like that."

And now what? I think. He went willingly because he thought it would be easier for him to get us access from up there, to dig up some proof of the Tribunal's dirty history, their genocidal plans. But by some miracle he's already accomplished the first part. And what could a fledgling cadet learn that we can't glean for ourselves now that we have access to their systems? Which means now he really is nothing but Whitlock's contingency plan, something for the Tribunal to use against me.

"We need to get him back," I say with finality.

Adam purses his lips. "I think I know someone who might be able to help."

"THIS STILL SEEMS LIKE A DUMB IDEA."

"So you've said," Adam replies drolly. He holds the door to Sundry's open for me. As I pass in front of him, I reach up to tuck an errant lock of golden hair back under his cap. He pulls the brim lower over his face, shadowing his ocean-blue eyes.

"Remind me again how you know these guys?" I lower my voice to barely more than a whisper as we walk down an aisle toward the back of the store. Mr. Sundry hums to himself behind the register, his back turned —unbothered.

"Am I not allowed to have friends? Did you think me so incapable?" Adam flashes me a grin, planting his palm on his chest in a mocking heart-grab. For the first time in the days since Mica left, I find myself wanting to smile back.

I nudge an elbow into his ribs. "I've seen firsthand how charming you can be. I just don't know how you had time to make new friends whilst hiding out."

"Three months is a long time." He shrugs. "I had time to kill, and no man is an island. I needed to make connections if I was going to find a way back up to Korbyllis to get to you. And once the initial hysteria after your, er, departure died down, it wasn't so terribly difficult to sneak around town every once in a while—cautiously. The tunnels made it easy enough to get here, and the Tribunal thinking I'd taken off with the rest of my team worked in my favor . . . in that regard at least."

I frown at him. I know he is still hurt by his team's departure—their decision to prioritize their mission over retrieving me. I don't hold it against them though, even if I did help them escape. They had been held for weeks. Whitlock and the Tribunal were convinced that they were the key to their stalled skycity conversion project. They forced them to labor —and who knows what else—against their will. What goes on behind closed doors at the behest of the Tribunal . . . It's why I'm so desperate to get Mica out of their clutches. "Still seems unnecessarily risky," I say.

"Some things are worth the risk. Especially if it meant having a single shot in hell of saving the girl I—" He cuts himself off with a clearing of his throat.

Something warm and fizzy stirs in my chest—it's not an unpleasant feeling.

"Besides, how else would I have reconnected with Mica?"

My steps falter at the mention of my brother's name spoken aloud.

That warm feeling fizzles right out, icy steel taking its place. The divider between my memories and my nightmares has been thinner than ever since Mica left—I'm staying tethered to my sanity by a few delicate threads. I go over them, again and again, in my mind: The relief of receiving Mica's first communication to us. Falling asleep to the sound of Adam's steady heartbeat under my ear. Each and every chime of Adam's datapad as it works overtime, scrubbing through Tribunal files and correspondence. The way Adam held me tightly against his chest that first night, as if he sensed the dreams that would come for me.

The way he's held me every night since.

I'd nearly had a panic attack when he told me we needed to leave the apartment in order to meet up with the people who could potentially get us to Mica. He'd offered to go alone. That just made me panic more.

"Together," I'd told him. "We stay together."

"Always," he'd replied.

Adam tenses at my side. "Breathe," he murmurs. "He's okay. He's getting settled in. In his last email, he said he was being treated the same as all the other cadets. He even likes his roommate. Remember?"

I look at him pointedly. He gets my meaning—emails that are almost assuredly being monitored by the Tribunal are hardly a trustworthy source.

"In his last *communication*"—this time I know he's referring to the messages dispatched via Adam's earpiece—"he said that nothing seemed amiss, but he's staying on guard."

We reach a door at the shop's rear, tucked behind a pair of diagonally-angled storage shelves. Adam turns back to face me, reaches for my hand. "We didn't know then half of what we know now. Now, there are people who can actually help. And . . . we're together this time. That has to count for something." He toys with the ribbon around my wrist. I've worn it every day since he tied it on me in the biodome. Another tether.

"Forgive me if that doesn't bolster my confidence. We don't have the best track record, you know."

"Oh, ye of little faith." Adam swings the door open and ushers me through.

Darkness swallows me.

"Shit," Adam mutters from nearby. "Where's the—" His words are cut off with a muffled grunt, his hand ripped from my own. A scent, sharp and pungent, pervades my senses as rough, callused hands grab me around my upper arms. Something soft presses against my face—covering my nose, my mouth—and the smell gets stronger.

My last instinct before everything fades into black is to laugh.

TEN

MY BLOOD HAS CEASED PULSING through the rest of my body. It must have, because it's all pounding against my head. It hammers in my ears, vibrates in my temples, throbs at the spot where my skull meets my spine.

What. The. Hell.

Something has my brain in a vice. Everything is fuzzy, hazy. Time feels like some foreign, unknowable thing—how long was I out? How long have I been here? Seconds? Minutes? Hours? Days?

I suck a slow breath in through my mouth. Then another, through my nose. The air is stale and a little humid, but there's not even a lingering hint of the cloying, acrid fragrance of whatever the hell was used to knock me out.

I take a moment to assess my situation.

I'm seated, my hands bound behind me, my feet dangling from the chair on which I'm perched. Or, I suppose, it could be a bench, or a table-top, or a cliffside precipice. I have no way of knowing, since when I crack my eyes open—first one, then the other—I find I might as well have kept them shut. I can't see a damn thing. It takes my muddled mind entirely too long to realize it's due to the piece of fabric currently wrapped around my eyes.

I tilt my head back and wiggle my head—back and forth, side to side —wincing with every additional throb of my head as I try to shift my blindfold down. Victory surges in my veins when it slips down over my ear on one side—just enough to offer a sliver of light if I look straight down my nose. I have a view of sad, gray flooring but I'm unable to maneuver it further before muffled voices sound nearby and I freeze.

"It was idiocy to bring her here." The voice is masculine, gravelly. Familiar, but I can't place it. "You're jeopardizing everything—it's hard enough to cover *your* tracks. I highly doubt that Whitlock's precious little informant goes anywhere without guardsmen being far behind. How long until they come looking for her? If she knows about us, she can tell *them* about us. She will wreck everything."

The hammering in my ears is suddenly a raging drumbeat. *WHOSE precious little WHAT now?*

"I've told you before and I'll tell you again"—my stomach leaps into my throat because I'd know *that* voice anywhere—"Terra is nobody's *spy*." Adam grates out the word.

The drumbeat morphs into a roar of wrath. How could they possibly think— In what universe would I *ever*—

"Explain to me again, then, her huge payoff from the Trib. Where she was for months. How, even after blowing every credit of said payoff, she still cashes in more than the rest of us each Collection. The timing of these new scav restrictions—the ones that are crushing the rest of us—is awfully suspicious, isn't it? Restrictions that never seem to impact her."

I swallow hard, trying to tamp down the flames kindling deep within me at his accusations. I want to jump up, yell, defend myself against this asshole who thinks he knows one single damn thing about me. *I didn't get away with a thing. I was trapped in a goddamn mental prison for those months. I earn more because I'm a good scav and I work hard. The restrictions aren't my fault and you don't have a clue what it truly means to be* impacted *by the Tribunal.*

"I told you where she was, what she went through," Adam says darkly.

"Then explain why the Trib would bother returning her here, why they wouldn't simply *disappear* her—dump her in a pit somewhere, incinerate her and leave her ashes in the wind, sink her to the bottom of the ocean—given what you claim she knows. Unless it's because she struck a deal with them. Because she's helping them in some way."

"And you call *me* idiotic," Adam scoffs. "I've told you the whole story. It's up to you if you're going to believe it—I can't force you."

"*If* any of what you told us is true." The man puts an obnoxious emphasis on the "if" and that crackling fire inside me wants to rage in Adam's defense too. For a moment, I wonder when my trust in him solidified to the point of instinctually wanting to defend his honor. I suppose your baby brother being forcibly recruited by the Tribunal really helps put things in perspective.

"You wouldn't be the first person to have trouble accepting it. But I've been nothing but upfront since the beginning—both about what I want and what I'm willing to do to get it."

My inner flame snuffs out. This guy knows about Adam? Like, *knows* knows? Why would Adam tell him? It's clear we're not dealing with some honorable humanitarian here. Even if this guy has the connections or the clout to get us to Mica, I wouldn't trust him with the kinds of secrets Adam is crafted from.

The man is tenacious. "It doesn't add up. You're seriously trying to get me to believe she's not working for them when she's back barely a month before her brother gets a free ride to AAMRE? When her entire family gets to go skyside?"

"Come now," a third voice chimes in—a smooth baritone, older. Have I heard it before? "You should know better than anyone that isn't always a blessing, Emery."

Emery? Emery Garren? A few flashes of memories run through my mind—snippets. The same head of reddish-brown hair that I saw at Sundry's last week, only this time I'm staring up at it from behind while we wait in the Collection line. Then, a smattering of applause mixed with hushed schoolgirl giggles from when Emery spoke to our class. A few years older than me, he was one of the rare students from Sixteen who got a scholarship to go to a skycity university—a real scholarship, not this pile of thinly-veiled excuses they used to take Mica.

Emery ended up coming home without his degree—and without any reasons for it. He just . . . left. Returned to the scav life and that was, well, that. It's not such a unique story amongst the few from Sixteen who get the chance to head skyward. Most of them fall right back down to Earth before too long.

Wonder why, I think, not really wondering at all. I already have a hunch why someone from Sixteen might not have made it too long *up there*.

I sulk inwardly. I don't want to feel bad for Emery. I bury the shard of sympathy creeping in—thankfully, my indignation makes it easy. There's a dash of sheer bewilderment there too, because *seriously*? *This* is who we came to meet? How is *Emery Garren* supposed to help us get to Mica?

The hinges creak on what must be the world's rustiest door, and Emery's next words filter in loud and clear. "Regardless, she shouldn't be here. We ought to dump her topside before anyone comes looking." He says it casually, like it's a suggestion on what to eat for dinner.

Adam snarls, and though I know it's the last thing I should care about right now, the sound soothes the place in me where fire was sizzling moments before. "If you want my help, you'll shut your mouth right now, Garren," he growls.

Emery's fuming inhale tells me he'd rather do anything but—he's ready to keep arguing. He wants to keep making his case for getting me out of here. I think about the contempt in his glare when he saw me at Sundry's. Whatever secrets he's hiding here—wherever "here" is—he doesn't want to risk the Tribunal finding out, and for some wild reason, he thinks that's at risk because of *me*.

It hits me then that I never quite realized the depths of folks' loathing. The real reason people have been so spiteful since I came back to Sixteen. They don't simply think I'm a bad sister or a bad neighbor—the kind of greedy, irresponsible person who neglects their little brother and wastes their windfalls by gambling it away.

They think I'm a traitor.

***

THE DOOR GROANS as it swings fully open and three distinct sets of footsteps make their way over to me. A shadow crosses over the splinter of sight I have at the edge of my blindfold.

A sharp intake of breath. Adam's. "What *is* this?" he hisses. "You— You tied her up? Knocking her out wasn't enough?"

A kind of tutting sound comes from the third man as he approaches me. He's been quiet—not that I imagine he could get many words in between Adam and Emery arguing—but there's something about him. His presence is somehow familiar.

"You can't blame me for being cautious," Emery says. His voice is higher—defensive. As if he knows that trussing me up like a common criminal was maybe, kind of, possibly, a little bit unnecessary. "Not like we could risk our location getting back to the—"

"Accuse her of working for them one more time, I dare you," Adam cuts Emery off, seething. "Untie her. Now."

There's a sputter of protest, but someone shuffles behind me and a moment later, there's urgent pressure on the bindings at my wrists— tugging, unknotting. A sigh of relief gathers in my chest, waiting to be expelled at the thought of being released, but it deflates a moment later. All thought leaves my mind as the unmistakable sight of a white guardsmen boot overtakes that small slice of my vision. My heartbeat is a wild, sonorous thing, and I am almost certain everyone in this room can hear it.

A guardsman? Why? My thoughts are frantic. That's who I'm being held by? Did Adam know? Did he bring them here? Did he . . . betray me?

No. Think logically, Terra, I tell myself. *They've been arguing about not wanting the Tribunal to find them out. There's something else going on here.* I mentally shake away the notion in an attempt to untangle my thoughts. I notice too late that my head is shaking in reality too.

"Oh ho," says the quiet man—no, the quiet *guardsman.* "Guess you've finally decided to join us."

"Terra?" Adam's voice in my ear, even upset as he is, is a summer breeze—warm and welcome. The blindfold is pulled from my head, tears instantly springing in my eyes due to the sudden brightness.

I blink.

Blink again.

Blink three times.

My vision widens and narrows as I take in my surroundings. Large metal crates are stacked all around me, under me. The ceiling is low, rounded. And as my eyes adjust, I realize it's not actually that bright in here. Lamps are scattered around us, but there's not a window or other source of natural light to be found.

"Where am I?" My voice is raspy, my throat dry. How long was I out for?

"It's been a few hours," Adam says, and for the second time I realize my inner thoughts are not actually so inner, after all. "I'm so sorry, Terra. I didn't know they were going to do this." With another slight tug, my arms are free. I rub at the noticeably raw skin on my wrists, the red marks from my bindings glaring up at me.

I, in turn, glare at Emery Garren. He shifts nervously. Good.

"Allow me to be the first to apologize, Miss Rhodon," comes the third man's voice.

My brain takes an extra long time to reconcile the person in front of me with my current situation. "Brant?"

"Hello, Terra." The guardsman's eyes blaze with a sincerity that makes me instantly uncomfortable. I stare back, gold-flecked brown meeting emerald green, in total disbelief. More flashes, more memory fragments—a guardsman's gloved hand on my shoulder as he escorts me home from a life-changing Collection Day. Stern looks and hushed warnings whispered in haste: *Don't ask questions. Keep your head down.*

Consternation must be written across my features.

"I can only imagine what you must be thinking. You must have questions," Brant says.

Adam snorts at my side. *No shit.*

"Maybe a few—considering the last time I saw you, you were shipping me off to Korbyllis armed with nothing but some advice to bullshit my way out of captivity." I glance between him, Adam, and Emery. "It seems like you are already aware of how that all turned out."

Brant's throat bobs. "I believe what I told you was to maintain your story. Get them to believe you didn't know anything."

"And as I told you then, I *didn't* know anything. I *did* stick to my story. It didn't make a difference." At least, I think I did. The memory is hazy, the conversation unclear. "Take it up with Inquisitor Wolfe if you don't believe me now."

Guardsman Brant winces. He physically recoils. "There is much I wish could have been different."

Stay strong. Your father would want you to be. Those were his last words to me before I was ushered to the capital.

"That day, the last time we spoke, you said . . . How do you know my father?" I ask. Adam tenses with surprise at my side.

"From the guardsmen corps," Brant says quickly. Maybe too quickly. "We were stationed here together, before."

Before.

Something indiscernible flashes across Emery's face. "Is this little reunion finished? Because we have more pressing issues at hand. Like what we're going to do with *her*."

And just like that, fire sparks in my veins once again. Adam opens his mouth, presumably to tell Emery where he can stuff it one more time, but I beat him to it.

"What *you're* going to do with *me?* Are you kidding me? How dare you. How *dare* you. I didn't *ask* to be here. I don't even know where the fuck *here* is. I'm not some double, triple, quadruple agent who's been brainwashed into reporting on whatever it is you have your hands in."

Adam looses a low whistle. "Guess your voice carries, Garren." Emery scowls at him.

"You honestly think I would work for *her*, that I would do anything for *them*? They *stole* Mica. Screwed with my memories. They tried to *erase Adam* from my mind." My chest heaves, head pounds as I leap from the crate I've been seated on and land squarely in front of Emery. Adam sweeps up next to me, his hand a steadying force on my lower back.

"Do you know what the Tribunal does? You think you know what they're really capable of? They *shot me.* Tortured me for *three months*. I still don't know the extent of what they did to me. I get flashes every now and then. Flashes that might be real—but they also might be fake memories they put in my head. It's a living *nightmare*."

Adam stiffens. His fingers, splayed across my lower back, tighten. "It's okay, Sunburst," he murmurs. "You're okay."

But I'm not done. The words flow out of me like a geyser. "And when they finally—*finally*—let me go, convinced they've messed me up enough to well and truly cover their asses, I come home only to find myself surrounded by people like you"—I shove a finger into Emery's chest—"who treat me like I'm a goddamn leper. You were so quick to take their lies at face value. So who's really the one wrapped around their finger?"

Emery stumbles back a step, and I highly doubt it's from the strength of my finger jab.

"That's enough, Terra," Brant interjects. "I believe you've made your point."

"You don't know what you're talking about," Emery grits out.

"I know enough." I turn to Adam. "This is who was supposed to help us? These are your *friends*?"

"There's more going on here than you realize," Brant offers.

I whip my gaze to him. "Was I talking to you?" He presses his lips into a hard line.

"Terra . . ." Adam's tone is soft, but I can sense the reprimand lingering under the surface. I was already teetering on the edge; it sends me right over.

Twelve weeks of imprisonment. Months of public condemnation. Eighteen years of barely living on this dusty, rotten planet before that. Dead mom. Deadbeat dad. Gran. Mica.

Mica.

Every sad second of my history, every look of disdain, every whispered judgment, every life-altering revelation layers on top of one another in my mind. It's more than any one person could be—should be—expected to take in stride. A great, thrashing beast rises up from deep within me. I can't keep it at bay.

I don't want to.

I stalk toward Emery, disgust still plastered across his stupid, smug face. I place my palms against his chest and push. Hard.

"Stop."

I don't stop. "All this debate about whether or not I'm going to sell your secrets to Whitlock. Why would the Tribunal need me? Seems like they're doing a perfectly good job getting you to dance how they want all on their own."

"Terra, breathe," Adam says from somewhere far away.

I push again.

"I said, stop." Emery grabs my wrists, pinning them down, and I hiss at the pressure of his calloused fingers on the raw skin where I was bound.

You already have a headache anyway, I remind myself. Then, I rear my head back and slam my forehead into his nose.

ELEVEN

"FEELING BETTER?"

I glare up at Adam, pressing the cold pack harder to my forehead as I raise my middle finger to him. He looks down at me—blue eyes twinkling, an amused expression on his handsome face—and hands me a glass of water.

Emery is sitting across the room, his head tilted back, bloody bits of fabric hanging from each nostril. I snort. He looks *ridiculous*. It's very vindicating.

"Well, now that you two have gotten that out of your system," Brant says, the mirth in his own voice barely concealed. "May I be allowed to speak now?"

I huff out a breath, a muted affirmative. The action makes my head throb even more.

"Great, thank you. Now, it seems there are many things that we could chalk up to having 'gotten off on the wrong foot' here—on both sides. I think the best course of action is for both of you to sit there, nurse your wounds—*silently*—and allow me to do some explaining. Agreed?"

Emery grunts. I mirror the sound. Adam chokes back a laugh.

"Now, while I don't necessarily agree with Emery's methods, it is understandable he would be wary about bringing another new face into our midst. There is a lot of sensitive information and even more sensitive identities that could be discovered here. It would be absolutely disastrous should they fall into Tribunal hands."

"Where is *here*?" My voice is low, resigned.

Brant doesn't answer for a moment. I peer up at him, see the conflict warring on his face as he glances between Emery and myself.

It's Adam who finally replies. "This is the Underground."

Emery's answering intake of breath lets me know that name—whatever it means—is significant.

"The Underground," I repeat.

Brant nods. "We are a resistance. Working against the Tribunal. Against their . . . plans."

I glance at Adam. "You know, then."

"We know. We knew before your young man came to us. Or, at least, we suspected. He cleared up quite a few things for us." He gives Adam an appreciative look, and it's the stupidest, stupidest thing, but hearing Brant refer to Adam as "mine" makes my heart flutter, just for a second.

"But . . . you're a guardsman."

"Indeed."

"So, don't you—Haven't you been—" I suck in a quick breath. "Aren't you on their side?"

Emery's derisive snort from across the room makes me wonder if it was a dumb thing to say.

Brant chuckles. "Shocking though it may be to hear, there are many skydwellers who do not, in fact, support the disparity between terrestrials and ourselves. And even more who would be truly horrified were they to learn about the extent to which the government has gone to maintain it."

"You're talking about the Skyfall. The plague."

He nods. "I am."

"So, why haven't they?"

"Why haven't they what?"

"Haven't they *learned* about it? Why haven't you told everyone? If you know the truth, you—"

"Same reason we didn't tell anyone, Sunburst," Adam says gently.

"You don't have proof," I say.

"We don't," Brant replies. "But we believe we know where we can get some." He lets that sink in for a few seconds before continuing. "I can't tell you how sorry I am that you and your brother have been dragged into all of this. It's not fair to either of you, and it's certainly not what—" He cuts himself off. "The simple fact is, we need each other's help. You need our help to get up to Altara and retrieve Cadet Rhodon."

I glower at the reference to Mica as a cadet. It may be true, but I hate it. If Brant notices, though, he doesn't let on. "We can do more than help you get him back. We can help you—all three of you—get *out*. For good."

"And in exchange?" I say, skepticism oozing from my every pore.

"And we need your help to retrieve something that could very well be the singular thing to cut the Tribunal's legs out from under them."

"There's nothing under them but us. They float in the freaking sky," I mutter. Someone chuckles in response. I'm not sure who. "Why me?"

"My question exactly," Emery grunts. Brant shushes him. I grin.

"To be fair, it's not so much that we need *you*. No offense intended, of course. We need *him*." Brant looks at Adam, eyebrows raised.

"You know about Adam too." It's not a question.

"They know enough," Adam says, and I make a mental note to ask him what exactly that means later.

"He's the only one who can recover what we need."

My brow furrows. "That's all well and good. But that makes helping you Adam's decision. And so, again, I have to ask: why me? Why am I here?"

Adam crouches down next to me. "Together. Always." His voice is a whisper against the shell of my ear, the words for me alone. My chest tightens.

"Can we have a minute, please?" I ask Guardsman Brant.

"Of course." He motions to Emery, who groans in protest but hobbles out of the room after him. The door creaks as they shut it behind them.

I drop the cold pack from my forehead and interlace my fingers with Adam's. They're searing against my icy, numbed skin. I relish the heat, the feeling. He and I erupt at the same time.

"I'm sorry—"

"Sorry, I—"

I laugh, lifting our joined hands and pressing a kiss to the back of his.

"Well, since we've established we're both sorry, can we move onto the big stuff? Kinda feels like we don't have a lot of time to waste here."

Adam takes a seat on the ground next to me and nestles my head under his chin. "Couldn't have said it better myself."

"Are they legit?" I murmur into his collarbone. His heartbeat is a comforting rhythm in my ear. My headache is finally subsiding.

"As far as I can tell. Before, when I first made contact with them, my only goal was getting up to Korbyllis, to free you. I didn't know the extent of their operations, I just thought they might be able to get me on a cruiser, get me skyside. I'd planned on figuring out the rest myself."

My grip on his hand tightens.

"When I reached out this time, they already knew what I was coming to them about. They knew about what happened with Mica, a little bit about your role in this, a little more about mine. I helped them fill in the gaps."

"So, they do know. About you. About . . . where you're from."

"They know as much as I was able to tell them," he says, and there's a tinge of sadness to his voice.

"Do they know about your team? Your people?"

"They don't know the specifics, they don't know who Charlie and Luke are, who Tom is. But they know they're coming. I explained that it's not for any destructive reasons, though. They believe me."

"Ouch." I slap my palm over my heart.

"No, I'm not—"

"I'm kidding. I deserve it anyway. You shouldn't have to work so hard for my trust, not after everything we've been through. I'm sorry about that too." As I say the words aloud, I know that I mean them.

Emotion glistens in Adam's iridescent eyes and my skin pebbles with awareness. His throat bobs. He draws a slow breath, like he's readying himself to say something . . . momentous. Then, a cough sounds from outside the door and he blinks, as if remembering where he is, the matter at hand. "I'm not sure how the Underground feels about the situation with my people. I do believe it's not their immediate concern. That may change. But for now, the Tribunal is a far more pressing threat."

"They want to bring them down," I say.

"Amongst other things," Adam confirms.

"Do they want to be in charge? Who even is at the top of their leadership? I'm guessing *Emery Garren* isn't their top brass."

Adam's chest shakes with a silent laugh. "That asshole. I don't know why he's decided to hate you so much, but whatever he thinks you did, whatever has his panties in a twist over you, I bet he'll think twice before antagonizing you again."

"Let him try," I say with a smirk.

"I'd pay to see it." I can feel him grinning against my hair.

"What is their long-term plan here anyway?" I ask. "We—you—find them their magic, irrefutable proof or whatever, they use it to take down Whitlock and the Tribunal and—then what?"

"I honestly don't know." He curls his finger under my chin and gently tilts my face up. "Right now, I'm not sure I care."

"They could end up being worse," I say.

"They could," he agrees.

"And you're still willing to help them? For Mica?"

"Without hesitation," he says, and it breaks my heart a little. I close the distance between our faces, pressing my lips against his with the kind of reverence I hope he knows he deserves. This man, so far from home, who has somehow become mine.

We have somehow become each other's.

TWELVE

"OKAY, WE'RE IN."

Brant observes me with an expression I'm not quite sure I can place. Almost like . . . pride? It inexplicably has something prickling at the back of my throat. I swallow the feeling as best I can.

"What do you need us to do?" I ask.

He gestures for us to follow him. Emery trails behind us as we exit into a narrow corridor. Like in the storage room, the air here is a bit musty, slightly damp, and carries a faint, earthy tang. Lamps dangle overhead every few yards, casting dim light across the hallway—notably similar to the maintenance passages I've been using to visit Adam.

"We really are underground," I remark.

Emery's answering snort has my face turning red, but Brant chuckles. "The Director appreciates a good double meaning."

"You're not . . . in charge?" I don't know why it surprises me. Maybe it's the way Brant seems so clearly to be Emery's superior—an observation that has already brought me much joy. Though I suppose the leader of a literally-underground underground resistance probably wouldn't have time to mess around with mid-tier guardsmen duties.

"I'm taking you to meet her now. She'll be able to explain your mission . . . amongst other things."

We round a corner and pass through a set of doors into a cavernous room. The hallways we passed through had been empty, but at least a dozen people bustle about here. Anticipatory energy crackles through the room.

A raised platform with a large, round table, sits in the center, a variety of documents and technological devices spread across its surface. A figure stands at one end, exchanging words with a trio of resistance members who all wear serious expressions.

Brant guides us toward the platform, and as we approach, the figure looks up. I'm unable to stifle my gasp as Zira Coal locks her sharp gaze on me. Her coarse, tight curls are more silver than black now, but Yttria and Juniper's mother still has the same sharp, angular face, the same warm, tawny skin, the same piercing black-brown eyes. They bore into me as if they see right to my very bones—the same way they did six years ago. From that tangled place in the back of my mind, the memory surfaces—sharp and vivid.

THE SUN BEAT *down as I walked home from school, spurred on by the rush of excitement I felt at the prospect of showing my father the present Yttria had given me that day. My best friend gifted me a booklet of homemade coupons— twelve of them, for my twelfth birthday. One to be exchanged for anything I wanted out of her lunchbox. One for a free hair styling session—she was always so much better at braids than I was. One for a hug—anytime, anywhere.*

Dad had been so down, so distracted. He usually got like that around the anniversary of Mom's passing, but lately it was extra bad. He hadn't even wished me a happy birthday before I headed off to school that morning. I was sure he'd have something special planned for me when I got home, though. He wouldn't have simply forgotten.

The apartment was quiet as I walked through the front door. All the lights were off. Nothing unusual—Dad wasn't due to be home from his shift for a couple hours. Gran would be coming over for my birthday dinner soon. I was settling myself on the couch when the faint murmurs of conversation drew me toward my father's bedroom.

The door was ajar—a narrow slice of light fell over my face as I peered into the room. I'm not sure why I felt like I had to be quiet, like I had to stay unseen. The feeling only got stronger as I took in the scene in front of me through the crack in the door. My father and Mrs. Coal—Zira—Yttria's mother. They were seated next to each other at the edge of my parents' bed, their jackets discarded next to them. Their voices were hushed but whatever they were whispering about sounded urgent. Sounded . . . secret.

My father's brows were furrowed, but Mrs. Coal's sharp, stern features were softened by an expression I could only describe as one of concern. And it wasn't just their expressions that caught my attention. It was the way they were sitting, so close that their legs were pressed up against each other. The way their heads were bowed, almost reverently, their foreheads nearly touching. My father held something in his left hand, while his right rested on his leg. Her fingers were lightly brushing her own thigh, as if she had abruptly pulled her hand back.

I don't remember how long I watched them. I couldn't make out exactly what they were saying, but it was clear that I was intruding on something . . . intimate.

I didn't like that. Not one bit.

When Mrs. Coal reached back toward my father, I knew I didn't want to see whatever was going to come next, but I didn't mean to stumble. Didn't mean to fall against the door, pushing it open. Definitely didn't mean to do it just as Gran came up behind me, her hands clamped around a cupcake with pink frosting. I didn't even hear her come in.

I remember the way Dad and Mrs. Coal had leapt apart. The shocked breath Gran released. The way the cupcake fell, frosting-side down on the floor. I remember the way Mrs. Coal dashed out of our apartment, my father's angry expression, the shade of my grandmother's face—vermilion—as she laid into him.

"She's married, Auron. What is wrong with you?"

"Whatever it is that you're thinking, Celestia, you're wrong."

"Her daughter is Terra's best friend. What do you think this will do to her when this gets out?"

"It won't do anything, because nothing is going to 'get out.' Especially if you don't go around flapping your gums about things you don't understand."

"Don't you talk to me that way. You may be my son-in-law but—"

"Then don't give me a reason to."

And with that, he raced out after Mrs. Coal.

In all fairness, I don't think Gran meant for it to get out. Maybe someone else saw Mrs. Coal running out of our apartment, saw Dad chasing after her. Or maybe Gran did say something. Maybe she confided in just one person, one friend she thought she could trust. But this was juicy stuff for the West Q. And maybe that friend—and I'd bet ten credits it was Gem Kuipers—just couldn't help herself. Maybe she told another friend. And so on, and so forth. All I know is that the scandal had spread like wildfire through Genesis X-16 within days.

Arc and Zira Coal separated the following week, and Yttria . . . Somehow Yttria knew exactly who to blame. She never forgave me for it. Her sister Juniper, well, she was still young. She was simply confused.

Just like Mica was, when Dad left a month later and Gran moved into our apartment. When the dust settled and he stayed gone.

"*SHE'S* THE DIRECTOR?" My voice jumps an octave and Emery scowls. Adam just looks at me with a puzzled expression.

"Director," Brant says respectfully, inclining his head.

"Brant." She acknowledges him with a warm nod before turning her attention to Adam and me. "Hello, Terra."

"Ma'am," I manage to eke out. At least she managed to call me by my actual name instead of the adoring epithet that Yttria took up after everything went down. I imagine after hearing me referred to as "Terror" for the past six years, it's a tricky habit to break.

She scans her eyes over me, and I have the distinct feeling of being evaluated, judged—appraised like livestock. I don't think I breathe again until she passes her laser-gaze onto Adam.

"I'm Director Coal," she says, extending her hand, "but please, call me Zira. I've heard a lot about you."

"All good things, I hope," Adam says, attempting that charming, lopsided grin of his as he shakes her hand.

Her lips twitch into a brief smile. "Mostly. We are grateful for your assistance. I know there was some . . . resistance to the idea of helping us last time."

"It wasn't personal. Just didn't actually end up needing to trade favors after all. But this time it's . . ." He flicks his gaze to me. "It's different now."

Zira nods and turns back to me. "I understand you're eager to get your brother back, Terra. We want to help you do that, but as Brant mentioned, we need your assistance with something first."

"Anything. Tell us what we need to do."

She gestures to the table, where a detailed map of an area I don't recognize is spread out. "This is Intheria, or rather, what's left of it. As you know, it was quite the bastion of scientific achievement . . . before it fell. And civilization with it. But within its depths, the city still holds something we need—schematics that can help us understand the propulsion and suspension technology keeping the remaining skycities afloat. They may also contain critical information related to the Tribunal's resurrected conversion project."

Adam leans in to examine the map, and I appreciate the momentary reprieve so I can try and stop my head from spinning. Intheria—the lost skycity. The conversion project. The weight of this mission suddenly feels extremely heavy.

"You really think these schematics are still there—still salvageable—after all this time?" If my question comes across as rude, neither Zira nor Brant react that way. Emery, unsurprisingly, lets out an audible, irritated sigh.

"We have reason to believe they are. With contamination concerns due to the plague, plus Intheria's remote location, the ruins have remained largely untouched."

"But what about looters? Raiders? Plus, are you seriously suggesting the Tribunal has left valuable intel, unrecovered, for this long?"

Zira darts her eyes to Adam, a look of hesitancy flashing across her face so briefly that I wonder if I imagined it. "We don't believe this particular intel would have been able to be recovered, even by the Tribunal. It's why we require Adam and his . . . particular skill set."

His skill set? I purse my lips as I contemplate her meaning. Does she know about his FX? Or is she referring to advanced Dissidian technology? I suppose either way he is uniquely qualified.

"These schematics are singularly important to the Underground," she continues. "It is imperative that we retrieve them."

"And in return, you'll help us get Mica back," I say, wanting to be absolutely clear. "And you'll help keep him safe."

Zira meets my gaze, her eyes unwavering. "Yes. We have contacts in Altara who can assist with his extraction. But we need those schematics first."

I glance at Adam. "Intheria . . . Well, I can honestly say this is not something I ever thought I would be tasked with doing. I never thought I'd lay eyes on the city's silhouette. It's so far from Sixteen."

"It is not a small undertaking, we know." Her eyes soften. "And it's not one for which we ask for your help lightly, either."

"It'll take ages to get there," I say. "How am I supposed to do that? I can't up and leave. They'll . . ." I swallow audibly. "The Tribunal will know something is up if I disappear for days."

"We did consider this, and admit it is a complication. One that would have made it easier if Adam had been willing to undertake this mission alone." She clears her throat. "However, it's been made perfectly clear that without you, he'd be most decidedly *unwilling*."

"Together," he whispers, the word like a caress on the shell of my ear.

I meet his cerulean gaze and take his hand, hoping he understands. *Always.*

I drop my other hand to my hip. "So, then, back to the issue . . . what am I supposed to do here? Granted, my surveillance has *seemed* to lighten up significantly since they took my brother, but I'm sure a multiple days-long absence will still be noticed. They can easily send someone to check up on me. And that puts Mica at risk. So, are we shit out of luck then, or . . . ?"

Brant attempts to cover his bark of laughter with a cough. "Fortunately, a stormfront is due to sweep in late tomorrow. A big one. Should keep everyone indoors for the better part of a week."

"Oh sure, another acid rainstorm heading our way—so very *fortunate*," I mutter.

"In this particular case, yes, it is," Zira says. "But it also means we don't have any time to waste—you two will need to leave in the morning if we're to take advantage of this well-timed excuse."

"Feels like there's a lot riding on 'shoulds' here. The storm *should* hit. It *should* keep everyone indoors. What if it doesn't? If it risks Mica's safety . . ."

"Not even if it's our only way of getting him back?" Adam says, his voice soft.

I bite the inside of my cheek.

"We have connections in Korbyllis that can help cover for you if need be," Brant offers.

I arch a brow. "What kinds of connections?"

"You'll just have to trust us," Zira says in response to my clear skepticism. "Just like we're trusting you two with this mission."

"You don't have anyone else *to* trust with this mission," I remind her.

She ignores me. "We'll ensure our Altaraan cell is aware of the situation and extends extra protections to your brother, as well—should the need arise."

"I'll give you a detailed briefing on what to expect, specifics on what we're looking for," Brant says. "We have resources to help you navigate the area, and, of course, will supply you with everything that you'll need. You won't be going in blind."

"You all are . . . organized. I—Thank you." I notice Emery skulking by the opposite wall. "You've been awfully quiet over there. Anything to add?"

"The UO needs you, doesn't mean I have to like it," he seethes.

"UO?"

He rolls his eyes. "Underground Order."

"Ah," I say. "That it? No final jabs? No advice?"

"Uh . . . Don't screw this up."

Now it's my turn to roll my eyes. Adam squeezes my hand supportively.

"So . . .?" Zira looks at me expectantly.

"All right," I say. "We'll do it."

She smiles, a determined glint in her eyes. "Good. It's a long journey, but I have faith in you both." She steps forward, something tender in her gaze. "Terra, I wanted you to know . . . your father, he—"

"Let's just get this done." I cut her off and bury the lump in my throat.

A sad smile appears on her face, but she nods. "Be careful out there. We're counting on you."

Adam and I make our way out of the room, Brant chattering at our front, Emery sulking at our back. Adam brushes my shoulder as he walks at my side, and I can't help leaning into it for support—physical and otherwise. I can still feel the weight of all that's happened, of what we're about to do, pressing down on me. But amidst all that heaviness, there's a flicker of hope.

We have a mission, a purpose, a path.

And we're coming, Mica.

THIRTEEN

"IT'S SO EMPTY OUT HERE," Adam says.

I nod. When I was a kid, I thought the world began and ended at the walls surrounding Sixteen. Then I became a scav and left the city limits for the first time. I never thought I'd be able to get used to how much space there was between the Western Fields and the mountains, the Southern Plains and the Dead Woods.

My worldview grew further—somewhat against my will—that day I was chased into the District ruins and realized how tiny my hometown was in comparison to the metropolises that once stood.

I'm certainly not in my hometown anymore.

Standing here, two days' journey from Genesis X-16, with not a single sign of civilization in sight for God knows how many miles, there's no evading how small I am. There are no buildings, barely any trees, barely any *roads*. Just endless landscape stretching off into the horizon.

It's absolutely freezing this far north too, which certainly doesn't help. The chill seems to seep right through the long, woolen overcoats and layers of thermal clothing that the Underground supplied for us. Even the air seems different up here—it's lighter, crisper, cleaner. If anything, it makes this barren wilderness feel more desolate.

I wonder if this is how Adam feels all the time. I'd imagine that venturing through the infiniteness of space makes one all the more aware of how insignificant we all are. I look up at him, his shoulders hunched against the cold, his breath emerging in visible puffs.

"Is this . . ." I swallow, my throat thick from sucking down breath after freezing breath. "Is this kind of what it's like up there?" I haven't asked Adam much about the logistics of where he's from, what it's like on another world, in space, none of it. Frankly, it's been too weird to consider, and knowing he probably wouldn't—couldn't, whatever—tell me anyway, I figured it wasn't worth the aggravation.

Adam meets my gaze, his blue eyes burrowing into mine. "Kind of," he says with a sigh, almost like he's confessing. "On the ship, whenever my brother and I would look out the window into the vast and empty blackness of space, you couldn't help but feel . . ." He trails off.

"Insignificant?" I offer.

"Yes, exactly. Tiny. Infinitesimal."

"Why 'kind of' then?" I prod.

"Home . . . where I'm from—"

"—Dissidia?"

"Yes, Dissidia. Space is big. Dissidia is . . . not. It's rather crowded, actually."

"Crowded? Like, the city you live in, on your planet, you mean?"

"Something like that," he says, his brow furrowed. "It was easy to start feeling . . . boxed in." His expression softens. "Tom and I didn't often agree on much, you know, but that was one area where we did align."

"What do you mean?"

"There's something about feeling so small that makes you want to . . . be bigger. We went about it in *completely* different ways, of course. Tommy had to become the biggest and best at everything. Never tell him I told you this, but it really was quite something to behold—the way he shot up in the ranks, curried favor with our higher ups. He's the youngest captain in Dissidian history, did I ever tell you that? He has this almost prescient ability to predict the things that need to happen, the moves he needs to make."

I pull my hand out from where it's been buried in my coat pocket and flex my fingers against the frigid air before reaching for Adam. "And what about you?" I ask, looping my arm through his.

He hesitates. "I think I just needed to be seen. By him, more than anyone. Which meant that while he was planning, plotting, and getting promoted, I was usually blowing things up."

I gape at him. "You mean that figuratively, right? Like, unraveling his best-laid plans for you."

"Sure." He grins. "But sometimes literally too."

I elbow him in the side with a snort. "You did tell me he was always getting on your case for being reckless. What you didn't mention is that you deserved it."

Adam laughs. "Exactly. So I can't even hold all the crap that he gives me against him." He pauses. "That he *gave* me, I suppose." Something despondent flashes behind his swirling cerulean eyes, and I tighten my grip on his arm.

"Adam, I—"

"He's still there, you know." He taps two fingers on his temple. "The voice in my head. That day, when everything went to hell . . . something hit the ship. Tore a hole right through our wing. We lost the conversion unit." He looks down at me knowingly. *That damn conversion unit.* "Ship was bucking like crazy. Tom wanted to make an emergency landing but we were flying too close to Korbyllis. Our mission was to stay unseen, undetected. If we had gotten picked up on Tribunal scanners . . ."

I nod understandingly.

"So, I said, 'Screw it.' I was going to *fix* things, I was going to make sure my team got out of there. Tom told me to stand down—gave me a direct order. But . . ." He takes a deep breath. "Sometimes I wonder if I make the decisions I do because he's guiding me, or if it's the exact opposite. Like, even in my head, I can't fight this need to tell him where he can shove it."

"Sounds like a pretty healthy sibling relationship."

He angles an eyebrow at me.

"Fine, maybe not *healthy*. But certainly not abnormal. Anyway," I say brightly, "I know a little something about being the mediocre sibling."

Adam places a kiss on my forehead, right at my hairline. "There's absolutely nothing mediocre about you, Sunburst. And you know it."

I smile despite myself, then glance back at the black transport vehicle, idling a few yards behind us.

When Brant said that the Underground would provide us with all the supplies we'd need, he wasn't kidding. The UO's connections and stockpiles clearly run deep. The transport was waiting for us the following morning, already loaded up with food, warm clothing, and a kit of tools and tech supplies for Adam. I'd thrown the tent, a couple of portable water filters and canteens, and a scant few personal effects into a duffel bag, but left everything else behind. Wouldn't put anything past the Tribunal, and I didn't want them immediately thinking I skipped town should anyone come snooping while we're gone.

"Stretched your legs enough, you think?" I say, anxious to return to the warm transport and get back on the road.

"Sure," Adam agrees.

Shivering, I cup my palms around my nose and mouth and exhale into my hands. A cloud of mist seeps out from between my fingers. "I didn't know it was possible for it to be this cold."

"That's because it's a million degrees by noon in Sixteen." Adam winks as he rubs my upper arms, the friction ushering warmth into my skin through the thick fabric of my coat.

"Well, I'll take a million degrees over this any day."

"You say that now. At least being this far north, we should be subjected to fewer of those insane rainstorms you get." He clasps his forearm—almost absentmindedly—as if he can smooth away the scar from his first run-in with acid rain in Sixteen.

"Small blessings," I say, arching a brow.

He grins. "All right. Let me carve out a road marker and we can get back on our way."

Staying off-grid to keep any Tribunal sensors from picking up on our position has made traveling a bit more involved than I suspect it normally would be. The UO provided us with maps and a general idea of where to go, but unfortunately, we quickly found them to be woefully outdated. Still, their guidance had been clear: Stay off the major highways and keep moving northwest.

There also isn't much of a functioning infrastructure left on the ground here—not this far from any of the other skycities. Signage is essentially nonexistent. The roads are unreliable. Some are so broken down and beaten up, we can't utilize them—another reason I'm grateful for the souped-up transport that the UO leant us, with its all-terrain wheels and the ease with which it navigates off road.

In an attempt to maintain our bearings, we've been locating discernible landmarks along our path, utilizing them as road markers for when we inevitably return this way. This particularly bleak stretch hasn't given us much to work with, however.

"How're you planning to mark our location this time? There's nothing to—"

"You may want to step back." Adam removes a fat black cylinder from the inside pocket of his coat and points it at the ground.

I comply, awkwardly shuffling backward, and Adam refocuses his gaze on the hard soil at his feet. He presses his thumb on top of the cylinder and a beam of bright white light shoots out from the bottom. I watch with rapt fascination as the laser blasts into the frozen ground, ripping a gash in the earth. Adam spins around, completing a wide circle with the laser before releasing his thumb. I assess his handiwork, the perfect ring he's carved into the dirt.

"Very, uh, symmetrical," I say, trying not to seem too impressed by this latest display of alien technology. At this point, I really *shouldn't* be phased anymore—this is, after all, what he probably used to carve out the pathways between the outpost, the maintenance passageways, and the tunnels outside the biodome. It's still hard not to be a bit dazzled, though. "But how exactly is this supposed to serve as a road marker? Nobody can see this unless they're standing right on top of it."

"So impatient," Adam says with a grin. "I'm not finished yet." He tucks the laser drill back into his pocket and laces his fingers together, flexing one hand against the other until his knuckles crack. He steps outside the circle and holds his hands out, palms down over the dirt.

He inhales deeply.

I wait.

Nothing happens.

Adam exhales in a huff, his breath nearly tangible in the frigid air, then breathes in again. The ground rumbles. Pebbles at my feet dance around each other as the shaking gets more intense. I look up with wide eyes to see Adam lifting his arms . . . and the circle of dirt lifting with them. It rises, rises, rises until it's cleared the ground—the base tapering down into a sharp point—an inverted cone of packed earth. With a grunt, he flips his creation, then drops it back to the ground next to the gaping hole he's just made.

Panting, Adam stumbles back as I move forward for a closer look. The laser did something to the dirt, giving it a crystalline finish—hard as rock but smooth as glass. The effect is not unlike that of a miniature mountain—at least eight, nine feet tall at its peak. Against this barren terrain, it's more than big enough to spot from a distance.

I release a low whistle. "Okay, then. Now *that's* a road marker." Awestruck, I trail a finger along the side of the crystal spire. This time when I shiver, I'm not sure if it's due to the icy bite it leaves along my skin or from the sheer impossibility of it all.

"I'm glad . . . you . . . approve," Adam says raggedly as he draws in a stilted breath. He's bent at the waist, his hands on his knees. His display of FX, impressive as it was, has clearly taken a toll.

"Take a breather, spaceboy." I tug on Adam's arm and draw him toward the transport. "I'll drive."

FOURTEEN

THE MILES PASS in a blur as I drive. My grip is white-knuckled on the steering wheel, Adam dozing in and out of consciousness in the passenger seat as the sun starts to dip. The heater hums softly, battling the brutal chill attempting to seep in through every crack and crevice.

I try to keep my eyes on the road—or what's left of it—and keep track of our surroundings. The terrain gradually becomes less barren as the hours pass, sporadic clusters of trees and the occasional dilapidated building breaking the monotony of the landscape. Too often, I find my gaze straying to Adam's form next to me, checking him over, making sure I can see the movement beneath his eyelids, the steady rise and fall of his chest. It seems like the strain of using his abilities has taken more out of him than usual, and I can't help but be concerned. I wish I'd taken the time to assess him more closely before shoving him in the vehicle, to make sure he's okay.

As if summoned by my thoughts, a structure appears on the horizon, casting long shadows against the setting sun. An old observatory, I think. Its domed roof is partially caved in, the surrounding grounds overgrown with straggly branched bushes, their leaves long since vanished.

I pull the transport to a stop and gently shake Adam awake. "Hey, I think I've found a place to stop for the night. Look."

He blinks and slowly follows my gaze. "We don't have to stop," he protests groggily. "Let's trade—I'll take over driving. I know you don't want to lose any unnecessary time."

My heart squeezes—he knows how concerned I still am about being gone too long, about the Tribunal figuring out I'm not in Sixteen anymore and taking it out on Mica. Despite the Underground's assurances, I'd spent the first few hours of our trip spinning out, imagining various worst-case-scenarios in extensive detail.

I bite the inside of my lip as I take in Adam's heavy-lidded stare, the sluggish way he rubs at his ocean eyes. The fact that he's so quick to prioritize assuaging my fears over the rest he so obviously still needs . . .

Right on cue, his head tips back with a yawn. A smirk plays on my lips. "Right, because you're so *clearly* back in tip-top shape. I'd rather not crash in the middle of nowhere."

"What would we crash into? You've managed to find the only building in miles. We'd have to have truly abominable luck to hit any—"

He cuts himself off when he sees the expression on my face. "Point taken."

The arctic air is a shock against my face as we step out of the vehicle. I wouldn't have thought it possible, but the temperature has dropped even lower.

"Maybe we should just stay in the transport," I say, trying to keep my teeth from chattering as Adam slings his pack over one shoulder. I reach into the back of the vehicle for my duffel bag but he bats my hand away.

"Doesn't hurt to at least check it out," he says, deftly grabbing my duffel and carrying it for me. "See if there's anything useful. Possibly find somewhere more comfortable to sleep." He makes a show of stretching before looping his arm around my shoulder and pulling me into his side. "Maybe it's not as cold inside."

I cast a dubious look at the observatory's sunken ceiling. "Forgive my skepticism."

"You? Skeptical? Never!"

I flick his nose. He laughs, and I already feel a bit warmer.

"Plus, if we want to make it the rest of the way to Intheria in the morning without any more pitstops, we need to restore some of the transport's power supply." He glances at the sky. "Moon's bright enough—it should be able to charge up a bit overnight."

"Weren't you just trying to convince me not to bother stopping?"

Adam grins. "Yes, well, since we *did* stop, I'm simply trying to be practical now."

The ground crunching beneath our boots is the only sound in the stillness as we make our way to the observatory's entrance. The front door hangs crookedly in the doorway on snapped hinges. I push it aside with a creak and moonlight seeps in to illuminate the interior—a cavernous, circular room. The walls, once adorned with what look like murals of celestial bodies, are faded, peeling, and streaked red with rust. Dust covers the floor, inches thick.

I pull out my flashlight and scan the beam across old equipment and furniture. Most of it is broken beyond recognition, though some pieces are miraculously intact—in good condition, even. As if they've been entirely untouched by time. What I imagine was once a grand telescope in the center of the room, unfortunately, is not one of them.

Adam drops our bags by the entrance, dust clouds blooming as they hit the floor. He moves over to a still-intact workbench and examines a set of ancient star charts. "This place must have really been something in its day," he muses, tracing a finger over one of the constellations.

"Yeah," I agree. The word exits my mouth amidst a silvery plume of vapor. "Though you were saying something about it not being as cold inside?"

Adam has the decency to look somewhat sheepish.

"I'm pretty sure my tears would freeze solid on my face if I were to start crying," I say.

"Well, good thing it's my truest goal in life to ensure there's far less crying in your future." His tone is bright and blithe, but something else shines behind his cerulean eyes.

"Collapsed roof and shattered windows aside, I admit it does help keep the wind somewhat at bay. Should be safe enough for the night. And hey, look—kindling." I point to a splintered pile of wooden shelves and rotted books.

"Small blessings, Sunburst," he says with that lopsided grin of his, and something warms further in my core.

I MAKE quick work of clearing space on the observatory floor and setting up the tent. Adam uses the laser drill—and explicitly *not* his FX—to carve out a fire pit so we can avoid freezing to death without risking the entire building going up in a blaze of less-than-glory.

"Whew," I say, dropping my fork into the empty can of D-B33F and setting it down. "Can't say that eating Rations straight from the can is my favorite thing, but it's still better than a bio-bar from your sustenance generator." Adam chuckles, his handsome features glowing golden in the flickering firelight, as I take a swig of water from my canteen and eye him surreptitiously.

Or, not so surreptitiously, as it turns out.

"You can stop obsessing," he says drily. "I am fine. You're the one who should be getting some rest now. Go lay down. I just want to check out what else is in here before calling it a night."

I make a small harrumphing noise, but can't deny the exhaustion settling over my bones now that I'm warm and full. "Fine, we'll *both* go lay down." I walk around the fire to where he's leaning against the telescope base and offer him my hand.

Adam releases what can only be described as a long-suffering sigh, but grips my palm without further protest. As I'm pulling him up, a small white flake drifts from above us and settles in Adam's hair.

"What is that?" I say, more to myself than to him. "Ash? Dust?" I drop his hand and move to brush the flake away, but it's already disappeared. I squint at the spot on his head where it had fallen, but see nothing. I'm still reaching toward Adam when another lands on the shoulder of his coat. This time, I see the tiny bead of moisture it leaves in its place when it vanishes.

"What is—" My hand freezes in midair as the realization hits me. I tilt my head back and look skyward, where dozens of tiny flakes are slowly floating down through the observatory's open ceiling.

It's rain. Frozen rain.

And it's about to cover us.

FIFTEEN

"OH, GOD." My eyes are pinned on the sky overhead.

Adam looks at me quizzically before following my gaze upward. His mouth pops open in shock as he sees the onslaught of white descending upon us. "Shit!" He grabs my arm and pulls me into a sprint, darting around the fire and toward the safety of the tent. We're not fast enough. I flinch as the flakes touch my skin—hitting the top of my right ear first, then falling upon my cheeks.

I brace myself for the pain.

But there's none.

A momentary sting of cold, and then nothing.

Between strangled gasps, I recognize that this strange frozen rain doesn't burn the same way the rain in Sixteen does. There's a trace of something biting and icy—but it's nothing like the searing pain I've experienced when precipitation descends from the sky.

The confusion stuns me in place. Time feels like it slows as a memory —it is a memory, isn't it?—emerges from that hollow place in my mind.

I was there when they hauled one of my fellow scavs, Feir, into the clinic that day. I can still hear him if I really think about it—the way his voice rang out in the most agonizing screams . . . and the most heart-breaking whimpers. He'd gotten caught in a downpour. The closest place he could shelter was the overhang of a nearby building, and it didn't cover him completely—part of his back and his entire shoulder were left exposed. The healers ended up having to cut what remained of his arm clean off. And they said Feir was actually one of the lucky ones—the burns had been so concentrated that they killed his nerves right along with most of his skin and muscle, so he didn't go into shock. Most people who get caught in the rain end up dying from the pain alone.

Is that what's happening to me? I think wildly. *Am I already so far gone that my body has simply given up on feeling pain?* I stumble, my boot catching on debris as more flakes hit me—this time landing on the tip of my nose—and without thinking I lift my hand to my face and touch it. I look down at my fingers, I'm expecting to see blood. To see my skin, bubbling and blistering. But there's only a tiny damp spot where the contact with the rain should already be eroding the pads of my fingers.

I shuffle to a halt as I attempt to process what I'm experiencing, even as Adam continues pulling at my arms to cross the final few feet into the tent's open mouth.

Tiny white flakes, not raindrops, are falling from above in slow, lazy waves.

When I look up, the night sky is full of wispy light gray clouds, not the threatening, dark swirls of navy and purple that I'm accustomed to seeing.

And every sensation on my skin is cold, not burning.

"Adam . . ."

"What are you doing? Get inside!" His voice is frantic, panicked. He releases my arms, dashing behind me so he can push me forward into the tent.

"No, Adam, look." I whirl around, forcing him to a stop. "It's not—it's just—" I'm at a loss for words. I simply brush a finger over his cheek, wiping one of the melted flakes away, and show him the moisture on my fingertip.

He stills, his eyes widening as he looks at my hand. Tentatively, he extends an arm toward the sky and catches a few flakes on his palm, studying them as they melt.

"Snow," he whispers. "It's snow."

"Snow?" I repeat, the word feeling foreign on my tongue. I've heard of it, of course. But growing up under the sweltering sun in Sixteen made it more of a myth than anything else. I certainly never thought I'd see it in my lifetime. And certainly never thought I'd *feel* it.

"How is this possible?" I wonder aloud.

"Must have to do with how far north we've come," Adam says. "The temperature—"

"Yes, I understand the *concept* of snow. I mean, how is it possible that it's not—"

"—eating through our skin?"

"Exactly. We should be two screaming piles of scorched flesh right now, shouldn't we?"

"You've got me. You're the one who's grown up dealing with murderous rainstorms all her life. And ostensibly, the precipitation here shouldn't be molecularly different from what you get in Sixteen. And yet . . ."

"And yet, all this is doing is making us, er, wet."

"Wet and cold," Adam adds.

"Wet and *freezing*," I say through chattering teeth. It's snowing harder now.

"Here, get inside." He ushers me into the shelter of the tent, settling himself on the ground and tugging me into his lap. He wraps his arms around me and pulls me against him, into the steadying warmth of his body.

I watch, entranced, as snow settles over the observatory—blanketing the floor, adorning the workbench with a wispy layer of white. Snowflakes sizzle into vapor as they fall into the still-smoldering flames in the firepit.

"It doesn't seem real," I say, my voice filled with quiet wonderment.

Adam tightens his arms around me and nestles his chin into the dip between my neck and shoulder. "It's beautiful," he murmurs.

"It is," I agree. "It really is."

We stay like this until the firelight begins to fade and we have to close up the tent's entrance to keep out the cold. Adam curls around me as we settle down on makeshift bedding, our coats draped over us like blankets, and I can't help but think that maybe—just maybe—our luck is finally changing.

"Adam?" My breath is visible in the frosty air but, surprisingly, I barely feel the chill.

"Mmm?" His voice rumbles against my ear lazily, like he's already half-asleep.

"I . . . Thank you. For doing this. For being here with me."

For saving me. For choosing me. For staying with me.

I shift in his arms, turning over until our noses almost touch. His eyes are open—combing over my face like they're trying to commit it to memory.

"What's wrong?" He brushes a strand of hair off my face, his fingers lingering on my cheek.

I pause. "Sometimes . . . I'm not sure if this is really happening," I breathe. "If this—if you're real."

"I'm real." He takes my palm and places it on his chest, right over his heart. "This is real. *We're* real."

"Tell me something good is waiting at the end of this," I whisper. "No matter how all the rest turns out, no matter what ends up going down with the Underground and the Tribunal and your people and *every-thing* . . . swear to me that we'll still be *us*. I can't—I don't—" I take a breath. "I don't want to lose you."

"You won't." He whispers it like a vow. "Terra, I—" He swallows, the air between us suddenly charged. "I swear it."

My heart stutters as I peer up at him through my eyelashes, at the swirling shades of iridescent color in his eyes—indigo, cobalt, sapphire, and cerulean. Like magnets, we draw together. Our lips meet. The kiss is soft, patient, tender—as if we're both afraid of breaking something fragile. As if we're afraid of falling too far into whatever this is between us.

I pull back—just for an instant—and there's something glistening in Adam's eddying eyes. I take a slow, deep breath, drinking in his stardust scent. His heart is a thunderous drumbeat beneath my palm as I rest my forehead against his.

Gravity stops.

Then his hand curves around the back of my head, drawing my mouth back to his.

And I let myself fall.

Suddenly, it's not cold anymore. The very concept of "cold" no longer exists. Even as we discard our clothing until there's only him and me, his skin and my skin, us and nothing else. Nothing exists outside this tent, outside of our bodies pressed together, outside of my parted lips and stifled sighs and the taste of him.

When I finally drift off to sleep—tucked safely against his chest, one leg draped over his—I do not have nightmares.

SIXTEEN

"SO, I've been thinking about it." Adam raises our linked fingers and presses a kiss to the back of my hand.

My lips curve up in a smile. "About what?"

"About *this*." He kicks at the loose snow at our feet as we trudge back to the transport. "About how and why it's not acidic."

"Oh?" With a squeeze, I release Adam's hand to shift my duffle bag on my shoulder, then bend down and scoop up a small handful of the frosty powder. I grin as it melts in my palm.

"The air's different here, don't you think? Less . . . heavy."

"Fresher," I offer.

"Exactly. Like there's less pollution, maybe? You said there aren't any settlements around here, right? This entire region's basically been abandoned since the Skyfall?"

I nod solemnly. "The plague hit the settlements closest to Intheria first —and hit them hardest. Not sure how many people even survived to do the abandoning."

"Perhaps without the settlements—without the recycling plants and processing facilities and transport vehicles and without people around here—the atmosphere up here has become somehow different. Almost like it has . . . reset?"

I chew on my lip, considering. "It would explain why the air feels—tastes—cleaner."

Adam darts ahead of me as we reach the transport, unlatching the passenger door and holding it open for me. A fragment of something bright flares in my chest as I toss my duffel bag into the backseat.

"It does make sense," I say. "I mean, God, even the sky seems bluer here. And don't the clouds seem whiter?"

"It would explain why this"—he stoops down and sweeps his hand over the ground, brushing the snow at his feet into two matching piles—"doesn't burn."

I'm about to climb into the vehicle, but Adam's sharp inhale has me halting my movement. I drop my gaze to where he's still squatting, to the swath of ground he's revealed beneath the snow. I gasp.

I couldn't tell last night, couldn't see it in the dark, but there's more than dirt and crumbling earth here.

There is *green*.

The revelation hits me square in the chest, as sharp as the blades of grass poking up out of the ground.

Things are growing.

"I think you may be right." My words are hardly louder than a whisper—a prayer—as I crouch down next to Adam. "But it's more than a reset of the atmosphere. More than the environment being different. It's . . . the earth itself. It's recovering. It's healed."

I run a hesitant finger along the grass and peer at Adam. His expression is a mixture of awe and apprehension, and the early morning light reflecting off the snow makes his cerulean eyes look more iridescent than normal.

"What do you think this means?" I ask him. I'm not sure why I do. He can't possibly know the answer. There's no way he can say what I most want to hear—that this means *everything*. That there's hope. There's life. That this planet isn't a lost cause after all. And maybe if the Tribunal knew about this, if we could make them understand . . .

I frown. Is there any scenario in which the Tribunal doesn't already know? Is it possible that their governance is so narrowly-focused, they haven't realized what's happening in these abandoned corners of the world? That they don't know Earth is capable of repairing itself? It seems wildly unlikely.

Which is why I wish, for a moment, I could take back my question. I don't want him to confirm what I already suspect—that the Tribunal *does* know. And that they don't care.

But Adam—wonderful, perceptive, knowing Adam—simply says, "Perhaps we'll find answers in Intheria."

———

THE CLOSER WE get to Intheria, the more I understand how unlikely it is we'll find any answers at all.

The Skyfall was an unmitigated catastrophe of the absolute worst proportions—I know this. I'd seen footage of the crash site before—in school, on television. But there's knowing, and then there's *knowing*. And there is no amount of knowledge that could have sufficiently prepared me for this level of devastation.

We're still a dozen miles away from the city itself when we start seeing the impact of the crash. The first thing I notice is the change in terrain. Gone are the rolling hills, the evergreen trees we passed. As if we crossed some invisible wall, suddenly there is nothing but . . . There is nothing. Any buildings that once stood here—any trees, any vehicles, any *life*—were obliterated by the blast wave. Any rubble or debris that might've once remained have long-since become ashes, scrambled in the winds of time.

The second thing I notice is far less subtle. Stretching across the barren landscape is a colossal rift in the earth. The fracture snakes its way through the terrain—a web of narrow, splintered fissures that meet to form a wide, jagged canyon. It comes upon us so suddenly, Adam has to swerve the transport to avoid careening straight into it.

But it's not until we finally approach the epicenter of the disaster—the city itself at the center of an impact crater miles-wide—that I find myself paralyzed by what I'm seeing. Adam wordlessly fumbles for my hand as he scans the road ahead, a muscle ticking in his clenched jaw. My pulse throbs in my throat as Intheria—wrecked, demolished, decimated— comes into view.

"I'd kind of assumed Intheria would be in similar shape as the District," Adam says. "But this is . . ."

"I know."

Intheria wasn't the largest skycity, by any means, but it was still a city. There were buildings and homes and *people* here.

Now? It's a graveyard.

Twisted metal beams jut out from the ground, the skeletal remains of buildings that once housed the most brilliant minds humanity had to offer. They rise from the rubble like ghostly sentinels. Vehicles lay crushed under fallen debris, their rusted metal mangled, half-buried under tenacious vines that have broken through the shattered city streets. Nature has started to reclaim this place, but I can almost hear the echoes of that day— the screams, the cries, the roars—as towers collapsed and the ground shook.

As the world ended.

"I don't know what the UO honestly thinks we'll achieve here," Adam says as the transport rolls to a stop in front of a squat building. It's halfway blasted apart, slumping inward as if bowed in defeat. "But this is as far as I can take this thing. We'll have to go the rest of the way on foot."

I nod sedately and move to open the vehicle door. Adam captures my wrist before I can exit.

"Take a few minutes if you need, Sunburst." His voice is soft, his face full of compassion as I blink up at him. It takes me a moment to realize my lashes are wet.

I shake my head. "I'm fine. Let's just get on with it. The faster we find what they want, the faster we can get back to Mica."

I don't add that I doubt there's anything left here to find.

SEVENTEEN

"THERE'S NOTHING HERE, EITHER." I levy a frustrated kick at the shell of an old computer monitor. It flies across the room and hits the side of a desk with a bang. "As with the other four buildings we've scoured, there isn't a single piece of tech that hasn't been completely crushed, looted, or desiccated into worthlessness."

Adam purses his lips as he walks over to a large computer hub embedded in the far wall—the only wall still standing. "This is the final location on the UO's recon list—there has to be *something* here worth salvaging," he says, pulling a small silver tool out of his pack and prying the console open.

"I knew this was a bad idea. *'Go to Intheria, Terra.' 'We want to help you, but we need your assistance first.'* I feel like such an idiot. The UO probably wanted me out of the picture and out of their hair, for fear I'd reveal their super-secret-operation to the Tribunal." I start pacing back and forth on the linoleum tile as Adam plunges his hand into the depths of the computer console.

"And now what are we supposed to do? If we go back empty-handed, there's no reason to think they'll stick to their side of the bargain. Though, granted, there was no real guarantee of that in the first place, was there? And how are we going to get Mica out when—"

"Shh," Adam says suddenly.

I look around wildly, expecting to see an intruder or some sign that the building's about to collapse under us. "What is it?"

"Hmm?" he replies. "Oh, nothing, I just needed you to be quiet. You were spinning out again. It's rather distracting when you start monologuing." He flashes his lopsided grin before moving to the other side of the console and ripping open another part.

I glare at him. "This is your fault too."

"Is it?" he says casually. "How do you figure?"

"Seriously? Am I the one who led my extremely beautiful and extraordinarily gracious friend into a super-secret cellar, only for her to get knocked out, tied up, and endlessly insulted by Emery-Freaking-Garren? It's not like the UO gave us a ton of options."

Adam grins. "*Friend*, huh?"

"All of that, and *that*'s what you're choosing to fixate on?"

"Why bother arguing with facts?" His eyes crinkle in the corners as his smile widens. "You *are* beautiful and gracious, and Emery *is* a douche— I'm still sorry about that."

He's trying to lighten the mood, get ahead of my intrusive thoughts, but it's not working. "Why are we here, Adam? Why did we agree to this? Why does the almighty Underground Order need *our* help so bad?" I'm becoming hysterical. Images flash in my mind: Mica standing at the front of a phalanx of warrior-kids, Prime Whitlock in a guardsman uniform barking commands at him, him and his fellow comrades moving in perfectly synchronized movements.

No. I shake my head. *Not real.*

Adam grunts, still hunched over the computer guts spilling out from the console. "You want to know why?" Adam's voice has an air of victory as he extricates his arm, gripping a sizable rectangular plate between two fingers. "Ask, and you shall receive."

The plate is paper-thin, green, and decorated with tiny silver squares, red buttons, and a thin gold filigree that forms paths along its surface. "What is it?" I ask.

"It's the motherboard."

"The what-er-what?"

"Do you really not know?" I had not particularly missed the way his voice flattens when he mentions something he thinks I should already know about.

I roll my eyes. "Should I?"

"You and Mica could not be more different," he says with a laugh. "This is basic computer stuff. The motherboard is like the backbone of the computer. Connects everything. Allows it to function."

"Here on *Earth*, computers have a CPM, not a motherboard." Even I know that much.

"CPM? Computational . . . Programming . . . Machine?"

I snort. "Central Processing Matrix."

To his credit, Adam seems to consider this. "Perhaps we're talking about the same thing. Trust me when I say that you all *used* to call them motherboards."

"Okay, so . . . now what? It has the data the UO is looking for?"

"Oh, no. This is totally useless for our purposes." He tosses the motherboard over his shoulder, letting it clatter to the ground without a second thought.

The baffled look on my face has Adam chuckling. "Then why—"

"Because where there is a motherboard," he says ominously, thrusting his arm back into the depths of the wall console, "there should also be . . . a hard drive." His final words are triumphant as he rips his hand back out, clutching a slim silver box this time. It looks a bit like a larger, more rudimentary version of the qube he gave to Mica.

Adam takes another tool from his pack and carefully inserts it into the side of the box. He rotates it slowly around the entire edge until he can ease the top half of the casing off, revealing a matte black interior and a shiny silver disc affixed to its center.

An impressed noise leaves my lips and Adam looks up at me.

"I'm a little scared to ask, but do you all even call them hard drives anymore?" Adam teases.

"Is it the same thing as a data core?" I ask.

"Seems likely."

"So, that has what the UO wants on it."

"Hopefully," Adam says. "As long as the data hasn't been corrupted or deteriorated too badly. But this place has been surprisingly well-preserved, given the state of the rest of the city. Maybe we'll get lucky."

I give him a pointed look.

"Anyway," he says, enunciating each syllable in a sing-songy fashion as he retrieves his datapad from his pack, "I'll see what I can glean from the drive."

"What *you* can glean?" I ask. "We're not taking it back to the UO?"

"Of course we are. But I think that after going through the trouble of trekking our asses all the way out here, we deserve the first look. Don't you?"

I can't argue with that.

"It might take a minute, but I should be able to decrypt and translate whatever's left on this thing."

I bite the inside of my cheek. "What are the chances that this actually has what we need though? The *one* drive from the *one* computer hub in the *one* building that hasn't been utterly pulverized."

"Oh, my faithless Sunburst," Adam says with dramatic flair, and I can't stop a smile from creeping onto my face. "Fear not. This is a two petabyte drive. Computers were likely all networked. I'm not making any guarantees, but odds are good that there's something here. There's a reason the Underground was so insistent on me being the one to come, remember?"

"Guess there's only one way to find out. All right, spaceboy. Work your magic."

EIGHTEEN

ADAM'S FINGERS dance over the datapad screen, the only sound besides the rhythmic crunch of debris under my boots as I pace—back and forth, back and forth. Adam glances up with a sigh, his eyes full of exasperation. Or is it amusement? Probably both.

I force my feet to still, but it doesn't keep the anxiety from leaking from me in other ways. The subconscious cracking of each of my knuckles, individually. The occasional deep inhale through my nose, as if I'd forgotten to breathe for a moment. The worried way I twist at my hair. Every beep, chime, and whirr of Adam's device sends bolts of hope and dread through me.

"Got it," he mutters at last. There's an exultant gleam in his eyes when he looks up. "We're in."

My pulse leaps and I nearly trip in my haste to return to his side. "What do you see?"

"It's miraculous, honestly. The data is in perfect condition. Completely intact. There are thousands and thousands of records here." I observe over his shoulder as Adam taps through folder after folder, bypassing an eternity of mundane, irrelevant files—data logs, technical reports, inventory records. Finally, he pauses.

Taps the screen twice.

And something shimmers to life as if it's pouring directly from his datapad screen, filling the space around us.

"This is . . ." My words fail me.

"It's Korbyllis," Adam confirms.

My eyes widen as I take in the holographic schematics—an intricately rendered design model that showcases the glittering capital skycity in all its original glory. I marvel at the intricacy, the details so painstakingly rendered, I find myself reaching out as if I can touch the miniature version of the city that has erupted around us. Adam pinches at the screen of his datapad and the hologram shifts as he zooms and scrolls through the interactive simulation.

There's the mechanical-looking underside, with its ion engines and gyroscopic stabilizers. The electromagnetic anchors and the gargantuan jaw-like doors that only open for shuttles flying in and out of the Skyline Transfer terminal. The atmospheric dome that encapsulates the city—the UV filter. They've even rendered it so that sunlight glimmers off the sparkling dyminium glass.

Something tugs lightly in the back of my mind, and suddenly, I'm no longer seeing sunshine glinting off a holographic model of Korbyllis's dome. I'm looking through the real one—up at a sky full of stars that twinkle over a blanket of darkest night.

Cosmic confetti sprinkled across the night sky.

I blink myself back to the present. Adam's lips are moving as he continues swiping at the screen. It takes a moment to reorient myself and realize they're forming words I might want to hear.

" . . .everything from the structural integrity of the platforms to the details of the propulsion and energy conversion systems. Given how much time has passed, these schematics are likely vastly outdated, and we won't know if they've made any improvements or changes. Though, perhaps the UO would? If they've managed to get access to the Tribunal systems. And if *we* could get access, then surely . . ."

Or, maybe I don't need to hear this, after all. It seems like Adam is just talking to himself as he works through his findings.

"But then, why would they have needed us to retrieve these if they had that kind of access already?" he continues. "Unless . . . this is information even the Tribunal doesn't have."

The lost city of Intheria, indeed.

I clear my throat. "When Whitlock had me up there, she said some things that make me think they may not." Adam shifts his gaze to me. "Have this data, I mean. She mentioned having some . . . technological limitations since the Skyfall. Since taking over from their 'forerunners,' as she put it—the government of old. I think the Tribunal has essentially been stuck in maintenance mode this whole time. Which is why—"

"—they wanted us so badly. Why they hunted us and forced Tom, Luke, and Charlie to—" He cuts himself off, clamping his jaw down so tightly I worry he'll crack a tooth.

I soften my voice. "And why Prime Whitlock was so royally pissed when she realized they'd—"

"Gone." The word drops from Adam's mouth, heavy and dense.

I gesture to the still-shimmering projection of Korbyllis surrounding us. "This is what the Underground was looking for, right? Is it only Korbyllis or . . .?"

"There's a separate drive for each skycity." He pauses. "They're all here. We have everything that Director Coal asked for."

"So what now? We take this back to the UO and hope they keep up their end of the bargain?"

His expression grows somber as he returns his gaze to the datapad. "Yes. Cautiously, though. I know you're anxious to get back but I'd like a little bit more time to parse through all of this. I need to duplicate it all to the datapad, at the very least, and this is . . ." He seems to consider his words carefully. "There's more here than I thought could possibly exist."

"I get it," I say, and I mean it. I do want to get back, give the UO what they want, and be on our way to Mica. He hasn't sent any messages through the communicator since we left, and if he's sending us missives in other ways, we won't know until we get back. We'll have been "off-grid" for nearly a week by the time we do, and there are still so many unknowns making me nervous. How long has the rain lasted? Have the guardsmen come looking for me? Are the Underground's "connections" good enough to protect Mica if they have?

But . . . I also recognize that whether we head back right this second or if I give Adam a couple of hours to research, little is likely to change. I can't imagine the Underground won't keep their word with this kind of information on the line. We made our terms clear, and Adam isn't stupid. He wouldn't hand these findings over to the UO without being certain they'll be able to get us to Mica. And the UO wouldn't risk Mica's safety before getting their hands on what they need. Regardless of what's going on back in Sixteen, worrying about it won't make a difference one way or the other.

So, you know. Just don't worry about it, I tell myself. Then I snort-laugh because *yeah, right.* Worrying is one of the things I do best. In fact, if tertiary examinations tested one's ability to overthink and their potential for continually screwing up, I would've passed with flying colors.

With another two taps of his finger, the cityscape around us disappears, and Adam starts scanning file after file again. Silently, quickly—*so* quickly. Words fly past my eyes in a near-blur, but even at the speed Adam is scrolling, I catch enough to get a sense of what he's digging through. What he's looking for.

Antigravity propulsion.

Orbital power transmission.

Cosmic field reinforcement.

"You're looking for the conversion plans," I breathe.

Adam doesn't slow down. More files, more schematic drawings, more folders, more labels, more words.

Office of Cybernetic Research.

Phase I Interstellar Conversion Trial.

Dissi—

"Wait, what was that?"

Adam is already several taps past it by the time the words exit my mouth. "Hmm? What was what?" he says, a little too innocently. Still swiping, still tapping.

"That folder I just saw . . . slow down!"

"Which folder?" It's another few seconds before he slows his fingers to a stop.

I narrow my eyes. "Like, six levels back."

Adam paws at the top corner of the datapad, and the screen backtracks—once, twice. "This one?"

I shake my head. "Keep going."

He obliges. "Here?"

Back and back and back he goes, revisiting the folders and digital drives and files he'd flown past. But it's not there.

"What are you looking for, Sunburst?" Adam's sympathetic smile has my cheeks suddenly burning.

"I don't—I saw—I thought I saw . . . Nevermind." I bite the inside of my lip, digging my canine in extra hard. To remind myself of what's real. *Wouldn't be the first time I thought I was seeing things, after all.*

Adam brushes my hand with his own before resuming his digital investigation. I drop to the floor next to him, no longer interested in making myself cross-eyed in order to keep up with him.

We sit in silence for a while, Adam continuing to sift through data while I do anything I can to keep my hands busy and my mind clear. I twist frayed lengths of computer wiring into braided bracelets. Draw faces in the dust that covers the floor. Construct tiny buildings out of pieces of surrounding rubble.

Finally, Adam shifts next to me, the movement so sudden I almost knock over the miniature Assembly Hall I've built.

"Look at this," he says, an emotion in his voice that I can't quite identify. Fascination? Concern?

I glance back at the datapad screen and find myself viewing something different than before—like he's crawled into an entirely new database. "This isn't at all what I was looking for."

"No," Adam says, angling the screen so I can more easily see. "But *look.*"

It takes me a second to understand what he's showing me. To take in the insignia at the top—a shield with three five-pointed stars, followed by a biohazard trefoil and a DNA double helix. To parse through the walls of text before my widening eyes. I take the datapad from his hands, my knuckles white as I read through the reports, the meeting notes, the emails.

As the gut-twisting realization of exactly how priceless—how *dangerous*—a discovery we've made here sinks in.

NINETEEN

THE TEXT on the screen is shaky, blurring together as I try to read it. It takes a moment for me to realize it's because my hands are trembling as I hold the datapad.

REPORT: Genesis Project
Level: Classified Report - TS/SCI
Project: Genesis Termination Pathogen
Lead Scientist: Dr. Evelyn Hawthorne
Department: Intherian Office of Biodefense Research
Date: October 14, 2348

Executive Summary
This report outlines the development and characteristics of the Genesis Termination Pathogen (GTP-13), a synthetic biological agent engineered to target individuals possessing a specific genetic marker. This document provides a detailed account of the pathogen's creation, mechanisms of action, and potential implications.

Objective

- Develop a pathogen capable of targeting humans with the genetic marker T-22.
- Ensure high specificity to prevent infection of non-target individuals.
- Establish a reliable delivery mechanism for widespread dissemination.

METHODOLOGY + PATHOGEN DESIGN

Vector Selection: The initial phase involved selecting an appropriate viral vector capable of rapid propagation and high mutation rates. The L2Z virus, a modified strain of the Zaire ebolavirus, was chosen for its efficiency in human-to-human transmission and adaptability.

Viral Engineering: Using CRISPR-Cas9 technology, the L2Z virus genome was modified to include a recognition sequence targeting the T-22 genetic marker. The recognition sequence was integrated into the virus's surface glycoproteins, ensuring the pathogen binds exclusively to cells expressing T-22.

Isolated Genetic Targeting: The T-22 genetic marker is a trait developed by prolonged exposure to Earth's surface environment, characterized by the phenotypic expression of brown eyes. This marker serves as an indicator of ground world residency and environmental adaptation.

Human Simulations: Ethical constraints have limited direct human testing. However, computer simulations predicted a lethality rate of 82%-85% in T-22 positive human populations, confirming the pathogen's potential effectiveness.

Delivery Mechanism: The proposed delivery mechanism involves aerosol dispersal using drone technology. This method ensures wide-area coverage and rapid dissemination. Preliminary field tests using inert viral analogs demonstrated effective distribution over a 50-square-mile area with a single deployment.

"IT'S JUST AS WHITLOCK SAID," I say. "They were going to wipe us out. Only us. Terrestrials. They came up with a way to specifically target us. Designed it to ensure minimal collateral damage to those in the skycities." Part of me had hoped she was lying. That she was spinning a tale to try and make her own disgusting, traitorous plans seem slightly less heinous in comparison.

Adam reads over my shoulder as I skim through the majority of the eye-wateringly extensive report—there's additional methodology behind the development of the virus, the in vitro and in vivo testing it underwent. I snort when I get to a section labeled "Safety Protocols," then snort again—louder—when I get to a flowery paragraph tucked under the heading "Ethical Considerations."

" 'A thorough review by an independent ethics committee is recommended before further development,' " I recite aloud. "Way to pass the buck."

By the report's conclusion, Prime Whitlock has some serious competition for Person I Hate Most in the Universe.

"Too bad this Dr. Evelyn Hawthorne has been dead for centuries," I say, surprising myself with the levity in my voice. "What I wouldn't give for a chance to lay into the person who masterminded the virus that nearly caused humanity to go extinct."

"You told me when we first met that skydweller eyes change color after enough time spent on the groundworld." Adam's voice sounds distorted. Maybe that's just because it has to filter past the anger pulsing from me in what must be palpable waves.

" 'The T-22 genetic marker is a trait developed by prolonged exposure to Earth's surface environment, characterized by the phenotypic expression of brown eyes,' " I read from the screen, frowning. "Yeah. Happens to nearly everyone, eventually. Can take years for the shift to be discernible, but spend enough time down here and everyone's eyes eventually darken—no matter what color they start as."

"Wonder what exactly it is about the atmosphere that does that," he ponders, my gold-specked brown irises meeting his iridescent blue ones as he catches my eye.

"Who cares?" I tear my gaze away, my voice sharp. "It doesn't matter. What *does* matter is that they put the time and resources into figuring out how to do this in the first place. The fucking *government* funded it—engineered a way to exterminate *billions* of humans. How could a single person go along with this? I guess it was okay because it was only supposed to wipe out people they didn't care about. Billions of *us*."

Adam sighs. Not a sigh of exasperation or irritation, but a deep, hollow, world-weary breath. "It's unfathomable," he says, and he gets that look about him that tells me he's choosing his words very carefully. "It doesn't make sense that people were just okay with this. Even amidst an entirely corrupt, self-serving government, there must have been folks who would've objected. Even with the highest levels of classification, even if they kept this study caged as tightly as possible, surely something would have gotten out about this. And there's no way that anyone who learned about this wouldn't have had an *extreme* reaction to it."

"I think you're severely underestimating people's capacity for self-preservation. Their aptitude for denial. Maybe somebody did leak it. But then the government would've swept in and made sure everyone understood that this was all hypothetical. Maybe they didn't like it, but they didn't think they would've been able to do anything about it anyway. Think about how the Tribunal is now, the control they exercise. Maybe the government back then was just as bad."

"No," Adam says darkly. "They were worse."

***

ADAM LEANS OVER ME, grazing the back of my neck with his fingers as he reaches toward the datapad. "Tap on that," he instructs, pointing to an icon at the bottom of the report. "A bunch of additional files are linked there."

A series of messages bloom across the screen—email exchanges between Dr. Hawthorne and one of her superiors, starting about six months from the date of the report.

To: General Marcus J. Harding, Director of Special Operations, IOBR
From: Dr. Evelyn Hawthorne, Lead Scientist, Genesis Project
Date: April 11, 2349
Subject: Ethical Concerns Regarding GTP-13 Deployment

General Harding,

Following recent discussions, I feel compelled to reiterate my profound ethical concerns regarding the deployment of the Genesis Termination Pathogen (GTP-13). While the pathogen's targeted mechanism minimizes collateral damage, it remains an instrument of mass eradication against individuals who possess the T-22 genetic marker, a.k.a. terrestrials.

The potential misuse of such a powerful biological agent is a grave matter that demands our utmost caution. The development of GTP-13 was intended as a scientific endeavor to explore the boundaries of genetic targeting. Deploying it in a real-world scenario crosses a line that should not be breached. We must consider the broader implications for humanity and the ethical precedent this sets.

Additionally, I must bring to your attention new concerns regarding containment. Recent tests have revealed unexpected mutations in GTP-13 that may compromise our containment protocols. These mutations have increased the pathogen's stability in the environment, raising the risk of unintended spread.

Immediate action is required to reassess and reinforce our containment strategies before deployment. Failure to address this could result in catastrophic unintended consequences.

Respectfully,
Dr. Evelyn Hawthorne

I BITE MY LIP. Okay, so maybe Dr. Hawthorne won't be inheriting the trophy for Number One Most Loathed from Whitlock quite yet. Can't be thrilled at the fact that she led this project in the first place, but at least it seems like she had second thoughts.

CONFIDENTIAL

To: Dr. Evelyn Hawthorne, Lead Scientist, Genesis Project
From: General Marcus J. Harding, Director of Special Operations, IOBR
Date: April 13, 2349
Subject: Re: Ethical Concerns Regarding GTP-13 Deployment

Dr. Hawthorne,

Your dedication to ethical science is appreciated but there are harsh realities to our current situation that cannot be ignored. The continuation of the human race depends on making hard decisions—ones that may seem morally ambiguous but are necessary for the greater good.

The recent delays in attempts to replicate the successful Phase I Interstellar Conversion Trial mean we can no longer rely on one single path forward to ensure humanity's survival. As such, deploying GTP-13 would not be an act of cruelty; it would be a regrettable but unavoidable step forward.

The immense overpopulation of the groundworld and subsequent resource scarcity makes T-22 positive individuals the most reasonable candidates for population culling. With the rapid acceleration of environmental collapse, increasing reports of groundworld UV filter failure, and lack of reparative funding, utilization of the pathogen will avert a more prolonged and agonizing demise for these individuals. It is, in the grand scheme, a kindness.

We have a duty to preserve a viable future for generations yet to come, wherever that future may take place. Difficult as it may be to accept, this is a necessary step in that direction.

General Marcus J. Harding

BLOOD PULSES UNDER MY TEMPLE. "Well, there you have it," I seethe. "They were doing us a *kindness*. It was a *necessary step*. For the *greater good*, don't you know?"

My eyes stumble over the words *Phase I Interstellar Conversion Trial* and I find myself curious about what exactly the General means. Delays in attempts to replicate its success? Does that mean they already successfully completed a skycity conversion? I'd conjectured that the reason Intheria fell in the first place was because they attempted conversion before they had perfected the technology. That was the reason Prime Whitlock was so eager to get her hands on Adam's team and their superior technology and advanced knowledge.

For some reason, the word I thought I'd seen earlier is suddenly poking at the back of my mind again.

"This is pure bullshit." Adam's furious voice derails my train of thought. " 'The immense overpopulation of the groundworld makes terrestrials the most reasonable candidates for population culling,' " he reads. "Like you're goddamn livestock instead of actual human beings."

Seeing the expression of disgust on his face actually helps tamp down the sharpest edges of my own outrage—misery loves company and all that. "It feels wrong to admit this, but I'm almost . . . relieved," I say. "This is what we've been looking for—hoping for—all this time, isn't it? This is *proof.*"

Adam threads his hand through his hair, *that look* on his face again. "More proof than I thought we'd find," he agrees.

My brows crease. "What do you mean?"

Adam clears his throat. "So, I think this is Dr. Hawthorne's user directory."

Not an answer, but okay. "You didn't know that before?"

"I didn't know whose directories I was accessing. Even if I did, it's not like I'd know which names were significant. I was just running keyword searches across the entire network drive. Picked the ones with the most hits to sift through. I suppose given her position and the projects she worked on, it makes sense that Dr. Hawthorne's was one of them."

I return my eyes to the datapad. "Looks like she sent one more email to the general."

To: General Marcus J. Harding, Director of Special Operations, IOBR
From: Dr. Evelyn Hawthorne, Lead Scientist, Genesis Project
Date: April 14, 2349
Subject: Re: Ethical Concerns Regarding GTP-13 Deployment

General Harding,

I understand the circumstances we face more than most. Even knowing the dire situation, I *must* stress that the deliberate extermination of a segment of our population, regardless of intent, is a *profound* ethical transgression.

We must seek solutions that do not compromise our humanity, and I am elated to report that there are, indeed, other avenues to explore. I implore you to consider the findings from last month's Planetary Sustainability and Preservation Authority report (attached), which details the unexpected ecological recovery phenomena observed in areas previously devastated by climate degradation.

This report is but one of many to come that are sure to illuminate new paths forward for humanity's survival—ones that will enable us to address our challenges without sacrificing our ethical and moral integrity—our very souls.

Beseechingly,
Dr. Evelyn Hawthorne

" 'UNEXPECTED ECOLOGICAL RECOVERY PHENOMENA OBSERVED,' " I read aloud. "Do you think she's talking about—"

"Like at the observatory," Adam says with a nod. "Open the attachment."

Automatically, I comply. "If this turns out to be another 200-page report, you have to read it to me like a bedtime story."

Adam chuckles. "Deal."

REPORT: Skycity Technology Impact on Earth's Ecological Recovery
Level: Classified Report - TS/SCI
Project: Ecological Recovery Analysis
Lead Scientist: Dr. Patricia Richardson
Department: Planetary Sustainability and Preservation Authority, Ecological Recovery Division
Date: March 21, 2349

Executive Summary
Recent investigations have revealed that Earth's ecosystems are exhibiting significant signs of recovery in regions devoid of human activity and technological interference, particularly in areas free from the influence of skycity technology. This report details our findings, hypotheses, and recommendations regarding the impact of skycities on Earth's ecological health and the necessary steps for ensuring the planet's long-term sustainability.

Hypothesis

Research suggests that the recovery is most pronounced in areas where there is a complete lack of skycity influence within a radius of approximately 600 miles. This report hypothesizes that the technology keeping the skycities suspended, specifically the anti-gravitational engines and associated electromagnetic emissions, appears to disrupt natural processes crucial for ecological healing.

KEY FINDINGS

- **Electromagnetic Interference:** The emissions from skycities are disrupting weather patterns and atmospheric stability, which are essential for a balanced ecosystem.
- **Particulate Matter:** The particulate emissions from skycity engines are altering soil and water pH levels. In regions without these emissions, natural pH levels are being restored, leading to healthier ecosystems.
- **Bioremediation:** Enhanced microbial activity in soil, crucial for decomposing pollutants, is more active in regions free from skycity influence.

THE REPORT CONTINUES, as the first one did, for many, many pages. Pages of observed phenomena and methodology dissection. Pages of conclusions and recommended courses of action.

I let the words sink in for a second. Then a few seconds more. Adam takes my hand between both of his own, like he's bracing me for the moment the realization hits. "This says that Earth is exhibiting signs of recovery in regions free from the influence of skycity technology," I finally say. "We were assuming it had to do with the groundworld, that the environment was starting to recover without the people and pollution from the settlements. But when this report came out, there weren't just settlements everywhere, there were cities—huge, sprawling metropolises."

"Like the District," Adam offers.

I nod. "And the skycities existed then too." He tightens his grip on my hand as I rake my eyes back over the report. "Electromagnetic interference, particulate emissions . . . The skycities themselves are responsible for the—how did General Harding put it? 'The rapid acceleration of environmental collapse.' They did this to us—to themselves. The skycities have been killing the planet."

TWENTY

"IT GETS WORSE," Adam says.

I nod—a sad, heavy sort of acknowledgement. I lay the datapad in my lap, gently pull my hand from his, and run my fingers through my hair. Resting my head against the wall, I close my eyes. "They knew. They knew even then."

"Knew, and made the active, conscious choice not to do anything about it." His voice is hollow.

"Why," I whisper. It's not a question.

"Absolute power corrupts absolutely."

I don't react. I'm still leaning back—eyes shut, lips tight. Wishing I could fall right into the wall and bury myself among the ghosts here.

"It's an old expression, it means—"

"I know what it means."

We don't say anything else for a long while. Eventually, I crack my eyes open with a sigh. "I think I'm ready to move on. We have a long way to travel in order to get this back to the Underground and I—I can't—I don't know if I . . ." I trail off.

"I understand, Sunburst," Adam says, his voice soft. "We've been here long enough. Give me a second to ensure the drive duplication is complete." He retrieves the datapad from my lap and begins closing out of Dr. Hawthorne's emails.

"Wait, what does that symbol mean?"

He glances to where I'm pointing at a small icon in the corner of the screen. "Means that file's locked."

"We can't view it?"

"You insult me," he says, mock-grabbing at his chest with one hand as he types something onto the datapad screen with the other. A mellow chime trills from the device. "More emails, looks like," he says.

From: [redacted]
To: Dr. Evelyn Hawthorne
Date: May 21, 2349
Subject: FWD: Re: Urgent: Meeting Request w/r/t Skycities' Environmental Impact

Ev—

This is what I was telling you about. Thompson doesn't care. Harding is a sycophant. None of them care. They're throwing all their resources behind new conversion trials. Won't even consider grounding the skycities, won't risk pissing off the higher ups or alienating their constituents (or, more to the point, their donors.)

We can't wait any longer.

T.

BELOW THE MESSAGE is a chain of email exchanges and memos with big red letters stamped across them that spell CONFIDENTIAL and TOP SECRET. The emails appear to be between the heads of the Planetary

Sustainability and Preservation Authority, the Intherian Office of Biodefense Research, and various other governmental entities.

"I was not being facetious when I said I was ready to move on," I grumble.

"Shouldn't have asked me to open the locked file then," Adam says with a shrug.

"Technically, I only asked what the icon meant."

"And then implied I couldn't unlock it. What did you expect? Anyway, you reading this or do you want a summary?"

I smack his arm—more lightly than he deserves, but I'm grateful for the break in solemnity that's been hanging over our heads since we arrived. I start to read. "Yeesh, I thought General Harding sounded like a dick, but this Secretary Thompson guy really gives him a run for his money, doesn't he?"

Adam scans the signature line from one of the emails and promptly rolls his eyes. "Secretary James Thompson, Planetary Sustainability and Preservation Authority. Sounds like a fancy misnomer given they don't seem particularly bothered to try and *sustain* or *preserve* anything other than their own hides."

"Ahem." I summon a memory of Prime Whitlock, doing my best to affect her graceless condescension as I drop my voice an octave and begin narrating from one of the memos. " 'The political and social implications must be considered, as our constituents have grown accustomed to a certain quality of life. Forcing a return to the groundworld would lead to widespread discontent and is an unacceptable solution.' What a load of crock. Hello, there were already people living on the groundworld, *asshole*."

"Sounds like Dr. Hawthorne and a group of some other scientists were trying to convince Secretary Thompson to call an emergency meeting with several other agency heads."

I continue scanning the exchanges. "Key reps from the Urban Development and Technological Advancement departments, the IOBR Director of Special Operations—that's Harding, I think—and the Skycity Tri-Council."

"Tri-Council, huh?" Adam says. "Sounds abysmally familiar. Precursor to the Tribunal?"

"Precursor or *pre-curse?*"

Adam chuckles, a sound that feels like a small victory. "I see what you did there, Sunburst." He toys with the ends of a lock of hair that's fallen over my shoulder. "You're in a remarkably good mood all of the sudden."

A strangled laugh bursts free from the back of my throat. "Not sure I would say that. It's more like . . . I've finally soared past my threshold for this insanity. I'm merely no longer surprised. I don't think there's a single thing that could shock me at this point, in fact."

"Is that so?" He says, amusement twinkling in his eyes. Amusement . . . and something else. Guilt? "Sounds like a challenge."

I smirk. "If you can find something that shocks me—truly shocks me," I say, "after learning about our current government's plans to convert every skycity into spacecraft so they can ditch this dying planet, our *previous* government's fully-sanctioned, terrestrial-targeting virus, *and* that the skycities themselves are responsible for killing said planet in the first place, then yes. You would deserve a prize."

"What do I get if I win?"

I laugh. "You really think you have a shot at winning?"

"Humor me," he says, my favorite lopsided grin on his face.

"Well, what do you want?"

Adam leans closer. "I want a promise."

"A promise to do what?"

"Just a promise. To be redeemed at some future point. Could be today, could be next week, could be ten years from now."

I tilt my head to the side. "All this for an IOU? Really?"

His grin falters slightly. "You asked me what I want."

I sigh and bite my lip in a way I hope might possibly be construed as seductive. "And to think of *all* the things you could've asked for," I say suggestively. The hiss of Adam's sudden intake of breath is particularly satisfying. "Fine. Shock me, astonish me, stupefy me—and you can have your *promise.*"

"I'm going to hold you to that, Sunburst."

"You do that." I lean into him, bracing my shoulder against his chest. He shifts so he can wrap his arms around my waist, holding the datapad in front of me. "But don't say I didn't warn you. I'm genuinely not sure I'm capable of being surprised anymore. I'm so . . . tired. Being forced to peel back layer after sickening layer of our history and finding out how depraved people really are, time and time again, is exhausting."

Adam grazes the back of my crown with a gentle kiss. "I get it."

I glance down at the datapad. "All right, so do we think there's anything new that we can glean from the exchanges between these assholes, or are we thinking it's just more of the same?"

"Given how thoroughly unshockable you are now," Adam says, tickling me lightly at my waist, "I can't imagine there'll be anything groundbreakingly new. I admit, I'm curious about the first email, though—the one from 'T.' Who is this person who was so well-positioned that they were able to collect all these classified missives and send them to Dr. Hawthorne? They allude to a lot in their message—mentioning the conversion trials, GTP-13 deployment moving forward . . ."

"Not to mention the cryptic-ass way they ended it," I say. " 'We can't wait any longer.' What's that supposed to mean?"

"I'm not sure but I . . . Hmm." Adam swipes through the remaining communications that T. had bundled together. "Check this out," he says, pointing to a now-recognizable icon on the screen.

"Another locked file?" I ask.

Adam nods against my hair. "A video file this time though."

"A locked file within a locked file? The mystery thickens."

"Perhaps there's still something *shocking* for us to learn," he teases.

"We'll see," I say, a smile dancing on both sides of my mouth despite being in this crumbling room, this dilapidated building, this fallen city. Despite the devastating truths we've unearthed, and the way it feels dangerously like now we are tempting fate. "We'll see."

TWENTY-ONE

A WOMAN *in a white coat sits behind a disorderly desk. Her ice-blue eyes are framed behind thick-rimmed glasses, and dark blond tendrils are swept up in a messy pile atop her crown as she leans back in her chair. A crystal decanter and a short glass sit on the desktop in front of her, both filled with the same amber liquid.*

The woman draws a deep breath, her face etched with a confusing mix of emotions. Nerves, trepidation. But also the hardened edge of resolve.

"My name is Dr. Evelyn Hawthorne," she says into the camera. "I am a scientist employed by the Intherian Office of Biodefense Research, and am Lead Scientist of the Genesis Project. Today's date is May 21, 2349. I am recording this video to document my profound horror and opposition to the planned deployment of the Genesis Termination Pathogen, also known as GTP-13.

"When I embarked on this project, my goal was purely scientific—to explore the limits of genetic targeting and its applications. Never did I imagine my work would be twisted into an instrument of genocide.

"The pathogen we've created is designed to target individuals with the T-22 genetic marker, a trait developed solely by those who live on the Earth's surface, the so-called 'groundworld.' To speak plainly, it has been engineered specifically to target terrestrials."

Dr. Hawthorne takes a brief pause, looking away from the camera, as if she's collecting her thoughts—or perhaps steeling her nerves. She raises her glass to her lips and gulps down half her drink before continuing.

"Our leaders argue that this is a necessary step for the greater good, to preserve resources and ensure the survival of humanity. But what they are proposing is nothing short of mass murder, a culling of innocent lives based on the discriminatory, bigoted divide between skydwellers and terrestrials that, I'm ashamed to say, I have only helped widen with my work.

"Unlike some of my esteemed colleagues who have, in fact, done the opposite. The discoveries unearthed by Dr. Richardson and her team might very well be the key to finally healing this great rift in humanity—to healing the very planet. There is much we now understand about the ecological degradation of the groundworld—how it came about and, infinitely more importantly, how to stop it. Possibly how to reverse it altogether."

Dr. Hawthorne plants her hands on the desktop in front of her and leans closer to the camera. There's a tremor in her voice when she speaks again. "I have brought my grave concerns to leadership, only to be met with dismissal and derision, time and time again. Unsurprisingly, I suppose, it appears our government officials are more concerned with appeasing those who line their pockets than with doing the right thing. They are unwilling to sacrifice the comforts and disrupt the status quo of their skydweller patrons, even in the face of leaving this horrific—and, we now know, unnecessary—legacy.

"But I cannot in good conscience remain silent. History will judge us not by our actions, but by our willingness to stand up against such atrocities. I am terrified by the ethical implications and the dark precedent this will set. What kind of world are we creating if we justify genocide as a means to an end?

"Terrestrials are guilty of absolutely nothing other than existing in a world that has left them behind."

"I will not remain silent, nor still. There may be limits to what I'm able to achieve—but thankfully, I am not alone. There are others, determined and resourceful, who know the truth. And together, we will do absolutely everything in our power to keep GTP-13 out of the government's hands and levy public pressure to get them to see reason.

"If you are watching this, know that there are those of us who are fighting against this atrocity. The future of humanity depends on the actions we take today."

She pauses again. Drains the rest of her drink. Adjusts her glasses. Then looks directly into the camera, and it feels like her eyes pierce directly into my soul.

"This is Dr. Evelyn Hawthorne, and I refuse to be a silent accomplice to crimes against humanity. History is watching. Join us."

"GUESS her moral compass won out in the end," I say, blinking away the prickle in my tear ducts. "She didn't reveal anything shocking, given what we already know," I continue, "but there's still something . . . . chilling about hearing it spoken. Having it summed up so plainly."

I feel the hair on the back of my neck part as Adam expels a sharp breath.

"Do you think she ever got her message out?" I ask. "Do you think there were people organizing, ready to stand up for us?" *Before everything went to hell?*

"I'd like to think so," Adam says. "But even if she did, even if there were . . ."

"It was too late. She recorded that video on May 21, 2349. A month before the Skyfall." I pause. "Do you think Intheria falling was related to this?"

"I don't know," he admits. "If the Tri-Council was anything like the Tribunal is now, I certainly wouldn't put it past them to enact some kind of insane countermeasure to bury dissenters—literally."

"I thought maybe the Skyfall was the result of a failed conversion attempt."

"That seems plausible too. Unfortunately, I don't think we'll ever truly know."

"It's horrifying either way."

Adam nods in agreement before dropping the datapad in my lap and going to gather his tools. A spark of affection zips through my chest as he carefully avoids stepping on the sketch of Mica's scowling face that I drew in the debris. After he retrieves the datapad from me and tucks it away in his pack, he wraps his fingers around my wrists and hauls me to my feet in one smooth motion.

"Ready?" he asks me. "The UO's going to have a field day with this video."

"I hope it's enough." I take a final look around the wrecked room. "And I hope it brings Dr. Hawthorne a little bit of peace to know that, even if it was hundreds of years later and not in the way she had planned, she still helped."

"I hope so too," Adam says. "Let's go home."

WE MAKE our way back toward the building's entrance—or what's left of it. Getting into the computer room in the first place had been quite the feat. Returning from it appears to be another ordeal entirely. Walls stand at an angle, like books leaning against each other on a too-empty shelf. More of those thick, warped vines are wrapped around every discernable surface.

We're in the lobby, not far from the shattered front doors, when a deep rumble shakes the ground beneath us.

I exchange a worried glance with Adam. "Did you feel that?"

He nods, his eyes frantically scanning the deteriorating structure around us. "We need to move. Now." He grabs my hand and pulls me forward. The rumbling grows louder. Cracks race up the walls.

"What is happening?" I screech over the building's groans.

"Just run!" Adam yells. We sprint toward the exit, dodging chunks of debris as they rain from the ceiling.

Until the floor craters in on itself, right where I'm racing across it.

"Terra!" Adam throws out his hand and relief floods every cell of my body as my body seizes, suspended above the cavernous pit that just opened up underfoot. He grunts as he uses his FX to levitate me to the side. I've almost cleared the hole when a massive beam crashes through the ceiling above us, forcing Adam to leap aside.

He loses his hold on me.

I scream.

I plummet.

Wildly flinging my arms out, I grasp the thick stem of a vine that's curving off the floor before I fall into the void. My ribs howl in protest as my chest slams against the rim of the chasm, my legs dangling, the feeling of utter nothingness below. Dust and debris churn in the air around me—flying into my eyes, my nose, down my throat as I gasp for breath.

Adam calls my name from across the black pit between us. The beam blocks his path to me.

"This entire building is coming down," I say through gnashed teeth as I put every ounce of strength into maintaining my grip on the vine. My heart pounds in my chest. "You need to go."

"You're certifiably insane if you think I'm leaving you here," he bellows. "Hold on!"

As if on cue, my grip slackens and the vine slips, costing me precious inches. I cry out, desperately trying to hook my feet over the ledge, but the flooring crumbles away each time I find a foothold. Panic washes over me as I scramble with the vine, but I manage to hoist myself up enough to partially rest my torso against the ledge, offering my trembling arms a slight reprieve. It's precarious, though—something made all too evident when the building shudders violently a few moments later.

Debris rains down, clattering over me, around me, rousing a cloud of dust that settles on every inch of my skin. A speck lands on the tip of my nose and a memory lashes at me—visceral, powerful. For an instant, my fingers aren't being ripped raw as they clutch a spiky vine. They're tracing soft patterns in the divots between Adam's muscles. My arms aren't buckling under my own crushing weight, but are gently pressed to my chest as Adam moves over me. And my heavy breaths aren't born from adrenaline and the very real fear that I could fall to my death any second. They're the greedy gasps and sighs of someone who wants more —more of his touch, more of his warmth, more of *him*—as snow falls outside.

Then, as suddenly as it came upon me, the vision disappears. Reality crashes back in as another puff of detritus passes over me, flakes of ash and grit landing in my hair like snowflakes. The irony of it stirs something hot and wet in the corners of my eyes.

I want more, yes. More of that, more of *us*. It's so supremely unfair that I'm not going to get it.

Adam's voice is nothing but a string of increasingly inventive curses as he grapples with the beam. He is half-hidden behind it, but what I can see of his face is contorted with effort, veins popping on his neck. Fear lances through me. Is the beam pinning him down? He needs to make it out of here, needs to make it back to Mica. He needs to bring what we found to the Underground. He needs to tell everyone the truth.

He has things to do.

"Adam," I say, a sudden wave of resolve turning my voice into a strange, foreign thing. "Promise me you'll get Mica, okay? Promise me you'll get him out. When I'm—"

"You're the one who's supposed to owe *me* a promise, Sunburst. And I still intend to win it from you fair and square, so you'd better hold the fuck on."

My fingers slip further, my thin shield of courage slipping with them. "Adam, I—"

"Don't you dare. Don't you even think about saying it." His voice is thick.

My heart cracks. "I need you to know that I—"

"No." The word comes out as a whimper. "Not now. Not like this. Please." His arm curves around the side of the beam like he's reaching for me.

A sob breaks free from my chest. "It's not fair. How little time we got together." Tears stream from my eyes, mixing with the dust on my cheeks, turning into a sour sludge as it trickles into my mouth. "But you need to know, short as it was, strange and enraging and improbable as all of it was . . ." I draw a shuddering breath. "I wouldn't trade it."

"I can think of more than a few moments I'm positive you would trade," he grunts out, "but it doesn't matter because we still have thousands more ahead of us to make up for them."

"I lo—" I start to say, but at the same time Adam shouts, "I've almost—"

A crash cuts through our words.

There's a rush of air. Pain in both of my palms as the vine is ripped away.

Weightlessness.

A shout, a scream, a plea. Adam's? Someone else's?

Then, pain.

Then, nothing.

TWENTY-TWO

THE FIRST THING I notice is the cool, hard ground beneath me. It's quickly followed by a second observation, which is that *everything hurts.*

My head throbs, my body aches. But, hey, small blessings—it would appear I am alive.

"Sunburst, can you hear me?" A voice—warm, urgent, close. Adam. "She isn't waking up. Why isn't she waking up?"

"Give her a minute," another voice says. Deep. Male. Faintly familiar. "She collided head-first with a metal joist before I could stop her fall. Better than the bonecrush that typically awaits people who free-fall three stories down, but still—can't have been pleasant."

"And whose fault is that?" Adam sounds pissed. Why does that make me . . . happy?

"Gee, I'm sorry," says the other person, and he doesn't sound very sorry at all. "Should we go back in time and see how you two fare without my intervention?"

I feel a gentle hand grasping my own, fingers fluttering over my face. "Please, Sunburst. Please wake up."

Well, since he asked so nicely. I force my eyes open, squinting against the early morning light. Adam's face comes into focus—his beautiful eyes rimmed with red, relief flooding his features.

"You're okay, you're okay." His words are quick, sharp. Repeated as if he's the one who needs to hear them.

"I'm okay," I croak, my voice gruff—like my throat is full of the same dust I still feel coating my skin, my hair, my lashes. I try to move, but a sharp pain in my side stops me. I manage a groan, my fingers twitching.

"I know it hurts, Sunburst," Adam murmurs, brushing the hair from my forehead. "I'm sorry."

"What—what happened?"

"Kind of a long story." He threads his arm below my back and eases me into a sitting position, politely ignoring the curses I levy at him as the movement ripples through my battered body. "Well, maybe not that long. And only moderately interesting. It's a story about how I got my ass handed to me by a giant metal rectangle and had to watch you nearly plunge to your death while being unable to do a damn thing about it." His expression darkens. "But the important thing is that we got you out and you're okay now."

"We?" I follow Adam's gaze as he pins it on something behind my right shoulder. Turning my head, I find myself abruptly aware that the usual ratio of terrestrials to extraterrestrials has shifted—and not in my favor.

"Hello again, kid," Luke says.

"What—How—Luke?" I sputter.

"We have to stop meeting like this," he adds, a sheepish smile on his lips.

I search my mind for a retort, some quip, some wisecrack about how this is now the second time I've come to consciousness with him lurking over me. I come up blank. I simply stare at his kind, mildly weathered face. I take in the dark circles under his brilliant turquoise eyes, the additional streaks of gray that seem to have sprouted in his dark hair by his temples.

When I finally open my mouth, what comes out is, "You're supposed to be in space."

A grin spreads across Luke's face. "Aren't you glad I'm not?"

I glance at Adam, who seems like he's trying to stifle a chuckle. "Are we glad about that?" I ask, raising my brows—and immediately wincing. *Right. Pain. Lots and lots of pain.* Slowly—so slowly—I raise my hand to my forehead, where the pads of my fingers meet the edge of a soft bandage. My eyes drop to my body, where another bandage covers the entirety of my upper torso. It starts at my clavicle, wrapping down my ribs, and stopping above my navel. I grimace as I note that part of the bandage is stained with the muted brownish-red color of dried blood.

"How long was I out?" I ask, at the same time thinking, *I'm really tired of having to ask that.* A detached part of me realizes I'm not wearing anything other than this bandage-wrap bandeau beneath my jacket, but I can't particularly bring myself to care.

"Fifteen, sixteen hours, maybe," Adam says. My brows fly up. "You were out the entire night. Barely moved." The concern in his voice has my heart swelling.

"Except when you were writhing in obvious pain," Luke offers helpfully.

Adam scowls at Luke, but his expression softens the moment his eyes return to mine. "Had me pretty worried," he admits, handing me a water canteen. I take a long drag before pouring out a bit to wash the grit from my face and hands.

"He's trying to play it cool," Luke says, "but he was a total wreck. Never seen him like that before. I s'pose there's something about seeing the love of one's life plummet into the depths of hell that will do that to a person."

Luke pretends to recoil from Adam's glower, while I pointedly choose to ignore that remark—though it doesn't stop the sparkly feeling stirring somewhere beneath my bruised ribs. Finally feeling steady enough to risk the wrath of my neck muscles, I glance at my surroundings. We're inside a tent—not the same one Adam and I shared in the observatory, I note with gratitude. Don't need Luke's presence coloring those *particular* memories.

This tent is larger, more structured—the shimmery material it's made of is sturdier. A small table and single chair sit in one corner, with two identical silver packs propped against the legs.

"Where are we?" I ask, prodding at the thin bedroll I'm sitting on. I note another one rolled up against the other wall, next to what looks like a small assortment of cooking equipment.

"Welcome to my humble abode," Luke says proudly, spreading his arms wide in a gesture of hospitality.

"Your abode," I repeat, dumbfounded. "How? What are you doing here? I thought you all left. Went home. Back to Dissidia."

Luke and Adam exchange a look. "I did. We did. And then, we didn't. Adam and I were able to catch up a bit while you were"—he clears his throat—"sleeping, but basically, Tom, Charlie, and I were indeed able to get back to Dissidia after we escaped from Korbyllis and, er, parted ways with Adam . . ." Luke chews on his lip, looking appropriately chagrined. "But we were ordered to return, as we were unable to complete our original mission."

Fury stirs in my gut. "You had just escaped captivity and they forced you to come back?"

Luke shrugs. "There were still things that needed to be done. I don't know how much Adam's been able to tell you about what we were sent here for—"

Now it's Adam's turn to look ashamed. "She knows we were sent on a fact-finding mission. She knows we—they are on their way here. Unfortunately, I have not been able to provide many particulars. It's been . . . a point of frustration."

I scoff, readying myself to share exactly how much of an understatement that is, but Luke speaks before I get the chance.

"Mmm, I suppose that tracks," he murmurs. "The Admiral was rather thorough with what she ordered Tommy to *nix* us on. And your brother's nothing if not a stickler for the rules."

"When it comes to me, you mean." Adam rolls his eyes. "Somehow you always seem to end up on his far less prickly side. Convenient how often he seems to forget to *nix* you entirely, isn't it?"

"Perk of the job," Luke says nonchalantly.

"He and I share fifty percent of the same DNA. You'd think if anyone was going to be offered the privileges of his favor, it'd be his fucking brother."

"I would be concerned if you were his *fucking* brother, my guy. And maybe just a tiny bit jealous," Luke says with a waggle of his eyebrows.

With a flick of Adam's wrist, the rolled bedroll goes soaring at Luke's head. He catches it with a laugh before it collides with his nose.

"Don't be disgusting. There's a lady present, asshole." Adam shakes his head disapprovingly, but I see the corners of his mouth twitch.

"Apologies, my lady," Luke sketches a bow in my direction. "I'd forgotten how much I enjoy giving him shit."

My mouth would be hanging open if I didn't think it would make me pass out, given the way my jaw already throbs. I run my tongue over my teeth and wonder if the little jagged spot on my front molar has always been there.

"May this *lady* ask a question?" I ask demurely. Then, less demurely, "What the actual fuck are you two talking about?"

Luke's guffaw rings through the tent like a clearing bell, taking whatever tension had remained with it. "I knew I liked you from the first moment we met."

"Have a soft spot for injured, barely conscious humans, do you?" I say, the memory of my first encounter with Luke washing over me. The similarities in circumstance between then and now are not lost on me—both times involved someone with FX saving my barely conscious ass. Now that I think about it, my first run-in with Adam was eerily similar too.

Ugh. So embarrassing.

"You know, before you all swept in, my life was quite peaceful," I say, a teasing lilt to my tone. "It may be hard to imagine, given our record, but I actually used to go about my day without requiring extraterrestrial extraction from mortal danger."

"Extraordinary," Luke quips, and though I roll my eyes, I can't quite suppress my smile.

"Anyway, I don't know how much you and Adam were able to cover while you were catching up, but if he hasn't already mentioned it, the *lady* can get real annoying when she doesn't get actual answers to her questions."

Adam snorts, as if to say, *Hey, you said it, not me.*

"And so, once again, I must ask: What the hell are you going on about?"

"Easy, girl." Luke lifts his palms conciliatorily. "What, all that ribbing? Your man just doesn't think it's fair that the occasional scrap of extra special treatment from his brother often seems to end up landing with me."

I blink at him. "But why would you get special treatment from Tom?"

Luke looks at me expectantly. I glance at Adam, who shares a similar —though admittedly less amused—expression.

Oh. Ohhhh.

"Well, good for you two," I say, my cheeks warm. "But that's not what I meant, and I think you know it."

Luke's mouth curves up in a gratified smile. "Fine, fine. To finish answering your earlier questions, yes, we're at my campsite right now. We're not far from where I found your vehicle, on the outskirts of the city proper." He grimaces as if in recognition of the fact that you can hardly call this place a city anymore. "Given what happened during our last attempt, and all the time we lost from the, er, setback, our commander split us up this time. My assignment was to continue with our original assignment and reconnoiter the Intherian crash site." He pauses, taking in the no doubt gobsmacked expression on my face. "I know—what are the chances? Quite the coincidence."

"Not so sure I believe in coincidences anymore," I mutter.

"Anyway, I had already completed my objectives and was en route to the rendezvous spot when, wouldn't you know, I came across quite the peculiar sight. Imagine my surprise to see a Steklenbergian obelisk smack-dab in the middle of nowhere, about 800 klicks southeast of here."

"Steck . . . lenn . . . what-ian?" I garble.

"He's talking about the road marker I made," Adam breathes against my ear. He's shifted closer over the past few minutes and I barely noticed. I take one of his hands and snake it loosely around my waist, letting myself relax into him. I know it's probably all in my mind, but I swear, the pain radiating through my body eases as I lean against his chest.

"They're a thing from back home." Luke dips his chin at his former teammate. "Solid work on that one, by the way."

Adam looks like he's fighting a grin, and damn it all if I can't blame him. There's something disarming about his teammate—former team-mate, whatever. It's honestly annoying how much I already like him.

"I picked up your trail from there," Luke continues, "and—lo and behold—ended up following you right back to where I'd come from myself. Didn't expect to find you in the middle of a collapsing building, admittedly. Always did like keeping me on my toes, didn't you?"

"Right. Well, thank you again for the save. Your timing was *almost* perfect." With a featherlight touch, Adam trails his finger along the bandage wrapped around my ribs.

Contrition flickers across Luke's face as he kneels beside me. "We smothered your wounds with healing balm, but your injuries were . . . extensive. It'll probably be a good while before you're back to feeling fighting fit." He gingerly places a finger under my chin, pulls a small round tool from his pocket, and lifts it to his eye, tipping my head back to assess me.

"Pain aside, what's my prognosis, Doc?" I ask when his evaluation seems complete. "Am I going to live?"

"Appears that way." Luke grins widely. Behind me, Adam huffs as though he doesn't quite appreciate our flippancy.

"Excellent. Because I have another question."

"I see what you meant." Luke shoots a meaningful look at Adam. "Tenacious."

"You're telling me," Adam gripes. I pinch his forearm and feel him smile against the back of my head.

Luke turns his attention back to me. "All right, lay it on me."

"What did you mean, before, when you said Tom had—what was it? Orders to *'nix'* Adam? What does that mean?"

"Mmm. Nothing gets by you, does it?" Luke's usually mirthful eyes are suddenly filled with a serious sort of understanding that makes me shift uneasily.

My eyes widen in alarm as a thought worms its way into my brain. "He didn't . . . he wasn't, like, ordered to kill you, was he?" I slice my hand across my throat. They both erupt with laughter.

"Okay, guess it's not that, then," I grumble.

"How much do you know about how *fixing* works?"

"Luke," Adam warns, retracting his arm from around my waist and standing up.

I purse my lips, confused, as he takes a step back, his fists clenched at his side. "*Fixing*?"

"FX," Luke clarifies. "The advancements we've been subjected to?"

Ah. "Not much," I admit. "Just what I've seen. We haven't really spoken about . . . any of that."

Luke tuts knowingly. "I see."

"Luke, I—" Adam's voice is strained—pained? And am I imagining that he's put another few inches between us?

"Merely witnessing this conversation is activating the lock?" Luke asks, incredulity coloring his tone. Adam nods, his jaw quaking.

Concern furrows my brow. "What's—"

"I think your guy here could use a break," Luke says peaceably. "Surely you have, er, needs that you want to attend to?"

I gawp at him, my mind blank. "Needs?"

"I mean, you were unconscious for sixteen hours or so. Do you really not understand what I'm getting at?"

As if his words unlock some sort of mental barrier I had placed around my bodily functions for the past day, I'm instantaneously aware of said needs. The look on my face must be confirmation enough, because moments later I'm being helped to my feet and ushered out of the tent— armed with instructions from Luke on where to go, and his assurance that I'll receive answers when I get back.

The last thing I see before I exit the tent is Adam, sitting with his head in his hands, his hands on his knees, as Luke whispers something close to his ear. Knowing Luke as I do now—and it feels like I know him entirely too well given the short time we've actually been in each others' company —it's probably something wholly inappropriate and sure to piss Adam off. I duck out of the tent's opening, grinning at the thought.

WHEN I RETURN—RELIEVED, clean, and eager—the tent is empty. Something sour burns on my tongue as I register the fact that Adam and Luke are gone . . . along with both of their packs.

Did they leave me here? Alarm rips through me for a moment, until I see one of their datapads laying on the table, next to an assortment of food bars that have been laid out. *Huh, considerate.* I snag one, ripping the packaging open with my teeth as I sit at the table with a groan.

I let a finger fall on the datapad screen only to find my own face looking back at me as the device wakes up. I'm perched in Adam's lap, my expression caught halfway between an eyeroll and a smirk as he presses a kiss to my cheek. Despite the soreness radiating through me, I feel restless as I stare down at our picture, immediately flashing back to the moment in the biodome when Adam snapped it. Was that really only a couple of weeks ago? It feels like a year has passed, so much has happened. My gaze lingers on the way Adam's hand rests on my waist, the amused curve of my mouth, the satisfaction in his eyes. We look so thoroughly . . . normal. The thought makes me audibly snort.

Where did Mr. Normal go, anyway? I toss my gaze back to the tent entrance. Unsure how long it'll be until they return, I decide to review the reports Adam and I unearthed before a building tried to bury us under it. Recalling the way Adam navigated through the Intherian data drive yesterday, I swipe through until some of the icons and file names start to look familiar. I'm about to open Dr. Richardson's ecological recovery report again when my eyes fall over a single word and every cell in my body feels like it stills at once.

Dissidia.

If my body wasn't so stiff, I'd be jumping up in victory. Realizing I'm not crazy after all is a very validating feeling. "I knew it!" I shriek, before mentally cursing myself for being so loud. If Adam's behavior yesterday —and all the time, let's be honest—is any indication, this is not something I am supposed to see. I, of course, could not possibly care less about that. I would, however, prefer to snoop without interruption.

My fingers tremble as I navigate through the folder, skimming through file after digital file at lightning speed. I only slow down after coming to one labeled "Report: Phase I Interstellar Conversion Trial." The screen fills with text and images and I release a shuddering exhale—I hadn't realized I'd been holding my breath.

It's all here. Dissidia, not some city or region on a distant alien planet, but a skycity. Just like Korbyllis, Altara, Lexicon. Just like Intheria. Created, launched, and successfully converted into a self-sustaining spacefaring vessel right here on Earth.

I. Freaking. Knew it.

My face feels like it has gone completely slack—my jaw hangs open and I'm gaping like a cartoon character. The rapidly-changing emotions coursing through me have me feeling like one too.

"They needed to know it was safe. Safe to return," Adam had told me in

those initial moments after I'd regained my memories. *"My people. They're coming back."*

When I'd asked follow up questions, when I'd sought clarification, when I'd asked for any other nuggets of info pertaining to the mind-boggling bomb he dropped, he hadn't answered me. Hadn't *been able* to tell me anything more.

Past conversations and unanswered questions soar into the forefront of my mind—pieces falling into place like snowflakes drifting to the ground. How Adam never once referred to himself or his people as alien. How their technology is somehow lightyears ahead of our own, but their names are old-fashioned. How he speaks in anachronisms. His discomfort at me referring to him as having powers—the way he refers to his FX as an advancement, instead.

The flap of the tent opens and I hear a single set of footsteps pad over to me. "Terra?" The voice that emerges into the silence isn't the one I expected, but I'm so stunned I barely register it.

My shock, consternation, and awe must be written across my face as I rotate to face Luke, the screen of the datapad visible as it dangles from my hands. He drops his pack with a thud, his lips pressed together in a hard line.

"Oh, thank goodness," he says as he runs his palm through his gray-streaked hair. "I was worried you were never going to figure it out."

TWENTY-THREE

"I DON'T KNOW how Adam put up with it all these months," Luke says. "I found this entire charade to be thoroughly exhausting, and it's only been a day. I really do not give him enough credit."

"I don't understand," I say. I still haven't put the datapad down.

"Don't you?" There's a mirthful look on Luke's face, and for some reason, it enrages me.

"What is this, Luke?"

"C'mon now. You know what this is."

I inhale deeply, finally setting the datapad back down on the table. "Dissidia was one of the original skycities."

"Yes."

"It was converted. It's . . . out there, right now. In space."

"Yes."

"And that's where you're from. Which means, in reality, you're all from . . . here."

Luke's eyes brim with something I'm not sure how to define—not quite pity, not quite relief—as he nods.

Something inside me pops. It is also a bit undefinable, what I'm feeling. It isn't rage, nor dejection, but a sort of—

"Why would Adam keep this from me?" I ask. "After everything?"

"It wasn't his fault. It definitely wasn't his choice." Luke's reply comes quickly, like he's been anticipating this question. "Adam couldn't tell you directly because of the commands he's under. That's what being *nixed* means. He received commands that strictly prevent disobedience. Like, physically prohibit it. Another perk of the job," Luke adds, his tone bitter.

My mouth gapes for an entirely different reason now. "Forced compliance? That's horrible," I say. "Nobody should have that kind of power over someone else. Who issues these commands? Why would you all allow this?"

"Again, it's not really a choice. This is how it is up there. Dissidia is a peaceful place, in no small part due to the . . . occasional . . . appropriately allocated . . . *nixing*. Plus, our advancements are kind of a package deal—you don't get gamechangers like telekinesis and enhanced healing without a way to keep them from being misused. As for who issues the commands, only a select few can do so. There are clearances involved, tests, permissions, etcetera. Plus, the devices are DNA-coded so only those with authorization can use them in the first place. No worries about some rando being able to force folks to do something just for the hell of it."

I arch an eyebrow. Luke clears his throat.

"Yes, well. I definitely want to have a chat with Adam's darling brother once I rendezvous with the team. Even for him, seems like this was a bit overboard. Tom didn't only *nix* Adam from being able to relay mission-critical information—he couldn't tell you anything about our history, our technology, ourselves. Himself, really. I don't blame Adam for completely cutting off communication with us."

"He—" A sinking feeling in the bottom of my stomach—surprise and . . . something else. "When did this happen?"

Luke shifts his weight, his gaze falling to his feet. "After we escaped, after we'd had a moment to relish the fact that we weren't *there* anymore, that *she* didn't have us anymore, Adam wanted to go back for you. Understandably, of course. I did too but . . ."

"But it wasn't your call. And that wasn't your mission."

"I am sorry. Adam didn't, uh, he didn't take it all that well. You know Adam—not really one for taking orders lying down in the first place.

Especially Tom's. So, when Tom basically forced him to choose between you and us . . . Well, you already know the choice he made."

Inappropriate as it is, something akin to satisfaction spreads through me. I bite back any foolish notion of sharing this aloud.

"If Tom had been willing to let Adam go after his final 'screw you' to us, that might've been it. But . . . Tom was concerned that Adam's decision to stay behind made him a liability," Luke continues, heavyhearted. "He *nixed* him. And that was the last time we saw or heard from Adam." He swallows. "I've witnessed a *lot* of fights between those two, but . . . To say Adam was pissed would truly be doing a disservice to the word."

I hadn't realized that him not being in contact with his team was a choice he had made. Even with all that time spent solo in the biodome . . . He'd rather have been alone than risk Tom continuing to wield—abuse?— this control over him. The thought has that familiar fire starting to rumble deep inside me again.

"Adam went dark after that. Didn't want to risk receiving any NX updates, I s'pose."

"NX?"

"Neural-Xenoaugmentation. It's what the cybernetic technology behind the mandates is called."

"As opposed to FX," I muse.

"Exactly. That's Fracto-Xenoaugmentation. And then RX is what gives us enhanced healing—"

"Let me guess. Regenerate? Restore? Rejuvenate?"

"Close." Luke smiles. "Reparative Xenoaugmentation."

"That's a mouthful."

He chortles. "Hence, the acronyms. Big fans of acronyms, us Dissidians."

"So, Neural-Xeno-blah-blah-blah becomes NX, which becomes '*nix*,' " I say. *And FX becomes 'fix.' Got it.*

Luke nods. "Adam wasn't even able to *try* to tell you. He told me he's been working on figuring out a loophole, a way around the commands. It causes physical pain to do so, you know. But he did it anyway, over and over, because he hated not being able to give you the whole truth. The truth you've deserved from the beginning."

I think back to every time Adam's face screwed up with what I had thought was focus or concentration. The way he sometimes seemed to take ages to say only a few words, like the mere act of *thinking* was laborious. Regret blankets me when I remember how often my reaction was bratty and unappreciative. Even if I didn't know he was in physical pain, even if I wasn't aware of what was happening at the time, I could have been more patient. More understanding.

"He shouldn't have done that," I say, gritting my teeth.

Luke's expression softens. "From what I can see, I think there's very little he wouldn't do for you."

I push down the warm feeling spreading through my chest and search Luke's face. "And how is it that you're able to tell me these things? You're not acting like this conversation is off-limits."

"Because it's not. Not for me. Not sure if you caught what Adam was alluding to when you first woke up but . . . Tom has a habit of, er, forgetting to *nix* me. I don't think he likes exerting that level of control over me, even when it's strictly mission related. One of several reasons why leadership frowns upon interunit involvement." He shrugs at that last part, as if he couldn't possibly care less what his chain of command thinks about his relationship.

My eyes narrow. "So, Tom will give you a pass because you're sleeping together, but not his own brother?"

He purses his lip, clearly displeased with my characterization, but simply says, "Tom has always been protective of Adam. Is it so hard to understand why he might think of this as the ultimate way to keep his brother safe?"

I rap my fingers on the tabletop, contemplating.

"I'm not saying it's right," Luke adds.

"Well, now that I do know . . . What does that mean for Adam? I don't want to hurt him. Am I going to have to keep pretending like I don't know the truth?" The suggestion alone makes me want to weep.

"That's very considerate," Luke says, his top lip curling in an amused grin, "but, thankfully, wholly unnecessary. While you were snoring your life away"—I scowl at him—"Adam and I spent some time getting to the core of Tom's commands. We figured out that while he's bound against revealing new classified information, and while he's forced to do anything he can to prevent discovery"—I think about the way he had

skated past the Dissidian folder when I first glimpsed it in his presence—
"he is not forbidden from discussion with folks who are already aware.
The trick was just in, well, getting you there."

"I don't—Huh?"

"What, you think that your loverboy just happened to leave his
datapad behind, fully unlocked, with the key to you finally learning the
truth at your fingertips? It can be quite tricky to work around *nixed*
orders, you know. I'd like a little credit where it's due."

"What are you talking about?" The irreverent way Luke speaks is
usually enjoyable, but right now he has me more confused than ever.

"Adam couldn't reveal the truth. He couldn't even orchestrate a way
for you to find out on your own. Hell, he couldn't even bear witness to
someone *else* orchestrating you finding out on your own. Not if he was
actually aware it was happening. And I couldn't just shoo him out to tell
you myself right away, because he's not an idiot. He'd know. And thus,
the NX would know."

"Where is Adam right now?"

"He's retrieving your transport vehicle from the other side of Intheria.
Given his physical reaction earlier, when we were discussing the *possibility* of *talking* about our advancements, I thought it would be best to
keep him as far from this conversation as possible."

"I'm still confused," I admit.

Luke's face falls, just for a second. "Okay, fine, whatever. I guess the
particulars don't really matter. Excuse me for trying to get a little gratitude out of masterminding this shit."

I grin despite myself. "Oh, do forgive me, Most Noble and Charitable
One. Your kindness and benevolence truly know no bounds. You were
most definitely not motivated to help because you were annoyed with the
idea of me continuing to have tons of questions, I'm sure. Better?"

"We'll work on it," Luke smirks.

I bite my lip. "Well, dang it," I say after a moment.

"What now?"

"I lost Adam's bet," I grumble. "I told him there couldn't possibly be
anything left for me to find out that would shock me. He's going to be
absolutely insufferable about it now, isn't he?"

Luke laughs. "Now that's a bet I'd take."

TWENTY-FOUR

WHEELS ROLL over gravel outside and, after a minute, Adam steps through the tent's entrance. He locks eyes with me immediately—I'm still sitting at the table—and the beautiful concern beaming from his cerulean eyes moves something deep within me.

"Right, that's my cue," Luke says. He offers me a mocking salute that has my grin widening, nods at Adam, and steps outside.

The air in the tent feels thick as Adam and I watch each other for a long moment. Several times, he opens his mouth, as if to say something, before closing it again.

"So," I say, putting him out of his misery. " 'Spaceboy' is a bit of a misnomer, as it turns out, eh?"

The relief that breaks out across Adam's face is a wave of cool water cresting over me. "You know."

"I know," I confirm.

He crosses the tent, closing the distance between us, and coming to kneel by my side. "You have to know how much I wanted to tell you absolutely everything. How many times I wish I could've given you a straight answer and—"

"I understand. Luke explained." I cup his cheek. "I get it."

Adam leans into my palm. "I'm sorry," he says.

I shake my head—it only twinges a little bit, like with this final layer of secrets between us finally being peeled away, my body feels lighter. It's a different kind of healing. "There's nothing to apologize for. You didn't have a choice. If anyone should be sorry, it's me. You've saved me so many times and you told me as much as you could, when you could, and I was such a bitch about it and I—"

"Hey now." He turns his head to kiss the inside of my hand, ceasing my babbling. "None of that."

"We can talk about it now?" I ask.

"We can talk about it now," he confirms. "Feel like going for a walk?"

LUKE IS LOITERING around the entrance to the tent when we emerge. "That didn't take long," he says, his brow arched. "I'd been led to believe you have quite the penchant for melodrama, T."

I glance up at Adam, who gives me an innocent look.

"I mean, where's the screaming and the crying and the dramatic makeup s—" Adam punches Luke's shoulder, cutting him off.

I laugh, sticking my tongue out as we walk past. "Don't wait up."

Adam and I walk for a few minutes in silence, our hands linked between us. My body whined a bit in protest when I first started moving, but every step I take has me feeling stronger, looser. The brisk chill in the air is calming, somehow, as well. I inhale deeply. "I know you tried to tell me. The second I . . . When I woke up. When you brought back my memories. You told me, 'They're coming back.' "

Five, maybe ten, seconds of excruciating silence pass before Adam says, "Back *home*."

"Because you're human." It's not an accusation. It's not a condemnation. It just . . . is. And for the first time since we met, I feel like we are finally *us*. It's a good feeling.

"Whenever you're ready, I want to hear it all," I say.

Adam sucks in a long, steadying breath before bringing my hand up to chest-height and flipping it so my palm is facing up. He begins tracing the lines in my skin—slowly, tenderly—as we tread through the open field surrounding us. We carve a parallel path to one of the large impact gorges, where the ground's been cleft open, splintering out from the city.

"This planet has been dying for a long time," Adam says. "Things were dire long before the skycities even took to the skies—resources drying up, ice caps melting, base temperatures across the globe increasing. I know you probably think that a government is good for nothing but corruption and cruelty, and based on everything you've seen, you have good reason to believe so. But it wasn't always like that. At first, people wanted to do the right thing. The world's governments tried to figure out a way to save the planet. It was unifying—every seat of power on Earth working toward a shared goal.

"It led to a golden age of innovation and advancement—technology the likes of which had previously existed only in science fiction. New elements, new materials were crafted—strong enough to withstand acid rain, flexible enough to craft into encapsulation domes that could protect entire towns. Self-sustaining biological environments where plants could flourish, where life could grow. Propulsion systems capable of supporting aircraft as big as a city. Sound familiar?"

It takes a second to realize he's waiting for me to respond, to react. I murmur a noise of encouragement.

Adam continues tracing indolent lines across my palm. "This continued for hundreds of years. Humanity took to the skies. But the damage had already been done. And once they realized there wasn't a way to reverse the wounds that millennia of humanity had inflicted on the planet—or, I suppose, once they thought they'd realized it—that goal shifted. It no longer became about saving the planet, but about preserving the future of its people.

"So, they took the next step toward ensuring humanity's survival. Not just keeping a city afloat in the sky indefinitely, but one that could traverse the next frontier. One that could take us to the stars, put us within reach of resource-rich asteroids. One large enough to house the equipment needed to extract those resources. To give humanity a chance —to turn the page on our next chapter." His finger stills on my palm.

"And that chance was Dissidia," I say.

He hums his confirmation. "Conversion is possible," he says. "You're looking at living proof."

"How is it that nobody knows about this, though? If Dissidia was a city like Intheria or any of the others, I—"

"It's been a long, long, long time, Sunburst. And when Intheria fell and the plague broke out and . . . Well, I think the folks who survived had their hands full for quite a while."

My expression darkens. "It would almost feel like justice that their plans failed so miserably, had it not brought down billions of innocent people when they did."

"That may have had something to do with it too," he says, a pensive expression on his face.

"What do you mean?"

"Dissidia wasn't here when the Skyfall occurred, of course. But we learned about it. And we would've come back, would've been here to help, but . . ." We slow to a stop.

"But what?"

Adam swallows. "Growing up, learning Dissidian history, they'd tell us that we couldn't return because of the plague, because of the concerns of contamination and having to preserve our own tiny subsect of humanity. I don't know," he sighs, "maybe that's true. But . . . seeing Dr. Hawthorne's video reminded me of some other things I heard growing up. Things that they didn't officially tell us."

"Things like . . .?"

"Like how we *must* have known about the Genesis project. About the pathogen. About the plans—ahead of time. And maybe it's because Dissidian leadership was so disgusted with the plan that they decided they wanted no part of it . . . or maybe it's because they wanted to punish the ones who did survive. To leave them to their fate."

"Either way, it's not a great look," I say.

"It's not. Certainly nothing I'm proud of. Especially not after seeing how it is down here, how life has been for you." He drops my hand, like he's too ashamed to keep holding it. For the first time since we began traipsing along out here in the chilly weather, I feel cold.

I pull my jacket around myself more tightly, fisting the material over my clavicle. "Don't cry for me, spaceboy. We can't change what's in the past. And at least now we have hope. Hope that things might change. That it might not always have to be the way it has been."

Adam shrugs, thrusting his hands into his pockets with a sad smile.

We continue walking, the silence growing heavier, the air colder. Eventually, I can't take it any longer. "So, you really aren't going to gloat?" I say, eager to replace the forlorn look in Adam's eyes with something else —anything else.

"Gloat?" he asks.

"I lost the bet," I say, sticking my bottom lip out in an obnoxious-looking pout.

It does the trick. "Is that so?" Adam beams.

"Loathe though I am to admit it, I have, once again, been shocked," I say. "You can consider your promise won."

"That didn't take long," he says with a smirk.

"What are you going to make me promise you, anyway?" I wrinkle my nose. "Nothing sketchy, right?"

"Tsk, tsk. You'll just have to wait to find out."

"*Nothing sketchy, right?*" I repeat forcefully.

Adam laughs. It really is a wonderful sound. "Nothing sketchy, Sunburst."

"Hmph," I say, irritated but satisfied. "I guess I do have one more question," I add after a moment.

Adam's eyes crinkle at the edges. "I would've been disappointed if you didn't."

"Why now? Why would the Dissidians want to return now? If you've been successfully living out there for so many generations? Earth certainly isn't in any better shape now than it was when you—er, your ancestors—left."

He stills, his expression shifting into a mix of worry and something that looks the tiniest bit like fear. "Remember how I told you that it's crowded back home? Well, it's more serious than that. Dissidia is legitimately running out of room. You can only expand the city so much when beyond the encapsulation dome there's just the infinite void of space, you know? Overpopulation has become a huge issue, and despite measures being put into place to help slow things down in that department—"

"What kind of measures?"

"Population control ones, primarily. Rules around having kids. Enforceable ones." His eyes narrow. "Tom and I being natural-born brothers? It's rare. There's a whole laundry-list of criteria that folks have to go through in order to be approved to procreate these days. Admiral Meers and our parents have a long history though, so . . ."

Discomfort writhes inside me. How many more ways can Dissidian leadership control its people? I swallow down the remarks I'd certainly love to say to this Admiral Meers person. "So, your fact-finding mission wasn't just for sentimental reasons. You came back because Dissidia is failing."

Adam nods slowly. "We're in a race against time at this point. We came back to see if Earth was still habitable, what the situation was here, whether there was anything to return to. And now that they know there is . . ."

"They're coming back." I say it with the same inflection he did when he first said those same words to me, months ago.

"I did try telling you before, you know, when you asked about why my people were returning. You were worried they were coming to—how did you put it?"

"I believe 'straight up annihilate us' was how I phrased it."

Adam grins. "That's right. Our—their—goal truly is to reintegrate with Earth. It's supposed to be a homecoming, not an act of war. The last thing the Dissidians would want is to endanger more innocent human lives at this point. But I fear their intentions are only one half of the equation, because—"

"Because the Tribunal is not going to react well to Dissidia's return. Even if they know its origins—which, based on how Prime Whitlock spoke about you all, I don't think is the case—they'll see it as an invading force."

A solemn nod from Adam.

"What we saw in Korbyllis was such a tiny fraction of the forces at the Tribunal's disposal too. Even considering Dissidian advantages . . ." I recall the lines of guardsmen sent to intercept Adam's team when we made our escape from the capital. The way the four of them took down a dozen guards with ease.

"It would still be a bloodbath," Adam agrees. "On both fronts. Which is why we can't let it get that far."

I shake my head—my mind is racing. "And how, exactly, do you propose we accomplish that? What are *we* supposed to do about it? This isn't our job—it's too much, Adam. We're just two people. Three, if you count Mr. Inappropriate back there." I jut my thumb back in the direction of the tent. "Four, if you count Mica and—" I stop short. *Mica.* "How far away was Dissidia when you first came here? How quickly are they able to travel? When will your people get here?" I ask, panic lining each word.

Adam's brows shoot up at my sudden franticness. "I don't know exactly. The fact that Luke and the others were able to turn around and come back to finish out their missions so quickly leads me to believe that they're not too far off."

"So, what are we talking about here? Days, weeks, months? How long do we have to get Mica back before . . ."

Before my little brother gets dragged into someone else's war?

Comprehension dawns on Adam's face. "Luke would know better than me. Let's head back. We can hit the road immediately—we've been waylaid long enough."

I nod in agreement. It's time to bring him home.

TWENTY-FIVE

"REMIND me why I agreed to tag along with you lovebirds?" Luke's voice rings out from the back of the transport. I straighten in my seat, rubbing at my forehead—I'd been leaning against the window, staring out at the surrounding landscape for so long, it had begun to get sore.

It's been strange, doing this trip in reverse. Like seeing the earth decay all over again. Devastating as it had been to witness the state of Intheria, with nature returning, with the land reclaiming itself, there had been something . . . hopeful about it. Inspiring. But as we've driven back toward Sixteen, there have been more signs of life—of people, of civilization—and fewer signs of, well, *life*.

"You tell us," Adam replies, shooting me a grin. "We told you we needed to head back and report what we found to the UO. Terra's brother is—well, it's complicated. But we need to get back. You're the one who got all pouty about it."

"Sorry I wasn't thrilled at the thought of saying goodbye again so soon. There's still a lot for us to catch up on. And whatever happened to gratitude? It's not like I saved your girlfriend's life or anything." Luke crosses his arms petulantly. "I'd have thought you'd be glad of the company."

"Of course I'm grateful for your help. It's just that I was supremely happy with the company I already had," Adam says, glancing at me in a way that has heat rushing to my cheeks. Let's be real, I wouldn't have minded the extra alone time either.

Luke groans, snapping me out of my wandering, increasingly inappropriate thoughts. "I don't know if my blood sugar can handle him like this, T. He never used to be this sappy."

Adam rolls his eyes.

I grin. "Perhaps both of you need to think of this as a chance to make up for lost time. Quality bonding time between old pals, with the bonus of getting to know yours truly without the threat of death and dismemberment hanging over our heads."

Luke snorts. "Because nothing says 'quality bonding' like being crammed into the backseat of a transport vehicle."

"And once again, I'm forced to remind you that you were perfectly free to go your own way," Adam fires back. "Could be heading to the linkup point and meeting back up with the rest of the team as we speak. You'd be moving a hell of a lot faster out there on your zoomer, that's for sure. And it'd be much more peaceful in here," he adds under his breath.

I choke back a laugh, glancing back at the zoomer in question, at the handlebars poking up from the trunk. Luke said it can cover twice as much distance as a traditional vehicle in half the time. Really puts that ancient motorbike of ours to shame.

Luke looses an irritated sigh but that upper lip of his curls into the beginning of a smirk. "Fine, fine. Let's keep moving. The sooner we get there, the better. I just need to update the rendezvous team so they can find a point closer to—where are we headed again?"

"Genesis X-16," I tell him over the trill of his datapad. He's already making the call.

"Are you okay?" I ask Adam, not missing the way he's gone rigid in the driver's seat.

"Fine," he grunts out.

I try not to roll my eyes. "Clearly."

"It's okay, man," Luke says, evidently more tuned into the reason behind Adam's sudden shift in mood than I am. "I'm just going to check in with Charlie."

Now I'm the one to stiffen.

"Luke, where the hell are you?" Charlie's irritated voice fills the vehicle, though it's easy enough to detect the layer of concern underneath. "I thought you were going to beat us here. How far off are you?"

"Hello to you too, love," Luke replies smoothly. "Bit of a change of plans. I picked up some stragglers on the road."

"What are y—" Her voice cuts off as I peek around the headrest—just in time to see Luke swivel the datapad so that I'm face-to-face with a pair of violet eyes narrowed beneath a stern brow.

"Hi," I offer weakly. Charlie's red hair is pulled back in a tight bun on the top of her head, making her expression look even more severe—if such a thing were possible.

Luke continues rotating the datapad, turning it to give Charlie a glimpse of Adam before I'm able to take in her reaction. "These two have managed to stay rather busy since we saw them last," Luke says amiably. "Ran into Adam and Terra on my way back from Intheria, if you can believe it. Saved their lives a little—no biggie. But between that and the fact that we've been incommunicado for months, I decided it was prudent to stick with them for a bit longer."

If Charlie is surprised to see Adam or myself, she doesn't let on. "Of course you did," she scoffs. "So basically, you're ditching your mission to hang with your bestie and his little—"

Luke's gasp cuts her off before she's able to fire whatever shot she had lined up for me. "You wound me, Charlotte," he says with melodramatic flair. If diffusing tension was a competitive sport, I have no doubt Luke would be a gold medalist.

Charlie huffs in response. I may have only spent about half an hour in total with the woman, but I still remember the visceral way she'd reacted to Adam calling her by her full name.

"First of all, I would never abandon my mission." Luke darts a guilty glance toward the front of the car, his eyes lingering on Adam for a moment before his typical blitheness takes back over. "I've already forwarded all of my observational data. And given the predilection these two appear to have for life-threatening danger, they are clearly in need of an escort. I'm just doing my civic duty here."

"I'm sure," she says drily. "What do you think Tom's going to have to say about that? Hell, what do you think the Admiral's going to do when she finds out?" Adam's grip tightens on the steering wheel.

"A bridge to cross when we come to it. It'll be fine. I'm not being completely self-serving, I swear. Adam has made important connections with a movement here on the ground that could be advantageous for us as well. A resistance movement against the Tribunal. Well established. Deeply entrenched. Even the Admiral, surely, can see the benefit in that."

My ears perk up at that, but I don't interrupt them.

"Fine, whatever. Far be it from me to give you orders. I'm not *her*. Just make sure you don't get yourself killed okay? I'd hate to have to be the one to deliver *that* message to Tom. He's been anxious enough waiting for your arrival."

This time, I anticipate Adam's reaction to hearing Tom's name and place my hand on his knee, stroking it soothingly.

"Right. About that . . ." Luke says. "How do you feel about being the bearer of a request instead? I need to move the rendezvous point."

She takes a long moment before replying. "Move the rendezvous point. Where we already are. Where we've been waiting for you."

Luke flashes a wide grin.

Charlie sighs. "Fine. Send me the coordinates of where you're headed. I'll map out a point to meet up and send you confirmation once I talk with Tom." There are some tapping and rustling noises, and when she speaks again, her tone is softer. "Please be careful. If you're heading back to . . ." She clears her throat. I imagine she's thinking about the last time their team was in the vicinity of Genesis X-16. When they were captured by the Tribunal.

"Always am," Luke replies. "Thanks, Chuck."

"Stay safe." She pauses. "You too, Adam."

"THIS SILENCE IS DEAFENING," Luke complains.

I can't say I disagree. Adam has been quiet since Luke and Charlie's conversation ended, and despite my gentle inquiries and all of Luke's callous prodding, he hasn't seemed inclined to explain why. "Surely you can't be this pissed about me contacting Charlie. They needed to know why I wasn't coming to link up with them."

"It's fine," Adam grunts.

"You don't seem fine," I say. "What happened between you and your brother? Luke mentioned—"

"Don't drag me into this," Luke mumbles.

"Please. You dragged yourself into this," I remind him with a roll of my eyes. I reach for Adam's hand, pulling it into my lap as he adjusts his grip on the steering wheel. "Tell me what's wrong."

The silence stretches on long enough that I really believe we won't be getting any answers out of him. Finally, his hand tightens on my own. "The last time I spoke to Tom, it was . . . He *nixed* me, yes. He locked me down, forced me to keep things from you. And we both . . . Things were said." He glances at the rearview mirror, his eyes searing into Luke for a split-second. "Things were . . . more than said. I worry about what will happen when I see him again. About it happening again."

"Hey man, I—" Luke starts. I cut him off with a sharp look.

"I don't want it to happen again," Adam continues, resolve blazing in his eyes even as he returns his gaze to the road ahead. "I didn't really care before, you know? Nixed orders were a part of life. I never felt like they were used for anything but what was necessary. Kept us on mission. Kept things under control, but not in a bad way. Kept life going. But now . . ." He threads his fingers through mine. "I don't want anyone else deciding what I can do, what I can say, who I can say it to. I don't want there to be secrets between us again, Terra—not ever. I never want to feel that kind of . . ." He shudders. It sends a splinter straight through my heart.

"Then you won't. We'll figure something out. You don't have to talk to him again, even with . . ." I trail off, the understanding sinking in that even were that possible, Tom is Adam's brother. Despite what may have happened, it's hard to imagine a scenario where Adam would truly be happy having cut him out of his life forever. And even if he could, Tom is not the only one in the universe capable of *nixing* Adam. What happens when the Dissidians arrive? When this mysterious Admiral comes back into the picture?

I take a shaky breath. "Okay, the truth is that I actually don't know what we can do about it. I'm admittedly in a little over my head here. But together, there has—"

"There might be a way," Luke interjects. Adam goes quiet again.

I twist in my seat. "What do you mean?"

"There might be a way to prevent Adam from being *nixed* again. Ever. But it's not without . . . consequences."

I wait for him to continue. Impatiently. "Well?"

Luke sighs. "There's a way to bypass our cybernetic enhancements. It would remove the NX but—"

"—it will also nullify the rest of my advancements," Adam finishes for him. "No more NX, but no more FX or RX either."

Surprise rocks through me. "No more telekinesis, no more healing?"

"Yes." Luke's voice is tight. "It's kind of like short-circuiting his brain. Just for a second. To neutralize the nanotech buzzing around in there."

I frown. "That sounds dangerous."

"It's not . . . *not* dangerous," Luke says.

Adam's jaw tightens. "It would be worth it. I'd rather lose my abilities than be controlled like that again."

"Adam, no," I protest. "There has to be another way."

He shakes his head. "I would be lying if I said I hadn't already thought about it," he says. "Many times over the past few months, if I'm being absolutely honest. Especially once I got you back." He looks at me meaningfully. "But I couldn't do anything about it on my own. For what I suppose are obvious reasons, it requires another Dissidian of a certain rank and advancement level and—"

"—and lucky for you, you happen to have one at your disposal," Luke finishes for him. "If you're serious about this, though, Adam, we should consider getting it over with sooner rather than later. The procedure will take a toll on you, and you'll need time to rest and recover. Especially considering—"

"—that I won't have RX helping me on the other side. Got it."

"Are you sure about this, Adam? Like really, truly, one hundred percent sure?" I clutch his hand like it's the only thing keeping me tethered to this vehicle, this world. He is already slowing down, pulling off the road.

He puts the vehicle in park and turns to face me. "Never been surer, Sunburst."

TWENTY-SIX

"HERE." With a thud, Emery drops a black duffel bag at my feet. No, not *at* my feet—*on* my feet. It's heavier than it looks, and I scowl at him as I extricate my boot from underneath. I'd thought that upon returning from our relatively successful mission in Intheria, he'd been slightly less rude to me. Less *outwardly* rude, at least. But perhaps that's because the top position on Emery Garren's list of Most Annoying People on Planet Earth has been usurped by the newest member of our merry gang.

"Watch it," Luke says warningly from behind me. "You nearly took her foot off."

"Or what?" Emery hisses. He was not particularly pleased to find we returned from our mission with more than data in tow.

"You sure you want to find out?" Luke smirks. They've been at each other's throats since the instant we returned to the Underground's base. If I didn't already know about Luke and Tom, I might wonder if there's something else going on here. Then again, maybe that's just Luke. There's no denying the man's got chemistry—the explosive kind, for better or worse—with everyone he meets.

I cast a sidelong glance at Adam, as if to say, *Not this again.* He responds with a half-hearted grin that doesn't reach his eyes, and I frown. Watching Luke conduct the advancement bypass on Adam had been difficult, but it's been even more challenging witnessing the significant after-effects.

Unlike me, after nearly falling to my demise, Adam doesn't appear to be physically hurt. Rather, for the majority of the three days since we returned, it's like he's been operating under some sort of fog. He tries his best to hide it, but I see the way his face screws up every so often, the way he pinches the bridge of his nose or rubs his fingers over his temples when he thinks I'm not looking. I see the far-off look in his eyes, like he's searching for something. Like he's trying to remember something he thinks he might have forgotten.

Unfortunately, that's a feeling with which I am entirely too well acquainted.

Luke's been assuring me that it's normal, but he also admitted that this isn't something he has a ton of experience with. It's not like good soldiers go about short-circuiting their teammates' brains on a regular basis, after all.

Brant walks in, interrupting Luke halfway through spitting a particularly sharp insult at Emery, and hands me a thin gray folio. "This has all the paperwork you'll need for when you get up top—you'll need to be extra careful when sneaking out of the cargo area."

"You get caught, you're on your own," Emery chimes in, so dismissively that it's all I can do not to join Luke in staring daggers back at him. I manage to bite out a sound of acknowledgement instead.

Brant turns to Adam. "The duffel bag contains the rest of what you need—clothing, food—as well as the items you requested."

Adam nods mutely.

"What items?" I ask.

"You'll see." Adam picks up the duffel and hoists it over his shoulder before extending his hand. "Thanks Brant."

Brant takes Adam's hand, but shakes his head. "We should be the ones thanking you. The schematics and additional information you recovered are going to make all the difference here."

A scoff slips from my lips and Emery's gaze narrows on me. *Whoops.*

"What?" he says.

"Nothing," I say, trying to wipe the skeptical look from my face. He is clearly unconvinced. I sigh. "It's just that if you needed the two of us in order to turn the tides of whatever it is you all are planning here, I'm not sure how much of a fighting chance you ever really had."

Emery opens his mouth, ready to shoot back something nasty, but Brant speaks first. "You might be right. But we certainly have one now. And we'll have even more of one, shortly. Something else we owe you two gratitude for." His earnestness twists something in my gut, and my face flares with embarrassment for being so disparaging. Maybe putting some distance between the constant squabbling between Emery and Luke will be good for me. Not sure I like the energy I've been picking up from them. Though to be honest, I'm also not sure what state this place is going to be in when we return since Luke is staying behind.

The information we'd brought back from Intheria turned out to be useful beyond what the Underground had even hoped. We got them the schematics they asked for, yes, but with additional proof that the skycities were directly responsible for keeping the planet in its rotting condition, the next course of action became clear.

The skycities need to come down—literally.

With assistance from Adam and Luke, the Underground has already managed to reverse-engineer a way to take over the skycities' suspension controls. With each skycity's controls locked on separate circuits—an understandable security measure—they need a backdoor in. With access, however, they'll be able to wrest control of the city's systems, and initiate a safe, gradual descent back to the ground.

It's why they asked us to give them a few extra days before we could finally go up to Altara—they wanted our help again. And with what I had just found out, I was more than willing to give it to them again.

Luke trails behind us as Brant walks Adam and me out to the loading dock, where we'll board the transport trailer that will smuggle us up to Altara.

"Director Coal wanted to see you off, but she's been called away," Brant says when we arrive at the trailer, Adam having fallen back to speak with Luke. "She asked me to convey her gratitude for your assistance, and to wish you the best of luck in retrieving your brother. We all do." He extends his hand and when I go to shake it, he pulls me into a brief—and surprising—hug. "I know it threw you last time, but I have to tell you," he says as he steps back, "your dad would be proud of you, Terra. So proud."

I force myself to swallow the lump forming in the back of my throat. "Do you . . . do you know where he is?" I say, cursing inwardly as soon as the words leave my lips. Why do I want to know? Why should I care? He's been out of our lives since I was twelve years old, for goodness' sake. So, why does it bother me so much that Brant seems to have known him better than I ever did?

Brant's expression turns sad. "I'm not sure it's my place to say."

"Right. I don't—Forget I said anything." I turn to wave at Luke. "See you on the other side. Thanks again for, you know, saving my life and all."

Luke flashes a wide grin at me and nods at Adam before I climb into the trailer. Crawling over storage crates, I locate a clear section of floor and settle in against the wall. Adam pops back into view a few moments later, dropping the duffel at my side and sliding down to me.

"Here we go," he says.

I shift uncomfortably as the transport roars to life. The trailer vibrates as we move, and I can feel every bump and divot in the metal flooring through the lining of my pants. It echoes through my still-sore body, setting my teeth on edge. I only last a few minutes before I have to stand.

"This is going to be a long trip," I mutter, rubbing at a particularly sore spot over my tailbone.

Adam chuckles as he rips open the duffel bag's zipper. "Here, this might make things a little more bearable for the next couple of hours," he says. He rifles around in the duffel before handing me a rolled up blanket. I unravel it, then fold it into a neat square, laying it on the ground like a cushion; it dulls the vibrations.

"Thank you," I say. "So, what else are you packing in there?"

"We don't need to mess with it all now," he says. "There's plenty of time."

My curiosity piques. "Mess with what?"

"I asked Brant and Emery if they could help procure a few things that would help us—well, help you—fit in a little better once we're up there." He sounds almost guilty about it.

Of course. A tall storage crate rests across the trailer opposite us, and my blurred reflection peers back at me from the metal casing. The details are fuzzy in the makeshift mirror, but there I am: brown hair, brown eyes, tan skin. And clothed in plain garb that hardly resembles the elegant skydweller fashions I remember from my quick tour of Korbyllis.

In my desperation to heal up and get on our way up to Altara, I hadn't really considered how much I'll stick out once we're up there. I think about the way folks' stares linger whenever a skydweller is spotted out and about in Sixteen—the way their upper-worldly beauty pulls focus. Something tells me that once I'm up top, people won't be staring at me with wonder and awe.

I bite my cheek as I turn my gaze enviously back to my blond haired, blued eyed companion. "I didn't really think this through," I admit. "Even with the right clothing, I doubt I'll make it fifty yards before drawing someone's eye. It's not like Altara is some big tourist destination. Someone's going to notice a terrestrial wandering around up there—and the last thing we need is anyone asking questions."

"Oh, ye of little faith," Adam says, patting my knee. "As if I don't have a plan."

"Care to elaborate? What kind of plan are we talking about here?

"The kind that's comprised of a multitude of things you're probably not going to be very happy about," he says, entirely too happily himself.

***

"IS IT READY YET?"

Adam shakes his head for the fifth time in the past twenty minutes, much to my chagrin. My head is starting to burn from the dye I've pasted onto my hair. "It's been over an hour," I whine. I prod at my tresses, piled messily on top of my head. I'm desperate to brush out the dye, to see it flake off and reveal the new color beneath—as Adam has already done. The smell is starting to get to me too—a pungent, sickly-sweet odor that feels like it might never fully go away.

I stagger a little on my feet as the trailer is transferred onto the transport shuttle that'll take us to Altara. We're officially skyward-bound.

"Five more minutes," Adam says. "You've got a lot more hair than me." He runs his hand back through his own freshly darkened locks. I marvel at how I'm already starting to get used to his new look. It was admittedly jarring at first, but now that the initial shock has settled, I can appreciate how the chocolatey strands frame his face, how they make the blue of his eyes seem even more vivid—something I didn't think possible.

"It suits you," I say, giggling as he tries to check himself out in the makeshift storage crate mirror. "You really embody that whole 'tall, dark, and handsome' thing now."

"Well, sure, 'tall' was a given," he says, that lopsided grin of his sneaking onto his face. "But handsome? I don't know about that."

I smack him playfully on the shoulder. "Oh, please, you can throw that fake-humility schtick right out of here. You know full well what you look like."

He scoots closer to me and leans in, careful not to touch my hair. "But what I think hardly matters. The whole point is whether *you* think I am. Handsome, I mean."

"I think"—I tip my face forward, close enough to kiss him, and lower my voice to a whisper—"that you are full of crap."

With a laugh, Adam sits up and plants a kiss on my forehead. "Go ahead and brush out the dye. It's probably been long enough." He glances down to the wide-toothed metal brush he had used on himself, resting on a nearby crate, and flicks his wrist as if to *fix* the brush over to me. The humor that previously lined his brow is gone in an instant, replaced by confusion, embarrassment, and anger at his momentary lapse. The emotions flit across his face so rapidly, they are nearly imperceptible. Probably would've been to anyone else—anyone who spent less time studying his features, who didn't know the typical set of his strong brow, his full lips, his sharp jaw.

I quash the desire to immediately comfort him, though whether it's because I don't want to embarrass him further, or because of the guilt I feel over him giving his FX up in the first place, I couldn't say.

Another moment passes, however, and he's schooled his expression into one of pleasant indifference as he hands me the brush. I smile in thanks and crawl over to the far end of the trailer. Bending at the waist, I tip upside down and start brushing through the monstrosity on top of my head. The dye, which was a dark, purplish color when I first applied it, has changed as it's dried, coating my hair a dull gray.

"This must be an attractive look for me," I gripe.

"Believe me, it is," Adam says. I look at him from between my legs to find him smirking at my doubled-over form.

"And here I was, thinking you were a gentleman."

"Just trying to make up for the utter lack of Luke-ishness on this part of our adventure. You know he'd never let this situation pass without comment. Besides, it's not really my fault. You're putting it out there—of course, I'm going to look. I'm only—"

"—human," I finish for him, a grin on my face as I resume picking at my hair. Slowly, the knots come undone and I'm able to brush through it —once, twice. Each time I rake the brush through my hair, tiny gray flakes fall toward the ground. They disintegrate into powder when they hit the floor—so fine I can barely see it by the time I stand back up.

"What do you think?" I ask, turning back around to face Adam.

I preen at the way his mouth pops open. "Whoa."

"Is that a good 'whoa' or . . ." I say, sauntering over to see the results for myself in the storage crate mirror. "Huh." My hair falls around my shoulders in loose, face-framing curls. The new color—a deep, luscious red—stands out against my white tank top like the last few blazing moments of sunset in a cloudy sky. "I thought the point is to be inconspicuous," I say with a frown.

"The point is to fit in," Adam replies.

I run my hands through my hair, not sure what I'm more astounded by—my appearance or the hair dye itself. The UO must have procured this product straight from one of the skycities, given the way it has somehow left my hair both silky soft and perfectly styled all at once. The stifling scent of the dye has dissipated as well, leaving nothing but a faint trace of something sweet and flowery lingering on my strands.

"Can't say I like the eyes much," Adam says as he surveys me, his eyes narrowing on the colored contact lenses that have hidden my gold-sparked brown irises under dark blue ones, "but the hair really is something." He lets out an appreciative whistle.

"Have a thing for redheads, do you?" I tease, then immediately wish I hadn't. Adam's laugh takes a little too long and is a little too awkward. All of the sudden, I'm thinking way too much about why my hair had to be *this* color.

"Not, ah, not anymore," he admits, rubbing the back of his neck. Discomfort ripples across my skin. I'd suspected there might've been *something* between Charlie and him in the past, but having it confirmed stings more than I expected. Although, I suppose, it does help make sense of how she's acted toward me since those first moments on Korbyllis.

"I was just teasing," I say, trying to mask the well of emotions churning in me with a casual shrug.

Unsurprisingly, Adam sees right through it. "It was a long time ago, Sunburst. Believe me, it was over long before our mission to come here."

"Right," I say, forcing a smile. "A long time ago." The words taste bitter in my mouth. I know it shouldn't matter—it doesn't matter, really. Everyone's entitled to a history. Lord knows Lee and I weren't exactly platonic. It's just such a stark reminder of all the things Adam and I still haven't talked about—all the things we haven't been able to talk about, before now.

"You're not . . . mad, are you?" Adam eyes me apprehensively.

"Of course not. There's nothing to be mad about. I'm just being . . . I don't know. I'm getting hung up on how I can lo—" I choke the word back down. Before, when I'd almost said it, I thought I was about to die. On the heels of complaining about his gorgeous ex is absolutely not the right time to pull that word out. "On how I can feel so close to you," I substitute lamely, "yet simultaneously still know so little about your past."

Adam's eyes widened a fraction at my almost-confession, the word I left unspoken, but all he says is, "No time like the present."

"Because every good 'getting to know you' conversation happens *after* you've both been on the brink of death a handful of times, right?"

"Kinda fits though, don't you think? New hair, new clothes . . ."

"New start?" I say coyly.

He wraps his arms around my waist, burying his face in my auburn hair. "Maybe I don't want an *entirely* new start."

I appraise the two of us in the makeshift mirror, our skydwelling doppelgangers staring back at us. "Me either, spaceboy," I sigh. "Me either."

TWENTY-SEVEN

"ASK ME AGAIN, Sunburst, and you'll be hammering the final nail into the coffin of my sanity. Yes, this is where Mica told us he would be. No, I'm not positive when he will be coming. He said that this plaza is on his unit's security route. Now, we wait."

I close my mouth, which had been open and poised with another question about just how sure Adam was that this was the place Mica had communicated with us. We hadn't been able to open a live communication channel while stuck in the transport trailer, but the information pieced together from Mica's back-and-forth messages gave us a loose plan for where to find him.

We're standing at the edge of the grand plaza at the Altaraan Academy of Military Refinement and Education, located smack-dab in the middle of the bustling skycity. The air is clean up here, the faint scent of ozone mixed with something floral wafting under my nose. I think wistfully of the crisp, wintry air near the Intherian crash site, and an ember of fury crackles in my veins at the knowledge that this city—and the rest like it—is what's preventing the rest of the groundworld from experiencing the same.

My eyes scan the plaza, looking for a familiar sweep of sandy brown hair amidst the sea of navy cadet uniforms. I wring my hands, sweeping my thumb over my palm and shuddering as it runs over my freshly scarred skin. In the trailer, Adam had been horrified at the sight of the incendiary device I pulled from my pocket, aghast at my intent to burn the skin—and thus, any identifying characteristics—from my hands. He didn't understand how easily a stray palm scanner could ruin our plans, how all the guardsmen carry them. Even disguised, we couldn't take any chances.

When we were stopped by guardsmen within minutes of us sneaking out of the shuttle bay's cargo area, just as Brant had warned, I felt vindicated in my decision. Thankfully, the paperwork the UO provided did its job. The guardsmen on duty didn't attempt to scan either of us—a fact that Adam was quick to point out afterward. But it would have been so easy for them to. And that's all it would have taken for this whole thing to fall apart before it had even begun.

I know he was simply concerned I'd done it for nothing. Just like watching Luke short-circuit Adam's NX had been hard for me, seeing me willingly hurt myself can't have been easy for Adam. But anything that had even the *possibility* of preventing us from being recaptured was worth it.

I was glad Adam had managed to keep his concern at bay long enough to assist me, at any rate. He might not have his advancements anymore, but at least that nifty little pot of Dissidian healing balm was still part of his arsenal. By the time the shuttle docked in Altara, my palms were whole and healed, and any formerly identifiable prints or creases are now obscured beneath a layer of fine scars stretching from the top of my wrist to the tips of my fingers.

Between my newly anonymous palms and our disguises, I feel an uncharacteristic glimmer of confidence in our plan. Beyond our hair and my new eyes, the UO had also set us up with appropriate clothing. We now perfectly encompass a couple of skydwelling civilians who might work on the AAMRE campus or live nearby. I glance at Adam, casually gliding my gaze over his fitted, dark blue suit with subtle silver embroidery. There's no denying it—the man looks *good*. I fist the skirt of my sundress—a flowing, emerald green that offers a striking contrast to my new hair color. For whatever reason, the combination works. Folks milling about the plaza glance appreciatively in our direction every now and again, no hint of suspicion or skepticism in their eyes.

That spark of hope flares brighter. We will make it to Mica. We will find a networked computer to get the UO a backdoor into the Altaraan servers. All three of us will get back to the shuttle bay and onto the ship that the UO has earmarked for our return trip.

We can do this. We will do this. We're almost there. I repeat the words in my head like a prayer until Adam's voice cuts through my thoughts. "There," he says, pointing to a small group of people entering the far end of the plaza.

I turn so I can get a better look, and Adam shifts with me, continuing to face me so as to keep up appearances. We're just two people, on a break, engaged in conversation. No secret Dissidian spies or terrestrial imposters here. Nope.

I try to keep my mannerisms as natural as possible, observing the group nonchalantly as they continue up the plaza's center walkway. There's about a dozen of them, a collection of AAMRE cadets, guardsmen, and a couple of folks in civilian clothing. They're heading toward the opulent structure perched at the north end of the plaza that I'd assumed was an administrative building of some kind. They draw closer and my stare becomes decidedly *chalant* as I rake my eyes over the approaching group to see if this could be the security unit Mica mentioned and—

Everything stops.

My breath, my heartbeat. Because there, marching forward, side by side with half a dozen other navy uniforms, is Mica.

Except, I almost don't recognize him. His floppy, sandy hair has been shorn into a short crop. His brown eyes are narrowed in a steely, assessing glare. And his physique . . . If I were a stranger seeing him for the first time, there's no way I would believe he's fourteen. No, he left fourteen in the dust four inches and twenty pounds ago. New muscles flex threateningly under the navy sleeves of his uniform and I find myself at a complete loss for words.

"Not . . . possible . . ." My voice is strangled in my throat, barely a whisper. What have they done to him?

"Stay calm," Adam mutters under his breath.

As if my feet are possessed, I move to close the distance between my brother and me. I've only taken a few steps toward the group when a firm hand clasps around my wrist.

"What are you doing?" Adam hisses, yanking me back. I whirl to face him, to shove him off me, to unleash the blaze that's been kindling in my chest—that's my *baby brother*, how *dare* he?—but the look on his face makes me pause.

It's a look of pure alarm.

Of fear.

For a moment, I don't understand why. Until I let my gaze fall back to Mica's unit, past the other cadets and the cadre of guardsmen, to the duo in civilian clothing I hadn't been able to make out before.

One is a young woman, her hair pulled back in a ponytail, tapping furiously on a tablet as the older woman next to her dictates. A woman with a sheet of chin-length auburn hair. Ice-blue eyes and rimless glasses. High heels that, now that I'm focusing on the sound, clack distinctively on the plaza pathway.

I watch in horror as my brother escorts Prime Morrigan Whitlock through the doors of the administrative building and out of sight.

"WHAT THE HELL is she doing here?" My thoughts are a frantic, tangled mess. Memories—real ones, I'm pretty sure—claw their way to the surface of my mind. Her icy stare. Her taunting laugh. The clacking of those godforsaken high heels.

For a minute, neither of us says anything. Adam stares at the doors that Whitlock walked through, his expression unreadable. "We have to follow them," he says, resolve threaded through his words. "We'll stay back, try not to draw attention. If she doesn't notice us, she won't recognize us."

I nod, swallowing the emotions bubbling up in me, and we slip inside the building. An extravagant lobby unfolds before us. Tall, marbled walls stretch up toward a high ceiling with a round reception desk in the center. I throw a quick prayer of thanks up when I notice Whitlock is nowhere to be seen, though as I peer past the reception desk,

I catch sight of a group of navy uniforms gathered at the end of a long, wide hallway.

Adam saunters up to the desk, the vigilance in his demeanor shifting into something more casual. "Excuse me," he says, confidence oozing from him as he casts a charming grin at her.

The receptionist, a perky young woman with straight blond hair and aqua eyes, glances up from her computer, doing a double-take as her gaze falls on Adam. "Can I help you?" I have to smother a snort at the eagerness radiating from her.

"I most certainly hope you can," Adam says, his voice lilting in a way that makes me want to smack the smarmy smile right off his face. "My, uh, colleague and I need to catch up with the rest of our party. They should have just arrived."

"Oh, the Tribunal delegation? They did, but I'm afraid they've already closed the conference room doors—the meeting has begun." She gestures down the hall, where Mica's unit and the guardsmen are lined up outside a pair of double doors. "You're welcome to wait here until they're finished, though," she says with a coy smile.

"Can't think of a more pleasant way to pass the time," Adam says with a wink, and I struggle not to roll my eyes. "But I think we should wait with the group. I'll see you on my way back out though." Her smile widens, and ridiculous as it may be, I have to appreciate Adam's suave maneuvering. She's letting us pass without a request for ID or asking us to sign in.

Adam and I fall in line a few paces behind some employees headed in the direction of the conference room. Heavy doors dot the hallway, bearing the nameplates of various academy employees, and in some cases, insignias indicating higher ranking administrative officers.

My eyes lock onto Mica as we approach, my heart leaping as recognition flares in his eyes. Recognition and . . . warning? He makes an obvious shift to look at the guardsmen lining the opposite wall from where he's standing, and I follow his gaze only for my blood to freeze in my veins.

"What the hell is *he* doing here?" Adam hisses into my ear as panic razes through me. Panic and something very much like terror as I find myself nearing the man directly responsible for the worst of my nightmares.

Inquisitor Wolfe.

TWENTY-EIGHT

I STOP IN MY TRACKS, my body paralyzed. I'm overcome with flashes of the time I spent under Wolfe's interrogation. Tiny orange pills being forced past my lips. A burst of bright, searing pain along my cheekbone. Glimpses of the most horrific images—real and imagined—rush through my mind. My mother's limp, lifeless hand. Mica and me, watching our home burn to the ground. Gran's funeral. Seeing Adam bleed out in front of me.

Little bird, Wolfe called me.

Bile rises in my throat as I realize Adam has been speaking to me, pulling at my wrist, urging me to move forward. I've stopped in the dead center of the hallway and my strange behavior is drawing curious looks and tittering whispers from the people around us.

I glance back at Mica, who is still staring at me in alarm. With the slightest movement, he jerks his chin to one side. His message is clear enough. *Get out of here.*

Wolfe stiffens, seemingly noticing Mica's expression and the fact he's looking at something. Mica averts his gaze, but the damage appears to be done as I see the side of Wolfe's head start to turn in our direction. Quick as lightning, I snag Adam by the wrist and pull him into the closest office, quietly shutting the door behind us.

"Do you think he saw us?" I gasp, my heart thundering in my chest.

"I don't know. I don't think so. But even if he did, without a good look at our faces, I don't think he'd have any reason to suspect anything. We're disguised." Adam says it as if to remind me and to reassure himself, but my heart plummets anyway. He knows as well as I do that the best disguises in the world aren't worth shit with Wolfe here. I spent three months being "outprocessed" in his interrogation lab—there's zero chance Wolfe wouldn't recognize me if he saw me.

I suck in deep, slow breaths as I press my ear to the door and listen for any commotion that might be happening back in the hall. When I fail to hear the thud of approaching guardsmen boots, my pulse starts to return to its normal pace. I pull back from the door and look around the office— the *empty* office—we've ducked into. The room is dimly lit, but warmly decorated. A plush, ornate rug sits under an imposing desk. Several filing cabinets lining the wall on either side of a small door. A closet or bathroom, maybe.

"How long until you think it'll be safe to get back out there?" I ask Adam.

"Not until whatever meeting Whitlock's in is over and they've left. I'm sorry." He stares at the floor, emotion etched into every furrowed line of his brow, and I am somewhat soothed by the fact that he seems equally frustrated with how close, yet still so far, we are from securing Mica.

"At least I got to see him in the flesh," I say, my throat thick. Adam pulls me into an embrace, resting my head against his chest. The steady beat of his heart calms me. "Got to see he really does seem okay."

"Better than okay, I'd say," Adam responds into my hair. "Whatever they put in their water up here clearly agrees with him—he's turned into a total tank overnight. The kid looks like a natural-born warrior now."

I peer up at Adam, frowning. "I think we both know there's nothing natural about his transformation," I say, though I'd be lying if I said I couldn't see the upside. He was already progressing in his self-defense skills at quite a clip, thanks to Adam's tutelage and our training. Now that he's got a physical leg-up, I feel much better about my brother being able to take care of himself. "Guess there's absolutely no way I'm winning in a sparring session against him now."

Adam's chest heaves with a silent laugh under my cheek. "We'll have another chance to get to him," he promises. "One with approximately one hundred percent fewer Tribunal Primes and psychotic Inquisitors involved. We just need to wait until we can contact him again."

Anxiety prickles in my gut and I pull back from Adam's arms. "We'll miss the Underground's pickup window if we wait too long, though. And that's assuming we can even get back in touch with him. If he can find some other window to slip away. Who knows how long—"

"There's still time," he says, cutting me off before I can spiral further. "Don't forget, there's one other thing we were supposed to do while we're up here. Maybe we're just checking off the list a bit out of order." He points at something behind me.

My brow furrows in confusion until my gaze follows his finger to where it's pointing—at the computer sitting atop the desk. Adam pulls a tiny external drive, no bigger than the top knuckle of my pinky finger, from the inside pocket of his suit jacket.

"The program Luke and I developed for the UO should only need a few minutes to download onto the server," he tells me as he plugs the drive into the side of the computer.

I walk around the desk to join him, frowning as I look at a black monitor screen. "Nothing's happening," I say.

"Appearances deceive, Sunburst," Adam says. "It's already running in the background. Luke will be notified once the download is complete, and then they'll be able to access the city's infrastructure control network. Easy, peasy."

"Don't jinx it," I hiss. "Nothing ever seems to be easy with us and you never know what—" A sound from outside the door has the rest of my words freezing on my tongue.

Clack. Clack. Clack.

"Shit!" I exclaim, looking frantically around the room as the unmistakable sound of Prime Whitlock's high heels intensifies. I run over and wrench open the door wedged between two rows of filing cabinets. A closet. Good. My heart pounds as I yank Adam inside and close us in just as the main office door handle starts to turn.

Adam and I hold our breath as the door opens. Through the thinnest crack where the door meets its frame, I watch Prime Whitlock strut into the office, someone I can't see trailing in behind her. My desire to snort in disbelief wars with my desperate need to remain quiet, because *of course*.

Of course, the one day we come to Altara is the day that Prime Whitlock and her posse are here.

Of course, the one person who's most likely to be able to identify me is part of her personal entourage.

Of course, the office we blindly picked to hide in is the same one she is walking into right now.

Of course.

"What's this about, Morrigan?" The stranger's voice is deep and carries a note of irritation—and something else that sounds hauntingly familiar. He crosses behind Prime Whitlock and takes a seat at the desk, too quick for me to glimpse anything other than the flash of a crisp navy military uniform. This is *his* office. "I thought you covered everything in the meeting just now."

"There are certain matters I prefer discussing in private," Whitlock says coolly as she follows him, and I almost groan in relief when the clack of her high heels is muffled by the carpet. I can only make out a fraction of the scene as they sit across from one another—the stranger's profile is nothing more than a shadowed silhouette.

I look at Adam in alarm, thinking about the tiny drive still stuck in the side of the computer. Of *his* computer. But I can't tell if the stranger knows anything is amiss as he sits at the desk in front of the very machine that's currently being hacked.

"What else is there? You've briefed the rest of the council about the Dissidians, you've issued your orders. Preparations are underway to mobilize all non-student military units."

My breath hitches and I shoot Adam a worried look. I guess the word's out on his people.

"I believe my orders were to mobilize *all* units," Whitlock corrects. "All means all, and includes the most recent cadet class."

"They're just students, Morrigan." The man's tone sharpens. "They're not ready. This is not their war."

"It's everyone's war, Commander," Whitlock replies coldly. "Were you not *just* in the same meeting I was? Did you not hear about the way our talks with the Dissidians fell apart? They're not backing down—they've refused all our demands and are coming anyway."

I swallow my surprise. The Tribunal and the Dissidians have already engaged in some kind of peace talks? Or, maybe 'war talks' is more appropriate, given what we're hearing. Does Whitlock know about their origins, their reasons for returning? Or is it as we feared and she assumes they're coming to invade?

Whitlock continues ranting. "I told their miserable leadership that they were welcome to return to this dusty planet if they just forked over what we were asking, but they remain less than inclined to share with us. They won't offer up a lick of tech, won't even provide their old conversion records. All we're asking is for them to pass on the same opportunities they were themselves given so long ago, but *no.* They're giving us no choice but to take it by force."

Guess that answers that.

Whitlock inhales sharply. "But you already know all this. And that is not what I wanted to discuss."

"Go on, then." Impatience oozes from the stranger—the Commander. His attitude is interesting, given Prime Whitlock's rank and clear seniority.

"I want to discuss the girl."

The anxious prickle in my gut explodes into a ball of spiky fear. Given our luck, I know better than to assume she's referring to some other girl.

"What about her?" Something softens in the Commander's voice. It's subtle, but maybe they aren't talking about me, then?

"Reports have surfaced from Genesis X-16 that she has not been spotted in some time. My investigators are now combing through footage from the past two weeks to figure out where Terra has been and exactly how long it's been since she was last seen."

Nevermind.

"I thought they were just getting over a week-long storm down in Sixteen," the Commander responds. The way his voice curls around the word 'Sixteen' stirs something deep in the recesses of my mind. "And *my* latest reports make it quite obvious she has a reputation as a bit of a recluse, especially since her"—he clears his throat—"brother left. I'll have my people look into it, but I don't find myself inclined to think anything particularly suspect is happening. She's just one girl."

Whitlock makes a non-committal noise.

"Anyway, I thought your monkeys thoroughly outprocessed any memories of what happened in Korbyllis—as well as all interactions with the Dissidians—from her." Adam slips his arm around my waist in support, and I'm grateful for the reminder that I'm not here alone.

"They did. They have." I bury the scoff that wants to burst free at the cool confidence in Whitlock's words. I wonder what she would have to say if she knew just how wrong she was. Part of me regrets the fact that I won't get to find out.

"So, what's the issue then?"

"The issue is that regardless of whether she has memories of it or not, her previous encounters with the Dissidians make her valuable—for at least one Dissidian in particular."

Adam's arm tightens around my waist.

"You think she is part of the reason they're choosing to return now?"

"I think we cannot afford to lose track of her, regardless of the reasons."

"And you expect me to do what about this, exactly?" the Commander says, a bitterness to his words that surprises me.

"Find her, of course," Whitlock says simply. "Secure her. Use the brother. You're the one who requested overseeing his enrollment. Commandant Ilken got bumped from his role as superintendent because you *swore* to be personally responsible for the boy. Now you get to do just that."

"I—" The Commander starts to say something that sounds like a protest, but he cuts himself off just as quickly. "Yes, Prime Whitlock," he says after a moment.

Satisfied, Whitlock turns on her heels and walks out the door. My lungs deflate a bit as the *clacking* dwindles, and I release the breath I'd been holding. The Commander lingers at his desk, but at least Whitlock is leaving. Hopefully that means Wolfe will be right behind her.

I squint at my watch in the near-darkness of the closet. We still have a couple of hours before the UO's return shuttle is due to leave. We just need to get back in contact with Mica and we might still be able to pull this off.

There is movement at the desk, and I tense for a moment as I wonder if the Commander is going to spot the drive, but he merely plucks something from a side drawer before standing. A thread of excitement whips through me as he walks toward the office door—he's leaving. We are actually going to get away with this.

He turns back toward the room one last time, as if he's taking it all in, appreciating the warmth and grandeur. The light falls on his face, allowing me to finally glimpse the face and features that have been hidden this whole time.

All at once, every ounce of air empties from my lungs. My hand is pushing the closet door open and my body is pouring into the room before I know what I'm doing.

The Commander goes rigid, his hand frozen on the door handle, stunned by the unexpected intrusion. My entire body trembles as I take in the expression of absolute shock on his face—older, more weathered than I remember.

"Terra," he chokes out after what feels like ten lifetimes.

I swallow hard.

He takes a step forward.

I take a step back.

"Dad?"

TWENTY-NINE

HE LOOKS different than I remember. The lines in his face are deeper. His once-bronze hair has all but faded to a silvery gray. But then, there's so much of him that's the same too. The same hazel eyes, streaked with flashes of green—their transformation to terrestrial brown having halted since he fled the groundworld—are lit with shock, concern, and something else. It's the same expression he had the time he discovered me half-buried in the dirt behind our apartment complex, when I was convinced I was going to dig myself straight to the other side of the world. The tiniest nugget of pride, perhaps, buried under his surprise.

His nose—my nose, high-bridged and narrow—flares with disbelief as he takes in the sight of the daughter he hasn't seen or spoken to in six years. The corners of my own mouth tug with disbelief, and I'm not quite sure if I want to frown or smile as my father and I stand there, staring at each other.

I'm not sure how much time passes before we break the silence. "How are you here?" he asks.

"How could you?" I ask at the same time.

"Terra, I—"

"Looks like you've been doing well for yourself, *Commander Rhodon*." The words are acid dripping from my mouth as I wander around the room, taking in the certificates, commendations, and accolades I hadn't bothered looking at before. His name is plastered across everything, and I want to slap myself for failing to notice it. I stop before a photo of him in his full Tribunal military regalia, shaking Prime Donovan's hand. "Made quite the name for yourself up here, it would seem," I continue, my blood igniting. "Are you curious to know what we've been up to all these years?"

"What are you doing here?" he asks, and with every word out of his mouth, I curse myself for not recognizing his voice.

"Because it hasn't exactly been a picnic," I say, ignoring his question. "I thought you were dead." He flinches. "Figured you must have died. Because why else, *how* else, would someone go six years—six *godforsaken* years—without even checking in on the wellbeing of their children?"

He winces as if I've slapped him across the face. Then, he moves closer. Adam's warmth seeps into my icy veins as he steps up behind me as well, and I've never been more grateful for his presence. The movement has my father finally realizing there's someone else in the room with us, and his eyes widen as he takes Adam in.

"You cannot be here," my father says, and I'm not sure which one of us he's speaking to. Whether he recognizes Adam as a Dissidian or just as my accomplice, I couldn't say.

"Does Mica know?" I blurt out. "Has he seen you? Does he know you're . . . you?" The questions feel stupid rolling off my tongue, but I need to understand. My brother was young when our dad left and goodness knows Gran didn't keep any pictures of him on display, but it seems silly to think Mica wouldn't recognize his own father. Even if he wasn't sure, he would absolutely recognize his name. He has the same one, after all. And Commander Dad here is clearly involved with the Academy in some sort of high-up administrative capacity. It feels improbable that they wouldn't have run into each other.

My blood starts to boil as I try to make sense of this—why he's here, what he's been doing all this time. Is he the reason Mica is here to begin with?

"Mica is aware of who I am," he says, and it feels like being struck. Mica's known our father was not only alive but was right here with him . . . and he didn't tell me.

"I—"

"You have to know that I never meant to hurt you," my father continues, returning his gaze to me, his voice low.

A sob races up from my chest, but when I open my mouth to respond, what comes out is a harsh, bitter laugh. "Ah, well, that makes everything okay then, doesn't it? Totally undoes the years of abandonment. Definitely makes up for the times I had to explain to my little brother—to your *son*—that you left, that you weren't coming back. To have to tell him over and over and over again, because he refused to believe it. The years we almost starved to death? Forgotten. You're off the hook, Pops."

"What? Starved?" To his credit, my father looks genuinely stunned. Enough so that he seems to physically recoil from this admission, leaving me even more confused as his shock morphs into anger. "Why? How? The money in the account I set up with Celestia should have been more than enough to take care of you all—and then some."

Now it's my turn to look flabbergasted, the mention of Gran throwing me off center. "What are you talking about? What money?"

"The account," he says, exasperation coloring his tone as he takes another few steps back into the center of the room. In the corner of my eye, I see Adam step next to the desk and unplug the drive with a sleight of hand. "Celestia didn't—"

"Gran died with a few hundred credits in our family account," I say with a shrug, like it's not a big deal. Like that wasn't a paltry amount for two kids with no source of income and no sense of how much it cost to simply *live*. Like her death didn't mark the crumbling of whatever normalcy—whatever happiness—we'd been able to maintain in the wake of our mother's death and our father's abandonment. "Turns out it's pretty challenging for even the most tenacious teenager to make ends meet. Would've been nice to know you were kicking around up here while we were—"

"I—That's not—That shouldn't have—" The weariness surrounding him seems to sharpen, and it's all suddenly focused on me. "You don't know what you're talking about. Everything I did—everything I have *ever* done—was to protect you and your brother," he says, and something inside me snaps.

"You son of a bitch," I hiss, my words coated with venom. "Maybe if you hadn't completely erased yourself from our lives, this wouldn't have come as such a surprise. You might've thought to check in on us, just once or twice. Though I suppose it's easy to lose track of time and ignore what's going on below while you're hiding away in your fancy perch up here."

My father clenches his fist at his side, opening his mouth as if to argue, but I don't give him a chance to interject.

"You say you were protecting us? Please. You cut yourself off from us so completely you didn't even know what happened to us after Gran died. You didn't care. No, whatever choices you made were for you alone." The words fly out of me, a maelstrom of anger and bitterness. Adam puts a steadying hand on the side of my waist and I press on. "You chose yourself over us when you blew up our lives by messing around with Zira Coal. You chose yourself when you left us. You chose yourself every time you decided to stay away—even after your fifteen-year-old daughter was suddenly forced to bury her grief so she could keep her little brother from passing out from hunger."

My father shakes his head. "That never should have happened. It never should have been like that. I set Celestia up with everything you could possibly need before I left. I've been regularly depositing credits into the account I created for you *for years*. She should have been using it, she should have told you—"

"You think that's what we needed? Money?" I spit, although I can't deny the fact that having access to this alleged mystery fund would have made things a hell of a lot easier over the past few years. I ignore the discomfort roiling in my gut as I wonder why Gran kept it from me. "We needed more than that. We needed our father. We needed *you*."

And there it is.

Loath though I am to admit it to myself, much less to him, it's the truth. And the reason it would have been better if he had just been dead all these years. I bite the inside of my lip to keep myself from spilling more of my truth to the father who abandoned me.

He goes quiet, emotion flickering in his eyes. "You have no idea how much I wish it could have been different."

The fight goes out of me. "Why couldn't it have been?" I ask in a small voice.

He just gives me a sad smile. For a moment, we stand there, the weight of all those lost years pressing down on us, and despite everything he's done and everything he represents, I find myself wanting to go to him. To wrap my arms around my father and cry until there's nothing left of this gaping hurt inside of me.

I don't, of course, and after a minute, Adam shifts next to me, his grip tightening on my hip. I turn to look at him and take in the sadness and concern written across his face. I get that he's worried about me, about how I'm feeling, but he also must be wondering what we're supposed to do now.

We've been caught, and it's my fault.

I should be more worried about that too, but for whatever reason, I'm not. Despite the fact that I'm standing in front of—and yelling at—a Commander for the Tribunal, I don't feel like we're in danger right now.

"We're here to take Mica home," I say to my father, breaking the silence.

He appraises me for another moment, then nods solemnly. "I understand."

My brows shoot up. "You do?"

"I tried my best to keep him out of trouble, out of her sights," he says, his eyes flicking to the closet Adam and I had hidden in. "But as I suspect you overheard, we are preparing for war. Prime Whitlock and the rest of the Tribunal intend to mobilize all available soldiers—cadets included. It's no longer safe for him here."

"I don't think it's all that safe for him anywhere," I mutter.

The sadness in my father's expression seems to amplify as he walks over to his desk, yanks a drawer open, and pulls something out. "Mica will be back in the barracks by now. It's two blocks over, en route to the shuttle station. Show them this at the front, say you're there to collect him on official business from the Commander. They won't give you any trouble."

"Won't they know you helped us?" I ask, though I'm not sure why the thought concerns me so much.

"Helped who?" he says with a sly smile, and just like that, I'm twelve years old again. "All I see are two Altaraan civilian employees who have been tasked with assisting me."

I stare at the badge in my father's hand boasting AAMRE's insignia—a shield emblazoned with an open book and two clashing swords, with a golden eagle perched overtop. As I reach to take it, my father inhales sharply, his eyes pinned to the silver watch on the wrist of my outstretched hand. My mother's watch.

"I was hoping you'd hung onto this," he says wistfully, tracing his finger lightly along the round clock face, and I wonder if he's thinking of the inscription on the other side. *To my wife, my love, my life.*

"What do you mean?" I ask, confused. "You're the one who pawned it when you left. I only got it back because . . ." I trail off, twisting to look at Adam.

"Pawned it, did I?" my father muses. "I suppose your Gran really wanted nothing to do with me after I left, did she? Maybe that's why . . ." He trails off, somewhat lost in his thoughts, but doesn't sound angry. He just sounds sad. "There's so much I wish I could say. So much I wish I could tell you."

"Come with us," I blurt out. I tug my hand back as my face reddens. "I'm sorry, I don't know why I—"

"Would that I could, my darling girl," he says. "But I still have things I need to do here. And if I go now, everything I've done to keep you and your brother safe will have been for nothing."

Adam places his other hand on my shoulder. "I'm sorry, Sunburst, but we need to go."

I nod at him, biting my lip to hold back the torrent of other things I both want and don't want to say. "Will we—Will I see you again?"

"There is nothing in this world that I would like more," my father says, and I purse my lips at the noncommittal answer as he pokes his head out the main office door. "It's clear. You should go."

"Sir," Adam says to my father with a dip of his head as he tugs me past him. My eyes lock on my father's in a silent goodbye, and we're gone.

THIRTY

FOR WHAT IT'S WORTH, my father was right. One flash of his badge and we were ushered right up to Mica's room. The force with which I crashed into him could easily have dislocated my shoulder, but after everything we'd been through, nothing was going to keep me from embracing my baby brother. Granted, I suppose I wouldn't be getting away with calling him that any longer. The skyworld soldier steroids that they must pump into the cadets here at AAMRE are alarmingly effective. Hugging Mica was like trying to hug one of the Dead Woods' petrified trees, he was so solid now.

My heart felt like it grew three sizes seeing Adam and Mica reunite as well—the bro-y way they slapped their palms together and clapped a hand on each other's shoulders calmed the waves of emotion surging inside me. I didn't bring up our father—I think Mica might've suspected I knew something, but I figured we'd have plenty of time to dig into our screwed up family reunion on the shuttle back down to the groundworld.

We just needed to get to said shuttle in the first place.

"We're cutting it pretty damn close," Adam says through gritted teeth as we speed-walk down yet another Altaraan sidewalk.

"We'll make it," Mica says, and my heart swells a little more. I can't believe I have him back.

Logically, I know it's only been a few weeks, but the fear I felt over his safety made every minute feel five times as long. I suspect the fact that he's suddenly built like a brick house and has the cool, collected demeanor of someone twice his age is contributing as well. Even in the civilian clothes he's changed into—having ditched his cadet uniform as soon as we cleared the campus—he exudes a new quiet confidence that I almost feel like I should be grateful to AAMRE for. *Almost.*

Mica slings an arm around my shoulder, and I bite back a scoff as I realize how easy it is for him. He's so much taller than me now.

"I like this," he says, threading a lock of my cherry hair between his fingers. "The eyes though . . ." His face screws up in distaste and I laugh as I catch Adam's eye and the "I told you so" glimmering there.

"Sorry I can't say the same, little brother." I run my hand up the short, buzzed hair at the back of Mica's neck, sticking my tongue out the way it pricks against my skin. "I'm not a fan. You absolutely should grow your hair back out." I attempt to ruffle the slightly longer crop on top, but it's cut so short and set in place with so much hair gel that I barely muss a single strand.

"Wasn't a choice I would've made for myself," Mica says, "though I can't deny how much easier it is to maintain. It dries in about five seconds. Pretty convenient."

"Mmm, yes, I'm sure it's quite timesaving. But tell me, how much time does using all that hair product tack back on?" I tease.

Adam laughs as we round a corner and the gleaming white shuttle station building comes into view. "Finally," he breathes, and a knot eases in my chest as I glance down at my watch. We made it with time to spare. I smile a little as I realize we won't have to sneak around in some cargo bay this time, either. Security is far tighter for those traveling skyward than vice-versa, and while figuring out a legitimate reason for us to visit the skycities—especially Altara—as terrestrials would have been tricky, skydwellers visit the groundworld frequently enough that it's unlikely to raise any eyebrows. Not with the papers the Underground granted us, at any rate.

"The transfer shuttle we are to board is docked in Bay 12. It's bound for the Skyline Transfer station near Genesis B-4, and the UO will meet us there," Adam says.

"We aren't going back to Sixteen." It's not a question, but there's a note of sadness in Mica's voice as he draws his arm from my shoulder that makes me want to explain.

"No, Mic, I'm sorry. It's not safe to go back there, even with the Underground's protection. Especially not after they realize we've both gone AWOL," I say.

"I get it. This is what we planned on doing all along anyway. Our chance for a fresh start." His voice is resolute, but I know he's thinking about Juniper and his friends. I understand. The idea of never returning to our hometown is bittersweet for me too. Life in Sixteen may have been a shitshow of epic proportions, especially in the past few months, but it was our home. The only home we'd ever known. With the only family we'd . . .

I draw my thoughts away from my father and focus back on Adam, who is speaking again.

"The UO has a satellite base near there, and after all we've done to help them, I've been assured they'll grant us passage to anywhere we want to go. Whenever we figure out where that is," he says.

"How unfair is it that you guys got to become resistance spies and all that cool shit?" Mica gripes, and relief washes through me at how thoroughly *himself* he's being.

"Language," I chastise warmly, and my brother beams at me. "And you were literally the definition of undercover up here, Mic."

"Yeah, but I didn't actually uncover anything worthwhile. Other than finding out our—" He cuts himself off with a swallow and that knot in my chest starts tightening again. Adam takes my hand to offer his silent support, and the three of us walk in silence the rest of the way to the shuttle station.

A WAVE of deja vu hits me as we make our way through the station. It's a mirror image of the one in the capital—a long, rectangular main terminal with a vaulted ceiling and individual hangars marked for each skycity destination. My eyes narrow as we pass the sign that says "Korbyllis," but I don't say anything as we make our way toward the entrance of the hangar marked for groundworld-bound travel. It's by far the largest one—it has to be, I suppose, in order to house the trash barges and other industrial transports that make the trip to the groundworld most frequently.

The crowds of travelers thin as we make our way toward the groundworld hangar, with most patrons clearly bound for one of the other skycities. The majority of people milling around the back half of the terminal are employees, their neon green uniforms nearly glowing as they go about their jobs.

Tension builds in my body as the memories from my last experience inside a shuttle hangar flood my mind. For a moment, it's like I can see the line of guardsmen that confronted Adam, Charlie, Luke, and me during our escape from Korbyllis. I can see Wolfe holding Adam's brother hostage at his front, the malicious hunger in his eyes as he'd tried to shoot Tom in the back like the coward he is. The phantom wound in my thigh pulses as I recall the way I'd jumped between them, feeling the bullet rip through my leg instead, remembering how I'd forced Adam to leave me behind as they'd escaped.

I blink, and the images disappear, replaced with Adam's concerned frown as he looks down at me. It's only then I realize how tightly I've been squeezing his hand.

"Just . . . remembering," I say, releasing his hand and cracking my neck as if it might help evict the lingering memories from my brain. My gaze flicks from Adam to Mica, who wears a similar expression. "I'm all right, guys, I just—"

A thunderous boom interrupts me, shaking the building. My eyes widen as the terminal lights up with screams and panicked movement. Multiple people have lost their footing and are now scrambling across the marble floor.

The initial boom fades almost as fast as it came, but it still feels like the terminal's foundation is vibrating, rattling my very bones.

"What the f—"

Mica's voice is immediately drowned out by a crack so loud, it's like the sound is coming from within my own skull. I whip around to find my brother's face frozen in horror as he stares at the ceiling. Following his gaze, I gasp as I see a web of fractures snaking through the vaulted glass.

"Get down!" Adam yells, pushing me against a wall as the ceiling shatters. Time slows, and for a moment, all I hear is the tinkling chime of the tiny, glittering shards as they break free.

For a moment, it's beautiful.

Then, it's raining glass, and the noises inside the terminal change from shouts of confusion and panic to screams of outright terror.

To *pain*.

"Mica!" I cry, and my heart leaps as my brother's hand wraps around my wrist. Adam has pushed him aside as well, and is covering us both with his body. Adam hisses in pain as shards of glass cut through his jacket—slicing into his arms, his back. Each wound feels like it is being carved directly into my soul.

Wails of agony fill the air and as I peek up from my position, crouched against the wall with my arms over my head, the first thing I notice is how the gleaming white marble walls and floors of the terminal aren't so white anymore.

They're streaked with red.

Adam's heavy breaths draw me back to him, and I reach up to touch his face as if needing to prove to myself that he's still here, that he's still alive.

"I'm okay," he grunts, though it takes all of two seconds for me to tell that couldn't be further from the truth. When I look up, I see the awning from one of the hangar entrances looming above us. Adam pushed us under the overhang to protect us from the falling glass, using his own body to cover the rest of us.

The sobbing around us intensifies and I have to force myself not to lose myself in the anguish of those surrounding us as I scramble out from underneath Adam to inspect his wounds. I choke on my breath as I take in the way his blood has mixed with the blue material of his jacket, creating a constellation of black stains across his back. When I draw my hand back, it is coated in his blood.

"You are not okay," I whimper, my voice hitching with the hysteria I'm feeling as vibrations continue to wrack the building.

"I will be," he says with a groan. "I'll heal and—"

"You don't have your RX anymore, Adam! Why did you do that?" I glance down at my body with the realization that not a single shard of glass made its way past my skin. A quick look at Mica tells me his condition is the same, but the relief that gives me is not enough to outweigh the guilt stabbing at me over how badly Adam was hurt saving us.

"You're really . . . going to scold me . . . about this?" His words are already becoming more labored, and fear strikes me right in the center of my body.

"We need to get out of here," Mica says. He wedges himself under Adam's shoulder, grabbing him around the waist to support his weight and help him shuffle forward. Adam inhales sharply, and I know he's trying his best not to voice his pain, but a low whine escapes as they start walking forward. "We're almost to the shuttle bay, we can still make it and—shit!"

With another sonorous boom, a huge metal beam falls right into our path, crushing the entrance to the hangar with our ride out of here. Mica is shouting about a change in plans but I don't quite hear him. My eyes are transfixed by part of a neon green uniform, dappled with red, visible underneath the beam.

"Terra!" Mica yells, and I scramble to help him support Adam. Something wet falls from my face onto my arm as I reach for him, and I realize belatedly that I'm crying.

We limp out of the terminal alongside dozens of other injured citizens. My heart shatters in two as a father pushes ahead of us, his arms curled around the body of his young daughter. She looks like she might have passed out.

God, I hope she passed out.

We exit the building but the ground is still vibrating. It hums like it's bursting with power.

"Quickly, Terra," Mica says, grunting with effort as he tries to take on more of Adam's weight. A third rumbling crash rolls through the air, and I brace myself for whatever is about to happen next.

"What is happening?" I cry, desperate for any explanation other than the stomach-turning truth I don't dare voice. Despite the answer that's already crawled up from the darkest parts of my mind.

Altara is about to fall.

THIRTY-ONE

THE SKY IS a haze of smoke and soot as we stumble away from the terminal's entrance, Adam's weight dragging on Mica and me. My heart pounds with every rumble, every tremor. My pulse feels like a countdown to the city's destruction, and my gut clenches with the very real fear that this is all our fault. The timing is just too coincidental.

"We have to contact the Underground," I say. "They need to know what's happening."

"They may already know," Mica says darkly.

I shake my head, understanding his meaning but unwilling to believe they would have done this on purpose. "There's no way. They want to ground the skycities, yes, but not like this. They don't want another Skyfall, they want to bring them down safely. This has to be an accident, a malfunction or . . ."

"You barely know them, Terra. You can't trust that they wouldn't do exactly this."

"Regardless, they're still our best bet of getting out of here alive, Mica," I scold, and he nods his begrudging agreement. The streets of Altara are in total disarray, filled with panicked citizens trying to flee the impending disaster.

"You guys snuck in through the cargo bay hangar at the back of the building, right?"

"Yes," I say, tightening my grip on Adam as another tremor shakes the ground.

"Okay, we go back that way. There's a chance the shuttle hasn't left yet, that it could still get out. And there should be a comms terminal in there we can use to contact the UO."

Before I can voice my assent, a deafening crack punctures the air. I fight against every instinct that's telling me not to look, not to watch, and force my eyes to lift toward the sky—toward the dyminium UV filter that domes the city.

Unlike the glass ceiling in the terminal, there's no spiderweb of splinters weaving through the glass. No, with an ear-popping, thunderous clap, a giant fissure guts through the center of the dome, right over our heads. It spans the diameter of the filter, splitting it like an egg. The temperature plummets as frigid air surges in from outside, thin winds whipping through the city now that the protection the dome provided from the altitude is no more. Suddenly, I'm not just shaking from the vibrations still rocking the ground.

I huddle closer to Mica and Adam for warmth as we turn the corner to walk the length of the building, heading to the back cargo entrance. A buzzing sound fills the air, and I brace myself for another shuddering boom, some new destruction to rain down on us. But when I locate the source of the sound, a hopeful gasp escapes my lips. Transport shuttles are zooming across the city, off to help evacuate citizens in need. I nearly cry out in victory when I see one dip down behind the shuttle station—exactly where we're headed.

Idly wondering how they mobilized so quickly, Mica and I continue to shuffle Adam toward our destination. "One thing at a time," Mica says, and I hadn't realized I had voiced my question aloud. "And another change of plans. Let's get our boy on that shuttle first, and then we can worry about exactly where they're evacuating everyone. And how we're going to contact the UO."

I nod emphatically, focusing on keeping Adam upright but bolstered by a new hope that we might just make it out of this alive. But with every partially collapsed building we pass and tormented cry we hear, a little bit of that hope gets carved away. There's so much damage, so much destruction—and the city hasn't even technically begun falling yet. Right now, we're still aloft in the sky, though the suspension system under our feet is clearly fighting for its life—for all of our lives—at the moment.

We finally make it to the end of the shuttle station, and my heart sinks as we round the corner and see a row of guardsmen lined up in front of the large evacuation shuttle fifty yards away. Masses of citizens are congregating around them, and the guards are triaging the injured and helping folks on board. I send up a prayer that in all the chaos, they aren't IDing anyone. Not that we have another option. We have to get Adam help for his injuries, and we need to get our asses away from this city.

"Sunburst?" Adam's feeble voice pokes through my crowded thoughts, and I slow us to a stop.

"Shh, save your strength," I say, exchanging a look with Mica that tells me he's just as concerned with how weak Adam sounds as I am.

"I'm ready . . . to call in . . . that . . . promise," he says, each word more strained than the last.

"Don't be silly, now isn't the time for that. It's just a little further."

"You . . . owe . . . me," Adam murmurs.

"Fine, what do you want me to promise?" I cluck, though my heart is gripped in a vice.

"Survive," Adam whispers, and a burst of strength ripples through my very soul, he says it with such conviction. "You have to . . . survive. No matter what happens . . . No matter what . . ." He trails off and my heart splinters.

I wave off all my instincts to dismiss him, to laugh it off, to protest that there will be plenty of time for this later. Instead, I simply place a tender kiss on Adam's cheek and say, "I promise."

WE'RE ABOUT to continue our labored slog forward when an odd sensation of awareness slinks down my spine. It has me shivering more than the icy air and roots me to the spot.

"I hope you're happy." Inquisitor Wolfe's cold voice slithers in from behind me, and every muscle in my body clenches at the sound. "I assume this is all your doing," he says, stepping out from the shadows of the shuttle station.

As if in slow motion, I pivot toward the guardsman who still haunts my nightmares, standing alone, his eyes narrowed on me.

"I liked you better the way you looked before, little bird," he says. Nausea roils in my stomach.

"What do you want?" I manage to spit out. A terrified tremor runs across my skin as Wolfe stares at me for a long moment before a wide, wicked grin dawns on his face.

"So you do remember," he breathes delightedly. "What a fascinating creature you are." He reaches toward me and Adam releases a low growl.

"Ooh, scary," Wolfe says with a smirk, but he draws his hand back. "Prime Whitlock will certainly be interested to learn that your memories are far more . . . intact . . . than we'd been led to believe."

"Inquisitor Wolfe, sir, pardon the interruption," Mica says, and my mouth pops open in shock at his inner soldier coming to the surface, "but Altara is about to fall out of the sky. Surely you have more important duties to take care of than preventing us from getting this injured man safely evacuated."

Wolfe's eyebrows shoot up as if he's just noticed Mica's presence. "Cadet Rhodon, I'm disappointed in you," he says with a click of his tongue. "I'd have thought our brightest, most promising cadet would be capable of making better decisions than consorting with traitorous filth."

Mica balks for a moment, like Wolfe's words hit their mark, and a bolt of panic slices through me as I wonder if I underestimated the Academy's —and the Tribunal's—ability to sink their claws into my little brother. Is it possible he might be feeling conflicting loyalties after just a few short weeks here? They've already transformed him physically, after all. And I'm more than aware of the kind of control they're capable of exerting over one's mind.

"All due respect, *sir*," Mica says in a tone that suggests anything but respect, "but there was never a decision to be made." My momentary spike of fear is washed away as he continues, his teeth gritted. "I'm where I belong. With my family."

"Though I suppose it's not much of an accolade to be the youngest cadet in thirty years when your admission was purchased with nepotism," Wolfe continues, ignoring him.

"Mica never asked to come here in the first place," I say, before cursing myself inwardly for taking the bait.

Wolfe's rotten gaze narrows in on me again. "And yet here he is! Throwing this generous gift from Prime Whitlock and the Tribunal right back in their faces. You could've gone on to do great things, my boy. Now look at you. An embarrassment to your father and to the Academy both." He sighs dramatically. "You brought this all upon yourselves, you know."

"Brought what upon ourselves?" I ask, my blood boiling.

"This," he says, gesturing broadly to the destruction surrounding us. "With your little act of espionage. Did you honestly think we wouldn't know someone was trying to access our systems? Do you really think we'd just let you take over, let you bring our cities down? Please. We have been here before. We've learned," he says, his eyes gleaming with malice.

"I have no idea what you're talking about, but we don't have time for this," I say, even as my heart sinks further at the realization that our stealth efforts have been for nothing. "Can you press pause on your cryptic bullshit until we're on the shuttle and he's getting the medical care he needs?"

Wolfe ignores me. "You all, on the other hand, do not appear to have learned a thing over the centuries. You should have known that we'd have a failsafe in place for the kinds of things you were trying to do."

My blood runs cold. "A failsafe? What are you—Are you saying you did this on purpose?"

"You cannot expect us to allow just anyone to wrest control of our own cities from us," he sneers.

"You'd rather let an entire skycity plummet to the ground and kill hundreds of thousands of people than allow it to be grounded peacefully? You're psychotic."

"It won't be hundreds of thousands," Wolfe says with a tsk. "Well, not hundreds of thousands of *us*, once evacuations are complete. But I suppose depending on where this place lands, it will still be quite the tragedy for the groundworld, to be sure. At least this time we won't have to worry about anything like that pesky plague getting out."

"This time?" Horror sparks through my veins. "You . . . You mean . . . You're talking about Intheria."

Wolfe's lips curl into a devil's smile.

"Intheria fell because . . . because of this failsafe?" I continue, trying to sift through everything I learned about Intheria in the weeks and months prior to the Skyfall. Trying to reconcile what Wolfe is saying now with what I've been taught my whole life.

"Intheria fell because some very small people got some very lofty ideas about what they thought was best for everyone," Wolfe says. "But reintegrating with terrestrial trash was never an option—not even as a last resort. Not when we still have so many . . . opportunities to explore."

"This is madness," Mica says sharply.

"Is it?" Wolfe shrugs. "I like to think of it as progress. Nothing unites people like a common enemy. Nothing motivates like tragedy."

"That's enough, Aros." My father's voice echoes over my head, and my mouth falls open as he approaches. I exchange a look with Mica, whose expression is indecipherable. I whirl around, my gaze shifting to the open doors of the cargo bay my father just emerged from, and it feels so ludicrous that I almost laugh. Was he waiting here for us? Did he change his mind about helping us?

Who's side is he really on? wonders the little voice in the back of my mind.

"Commander," Wolfe says, snapping to attention. I want to snicker at the way his spine straightens.

"I think it's time we took this conversation somewhere a little more private," my father says, glancing toward the line of guardsmen by the evacuation shuttle. They don't appear to have noticed us amidst the chaos of the evacuating crowd, but my father gestures to the open doors at the back of the shuttle station nonetheless.

Adam leans further into me and my arm is sticky with his blood as I continue clutching his waist to keep him upright. "Please," I beg my father, staring at the triage tent by the shuttle. "He's badly injured. Let me just take him to get help and I'll come right back here with you." A wild kind of desperation hacks at me from the inside—a fierce need to help Adam, to heal the injuries that are making him weaker by the moment.

Why did I ever agree to let Luke fry his NX? If he had his advancements, none of this would be happening right now.

My father simply continues to hold out his arm, directing us into the building, and I bite down on my tongue as resignation takes me. Adam releases a pained grunt as Wolfe shoves Mica's shoulder in an effort to be the first to follow the Commander's orders. My father instructs Mica to go with Adam next, and I reluctantly withdraw my arm from around Adam's waist as they move forward, cringing at the way my fingers stick together with his blood.

I move to follow but a gentle hand on my shoulder holds me back as my father slides his hand into his pocket and pulls out a small silver syringe. He surreptitiously places it in my hand without a word, then prods me forward. I clench it in my blood-stained fist before slipping it into my pocket. Whatever his game, I have no choice but to follow along.

THIRTY-TWO

THE SHUTTLE STATION'S destruction seems to have ceased after the hangar entrance inside the terminal collapsed. We exit the cargo bay into the main shuttle hangar to find it largely undamaged, but also completely empty. Dread settles in my core as I realize there's no shuttle in sight—the ride the Underground had secured for us is gone, leaving the hangar's retractable roof wide open in the wake of its takeoff.

"How would you like to proceed, Commander?" Wolfe says eagerly, spinning to face my father as he closes the hangar doors behind him.

My father arches a brow. "Proceed?"

"I fully recognize that these are your . . . progeny, Commander, but no one is above the law." He glowers at us, his gaze stalling on Adam, who is leaning on Mica so heavily at this point he's barely standing. "And they have been caught red-handed."

My father surveys Adam, noting the red footprints he's trailed into the hangar, the blood still dribbling from the gashes on his back. "If that's a joke about this man's current state, Aros, it's in poor taste."

"Sir, I would *never* joke about such things," Wolfe says, donning a wounded expression. It's all I can do not to roll my eyes. I hope my father isn't buying this bullshit. "Your daughter and son appear to have been working in tandem to sabotage the city of Altara and—"

"You said it yourself," my father cuts in, "they *appear* to have been. But to say someone has been caught red-handed implies a witness or some other irrefutable proof of committing the act of which they are accused. Do you have such proof, Inquisitor Wolfe?"

Hope sparks in my chest at his words.

"I—You—" Wolfe looks genuinely at a loss for words, and I smother the smile that's trying to creep onto my face. "Sir, their presence alone is proof. Your daughter has clearly broken through the mental wards placed on her by the Tribunal. Her failure to report the return of her memories is a criminal act in and of itself. And this man," he sneers at Adam," is a known fugitive. A Dissidian spy. A terrorist. And then there's the matter of your son's presence at the Academy—"

"—which was sanctioned by Prime Whitlock herself. If you have an issue with her decision, I strongly suggest you take it up with her," my father rebukes, and for a moment it appears as if Wolfe has been stunned into silence. Then something shifts behind his gaze and the expression that follows snuffs out my spark of hope.

Wolfe rolls his shoulders back and straightens his spine. "So I shall," he says with lethal calm. My eyes widen as his hand drifts closer to his belt and the weapons holstered there, and the phantom wound in my thigh throbs. "Your relationship with the suspects is clouding your judgment. Preventing you from being able to fulfill your duties as a sworn officer of the Tribunal Guardsmen Corps."

"You dare—"

"I will have to report this conflict of interest and your clear dereliction of duty to Prime Whitlock," Wolfe continues, speaking over my father's outraged protestations. "And maybe this time she'll actually listen to me," he adds with a grumble.

Wolfe's psychotic flip from brown-nosing underling to blatantly disregarding the chain of command has me reeling, and the words slip out before I can stop myself. "This time?"

"I *told* her not to let your father interfere during your apprehension in Korbyllis, but my opinion didn't carry much weight back then." Wolfe rakes his gaze over me, a wistful expression on his face that makes my stomach curdle. "I could have accomplished so much more with you if I'd just had the runway," he sighs.

My father roars a sharp reprimand at Wolfe, but I don't hear the words. My mind is spinning with this new revelation. I'd long wondered why they went through the trouble of wiping my memories and constructing elaborate cover stories for my whereabouts when it would have been much easier to just knock me off and dump my body somewhere. Was this my father's protection all along?

"The Prime will want to be informed of these new developments immediately," Wolfe says, "and as we don't have much time remaining, I suggest you contain these two criminals on your shuttle." He gestures blithely to Adam and Mica, and even I am rankled by his sheer insubordination. I suck in a sharp breath as the atmosphere in the hangar becomes heavy and stiff—despite the thin, frigid air rushing in from outside the wrecked UV filter.

"You're so far over the line, you can't even see it anymore, can you?" my father says steadily, glancing up through the open hangar roof to the splintered dome as if my thoughts summoned his gaze to it. For a second, I think he might be searching for something high above, but I blink and he's back to glaring at Wolfe with vicious focus. "You forget your place, Aros."

"You're the one who appears to have forgotten where your duties lie, *Auron*," Wolfe spits. "Place them under arrest and get out of this city while you still can. I will escort your daughter *personally* to see the Prime. After all, we have a lot of catching up to do, don't we, little bird?" he adds, leering at me.

Adam, who I wasn't even sure was conscious enough to be paying attention, suddenly jerks against Mica. "Over my dead body," he snarls.

"From the look of you, that doesn't seem too far off," Wolfe says, a savage gleam in his eye as he surveys Adam's wounds. "A small penance, given what you've done, Dissidian scum. Far worthier people than you have already lost their lives today."

"What *we've* done? It's what *you've* done! Those people lost their lives because of you," I cry. "You're all insane. You'd rather kill off thousands than have to face the moderate inconvenience of a groundworld life."

"Take it up with the Prime," Wolfe says dismissively, reaching for my wrist. I recoil, backing into my father. He sweeps me behind him, murder written on his features as he stares down the Inquisitor.

"Step aside, Commander," Wolfe snarls. "She was always supposed to be mine."

My father takes a fighting stance and my pulse quickens in anticipation of the blows that I'm sure are about to be exchanged. I'm rooted in place, stunned not by how rapidly this situation has deteriorated, but by the sheer fact that my father is here. That he's physically defending me.

At first, I think Wolfe is moving himself into a similar position—readying himself to fistfight his Commander for, well, for me. Nausea writhes in my belly at the thought. But then, so fast I'm barely able to track the motion, Wolfe snatches the stunner clipped to his belt.

"No!" I scream, the worst kind of deja vu sweeping over me as Wolfe fires two shots straight into my father's chest. He drops to the floor, convulsing wildly, each second an eternity. Finally, he stops, and it's like the world stops with him. Mica's face is frozen with fear as I crouch next to my father, holding my breath until I see the tiny movement of his chest. Proof that he's still alive.

"Time to go, little bird," Wolfe says smugly. He reaches for me again, and with a ferocity I didn't know I possessed, I grab hold of the terror in my veins and launch myself at Inquisitor Wolfe.

THIRTY-THREE

MY ATTACK TAKES Wolfe by surprise, and I manage to knock the stunner from his hand as I collide with him. The victory is short-lived, however, as his fingers dart back to his waist, yanking a small metal cylinder from his belt. He flicks his wrist and the cylinder extends into a long metal baton.

From the corner of my eye, I see Mica trying to set Adam down so he can come to my aid. My vision goes white as my legs are knocked out from under me with a savage swipe of Wolfe's baton. I crash to the floor, catching myself with my hands and rolling to my back. In one fluid move, I kick myself back up to standing.

Silently thanking Mica for every single moment he pleaded, cajoled, and otherwise dragged me into sparring with him, I fling myself back at Wolfe. I duck under the baton—already in motion again—and jab my elbow into his solar plexus. Before I can savor the moment, my right side lights up with bright, fierce pain as he strikes me again.

I suck in a sharp breath, my heart pounding in my chest, as the pain threatens to consume me. I may have landed a solid blow, but it's just me—partially trained and gangly limbed—against a fully-grown, fully-equipped guardsman.

"Who knew you were such a fighter," Wolfe sneers, gripping the front of my jacket, hoisting me up, and forcing me to meet his cold eyes. "Are you sure you're the same little bird who begged and begged me to stop offering you memories of your past? Visions of your future?" I claw at his hands, drawing blood with my fingernails as I try to break his grip, and he snarls. "I liked it when you begged, but lucky for you, I think I like it even more when you fight."

With a grunt of effort, he sends me flying into a stack of crates. They topple with a crash, and a pained whimper escapes me as a sharp corner pierces my abdomen. Something warm spreads across my torso and has the material of my dress sticking to my skin.

"Terra!" Mica cries, and I relish Wolfe's yelp as my brother rushes him, tackling him to the ground. Every part of my body trembles as I force myself back to my feet, terror-stricken as I watch Wolfe and Mica brawl. A clang vibrates through the air as Mica manages to knock the baton from Wolfe's hands, sending it skittering across the hangar. For a moment, impossible as it seems, Mica has the upper hand.

Then screaming fills the air, and I realize it's my own as Wolfe rears back, his fist connecting with Mica's face, and my brother goes down. He hits the floor head-first with a sickening crack.

"Now, where were we?" Wolfe growls. He dusts himself off before stalking back toward me.

"I'll never go with you," I say, my eyes on Mica's prone form, stoking the embers of anger inside me into a blazing fury. Wolfe's eyes narrow on me, and as I read the sick intent lighting them, I know I mean it. I know that I'd rather die here and now than let him get his hands on me again.

Wolfe seems to sense the shift in my will because quick as lightning, his hand is at his waist again. "Is that so?" He pulls something new from his belt. It's not a stunner or a baton. It's a knife—shiny, silver, and threatening death.

But not *my* death, I realize as Wolfe looks between the crumpled forms on the ground with maniacal glee. His gaze darts hungrily between them —Adam, Mica, my father, Adam, Mica, my father—like he can't make up his mind. "You really won't *ever* come with me?" he taunts, and my stomach clenches at the cruel slant of his voice. He's toying with me. "Not even if it meant saving one of them? All of them?"

Any words I might have spat back at him die in my throat as my eyes go to the three men lying prostrate on the hangar floor—my father, knocked out. Mica, wounded. And Adam—my heart fractures as I even think the word—*dying*. I look at the three men who have hurt and bled and sacrificed for me, the men who are my *family*, and my resolve cracks.

Like he can sense my wavering conviction, Wolfe steps forward. "Tell you what. I'll let you go. I won't even tell Prime Whitlock about you. All you have to do is pick which one of them you want to die instead."

Rendered speechless, I just stare and stare and stare at him.

"Quick, quick, little bird. If you don't make up your mind soon, the choice might just be made for you." He glances disapprovingly at Adam before moving toward the father I've barely begun to get to know again.

"Don't," I growl.

Wolfe raises his hands in a placating motion. "Huh. Never figured you for a daddy's girl, but fine. The brother then?" He starts to advance on Mica next, and though every muscle in my body burns from the effort, I race over to cover my brother's body with my own. "Don't you fucking touch him!"

Wolfe shrugs, infuriating me. This is all just a game to him. "And then there was one." He turns back to Adam's body, pale and limp, with a knowing smirk.

He's lost too much blood, the voice in the back of my mind informs me, as if I need the reminder. As if I don't already know how totally screwed we are.

His eyelids flutter open as Wolfe approaches, knife drawn, tutting as his shadow enshrouds Adam's body. The last bit of fire in me dies out. Adam made me promise to survive, but there's no surviving without him. Without them.

"Swear to me that they'll be safe," I say, my voice low. "Swear you'll get them out of this city, that you'll get them help, and I'll go with you. I won't fight you."

The victorious gleam in Wolfe's eyes makes me want to vomit as he reholsters his knife. "Would be a shame if you stopped fighting altogether," he says, and I suppress a shudder. "But you have my word. I'll have the guardsmen unit outside sweep in as soon as you leave with me."

At my look of alarm, he adds, "Don't be naive. Of course, they'll arrest your brother and the Dissidian, but their wounds will be treated. They'll be perfectly safe in the cozy holding cells they'll soon be calling home. As for your father, well . . . his ultimate fate will lie with Prime Whitlock. Why don't we go see her now?" Wolfe extends his hand. Fighting against everything my instincts are telling me to do—slap it away, spit on it, chop it off—I place my own hand in his with a resigned nod, and allow the bastard to pull me up.

Adam stirs as Wolfe begins to escort me back toward the cargo area's doors, and the whimper that slips out of him breaks my heart. It's a sound of pain, yes, but not just the physical pain he's feeling. It's also the sound of hope dying.

I pluck the contact lenses from my eyes with my free hand as Wolfe drags me past Adam. I want the last time I see his beautiful, brilliant blue eyes to be when my own are what's looking back. His gaze seems unfocused, so I don't know if he registers the three little words I mouth to him as Wolfe tugs me away, but I hope he does.

I hope he knows.

I slip my free hand into my pocket, closing my fingers around the syringe my father gave me, and wishing I knew what he had intended it for. Was I supposed to give it to Adam to heal him? Use it on Wolfe to stop him? Administer it to myself for some other reason?

I don't get the chance to pick apart my father's intentions, though, as the vibrations that have been ransacking the city this entire time suddenly intensify. My teeth chatter against each other as I attempt to stay upright.

"Damn it." Wolfe hauls me forward, and I bite my lip to keep from crying out at his painful grip on my hand. "Hurry up. We're out of time."

"Out of time for—" I start to say, but I don't need to finish my question. With another, now terrifyingly familiar, calamitous boom, it's like the ground gives way beneath us.

Gravity disappears for a split-second.

My feet lift.

And I'm slammed back down with knee-buckling force as the city falls.

THIRTY-FOUR

THE GROUND beneath us convulses with another violent tremor, and Wolfe curses again. "The antigravity propulsion systems have given out. It won't be long."

"Call the guards," I urge him, attempting to look back over my shoulder at Adam, Mica, and my father. "You have to tell the guardsmen to come get them now, before the—"

Wolfe ignores my plea, yanking me forward, and the realization hits me like a punch to the gut. Whatever his intentions might have been before the city began to fall in earnest, his promise to get the three of them evacuated and to safety is clearly null and void. Nobody is coming for them. He's leaving them for dead.

Fury and desperation surge through me as I wrench my hand from Wolfe's grip, the syringe clutched tightly in my other palm.

Wolfe's eyes are wide with surprise as he spins to face me, but he recovers swiftly, lunging at me with a vile savagery that has my heart leaping into my throat. I duck under his outstretched arms and launch forward, slamming my shoulder into his chest. The blow reverberates through my body, waves of pain pulsing from my abdomen and the injury still bleeding there, but it's enough to send Wolfe staggering back.

"I give you a chance, little bird, and this is how you thank me?" Wolfe snarls, feinting to the left before coming at me again. Somehow, he's unsheathed his knife again and I narrowly dodge the blade, feeling a rush of air as it slices past my face.

"I'm not your little bird," I growl, striking his outstretched arm with the palm of my hand and driving my foot into his knee. Wolfe grunts as his leg buckles, and I seize the opportunity to catapult forward and lock my arm around his shoulders. He emits a shocked yelp as I muster all my remaining strength to keep him in place long enough to plunge the syringe into his neck. Then, another cry fills the air, this time from me, as Wolfe stabs the back of my hand with his knife in a desperate bid to get me off him.

I rear back, hissing in pain as blood pours from my hand, but he's too late. The syringe is embedded in his neck, the plunger depressing automatically as it injects its contents into Wolfe's bloodstream.

"You bitch . . ." The knife drops from his grip as his hands go limp at his sides. His other knee buckles and he stumbles backward, his eyes glazing over before he collapses. His body twitches as whatever was in the syringe takes effect.

My breaths are ragged as I stare at Wolfe in disgust, clutching my bloody hand to my still-bleeding abdomen. The pain should be agonizing, but the adrenaline zipping through my veins blocks the feeling. I race back to Adam, Mica, and my father, leaving Wolfe convulsing on the floor.

"Adam! Mica!" I shout, dropping to my knees beside them. Adam is barely conscious, his breaths shallow, and terror grips my heart as I grip his hand in turn. I notice Mica beginning to stir and relief blows through me so viciously I nearly collapse. My father remains unconscious but his breathing has gotten stronger, and he appears to be otherwise unharmed by Wolfe's stun shots.

"What do I do, what do I do," I mutter, my thoughts manic. How am I going to get us out of here? Out of this? How fast are we falling? How much time do we have?

Frightened wails from outside the hangar cut through the noise in my brain, and I lift my eyes to the open roof above us. Evacuation shuttles are taking off in every direction, most of them flying directly out through the open chasm in the UV filter. Despair tears at my heart as I realize they're taking off with any chance we might have had to escape as well.

"I'm sorry, Sunburst," Adam's voice drifts up to my ears, and I look down at him with tears already brimming in my eyes. "This isn't what I . . ." He trails off, seeming to lose focus, and panic banishes the air from my lungs. His eyes fall on Mica, who is groaning as he props himself up on his elbows. "You two . . . have to go. Take your father, find a ship . . . Run. You have to . . . survive."

"You're out of your mind if you think I'm leaving you here."

"Terra . . ." The sympathy in Mica's voice makes my name feel like a blade slicing across my ear. He's upright now, able to take in how much Adam's condition has deteriorated, and the look on my brother's pale face shatters the remaining fragile pieces of my heart. He doesn't think Adam's going to make it.

"Please, Sunburst," Adam whispers. "Remember your promise."

Tears stream from my eyes as I raise his bloodied hand to my lips and press a kiss to it. "I love you," I tell him. "You're everything I ever wanted and more than I could've hoped for." My voice breaks as mental images crash into me. The way he looked the first time I saw him, hunched over as he tried to stifle the bloody nose I'd given him. The feel of his lips, soft and appraising, as he brushed them against mine the first time we kissed. The incandescently perfect fit of our bodies as we came together.

Adam's eyes, those pools of swirling cerulean stardust, burrow right into my soul. "I journeyed across the stars to find you. To save you. To be saved by you. And as long as you *survive*, you won't be leaving me here. Not really." He takes a shuddering breath, like he's drawing on the last scraps of his strength in order to speak. "There's no place in this galaxy you could go where I won't be with you. Always."

Even as Adam's words warm the block of ice that's taken up residence where my heart should be, a dark shadow emerges from the recesses of my mind. It feels a little bit like being reunited with a long-lost friend, and I don't bat it away as it sweeps across my consciousness. It's the same darkness that overtook me when Gran died, that pushed me to just . . . stop. To shut Mica out. To shut everything out. And as I look down at the man I love, at the life slowly ebbing from his eyes, I welcome it. I want it.

I want it to take it all away—this pain, this loss. I want to dive deep inside myself, locking myself away with my memories of Adam.

"Terra." Mica's voice is far away. As if being controlled by something else, I turn my head to see him crouching beside my father, trying to lift him. And I remember the way Mica had looked that day, so many years ago, when the hunger and exhaustion finally proved too much. The day I finally pushed through the haze of grief. The day I swore I would never fail him again.

I won't fail him again.

And I won't let everything Adam has done to keep me safe be in vain.

"I love you," I say again. Adam nods weakly as his eyes flutter shut, his chest continuing its shallow rhythm of sinking and rising as I release his hand. With a swipe of my bloody fingers, I banish the tears from my cheek and rush to Mica's side. I throw my father's other arm over my shoulder, and with a labored grunt, the two of us start dragging him toward the door.

"There has to be a shuttle out there somewhere," Mica says. "We'll find it."

I'm about to voice my agreement when a glint in the sky beyond the hangar roof catches my eye. I nearly drop our father as a shuttle flies *into* the city from outside the cracked dome. It looks different than the ones fleeing Altara—shinier, sleeker. My breath hitches as it barrels right for us, and I allow the tiniest spark of hope to pierce the darkness that's been threatening to smother me from within.

The shuttle lands inside the hangar with a dull thud. The grating squeak of hinges rubbing has never sounded so beautiful as the hatch opens to reveal a familiar face.

"What are you waiting for, a formal invitation?" Luke shouts at us, gesturing wildly. "Get your asses on board!"

THIRTY-FIVE

THE OPTIMISM on Luke's face is extinguished half a second later, his mouth clamping shut and eyes widening at the sight of Adam on the ground. He rushes toward his friend, and the wave of relief that crashes into me is so overwhelming that I almost don't notice Tom flying past us to join him.

Tom offers me a curt nod as he hauls his brother up and we all stumble on board. The shuttle is lined with jumpseats on either side of the cabin, and Mica and I flop into seats opposite each other as Adam and my father are laid on the floor at our feet.

Tom and Luke are a blur of motion as they perform quick assessments of Adam and my father. I've reclaimed Adam's hand, and Tom snorts as he has to step around me to roll Adam on his side. With a deft flick of his wrist, Tom uses his FX to cut through the seams of Adam's jacket, then proceeds to peel the crusted fabric from his back. I suck in air through my teeth as the shirt underneath—stained a dark scarlet—is revealed.

"How has he lost so much blood? Why isn't he healing?" Tom demands, and shame burns in my cheeks. I glance at Luke to find a similar expression on his face.

"He—His RX doesn't work anymore," I admit. Tom's eyes widen, mostly because of the revelation that Adam's healing ability is gone, but perhaps partially because I'm not supposed to know what RX is in the first place.

"It's true," Luke confirms as he wafts something under my father's nose—he starts to rouse within seconds. He coughs, rubbing the spot on his chest where Wolfe hit him with the stunner, and something in my chest eases.

"Dad," I breathe, my heart swelling as his eyes find my own.

My father's gaze darts manically around the cabin, landing on each of us in turn. He takes in the concern and relief pouring from Mica and me. The distinct displeasure on Tom's face. And Luke's expression of . . . Is that amusement?

"Cutting it a little close, wouldn't you say?" my dad quips at Luke. My brow furrows with confusion at the casualness of his tone, almost as if he had been expecting this. Before I can say anything else, though, Tom's sharp voice rings out again.

"What *exactly* do you mean when you say Adam's RX no longer works?" he asks me, accusation lacing every word.

"You *nixed* him, Tommy," Luke says, as if that explains everything. "You know Adam. Did you really expect him not to figure out a way around it?"

"Are we good to go?" Charlie's voice cuts in from the front of the shuttle. "This place is literally coming down, can we finish this later?"

"Yes," Tom replies, though his gaze is still laser-focused on me. "Get us on a trajectory back to Dissidia. We *will* continue this discussion after we get out of here."

"No." My father's voice rings clearly through the shuttle, his authority booming through me despite the fact that he's barely regained consciousness. "We cannot leave yet. There are still thousands of people out there."

"It's too late, Da—sir," Mica says, his tone grave. "We can't save them."

"It's *not* too late," Dad insists, getting to his feet. "The city hasn't reached terminal velocity yet. At that point, yes, it will be impossible. But as of this moment, there's still a chance to stop it."

"And how exactly do you propose we do that?" Luke asks.

"Take me to City Hall. It isn't far from here. The manual controls for the Altaraan city infrastructure are housed in a sub-basement there. I can manually re-engage the propulsion system and slow the city's descent."

"You can really do this?" Tom asks.

"I can," my father says. "I've trained for this."

Somewhat hesitantly, Tom nods his agreement, but my mouth drops open. "You can't seriously be asking us to leave you behind so you can—"

"What else would you have me do?" My father turns to me, steely determination floating in his hazel eyes. "Even disregarding all the people still trapped here in the city with us—what about the people below? This city is even bigger than Intheria. Think about how much more devastating its fall will be."

My breath catches as I consider what my father is saying. If there is truly a chance of him stopping this . . .

But what is a chance worth? the voice in my head asks.

"You can come back for me after—if I'm successful. But someone has to stay. Someone has to give these people a fighting chance."

"Why does it have to be you?" Tears pool in my eyes once again and I suddenly sound very young. "We just got you back."

My father's expression softens and something profoundly sad flashes across his face. "It can *only* be me. I have the clearance to get in, and I know how to engineer a slowed descent."

"Why? How do you know how to do that?"

"I—"

"Because this is what he's been working toward for a long time, Terra," Mica interjects.

"I don't understand."

"T, your father's the one who called us here," Luke explains.

"Dad has been an Underground plant for many years," Mica says. "Their highest-ranking informant."

I gape at my brother. "You knew this?"

"He . . . I found out when we reconnected at AAMRE." His eyes are fixed on Adam—whose breathing is already steadier and has color returning to his face even as he remains unconscious—as if to avoid making eye contact with me. "I'm sorry I couldn't tell you—didn't tell you. But it's why . . ."

"It's why he left," I finish for him, so many things seeming to fall into place in my mind as I take in my father's grim expression.

Everything I did—everything I have ever *done—was to protect you and your brother.*

Whatever it is that you're thinking, Celestia, you're wrong.

"Back then, when I . . . When I saw you with Zira Coal . . . You weren't having an affair," I say.

"No, I wasn't," Dad confirms. He clasps my hand. "I know this is a lot to take in, especially in such a short amount of time, but I need you to trust me."

"I hate to break this up," Charlie yells, her voice rife with annoyance, "but if we don't get moving here soon, there's not going to be anything left to save, including us."

Biting my lip, I nod with reluctant acceptance. Tom exchanges a look with my father, then barks an order to Charlie and the shuttle roars to life. We're airborne in an instant, jetting through the hangar roof and speeding toward the heart of Altara. Through the viewport, I watch as chaos continues unfolding below. People still litter the streets, scrambling to escape the doomed city.

Dad places a hand on my shoulder, warm and grounding, and I find myself leaning into his touch before wincing when the movement pulls at the gash in my stomach.

"You're wounded," Luke gasps, having noticed my reaction. "Why didn't you say anything?" He races over to me before using his FX to summon bandages and a tin of healing balm to his hand.

Within seconds of his dutiful ministrations, the sharp ache in my side eases, and I offer him a grateful smile. "Thank you," I say.

In classic Luke fashion, he bats away my appreciation with a joke. "Next course of treatment will be getting you a shower." He grimaces as he tries in vain to clean some of the blood and grit from my limbs. It takes a great deal of self-control not to purposefully decorate his pristine clothing with some fingerprint-sized red polka dots.

"We're approaching City Hall," Charlie announces. The building looms ominously against the backdrop of the collapsing city, but still appears entirely intact. Intact . . . and abandoned. No frantic screams from panicked citizens rent the air here. The self-important skydwellers working and residing in this part of the city must have been the first to evacuate.

Charlie hovers the shuttle right over the building, opening the hatch so my father can jump the final few feet down onto the roof.

"Get to a safe distance from the city," my father commands. "Feel free to loop back around in about, oh"—he checks his watch—"eight minutes or so. Provided all goes to plan." Tom, Luke, Charlie, and Mica all salute him, and some tiny part of me finds it amusing that military cordiality can be so unifying. Belatedly, I whip my hand up to my forehead in an awkward attempt to follow suit, and my dad huffs a laugh. "No need for any of that, sweetheart," he says.

I bite my lip at the endearment as memories accost me. He called me that for twelve years. Twelve years of 'sweetheart' and 'T-bird' and 'my girl,' followed by six years of bitter resentment as the nicknames disappeared when he did. Six years of disappointment and anger and hatred over his abandonment that I've held on to so tightly, I fear it's become a core part of my very being. And I'm scared of what might remain if I let go of it.

But I *want* to let it go.

"Come back to us, Dad," I say, my eyes burning.

"Yes," Mica agrees, stepping across the shuttle to take the jumpseat right next to me like he knows I need the support. Or maybe he does. "If it's not . . . If you can't get to the controls, or something goes wrong, or you run out of time, come back anyway. We'll wait, we'll come for you."

Something fierce and powerful flares in our father's eyes. "I couldn't be prouder of you both," he says. "I've loved you from the moment you took your first breaths in this world. I have many regrets in this life, but I'll never regret working to make this world a safer place for you. For trying to secure a future that's worth living. I hope, in time, you'll understand that." And with that, he hops off the shuttle and onto the roof, tucking into a swift roll to absorb the impact of his landing.

"Damn, your dad is cool," Luke says with a low whistle. Still reeling from the emotion behind his parting words, I don't even glare at him.

Our father disappears behind a door and Charlie pulls the shuttle back up into the sky, zooming through the crack in the UV filter, putting distance between us and the skycity. My breath comes in rapid, shallow bursts as I take in the scene from this new, exterior perspective. While we were on the ground, I knew the city had started to fall from the way gravity seemed to be yanked away for a moment, from the way the thin, freezing air whipped around us. But from here, from the outside, I am literally watching it fall.

Like a scene from a movie, or maybe a dream, the majestic city plummets through the sky before my eyes.

The minutes feel like hours as we circle the city. Even from a distance, City Hall is visible, and my heart feels like it's stuck in my throat as my eyes stay pinned to the building—waiting, hoping.

Then, the descent slows. It's so minute that at first, I'm not sure anything is happening. But as loud, tremulous blasts echo from the underside of the city, where the propulsion engines sit, my spark of hope fans into a full-on flame.

Another minute and the city levels out, hovering a hell of a lot closer to the ground than it previously did, but no longer in freefall.

"He did it," Mica whispers, awe in his voice, on his face. "He really did it."

"Go back, Charlie!" I yell, and though she sneers at the command—and the fact that I'm the one issuing it—we're back inside the dome moments later. The atmosphere in the shuttle is charged with wild elation, as are the streets below us as stranded citizens realize what's happened. Cheers erupt from every direction, and despite the wreckage surrounding us, I can't help but smile at the impossibility of what my father, Auron Rhodon, Tribunal Commander and Underground Agent, just achieved.

But the elation is short-lived.

As we approach City Hall and prepare to land so we can join my father, to assist him, to retrieve him, a final quake rips through the city. A crater opens up in the ground in front of the building, ripping the street in half before turning its sights on City Hall itself.

Time slows to a crawl and my cry is lost to the wind as I try to launch myself out of the half-open shuttle hatch, desperate to do something, to get to my father who's still somewhere inside.

I hit a wall of solid air instead.

Someone's FX holds me back, even as I claw at the invisible barrier until my fingers are bleeding. I'm helpless to do anything but watch as the ground splinters, as fissures spread in all directions. As giant, horrifying cracks race up the walls of the building. As the structure strains, like its very bones are being hewn apart.

And, finally, as the building collapses in on itself with a burst of sparks, leaving behind a plume of dust . . . and an irreparable silence.

THIRTY-SIX

I'M YANKED from the darkness. I blink my eyes open—once, twice—but the world around me is a blur of unfamiliar shapes and colors. White. White, I recognize. White, I know. The ceiling I'm staring up at from my prone position is white.

Panic grips me as I try to sit up, only for a wave of dizziness to force me back down. Dizziness, but not pain. I graze my fingers over my abdomen and a startled sound escapes me as I realize that underneath the gauzy clothing I've been dressed in, there's no sign of my injury. Not a scab, not a scar—not even the faint *memory* of pain, like the ghost of the healed gunshot wound in my thigh. Nothing on my stomach, and nothing on my hand, either. On *either side* of my hands. The place where Wolfe stabbed me and both of my palms are smooth and free of scars.

I suck down a shocked breath, noting idly that there's something different about the air. It tastes . . . sterile. Almost tart.

Where am I?

I comb through the shadowy tangle of thoughts and memories in my mind. The last thing I remember is seeing City Hall collapse with my father inside . . . and the crushing grief that followed.

My eyes immediately start to prick with tears, but I refuse to let them spill over—to let myself fall apart. There will probably be time for that later. For now, there are things I need to figure out. Where I am, where everyone went, and what the hell is happening, to start.

Gradually, my surroundings come into focus. In addition to the white ceiling, I find myself in a room with equally stark white walls. No window. One door. Stark, cold light beams down from a translucent panel in the center of the ceiling, and the faint hum of machinery fills the air.

I follow the humming sound to a monitor positioned next to me, then my eyes wander down the wires that extend from it to the pads on my clavicle, my temple, my wrist. My first instinct is to snatch them all from my skin, but a gentle voice breaks through the haze of my thoughts before I do anything.

"Terra?"

Mica's voice is soft, hesitant. Finally feeling clear-headed enough to be able to prop myself up on my elbows, I find Mica sitting in a chair at the foot of my bed, a stack of comics piled on a small table next to him. Immediately, my racing pulse slows to a steady beat, the sight of him filling me with relief. Wherever we are, it can't be that bad if he's here with me.

"Where are we?" I ask, my voice hoarse from disuse.

"After we lost . . ." He takes a moment, like he's composing himself. "After the building collapsed, you did too. Altara stopped falling but the city was wrecked. Adam was still super injured. We didn't know if we could . . . Tom thought it would be best if we just . . ."

"Spit it out, Mic."

"We're in Dissidia," he says, and my ensuing shock ejects all other thoughts from my mind. Only that one word remains: *Dissidia.* Adam's home. The original converted skycity.

"We're . . . in space?" I manage to eke out. Irritation flares inside at the realization that I'm finding myself floored by yet another mind-blowing turn of events. I really did think things would stop shocking me, I swear.

Mica nods, drawing himself forward to prop a pillow behind my back as I struggle to sit up further.

"How long have I been out?" I ask, biting back the "this time" that's on the tip of my tongue, because while I'm more than aware of the comical number of times I've now awoken in an unknown place after an unknown amount of time, Mica isn't. And he doesn't need to be brought up to speed on just how much of a joke his big sister is at this point.

"Couple days," Mica says. "You woke up a few times, but maybe you don't remember since they had to . . ."

"Had to what?" I ask, dread spiking in my veins.

"Sedate you," he says with a deep sigh. My panic fizzles out as I take in the palpable exhaustion leaking from him—his red-rimmed eyes, the concern carved into every crevice of his face. "You . . . weren't in a good place. Screaming, crying . . . and then out cold. They weren't sure why. Luke said your injuries weren't bad enough for you to pass out like that in the first place, but after D-Dad"—he stumbles over the word and my heart clenches—"you just . . . It was like everything caught up to you all at once."

Words fail me for a few seconds as I absorb what he's saying. "I'm sorry, Mic. I . . . I don't know what to say."

"I'm just glad you're back," he says, and I can tell he's trying to keep his tone light. "You scared me, sis. Adam said that you have nightmares sometimes, and that—"

"Adam's okay?" I ask, alarm lancing through me as I recall how close I'd been to losing him. How pale he was, how weak. Alarm and . . . guilt. Because I almost left him behind.

"He's stable." Mica's eyes flicker with a mixture of relief and sorrow as he takes my hand. "Tom and Luke are with him. I won't lie to you, it was close. But this place . . . They have the most incredible tech here, Terra. Even you would be impressed." The wonder dawning on his face is so pure, I almost smile. But I don't, because there's one more person I need to ask about.

"And Dad?" I whisper. I know the answer—I knew it the second I saw that building come down. But something in me needs to hear it confirmed.

My brother's face crumbles, and he shakes his head. "He's gone."

The way his voice breaks should've sent my tears tumbling, but they stay in, my eyes burning. "Why didn't you tell me about him?"

Mica's grip on my hand tightens, but it doesn't feel like a gesture of support. Not for me, at least. "I was going to," he says. "I was always going to. But he said . . . he said he had so much to make up for. He wanted the opportunity to tell you himself and . . . you were so angry. Always so angry with him."

"I had every right to be angry!" I exclaim. "And you did too. Frankly, I always thought you should've been way more pissed than you ever were."

"You did have every right. And maybe I did too," Mica says, a pensive expression crossing his face. "But from the minute I saw him—he met me at the station when I arrived, you know—I just . . . I don't know how to explain it. I trusted him."

I bite my lip but don't interrupt again.

"I wasn't sure how you would react to knowing he was here. I thought it might make you act . . . rashly." He releases my hand like he's giving me room to process.

I snort. "Who, me? Rash?"

The corners of Mica's mouth curve up with the hint of a grin, but it's gone a second later. "I didn't want you to jeopardize yourself, and once I realized he *was* trustworthy and that he was working toward the same things we wanted, I didn't want you to jeopardize that, either."

"You could have told me about all of it—his reasons for leaving, working with the Underground, everything."

"Even if I felt like I could get that kind of seriously scary-dangerous information to you safely, can you honestly say you would have believed me?" Mica counters.

"You really thought I hated him more than I trust you?"

Mica says nothing and guilt stabs through me.

"In the end, I . . . I don't think I actually hated him at all, you know?"

"I know," my brother says quietly. "He knew too."

The truth in that statement is the final wave that sends the tears streaming from my eyes. I let them fall, rivulets carving paths down my cheeks as I mourn the father I never really knew—never got the chance to know. The man who deceived and lied and, yes, abandoned—but for none of the reasons I thought. The man who sacrificed his past to try to safeguard his children's future. And I mourn the girl I was when he made the choices he did. The girl born of hatred and contempt for the life I thought I was owed. Because that girl doesn't exist anymore, either.

A soft knock on the door interrupts us, and we look up to see Tom standing in the doorway. "May I come in?" he asks.

I wipe at my cheeks as if it'll stop the stream of tears still falling from my eyes. "Sure. Just ignore this," I say, gesturing to my face. "I'm not sure how to get it to stop."

Tom smiles and it transforms his face into a near-perfect match of his brother's. Between the kind expression and the swirling cerulean eyes that so closely match Adam's, it steals my breath. "How are you feeling?" he asks.

"Physically? I feel pretty amazing, all things considered. A little dizzy, maybe."

"You are probably still a bit dehydrated, but I'm glad to hear that you're feeling otherwise well. How about, er, non-physically?"

That feels like a loaded question, if I've ever heard one, I think, unsure of how to even begin answering it. Eventually, I settle on, "I'm . . . managing." Then add, "Thank you for saving me—saving us."

The tiniest flash of something crosses Tom's face, and his countenance shifts. He's still smiling, but it no longer reaches his eyes. "Please. I'm the one who is long overdue to express *my* thanks. As well as my sincere apologies. You saved my life the day we escaped Korbyllis, Terra. You saved my brother in more ways than one. I made a bad call—several, really, when it came to you—and I'm sorry."

The lump that's suddenly formed in my throat makes it impossible to respond to Tom's unexpected confession, so I just nod.

"Adam asked us to let him know as soon as you were awake," Tom says after a moment. "Do you feel up to seeing him?"

"Yes," I say immediately, swinging my legs over the side of the bed so hastily that Mica doesn't have time to extricate himself before I've crushed his wrist under my knee. Tom chuckles as Mica swears under his breath, but a moment later, they're both helping me stand on shaky legs.

MICA and I follow Tom down a long hallway, my eyes darting around as I take in the architecture of the building we're in—a hospital or clinic, if I were to guess. The walls are pristine, the air smells of antiseptic, and that faint machine-like hum is ever-present. I do my best to take it all in despite how disoriented I am—not by my dizziness or wobbly legs, but by the sheer fact that I'm here.

Dissidia.

Despite hearing about Adam and Luke's experiences here firsthand, despite learning about its history and seeing proof of it in Intheria, in some ways, this place still seemed like a fairy tale.

Tom stops before a set of double doors at the end of the hallway. "He's in here," he says, pushing the door open. Inside, the room is brightly lit. The sun streams in from a large window and illuminates Adam's form as he peers out of it.

For a moment, I just relish his presence—the fact that he's alive, that he's truly standing here. His hair has been returned to its natural sunlit blond, and for the first time, I think of checking my own. Whoever's been attending to me has woven it into a loose braid, and when I draw it over my shoulder, my original dark brown strands appear.

"Figures you get a window," I say.

Adam turns toward my voice and the smile that breaks out across his face is the best thing I've seen in a long, long time. It is, perhaps, a little weaker than I'm used to, but there's no denying the joy that flows from him as he looks at me. "Hey there, Sunburst."

"Hey yourself," I reply, moving to his side and taking his hand. His skin is warm, and I can feel the strong beat of his pulse as I run my fingers across the underside of his wrist. "You're okay?"

"Better now," he says earnestly, those cerulean eyes simmering with emotion as he looks me over.

Remorse crawls up from my gut as I remember the words we'd exchanged when we'd both thought he was a goner. "I'm so sorry," I blurt. "I thought I was losing you. I thought you were . . ." I trail off, twisting my braid between the fingers of my free hand.

"There's nothing to apologize for, Sunburst," he says as he lifts his own hand to my brown ends, and I breathe out the anxiety I'd been holding thinking he might be upset at me almost leaving him. "Hope it's okay about the hair, by the way," he adds. "Mica and I thought that you might prefer a bit of normalcy when you woke up."

"Definitely okay. Not that anything about any of this is normal. I like the idea of you seeing, well, me, when you look at me."

"I always see you," he says, and when he squeezes my hand it feels like he's squeezing life back into me too.

"I was so scared, Adam," I admit.

His eyes soften, and he moves his hand from my braid to touch my cheek. "I know, Sunburst. I can't say I was feeling my bravest at that moment either, if I'm being totally honest. But I'm not going anywhere. Not if I can help it."

I have a sudden need for physical acknowledgment that he's here, that I'm here, that we both survived. I wrap my arms around the column of his chest, locking them tightly behind his back in a crushing embrace, and gaze up at him through my lashes. My head tips back in silent invitation. Adam's eyes flare with heat, and a moment later, his lips are on mine.

A cough sounds from behind us, and I remember that we aren't alone. I fight the urge to bury my face in Adam's shirt, embarrassment shining from my rosy cheeks as I turn my head to find Tom and Mica awkwardly standing in the doorway, averting their eyes.

"All good, Tommy?" Adam says, one side of his mouth curving up into my favorite lopsided grin. He turns me in his arms, my back to his chest and his hands wrapped around my waist as we face our brothers.

Tom nods. "How're you faring after the procedure? Headache still bothering you?"

Adam's grip on me tightens and irritation flashes over his face when I peer over my shoulder to look at him. "It's fine now," he says, his tone surprisingly curt.

"You let someone know if it comes back, okay? RX should have taken full effect by now, so that shouldn't be an issue any longer.

I whip my head back to Tom. "RX? What?"

My whole body moves against Adam's as he takes an enormous breath. "They reactivated my advancements to help me heal," he says.

"An infection was setting in—there was only so much we could do without . . . internal assistance," Tom adds.

"Just RX though, right?" I ask Adam.

A muscle ticks in his jaw. "It doesn't work that way, unfortunately."

"So you're telekinetic again?" Mica asks.

Adam nods. "And the rest," he confirms to me without having to ask. His NX is active again. I glance at Tom, who is looking contritely at the floor.

I wring my hands together, anxious at the thought of Adam being subject to the whims of his superiors again, his free will compromised. And after what he went through and risked by having Luke turn off his advancements too. My smooth palms rub over one another and a frightening thought crosses my mind.

"I didn't—You didn't—They didn't—" I stammer, a flurry of movement as I shove my palms in Adam's face, grab at my side where a scar should be, and gesture to my head.

Blessedly, it doesn't take Adam long to pick up on what I'm plainly freaking out about. "No, Sunburst," he says, his steady voice a calming force. "No advancements messing with that gorgeous mind of yours."

"Nobody's going to *nix* him, Terra," Tom says, though my skepticism must be written across my face because he is quick to add, "It was a condition of his agreeing to help."

Another whip of my head, because I'm not quite sure which brother I'm speaking to when I ask, "Help with what?"

Before either of them has the chance to answer, we are interrupted by the soft chime of a communication device. Tom pulls it from his pocket, a serious expression on his face when he lifts his gaze back to us.

"It's time," he says solemnly. "She's summoning us."

"She?" I ask, my eyes narrowing.

"Admiral Meers," Adam says, and I can't read the emotion in his tone. "Dissidian leadership. She's a big deal around here—"

"The biggest deal," Tom interrupts. "But meeting her is a good thing. It means she's open to hearing what you have to say."

"What I have to say about what?" I step forward. "I'm confused."

"Communications with the Tribunal have gone somewhat poorly," Tom says.

Someone snorts from the hallway. "If that's not the understatement of the century," Luke says, popping his head into the open door frame. "Your Prime Whitlock is a real piece of sh—"

"—work," Tom says quickly, looking at Mica. "A real piece of work, yes."

A laugh bursts from my lips. "She's not *my* anything. Unless we're calling her 'the bane of *my* existence.' And please don't feel you have to watch your language on his account," I say. "I think I stopped caring right around the fourth life-altering revelation. Or was it the fifth? Turns out, once you've lived through multiple shitstorms, your affinity for a well-placed curse word or ten goes up."

"Way the fuck up," Mica mutters, and laughter fills the room. Even Tom cracks a grin.

"Fair enough," he says with a chuckle. "Anyway, the Admiral wants to see you because our understanding is that you might have been privy to information from Prime Whitlock regarding their intentions toward us."

I look back at Adam, my brows furrowed in question. "I told them we overheard her speaking with your father, but that I wouldn't relay what we heard until I'd had a chance to talk to you," he says.

I loose a wobbly breath. "Okay. Well, if it's between helping the Dissidians and helping Prime Shitlock"—I shoot a grin at Mica and he beams—"then I think it's pretty obvious what I'm going to do."

Tom nods approvingly. "Let's go meet with her and Vice-Admiral Conroy, then."

At that, Luke groans. "Conroy's going to be there too? Shit."

"What's wrong with the Vice-Admiral?" Mica asks.

"Like I said, the Admiral is a good person to have in charge. She's tough but fair. Conroy is . . ." Tom trails off, like he's searching for the right way to put it. "Less understanding," he says after a moment.

"A douche," Luke says at the same time. Mica laughs.

Adam steps forward so he's at my side, his arm pressing into mine. "I'm with you, Sunburst."

I swallow, steeling myself as I exchange a look with Mica. He's chewing on his bottom lip with obvious nerves, but offers me a nod.

"Always," I say, and I follow Tom out of the room.

THIRTY-SEVEN

IT FEELS like it takes an eternity to travel to the location where we're to meet with Admiral Meers and Vice-Admiral Conroy. Part of me wonders if Adam hasn't instructed Tom to drive us down the scenic route, and I'm glad for it because this place is incredible.

If I could take everything that had me awestruck from the moment Adam swept me into the biodome underneath The District, and multiply it by the things that blew my mind when I was first brought to Korbyllis, and then double—triple, quadruple—it, maybe I would start to get close to explaining what Dissidia is like.

The city is smaller than Korbyllis, Altara, or even Intheria, but the buildings are things of beauty. Skyscrapers made from gleaming sheets of metal tower above us, vibrant greenery spilling down the sides from lush vertical gardens. There are sleek wind turbines constructed to both create and harness the artificial breeze that wafts across my skin. And as Tom drives us along, we pass underneath transparent, elevated walkways that crisscross the city.

Thin brown tree trunks topped with huge leafy fronds line every side-walk and dot the grassy divider running through the middle of each street. We slow to a stop at an intersection and I relish the feel of the sun streaming down from above, warming my skin. I know from my time in the biodome that it's not real sunlight, not exactly. Just like the endless sky stretching above us is not, in fact, so endless. If I look up and squint, I can recognize some of the same signs of artifice that the biodome utilizes to create its gorgeous, seemingly infinite sky. But to think that on the other side of this encapsulation dome is not the District's subway system, but *space* . . . I don't know how to wrap my head around the wild thought. This is so much more than I ever thought I'd see, and it's like I've set foot in an impossible dream.

Paradise, the small voice in my mind says as we round a corner and I catch sight of a pristine, shimmering canal curving through the city. It's lined with more translucent walkways—bridges—across which citizens stroll at a leisurely pace. They chat pleasantly with one another, unencumbered by whatever might be going on between warring peoples on another planet. Unbothered by the fact that they're heading there right now.

A pang of envy rips through me, though it's not the same feeling I had when I witnessed the haughty, debauched delight on the faces of the citizens of Korbyllis as they partied in the streets. No, I'm envious because these Dissidians just seem so at ease, so . . . safe.

Home, the voice says. And I can't explain it, but as I glance at Mica and the look of absolute rapture on his face, as I clutch Adam's hand in my lap, I know it to be true.

Finally, we pull up to a large silver gate, behind which a long driveway extends. A surge of fear grips me as I take in the palatial mansion perched at the end, flashing back when I was brought to a near-identical building in Korbyllis. Reason tells me that it is logical that the architecture within all skycities would resemble one another, and Dissidia was, in fact, a skycity, once. Adam squeezes my hand like he knows what I'm thinking as the gates open and Tom drives us up the winding path.

We exit the vehicle and stride right into the building, with Tom flashing his badge here and there and he, Luke, and Adam levying the occasional salute at passersby. Tom leads us down a hall, into an elevator, and down another hallway to a set of large, imposing doors. He takes a deep breath before pushing them open. The five of us step into a spacious room, dominated by a huge circular table in the center with a holographic display rotating on top. A closer look has me realizing we're seeing the same holographic schematics of Korbyllis that Adam and I recovered from Intheria.

At the far side of the table stands Admiral Meers in all her imposing glory. Adam, Luke, and Tom fall into a synchronized salute—*snap, clap, drop*—the moment they cross the threshold. I watch with fascination as the Admiral and Vice-Admiral, who is standing beside her, offer a simplified version in response before taking their seats. Tall and statuesque, the Admiral has coppery-blond hair pulled tight in a bun, while the man to her right is bald with thick, dark eyebrows that frame even darker eyes.

Admiral Meers sweeps her violet eyes over us and I swallow as they linger on me for several agonizing seconds. "Welcome," she says, her cool and authoritative voice finally breaking the intense silence. "Please, have a seat."

I belatedly realize that Meers and Conroy are not the only ones in here with us, and offer a weak wave to Charlie as she takes a seat next to the Admiral. Then I do a double-take as violet eyes as vibrant as the Admiral's narrow as they look me over.

Exactly as vibrant.

I glance at Adam, my eyes wide with the question, and he gives me a knowing nod. Charlie is the Admiral's daughter. Huh.

We take seats directly across from the Admiral and Vice-Admiral, Korbyllis a glittering ghost as it rotates between us. With a flick of her wrist, Admiral Meers makes the hologram disappear, leaving my mouth slightly agape as she addresses me.

"Thank you for coming so quickly," she says, clasping her hands on the table in front of her. "I understand you've only just awoken, so I do appreciate you responding with such haste. I did not want to delay any longer than necessary, given the important information I've come to under—"

"Why do you have the Korbyllis schematics that Adam and I recovered?" I blurt out, surprising myself, but surprising everyone else at the table more, judging by their reactions. Tom looks horrified, Mica seems confused, and Charlie rolls her eyes while Luke's are lit up like he's about to witness something truly gossipworthy. Adam's expression is one of vague amusement, and to her credit, the Admiral seems to share the sentiment. I relax infinitesimally.

"You do not interrupt the Admiral," Vice-Admiral Conroy admonishes in a booming baritone. The disdain on his face is veiled so thinly that I wonder why he bothers trying to hide it at all.

"Sorry," I mutter, my cheeks going red.

Admiral Meers waves her hand again, not to *fix* anything this time, but to dismiss Conroy's command. "Don't mind the XO," she says, a kind smile on her face. I catch Luke's eye across the table, and he mouths "Executive Officer" without me having to ask. I flash him a grateful smile.

"He forgets that you are not a member of the Dissidian military and unaccustomed to the way things typically go around here," the Admiral continues, inclining her head toward me before addressing Conroy directly. "Miss Rhodon may speak freely."

The XO-slash-Vice-Admiral-slash-asshat sits back in his chair with a huff and narrows his eyes on me, but doesn't say anything else.

"To answer your question, Miss Rhodon—"

"Terra, please," I say, and this time Tom audibly gasps at my interruption.

Admiral Meers chuckles lightly. "All right, Terra, then. You're quite observant to have realized that the schematics we were just viewing are indeed the same ones that you and Ensign Killian retrieved from the Intheria crash site. Lieutenant Prynn executed an agreement with the Underground Order on the groundworld, and they permitted us to examine all of their—well, your, I suppose—findings."

"*Prynn?*" I mouth at Luke, who shrugs and shoots a grin back at me.

"Which is quite a perfect segue to the matter at hand, and why I wanted to speak with you."

"You want to know what I overheard Prime Whitlock telling my father," I say.

"Just so," Admiral Meers replies. "It is my understanding that you have been privy to some potentially crucial information, and I would be very"—she clears her throat—"grateful if you would share it with us." I don't miss the way her violet eyes dart over to Adam, who has schooled his face into a neutral expression. Is that irritation I sense in her? Perhaps she's annoyed that she can't compel the information from Adam directly. I suppose it's a good sign that they're holding to their word not to *nix* him.

"Yes, Admiral. I did overhear Prime Whitlock discussing the Tribunal's plans with my father. I don't know how much you've been told about him, but . . ." I trail off, not wanting to make it seem like my father was party to Whitlock's heinous plans.

"I am up-to-date on the role your father has played," the Admiral says, and at first, I'm not clear if she's being critical or understanding. "I understand he made many sacrifices in order to help the Underground movement, including the ultimate one. He saved many lives when he stopped Altara's fall. I'm sorry for your loss."

I take a deep breath, attempting to banish the tears pooling threateningly in my eyes. "Thank you, Admiral. I . . . I'm still not sure it's fully sunk in. But he did work for years to try and undermine the Tribunal's plans as best he could. Some of those plans, Adam and I were able to overhear from the closet."

The Admiral's brows shoot up. "The closet?" she repeats, the corners of her mouth quirking up.

"Well, yeah. We had to stuff ourselves in there when we realized someone was coming into his office. Which is where we had hidden so that we wouldn't be seen by someone else in the hallway. Honestly, it's all just one big coincidence that we overheard anything at all."

Stop babbling, dummy, I mentally berate myself.

Out of the corner of my eye, I can see Tom shaking his head.

"Anyway," I say, drawing another breath to steady myself. "Whitlock talked about some, er, negotiations you entered with them. How they fell apart. She has issued commands to mobilize the Tribunal's military forces. She said . . ." I pause, chewing on the inside of my lip for a moment. "She said that they intend on taking you on by force so she can get her hands on the technology they need to replicate Dissidia's conversion."

"Sadly, this is not surprising. Their demands for access to our technology have been by no means unclear," Admiral Meers says. "But I will never allow them to get their hands on even the smallest scrap. Not after what they've done." She glances at Charlie, a fierce protectiveness gleaming in her eyes, and the back of my throat tightens at the display of motherly wrath. "They say they only want conversion tech, but I'm not fool enough to think they'd stop at that. They already know about FX.

What happens when they find out about our . . . other advancement capabilities?"

My blood freezes in my veins as my mind leaps to a scenario where the Tribunal has the ability to force NX on people—on everyone. To *nix* dissidents, to control the words and actions of their own people. Prime Whitlock could have the entire world in her talons with a few simple commands.

"So then, you are prepared to go to war with the Tribunal," Mica says, his voice quiet but enough to break me from the hellscape I was imagining. I wonder if he made friends during the weeks he spent at the Academy, if he's thinking of them. Prime Whitlock seemed all too ready to throw her youngest and most vulnerable soldiers right into the fray.

"We are. If that is what they intend to bring to us," Admiral Meers confirms, though it's clear she takes no pleasure in it.

Vice-Admiral Conroy, on the other hand, seems less opposed to the idea. "Typical human behavior," he scoffs, crossing his arms. "Destruction, chaos, and war seem to be all you're capable of." He turns to Admiral Meers. "We have more than enough firepower to eradicate the Tribunal's forces. They want a war with us? Let them start one. We'll be the ones to finish it. They won't have any reason to come after our tech and our knowledge if their precious skycities have been blasted from the sky."

Adam bristles beside me, and my own urge to leap across the table and smack some sense into this bald-headed jerk is strong, but somehow I manage to hold back. "I can't necessarily disagree with you that humanity's legacy is not much to be proud of thus far," I say, more calmly than I thought myself capable. "After all, the Tribunal would rather have another Skyfall on their hands than ground the skycities. They almost succeeded in doing as much with Altara, and stopping it cost my father his life."

Conroy's face softens slightly, though his arms remain crossed and his body tense.

"But surely you cannot think that a few bad people making bad choices is worth condemning hundreds of thousands—millions, even— over. To punish an entire people over the actions of a few? That kind of logic is awfully close to Prime Whitlock's," I finish.

"And there are plenty of good, decent humans who would never agree with the Tribunal's plans if they knew about them," Adam adds.

"Your perspective is skewed, Ensign," Conroy sneers. "Your relationship with this girl has compromised your impartiality. Of course you would say that."

Adam opens his mouth to refute Conroy's claims, but it's Charlie, to my utter surprise, who answers first. "Don't be stupid, *sir*," she says, and Tom sucks in a stunned breath through his nostrils. I guess nepotism is a universal beast, though, because Conroy doesn't fly off the handle at what even I know to be a clear impertinence. Being the Admiral's daughter must have its perks.

"Adam may have a . . . vested interest . . . here," Charlie continues, "but he isn't the only one who's seen firsthand the strength and resilience of these people." She looks me up and down again, but the usual air of pretension is missing. If I didn't know better, I'd almost think she's looking at me with respect.

Conroy huffs, but Admiral Meers seems to consider Charlie's words. "You make a valid point, Charlotte. As does Ensign Killian—the people do not know about the plans the Tribunal has, nor do they know about the true bloody history of their own world. Maybe it's time they did. If the Tribunal wants to wage war on us, the least we can do is open the eyes of their citizens. So they know exactly what they're being dragged into—and why."

Hope flickers inside me at her words. "If you've already been communicating with the UO, then you know that what we found in Intheria goes beyond some skycity schematics. We found proof of the origins of the plague, of the fact that the skycities themselves are keeping the planet from healing. I know there are plenty of selfish people out there who might not care enough, who might back Whitlock's conversion plan because the idea of slumming it with us terrestrials on the groundworld is just *that* abhorrent. But I have to believe there would be more who would not be okay with sacrificing our lives for their comfort. People like my father."

"And he wasn't the only skydwelling member of the UO by far," Luke confirms. "There are more undercover agents and informants sympathetic to the cause, they just haven't been able to recruit on a larger scale."

"Why not?" Admiral Meers asks, genuine curiosity lighting her face as Conroy grumbles beside her.

"Lack of proof, of course," Luke answers, "which is no longer an issue. The ability to get their message out en masse is, however."

"We could help with that," Charlie suggests, and that flicker of hope inside me flares into a dazzling beacon as I turn my gaze back to her mother.

Admiral Meers takes a minute to ponder everything we've shared. "Lieutenant Prynn, connect with our UO allies"—my heart leaps at hearing the word, even as Conroy visibly seethes—"and inform them of our willingness to assist. Set up a time and location to meet once we arrive on planet. Unfortunately, I do not believe that war can be avoided, but we will do everything we can to ensure civilians are kept out of the crossfire and reveal to the Tribunal's troops the truths they are sorely lacking." She turns to Tom. "Captain, ensure that battle preparations are underway. We need our soldiers to be ready at a moment's notice."

With a quick salute to their superiors, Tom and Luke exit the room. The Admiral glances at Mica, and I offer an encouraging nod before he skips off after them. Adam's hand finds its way to mine under the table as if to support me against the Admiral's violet-eyed focus.

"You truly believe the planet can be healed if we ground the skycities?" she asks me, and I'm momentarily floored at the vulnerability in her voice. "That there is some potential future where all of us—Dissidian, skydweller, terrestrial alike—can live in harmony?"

I bite my lip. "I don't know," I admit, "but I hope there is." I draw Adam's and my hands, our fingers intertwined, onto the top of the table. "I *have* to hope there is."

A gentle smile appears on the Admiral's mouth, even as Conroy's gaze narrows on our linked hands, and she nods, dismissing us.

"Perhaps we regular old humans are not simply creatures of chaos after all, hmm?" I say, my body turned toward Adam but my words meant for Vice-Admiral Conroy and the aura of distaste currently oozing from him. The disgruntled exhale I hear tells me he heard loud and clear, and I smirk inwardly as Adam and I rise from our seats.

"I suppose it's a good thing you two have formed such a strong attachment to one another, all things considered," Conroy's voice cuts through the room, something sharp in his tone that has me stopping before we reach the door.

"All things considered?" I say, my curiosity piqued despite the knot forming in my stomach.

"Considering the most pressing issue on *our* side of this war," he says, his voice dripping with condescension.

"Vincent," Admiral Meers warns, but Conroy barrels on, undeterred.

"Personally, I'll be fascinated to see how long it takes for a little half-terrestrial, half-Dissidian baby to be toddling up and down these halls." He purses his lips as he makes a show of looking me over. "There isn't already one on the way, is there?"

"*Excuse* me?" I roar.

Every muscle in Adam's body tenses, like he's preparing to fight Conroy. And maybe he would, were it not for the death-grip I'm currently exerting on his hand.

Conroy only leans back in his chair and crosses his arms over his chest again. "You didn't think that all of this—our decision to ally with the UO, to help you, to return to Earth in the first place—was solely altruistic, did you?"

"What is he talking about?" Adam asks the Admiral, whose expression flickers with something like discomfort. Or is it guilt?

"You are already aware of our population challenges," she says after a beat, her voice returning to the cool, authoritative one she initially greeted us with. "And the control measures we had to put in place."

"Yes, and I've explained them to Terra too. But what does that have to do with—"

"They worked too well," Conroy interjects, and suddenly the tight grip I have on Adam's hand is the only thing keeping me from slapping the smug expression right off his face. "Even after reversing the population control advancements, fertility issues have become . . . rampant."

I recall what Adam told me about how rare it is that Tom and he are natural-born brothers. How far Tom has been able to climb in the ranks despite his young age. "You tried to curb overpopulation, and instead created the opposite problem for yourselves," I say tightly.

"Just so. Our birth rates are in the negative," Admiral Meers says, and Conroy's eyes gleam with a cruel satisfaction as he sees the weight of this sinking in. "But," she continues, shooting a warning look at Conroy, "it's not *your* problem."

"How can you say that, Admiral? Combining Dissidian and terrestrial DNA could very well be the answer to *all* of our problems." Conroy turns to face Admiral Meers and juts his thumb in my direction, like I'm no longer a participant in this conversation. "She's even got some skydweller in her, from what I understand. Their progeny could be the literal embodiment of this *harmonic future* you seek. And they've already made an emotional connection. She's the perfect subject for this."

"Do I get a fucking say?" I shout through gritted teeth. Even Charlie, who has remained silent this whole time, balks at my tone.

The room falls into a stunned silence. My heart pounds in my eyes, outrage and humiliation rolling through me. Adam's face is a mask of fury, his eyes blazing with indignation.

"How dare you," I say, my voice shaking, though not from fear. It's from trying to keep my rage contained. *"How dare you.* I am not some test subject. You don't get to manipulate me into agreeing to some insane experiment so you can play around with my goddamn DNA."

"When it comes to our survival, I assure you, nobody is playing," Conroy says dismissively.

"You and Prime Whitlock really would get along," Charlie mutters, and Conroy whirls toward her with a sneer set on his face.

"That's enough," Admiral Meers finally speaks, her voice firm.

Conroy smirks. "Thank you, Admiral, I—"

"No. That's enough from *you,* Vincent. Terra is a valued ally, not an experiment. I can't believe I even have to say this, but her relationship with Ensign Killian is between the two of them alone. I have always valued your input, and so I have been lenient thus far. But not only are these issues that do not belong on the shoulders of this young woman, but they are ones that we should not be discussing *at all,* let alone here." The cold turn in her voice makes me think—not without a fair amount of glee—that their conversation is far from over.

Conroy's sneer fades, and I think I catch the slightest flash of fear before he dons a mask of indifference. "Of course, Admiral. My apologies," he says, not sounding apologetic in the slightest.

Admiral Meers turns back to Adam and me, her eyes softening. "I apologize, as well. Please understand that nobody holds you accountable for anything happening in Dissidia. Any issues we may be facing are currently secondary to the more pressing ones at hand. The ones impacting *your* home."

Home, that little voice in my mind echoes, and I clench my jaw. Because I do already feel a kinship with this place, like I might very well already belong, and that their problems *are* my problems. Not that I'm willing to pop out a bunch of kids for them, but I still want to help. There's no way in hell I'm letting Conroy know that at this point, though, so I simply issue a terse nod.

"Harmony clearly means different things to different people," I say, shooting a final cutting glare at Conroy. "But I think you and I are at least aligned in what it means for our future. For the future of the planet, and *all* its people."

I turn and tug Adam out of the room, not waiting to be dismissed again. The doors close behind us and I nearly collapse into him with the force of my exhale. I meet Adam's gaze as he stares at me like I'm the most extraordinary thing he's ever seen, and it immediately has heat building in my cheeks . . . and elsewhere.

"Let's go," he says. "We have a lot to figure out."

I pop up onto my tiptoes and plant a soft kiss on his lips. "We do. But we'll do it together."

THIRTY-EIGHT

I THOUGHT we'd head back to the hospital building where I'd woken up, but Adam leads me to a tall apartment complex within walking distance from City Hall. Greenery frames the entrance doors as he ushers me inside, then into a glass elevator that shoots us twelve stories high.

"This is where you live?" I ask as I take in his modest apartment. It's not the apartment itself that is leaving me incredulous, but just the fact that this place exists. Another reminder that Adam had a home and a life here. That it's real. That he's *real*.

"Tom and I live here together. I wish I had more privacy for you, but as you already know, living space in Dissidia is a bit of a limited resource right now."

The apartment is clean, tidy, and relatively bare, as I suppose I would have expected. A beige couch faces a wall that houses a built-in viewscreen, with a small kitchenette and dining table on the other side. Past that, there's a short hallway with a couple of doors on one end. Nothing particularly exciting, nothing that should scream *Adam* at first glance. But I still feel him in every part of this space.

"How long has it been since you've been home?" I ask, knowing the general answer already, but at a loss for how to process this place otherwise.

Adam takes a moment before answering. "Six months, give or take?"

I swallow. "And how does it feel to be home?"

"Somehow, like it's never felt more and less like home at all," he says with a smile, and something warm bubbles up into my chest.

"I know what you mean," I reply, stepping further into the apartment. I stop to look at a digital picture frame that's hung at the entrance of the hallway, mesmerized by the photos rotating in and out of view. Tom and Adam as kids, arms slung over each other's shoulders. Then one with Luke and Charlie joining them, all of them a few years older, clustered together in school uniforms like they're celebrating a graduation or some other milestone. The next photo is of a group of four as well, but Luke and Charlie have been replaced by two adults. A woman with golden hair pulled back in a low bun smiles down at the two boys as a man with gleaming cerulean eyes grins at the camera.

"Your parents?" I ask. Another thing I never really bothered thinking about too much, and guilt gnaws at me. Was I really so damaged by my own parental history that I never even thought about the people who raised Adam?

"That's them," Adam says lightly, like he's not quite sure how to formulate his response.

"Where are they?" I plant a reassuring smile on my face and Adam visibly relaxes.

"Oh, they're around. Not active military any longer, so they live in a complex across the city. Dad's a security consultant and Mom works at the hospital, actually. You'll meet them sometime. If you want," he adds hastily, and his thoughtfulness has that warm feeling inside me blooming.

"I want," I say, and Adam's answering grin is so broad, so endearing, I want to kiss him.

So, I do.

It's short and sweet and heartbreakingly normal.

I could get used to this.

"Tom's room is over there," he says, pulling back for a moment so he can point down the hall. "And the couch pulls out into a bed where Mica can sleep. That is—I mean—I don't want to be presumptuous, but—Just saying, if you're good with . . ." He trails off, his eyes darting to the door next to Tom's, which I assume is his own bedroom.

Laughing, I prance down the hall and right through the door he indicated, too giddy to contain my excitement even after the harrowing meeting we just endured. "You mean we won't be sleeping on the floor of a storage trailer, or in a dusty old observatory? We're not going to be chained up or tied up or plastered with little wires that connect us to monitors? This is a dream come true." I flounce onto the bed, disrupting the neatly made covers.

I squeal as Adam comes bounding in after me, pouncing and pinning me to the bed. "I think I know a little something about dreams coming true," he says, nuzzling my neck.

"That was cheesy." I sigh contentedly and wrap my arms around him. "Do it again."

He laughs into my collarbone, his breath sending goosebumps across my skin. "You really want more cheese?" he teases, his fingers tracing delicate patterns on my upper arm.

"Give me your absolute worst."

He lifts his head until his face is hovering over mine, his lips a hairsbreadth away from my own. "You are the sun in my sky and the moon in my night," he murmurs.

"Not bad," I say with a chuckle. "But I think you can do better."

He smiles back. "How about . . . My heart beats for you. Your voice is a melody that I never want to stop hearing," he whispers.

"Okay, you're pretty good at this," I admit, breathing in his stardust scent. "Anything else?"

Adam pauses for a moment, pulling back so his perfect cerulean eyes can sear straight into me. "You are my home," he says as if it's the purest, simplest truth.

I swallow thickly. "Well, that's not very cheesy at all, is it?" I say breathlessly, before finally pressing my lips to his. The kiss is slow and unhurried, tentative and testing. So much has happened in such a short amount of time, and I can tell how careful he's being, how controlled. Like he doesn't want to push me, doesn't want me to break.

But I don't want control.

My breath turns ragged as I tangle my hands in Adam's hair, pulling him closer, closer.

I need to be closer.

I rake my fingers down his back, my nails digging into his shirt as if I might rip the fabric from his form. Adam seems to understand my urgency, and with a flick of his wrist, our clothes are on the floor. I idly wonder why we haven't been making better use of his FX all along.

"Are you going to *fix* me?" I challenge as I roll onto my side, pressing my chest against his and relishing the warmth of his skin on my skin.

"You don't need fixing," he groans, his teeth grazing my earlobe and sending shivers down my neck. "You're perfect."

With that, I lose myself in the sensation of our bodies coming together. In the way he feels pressed against me, all heat and strength and electricity in his touch. In the way his hands slide up my side, his fingers grazing the places where my injuries used to be. They skate over my thigh, my ribs—like he's worshiping every repaired inch of me.

The world outside fades away, and I don't think I'd even notice if his datapad started chiming, or Tom came home with Mica, or an earthquake threatened to topple the very building we're in. There's nothing here, no one else—only us. Together. Always.

"SO, where's *my* cheesy declaration of love?" Adam teases, stroking long lines up and down the side of my body.

"I thought we've long since proved that you're the wordsmith here. I could barely muster more than an 'I love you' when you were dying in front of me," I pout.

"But from you, those three words are like a sonnet. I'd take them any day. Preferably without the dying part, naturally, but still."

I groan melodramatically. "See? Even when you're giving me crap, you're good at this. Not all of us were born to wax poetic, but it's so not fair that I—"

He swallows the rest of my complaint as he brings his lips back to my own. When we finally break apart, Adam rests his forehead against mine, his eyes closed. "I've missed this," he whispers. "Joking. Talking. Just being with you, without worrying about what's going to happen next."

"I'm always going to be a little bit worried about that," I admit, running my fingers through his hair in soothing, repeated strokes. "But

I've missed this too. Missed you. It feels like we've never had the time to just *be*." I bite my lip, thinking of all the things I wish we'd had the time for. All the things we were robbed of. Time to get to know each other without threats and leverage and clandestine missions looming over our heads. Time to meet each other's families the right way.

"It doesn't feel fair, does it?" he murmurs, before kissing away the single tear that's slipped down onto my cheek. I didn't even realize I'd started crying.

We stay like that for a while, wrapped up in each other, savoring this rare chance to *be*. But eventually, reality starts to creep back in around the edges, puncturing our perfect moment of peace. And when I adjust myself to get a better look at Adam's face, I can see the worry lines forming on his forehead. I sense the tension returning to his shoulders.

"What's wrong?" I ask, continuing my idle stroking of his hair.

He sighs and pulls away to sit up at the edge of the bed. "I keep thinking about the meeting."

"Yeah. I do too." I swing my legs over so that I can sit shoulder-to-shoulder with him, drawing the sheet from his bed around me as all the warmth we just generated together gives way to the memory of the Vice-Admiral's cold words.

"Adam," I say, breaking the silence that's fallen over us. "I asked you once to swear to me that no matter what went down, that we would still be *us*. That there would be something good waiting at the end."

"I remember," he replies. "But we aren't at the end yet."

"I know. But this is good."

"Yes." He links his fingers with mine. "And this is real."

I lean my head on his shoulder. "Then screw Conroy and everything he said."

Adam chuckles softly and brushes a strand of hair away from my face with a gentle touch. We sit there for another minute before I draw in a deep breath.

"Adam?"

"Yeah, Sunburst?"

"You're my home too."

THIRTY-NINE

THE DAYS that follow are a whirlwind of activity as Dissidia continues its steady trajectory toward Earth. With our personal uncertainties momentarily set aside—as long as Vice-Admiral Conroy stays out of my line of sight, that is—we throw ourselves into preparations.

Luke has been in nonstop meetings with the UO as they work tirelessly to prepare for our arrival in addition to continuing their work against the Tribunal. I get pulled into the occasional meeting, though I prefer to stay out of it as Luke and Emery's bickering takes up an inordinate amount of time that I feel could be put to better use elsewhere.

The UO has been plenty busy on the ground too. With the Dissidians' help, they've managed to start mass dissemination of the Intherian reports, as well as Dr. Hawthorne's video confessional, to terrestrials and skydwellers alike. It's a slow victory, though, with immediate responses from the Tribunal each time, dismissing the allegations as propaganda and disinformation. The irony of them being the ones to make those claims is not lost on me.

Factions seem to be emerging in the skycities, with some eager to join the Underground's cause, and others . . . Well, I can't say I'm surprised that there's still a large contingent who'd prefer to maintain the status quo. It's also clear that the Tribunal will be doing everything they can to support said status quo, and with the added security and restrictions now placed on skybound, and even inter-sky travel, the UO is finding it increasingly more difficult to get a foothold in each city.

There are also troubling reports of the Tribunal detaining and capturing UO members. I don't know how much of it is to be believed, because I didn't think that there were that many undercover agents to begin with, but it appears that Whitlock has taken an 'arrest now, talk later' approach.

"We have to do something more impactful," Charlie says, an hour into our fourth strategy meeting in as many days.

"Terrestrials on the ground are up in arms and ready to fight over all the secrets the Tribunal has been keeping, the way they'd rather ransom the planet's health than equalize the two halves of humanity. But the skydwellers are burying their heads in the clouds. It's too easy for the Tribunal to dismiss the reports and the video we've been circulating as fake. We need to take it further."

"What did you have in mind?" Admiral Meers asks her daughter.

"We use Altara as an example," Charlie replies. "Show everyone real-time proof of the damage the skycities cause, and that we can reverse it."

"Why don't we just get boots on the ground back near Intheria and showcase what's already been happening there?" I ask. "Seems like it'd be both easier and faster."

"Intheria is so far north that the ecological development of the area is stalled by the climate," Charlie says. "It makes it hard to showcase the planet's return when any fauna and flora is buried beneath three feet of snow."

"The existence of the snow itself should be enough to convince virtually any terrestrial," I mutter.

"Right, but it's not the terrestrials who need convincing," Mica pipes in.

"Word from the UO is that the Trib has set up some pretty significant guardsmen forces surrounding the Intherian crash site anyway," Luke adds. "I think they figured out where we found the reports," he deadpans.

"The UO also informs us that Altara's new lowered altitude is having a significant adverse effect on the area surrounding it. Far more immediate and severe than previously thought. People in the nearby settlements can attest to this, and if we want to prevent an imminent ecological disaster, we need to intervene," Charlie says.

"Why didn't you just start with that?" I ask.

Charlie rolls her eyes.

"I've been speaking with our biological engineers, and they think we can reverse-engineer the skycity suspension systems—you know, the things that are basically single-handedly responsible for the excess degradation of the planet—and convert them into carbon capture generators instead," Tom says. "A kind of reverse-conversion, compared to what was originally done to get the cities launched in the first place."

"Altara is already evacuated, so the risk to civilians in messing with the suspension systems this time would be minimal," Adam muses, and I know in an instant that he's on board.

"And the UO indicates that there is no significant show of Tribunal forces currently planted there. They're too busy helping the Altaraan evacuees," Luke says.

Admiral Meers looks at each of us like she's carefully weighing everything being said. "We're still a couple days from entering Earth's atmosphere," she eventually says. "What kind of timeline are we talking about here?"

"We should send an advance team to Altara immediately," Charlie responds. "A shuttle can travel back to the planet more than three times as fast as the rest of the city. Tom, Adam, Luke, and I should go, along with a small security detail, and, of course, the biological engineering specialists. We'll rendezvous with the Underground, secure the area, run diagnostics, and get a head start as we wait for you to arrive."

I clear my throat. "Aren't we forgetting someone?"

"Make that two someones," Mica adds before I shush him.

"Terra," Tom starts, his voice low and kind, and I know exactly what he's going to try to say. So I don't give him the chance to say it.

"I get that Dissidia as a whole is pretty fantastical, but you're truly living in a fantasy world if you think for a second you're going back without me." I glance at Adam, who gives me an encouraging nod.

Vice-Admiral Conroy, who's been sulking in silence, decides this is the time he's finally going to speak up. "You are not a member of the military, nor do you have the requisite training," he says, throwing Admiral Meers' previous words back at me.

"I may not be military, but I have something just as important: experience and knowledge. Adam and I have been involved in every part of this —together—from the beginning. Without us, you wouldn't have half the intel you do. I mean, for crying out loud, most of you wouldn't even *be here* were it not for me."

Tom exchanges a sheepish look with Charlie and Luke.

"I don't say that to make you feel bad," I add quickly. "Just to point out the facts. My arrest by the Tribunal was the catalyst for everything that went down in Korbyllis, the most important result of which was the three of you getting out. And if taking a gunshot meant for one of you doesn't make me an honorary member of the team, well, then . . ." I trail off, not quite sure how I was planning on finishing that sentence. Fortunately, my message appears to have landed anyway, and I think my heart might burst with the way Adam, Tom, Luke, and Mica are all looking at me. Even Charlie seems to have tossed her irreverent attitude aside for the moment, and I swear there's a glimmer of pride in her eyes as she observes me.

Conroy opens his mouth to argue, but I cut him off. "The bottom line is, I've been a part of this fight since the beginning. Let me see it through to the end."

Adam beams as he mouths "wordsmith" at me, and I can't help but grin. "If anyone deserves to be part of this team, Admiral . . ." he says, turning to Admiral Meers with that lopsided smile on his perfect face.

Tom nods. "We need every advantage we can get. Terra's unique history with Prime Whitlock could prove invaluable as well."

Admiral Meers considers for a moment. "Very well. Ensign Killian, I assume you are prepared to take responsibility for her on the field? From this moment on, she is under your charge. Your responsibility . . . or liability."

Adam looks entirely too delighted at that description, and I elbow him in the rib before he can make an inappropriate remark. He coughs, then garbles out a polite, if hasty, acknowledgment. "Of course. Thank you, Admiral."

Mica steps forward eagerly. "And me? What about me?"

This time, Admiral Meers shakes her head outright before offering Mica a small smile. "You're braver than many of my own soldiers, but I'm afraid I have to put my foot down here. Unlike the Tribunal, we do not believe in sending underage cadets off to fight our battles."

"Oh. Right." Mica looks so crestfallen that I almost want to make a case for him to join us too. But I know he'll be safest if he stays back with the rest of Dissidia. The last thing I want to do is jeopardize his safety again.

Admiral Meers seems just as affected by Mica's disappointment as I am, because a moment later she adds, "How about you help me coordinate from here? If this team expects to accomplish their rather lofty goals, they'll need our support. You can be my personal assistant for the duration of this mission."

Mica's eyes light up, and my heart swells with gratitude.

"Time is, unfortunately, of the essence," Luke says, stepping forward. "So if we're going to be attempting this, we need to get going—like, yesterday."

Adam nods his head once—slowly. Then again—with conviction. "Consider us gone."

FORTY

THE SHIP'S ENGINE HUMS, reverberating through my body as I stare out the small viewport at my side, my breath catching in my throat. The vastness of space unfolds before me, an endless sea of stars and darkness that even after hours and hours of travel, still seems so impossible. Having been unconscious for the trip *to* Dissidia, I wasn't prepared for what the journey through this awesome infinity would be like.

It's one thing to know about space, to hear about it, to see it from afar. But quite another to experience it. The sheer magnitude, the quiet beauty—it's overwhelming. Adam was right. There's something about space that makes you feel . . . small. But somehow, also . . . important? Because even if I'm just one single speck in the grand scale of the universe, so many things had to happen for me to be right here, right now. So many seemingly insignificant choices and occurrences all came together to bring me to this point.

For a moment, I forget about our mission, the stakes, the Tribunal, everything.

I'm just a girl staring into the infinite.

Adam's hand finds mine and gives it a reassuring squeeze. "It's incredible," I whisper.

"It is," he replies, though when I turn to look at him, his eyes aren't on the viewport or the scene outside.

He's just looking at me.

"Preparing for atmospheric entry," Tom announces from the cockpit. "ETA fifteen minutes. Brace yourselves."

I break from Adam's piercing gaze, returning my eyes to the viewport and the renewed sense of awe that overtakes me as Earth comes into view. The other ship, carrying the biological engineers and the majority of the security team that's been assigned to accompany us, passes into my field of vision, barely more than a silhouette against the backdrop of the planet.

Our ship tilts slightly, and pressure builds against my chest as we accelerate. The stars outside the viewport begin to blur as they're replaced by the growing sphere of Earth, and my heart starts to race. We're really going back.

My eyes roam the cabin, observing the others as they make their final preparations. From their jumpseats, Charlie reviews schematics on a holo-display, while Luke does a final gear check. His eyes shutter a half-second before we pierce the atmospheric barrier, the ship quaking.

The view outside shifts dramatically in an instant. Flames lick at the edges of the viewport, and I nearly let out a panicked shout when I glance at the other ship and see its entire hull ablaze. It takes a fear-frozen moment before I remember this is what's supposed to happen, that the friction of our rapid descent is what's creating a fiery halo around both ships. It does little to assuage the dread building in the pit of my stomach, though.

I grip the armrests of my seat, my knuckles white. Despite the shuttle's systems doing their best to compensate for the turbulence, it's impossible to ignore the sensation of being hurled through the sky at breakneck speed—exhilarating and terrifying.

"Hold tight, everyone," Tom's voice crackles through the comm, calm and steady. "We're almost through."

The flames outside the viewport subside, replaced by a hazy, cloudless blue sky. I take a deep breath as the pressure against my chest lessens, the sight unfolding before me somehow both familiar and entirely alien. Most of what I can make out is a drab sea of brown, a marred landscape between the edges of the oceans, but the patches of green I observe from my small viewport make me wonder how we've gone so long thinking the entire planet was dead. From up here, you'd never know how desolate it is on the ground.

Until Altara comes into view, that is.

The city floats just a few hundred feet above the ground, casting a dark shadow over the earth. The ground below is not just dust and desert. It's as if life is being actively siphoned from it. Blackened veins stretch across the terrain, burning through the earth like a web of vicious scars.

"It's already done this much damage? This quickly?" My voice comes out as a whisper.

"The electromagnetic emissions from the city's anti-grav engines are too focused, too strong at this height," Luke says.

"Like I said, ecological disaster," Charlie chimes in.

"The rendezvous point is just on the other side of the city." Tom points ahead through the front viewport at something I can't quite see from where I'm sitting. "We'll—wait." *Beep. Beep.* The panel in front of him lights up. "Something's not right. I'm picking up signs of a skirmish."

The ship glides smoothly as the ground rushes up to meet us, the other ship descending with a mirror trajectory, and my eyes widen at the scene that unfolds before us—the *battlefield* below us. Flashes of energy weapons and the glow of advanced combat drones light up the field surrounding Altara as Underground forces engage with Tribunal troops.

Explosions pepper the ground, resonating through the ship as we sail closer, zipping between plumes of smoke and debris. I can see the silhouettes of soldiers darting between makeshift cover, their forms briefly illuminated by the beams of energy weapons.

"Did we know about this?" Charlie shouts across the cabin, her voice tense.

Luke taps frantically on his datapad screen. "We've received nothing from the UO," he says. "I'm trying to get a hold of them now. Either this just started and they haven't had a chance to contact us yet or—"

"—or the Tribunal has been jamming their communications," Adam finishes. "They're trying to keep them from getting to the city."

"Do we just keep going past? We could fly straight into Altara from above," Charlie suggests.

"And leave the UO on the ground to fend for themselves?" Luke says, a touch of alarm in his voice.

"Huh, who knew you actually cared," Emery's dry voice crackles in from Luke's datapad, his reddish-brown hair sweatily plastered to a dirt-streaked forehead, as his face appears on the screen.

"Talk to us, Garren," Adam says.

"They surprised us. Dropped in overnight and smoked us out. And now they hide behind their holographic barriers, deploying drones and firing long-distance bolts at us."

"Cowards," Adam says.

"Bastards," Charlie adds.

"How did they know you were here?" I ask.

Static crackles across the datapad. "We're not sure. Communication interception, maybe? Hardly matters now. We're trying to cut through their western flank, but they've been making a push for our—*shit!*" An explosion sounds—I hear it on Luke's datapad first, then feel it echo through the ship itself.

"Emery!" I cry. Luke curses. I cram my head against the viewport, trying to get a better view of what's happening on the ground. My mouth freezes open as a Tribunal assault team fires at a cluster of Underground vehicles, haphazardly arranged in a defensive perimeter around a group of tents. The UO team is laying down suppressive fire, and I think I catch the briefest flash of reddish-brown hair through the smoke.

With a shudder, a series of shots rattle off from our ship—*rat-a-tat-tat*—and where the assault team was standing a second ago, there's nothing but a smoking hole in the ground. Charlie whoops from the front of the ship.

Holy shit.

We land in a clearing behind the perimeter we just helped clear, the ship's ramp lowering with a hiss as the sounds of battle flood into the cabin. The acrid smell of smoke and burning circuits fills the air, along with something wet and metallic that makes my stomach turn.

"They need help," I say, unstrapping myself from my jumpseat. Through the ship's open hatch, I see the other ship has landed nearby, their crew already disembarked. Tom, Luke, and Charlie are halfway down the ramp, on their way to join them, but a strong set of fingers tugs on my upper arm before I can catch up.

"Not you, Sunburst," Adam says. Before I can explode with indignation, he adds, "I need you to hang back and provide cover from the shuttle. It's too dangerous for you to be out there on the front lines."

I open my mouth to protest, but he holds up a hand. "You know I think you're capable of anything, but you're not a trained combat fighter and this is real shit. Stay here. Be our eyes in the sky while Ensign Davis flies." Adam motions to a soldier from the other ship, and a person with a slender face and pitch-black hair shorn in a close pixie jogs over. "We'll be counting on you to cover our backs."

I glance at the battlefield, still lit up like a fireworks show, then back at Adam. *Damn it, he's right.* Reluctantly, I nod. "Fine. But you'd better come back in one piece."

Adam shoots me that lopsided grin of his, a flash of his typical bravado. "Always."

Ensign Davis positions themself in the cockpit and gestures for me to join them in the co-pilot's chair. We're back in the air a few minutes later. Through the viewport, I watch as Adam, Tom, Charlie, Luke, and the others from the second ship make their way toward Emery's position on the field. Davis keeps the airwaves open so we can keep in constant contact with the team through their communicators, and my heart races as the sounds of battle grow louder the closer they get. I try to focus on the task at hand, my eyes rotating from the viewport to the radar systems and back again as I attempt to help the team navigate through the mess below us.

I'm not nearly as helpful as I wish I was, being untrained in reading said radar systems, but Davis is a force to be reckoned with. They anticipate drone movements like they're nearly clairvoyant, and seem to know just when to cut through Tribunal forces as we provide cover fire for our own advancing team. I translate their commands as best I can when needed, and otherwise try to stay out of their way. Instead, I keep my eye on Adam as he and Charlie fight side-by-side. I marvel at the way the two of them use their FX to create a barrier against the Tribunal's shots while the other Dissidian soldiers provide cover fire from behind.

Stretching my neck so I can get better visibility of the scene on the ground from the viewport, I notice Tom and Luke running perpendicular to the rest of the team. "What are they doing?" I ask Davis, who doesn't respond as they swerve the ship to avoid a blast from a Tribunal air cannon below. A second later, the cannon explodes, and I have my answer.

"We're almost through," Tom's voice crackles through the comm. "There's just one more contingent of Tribunal forces to deal with."

"Copy that," Davis says as they adjust the ship's targeting systems. "We're clearing a path now." *Rat-a-tat-tat* goes our ship, and our team surges forward. I lean back in my seat, ready for the heady mix of relief and exhaustion that I know is coming. The UO encampment is safe, and we've given the Tribunal a taste of their own medicine.

Just as I'm about to relax, an alarm blares through the shuttle. Red lights flash, and the ship jerks violently. "What's happening?" I ask Davis, my heart leaping into my throat.

"They had another goddamn air cannon," they grit out.

There's another fierce jolt of the ship and my insides twist inside out as we go into a tailspin.

"We're hit," they shout into the comm. "Ship's going down!"

"Davis, what—" Tom's voice responds, but whatever he was planning to say is cut off by Adam roaring my name.

Panic grips me as Davis struggles to regain control of the ship, and I can do nothing other than tighten my grip on the straps keeping me locked in my seat. My eyes are frozen open in fear as the ground rushes up to meet us.

"Brace for impact!"

We crash with a bone-jarring thud, throwing me against my restraints. Pain lances through my body, a stroke of lightning that burns a path down from the back of my neck, and everything goes black.

FORTY-ONE

THE WORLD IS a blur of darkness and muffled sounds as my senses slowly claw their way back to awareness. I force my eyes open and blink blearily in the brightness.

I'm still strapped into my seat, my arms and legs dangling awkwardly in front of me, my full weight born by my restraints. My view from the cockpit is distorted by cracks in the viewport, but based on the dusty brown nothingness that surrounds us, I suspect we nosedived into the ground. The ship is perched at an angle, sparks lighting up the cabin from behind me.

Groaning, I try to move, my muscles protesting. I manage to release the buckles of my restraints and fall forward, catching myself on the console as pain rockets up each of my arms.

"Davis?" My voice is hoarse, barely a whisper. I turn my head, blinking through the haze, and find them slumped over the controls. Relief floods through me as I see the shallow rise of their chest—they're unconscious but alive.

I fumble for the comms panel, which is beeping and blinking rapidly. "Can anyone hear me? This is Terra. We've crashed. Davis is down."

Static sputters on the line before Adam's voice cuts through. "Thank goodness. Are you hurt?"

"Just a little banged up," I say, wincing as I roll my shoulders back to make sure that's true. "But Davis is unconscious."

"I'm coming to you," he says, the conviction in his voice loud and clear even through the damaged comm. It settles some of the churning in my gut. "You crashed on the other side of the perimeter, so stay hunkered down. We're still trying to take out the last of their drones."

"Copy that," I say, my voice steadier than I feel. Last I'd seen, there was still a sizable Tribunal force left on their side of the UO's makeshift perimeter. Hopefully none of them are too concerned with our downed ship, but I'm not taking any chances. I carefully release Davis from their seat, checking them over for bleeding before gently laying them to the side on the ship's cabin floor. I then take the stunner that's strapped onto their jumpsuit and wait.

I'm still crouched by Davis when the comm crackles back to life minutes later. "Terr . . .Get . . .Come . . ." Adam's words are garbled and keep getting cut off by static as I run back to the dashboard—as if I might somehow establish a clearer connection. Just as I reach the console, the earsplitting crunch of twisting, grating metal fills the cabin. I duck down, hiding my body between the two cockpit chairs.

The ship's hatch door is wrenched away and the sound of heavy boots stomping up the ramp has my blood freezing solid in my veins. Somehow, I know it's not Adam. It's not the UO.

"I shot a bird out of the sky," a cold, calculating voice slithers through the cabin. "Come out, come out, little bird."

It's Wolfe.

I sink further back into the shadow of the dashboard, my finger on the trigger of the stunner at my side. A vision of his convulsing body, the way it was as I left him in Altara during the fall, flashes through my mind. I don't know how he survived or how he knows I'm here, but I burrow into my body as close as I can. Maybe if I stay silent enough, hidden enough, he'll think he got it wrong.

The comm sputters to life again, the line clear enough this time to damn me as Adam's voice cuts through the silent cabin. "Terra? Terra. Report!"

"I knew it," Wolfe murmurs, and though he's clearly only speaking to himself, panic races through me as I realize how close he is. I clamp a hand over my mouth as if I might force my breathing to slow and my heart to stop thundering.

"Little bird, where are you hiding?" he taunts, the cruel melody of his voice sending shivers down my spine. "You can't hide forever." Wolfe's footsteps pause, and I hear the soft rustle of fabric as he searches the ship. My heart clenches at the thought of Davis lying defenseless on the cabin floor, and I glance at their vulnerable body just as Wolfe's boots come into view next to them. Suddenly, the stunner in my hand feels woefully inadequate.

"Oh ho, who's this?" A hot spike of anger rears up inside me as he kicks Davis in their side, though it's quickly replaced by fear as he crouches down. He's at my eye level now, and with a simple turn in the right—or wrong—direction, he'll be looking directly at me. But he doesn't. Instead, he bends closer to Davis, using two black gloved fingers to turn their face for a better look at them.

The predatory gleam in Wolfe's eyes has my hackles rising. I have no idea how far Adam is, or if anyone else is coming. I have to draw Wolfe's attention away from Davis, and the easiest way to do that is by showing him exactly what he wants.

Now or never.

With every ounce of stealth I can muster, I peer out from between the seats, my eyes locked on Wolfe as I raise Davis' stunner. As if he can sense the target on his back, he whirls around, the movement so quick and startling, I squeeze the trigger.

The shot hits Wolfe in his side, and he falls forward onto his hands and knees with a grunt. But instead of going down, his head pops up, eyes blazing with fury as they find me. I'm already moving, racing toward the exit, but even after that stun shot, Wolfe is fast.

"You'll pay for that," he snarls, lunging at me.

I fire at him again, but he dodges, the bolt barely grazing his arm. He's on me in an instant, knocking the stunner from my hand and slamming me against the cabin wall. Pain explodes in my shoulder, but I grit my teeth, refusing to give him the satisfaction of my scream.

"Should've killed me when you had the chance, little bird," he says, a manic glint in his eye that might have had me quivering in fear if I wasn't already shaking from the adrenaline coursing through me.

"Yes, I should have," I spit. I clutch my shoulder as I try to duck under his outstretched arm, still aiming for the exit.

"Would've, could've, should've," he tuts. He catches me before I've made it more than a few steps past him, crushing my arms against my torso with an iron grip. "Now, if you wanted to get out of here, all you had to do was ask." I struggle against his hold, kicking and thrashing, as he drags me toward the open hatch.

A sudden burst of gunfire erupts outside, and Wolfe freezes just before we reach the opening. His grip loosens just enough for me to wrench free, and I stumble back, falling to the floor. Wolfe curses, and I look up to see Adam and Tom charging inside the ship, weapons drawn.

"Get away from her!" Adam roars, raising both arms and using his FX to knock Wolfe onto his back. Wolfe snarls as he rolls to the side, diving for cover behind the row of jumpseats lining the left side of the ship. I scramble over to Davis, looping my arms under their shoulders and pulling them into the cockpit area to shield them from the crossfire as shots ring out across the confined space.

Adam's eyes never leave Wolfe as Tom catches my eye from across the cabin. "Stay down," Tom commands. "We'll handle this."

I nod, my heart pounding. I can see Wolfe's chances aren't good, but past precedence has proven he has an uncanny ability to beat the odds. Adam keeps Wolfe pinned in place as Tom moves to flank him from the side. Wolfe releases a series of panicked, directionless shots from his stunner, the bolts bouncing across the cabin. One happens to ricochet off a panel, and I cry out in surprise as it lances my arm. The distraction loosens Adam's hold on Wolfe. With a roar of defiance, he breaks free entirely, twisting to lunge at Adam. He knocks his arms aside and before I've fully comprehended what's happening, the two are grappling in a brutal hand-to-hand struggle.

"Tom!" I scream, but he is already moving, closing the distance between them. He tackles Wolfe, pulling him off Adam and slamming him into the cabin wall. Wolfe roars, thrashing against Tom's hold, but Adam is there in an instant to deliver a swift, precise blow to the back of Wolfe's head.

Wolfe crumples to the floor, unconscious, and the cabin falls silent. The only sounds that remain are our heavy breaths and my blood pulsing in my ears.

Adam rushes to my side. "Are you okay?" he murmurs, his voice shaky with relief as he helps me stand.

I nod, clinging to him. "I'm fine. Davis is the one who needs help."

Tom kneels beside Wolfe, securing him with restraints. "We need to get out of here before more of them show up."

Adam steadies me by looping his arm around my waist. "Can you walk?"

"Yes," I say, wincing slightly as my injured shoulder and arm make contact with his chest. Dust settles around us as we exit the ship's wreckage and make our way through a battlefield that is significantly less chaotic than it was before we crashed. I take a deep breath—it appears the UO has fought the Tribunal back, at least for now.

Tom follows closely, grunting from exertion as he uses his FX to tote both Davis and Wolfe behind us. We make it a few yards from the ship when a drone passing overhead makes us stop and take cover beside an overturned vehicle.

"Damn it," Tom mutters, tearing a strip of cloth from his shirt to bind a wound I hadn't noticed on Davis. "We need to get them to a medic."

"And I have a few choice words to share with this one once he wakes up," Adam says, motioning toward Wolfe. "Let's take them both to the Underground encampment."

THE SOUND of Wolfe's face colliding with Adam's fist is immensely gratifying, I admit.

"Try again," Adam sneers. The Underground tent that we commandeered for this interrogation sways as a rogue wind passes through. "What is Whitlock planning? Where are the rest of the Tribunal forces?"

Wolfe spits blood onto the floor at Adam's feet. "Such a brave little soldier. But what makes him think I'm going to spill the answers he seeks?"

Tom steps up next to his brother. "Tell us what you know, and we'll be lenient—which is far more than you deserve, and I think you know it."

"I don't know much, but you know even less," Wolfe says, a sing-songy quality to his voice that makes my stomach queasy.

"Why bother keeping your secrets now? You lost," Adam says.

"Did we?" Wolfe replies, a self-satisfied smirk on his face. "The little soldier asks the wrong questions. Regardless, you won't be getting answers out of me this way."

"Fair enough," I say, summoning all my remaining scraps of confidence as I step forward.

Wolfe has the audacity to smile like he's genuinely pleased to see me, and I swallow down bile. I make a point of taking in the cuffs clamped around his wrists and ankles, the chains binding him to his chair. I look at Adam and Tom, and the Dissidian soldier standing guard at the tent entrance.

He's completely restrained, I remind myself. *I'm safe.*

I take a second to will my voice not to shake before continuing. "You are the expert here, after all. Maybe it's time we take a page out of your own book, Inquisitor Wolfe," I say, pulling a small plastic bottle from my pocket. "You didn't have many items on your person, but you did have this." I flip the lid and give the bottle a shake, the small orange pills inside rattling satisfactorily as I pour one into the palm of my hand. Even more satisfying, though, is the way Wolfe's eyes widen in recognition of what I'm holding. "The first time you forced me to take one of these, it brought me back to the absolute worst day of my life. It was like I was living it all over again. What will it force you to relive, I wonder?"

"I don't—"

"You don't what? You don't want to take it? I didn't want to either. I'm sure none of the people you've tortured with their own memories, whose minds you've messed up, wanted to. That didn't stop you, though."

I glance at Adam, whose awestruck expression only bolsters my boldness, before approaching Wolfe with the pill pinched between my fingers. Wolfe struggles against his restraints, and the sudden violence in each of his movements as he bucks his body back and forth almost makes me drop the pill. Thankfully, he's well-secured and I'm well pissed off—enough so that before I fully comprehend what I'm doing, I've grabbed a fistful of his hair in my hand. Power surges in my veins as I pull his head back, the architect of my nightmares finally at my mercy. "Last chance, Inquisitor."

Wolfe starts shaking. Trembling. At first, I think it's with fear. That the reality of what he's done to me and so many others is finally catching up with him. But a strangled kind of cackle emerges from him, and I realize he's actually shuddering with laughter.

"He truly is insane," Adam says. My grip on Wolfe's hair loosens.

"You think anything I say is going to make a difference? You think one of those little pills is going to change a damn thing? She'll be there any minute. We'll all soon be ash." Each of Wolfe's sentences is punctuated with a bone-chilling laugh.

"Who will be where?" I demand.

Wolfe's laughter dies down as his beady blue eyes lock on my own, mania flashing in them. "Tick, tock. Time to fly away, little bird. Prime Whitlock gets what she wants, or nobody gets anything at all. Tick, tick, tick."

"What are you—"

"Sir!" Another one of the Dissidian soldiers bursts through the tent entrance. "Our scanners picked up a Tribunal shuttle headed into Altara."

Tom wastes no time following the soldier back out.

"Don't say I didn't warn you," Wolfe sings. "Ash and dust, dust and ash. Better to turn the city to dust than let it fall into your hands."

"The city . . .?" I look up, as if I can see Altara looming overhead through the top of the tent. "She's going to . . ."

"Tick, tick, boom," says Wolfe, and with another savage buck of his body, he rips his hair out of my grasp. He jerks his head to the side, then lurches forward toward me with a chomp of his teeth, and I leap back, thinking he means to bite me. But then I hear a cracking sound come from inside his mouth, and the wide smile on Wolfe's face falters as his body starts to convulse. Pinkish foam oozes out from the corner of his lips and that manic, deranged spark in his eyes goes out.

"Holy shit," Adam says. "He killed himself."

Shock threatens to root me to the spot as I stare at Wolfe's lifeless body slumped over in his seat, but his final words won't stop rattling around in my brain.

"I think Prime Whitlock is planning something really terrible," I tell Adam.

" 'Tick, tick, boom,' " Adam repeats, horror written across his face.

"We need to get up to Altara. Now."

FORTY-TWO

ALTARA IS A GHOST TOWN. The abandoned city seems to echo with each of our footsteps as Adam and I race through the streets, hearts pounding. Tom was going to bring us straight to where we tracked Whitlock's shuttle, but a half-dozen Tribunal drones had different plans. He dropped us as close as he could before drawing them away, leaving us to race across the ruined city to reach City Hall on foot.

Or what remains of it.

My heartbeat stutters as the place that claimed my father's life comes into view. The first thing I see is the Tribunal shuttle, parked just in front of the square that used to host Altara's grand City Hall building. Then, the destruction just beyond—jagged fragments of concrete and twisted metal beams sloping inward, a ring of rubble that leads down into a cavernous pit of debris where the building collapsed in on itself.

And there, standing right on the edge of the pit, is Prime Morrigan Whitlock herself.

The usual picture of cold elegance, there's something off about her at this moment. Her usually sleek, auburn bob is disheveled, her ice-blue jumpsuit is wrinkled. She isn't alone; the petite, young woman we saw with Prime Whitlock at the Academy is next to her, looking nervous, and a pair of fully armored guardsmen stand a few yards behind them.

Adam pulls me behind an abandoned vehicle, his sharp eyes never leaving Whitlock or her entourage. "What's the plan, Sunburst?" he whispers.

"We need to get closer. Wolfe wasn't exactly forthcoming about what exactly she has planned, but the fact that she's here at all is proof enough to me that his deranged rantings weren't totally made up. If she's planning on blowing up the city, she has to have some kind of device on her. We have to get to her before she triggers it."

We creep forward, using the debris as cover, until I can hear Whitlock's voice, sharp and commanding. I peek around the corner of the building we're crouched next to, finding Whitlock holding something in her hands as she faces the young woman. She looks terrified, her eyes darting around as if she might bolt any moment.

" . . .must ensure the device is set correctly," Whitlock says. "The suspension core is weakened, but it will still be powerful enough to level the city. We'll crush the resistance forces below and send a clear message to the rest of the world once we tell them exactly who was responsible."

"What do you mean, ma'am?" the young woman squeaks out.

"For crying out loud, Posey. We blame the Underground, of course. It's just what we need to put any lingering support for them to bed."

"And . . . and you're sure this is the only way to do it? It just seems so . . . wasteful. Much of this city can still be salvaged. So many citizens have been displaced, and I know they have hopes of one day returning to their homes here and—"

"Do I pay my assistant to question me, Posey? Or do I pay you to *assist* me?" Whitlock's icy tone cuts right through Posey's words.

"Yes, Prime Whitlock. I mean, I'm sorry. I mean, I'm here to assist you."

"Good. Now, hold this while I double-check the parameters. We don't want this thing detonating before we're good and ready. But be careful, it's already armed."

Posey looks like she might throw up, but takes the device from Prime Whitlock's outstretched hands.

Adam tenses beside me. "We have to move now," he whispers. "Get close to the girl. I'll distract the guards."

I hesitate. "Shouldn't we wait for Tom and—"

"No, we can't delay. We need to get that device away from Whitlock—Tom will track us down."

As much as I'd love to argue further, I know we're already running on borrowed time. I squeeze his hand once before we slink off in opposite directions.

I circle around, staying low and quiet, ducking behind the gigantic pieces of debris that litter the ground. Posey's back is to me, her attention focused entirely on Whitlock standing at the pit's edge. I'm almost to her when one of the guards abruptly shifts, his gaze sweeping over the exact broken stretch of wall I'm hiding behind.

I freeze, barely daring to breathe as I press my body closer to the wall. The guard takes a single step in my direction, his stare laser-focused on my position, and I know I'm only seconds from discovery.

Suddenly, a loud crash echoes through the square, and the guard whirls toward the source of the noise. My heart lurches as Adam steps into view, having knocked over a pile of debris to draw attention to himself.

"You!" Whitlock snarls as she spins in place to face him. "You just won't die, will you?"

Adam smirks. "Sorry to disappoint."

The guardsmen rush Adam's position, their stunners raised. With Whitlock's wave of command, they both start firing bolts at him. Adam dodges, rolling to the side just as the ground where he stood explodes in a shower of sparks.

My heart clenches with concern, but I won't let Adam's distraction go to waste. I sprint forward, grabbing Posey's arm and clamping a hand over her mouth before she can call for help.

"Shh," I tell her, pulling her back behind the wall I was previously hiding behind. "We want to help, Posey—it's Posey, right? Can you stay quiet, Posey?"

Her wide, light blue eyes meet mine, and after a moment, she nods.

"I don't think you want Prime Whitlock to blow this city up, do you?" I release her, gesturing to the device in her trembling hands.

"I never wanted any of this. My parents got me a job as the Prime's assistant because they thought it would be good for my career, but she's

—" She cuts herself off, as if afraid of what she almost let slip. "This is just not what I signed up for."

"Believe me, I understand. And what Prime Whitlock wants to do here . . . there's no reason for it. Everything that the Underground is telling folks? About the skycities and the planet being able to heal? It's all true. We have an opportunity to repair our world—to make a better one, for all of us. But the Tribunal is so scared of losing power that they're willing to risk everything and everyone just to keep themselves on top."

I chance a look around the corner at Adam, his movements a blur as he dodges the guardsmen's attacks. He occasionally counters with a strategic strike of his FX, but I can tell that he's using evasive maneuvers to keep their attention on him. Prime Whitlock doesn't appear to have noticed Posey missing yet, but I know it's only a matter of time before she does.

"Can you disable it?" I ask Posey, nodding toward the device.

She swallows hard. "I don't—I don't know. It's complicated, but I've seen Prime Whitlock use it. She still has the detonator on her, but maybe I can disarm it?"

"Do it. We don't have much time."

"She'll kill me if she finds out."

"No," I tell her, a lethal calm in my voice. "She won't."

Posey pauses, biting her lip, as she watches me for a moment. Finally, she nods. She crouches with the device in her lap, poking at a series of buttons until a keyboard unfolds from one side. My eyes dart between Adam, still fighting, Prime Whitlock, her attention locked on him, and Posey, her fingers flying over the keypad.

"Please, hurry," I urge.

"I'm trying," Posey mutters. Finally, there's a sharp series of beeps, and a green light on the interface switches off.

"Best I can do," Posey says, handing the device over to me. "It's not completely deactivated, but Prime Whitlock won't be able to detonate the device without rearming it first."

A scream of rage draws my attention back to the scuffle. Whether Prime Whitlock's detonator alerted her to the device's change in status, or if she's finally noticed Posey is no longer where she left her, it's clear that our time is up.

"Run, Posey," I tell her. "Run and hide. We'll come find you."

She hesitates for half a second, then she's gone, disappearing into the shadows. I turn my attention back to Adam, and a chill runs down my spine as I watch him misjudge the distance between one of the guardsmen and himself, stumbling as he tries to sidestep his advance. The miscalculation costs him, and I have to hold in my scream as the other guardsman comes up from behind, pinning Adam's arms behind him.

"Where is she?" Whitlock spits at Adam as she stomps toward him. "Where is my device?"

"Mmm, afraid I don't know who or what you're talking about."

Red flares across my vision as Whitlock slaps him across the face.

"I know you disabled the timer on the device, but don't think for a second I'm not still willing to detonate it. It won't have *quite* the same impact as my original plan to blow up the suspension core, but wherever she is hiding, it'll still do a nice chunk of damage."

Shit. Posey disarmed the timer, but not the device itself. I need to get the detonator away from Whitlock. I need to help Adam get free. Preferably both. Preferably now.

"This is madness," I say, stepping out from behind the wall.

Whitlock's eyes blaze with a fanatical glee. "I was hoping you were around here somewhere, Miss Rhodon. Inquisitor Wolfe informed me of you slipping your outprocessing—I'd be impressed if I didn't find it so irritating that you keep popping up where you don't belong." She darts her eyes between Adam and me. "Seems no matter what we do, you two just can't seem to stay away from each other."

I hold the device up as I walk toward her. "If you detonate this now, you won't just fail to accomplish your goal, you'll kill yourself and everyone here."

"So be it," Whitlock says with a dismissive wave of her hand. I don't miss the look that the guardsmen exchange with each other. "I'd rather die than see you win."

"You're insane. This is bigger than me," I say, taking another step toward her. "The second we uncovered the real history of the Skyfall and what the skycities have done to the planet, it became bigger than any one of us. There's no stopping the truth."

She scoffs. "Centuries of cultivating a near-perfect world won't be undone by one little groundling. As if one pathetic girl, from pathetic, weak, parents, can bring down the Tribunal? Your father was such a disappointment. And look where we are—his sacrifice won't even have meant anything in the end.

"You see, this isn't about power or control. It's about survival—the right kind of survival. You want to drag us back to the ground, to a world that's already dead, when there's proof that humanity's next chapter is out there!" She points a long, manicured finger to the sky. "I've seen the data. Earth is a wasteland, and you would doom us all to live on it until our last, crumbling breath."

"You can't be serious," I say. "If you've seen the reports, you must know the truth. The planet can heal—we can *help* it heal. It's the skycities you so desperately cling to that are killing the earth, not the other way around."

"Propaganda!" Whitlock shrieks. "Lies! Seditious fraud! Fabrications by the Underground Order to undermine the Tribunal's authority. A clear attempt to wrest control of the skycities, to take our technology and advantages for themselves."

"You're deranged," Adam says. "And a damn hypocrite."

Whitlock looks genuinely taken aback. "Hypocrite?"

"Yes," I agree, "Remember the Dissidians? Does that ring any bells? The only one trying to steal technology and take control of things by force is you."

"Just another reason to stay true to the plan. Our people are divided, now more than ever. Without the Underground sowing the seeds of doubt and resentment, our people will come to understand. They will place their faith in us again. We need that unity—we are on the cusp of war, after all."

"A war *you* orchestrated!" I cry. "You're willing to let thousands of your soldiers and citizens die just to prove a point. The Dissidians don't want to fight. They just want to come *home*."

From the corner of my eye, I see the guardsmen exchange another look.

Adam tenses his body, like he's getting ready to bolt, and it has me wondering if their hold on him is no longer quite as iron-gripped. "You're mad," he says.

Whitlock begins to laugh—a harsh, maniacal sound that echoes through the square. "You call it madness, but I think it's just common sense. Now, give that to me." She points at the device in my arms, her eyes wild.

I shake my head, heavy with the realization of just how far she's fallen into her own twisted point of view. She's beyond reason, beyond saving. And I don't think I'm the only one who realizes it.

"Let him go," I turn to the guardsmen. "My father, Commander Rhodon, was a lifelong guardsman and a good man, who fought his entire career against this kind of corruption. Do you really think your fellow citizens would agree with this insanity? Or do you think they would want to work toward a true future, one that skydwellers and terrestrials can have—together?"

Whitlock's laughter turns bitter. "A future? There's no future down there. Only death. You're too blind to see it."

A sudden flash of light has me shielding my face as Whitlock lets out a scream of rage. When I lower my arm, I see one of the guardsmen crumpled to the ground. Tom emerges from behind a pile of rubble, his weapon raised.

"About time," Adam mutters, taking advantage of the distraction to break free from the remaining guard's hold. He ducks and rolls, retrieving the fallen guardsman's weapon as he rises to his feet.

Whitlock's eyes flick between us. "This isn't over," she snarls, raising her hand, a small device glinting within—the detonator. "I'll see you all burn."

"No!" I shout, lunging forward. But Adam is faster, a blur of motion as he dives toward her. With a flick of his wrist, the detonator flies from her hand and skitters across the pavement. It lands near the edge of the pit just as Adam tackles Whitlock to the ground.

The remaining guard hesitates, clearly torn between his duty and everything he's just learned. Tom takes advantage of his indecision, firing a warning shot at his feet that sends him scrambling backward, hands raised in surrender.

I rush to the edge of the pit, retrieving the detonator. "This ends now,"

I say, my voice steady despite the frenetic energy coursing through me. "It's over."

Whitlock stares at me, and I see the moment her defiance starts crumbling into despair. "You're making a mistake," she whispers. "A terrible mistake."

"We'll see about that," I say, signaling to Tom to secure her. He moves forward, binding her hands with a zip tie, his expression grim.

As we pull Whitlock to her feet, Posey reappears, her face pale. "Is it over?" she asks, her voice trembling as she deliberately stays behind Whitlock, out of her line of sight.

"Not yet," Adam replies, his eyes scanning the horizon. "We need to hightail it before any potential reinforcements arrive. But we've stopped her from blowing this place up, and that's what matters."

Posey nods, relief flooding her features. "Thank you," she says, her voice barely above a whisper.

"No, thank *you*," I tell her. "You saved lives today."

We reach Tom's ship and get the guardsmen and Whitlock aboard, her icy eyes still burning with a manic sort of rage. The sky is painted with dawn's first light as we soar back to the Underground encampment, where questions and decisions and deliberations await us. But for now . . .

"How're you doing?" Adam asks me, his hand on the small of my back as he looks me over.

"Been worse," I say, my voice a bit hoarse. "You had me worried for a second back there," I admit.

He plants a kiss on my temple. "All's well that ends well, Sunburst."

I nod, tears stinging my eyes as I lean into his comforting warmth. "From your lips to God's ears, spaceboy."

FORTY-THREE

A SEA of anxious faces greets us as we step off the ship. Luke rushes forward, his eyes scanning us for injuries before settling on Whitlock, still bound but miraculously silent. "You did it," he breathes, a mixture of awe and relief in his voice. Whispers run rampant through the crowd of gathered UO members at the sight of one of the Primes of the Tribunal in custody.

"We did something, all right," Adam grunts, ushering Whitlock and the guardsmen off the ship. "Not quite sure what this is going to mean in terms of that war we're trying to avert, but at least we've curbed the scheming of the most homicidal of the Primes."

Tom steps forward, a grim smile tugging at his lips. "The UO will secure her. We need to debrief the Admiral and figure out next steps."

Emery approaches, looking smug, and despite his more asshole-ish tendencies, I'm relieved to see him unscathed after the battle. "Allow me to escort you to your holding cell, Prime Whitlock. I believe I know several people who are just dying to chat with you."

I watch them walk away for a minute, then turn to Adam. "How long until Dissidia arrives?"

"Two days, give or take," Adam replies.

"What do we do until then?" I ask.

"What we said we were going to do," Tom says. "Prep for their arrival, run diagnostics, and get ready to turn Altara into the shining example we're all hoping it will be."

Charlie runs up and slaps a palm on Adam's back before facing Tom. "The engineering team is ready to head to Altara and start preparations for the reverse-conversion as soon as you deem it, Captain."

"You have excellent timing," I say, grinning at Charlie. Her returning look of puzzlement melts into grudging acquiescence, and a prickle of pride runs through my chest. Maybe I'm making progress with that one after all.

"I suppose we will be adding a few additional items to our task list," Luke adds. "Helping with repairs and providing medical attention to the UO as needed, given the scene we stumbled upon."

"Goodness knows this would likely have been a very different situation had you all not come when you did," a familiar voice chimes in from behind me.

"Brant!" Before I'm fully aware of myself, I find myself drawing the ex-guardsman into a firm hug. His chest shakes under my grip as he chuckles. "Sorry," I say self-consciously, stepping back. "I'm just . . . I'm glad to see you. That you're all right."

"I could say the same thing," he says. A charged silence falls between us, and Adam, Tom, and Luke make an awkward show of shuffling away. Brant and I try to break the silence at the same time.

"Brant, I—"

"Terra—"

We laugh, and Brant gestures for me to go ahead.

"I don't know how much you know about what's happened since we saw each other last," I start. Has he already heard about my father? Or am I about to be the bearer of bad news?

Brant hesitates for a long moment. "I do know. What happened with your father . . . I'm so, so sorry, Terra. I wanted to be able to tell you so much more, about what a great man he was, about everything he was doing, everything he'd done . . ."

I ignore the twinge at the back of my throat. "It's okay, Brant. I get it. Honestly, I just wanted to say thank you. I know you didn't feel like you could say much, but I think . . . I think that the little bits you did let slip helped me understand, helped me believe him more readily. And given how little time we ended up h-having"—I swallow thickly—"it made a difference. So, thank you."

"I wish you could've known more of him."

I sigh. "I do too. At least Mica got a little extra time with him these past few weeks, even if I didn't know it. He had so few memories of him from before he left. I've got a lot of feelings to untangle from the memories I have, but I know I have some good ones."

"That sounds like an admirable goal," Brant says. "And anytime you're in the mood for some stories from the Academy or your dad's early days on the force, you let me know, okay?"

I smile. "I absolutely will be taking you up on that."

TURNS OUT, it's not so hard to divert a war effort when the primary warmonger is cut off from their platform. With Prime Whitlock in custody, it became devastatingly obvious just how skewed the power balance within the Tribunal had become. Primes Laraby and Donovan were barely more than figureheads and were either unaware of or unconcerned with everything Whitlock had her hands in. I'm not sure which is worse.

Either way, once Dissidia finally arrived, the rest of the Tribunal was quick to wash their hands of Whitlock's involvement and intentions. It probably helped that with all the evidence we gathered against Whitlock —not to mention the direct confession Zira Coal was able to get out of her —they needed someone to take the fall for the corrupt and tyrannical plans that had been underway.

While I can't say I trust that what's left of the Tribunal has anyone's best interests in mind other than their own, they at least seem like they'll do an adequate job maintaining things, for now. After all, there's a new world order to figure out—an entirely new fabric of society to weave, composed of Dissidians, terrestrials, and skydwellers alike. A tapestry of humanity coming together in a way that once seemed like an impossible fantasy.

It was a bit surreal to see how smoothly reintegration talks between the Dissidians and the rest of us went. With the backing of the Underground and a bit of careful media planning, the Dissidians were able to explain their origins and desires to return to Earth, as well as confirm their ability and desire to help. They encountered little resistance, even in the skycities, after Prime Whitlock's deceptions were revealed. I didn't want to jinx anything, but it seemed like our luck had finally changed, after all.

In the days that followed Dissidia's return, the priority became figuring out a transparent, long-term plan for grounding the skycities. The reverse-conversion of Altara was promising, but it would take time to see results both visible and compelling enough to quell the concerns coming out of the rest of the skycities. So, Dissidia itself became the prime example of what a controlled, deliberate skycity grounding might look like.

The Dissidians ended up settling the city into a great stretch of land not too far from Genesis X-16, much to Mica's utter delight. When I'd asked Adam about what had influenced the decision on their ultimate location, he parroted something about the practicality of being relatively close to Korbyllis—for all that traveling to and fro for negotiations, of course. He also said something about the symbolism of being near the District—which, as it turns out, was where the old groundworld government was based.

I'd patted Adam's cheek, smiled, and nodded, as if I didn't know there was a little something more to it than that. However he pulled it off, I was grateful.

One Month Later

THE SUN IS JUST SETTING on the horizon as Adam and I stand on a hill, overlooking the commotion of the city below. With the encapsulation dome taken down, Altara looks like any other city. Well, any city undergoing major rebuilding efforts. Even with Dissidian technology at our disposal, we've barely cracked the surface of the repairs that need to be done, but the air is filled with the sounds of construction and laughter, and I find myself filled with the most rapturous sense of hope.

"We've come a long way," I say, leaning into Adam's side.

He wraps his arm around my shoulders, his gaze fixed on the cityscape in front of us. "And we have longer to go," he admits. "But it feels pretty good, doesn't it?"

I turn to look at him. "What does?"

"To feel like we're heading in the right direction for once."

I nod, nestling my head against his shoulder, a feeling of peace settling into my bones. "It does."

Adam plants a kiss on the crown of my head. "You ready for this?" he asks after a minute.

I inhale sharply through my nose. "I guess. Still not sure why they wanted me to make this speech," I grumble, smoothing the fabric of my long sky-blue dress and self-consciously tucking a tendril of hair behind my ear.

"As if there was any other choice, Sunburst," Adam says, his voice full of warmth as he takes my hand and leads me down to the group gathered at the base of the hill. "It could only be you."

As we draw closer, I recognize some of the faces in the crowd. Admiral Meers, Charlie, Tom, and Luke are at the front of a large contingency of Dissidians, and I even think I see Vice-Commander Conroy's bald head poking out from the crowd a few rows back. Next to them is Zira Coal with her daughters, Yttria and Juniper, leading an even larger group of Underground members and local terrestrials.

My eyes burn as they roam the crowd, which only seems to grow with each passing second, my heart swelling as more familiar faces appear. Ones from my past, present, and future, all standing before me—Brant, Emery, Ensign Davis, Copp, Mr. Sundry. Even some of my fellow scavs from Sixteen have made the trek out here to pay their respects. Surprise flares in me when I notice a few of the guardsmen I'd had run-ins with— Akryn, Trimble, Clay—standing near the back of the crowd.

Finally, my gaze lands on Mica, his shoulders set with pride as he stands next to a huge Steklenbergian obelisk. Adam and Tom had worked tirelessly together all week carving it out, and the sight of my brother standing guard next to it is what finally does me in. Tears spill from my eyes as I take my place next to Mica, placing a reverent hand on the obelisk which has been painstakingly carved with the names of every person lost when Altara almost fell.

Adam's gentle hand brushes my cheek, wiping the tears from my face. I take a deep, steadying breath as I turn to address the crowd.

"I like to think I know a little about loss," I say, my voice shaking. "I lost my mother when I was a kid. Lost my dad when I was a bit of an older kid." I pause, my eyes finding Zira Coal's piercing ones, and offer an understanding nod. "Lost my Gran, lost our money, lost my mind . . ." I hear Luke chuckle from somewhere in the crowd, and it bolsters me. "And then, as you all know, I lost my dad again." Mica slips his hand into my own, and I give it a squeeze.

"I do not say this to elicit your sympathy. But rather, to say that when I stand here with you, I know what it feels like to have lost." I run my hand over the names carved into the obelisk, my fingers tracing the lines of one particular name, and Adam steps closer to me. "But I also know what it feels like to be found. I know what it is to hope.

"We stand here today, united by our shared loss and our shared hope. We paid a heavy price, but have also found strength in each other. We have proven that the best of humanity can be found when we come together. That we can *over*come, we can rebuild, and we can be better— together." I pause, taking a deep breath. "And because of this, future generations will live in a world united, no longer divided by ground and sky. No longer terrestrial versus skydweller, no longer Dissidian versus, well, however you all used to refer to the rest of us." Low laughter rings out through the crowd.

"So, we honor and remember those who were not able to see this dream become a reality with this memorial—as we will with our actions and words every day," I finish.

For a moment, I'm not sure if they realized I've finished speaking. Or if, perhaps, I've said something wrong. But then I see the way each and every head in the crowd is bowed, their eyes closed, the air thick with our collective grief and resolve for a hopeful future, and my heart swells again.

"Together," I say, my voice thick.

"Together," the crowd echoes back.

EPILOGUE

ADAM

Six Months Later

THE STREETS below bustle with the sounds of life—laughter, music, and the hum of activity. It's still hard for me to reconcile the Dissidia I grew up in with the city I live in now. With the ability to grow past its previous limits, the city's only become more vibrant, more lovely. Funny how much a little extra space and a lot less panic does for the human spirit.

"Hey spaceboy, stop daydreaming and get over here." Terra's voice, bright and melodic, pulls me from my thoughts. She's setting up some snacks and drinks on a table further back on the rooftop terrace, a playful smile adorning her gorgeous face. "The crew's almost here and I need your help."

A grin creeps up one side of my mouth as I wrap my arms around her from behind. "You mean, you require my excellent taste-testing skills, right?"

She swats at my arm as I reach around her, aiming for a small, square, fluffy bite of something delicious-looking. "Wrong," she says with a laugh. "More like, I need you to go back inside and get the ice chest from the apartment."

Before I can respond, the rooftop door bursts open. Mica rushes in, still wearing his Dissidian school uniform, followed by Luke, Tom, and Charlie. The buzz of chatter and clinking glasses quickly fills the air as everyone gets settled.

"Hardly seems fair that you two get a view like this," Luke exclaims. "Explain to me again, Tommy, why you gave them dibs on this apartment?"

Tom laughs. "With the amount of time you spend traveling from city to city, Liaison Officer Prynn, you'd hardly have time to enjoy the view anyway."

"Ooh, *Liaison Officer*, huh? So, it's official?" Mica asks Luke, who offers a demure nod in response that has everyone cackling.

"Modesty, thy name is decidedly *not* Lucas Prynn," Charlie snorts. "But yes, Admiral Mom made it official last week, so say hello to the newest official Dissidian member of the Unity Council. As if he weren't already insufferable enough."

"All right, everyone, help yourselves," Terra says, gesturing to the table.

The conversation flows easily as we catch up. Mica is in particularly high spirits, happy to share his latest stories from school and his plans for his next visit to see Juniper back in Sixteen. Terra quizzes Luke about his new position, excited at the thought of getting to work together more now that he's officially part of the Unity Council like her. I throw in a few comments on how resettlement efforts in Altara have been going. And Charlie seems perfectly content needling Tom about his new promotion—and the fact that he now reports directly to Vice-Admiral Conroy.

"He may be training you to be the new XO, but I still think you having to put up with his bullshit is a fitting penance," she says, taking a sip of her drink. "You know, for *nixing* Adam so extremely only to then be generally insufferable about him leaving."

I grin appreciatively as Terra giggles—my heart soars with the sound. "You tell him, Chuck," I say, raising my glass in Charlie's direction.

Tom scoffs. "I thought we'd moved past all that. And the Vice-Admiral is honestly not so bad when you *actually* follow protocol and act with respect and—"

Charlie cuts him off with a dramatic groan, rolling her eyes, and everyone laughs.

"So, Adam," Luke says, nudging me with his elbow. "I take it from how thoroughly edible this spread is that you had absolutely nothing to do with its preparation this time?"

I smack my palm over my heart. "You wound me, sir. That was one time, and I—"

"—nearly killed off all our taste buds for an entire week," Terra interjects.

"Traitor," I accuse, and she squeals as I grab her by the waist and pull her into my lap.

"The lady speaks the truth," Luke says with a shrug.

Terra pats my cheek, grinning up at me with such earnest amusement, my heart might just about burst. Hot damn, I love this girl. "It was a valiant effort, spaceboy," she says. "And it certainly made for a memorable evening."

I groan. "Fear not, friends, I'll be leaving the cooking to this one for the foreseeable future."

"Everyone has different talents," Charlie says with a smirk. "Yours clearly lay outside the kitchen."

"True. Like in the bedroom," I say, a devilish grin on my face as Terra yelps and swats my arm again.

"Adam!" she hisses, darting her eyes to her brother. Mica retches loudly.

The rooftop erupts with laughter. With a roll of her eyes, Terra's back to smiling, which only broadens my own grin. There's nothing that makes me happier than seeing the easy delight in her eyes these days. She deserves it.

She deserves everything.

The night eventually winds down, and we say our reluctant goodbyes to our friends as they go their separate ways—Mica back to the dorms, Luke and Tom back to their place on the other side of the city, and Charlie off to wherever it is she's been hunkering down these days.

Terra snuggles into me as I lean back in my chair and wrap an arm around her shoulders, feeling the calming rhythm of her chest rise and fall.

"I'm not sure I believed this would ever really happen," she whispers suddenly, her breath sending a shiver down my skin.

"What would happen?" I ask, my voice low as I pull her in closer.

She pauses. "Just . . . this. Life. A real life."

When I peer into her beautiful face, tears brim the edges of her perfect, gold-burst eyes.

I shift her in my lap so I can reach our drinking glasses on the table in front of us, handing one to Terra before I settle back in my seat. I tip my glass toward hers.

"To us," I say. "To life. Our life, together."

She raises her glass to meet mine with a clink.

"Always."

ALSO BY GRETCHEN POWELL FOX

Smoke and Scar

Splintered Kingdom *(coming Fall 2025)*

ABOUT THE AUTHOR

Gretchen Powell Fox spent her childhood in far-off places—literally and figuratively. She grew up with her nose buried in books and her feet on foreign soil. Both, she found, were essential in forming her deep fascination with stories.

Now, she crafts fantastical and futuristic worlds—along with the fiery heroines destined to change them for the better.

Her creative process involves copious amounts of Sour Patch Kids and sleeping fitfully. Her many interests include Taylor Swift, polka dots, reading fantasy novels, and playing the ukulele.

She lives in Northern Virginia with her husband and two wild, wonderful children.

Find her on social media @gretchenwritesbooks and visit her website at gretchenpowellfox.com.

www.ingramcontent.com/pod-product-compliance
Lightning Source LLC
Chambersburg PA
CBHW050058120726
47904CB00004B/1136